THE M
WITH
THE GOLDEN ARM

The Tales and Adventures of Jonathan Owen

RICK THOMAS

Trafford

Best wishes
Jamie

Cover painting by: Rick Thomas

All characters depicted in this publication are fictitious and any resemblance to real persons, living or dead, is purely coincidental.

Order this book online at www.trafford.com
or email orders@trafford.com

Most Trafford titles are also available at major online book retailers.

Note for Librarians: A cataloguing record for this book is available from Library and Archives Canada at www.collectionscanada.ca/amicus/index-e.html

Printed in Victoria, BC, Canada.

ISBN: 9781-4269-1438-6 *(sc)*

Our mission is to efficiently provide the world's finest, most comprehensive book publishing service, enabling every author to experience success. To find out how to publish your book, your way, and have it available worldwide, visit us online at www.trafford.com

Trafford rev. 8/12/2009

www.trafford.com

North America & international
toll-free: 1 888 232 4444 (USA & Canada)
phone: 250 383 6864 • fax: 250 383 6804

About Rick

Rick Thomas was born in Cardiff, Wales in 1944 and immigrated with his parents to Canada in the 1950s. In early life, he attended school in Victoria, British Columbia and the Vancouver School of Art in the 1960s. He retired from the Government of BC a Cartographic Scientific Technical Officer and graphic artist, mapping and illustrating ecosystems, animals and plant life of British Columbia. Rick is a painter, graphic artist, set designer, writer and fitness instructor. He has a daughter, Kim.

He traveled sixty thousand kilometers over five years writing and drawing about crime, adventure and a fictitious personality, Jonathan B. Owen. Rick lives in the Pacific Northwest.

About Jonathan

Jonathan B. Owen, criminal and madman, lives his life between two worlds—a dubious reality and a scary fantasy. No in-between like you and I. Never awe struck by the ordinary; he's in a place many would like to be—alone, far from mediocrity and our own crowd. If not running from the law or pursuing a woman, he is wandering the world—slipping around a corner, dancing up a street or falling over a hill.

Wandering through tropical countries he encounters souls, cultures and gods; countries open their villages, cities and temples to shake and rattle him. He stands his ground keeping them at arms length, holding off temptation, protecting himself from harm but sometimes he takes flight for his life. He is brave when the fight is needed especially twelve feet up on the neck of his Thai elephant or in pursuit across Cuba of a Garifuna woman. He is a rich man making a wave through a sea of desperate people. His fear is being possessed by it all—forever to wander. He floats from place to place not knowing where he will land but that is where the excitement begins; in the dust that covers his sandaled feet, in the searing sun that bakes him into one with the earth.

Lost in the beauty of a young criminal woman, the psychotic frenzy of a lover or the embrace of a refugee family he copes the best he can.

Gods, animals, men, women, assassins and thieves drive his ego to wits end. There is no journey here, no grand design and no cheap excuse, just a manic curiosity—a walk over ghosts and bones. No worry of the danger he courts—in the end there is redemption and the knowledge he lived. Look deep—he is as naughty as you.

Dedication

There is a group of children who make a living selling books to tourists at The Bayon Temple in Angkor, Cambodia. It is a hard life with an uncertain future for them but they face it with laughter and optimism. They were an inspiration to me. Through them I look at the world quite differently. I dedicate book four to them—the rest, to all my friends around the world.

Acknowledgements

I would like to thank Victoria Hasler, Scott Geritty and my daughter Kim Denness Thomas for their editing and advice. Many thanks to all of those at home in Victoria who emailed words of encouragement when I was on the road in Asia, Europe, Central America and North Africa struggling with Jonathan Owen.

Rick Thomas
Victoria, British Columbia

One

JONATHAN OWEN, SILVER BULLET AND BANK ROBBER

Canada United States Mexico

Terror, tragedy and madness await Jonathan B. Owen on his five-year adventure. He is not afraid or in awe of where he has been or where he is going; he is looking for something new each day and what that is – he doesn't know. Jonathan is on his way home – a five thousand kilometer drive; home for a rest only to be on the move again to other countries and adventures.

The Bullet roared north on the Pan American Highway. The silver gray Jeep will climb the Sierra Madre; rumble through Mexican towns and cities; roar across deserts and jungles to the border of Mexico and dash up the United States and into Canada.

In Bullet's cargo boxes are the rag doll images of the Zapatista National Liberation Army. His painting of Quetzalcoatl wrapped in a Mexican blanket is strapped to Silver Bullet's cargo boxes. In the passenger seat next to him is the ghost of Bank Robber.

Down a Continent and up a River to The Market of Bucerias

"Damn black, witch, bitch. She gave me the eye!" Jonathan yelled as he slipped on a slime-covered rock while crossing the river. He went down on his back into the muddy water and muck. Cursing he managed to hold his bags of groceries out of the mess. Barbara, all two hundred plus pounds of her grunted and reached down, grabbed him by the palm trees on his shirt and helped him to his feet. Timothy roared with laughter, threw his market load into Bullet and opened three beers. They climbed into Bullet with their bundles and drove up the river. Drunk and in celebration they sang an old cowboy tune as they went—Timothy led the chorus. Ever since he rode in Bullet he could not get some old television cowboy sidekick's image of the Jeep out of his mind.

Jonathan drove out of the river up the bank onto Francisco Madero. He tried to kill any chickens on the road that got in his way but they were too quick for him, they were always too quick for him. They arrived home safely to the pool, flowers and lizards. Timothy took on the role of food prep and Barbara and Jonathan jumped into the pool. Her Rubenesque body created a small tsunami as she landed. Timothy made some fabulous salad sandwiches, which they washed down with beer and at the edge of the pool the three held a ceremony setting their caged birds free. Hot and comfortable, the trio fell asleep in lounge chairs under fluttering palm trees. Birds chirped and sang in the bougainvillea that climbed the wall beside the pool. Big Bob the iguana scurried under their lounge chairs on his way to his hibiscus tree. Jonathan dreamed of the day's events and his journey to this little place on the edge of Mexico. In the distance, across the footbridge and town square the trio could hear the ringing of the Church bells calling her children to prayer.

A month earlier in Canada, Jonathan drove out of his sleeping village in his Jeep, Silver Bullet that perhaps in its way is as old as he. Leaves fell from the towering maple trees that grew along the manicured boulevards of the village. Like parchment, they had turned to gold and rust; the skies were steel gray; the temperature was dropping daily; winter's shroud had arrived and he was glad to be leaving. The Bullet and Jonathan had a long way to go and into dangerous places. It was time for him to leave his home for Mexico—five thousand kilometers away.

Jonathan had retired from his government job a few months earlier. In his work he felt privileged to be part of a process of building harmony, understanding and balance in the human and animal world. Someday far away in the future, a group of scientists and technicians will come across electronic disks and make something profound and helpful for the planet.

He will be forgotten. His work outside of his employment he knows will survive; he painted it and signed his name at the bottom. It was real and tangible like the ancient works painted and carved in rock on Maya, Toltec and Aztec temples.

There is not much that makes Jonathan stand out in a crowd, physically, he is medium height and weight but stronger than most from working hard in the gym. In looks and physic he is Germanic even though he is Welsh by ancestry—his skin fair, eyes blue and hair blonde. He is arrogant on occasion, and he knows this, but it gives him the audacity not just to experience life, but to grab it, shake it and take risks.

There were only a few women in his life that went where he did but the chaos was too great for them and after a while they left him for a more stable world with other men. There is a woman who could follow him, or was it the other way around? Tula, is her name, the darkest creature he has ever met. She will play a terrifying role in his tales and adventures to come.

He wandered up one of the spurs of the market and something familiar and frightening caught his boozy eyes. Tucked in between two stalls against a whitewashed wall sat an old wrinkled woman in black, her face and arms brown from the sun and her heritage. An embroidered piece of black fabric lay across her head. Her bony sandaled feet were tanned and dusty in contrast to her white manicured toenails. Deep, black, shimmering, curly hair cascaded down her shoulders and large silver hoop earrings peeked out from the dark. Her face was tanned bronze patina, not wrinkled but coarse lines running across and down her jaw. Black pupil eyes against white clean eyeballs were set deep beneath her forehead where wisps of black curls hung. Her thin nose and high cheekbones were taut and reflected the sun; her lips, with a hint of glossy red cherry lipstick, were still full. The top buttons of her blouse were undone to her mid chest exposing a tanned cleavage. A silver cross of jewels hung upside down; it shone against the ample flesh of her breasts. Her long bony hands and fingers ended in gleaming white nail polish. They gestured as she spoke, flashing silver rings and wrist bracelets. Under her black dress and blouse was a beautiful woman, probably younger than him. The old woman sat on a stack of leather-bound Bibles and leaned back against the wheel of her small handcart—weathered to almost black. The wood of the cart was decked out in crosses and symbols, faded now from years of travel.

The witch was a tarot card reader and she quietly mumbled, drawing pictures in the air while conversing with a young girl breast-feeding her fat round baby. The old crone and girl were closely huddled together in deep and serious conversation. In front of them on a red and black striped blanket was a skull on top of some bones that looked like femurs. He knew the bones were real and God and she only know where they came from. A candle was burning on the skull; it dripped wax over the eye sockets—very theatrical. Surrounding the bones were the tools of witchery: a pile of shiny stones; dried carcasses of frogs and lizards; crosses of different sizes; bottles of potions probably for love or to bring back an adulterous lover or husband; old coins; small cheap plastic statues of deities; dirty worn faded pieces of paper with written inscriptions; knife blades scratched with crude pictures; small piles of bleached chicken and rat bones with cheap jewelry mixed in; tarot cards; colourful sea shells; and painted terra cotta pots burned incense.

The young girl was cross-legged on the blanket dressed in red pants her black blouse opened wide for her baby to feed. Her milk was smeared across her bulbous breasts. Her long hair was pulled back straight from her heavily made up face and she showed an intensity of concentration as she leaned forward over her baby taking in every word and gesture of the old dark witch.

This is too much of a picture for me to pass over; he mumbled through his drunken haze—it's just too much. He crouched down to their level and snapped the photo he wanted. She heard the click and the old woman slowly turned her head to him and looked deep into his eyes. He had experienced this menacing look before, she was an anathema to him—a real bitch and sexy—straight from hell. This is not good, he thought, "Thanked you." He nervously responded—they stared. He rose and almost fell but caught himself. He left them to their charade.

Tim, Barb and Jonathan would be making lunch later beside the pool—he was hungry now. At one of the street cafes he sat down and ordered a small sample of red snapper fried in butter and garlic, from a portly woman in a yellow and red-stripped apron. The cook's gray hair was stacked on her head and from her round face came a wide encompassing smile. Her huge breasts bulged out the top of her dress and filled up most of the space in her little establishment. A skinny, frightened—looking man squeezed into the place to assist her and Jonathan wondered if he was her husband. He must be—he looked frightened. The cook's stove was half of a steel forty-gallon drum filled with hot coals over which she barbequed fish and vegetables on a stainless steel grating. A deep fryer made from a large pot welded to a truck tire rim placed on bricks with a coal fire beneath, fried her fish and chips. At the back of the eatery a young woman at a table prepared the fish for the barbeque and deep fryer. There were freezer chests full of fish for sale: tuna, perch, swordfish, shark, bass, shrimp and huge prawns. The fish were caught during the night or in the early morning and trucked to the market from fishing villages nearby. Off to the side was a young boy; his black hair well oiled, he played guitar and sang love songs as a young girl with love in her eyes melted into his dark face.

A short time ago he had crossed the border between Canada and the United States at the Washington State Peace Arch and drove down Interstate 5—the route to freedom and tropical paradise. Nervous and apprehensive there was no turning back, no matter what happened. He had committed himself to this adventure and he was going to follow the challenge through. He had a long drive ahead of him in the Bullet who was now getting on in years. Hell, both of them were getting on in years. Bullet is a Jeep; a powerful beast of rubber, canvas and metal—an extension of him. After many hours on the road Jonathan calmed from his anxiety of what he was leaving behind: all the damn rules, regulations and guidelines that Canadians have to live by and obey.

Interstate 5 with its fast food outlets, motels, gas stations and warehouses can be boring for the traveler. Their monotonous signs flash on high steel poles like giant cocktail swizzle sticks puncturing the American landscape. They are beacons of welcome; comfort zones for those on the road: truck drivers, businessmen, families on the move or vacationing bachelors like Jonathan going to a Mexican party. The highway had a pop-culture look, a video game with images suitable for an exhibition at the Museum of Modern Art. You can love it or hate it. He spent the night in Medford, at an America swizzle stick motel, he used a swizzle stick station to fill Bullet's tank, and had breakfast at a swizzle stick fast food franchise with a number of enormous Americans.

The local pancake house was a shocker; he had never seen so many overweight people stuffing down huge platters of pancakes, waffles, eggs, steak, potatoes and fruit. The entire mess was covered in syrup and butter. Several cups of coffee and juice were nearby. Wow, he thought America has a giant food celebration in constant motion, a culinary orgasm of immense proportions. He took a booth across the aisle from a site of unexpected beauty, a woman—a gorgeous rotund woman. Auburn hair cascaded over her tanned strong shoulders. Her face, cherub like, was painted in soft makeup; her lips, large and full, shone from a natural coloured lipstick—beautiful and ample—a Raphael cherub. She wore a simple short, black sleeveless dress that showed the cleavage of her sun baked, firm, enormous breasts. Much of her body was exposed, with no signs of cellulite or stretch marks just beautiful healthy flesh covered in clear flawless skin. Her feet were large and thick, her toes powerful balls of muscle and flesh capable of carrying and maneuvering her huge body. Her legs were massive; the muscles firm and strong; thighs large and broad, surprisingly arrived at a relatively small waist. She sat erect and attentive talking to her friend who was also of the same stature.

Was this woman the wave of a new beauty in America? Jonathan wondered. She noticed him looking at her; she smiled and heaved her breasts up as she shifted her mass across the red vinyl upholstered booth. Would the Peter Paul Rubens, baroque woman of the seventeenth century become fashionable again in the world? He could see her on the cover of some glamour magazine in a pinstriped suit standing at a conference table of some America corporate enterprise—a look on her face and physical demeanor that could snap the spine of any corporate mogul.

He ordered the kid's size pancake breakfast. And when he finished he said goodbye to the American goddess as he passed her booth. She was warm, sensual and smiled a goodbye. He wished he could have stayed.

He saw his first palm and cypress trees before entering Sacramento. Excitement took hold of him; he pulled off the highway and changed into a tropical garish shirt; then roared Bullet down the highway that hugged the skyscrapers. He drove south for hours through the broad flat country of vegetable farms to below the city of Bakersfield. There he left the Interstate 5 behind and Bullet sped east on Route 223 to Interstate 40, which would take him across the desert into Arizona.

Slowly the country became bone dry, the vegetation changed to cactus, the wildlife stung and the sky became huge as the mountains ran off into the distance. Inside Bullet the temperature rose. Jonathan sweated his way to Tehachapi to find the local swizzle stick was full, he found cheap digs near a rail stop on the edge of the Mojave Desert. Yellow, green and black locomotives rolled through town blasting their horns and waking tired travelers. It was a bad night for him.

In the morning he dressed in as little as possible to drive across the anvil hot Desert. He opened the side and rear windows of Bullet and stocked her with gas, oil, fruit, water and diet pop from a fat and cholesterol packed minisuper truck stop. The days ahead would be long and dry.

Jonathan found the Mojave Desert to be a mysterious place and that people actually live there baffled him. He guessed it is the military presence, for along the highway are signs shouting their existence. Suddenly out of the desert's sky six thundering jet fighters flew low in formation; practicing a bombing run on some poor rabbit terrified from their roar. In the distance to the south was Antelope Valley, the former Marine Corp Air Station, the desert airplane storage facility for aircraft of every description. The magnificent and genius objects human kind created and built only to be discarded; allowed too decay out there in that lonely dry, hot and hostile place. A sign read Military Logistic Center. What the hell could that be? He wondered.

A small sign popped up on the highway and Jonathan realized he was running next to a sacred part of America, Route 66 America's Main Street—the highway from Chicago to Los Angeles that Jack Kerouac and John Steinbeck made famous. Kerouac's Mother Road was the route Americans drove west to seek their fortunes. Today nostalgia buffs drive the highway of dreams with the ghosts of Kerouac and Steinbeck in the back seat.

A sign on the route advertised, Forty Mule Team Borax products. In the 1800's huge wagons driven by two men and pulled by forty to sixty horses and mules hauled Borax from Death Valley in the north, south to Barstow through the inhospitable desert. People making a living in the hot and dry desert was something to be admired, the climate can make you old very fast and kill you. Many stories, mostly erroneous adventure pulp, were published about these tough men, their environment, wagons and horse teams. They became a part of America's folklore told in movies and television—adventurers that America wanted in the '50's and '60's.

At the desert town of Needles his highway left Route 66. He picked up the two-lane Highway 95 south to Blythe that put him onto the Interstate 10 to Casa Grande, Arizona and his friend and Bullet's mechanic Bill. Silver Bullet and Jonathan would get a two-day rest before entering Mexico. Bill Dunsworth is a snowbird and had been Silver Bullet's mechanic for years. Back in Canada, he made her ready a few weeks prior to his journey to Mexico. Jonathan stayed with Bill for a few days and relaxed and acclimatized the best he could, which was a challenge as the temperature was always over one hundred five degrees and the humidity unbearable. Bill checked out the Bullet and found her worthy of the trip ahead.

He said goodbye to his old friend Bill and continued his way south through Tucson and entered Mexico via the towns of Nogales, which span the United States and Mexican border. This was major for him; he was leaving the protection of American and Canadian safety nets and entering a place of uncertainty. It was a country of foreign language and culture; a place that if anything goes wrong—help may not be there. He stroked Silver Bullet's dashboard and gently asked her not to break down.

There is a contrast in the fabric of the two Nogales's, one a well organized American town, the other a bustling frayed Northern Mexican hamlet; a community of colour: cars and pickup trucks full of people going somewhere; music blasting out of bars and cars; and markets filled with dark people selling strange vegetables and fruits. Red sun burned tourists argued deals at souvenir shops strung out along cobbled dusty streets.

On the Mexican side Jonathan pulled into a Pemex gas station alongside a huge rusting tractor truck pulling a flat deck trailer with cages stacked three high. Each cage held three full-grown pigs. The two hundred porkers were on their way to a farm or meat market. The stench of excrement filled the air as the driver hosed the beasts down to cool them. There were squeals of displeasure from the porkers as they stepped on one another, trying to get at some of the cool spray. A brown river of excrement ran off the flat deck down the cobbled street into a drain. Jonathan drove away to the Mexican customs and immigration thirty kilometers down the highway. Clearing them was slow. He bought Mexican insurance, two hundred dollars for his five-month stay in Mexico—enough to buy his way out of jail if he was in an accident.

Jonathan crossed a large expanse of the Sonora Desert, a dry hostile place that extends hundreds of miles into Mexico and north across the US border into Arizona and Southern California. Several times he drove past strange ragged people; their clothes filthy black from dirt and dust; their exposed faces and hands burned a deep brown from the sun. The black shadows flashed the whites of their eyes from bowed heads and long matted black hair. One of the shadows dropped his pants to expose himself to passing motorists. Death for these derelicts, Jonathan thought could be an insect bite or broken ankle.

Slowly the landscape turned into the agricultural plains and jungles of the Mexican Pacific Coast. The countryside was a riot of flowers and animal life. The air was filled with butterflies that migrate to Mexico—hundreds of billions from across North America. At night huge bats pursued giant locusts and other flying insects that crossed his headlights. A time he should not have been driving. For two days he drove across fields of corn, wheat, tobacco, vegetables and coffee. Every few kilometers were breeding sheds for cattle, pigs and chickens that he could smell before he could see them. There are one hundred and ten million mouths to feed in Mexico, thirty million in Mexico City. That's a lot of pig trucks on the road.

It cost him thirty-five dollars in legal tolls to get to his destination of Puerto Vallarta and since Jonathan drove on the wrong highway between Mazatlan and Tepic; he spent another ten dollars in local tolls. Drugged and desperate looking bandits, who felt they had a right to their share of Yankee and Canuck dollars, pushed tin cans in his face for donations. For some, it is the only way for them to stay alive. There are no safety nets of unemployment insurance; welfare or pension plans in Mexico. If you don't work and make money or have an extended family to help you—you starve.

On the short drive from Tepic to Puerto Vallarta, he witnessed the aftermath of accidents. In a small dusty town in a gas station was parked an eighteen wheel tractor truck and box trailer; its sides ripped open. Red blood painted the gash from the bumper to mid way down the trailer; the metal peeled away exposed the trucks structure and cargo of cardboard containers. Whatever side swiped the truck took the driver with it—the front seat was torn in half.

South of Tepic on the mountain highway meandering down through the coastal jungles to Puerto Vallarta, service trucks were parked on the shoulder. The road barrier was a misshapen length of metal; a twisted end ripped from its metal post rose menacingly into the sky. A tow truck's cable was hanging taut over the cliff. Jonathan cautiously drove by. On the side of the highway he saw rusting wreckage of cars and trucks buried in vines and flowers. They lay quietly twisted and broken—monuments to disasters and shattered lives.

Suddenly Bullet and Jonathan broke through the jungle and onto the highway that follows the Bahia de Banderas—the giant bay and its thriving tourist industry. They roared through a military checkpoint; drove past the towns of Bucerias and Mezcales and into the gated compound in Nuevo Vallarta to Mary Jo and Poncho's townhouse. It was good to see Mary Jo again; it had been years since they last talked. She was once married to a friend of his in Canada, their union eventually dissolved and Mary Jo fled to Mexico. She and Poncho live in a palatial quadrangle of concrete stucco townhouses brightly painted in pastel colours with a swimming pool in the center of a courtyard. The complex is surrounded by high walls, steel gates and patrolled by security guards. Outside the compound is a new town of several thousand people, pretty and new but Jonathan could see it would become a ghetto in the future; its youth in gangs ravished with drugs.

After a week of acclimatizing and fantastic meals cooked by Poncho it was time for him to find his own place. Mary Jo and Poncho wanted him to stay longer but he is a bachelor and independent and he needed his own space. Poncho and Jonathan went looking in the little town of Bucerias north of Puerto Vallarta for suitable long-term accommodation for the winter.

Bucerias, Place of the Divers, is a small seaside town, nineteen kilometers north of Puerto Vallarta—population about five thousand. His cottage in the well-to-do part of town was comfortable, clean and quiet. His neighbors were the middle class from the outside and the rich from the interior of Mexico. The poor section of town across the highway was dirty with freaked out street dogs and roaming chickens. Wandering horses, donkeys and burrows made their home in garbage filled empty lots. In the dry season the dust and stench of death are typical of this part of Mexico.

He rented a one bedroom cottage two blocks from the surf on an old estate with a pool, gardens, palm trees, lizards, humming birds, bats, canaries, frogs, toads, weird insects and maid service. The water, gas, and garbage delivery trucks drove by each day giving out distinct noises and when you heard the right sound, you ran out into the street to buy what you needed. His cottage had a bedroom, bathroom and an outdoor kitchen, the windows and doors where wrought iron protected.

The landlord's daughter, Angel, a cute cherub girl of twenty, lived above his cottage in a little suite with a balcony overlooking the street. Angel loves Bucerias and her alcoholic boyfriend who has a nowhere job at a pizza delivery service. The two lovers have a beautiful Shakespearian relationship. Out on the street late at night under the light of the moon and the star Quetzalcoatl, the boy would whistle gently like a tropical bird, she would come out on the balcony and they would whisper words to each other. Sometimes she would let him in, other times he came to say good night and then would just go home. Angel's father had no patience for him and would raise hell if he caught the boy near the place.

It had been a long, hard and fast ride but Jonathan found what he was looking for—a cottage, a pool and a few crazy friends.

Timothy came up behind Jonathan and grabbed him by the arm and said, "You're a goddamn good man for bringing us to this place. We would never see this kind of stuff if it weren't for you. Let me buy us some drinks."

He and Barbara pulled him into a hole in the wall cantina and ordered shots of tequila with beer chasers. A burly bartender/owner was full of smiles in his packed little cantina. He does well on market day. His son and daughter, about the ages of eight or nine, wait on tables—their little hands were out for tips at every opportunity—their big brown eyes tug at your heart.

"Jesus!" Timothy said, "The old man would be arrested back home for using child labor."

"There are no labor laws in Mexico, everyone can and does work," Jonathan said, "its all family." They toasted each other and mused about their governor and their American friends, and his Canadian ones back home, "I can see them now," Jonathan toasted, "huddled under the outdoor heaters at the coffee shop in the wet, cold winter."

Quite pickled with cold beer in hand, they poured out of the cantina and continued to explore the market. Timothy and Barbara went off to the hardware section, which was a spur off the main market road. Timothy liked mechanical stuff and he would find a great selection of it: fridges, stoves, machetes, motorcycle and car parts, coloured poly rope, drills, saws, stereos, safety equipment, chisels, cell phones, bikes and washing machines. Years ago, when Jonathan visited the markets, electronic technical merchandise did not exist. Everything is available now.

Timothy and Barbara, a loveable fat couple from a town near Atlanta Georgia, were Jonathan's neighbors at the Hacienda. He met them at the pool and the three struck up a friendship. Home for the couple is a small town in mid West America and, apart from the time Timothy attended university, they both have lived there forever. They are the town's parental guidance: Timothy, the town's engineer, takes care of the roads, electrical power and plumbing, and Barbara works in the municipal hall as a clerk processing the town's accounts. Their three children are grown and have their own families; they do not travel to Mexico with them anymore. Like Jonathan, Tim and Barb exercise their freedom to play in the tropics. They plan to live in Mexico during the winter months, away from the Canadian cold fronts that travel down and deep freeze their home in America.

The trios split up to do their own shopping and agreed to meet at one of the greasy smoky restaurants later. Jonathan wandered under the blue plastic sheeting strung across the road to protect the hawkers, farmers and the goods from the sun. Chickens and pregnant dogs were underfoot and young girls' breastfed their babies at the back of the booths—babies feeding babies. Five women beautifully dressed in black, pink and white dresses strutted down the street. Their brightly coloured blouses were shot with designs of baroque swirls and flowers; their feet in polished leather sandals. Their black lacquered hair was pulled back from their faces and tied in the back with jeweled clasps. Makeup was heavy and severe on their faces, especially their large fleshy red lips. One carried above the group a golfer's umbrella to protect them from the sun. They elegantly paraded and glided across the market chattering like tropical birds as they strode up the hill to Sunday Mass. He loved the quality of these people around him, clean, proud, heads up, shoulders back, smiling, happy and confident. Each day—a great day.

Groceries are delivered to the market in the morning from the east up of the valley. Tons of merchandise arrives in large paneled red, green and white trucks; horse drawn wagons, cars and pickups. They burst with vegetables, fruits and many strange looking growths that Jonathan did not recognize. Boxes are scattered on the dirt road under the sky blue canopies sagging under the heat of the day. There is no lack of food; fruit, vegetables, nuts and meat grow and flourish everywhere. Eggs, goat cheese or avocadoes—those items you ask for.

Jonathan saw Timothy and Barbara having a good time going through the vegetables and fruit. They could be at home at their local supermarket except here is the freedom and simplicity experienced when shopping at an open market. Its fun and feels like you're getting a deal—which you are, since there is no overhead for the vendors. The meat Jonathan stays away from; half a cow skinned and covered with flies looks awful lying in the back of the local butcher's blue pickup. The street dogs lick up the blood as it drips from the tailgate. You just don't know when the beast was slaughtered. It's all perfectly good meat and it's the same truck that delivers to the grocery stores and restaurants all over Bucerias but white folk, like him, are used to the anonymous packaged meats in refrigerated counters back in their comfortable hometowns. When you order a steak in Mexico you don't know the route it has taken to get to your plate. Sometimes it isn't even a cow—it's a horse. After a few beer he did buy a pork rind once, a big half meter square chunk and he didn't care where it came from or looked like, besides over the years in and out of Mexico his stomach has turned to iron and his immune system is overloaded with anti—whatever you call those things that kill the bad stuff in your blood.

Makeshift kitchens and eateries of bright umbrellas, plastic chairs and tables were huddled together serving, chimichanga, tortillas, enchiladas, chicken, fish and tacos. Big cauldrons of stew bubbled and boiled, chicken, pork, radishes, onions and spices of oregano, salt and lime added flavor. Noise, smoke and smells filled the streets and neighborhood.

Jonathan photographed mothers and kids, belts, bags, dogs, chickens and tables full of colourful junk; wooden and plastic horses; dolls dressed in garish outfits; stacks of bright wool and yarn; and rip-off sandals and shoes with designer names

A jeweler, dressed in white with a red bandana around his neck, approached him with his black leather jewel case open displaying, cheap, silver rings, hash pipes, necklaces, bracelets and watches. Since he was in no pain and felt he needed a present for himself he bargained for a Rolex watch and got the vendor down to ten dollars Canadian.

The vendor said, "I have the real thing here for twenty five."

Jonathan had a drink of beer, burped and went on his way. This was the fifth Rolex watch he had bought. All were the same price no matter where he went—around ten bucks.

Timothy and Barbara, loaded down with their shopping, joined him. Both were feeling the Tequila and beer. The threesome decided to call it a morning and they stumbled down the market road to the river, and Silver Bullet. Barbara was loaded down with a large bag of fruit and two round wire cages, one contained a green, yellow, red-beaked tropical bird and in the other, two sweet little finches. She named them after her kids and babbled to them—tears in her eyes. Tim staggered carrying bags of vegetables, a geologist's hammer and a box of beer. He rambled on that now he had the tool to finally pursue a hobby he had always wanted—smashing rocks to see what was inside of them. Jonathan carried four bags of veggies and toiletries. They arrived at the river. It was time to get home and make lunch.

Jonathan moved into this tropical environment and chaos to begin his new adventure of retirement and he had no idea how to handle it—he would take life as it unfolded and not ask why. Profound events would become ordinary and matter-of-fact; the astonishment of nature is after all, natural. Life would become entertaining, exciting, overwhelming, mysterious, tragic and dangerous in the years to come. This little place on the edge of the world with its market, festivals, friends and camaraderie will be the starting point to learn of another grander world.

Over The Mountains and Into The Future with Bank Robber

He was well into his Mexican stay when he met the woman he would come to call Bank Robber. He was contemplating a painting at a gallery in Old Town PV. It was mythological, whimsical and dramatic—a green God-like creature with deep coal-black curly hair—round beady eyes jumped off the canvas at him.

Somebody behind him said in an accent he did not recognize, "Not a bad piece of work, don't you think?"

He did not turn around but blurted an arrogant reply: "Yeah but the artist could have picked a better suite of colours than the dominant pastel greens with a pink discord landscape. It looks like a bad Gauguin. It turns the composition sour, which doesn't do the powerful personality of the creature justice. He is a dramatic, Mexican mystical and magical character full of power; a bold ancient hero that should be painted in primary colours."

"Cocky bastard, aren't you?" she said.

Jonathan turned to see where the sarcasm was coming from. A pair of smiling, naughty-looking, bright white eyes with deep black pupils, curly cascading black hair, tanned, buxom, round hipped, long legged, in her ripe twenties, a thin tiny short canary yellow dress held up by ample breasts and spaghetti straps with just enough length to cover her upper thighs and no hint of underwear—greeted him. She looked at him and smiled a giggle, spun on her cute, sandaled, tanned feet with bright red painted toes nails, and walked out the door. She glided gracefully through the crowd on her way to another gallery down the street. He watched her walk away and remembered another time and another place when he was a young man. He thought of what he might have done with the opportunity. He sighed and went back to his glass of red wine and pictures.

A regular email home to friends and daughter needed to be done; the Internet he used was at the local realty company. The day was like any other, full of surprises but this day was to become the turning point of his stay in Mexico; because she, the one who called him a cocky bastard at the gallery, was doing her email and looking more beautiful and naughty than he remembered. He had more than a sexual attraction to this young woman; besides her beauty she was sensuous, intelligent, confident and open. But something about her told him she was dangerous. He was drawn to the dangerous and beautiful; he liked beauty close to him—danger came along with it. They struck up a conversation and immediately became friends—comfortable and available. Her dark eyes never left his when they talked—no coyness, no shyness.

They decided to hang out together and planned a few trips around the bay. She didn't have a car so he was a convenience for her to see more of Mexico. He sensed he was going to be used but he didn't care—he would use her too. He drove through valleys and over mountains with her long, tanned bare legs laid up on the dashboard; her bikini draped over the rearview mirror—a beautiful sight. Her last name he forgot or maybe never knew it but she would soon have the handle, Bank Robber. She would become a friend, partner and a tragedy in adventures with Silver Bullet and him.

There is a little Mexican town with a beautiful beach off the side of a bumpy, dusty road north outside the Bahia de Banderas—about twenty minutes via Silver Bullet from Bucerias. The houses along the cliffs are brightly coloured with mosaic-decorated copulas. White, pink, orange, blue, yellow and green plastered privacy walls covered in bougainvillea and other exotic flowers surround the properties but leave the beach side open to the Sea of Cortez. They are homes for rent, small resorts and condominium clusters. Palm trees grow and flourish everywhere, their feather fronds, flutter in the gentle breeze blowing in from the sea. The beach stretches out for a kilometer from a parking area high on a cactus festooned cliff that juts out onto a beach. The cliff is a volcanic tailing of pillow lava that ran into the sea millions of years ago; mosaic tiled stairs descend from the parking lot to the beach that runs south to the jungle, a rocky outcrop of boulders and heaps of broken white coral. The point of land is property that was grabbed by the government and northern investors from the fishing families who lived there for a thousand years.

Ghost crabs scatter about the sand and dive into their burrows when alarmed, while mechanical steel black, green and red, razor-trimmed crabs clatter about on the pillow lava cliffs. Waves crash over them but they keep a foothold. Pelicans cruise the beach like airborne police and black vultures roam for carrion. A few times a year, whales, after completing their life, wash up on the beach. There is plenty of food to go around for the flying and crawling creatures.

This was the place where he bought Bank Robber and the place she got her name; the only name Jonathan remembers her by. They walked the beach and talked about their lives.

"What was life like in North Africa," Jonathan asked. He laid out a bright Mexican blanket.

"Very comfortable," she said, I was never in need of anything. Lot's of money but I don't know how much. Dad never told Mom and I how much we are worth. To him that was something crude—old school—something not mentioned."

"Lucky you, my family always knew how much we had. Sometimes it was not much, other times nothing."

"Your rich now, look where you are," she said.

"Yup, for years I dreamed of this and now it's here," he put his arms around her, "Where are your parents now?"

"They are divorced but still do business together."

"What's the biz?" He let her go.

"Import/export, antiques, fine art and money. The money is secret because it's laundered. That's where I come in. Mom and Dad do the arts and I do Dad's client's currency."

"What do you mean?"

"I work in a bank in North Africa, a bank my father's clients use to launder their cash. I skim of the top when I do the currency exchanges and receivables."

"Christ, isn't that scary. Aren't you afraid of being caught."

"No, not at all, my clients know what I do and they don't mind since they make far more cooperating with me. Let's say we are partners. I don't take much anyway. I am not greedy."

"You shouldn't be telling me this."

"It doesn't matter. What good would it do for you to turn me in? There would be no reward."

"I'm not thinking of anything like that. What does your parents think about what you do?"

"They are divorced. Mom doesn't know what I do and Dad is my lover. That's why they divorced."

Jonathan looked at her in disbelief: "Ah, come now! Your lover?"

"Yes, since I was a young teen."

"Again, maybe we shouldn't talk about such things—incest—bank robbing."

"Very well," she said and stood up and took her shorts and top off and ran into the water. Jonathan stripped down and ran after her. Waves crashed over them. "I've never had a long-term intimate relationship with a man my age," she said with her head just above the waves.

"No boy friends? A woman as beautiful as you? I can hardly believe that."

"Once I enjoyed the company of a good friend but he was mistreated as a child. We were in love but it was too difficult because of our past. We behaved badly, like animals; we decided not to be lovers, just friends. What about you? What was your past like?"

Jonathan shared with her his life with his father who suffered from Post Traumatic Stress Syndrome from World War II: "Mom was a good woman, bought up wealthy only to marry my poor dad. Dad tried to fit into peacetime society but he found it very difficult. He drifted to the end of his life an unhappy soul. He made my mom unhappy and me too—in my younger days. But you know I completed that package of life's passages. I wrapped it up and put it up on the shelf with all my other stuff—good and bad. We have to forgive and let wounds heal in the end."

Bank Robber looked at him curiously as though she didn't quite get what he said. She had a different outlook and agenda, this beauty from North Africa.

"What about women?" she asked sputtering water—a wave hit her in the face.

"Come and gone over the years. Half I can't remember now."

"Was there a special one?"

"Yeah, a crazy lady that was very different from me. I loved her with all I had in me but she became too dangerous."

"Where is she now?"

"Don't know, and don't want to know" and he walked out of the water up the beach to their towels, "Hey, Bank Robber. Do you want to go into the jungle tomorrow?" he shouted back to her.

"Yeah, let's do that," she said laughing, "I like that—Bank Robber—as she walked out of the water to him. He wrapped a towel around her and patted her dry. She pushed her chest out to him: "Are you going to make love to your Bank Robber, Jonathan?"

"Oh, I'm too old for you and you're too beautiful. He bent down and patted her legs dry, "I would fall in love with you and then have to put you on a plane home in a couple of weeks. I would spend the rest of my time in Mexico pulling my hair out. Or spending the rest of my life on a camel wandering North Africa looking for you."

She laughed, quickly kissed him, "You're an attractive old man." She ran back to the water, and dove into the surf. And he thought. That was fast. Make love to you—not on your life—after all the boys you've been through in the village. You're just a little con girl in the tropics. "Oh hell, who knows what to believe and who cares," he whispered and he ran after her.

Beer, Bandits, Cops and Apparitions

Café Bucerias was the place Bank Robber and Jonathan could slip into, put their feet up, drink pop or beer and chat with the inmates—for this was their second home. They ate western and English style food here when they tired of the Mexican fare. The café was a source of information and a resource for emergencies that would come up now and then. The establishment serves as local pub, restaurant, tour guide, merchandise store, property management and anything else that is needed. The cafe was most of all a place with friends and camaraderie, a place full of stories, a place to start adventures.

The premises proper of the cafe is an adobe brick and plaster Spanish-style house converted into a bar with roof extensions jutting out at odd angles strung with Christmas lights, sports memorabilia and pennants. The café's menu postings are a snowdrift of eight and a half by eleven computer generated paper signs fluttering in a breeze created by floor fans. The fan's feet have been removed and the bodies hang at various angles on the ceiling beams like giant wounded insects. Gaudy signs on the street, painted in primary colours, advertise the owner's services and products. The electrical system is a cobweb of extension cords emanating from an over used electrical box whose fuses blow up frequently. Television sets are hung high in the corners with an assortment of recording devices hooked up to two huge satellite dishes on the roof and a cable system that hasn't been invented yet. There is a leaning satellite wired jukebox on the patio dining area that is cable programmed but it plays old tunes since the bar hasn't upgraded its license to play the latest and greatest. It doesn't seem to matter to the clientele.

The café is owned and operated by a fifty year old blond burly soccer player from Liverpool named Wolf who has football games constantly playing on the numerous televisions. He left the bad neighborhoods of Liverpool in the UK behind; the city was too difficult and hard to make a decent living. He fills the bar with his presence and sweats until soaked from working and philosophizing at a constant and frantic pace. He takes full command of his enterprise and runs a tight operation expressing that it's all for his wife and daughter. He is a good man, Wolf—honest and fair.

He told Jonathan and Bank Robber: "If you are entrepreneurial, you can make a living in Mexico; if you aren't then your pay is about five dollars a day—starvation wage. You can never save money so when the time comes to leave Mexico you have to borrow to get out." Many owe Wolf money.

Chickens run free in Bucerias and some have learned to live in trees. They are irritating in the morning at first light and often—all night. The local stores and the cafe have slingshots for sale and with a little practice you can become quite efficient at dispatching or keeping the cockerels away. Wolf uses an air rifle to shoot the local roosters that gather around his house and business. He advises all who are having chicken problems that he has a friend that will do away with the pests for fifty pesos each.

"Want to go up into the hills today?" asked Jonathan over a late breakfast with Bank Robber, "Its just a short drive up the coast to Alta Vista."

Wolf overheard them: "Now Jonathan my friend, don't you go poking your bloody nose around up there. The damn place is dangerous—people disappear. There are dope farms up in those hills—real bad-asses with guns. They'll shoot you and keep your little princess for a while before selling her off to the gypsies." Wolf and Jonathan broke into laughter.

"It's not dangerous—is it—you guys?"

"No, no," Jonathan calmly said, "There won't be a problem," Wolf and Jonathan looked at each other cautiously, "we'll be okay."

Tourists do not go to the hill villages and mountains unless on a supervised adventure tour since up the valley, as Wolf said, is drug country. The special unit of the federal police, a security force that deals only with the extreme, murderers, drug lords and growers, stopped them on the road. They were a dark crew—dressed in black with gold lettering. Huge white teeth smiled menacingly at them. The commander of the group was a large man and appeared to weigh about as much as a small car, his demeanor invoked terror in his subordinates. On a gold plate above his breast pocket was etched Bernarda S. Perez.

"I cannot speak your language." Jonathan said with a giggle.

Commander Perez folded his arms and leaned back on his truck; a subordinate took over asking Jonathan for his driver's license and insurance. The young officer wrote down his name and license number in his black notebook. He returned the documents to Jonathan—Commander Perez said nothing and waved them on. The police knew they were just a couple of tourists out for a joy ride. This would not be the last time Jonathan would run into the commander.

"God, they looked scary!"

"Yeah, those boys in black and gold are there to make arrests or get their payment and share of the goods from the growers. How naive he was, as he would find out. They were also around to protect those coming into the area from bandits, murderers and thieves.

A couple of kilometers past the blockade they stopped at a bleached white high walled, wrought iron gated cemetery filled with beautiful architecture built to house the dead. The little village occupied about two hectares with many generations of local families crowded together. Their lives were spent in the green lush hills and jungles. When they lived they did not travel much and when they did, it was a few miles to another village on a religious holiday, wedding or funeral. This place was something else, quite, beautiful and dignified, full of tradition and ceremony he thought, and he took Robber by the hand.

The graveyard was, ironically, full of life. The jungle moved in below high old deciduous trees and filled the graveyard with yellow, white and red flowers that grew shoulder high, dozens of species of butterflies of all colours and patterns fluttered about. Huge yellow and black bees, Dipper dragonflies, Katydid and Nebraska Cone-head grasshoppers chirped about the place. Great Southern White and Giant Swallowtail butterflies as big as small dinner plates fluttered on delicate wings. Monster-sized mosquitoes buzzed like little fighter planes everywhere and fleas jumped out of the grass to eat Robber and Jonathan. Colorful tropical birds flew in the trees above, they whistled and sang, making a fuss about the intruders in their Eden. Spiders clung to the walls of mausoleums—huge ugly things but they had the right to be there, to eat and be eaten like all the other inhabitants. All the creatures had a place in the food chain. In a mausoleum a black and green rock lizard scurried up a wall out of the way.

"Are there snakes here?" Robber asked.

"Maybe," he said. He did not know—he was a stranger too.

Some of the grave markers were just a few sticks wired together; others were carved granite topped with the caste statuary of the Virgin of Guadalupe. The graves were festooned with artificial wreaths that had faded with time and the sun; some were still in their plastic wrappers. Framed photographs of loved ones, sun bleached and barely discernable were mounted on some of the mausoleums and headstones. They were the faces of lives lived long ago but not forgotten; fore every year the village of the dead would be weeded, painted and adorned with flowers. Food and drink would be consumed as relatives gathered to celebrate their dead relatives during *Day of the Dead*. Those spending eternity in the white painted village have company and visitors, and the view from the cemetery's slopping sides is supreme; a panorama of marijuana, mangos, pastures, cowboys, children, cops, bandits and banana plantations sweep out to the distant azure Sea of Cortez.

They got back into Bullet and drove into the mountains to the village of Alta Vista. There they wandered about discovering themselves and a little beautiful piece of Mexico.

"Tell me about the Virgin, Jonathan."

"Okay, on the way home we'll stop at a place I visited a few years ago. The place will explain it better than I can. We'll visit the apparition of the Virgin of Guadeloupe." They left the hills, drove back to the coast, to an icon and dinner in Sayulita, a fishing village.

They drove through the village and parked at a primitive adobe hut on the hill on the south side; no one was around but the door was open and the inside was ablaze in candle light. They ducked under the overhanging thatched roof and low-beamed door and entered the dirt floored hut into what was, at one time, the kitchen. The home was a tiny little place built of mud and rotten palm fronds. It was separated into two rooms by a tattered bed sheet. A refrigerator and a bed were visible through a tear in the sheet. They stood in silence; he took her hand and whispered to her what he had learned from friends about the Virgin of Guadalupe.

"In December 1531 a poor farmer, Juan Diego, came across a vision on a hill north of Mexico City. He saw a brown skinned Maya/Aztec version of the Virgin Mary glowing before him. The vision commanded Juan to go to the local Bishop and ask that he build a shrine to her on the spot where she stood. Juan did as he was told but the Bishop would have nothing to do with the simple farmer. So Juan went back to the vision and reported that the Bishop refused his request. The vision gave Juan Diego a bundle of roses wrapped in a cloth and told him to go back to the Bishop and try again, and this time give the roses to the Bishop. There were no roses growing in Mexico at the time of the early Spanish occupation and the Bishop was astonished to see them. He was not only surprised by the roses but by an apparition on the wrapping cloth; an image of a dark skinned woman in prayer with a halo above her head. The Bishop ordered the church built and soon others were built throughout Mexico.

"To this day, after five hundred years, the Virgin of Guadalupe is the loved patron saint of all who live in Mexico. The Indigenes, Méstizos, Negros and Creoles adore her because she is dark like them and represents everyone in Mexico—all are to have a place in heaven. She is very important to the culture of the Mexicans she blends the ancient past of Maya and Aztec religions with Christianity. She is the spiritual unifying force of Mexico."

Against a wall fashioned from straw and palm fronds was an altar with pictures, flowers, Bibles, candles, and crosses. In the center was a cookie tray decked out with lights and filigree. On the tray was an image of the Virgin of Guadeloupe, or so people have interpreted the stain.

Jonathan went on: "This apparition appeared one morning about three years ago, when a husband and wife were cooking. When they removed cookies from the tray, the stain appeared. There are other apparitions that have occurred over the years, in most towns and hamlets of Mexico. It seems that anything that looks like the shape of the Virgin becomes an apparition and these are always discovered by the peasant folk, who are extremely poor and whose education is limited or non-existent. Most people in Mexico give their support to the families with apparitions; it instills good and moral values, which are evident everywhere. It's too bad that these values don't filter up to the rich and powerful, where most of Mexico's corruption festers."

The two pilgrims dipped into their pockets and pulled out some paper pesos; rubbed the money on each other's heads for luck and placed the offerings on the altar.

"Let's go home." she said as she leaned against his chest and closed her eyes.

Four Deaths in the Afternoon

Jonathan read the poster on a light pole in the town square of Bucerias:

CORRIDA DE TORO

PLAZA DE TOROS "LA PALOMA"

PUERTO VALLARTA

MIERCOLES A LAS 5:00 P.M.

SENSACIONAL CORRIDA DE TORO CON LOS MATADORES

He entered the bright white plaza, walked across the cobbled courtyard and passed under an immense black metal cutout of a bull. It stared defiantly across Francisco M. Ascencio to the gleaming white cruise ships docked at the marina. He walked toward the stairs that led to the bullring. Before he got there a woman with her daughter in tow screamed and ran into him. A big Mexican held two beautiful Green Iguanas out to them. Mom and daughter had a fit. The father and Jonathan calmed them down; they were soon laughing and wearing the beasts on their shoulders while Dad took pictures.

The family was from San Francisco and they became friends with Jonathan immediately. He was an island of normality to them; they were so far from home. Worried that something like an Iguana could terrify them, he warned them of the events to come and that the bullfights were not a sport but a recreation. The bulls have no chance of surviving the afternoon even if the matador gets injured and cannot continue. The bull would be killed and butchered out of sight, behind the stands. They had no idea that they would experience four deaths in the afternoon. They were naive and thought that if the bull did a good job he would be set free to live a happy life, smelling daisies under a fig tree in some beautiful field like a cartoon character from their childhood. They would sit beside him the entire event.

At four thirty the band struck up in the courtyard; sixteen Mexicans in their dress whites played drums, flutes, guitars, trumpets and trombones in a very tinny lively gay Spanish style full of joy and celebration. Colorful people poured into the whitewashed courtyard. Hawkers carried buckets of beer and shouted, Viva Mexico! Others hawked pistachio nuts, t-shirts and posters. The band blasted for twenty-five minutes as a thousand spectators took their seats. The San Franciscan family and Jonathan sat below the band and the judges on the shady side of the ring. Latecomers would be in the sun side. The arena was painted white and the seats were a light gray; down on the sand between the bulls, matadors and assistants a blood red hoarding of heavy timbers formed a ring of protection.

There was a diversity of people in the audience; young couples perhaps newlyweds off the cruise ships; boisterous white boys sloshing back beer, and single girls attracted by the testosterone—their breasts and thighs strained against their clothing. Some middle aged and older couples had the look of bullring experience in their demeanor. And then there were the young Mexicans; beautiful men and women that floated and pranced into the arena, some of the women carried flowers to throw to their favorite matadors. There were a few older Mexican men who looked like they owned the place or the bulls. Everyone in the arena was bright and beautiful in the hot blazing sun; all chattered and made themselves comfortable.

A few minutes to the hour the judges entered the bullring followed by the band—they took their places. A trumpet player took a position on the opposite side of the ring, he announced with a blast the pageant would begin. The trumpet solo was very lonely, dramatic and impressive. The sound of a distant trumpet touches the soul; the sound is the bull so far from all of them, lonely, from another world, another time. There was pride, power and sadness in that trumpet's sound and it filled the arena.

The stage for the entrance of the participants was set. Large red doors in the hoarding swung open and in walked four matadors with their right hands over their hearts. Their assistants, bandoleers and horsemen, followed the matadors. And entering last was the maintenance crew with a Belgian horse and harness. Hung from the rafters at the back of the entrance to the arena were pulleys and other gear that would come into play later in the day. They were hidden and seen only when the doors were open.

The parade went on with great fanfare: the blast of horns and drums and the roar of the bloodthirsty audience. Everyone took their positions behind the heavy red wooden hoarding of the ring; the matadors checked their equipment and appearance. The more senior matadors and family members assured the fighters that they would do well in the event. All eyes behind the hoarding looked up to the judges for the signal to start. The judges nodded their approval, a metal door opened and a massive, ferocious, black bull charged into the ring. The audience sucked the air right out of the bullring as they gasped in anticipation.

The bullfight is one of very few events to start on time and it was five o'clock, time for the first Lidia, or first encounter to begin. On the side of the first bull was 76 painted in white—numbered for accounting purposes. Like all bulls that come to the ring he was four years old, five hundred kilos and one and a half meters at the shoulders; these bulls are strong for their breed because of the massive neck and shoulder muscles. 76 had spent most of his days quietly and undisturbed with others of his kind on twenty five thousand hectares on the plains of Guanajuato. He was never treated badly nor had any reason to fear for his safety but inside him were ferocious genes passed down to him. His heritage had brought him to this place and the matador that would kill him. The breed and genes of these bulls would not survive without the bullfights of the world. He is just too vicious a beast to have around. 76, full of arrogance, charged around the ring after the matador's assistants who displayed their capes to him.

The bullfight is in three parts: the stabs by men with lances on horseback, the bandoleers with knifed tipped sticks and the matador and his sword. The matador, in his beautiful white and gold suit of lights, assessed his bull's temperament from the hoarding. He watched noting his unique movements. Knowing such things would keep the matador alive. The matador came into the ring and performed the cape maneuver with number 76 and they got to know each other as they moved about. This went on for some time and the audience clapped and shouted, Ole! at the appropriate moment and Mom and Dad and the kids were delighted. Even though there was a noticeable trickle of blood running down 76's leg from a tag with a small six-inch flag imbedded in his shoulder muscles.

The matador went behind the hoarding and the gates opened to a blast of horns and in rode two picadors to perform the stabs. Their horses were blindfolded and draped in heavy leather armor; the riders wore stainless steel armor on their legs and feet. They carried lances with short knives at the business ends. 76 charged the first horse; diving into its side he lifted him into the air. The horse frothed at the mouth and screamed in fear. He was unaware of what was bothering him. The lance blade went into 76's back a short distance and severed his neck muscles. He bellowed and roared—his heart rate pounding, he pumped thick blood out of his wound. 76's head was now lowered and he was unable to raise it with much force. The horsemen were satisfied with the situation and left the ring and 76 to the matador who signaled for his assistants to place the banderillas. Their weapons were six; twenty-six inch sticks coloured with paper frills with short barbs. The assistants held the banderillas above their heads, ran to the bull, and between the bull's horns, drove the barbs into the bull's back. All six were placed in the shoulders—two at a time. 76 now became enraged, shaking loose some of the banderillas. He frothed at the mouth and was bleeding badly from his back.

The audience could see the heart pump the blood out of him and down his flanks where it coagulated in rivers and stained the sand of the ring. Jonathan turned to the San Franciscan family and they were white and silent; the girls had tears running down their cheeks. There was a strange look of fascination on their faces.

Number 76 was a celebration as he waited in the ring and the matador raised his hat to the judges for approval for the third of death—the final act. Approval was given and the matador threw his hat onto the sand. The bull and matador jostled with each other for a few moments, but not for long. The bull's head drooped, the matador raised his sword and lunged between the horns and delivered the killing thrust between the shoulder blades and down through 76's body. Blood bubbled and gushed across the back of the bull that bellowed with rage throwing up his stomach contents and spurting blood and saliva from his mouth. The bull accepted his fate and the life drained from him. The matador's assistants entered with capes. 76 charged back and forth between them in a last gesture of defiance but the sword cut his insides to shreds from the movements orchestrated by the assistants. His legs buckled and he collapsed but kept his head raised. An assistant quickly moved in with a short knife and cut 76's spinal cord at the base of the skull. 76 died—the encounter was over. For a moment the crowd fell silent.

The matador bowed to the bull and to the audience who applauded and cheered him for the quick and efficient manner in which he performed his art. The judges also approved and before 76 left the ring his ears were cut off and presented with hugs to the matador who promptly threw them to a woman in the audience. The horse with a harness, came in and dragged 76 away. The clean up crew came on and cleaned and raked the blood from the sand while the band blasted on and Jonathan bought beer and pistachio nuts. Half of the audience left in shock.

For some this was too much, they left the bullring—some crying. Those who act so tough and dispassionate towards what they are about to witness are usually the first to leave. Others, like the San Franciscan family, learn about this ancient ritualistic encounter between man and beast and go away with a new appreciation of life and death.

The second bull was number 73, a black and gray beast and events did not go well. The matador, in his blue and white suit, at the moment of truth could not kill him on the first lunge so his assistants had to retrieve his sword out of the bull three times. The bull refused to go down and the crowd got very angry and yelled at the matador to finish. Finally 73 dropped and in came the horse and harness to drag him out of the ring but the horse spooked and the harness tangled in the horse's legs. The crew tried its best to straighten things out but each time the horse could not handle the situation and the crowd stood and jeered and the band blasted away. A pickup truck came into the ring and number 73 was dragged out. The audience yelled, Toro, Toro, Toro, for him but he could not hear them.

The third bull was number 78, his matador was dashing in his white, green and gold suit of lights. He was skinny kid, about sixty-five kilos, who handled himself gracefully and with a look of compassion on his face for his bull. A bad incident occurred when, during an encounter, he moved too close to the horns and was thrown on top of the bull. He slid down its back and onto the sand; the audience was on its feet in anticipation of the matador's death. He was covered with 78's blood. The assistants immediately distracted the bull and the matador retreated to the red hoarding to be counseled by his mentors. They offered him rags to wipe the blood away but he would have none of that and strode back into the fray with 78. He finally killed him with one thrust of the sword.

The matador was visibly shaken; fear was in his eyes and the boy, whom he really was, showed on his face. The pickup drove into the ring and dragged 78 away. The cleanup crew came on and did its business.

The fourth encounter was the wildest of all. 75 charged into the ring and jumped over the hoarding into the aisle that the matadors and assistants use. They jumped into the ring out of the way of the raging bull that dug his horns into the equipment and tossed it into the air. The crowd was on its feet cheering and singing, Toro, Toro, Toro! The bull made a mess but was led back into the ring. The matador had a monumental task ahead of him and fear showed on his young face. Twice he was thrown into the air and he limped during the rest of his time with 75 but alas, it was all over soon enough and number 75 was dragged out by the pickup. Four deaths in the afternoon had ended.

By the end of the fourth bull it was dark and Jonathan said goodbye to the San Franciscan family who said how much they enjoyed the whole spectacle. The young girl who was terrified at the sight of the Iguanas and cried for the first bull was so excited about the event that, "...she couldn't wait to get back to school and tell her friends what she had seen."

Downstairs in the Bullring's courtyard the matadors assembled to be congratulated by friends and family. They all looked so young and very beautiful in their suits of lights. Some had not washed the blood from the bodies; they displayed their signs of courage. They were all courageous that day—matadors and bulls. Their families beamed with pride. The young girls gathered around them and giggled and had their pictures taken with their favorite matador. Bank Robber would have loved this part of the bullfights and he wished she were there on his arm witnessing this other culture—this strange celebration of man and beast. He missed her.

He made his way out of the bullring and walked down the road to Silver Bullet. He passed the service entrance to the ring and a large steel door was open. In the dim light he could see a black figure of a bull being hoisted by pulleys—figures milled around him. It was 75 about to be prepared for the market tomorrow. A young man moved out of the dark, looked at Jonathan, and slowly closed the iron door.

San Sebastian

Bank Robber and Jonathan went many places in the states of Nayarit and Jalisco. Swimming and bodysurfing at Sayulita and Higuera Blanca and exploring the little villages high in the dope growing country of Alta Vista were their adventures. Wherever they went in the hills, beautiful dark people came out of their homes to stare at the strange couple. Women proudly displayed their babies to them. Silver Bullet could get them into private places. Naked, they swam in the rivers and streams of the jungles in the backcountry of the Bahia de Banderas.

They agreed to be good company and would try to keep it that way. She went to places in the physical and spiritual world with him and her young mind ate everything up especially the things he told her about his past experiences. She loved his stories even though she would say he was—full of crap. The heat of sexual desire between them became intense at times especially when they slept in the same bed together. He understood that she felt safe and confident with him. He was old and had nothing to hide—she trusted and loved him.

It is fifty-one kilometers from Puerto Vallarta to San Sebastian but it takes three and a half hours to reach it by Jeep. Bank Robber and Jonathan set out early one morning; they did a maintenance check on Bullet and gassed up at the local Pemex station in Bucerias. The right front tire was a little low on air so he gave it a boost with the air pump and the radiator's pipe work was a little damp but that did not worry him. They rolled down the highway 200 and caught the road east at the end of the Puerto Vallarta Airport runway to San Sebastian. The temperature was in the nineties and the humidity was appalling so they kept their clothing to a minimum: sandals, shorts and his gaudy Hawaiian shirts. Silver Bullet's canvas top shaded them from the sun; regardless they would both be drenched with sweat in no time as the morning sunburned relentlessly. They drove through Las Juntas, Ixtapa and arrived in the square and market of Las Palmas where he bought food and water.

Standing between some market stalls was a very old withered woman dressed in black, an embroidered shawl partially covered her head and wrinkled face. She was respectfully begging and he gave her a few pesos to ward off any bad luck or curses. She smiled her approval and he sensed a look of remembrance in her face as her eyes roamed over Robber's body.

Across the street from the market was a double bell tower cathedral of terra cotta brick. Baroque, filigree wrought iron bar work protected the windows and doors. Tall spiked iron fencing and gates cordoned of the front courtyard. In front of the cathedral on the busy main street waited a funeral hearse and two white pickup trucks filled with flowers. Holding hands for reassurance, they were strangers in this place; they entered the edifice and quietly watched the proceedings. It was the end of the service, the Mexican folk wheeled the coffin down the aisle and at the door eight husky men hoisted it onto their shoulders. A ten-piece band of drums, guitars, sousaphones and tubas started up a funeral dirge. There were many tears as the coffin was loaded into the hearse and as it moved out, the traffic on the road backed up to let the procession through. A cowboy on horseback carried a rooster symbolizing the deceased's hobby or business with cock fighting. Whoever it was that was being taken to his last resting place had many relatives, evident by the tearful but joyous procession.

They returned to Bullet and went their way. A few miles down the dirt road they came upon a white and flower-festooned cemetery in the middle of a cornfield. He pulled Bullet into the dusty parking lot; he was excited because he wanted to tell Robber a story about the Day of the Dead and how it is celebrated in Mexico. Alas, the hearse, band, relatives, backhoe and flower truck arrived. Faces stared at them, as white folk are not usually around these country parts of Mexico, let alone attending a funeral so deep in the farmlands of Nayarit. In respect for the family, they left and drove east to the jungles and mountains.

Bullet and her cargo followed the beautiful Valle de Banderas through tiny communities, crossing rivers and deep ditches, the road became rougher as it rose into the foothills and the jungles of the tropical deciduous forest. This bioclimatic zone is host to an enormous variety of wild vegetation: hydromorphic fig, lianas, orchids, acacia, mesquite and Colima palm. Entangled in all the abundant rich plants are red, orange, purple, pink and white flower covered vines. They hang dozens of meters down the cliff faces to the valley floor, covering bushes and trees that turned the scene into an old Tarzan movie poster. Robber, the thick green jungle and Jonathan sweated in the heat and humidity.

They were in the Sierra Madre Occidental where mountain lions, jaguars, coyotes, ocelot, margay, jaguarondi, mule deer, rabbits and rodents make a living. The big cats are rare and since they are night creatures they are never seen. Beautiful hawks, eagles, toucans, macaws, parrots and parakeets thrive in the jungle canopy and high overhead are graceful frigate birds and turkey vultures. Lizards and snakes abound in the jungle undergrowth. On the way up a canyon a big fat black iguana ran in front of Silver Bullet, it darted up a tree only to jump off into the bushes as there was another iguana in the same tree that was furiously bobbing his head. He was ready to fight for his territory. Robber squealed with delight.

The insects were big and nasty, there were huge colourful spiders with abdomens as big as your thumb and legs the length of your outstretched fingers. Their massive web orbs thrown five meters from tree to tree can catch a small hummingbird. Bank Robber and Jonathan rubbed their bodies with insect repellent since mosquitoes; flesh-eating flies and fleas were plentiful.

The jungle rose in elevation for a few thousand meters to the semi desert grasslands. The area was prime habitat for people, coffee, tobacco, cattle and the cultivation of blue agave for the distillation of Tequila. Big Brahma bulls stood in the middle of the road just to look and stare at the Bullet; however, they soon got bored and moved on. The bulls were gentle animals, not like the ones from the bullring.

As the road became steeper, rougher and narrower he put Bullet into four-wheel drive and they clawed and bounced their way over mud banks and rivers. They rapidly gathered altitude a few thousand meters up the Sierra Madre. The road was so narrow in places the body of Bullet rubbed the cliff face. "This is nuts!" Jonathan said. They looked down into a landscape completely engulfed in jungle a hundred meters or more below. Robber and he would disappear from the face of the earth if the Jeep were to roll to the bottom of the canyon. No one would know for days they were missing, as neither of them told anyone where they were going. The jungle would soon claim them; those great big spiders would crawl through their eye sockets. Robber was very casual about all this, half naked, feet up on the dash, chewing on beef jerky, soaking wet, not wearing her seat belt and quite pleased at the thought that they could disappear. She was the epitome of no fear, a woman of adventure, young and romantic. He had known many others like Robber in his life for most of his time has been in bachelorhood.

They were hungry and wet from the heat and humidity—they pulled over onto an outcrop used for passing vehicles. Lunch was to be on a high precipice overlooking canyons and jungles with all their beauty and terror. They could see for many kilometers across the foothills and mountains and the cliffs that dropped down into rivers of rapids and waterfalls—green, blue, lush, wet and misty.

Bank Robber, chewing on beef jerky, rambled on about her future plans of going back to university, getting a job, getting rich and hiring Gringo Jonathan Tours via Silver Bullet, to take her to exotic places. They laughed at the possibilities and he apologized that he would have to decline any such deal. Fortunately they didn't talk too much about exactly what university or where she came from in North Africa and he made it clear he didn't want any more information than he already had. He didn't even know her last name. She had his email address and he didn't know if that was wise or not.

She held his hand when he wasn't changing gears, "You've been to many places and done a lot of things in your life because you're old—"

"Thanks."

"No—no—that's not derogatory or anything like that! It's just that I want to experience the things you've done. Where should I go?"

"That's up to you honey, don't rush your life. You don't know it yet but coming here you have started one of the many journeys of a new life.

Hey, you're only twenty-six. There is a passionate place in the world for you out there, keep your head up and your eyes open. In time you will come upon it and it will thrill and awe you, a place you will be become familiar with, remember, and be close to forever. It's like a person whose passion is hiking or mountain climbing. They might want to hike the trail from Katmandu to base camp on Mount Everest, or divers with a love for marine life might want to explore the reefs off the Yucatan. For me it was Florence, Italy."

"Why there?"

"I'm an artist and in Florence there is some of the great art of the world and parked up here on this dirt road overlooking the jungle reminds me of a place in Florence that also overlooks a magnificent scene. I was there a few years ago on a pilgrimage, as a student in art school, I promised I would take and I did. Even if it was forty years later"

"A jungle in Florence?" she laughed.

"Yeah, sort of," he said, "the jungle of the city's buildings are on narrow streets where you can get lost. The city is beautiful architecturally and filled with wonderful art and ghosts. As a matter of fact, you see it all from a parking lot just like this little piece of dirt right here. Down there in the jungle are insects, plants and animals building homes for their young; architecture of bird's nests, bee hives, mud casings in trees for ant colonies, termite mounds, bat caves, tangled trees and epiphytic plants living off each other in a symbiotic relationship—a thriving living organic mass. All those living organisms are building a natural city for themselves under the hot sun and fed by summer rains. Some trees are fortified with spikes over their trunks, some ooze a poisonous sap that can become an irritating rash if touched; spiders, ants and snakes lurk about full of poisonous fangs and barbs; the big cats kill with claws and fangs. All the life down there is guarding its own little spot on this earth and each has a special place in the food chain—all eventually becoming food for others.

"So what was it you saw in Florence?" she said as she bit into an orange.

"Well, honey, I spent an incredible time there. It's a Mecca for art lovers; artists must visit Florence sometime in their lives. One day in particular I walked in the footsteps of intellectually great and powerful people. I walked among Renaissance men and women: Michelangelo Buonarroti, Lorenzo de Medici, Leonardo da Vinci, Giotto di Bondone, Cimabue, Masaccio, Botticelli—

"Whoa, enough! Too much, I don't know those guy—"

"Sorry, they are just a few of the famous that left pieces of themselves in that fantastic city." He reached behind him and bought out and orange and water bottle from his backpack. "Like the sweat on me now, they were in my shoes and my clothes. I could feel them all around and walking through me. Pampered, condemned, worshipped and revered they were the celebrities of their time. These citizens of Italy were giants of history; these were the tigers and lions of the day, the top of the food chain in old Florence. The way we look at the world today, the way we judge the guilt and innocence of others, socially and politically, has been passed down to us from Renaissance society, like it or not. These people made something with their hands and hearts and put their names to it— they will live forever.

"Out of the darkness comes light; Machiavelli's work The Prince has always been a condemned and hated work but after you read it you know how to screw someone politically or, on the other hand, you recognize when someone is screwing you. He was unlike Savonarola who denounced oratory and poetry as the devils work. They burned him. The closer you get to knowing and positioning where you are in the world; the better you do in the food chain."

"You talk like my dad sometimes. He knows about the world to," Robber said practically in his lap—biting into an apple.

"Did you wash that with some bottled water?" Jonathan inquired pointing to the apple.

"No!" she replied.

"Stupid," and he handed her his water bottle, "Wash it. It's time for us to move on."

"Just a minute please," and Robber jumped out of her seat and squatted behind the Jeep, "there let's go," she said on her return, "thanks for the stories Jonathan," and she leaned over and buried her face in the flesh of his bare arm, "you smell good," and in the same breath, "do you do drugs?"

"When I was young I experimented like most of my generation. Why do you ask?"

"Your imagination is very vivid."

"I think sometimes that's my malaria drugs speaking."

"What!" and she sat up in her seat and looked at him, "what do you mean?"

"I was in Panama a few years ago on a trip. I took malaria pills once a week for two months. There is a ban on those pharmaceuticals now. Anyway, I had hallucinations. I'd lay in bed in the morning trying to figure out if I was awake, asleep or dead—it was weird, totally irrational. Ever since those pills, my brain has been a little odd."

"You're not dangerous—are you?"

"But of course," and he reached over and squeezed her thigh and gave out a hollow laugh. She screamed, giggled, squirmed and ripped on a chunk of beef jerky.

They drove across the plateau, the jungle was behind them and they saw agave farms, Brahma bulls, chickens, and wild-eyed Mexican men and boys. Along the road was the stench of rotting garbage, dogs and animals.

They arrived at a small town ten kilometers before San Sebastian, a service center for vehicles that maintain the roads through the jungle and mountains. They stopped and asked six beer-drinking men lounging in an open-air cantina for assistance to fill the tire that was low. The boys had chickens nestled on their laps; fighting cocks that they stroked affectionately. Blank stares from big drunk, drugged eyes and angry faces came back at them followed by some snickers, whispers and giggles. The boys were having fun at Robber and Jonathan's expense. One of them in filthy coveralls with an ugly scare across the left side of his mouth, acted like the leader of the group. He carried a fighting cock under his arm—it had crapped down one leg of his pants. The group walked over to the Jeep stroking their chickens and talking in Spanish.

Jonathan had seen this look, a look of jealousy toward gringos for what they possess and the lifestyle they enjoy in a far away place—a place forbidden to them. He reached down between the seats to check if his steering wheel security bar was there in case he needed it to fight them off—it was. He wasn't scared of the Mexicans; he may be old but he was fit and agile as a deer and they were drunk. If they didn't have guns he could take them easily. He knew what they were thinking; what was this older gringo doing up here in a Jeep with a young half naked woman sucking on pop and chewing beef jerky? To break the tension she reached over and took Jonathan's head in her hands and kissed him hard on the lips. The act intimidated the Mexicans—public affection is not common. It is seen on beaches and in bars but not in some small little town up in the mountains. They were not going to get any cooperation from these mountain men so he rammed Bullet into first gear, waved goodbye and they were gone—bumping across the plateau, laughing all the way. In the rearview mirror he saw the Mexicans shouting obscenities, laughing and throwing their chickens in the air.

Soon they were driving on a cobbled road into the little town of San Sebastian. It was postcard perfect right down to the folks hanging around the town square in their cowboy hats, big belt buckles, jeans and boots. Their horses were tethered to the handrails of the town hall's veranda. Jonathan parked beside them. He checked the tire and it was okay for now but he discovered the radiator was leaking. They went to explore the old village.

San Sebastian del Oeste (Saint Sebastian of the West) is a simple hamlet of whitewashed stucco adobe buildings, ochre terra cotta-tiled roofs, and wrought iron secured windows and doors. The church bell tower above the cathedral on the town square dominates the one and two story architecture. The streets are cobbled and lined with stone fencing covered with dark green algae. The scene reminded Jonathan of the small villages in Europe, and rightly so, as San Sebastian is a Spanish colonial town.

He had read in his guidebooks: for thousands of years this area was known as Ostoticpac, which means hollow in the highlands. The Texquines, a Nahuatl Aztec speaking people who grew cotton, corn and vegetables, and mind gold and silver in the hills flourished here. In the sixteenth century the Spanish renegade Nunu de Guzman robbed, killed and raped the peaceful Indians. As in the rest of Mexico the indigenous population died by the millions from overwork and the white man's diseases. Those who survived and generations to come, became slaves for the next three hundred years raising cattle, working the mines and farms, and making the Spanish rich and greedy. After the Revolution of Independence from Spain, dreamers came from around the world. They sought gold and silver until the mines played out and now only a thousand or so inhabit this beautiful colonial town nestled in the Sierra Madras.

Bank Robber and Jonathan walked hand in hand; she leaned against him whenever she had the opportunity, and glanced lovingly at him with dark eyes—the place and time were starting to overcome her. They had a lazy and peaceful time up in the mountains. They wandered the winding streets and explored the little village, remote from the modern world that is in such chaos.

They watched a young dark-skinned mom give her plump round babies a bath in an enamel basin on the front porch of her home, dogs slept nearby, hens and roosters made a living in the dirt squawking and complaining and fat white turkeys gobbled and clawed. Over a rock wall a donkey stared and snorted his approval, he was just happy to watch the goings on.

They listened and managed to interpret a conversation of the farmers and cowboys in front of the Municipal hall who discussed the latest news about some piece of equipment that is on order to pump water to a nearby agave field. The new piece will work much better than the one they bought eighty years ago. Cautiously others whispered about a cockfight to be held in a nearby town. Young girls and boys gathered in the streets giggling and teasing each other, repeating the game of love that has played here generation after generation. No one rushes in San Sebastian; the days are long with not much to do but take in the beauty and rhythm of life.

Robber was overcome, she said, "Will you be here for me if I call for you? I want to be that woman we saw with her babies and animals. But with your babies."

He didn't answer.

A Visit with Montezuma

Jonathan liked Bank Robber because there was a lot about her that was in him—a fighter with no tolerance for mediocrity and boredom. He felt her harshness when they were confronted by the Mexican boys; the adrenalin pumped, he felt they were a unit—partners—soul buddies and when she kissed him he felt true affection and passion from her. Since he was older he was in control of his life, not so for Robber who was always careless about sex, her eating habits and cleanliness—the major things that can screw you up. He reminded her to wash her hands before eating and to watch what she ate. Eating off carts in the street is fine for Mexicans who have built up a tolerance for the parasites and bacteria that abound. It's different for white folk from the north. Montezuma's revenge is true and he hits thousands daily, when right off the plane they become run down from too much drinking and eating spicy cuisine. Robber did not listen to Jonathan's advice; she treated the criticisms as fatherly, ate bad food and didn't wash before she ate. She got angry at his patronizing ways about her bad habits.

They had spent the day wandering in the little town of San Sebastian, ate the local cuisine, took pictures and drank pop and water. Early in the evening Jonathan checked them into a hotel on the corner of the central plaza. They went to their room.

"Jonathan, I'm tired and my stomach is a little upset—I'm going to bed."

"Oh Jees, I hope you're not sick—can I get you anything—"

"No, you go and have a beer—find yourself a woman."

"Are you sure—?"

"Yeah! Get out of here."

"Okay, I'm off for a few beers. I won't be late."

On the way out he thought and giggled, he needed to be away from this beautiful, hot, sweat covered, practically naked young woman that was constantly coming on to him. He thanked God his hormones were not raging as they were in his youth. On the other hand, the gods of Mexico would be upset with him for not jumping in.

At the local cantina he made friends with the bar owner, Emilio, who spoke very good English. He had learned the language of commerce down on the coast when he worked in a timeshare operation. Emilio introduced Jonathan to the leathery cowboy locals; some could speak just a few words of English. He was soon bored of them, as it was a struggle to communicate and he found himself buying beer for everyone. He decided to go back to the hotel. He stopped at a grocery store next door to the bar and bought a twelve-pack of beer. The town was now dark. Only the stars, moon and Quetzalcoatl lit the streets.

He entered the hotel quietly; the night caretaker was asleep behind the front desk. Up the stairs to their room he crept and rolling down the hall came a terrible stench. The door to their room was ajar; he entered quietly thinking she would be asleep but he found her kneeling on the floor naked and violently throwing up. She had defecated everywhere; over the bed sheets, pillowcases, floor, walls leading to the bathroom and everywhere in the bathroom. It was a terrible stinking mess and he retched but managed not to vomit. He helped her to the toilet, which she hugged like a long lost buddy. He placed a towel under her to make her comfortable and went next door of the hotel to the drug store—waking up the caretaker on the way. It was closing for the night but he managed to get the attention of the sales woman, who lived in the back, by banging on the door. She came out in her nightgown grudgingly. He purchased a bottle of pink medicine, aspirin and anti-diarrhea—remedies to plug both ends and relieve the pain for poor Robber. He rushed back to the hotel to find she had crawled back to the bedroom after turning herself inside out.

"For God's sake woman!" he whispered harshly at her in frustration, "I told you, I told you!" Gently he moved her back into the bathroom and she threw up on him from both ends. He sat on the floor and wondered what the hell to do next—he was drunk and tired. He waited a few moments to catch his breath then, after empting his pockets, he got them both into the shower. He washed his clothes while they were still on. Fortunately all he had on was shorts, underwear and a t-shirt that would easily dry by morning—he thought. · Her clothes were draped neatly on a rattan and leather chair in the bedroom—clean. He sat in the warm shower with delirious Robber until the water ran cold and turned it off.

"You funny girl, I told you so," he said and gently wiped the hair from her eyes.

"Go to hell!" she slurred, hugging him close.

"Now don't go anywhere. I've got to clean up the mess," he laughed at that statement.

After pulling himself from her he wrapped her in a towel. Leaving her in the shower stall he stripped, wrapped himself in a towel and went downstairs for fresh bedding.

The caretaker was not pleased with him for waking him up but he cooperated.

"Loco gringo," he muttered as he went into the back of the lobby and slammed the door.

Returning to the room he remade the bed and let Robber sit in the bathroom for the next hour with a towel around her. He read his tour guide and consulted his maps for the following day's journey.

An hour went by and Robber seemed to have emptied herself. He made her drink a few gulps of the pink stuff; the anti-diarrhea and aspirin she would need in the morning. In her fevered state she protested everything. She sat shivering in the shower stall raging at him.

"You asshole! You don't get it, do you, Jonathan—do you?" she said accusingly. Her red bloodshot eyes glared up at him; her wet black hair pasted strands across her face, down her shoulders and breasts. Her face was red and swollen and her mouth, a wet menacing mess. She was not the beautiful young affectionate woman of a few hours ago.

"What honey?" he said innocently, keeping back the laughter. He was not going to get into an argument with this creature that he had not seen before.

"I have always done my own thing. You didn't understand anything I've said to you! You've been acting like my father! My father didn't fuck me, I fucked him!" With that said, she giggled and broke into laughter.

Jonathan felt naive, for a moment the raging upset him, it made him feel stupid so he dismissed it and attributed it to her condition. She laughed and mumbled more about her father but it was too garbled for him to make out. He felt sorry for her but couldn't help but break into laughter, suddenly it sounded so comical. Sometimes a bad situation can be that way. She was delirious but alive and getting stronger. Tough little girl, he thought and he packed her up in his arms like a sack of flour and put her to bed. He stuffed a towel between her legs and one under her head to protect the pillows and sheets in case an attack came on. He cleaned the floor of excrement with the soiled sheets and pillowcases and put them in the shower and gave them a rough wash. He opened the window and turned on the overhead fan. The room was relatively clean, in order and the smell going away—except for her bad breath. A sweaty feverish Bank Robber had settled down. Still a bit delirious from the fever, she rocked her head back and forth, kicked the towels and sheets away and with her eyes almost closed, she asked him for a story.

"Tell me about that Quatso - Quat—you know—that mythological God you keep talking about," she slurred.

"Quetzalcoatl?" he said.

"Yeah, that guy—God."

He carefully laid her clothes neatly on the floor and made himself comfortable in the rattan and leather chair. With a crack and fizz he opened a beer and began a bedtime story for Robber. She lay naked and squirming, taunting him—he turned the chair to face the window.

"Quetzalcoatl was first a Toltec, human, a mortal King who walked the earth a thousand years ago. Of great intelligence, he was a benevolent leader of men and one who did not approve of ceremonial human sacrifice that was a common practice—"

"Boring!" she groaned.

Jonathan went on: "He preferred the sacrifice of butterflies and reptiles. Like all mortals he could sin and Quetzalcoatl did. He had an incestuous relationship with his sister that he was coerced into by a crowd of evil priests. He banished himself from *The World* and left on a boat of serpents on the ocean to the east, never to be seen again. But it is rumored he will return after a thousand years, perhaps in 2012 when we will all die—"

"What do you mean—when we all die?"

"That's the end of the Maya/Aztec calendar," he replied in a matter-of-fact tone, "the end of the world."

"Oh—oh—I feel like shit," she groaned.

"His last words were like many of the persecuted gods of the ancient and modern world, *I will return*. Legends grew over the entire country around this man and the indigena nations turned him into a God and called him by many different names—"

"I don't know if I will return," she groaned.

"The temple dedicated to Quetzalcoatl built in three hundred BC in Teotihuacán is one of the most beautiful in Mexico. It is covered with huge stone feathered serpent heads with menacing fangs and flower petals surround them like collars of sunrays. Quetzalcoatl is revered to this day in Mexico as the most loved deity of the ancient gods. The brightest star, the one we know as Venus, is Quetzalcoatl. See that one out there—that star," he said, and pointed out the window into the western sky. "That's him—he's looking for a way home." She attempted to get up to see but fell back onto the bed.

"Will he ever return?" she asked and she threw up a pink mess into a towel, "sorry."

He replied: "Some say he did return in the form of the Spanish army that decimated *The World* in 1519; the year of a Great Cycle in the Maya/Aztec calendar. Some believe he is still out there struggling to get home from his adventures in the far corners of the earth and sky. He is everywhere: in the streets, in the stones, in the trees and inside the hearts of you and me. What will he do on his return? Well..."

She was asleep, snoring loudly and he was exhausted. He removed the soiled towel, draped fresh ones on her and climbed in, clothed, beside her; pulled the sheets over them and fell into dreamland. He awoke a few hours later, jarred from sleep by a dog crying and barking in bed with them: "Damn malaria drugs he muttered—the dog went away.

He was awake and it was past one on his Mexican Rolex. He opened a beer and made himself comfortable in the rattan and leather chair, his feet up on the bed and he watched his naked friend sleep deeply. She would be fine by morning, knowing her, he mused—she was a tough little nut. She had thrown the sheets and towels from her and she lay in the light of Quetzalcoatl and the basket moon beaming in through the west facing, iron barred window behind him. She was Francisco Goya's *Naked Maja*; she had the long neck of a Modigliani woman; the firm rock breasts and belly of a fine Rodin; the stubby high arched feet from Picasso's *Guernica* and

Courbet's *The Origin of the World* glowed between her thighs. The light shone across her body, the shadows of the iron bars held her against the white bed sheets. She was beautiful and he remembered his girl friend, Tula, of long ago and the times he had spent sitting in the moonlight looking at what he loved and cherished. If it was possible he would love this woman also but his youthful years had passed that her energy and youth would demand. She would belong to another some day and have his babies and grow old. He knew he would be long dead and forgotten by the time she had grandchildren. If he was lucky he would have someone in his old age but he was not worried or in any hurry to fill that gap. There are more beers, adventures, robbers, bandits and magical places like Mexico to explore before he joins Quetzalcoatl. He yawned, sighed, stripped and climbed into bed. He held Robber's naked body next to his. He slept and dreamt of giants painting the ceiling of the Sistine Chapel.

The morning sun climbed over the craggy eastern Sierra Madras and shone down on the village and a tired haggard Jonathan. His clothes were wrinkled and still damp—Robber's were clean and fresh.

"It won't happen again," she apologized, "I've learned my lesson and I'll watch what I eat from now on," faking a whimper, "did I say anything about my dad last night?"

He laughed and leaned against his backpack in the gutter in front of the hotel and said: "Why don't you have some kind of hangover—or something? For me it takes days to get over what you went through and I get skinny doing it. Why is it you look like that and I'm looking like this?" as he pulled on his wrinkled shirt.

"What did I say about my dad?" she said with urgency.

"Just that you loved him, honey—just that you loved him. Now let's go for breakfast." he gently replied, struggled to his feet and took her hand.

His clothing would straighten out in the heat and humidity, and he would find his energy after a breakfast of scrambled eggs, bacon and coffee at the local pub. Robber was empty and starving, she inhaled the same breakfast but with eggs sunny.

They spent a few morning hours in San Sebastian wandering the streets and alleys before they headed down the dusty road to Compostela and to the Valleys of Volcanoes. He loved to tell stories like those he had told of Quetzalcoatl and Robber loved to hear them. They contained true facts about the real world; the same method the ancients used to pass on their knowledge. He embellished his a little.

"2012 is the end of history here in Mexico and maybe the world," he said.

"What do you mean by the end of the world?"

"As I told you last night. You probably don't remember; the calendar ends that year—there is nothing beyond 2012. Do you want to know what is going to happen?"

"Yeah, give me the bull."

As they roared and bumped across the plateau towards the volcanoes, Jonathan told a sad story of a gentle loving Mexican family who live in the future:

"Romero Diaz was sitting at his desk when a red flashing message was broadcast on his computer monitor. Something was urgently wrong. He had felt it in the morning over breakfast with his wife, and he had seen it in the face of a church beggar woman the day before. Something was about to happen and he could feel it in his indigenous Huichol being. The message that flashed on the monitor was, *Cataclysmic event imminent, instructions to follow*. Something ancient was going to happen today, something that had impacted his past and would fulfill his destiny as an indigenous person of Mexico.

"The early warning system had been broadcast from the United States Geological Society Weather and Seismic Early Warning Station south of Vera Cruz on the Gulf of Campeche. The warning was sent to inform the world and instruct the Mexican population to prepare for a possible cataclysmic event. An earthquake, tsunami, hurricane or exploding volcano was happening somewhere in Mexico. Romero started to shake for some reason. He looked into his small aquarium and knew it wasn't him for he saw shock waves forming in the liquid around the rim of the tank. Earthquakes were rumbling across the center of Mexico without warning, which was an unusual since new technology planted across the country predicted seismic events well ahead of time.

"He put on his 3D Geographic Information Systems audio-visual helmet and pulled the goggles over his eyes and opened the keyboard in the left arm of his chair. He activated the joystick in the right arm and Romero entered his world of mathematical images, looking down in real time on a digital elevation model, and satellite images of central Mexico's terrain. With a few keystrokes he activated a three dimensional white grid of light that was geo-referenced to thousands of seismic stations. The computer integrated both sets of data and gave him the power to fly in a digital world over the landscape of Mexico. The stations came up as glowing red pinpoints on the white grid. With his joystick he moved from his location at Guadalajara and flew over the central plateau, past the Sierra Madre Oriental Mountains and down to the east coast. He stopped and hovered a hundred kilometers above the Vera Cruz stations. Romero typed in a code that changed the resolution of the grid, exaggerating and illustrating the shock waves and movements of the earth as they were taking place.

"As the software kicked in he saw a startling sight; the grid and seismic points along the eastern boundary of Mexico had faded out and the edge of the grid had become an arc several hundred miles wide, curving up on its edge like a wave moving west. He refreshed the screen to make sure he wasn't seeing an electronic anomaly created by the information system—everything came up the same. Using the thumb button on his joystick, he double clicked on one of the seismic points and up flashed the Richter scale rating. It was at its maximum before it faded away: eight point eight—the energy of six million tons of TNT. Typing a reference code into the keyboard to create a point, he placed the cursor on the edge of the wave. A quick calculation by the computer told him the wave was traveling at several hundred miles an hour and would reach Guadalajara and Romero very soon. He quickly keyed in the emergency response code broadcasting to the world confirmation of the emergency broadcast. He called his wife but she was not home. Romero Diaz was about to die a death like many of his ancestors before him. Do you understand me so far?"

"Yeah, except for the tech stuff, I understand most of it. Go on."

"Good—now—Maria, Romero Diaz's pregnant wife, had just returned to her shop studio after dropping off their two boys at school. She went shopping at the local fabric manufacturer for some upholstery fabric before returning home. Touching the doorknob to the shop it rattled faintly, enough to startle her but she dismissed it. As she turned the doorknob and entered the shop, she heard the phone ring, so she laid her parcels down on the kitchen table and walked towards the phone—she reached to pick it up. It was the last thing she ever did."

"Tell me a bit about them, Jonathan, please." said robber as Bullet roared down the highway past farms and jungle. They had a couple of hours to fill.

"The couple met and fell in love in the library restaurant in San Miguel de Allende. A week after he met Maria, Romero paid a formal visit to her parents and asked her father, her mother was sitting close by, for her hand in marriage. Romero had to return the next week for his answer; in the mean time an investigation of Romero had to be carried out. His credentials as a decent human being; the prospects of him becoming a supporting father and an honest husband were confirmed by the family lawyer, priest and powerful business partners. With great rejoicing for the young couple, permission to marry was granted but a wedding would take place only after a year of courting in the presence of the families and work performed by Romero for Maria's father."

"That's a little much, don't you think?"

"You have to understand Maria is from a family that extends back twenty thousand years—in recorded history, many hundreds of years to the founding of the city San Miguel. The family had managed to survive and to hold on to their land and fortune through Mexico's tumultuous history: raising cattle, show horses, growing tobacco, agave and corn and adapting to their time and politics. So there's so much at stake here. Understand?"

"Yeah, go on."

"Maria attended the Institute Allende Art and Language School and had achieved her Master's degree in interior design with the ambition of opening her own studio—"

"What about Romero," queried Robber, wriggling in her seat, "tell me about him." She had no interest in the woman of the story.

"Christ, I'll never finish!"

"You will. Do you want a beer? There's some left in your pack."

"Yeah, please." She reached into the back seat and pulled two cans from his backpack and opened them. She pulled a kerchief from her pocket and wiped the tops and handed him his beer.

He noticed. "Good for you," and he rested his hand on her brown thigh. He went on with the story.

"Romero was born in Guadalajara of Huichol ancestry; a family of many hundreds of indigenous people. He attended the University of Mexico getting a degree in geophysics with plate tectonics and vulcanology as his specialties. Maria's family was catholic so Romero and Maria were married in the vast pink stone Gothic San Miguel Archangel cathedral. With the cathedral bells ringing, the newly weds made a grand parade around the cobbled streets of the town square. A Mariachi band led the couple to the delight of parents, relatives, friends, town's folk, and American and Canadian expatriates. The wedding reception was held in the Culture Center under the mural of the independence fighter, Allende, painted by Siqueiros. Both families filled the courtyard and balconies with over a thousand guests and all bought food, drink and gifts. The reception lasted until the sun came up.

"The couple lived apart for a year, attending to their education, to the consternation of their parents who believed Maria should give up her career ambitions and attend to Romero. But the couple would not have old-fashioned ways and customs interfere with their career paths—"

"Good for them," Robber jumped in.

"After graduation the couple moved to Tlaquepaque, a very old neighborhood of Guadalajara, home of artists and craftsman. Romero took a position with the International Geophysical Assessment Cooperative, a partnership between most of the countries of North and South America. They created the early warning system.

"Eventually they had two boys and lived above the spacious studio shop that Maria created. The family attended services on Sundays and worked for the local Red Cross volunteer organization that supported the poor and the orphans of Guadalajara. At each Sunday service they prayed to God for a girl child and gave pesos to their two young boys to give to an old woman who bore the weight of Mexico in her eyes. She begged in the palm-festooned plaza at the entrance to the church. She wore a faded black dress and shawl over her head to protect her from the sun; her crippled body rested on legs, which were laid back beneath her body in an awkward and painful position. She always gave a toothless smile and blessed the family, wishing for Maria a baby girl and a healthy birth. In recent weeks the old woman did not smile and had worry and fear in her eyes. So now I get back to the story—okay?"

"Okay."

"On Romero's desk was a photograph taken of his family beside the fountain monument to Quetzalcoatl below his office. Alongside the photo was a graduation gift from one of his sisters, a small Huichol fabric art painting of a blue deer, an animal sought and seen only by those Huichol during the ceremonies with the sacred peyote plant. Romero often wore a white shirt embroidered with traditional symbols of his ancestor's homeland. The indigenous populations were flourishing, growing and their numbers had surpassed the time of the Spanish takeover."

"I love your ramblings," she bent over and kissed his shoulder and he removed his hand from her thigh, changed gears and put his hand back.

"Romero was feeling uneasy. He was anxious about the shaking of the building that was becoming more pronounced but he kept the 3D helmet on and watched the progress of the terrestrial wave and talked to the hysterical staff filling up his office. He fielded the phone calls from politicians and news media from around the world. He called Maria but there was no answer. The building started to rattle and shake. He told the office staff to go home to their families. Not taking his helmet off, he wished them luck and God's speed. He reached out his hand, which they took, squeezed hard and left. He watched the wave expand and roll across Mexico, the grid and seismic stations disappeared as everything was being destroyed. The wave was near and he removed his helmet and laid the phone down after calling Maria for the last time—the line was dead and he felt terribly alone. At his desk, facing southeast towards his home and family, he saw the Plaza Tapatia with its monument to Quetzalcoatl, the huge market Mercado Libertad and the orphanage with its treasured Orozco paintings.

"Romero saw something awesome on its way to Guadalajara, a massive wall extending north and south into the horizon. A gigantic cloud of dust, like a wave on an ocean was traveling towards him at a tremendous speed. Very soon the source of the dust was in sight; buildings collapsed in the wave that was the ground itself. The Mercado Libertad exploded as the wave hit its southeast corner. The orphanage collapsed and the dome holding Orozco's magnificent painting *The Man of Fire* came crashing to the floor, disintegrating into dust—everything became dust. The wave swept across the Plaza—tile, concrete, debris and dust exploding into the air. The monument to Quetzalcoatl tottered as the wave hit its base raising the giant edifice up and towards Romero's office building. Romero dropped his eyes from the disaster to his desk; the portrait of his family and the blue deer beside them stared back at him. Romero's world turned from blue to bright white light and he was gone.

"The news flashed around the world to newspapers, radios and televisions:

"35 MILLION OR MORE DIED TODAY. A northwest shift along the Acapulco Fault in a section of the Caribbean Continental Plate and the North American Plate of Central Mexico has created the greatest natural catastrophe in recorded history. The United States Department of Defense's satellites monitoring the thousands of seismic stations across Mexico made measurements of the continents movements. The caldera of the Bahia de Banderas and surrounding mountains and valleys has bulged out east and north 110 kilometers. The caldera emptied and is now an active volcano 900 meters above sea level and rising.

"Tsunamis have flooded cities and lands killing hundred of thousands, perhaps millions, along the shores of the Pacific Ring of Fire. The dust and ash cloud in the stratosphere above the Tropic of Cancer has formed a debris belt around the world and it is spreading south and north.

"The International Weather Network broadcasted that climatic conditions are expected to change drastically for the next few years, as volcanoes reaching from coast to coast in Central Mexico actively spew billions of tons of ash each hour into the atmosphere.

"Financial institutions around the world have collapsed and have closed their doors for business until further notice.

"The president of Mexico, Don Pedro Cardenas, his cabinet and eighty percent of Mexico's civil service are presumed dead; acting president, Julieta Davalos, who is attending a conference in Paris commented: '...something moved up against the continent just south of Vera Cruz shifting the central Mexican land mass west'.

"This was in the year the Maya calendar ended and the return of Quetzalcoatl—2012."

"That is a sad story," Robber said, "do you think that will ever happen?"

"Yes, maybe not in Mexico and not in your lifetime but it will. There is strong evidence that my story can come true. Scientists are conducting research around the world and are discovering such catastrophic events like my story have taken place."

"It sounds like that god of yours was responsible."

"Yeah, a little drama on my part. My stories can't be all science. Hey look, honey we're here." Out of grassy plains and farms rose sleeping black volcanoes.

Valley of the Volcanoes

"Hey Jonathan—how is it you know so much stuff or is it all bullshit? Want another beer?" Bank Robber asked as she reached under the backseat where more were stashed.

"Yes, I'll have another—no bullshit, Robber. You get that way when you get older, all the trivia of life and experience jambs up in the brain and you have to get it out, and that's the reason for the stories. The stories I tell you are surface though, the romantic side. The other side of the stories is the academic side, full of statistics, definitions, tables and data, the stuff of science. As you get older you'll take in an incredible load of information. Do you get what I mean?"

"You're so full of it." she said lovingly.

"Yeah, I guess—but isn't it fun, and your still young."

They sat quietly close together, sipping their beer, on the floor of an observation platform overlooking the huge black lava tailing of a volcano. Bullet was parked below them on the highway built over the black mass. For Robber her friend's stories were becoming quite real to her. Romero and Maria became Jonathan and Bank Robber. Suddenly she knew she was in love with him or was it the need to have someone like him and raise a family—she was confused. She wanted the world to go away and leave them to scratch out a living on a farm between the lava flows or behind the algae covered stonewalls of San Sebastian. The romance of Mexico and her biological needs where overwhelming her.

Jonathan's thoughts were different as he looked over the burned landscape. His mind was home planning a criminal act. He was shocked at the ideas going through his mind but he could not resist them. He blamed the dilemma on the malaria pills he once had to take.

He put his arm around his friend and held her tight to him: "We should start heading home, honey."

"I know. But I don't want to leave. I love it here with you."

They left the volcano valley and drove the radiator-and-tire-troubled Bullet to Bucerias. Apart from Robber's horrendous night, the two of them had a couple of good days and believed they had learned a lot about each other and Mexico. She reached into his backpack and pulled out his CD player, which he hadn't used since coming to Mexico.

"Do you mind?"

"No, go ahead." She rustled through his CDs strewn through his backpack.

"Hey, everything is opera. I don't understand opera."

"You don't have to understand it. Try Madama Butterfly by Puccini," he said, "it's simple and light not heavy like German stuff." She put in the CD and laid back with her feet up on the dash. On the way home, her hand never left his thigh. Eventually Bullet kicked up the dust down the cobbled Avenida Cárdenas to her apartment. He noticed tears coming down her cheek.

"What's the matter?"

"The damn opera. I couldn't understand a word—it was so sad. What was it about?"

"It's about a naval officer, Lt. Pinkerton and a Japanese fifteen year old Geisha, Butterfly, whom he purchases and marries. He goes home from Nagasaki leaving her not knowing she is bearing his child. She is poor and with her friend Suzuki, they struggle for three years waiting for him. She stays faithful and longs for his return. When he does return, with his new wife, it is only to take away the child he recently found out he had. Butterfly is heartbroken and commits suicide."

"Wow, I could feel that in the music."

"Sometimes just hearing is enough."

"Thanks for the wonderful trip—I think I love you. Will you sleep with me tonight?" she said as she grabbed her backpack and jumped out of Bullet.

"No honey, not tonight and you don't love me, it's your youth and Mexico speaking. We are friends—remember?"

"Thanks, Jonathan, let's go into PV on Friday." and she waved goodbye.

The next day Bullet's tire went flat and when Jonathan changed to the spare, the tire rim rested on the brake housing and the car would not roll. The spare was useless—for fifteen years he did not know it didn't fit the Jeep. The gods were with them among the volcanoes and the Sierra Madras.

Friday rolled around and Bank Robber and Jonathan went shopping in downtown Puerto Vallarta for something made by the indigenous Huichol, like fabric or bead art. They found a store near the town square.

"Wow!" Jonathan yelled to Robber as he picked up the black fabric doll from the window display. He read to her the attached label on the rag doll:

"Receive their voice, which, although far away, says: Greetings, workers of the sea and of the land! The Zapatistas follow you in their struggles! With you there will be a country and future for all some day! Without you, night will continue to rule these lands!"

"The Zapatistas are alive and well right here in PV—Jesus! I read about these people in Oppenheimer's book, *Bordering on Chaos*—look! It's only twenty bucks Canadian. I'll give her twenty five."

"What?" Robber said with a screwed up face.

"The extra five is for the cause," he said and he paid the clerk the pesos.

"What's the big deal about this thing," she took it from him for a closer look, "it's made of black—kinda' dirty rags."

"Yeah, and put together by some poor soul down south in the state of Chiapas trying to make a living in a hostile and oppressed place—dangerous too," he said taking back the doll and holding it close. Then he held it up for her to see: "This is sub commander Marcos with a rifle in his hands wearing a ski mask, and this figure here riding on the back of the horse holding onto him is Roselia. They always wore black. These were important people—back in '94 on New Years Day they led the fight against oppression imposed by the rich, the government and military. The Zapatistas raided and captured some towns in Chiapas and handed over the land from the rich to the poor; kinda' like Robin Hood and Maid Marian. Roselia became a hero when several hundred soldiers approached her community—she drove them off. I think Marcos is still hiding out in the mountains.

Bank Robber bought herself a small Huichol string painting of a blue deer in remembrance of Romero and Maria. They left the shop and walked down the Malecón to a restaurant on the corner and took a table on a wrought iron balcony overlooking the palm trees, beach and the Bahia de Banderas. They ordered food and beer. Robber pulled out the rag doll from its bag and a small piece of paper came out with it.

"What's written on the paper?" he asked.

She read the script:

"No longer are they ashamed of the color of their skin. They are proud to see that they are the color of the earth.

They advised them to be prudent and to sign the peace agreement. They said the government would finish them off in hours or days, at the latest, if they didn't sign for peace ... They asked them to prudently surrender and live ... Who could live with that shame? Who trades life for dignity? Such sensible advice was useless ... All afternoon they talked in the Committee. They tried to find the word 'surrender' in some language but they couldn't. It doesn't translate into Tzotzil nor into Tzeltal and no one remembers that word in Tojolabal or in Chol. They spend hours trying to find an equivalent ... Someone arrives with rain pouring off the cap and the rifle, 'Coffee's ready', they tell them. The Committee, as is customary in these parts, takes a vote to see if they'll have coffee or continue trying to find the equivalent of 'SURRENDER' in the language of truth. Coffee wins unanimously. NO ONE SURRENDERS. Will they be alone?"

Subcomandante Insurgente Marcos.

They ordered chicken fajitas; coffee and ice cream on apple pie, people watched and made small talk for the next hour. The hot tropical sun shot between the palms lining the Malecón—roasting them. They drove home to Bucerias and he reflected on how pleased he was that he had come across black Marcos and Roselia on horseback and connected with modern Mexico. For him, every day is a new day and God knows what will come down the street and bite him in the butt.

"Oh no," Robber whispered, "look, there's a dead horse over there." And she pointed out the jeep to a body lying on the side of the highway lane going into town.

"Let's go have a look," Jonathan said and he pulled the jeep into an emergency road that took them to the lanes going back to PV. He pulled over onto the highway shoulder and parked next to the body.

Her coat was a faded light ocher with a straggly auburn mane and tail; a white spot was the only other colour, or lack of it, forming a star on her forehead. Her large eyes were brown, glazed and vacant—frozen in the terror of her last seconds of life.

"It looks like she has lain here for some time. See how her belly and chest are distended from the gasses building inside her," Robber said quietly standing close to Jonathan.

"I can see damage on her body—wear marks of harnesses, bridles, saddles and there," he pointed to marks on her flanks of abuse from whips and stirrups, "but there's no breakage of the skin from the accident that I can see.

"I guess the injuries that killed her are internal. Look at the pool of dried blood by her mouth in the dirt. What shall we call her?"

"How about Lucy?" Jonathan said.

"Why Lucy?

"She has red hair and that's the first name to come to me." A worn-out abused creature, Lucy was just one more wreck on the highways of Mexico.

"Let's get outta' here. She smells real bad," Robber, said, "God, the smell of Mexico gets to me sometimes."

They would continue to see and smell her over the week they would come and go to the city. Traffic kept the vultures away; the city's highway crews did not go near her. No one claimed her or cared to bury her. But one day someone did come by and dragged her away. Her burial was not in the ground—she would nourish others. She was left in a cultivated field nearby. In a short time her belly was flat and her legs level with the field. Black vultures and turkey vultures ate her during the day. Night creatures were out for their share after the birds had left. In a week Lucy was a skull and a sheet of leather baking in the sun. Soon that would be gone and she would return to the earth from whence she came. The farmer would grind what remained of her into the dirt of his field.

The Three Graces

Jonathan stretched out, a little drunk, on his beach blanket in front of a restaurant at Boca de Tomatlan. The heat and beer made him sleepy. He propped himself up and checked on Bank Robber who was out in the water swimming among the fishing boats and children—she was happy. Three women from the nearby sandbar ran into the water and joined them—giggling and laughing. They were women that reminded him of a day in his past and of the Three Graces painted by Botticelli. As he drifted into sleep the chaos of that day came back to him.

Three Graces, getting drunk on beer, lounged on a blanket under a red umbrella on a sandbar. The hot sun was high noon and heating up the day on the river estuary. Two children played in the surf that crashed into the fresh cool waters of the river. A slight breeze blew in from the west off the Sea of Cortez; the palms leaned into the bay against the blue sky. Brown pelicans dove into the fish-rich waters of the bay and high above them were frigate birds ready to rob them of their catch.

White and blue fishing boats came and went, some tied to rocks on shore, others pulled up onto the beach; their nets spread out on the sand to dry and be repaired. The fishermen were busy at their labor; their muscular arms, legs and hands flexed. Their faces shone leathery and handsome from the work, sun and sea.

David and Jonathan sprawled back in their plastic chairs sucked on beer, chewed beef jerky and pepperoni sticks. Through sunglasses they surveyed the scene. It was siesta time for the smart Mexicans and residents; play time for the likes of the Three Graces, David and Jonathan.

"So, what do you think?" David mumbled.

"Yeah, I think we should do it," a lazy voice replied.

"Senior," David called the waiter over, "tres cervezas por favor," as he pointed to the Three Graces.

"Si," the waiter said, "they are much drunk."

"Sounds good," David, remarked, "so are we." They all laughed.

The waiter walked across the shallow fresh water inlet to the sandbar with beer and limes on a tray. He bent down to give each woman her drink and pointed to where they came from; each one took her drink and toasted David and Jonathan, from the distance across the inlet.

"Let's give them some time," Jonathan said and they both laid back and ordered another beer. After a short time a longhaired bearded hippie at a table next to them ordered three more beers to be delivered to the three women. He to had noticed the girls were having a good time. He decided to deliver the beer himself. He winked at David and Jonathan; they laughed and the trio strolled across the inlet to the sandbar.

"Buenas tardes, ladies," Jonathan said.

"Buenas tardes, guys," a weatherworn tanned American woman

replied. The Hippie handed them a beer each, which they profusely thanked him for. Introductions went around but Jonathan would never remember their names. All were quite drunk and their pasts came out to haut them. They would soon get other names.

The American woman, Vegas, came from Las Vegas of course; she owns a beachfront townhouse a few miles towards PV. Her youthful years had gone, her long thin body and colour showed signs of life's wear and tear. For years she was a black jack dealer in the casinos of Las Vegas; the all-night shifts and parties weathered her—so had the tropical paradise. That day, out on the sandbar, she still had some beauty and spunk left as she paraded for them and played with the children. Her drunken language was crude and she cursed constantly. She said, in the seventies, she worked in music studios in Los Angeles as a session singer for recording artists. Her clients were very big in the biz. She and her record producer Mexican husband, dead long ago from heart failure, bought a townhouse in the early eighties when land was cheap in paradise and the choices plentiful. Now she spends a few months in Las Vegas each year, but most of her time in Mexico teaching black jack to dealers for the Mexican government's casinos that Jonathan didn't know existed.

Houseboat was a good-looking blonde of forty years who took a fancy to Hippie. She lived on a boat at a marina in a bay north of Seattle, Washington and worked as the manager and partner in a popular floating fish and chips restaurant. Separated from her husband of twenty years, she came down to Mexico for some R and R and to grieve her loss. She worked too hard at her job, keeping long hours, and her husband drifted away to a younger more attentive woman. Her bitterness showed in her face and demeanor. Vegas and Houseboat were buddies from grade school in Bremerton, Washington. They lost touch in their' 20s, each going off to pursue careers and men. Now alone again, both get drunk to drive away the ghosts of their past.

Chicago was the third of the Graces who is an alcoholic. A Mexican woman, she is married to a wealth man in Chicago. They had two children—the boy and girl that play nearby in the surf. Chicago is in her 30s but looks older, the ravages of booze and smoking show on her bloated face. Her body is square—a large torso with thin arms and legs. She has not seen her husband in years but money is put in a bank account every month to support the kids and supply the liquor she consumes.

Drunken Chicago was in an uproar over her young son who had taken the keys to her car. Playing catch with his sister, he lost them in the sand of a restaurant. The Three Graces had spent some time looking for the keys but it was hard work so they did the next best thing, do it later, and got comfortable on the sandbar to drink the day away.

The clan of six had a couple of good hours out there on the sandbar;

they watched the fishing boats return from the sea with their catch, and the tourists who arrived for the afternoon. The kids did not hang around; they would rather not be around their parents, especially at the beach. The waiter hustled back and forth across the inlet with drinks, chips and salsa. The six got to know each other a little too much.

Eventually, drunken David got into a terrible argument with Chicago over what to do about the car keys and the girls who were stranded there in Boca de Tomatlan. He took her by the hand, and with her son, they went to search for the keys. Why David was so worried about the damn keys Jonathan could not understand. David was a stationery engineer, highly technical and professional, which made him anal about how things must be. He organizes, plans and puts himself in charge.

Hippie passed out from the heat and beer and from listening to Houseboat's tirade about men—only she was really raving about her lost husband. She kept up a howl to a body that could not hear. Vegas and Jonathan had a good time drinking beer, telling lies and stories. He liked the wrinkled old crone.

Time lazily moved on and those left conscious on the blanket decided to eat some of the local fare; Vegas wanted to go to a hole in the wall up the beach. Houseboat and Jonathan declined and said they would meet her later after they ate a little something at the restaurant where a drunken Chicago, her son and red faced furious David, grubbed in the sand for the lost keys. David could not take much more abuse and he was drunk and, discombobulated, as he later put it; he was going to take the next bus home to PV. Chicago told him to fuck off and not come back to her country again. That was that—David was gone.

Hippie was down on the beach asleep guarding the blankets and umbrella. Chicago, Houseboat, the kids and Jonathan dined on right-off-the-boat grilled fish over an open fire pit while Vegas was up the beach in a hole that billowed smoke and fire. The catch of the day, that Jonathan could not pronounce, was delicious washed down with beer and they were well into their meal when a tall, thin white fellow walked up to their table and told Houseboat she would have to move her belongs that evening from the cottage that she was renting. Her time was up and new tenants would arrive at midnight; the place had to be cleaned. Houseboat went into shock. It would be very inconvenient to pack at this time. Confused, she went back to eating only to have her top denture plate break in half. There was cursing and swearing and she disappeared leaving Chicago trying to get a hand up Jonathan's shorts.

"Okay," Jonathan said, summing up the situation, "It's time to find Vegas."

Chicago's two kids headed back to the beach and found some friends and their parents. They came back and said, they would go home with their pals and they would leave Mom to figure out how to get the car home. In a drunken sarcastic slur she thanked them and sent them on their way. The clan had become smaller. Up the beach staggered Chicago hanging on to Jonathan for support and lust. They found Vegas chomping down on yellow roast chicken in the hole in the wall.

The cook-owner was a dark, huge smiling white-toothed Mexican woman wearing a bright flowered apron over black pants and t-shirt. She stood at her wooden cutting table with a menacing cleaver; her big strong arms, the size of a man's thighs, cut up chickens and smashed the halves flat. From bottles and terra cotta bowls she spiced and drenched the chicken with cooking oil and threw the yellow-coloured chicken on the half-barrel barbeque behind her; smoke billowed and the fire spat and crackled as the oil hit the heat.

Her kitchen and dining room were constructed of cement brick, three meters high on three sides and open to the sea on the forth with a thatched roof above festooned with pots, pans, bags of fruit and strings of chilies. On top of one wall was, what looked like, the carcass of a cat. In one corner, cooking fuel and water bottles were on the sand floor under a small table covered with cutlery, napkins and condiments. Alongside the table was a freezer chest with soft drinks and beer. One plastic table with a yellow tablecloth and four chairs was her dining area.

Along one wall was a low wooden bench where six Mexican boys and girls sat, all less than ten years; they were full of laughter and giggles, ferociously eating chicken.

"My chillen," the cook said to Jonathan. She beamed with pride.

The children were filthy from playing in the sand and dust all day; some of their noses were running and their little faces and hands were covered in grease and food. Their big brown eyes never left the drunken customers. Four beach dogs, brown and white mangy bastards to Jonathan, chased each other in and out of the hole, around the customers and under the cutting table; wanting to play, they jumped on Jonathan. He noticed fleas jumping and racing along the miserable canine's backs and there were bigger looking things crawling on their legs and tails. A rooster was under the cutting table fussing around the cook's feet and squawking at the dogs. Flies and wasps were everywhere. The kitchen was from hell; filled with smoke and the smell of burning chicken carcasses; the noise of barking dogs; the squawking chicken; kids yelling, fighting and laughing; sizzling and crackling oil, the banging meat cleaver against chicken bones and the crooning of two horny drunken women. Jonathan staggered outside the kitchen and looked with raised arms to the sky and shouted, "Thank you Lord, thank you."

A Mexican construction worker from a building project nearby entered into the madness, "Senõr, I'm looking for owner of white car," and he pointed to Chicago's vehicle, "it parked in way my truck. Please to move it."

Jonathan explained to the workman, the best he could using a few words and hand gestures, "That owner," pointing to Chicago, "lost her car keys, "all too drunk to take care of it."

"Have to move car!" the worker said, getting angry.

"Okay—okay—uno momento," Jonathan felt obligated to fix the situation and went down the beach and recruited help to lift Chicago's car out of the way. He managed to get three sturdy fellows and with him that was four and three workmen made seven. They all heaved one end of the car at a time and moved it a couple of meters up against a building making enough room for the worker's truck to squeeze by. He bought his volunteers a beer and they went back to the beach. Jonathan went back to face the duo in hell's kitchen.

"Enough," Jonathan said, "goodbye ladies." They decided that they were also finished and would leave—on his arms. After paying their bill and a few coins to the kids, they left for the beach and picked up their gear—the hippie was gone. Beer in hand, they staggered up the cobbled hill to catch the next bus to PV. Supporting each other they boarded the bus and took a seat for two but both women insisted on sitting with him—they squeezed in together. The bus rumbled and banged with every pothole down the highway; the gears ground with every shift the driver made.

The girls begged him to come and stay forever and he declined saying that he must return to PV and Canada—alive. The women were very drunk, they laughed and talked like screaming seagulls and groped him. As the bus approached their stop he stood up to let them out; they grabbed his clothes trying to pull him down the aisle and off the bus. The passengers were very amused—the women were going to take him home. He pulled back but they insisted. The bus driver saw the mess and came to his rescue helping him get untangled from the hellions. The driver and Jonathan managed to get them off the bus—he kissed them goodbye; the passengers cheered and the bus moved on to PV. He watched them through the back window, blowing kisses and waving. They disappeared as the bus rolled down the winding highway. Jonathan knew he would never see them again. Such is the way for travelers.

"Jonathan, Jonathan, let's have something to eat," Bank Robber said bending over him and caressing his chest, "Why the big grin? Were you dreaming?"

"Yeah," he said and he reached up and took her head in his hands and drew her to his lips and kissed her.

"Where did that come from?" she said with surprise.

"There's a little hole in the wall place I know just up the way. If it's still there and you like what you see—we will do lunch."

"Why are you laughing?"

"Oh, I have a story for you." He took her by the hand and led her up the beach—he started the story of The Three Graces.

A Waste of Angels

A massive green, white and red striped garbage truck thundered its way from Puerto Vallarta up the lush Valle de Banderas; up through potholed river roads, dodging chickens, dogs, tin shacks and dark skinned Mexicans. It rumbled into a ravine and up a steep driveway past a security gate and onto the dump. In low gear, straining under its weight, it's engine roared up the hill of human waste and garbage one hundred meters high. The monster machine backed up and with heaving hydraulics, opened up its rear end and ejected its load of garbage from the city by the sea. Children scattered out of the way and when it finished they scrambling like insects into the heap. This was the bottom of the food chain; a universe far removed from Jonathan's.

He had driven up onto the heap through the back service gate. He parked and jumped out. A boy and a girl cowered behind a rotting sofa out of the sun and as he came near they froze. He noticed worms under the skin of the little boy's feet. With huge black eyes they looked at him in terror. It was as though they had never seen a blonde, white-skinned human before. White people do not come to this place; for all they knew he could have been some monster from the bowels of the dump. Others were quite astonished at him, a blonde white man in a Jeep on top of this hell hill—their home.

Thousands of birds dove and swooped looking for scraps around the fresh dumped garbage. Flocks of vultures, cattle and snowy egrets, doves, grackles, sea gulls and black birds formed columns hundreds of meters into the blue sky. Horses, bulls, donkeys and burros foraged in the rot and stench.

The recyclers, dove into the heap of waste and human excrement with metal hooks; digging for their gold—tin cans, metal scraps and plastic bottles. They work fifteen-hour shifts among the birds and animals to package in huge industrial plastic garbage bags, tons of recyclable refuse for a few meager pesos. They are burned black from the sun, tattooed and filthy.

"Ola!" shouted a dark figure seated with two other men drinking beer, "you come for visit?" he said, rose, came over to him, reached and shook his hand. "My name is Alejandro, and yours?"

"Jonathan Owen."

"Nice to meet you." He spoke English with some authority and showed off in front of his friends and workers by making conversation with Jonathan. They talked and Alejandro begged, which made both of them uncomfortable. He needed money for his family that lived on the edge of the dump and wished for a new job in the glittering hotels.

"Get in the Jeep Alejandro and tell me about you and all this," Jonathan said and made a sweeping hand gesture across the dump. "Wanna' beer?" and Jonathan reached in his backpack behind the driver's seat and pulled out two cans and opened them.

"Thanks," said Alejandro. He jumped into the passenger seat, "I grew up in downtown PV and did jobs off the Playa Los Muertos hustling tours, trinkets, blankets and drugs. Sometimes I crewed on fishing boats from the fish market at the north end of the Malecón."

"Yeah, I know that place—"

"I met my wife, Maria Guadeloupe, on the beach when we were young and beautiful," he laughed and Jonathan chuckled, "before we knew it, we had five children before I was twenty-five. We lived a good life for a while but I could no longer hustle enough money to support my habit and growing family. I did time for trafficking cocaine and I wanted to run away when I got out. But I couldn't, I love my Maria and kids," he looked off into the distance, "her family took us in."

"How did you get here?"

"I came up on the heap one day to help a friend and found it was easy money, so I stayed. Now I can't get out. This is it for me. I hope my kids do better."

His youthful tanned tattooed body no longer looks as passionate as it did on the beach—a far away memory for him. His body is scarred and thin, his black hair no longer has a luster, his eyes are glazed and his speech slurred. He and this place were overwhelming for Jonathan to be sorry for—it was just scary.

"You *rico*?"

"Yeah, I guess I am by Mexican standards. May I visit your family?" Jonathan asked.

"Of course. We live in our house a half a kilometer to the right of the gate as you leave. You can't miss it; we have the Virgin hanging over our table." He got out of the Jeep,

"You come again?"

"Maybe—I don't know. We will see. Goodbye Alejandro and good luck."

He drove out of the dump, down the dirt road looking for Maria. It didn't take long, she was with her children around a table covered in flies; above the table was a bed sheet with an image of the Virgin of Guadeloupe just as Alejandro had told him. The image was appropriate, he thought for the Virgin is the patron saint of the poor of Mexico. Other shacks nearby displayed similar but smaller altars. Jonathan introduced himself to Maria and her children. He waved his camera in front of her, "Take picture?"

"Si," she said and gathered her children around her. A couple of chickens came out from under the table and joined in.

Their home was made from concrete blocks, cardboard and plastic sheeting. Where the walls started and ended was an architectural mystery. The family slept on urine stained filthy mattresses, a gas stove was in a corner for cooking and heat and their toilet was a pit out back. They had an electric washing machine and dryer that a friend had managed to make operational. Their little plot was decorated with Christmas lights, plastic flowers and anything and everything that glittered. A layer of gray dust covered everything. Electricity came from a nearby tap into the local system by means of wires thrown over the bare municipal power grid, as Jonathan had seen done by the vendors in Bucerias. Water and gas was purchased from the local delivery trucks that rumbled down the dusty road everyday.

Maria is still beautiful and dedicated to her husband and children but her future is uncertain. Death will be by disease, injury, murder or old age at thirty-five—but who really knows. Inevitably it will continue to be trouble, strife and misery. She keeps a home the best she can. How do you keep your family clean in a place that is encrusted in dust and flies with garbage trucks rolling down your dirty, dusty road every fifteen minutes? Impossible, this is damn heartbreaking, he thought. In the naked trees nearby, crouched hundreds of black turkey vultures—watching and waiting.

He took pictures of Maria and her children and they enjoyed posing for him. He pulled a couple of hundred pesos from his wallet and gave them to Maria and she thanked him and crossed herself. He said goodbye, left the family and drove down the back road to the highway north to his cottage.

On the way home he passed a white pickup truck. In the back was a huge white and brown faced, sleepy-eyed Brahma cow that weighed more than the truck. The cow stood erect and stared at him as he pulled up close to pass. She was being transported to the slaughterhouse that was near the dump and she had defecated a watery brown mass over the back and sides of the truck; a defiant gesture she had no idea she had performed. What next? Jonathan laughed. Something bizarre everyday happens for him as the circus of life in Mexico rumbles by.

At home he showered the filth away, put his clothing in the laundry basket, dressed and washed the Jeep's steering wheel, driver's seat and gearshift. He walked to Café Bucerias to meet Robber for the evening. He had many questions for his friends and a soul-moving day to think about.

What he saw and experienced nagged at him that night and next morning. He decided to buy some groceries for his new friends in the wasteland. Robber wanted to come along after seeing his digital photos. She wanted to give something back to this country and to help Jonathan, because she cared for him. She knew what he had seen worried him. He warned her of the filth and degradation she would see and she scolded him for being fatherly.

They would be leaving Mexico in a few weeks and they felt strongly about making some contribution, however small, to the Mexican community. The act of charity spreads and together they hoped their little one would also. At the Super-Mini-Market in Mezcales just down the highway from Bucerias they bought cucumbers, tomatoes, peppers, chilies, limes, cauliflower, beans, red and white onions, oranges, canned tuna, soap and two cartons of milk—enough for a week of healthy meals. They loaded the food packages into Bullet.

They drove the backcountry road to the dump and arrived at Maria's ramshackle home. A small game hen was tied to a metal pipe, a rooster pecked away in the family's outdoor cement sink and a number of chickens and a goose roamed around the family's outdoor dining room. The ever-present vultures were perched in the trees above. Maria came running out with the kids and gestured to him about taking more pictures. Alejandro was not to be seen, he was in the dump or sleeping off the day inside the shack. They gave up their bundles of food to the family, placing them below the Virgin of Guadeloupe on Maria's plastic dining table. After shooing some chickens and the goose away they took some photos. Robber had a simple conversation in Spanish with Maria. She was emotionally touched by the Mexican experience—her eyes glowed with tears. Wow, he thought I haven't seen this in her. They wished Maria and the children luck for the future and he rushed Robber away from the sad place, leaving Maria and her brood behind and an uncertain future but grateful for the offerings.

Jonathan drove to the back of the dump and service entrance he used the day before. To the top of the hellish place, in low gear, they roared. Bank Robber was crying. He stopped and rushed around to the passenger's seat. She was in need of someone to hold onto. She kissed and held him for a few minutes.

"Oh Christ, I've seen this all before in Africa. I still can't get over it. It's always a shock."

"I know honey. We'll take a few photos and get out of here. Are you okay now?"

"Yeah, I'm fine. Thanks."

She took photos of the dumps wildlife and children who were all over her, trying to pull her out of the Jeep. They drove across the acres of misery and abundant life, waving to the children and workers who waved back. Each time they parked Bullet, dogs would lie beneath her for shade; there are very few places on that man made mountain to get out of the sun.

They had enough. They drove down the garbage mountain and out the main gate and sat in silence during the journey home. They both felt the need to wash off what had crept over their bodies. Down the highway was his cottage with its garden, pool, lizards and maid service. They got home, stripped down and went for a swim. He floated on his back and looking up at fluttering palm fronds against a giant blue sky—he felt so relieved he was a visitor.

The Virgin's Flowers of Fire

By midday Jonathan had guzzled a few beers at the Café Bucerias, and organized himself for the festival in the town square. He walked across the purple pedestrian bridge over the dry filthy riverbed, where among cats, dogs and geese, were roosters and their hens clucking and scratching. Today he would witness their relatives do battle. The footbridge joined up with painted houses adorned with flowers and lovers; large statues of men and women leaned toward each other, whispering. Some were carved in wood; others in ceramics festooned with mosaic. Chac, the rain god, crouched among them.

He walked up the road that runs through a souvenir market past the library and an American coffee shop. He came onto the square with its church, shops and restaurants. The road continued on to the northern neighborhood of Bucerias.

Several acres of the town and the square had been transformed over the past week. A traveling market industry had come to town of souvenir shops, food stalls and gypsy wagons. Makeshift restaurants, trucks that spilled their goods out their backs—everything spilling out and filling the cobbled streets in a riot of smells, colour and sound overpowered the small town. Balloon and candy men, hawkers, fortunetellers, shaman and carnies selling rides on fantasy machines, plied their trade. Large painted signs strung between the palms invited everyone to the celebration. The Church, the dominant building on the square, held services for those who need comfort, for those to be wed and for those to be buried. The priest is a busy man.

Residents came from the communities of La Cruz de Huanacaxtle, Las Palmas, Mezcales, Ixtapa, Valle de Banderas and San Jose del Valle. There were boys with shining, greased, black curly hair combed forward onto their faces; dressed in their best jeans, boots and shirts. They escorted young girls in tight revealing clothes displaying their sexuality; they performed like peacocks, dancing that wonderful primal dance Jonathan fondly remembered. Middle-aged mustached men in cowboy gear from the farms and businesses strutted about the place like cocks in a barnyard—wives and mistresses where off gossiping. There were the old couples, dignified and leathery, full of grace and beauty with their extended families—respected by everyone. Young mothers of fifteen and sixteen in groups cradled or pushed their babies in wheelers and chatted about how gorgeous their babies are; proud of the life they have given. And the babies—there were hundreds of them dressed in their finest. The baby boys were dressed like their fathers in jeans, cowboy boots and hats; the baby girls wore pink frilly dresses, white socks and shoes with ribbon bandanas and flowers in their hair. These people were richer than they knew, thought Jonathan.

A flotilla of fishing boats was supposed to arrive from La Cruz Huanacaxtle, a fishing village, just a few kilometers north on the curve of the bay. But that didn't happen until later—no surprise. Jonathan ran into Timothy and Barbara, he joined them and they lounged around drinking beer at a beach restaurant on the edge of the square. They heard a small band play up the beach—it approached the restaurant.

A parade had begun led by two women who held a sign aloft, a pledge of the local fishermen's devotion to the Patron Saint was written across it. Three virgin children in a small boat carried by fishermen followed them and following them was a child dressed in blue satin standing on a platform carried by four men—everyone stood in respect. She was an angel, her hands clasped in prayer. She wore a halo of gold—the Virgin of Guadeloupe. Behind her came the player of Jesus himself, dragging a large wooden cross. He wore a blood splattered bed sheet and a crown of thorns about his head. Beating him, with hawser lines from their boats, were four fishermen dressed in their yellow rain gear. A choir of men, women and nuns followed the procession singing a Catholic song.

Waiting to greet them at the steps of the Bucerias Malecón were two-dozen Aztec children dressed in shimmering blue and white capes with headdresses of white feathers. They escorted Jesus, the fishermen and the punishers up the beach to the stairs and onto the square. The escort delivered them to the priest who was waiting with his flock of more than a thousand in the church. Thousands more spilled out onto the streets. The bells peeled in the church tower to summon everyone to the holy blessing. The innocence and devotion of these people shot through Jonathan.

He had to look away and catch his breath for fear of breaking down. There were thousands in the square watching the ritual and many had tears in their eyes, some openly weeping. The most devout fell to their knees and crawled along the cobbled road to the church. The priest, the most powerful man in Bucerias, embraced and performed a ceremony that blessed them for their devotion. He wished the fishermen a good catch, safety and God's speed in the year ahead. He blessed his flock of thousands that day.

A flotilla, bobbing and glistening in the high sun from La Cruz de Huanacaxtle, was spotted far off in the bay. There were about two-dozen blue and white outboard motor-driven fishing vessels carrying passengers. One large vessel carried a Jesus on a cross attached to the housing—this Jesus represented the fishermen from their village. The flotilla was festooned with crosses of orange, white, blue and balloons, and flowers. The boat was packed with apprehensive village citizens with a few tourists thrown in for ballast. The wind was strong and the tide was high; a steep climb to the beach made the situation mean and dangerous. At the signal of a self-proclaimed official on the beach, each boat made a run for it at full speed and the boats flew over the breaking surf and onto the beach. Immediately a crew of spectators, Jonathan included, hauled the boats up onto the high sand. Some boats came up a little too slow and waves broke over their sterns flooding the craft, which evoked howls of laughter, confusion and chaos. Everyone got into the act, heaving the boats up, helping the passengers out, taking the motors off and tipping the crafts over to drain. Last to arrive was Jesus who is traditionally tied to the cross but the year previous his handlers dropped him face first onto the road. He suffered some bad bruising so they let him free this year. The two-dozen little Aztecs escorted Jesus and the fishermen across the square to the church and the priest for their blessing.

The passengers quickly headed for the nearest bar to settle their nerves.

On the Malecón, next to the square, a mariachi band struck up its tinny, brassy cacophony of Mexican marching songs. Down the street came riders on big horses, twenty of them, dressed in their finest gear—dress pants; blue, white, beige, silk, embroidered shirts; cowboy boots made from lizard skin; monstrous brass belt buckles and wide, brimmed sombreros. They looked like the revolutionary bandits of long ago, Emiliano Zapata and Poncho Villa.

Two young girls were with them; they rode cross saddle with confidence and grace. Both were dressed in beautiful embroidered long blue dresses trimmed with little red bows; on their heads were feminine sombreros. They sat in the saddles made and burnished of the most expensive leather; their groomed horses were magnificent. They were real cowboys that work on the ranches and farms in the valley, not just men and women dressed up as weekend warriors. As the band played the horses danced, moving side-to-side tucking their heads down and prancing from hoof-to-hoof.

The cowboys rode around the square and side streets drinking beer, flirting with giggling young mothers and giving their babies rides. They all sat straight on their prancing horses in their beautiful embellished saddles, blankets and gear—handsome, proud and arrogant.

The crowd had warmed up on the square: the two Jesus and fishermen had been blessed and were in a cantina drinking, laughing and recounting their ordeal; the riders were out and about; the beer from the bandstand stall flowed faster and faster, and more people arrived every minute by taxis, bus and on foot.

The police at the edge of the square with their new truck beamed with pride, their relatives and friends were there. People sat and moved about on the lawns, sidewalks and fountains eating cotton candy, candy apples, roasted corn, hamburgers and hot dogs. Dark hair pulled back, mustached, swaggering, buxom, shapely, clean, big eyes, and healthy—all lovely Mexicans filled the place to bursting. Drinking was heavy and many got drunk, put in taxis and sent home. The skies became darker as the sun dove into the bay to the cheers and clapping of everyone.

The stage acts in the square got underway with a pageant to select Miss Bucerias. All of the young women deserved to win and they all did; their parents, relatives and boyfriends beamed with pride. Drums became louder and more aggressive and the band blasted away from the bandstand.

A conch shell sounded a distant lonely blast; it summoned the crowd to a stage on the edge of the square. Ten ferocious Aztec men and women dancers in feathered headgear, war makeup and armor stood under amber and red lights. Flaming torches lined the stage, some held aloft by the performers. Drums sounded, conch shells blared and the dance troop performed a fire dance, working itself into a sexual frenzy of light and colour. The hot coloured lights and flames glowed across the dancers' legs, arms and faces; their muscles taught under the strain of the dance; their bodies vibrated, rattled shells and flashed the colours of the long pheasant feathers shooting out from their heads. A knowing look appeared on faces in the crowd. Silent, mesmerized with eyes wide open, they sucked in the primitive ritual. Jonathan watched with fascination; these people had been here before in ancient times. They all knew where they had come from; in their eyes and the sounds around them was their pagan ancestry—sensuous and brutal.

The dance performance over, the cockfights were to begin in an arena nearby. Jonathan felt exhilarated from the day's events and went in search of the arena to learn about fighting birds. He would enter this other world of the cockfights—a world that would eventually haunt him forever.
Cockfighting in Mexico and other countries are gambling entertainment, legal and licensed by governments but there are many dangerous illegal tournaments around the bay area, some of which Jonathan attended. The audience was made up of a society with disposable cash: local mafia bosses, drug lords and regular families of mom, dad and the kids just out for an evening of entertainment. The cock handlers and owners are cowboys, politicians and ordinary folk who have ranches, farms and businesses in the agricultural areas around Bucerias.

The local operation is legal but floats around town, so a local hot dog vendor gave Jonathan a lead to find the arena. At the fish market on the Malecón he talked to the boss of the cockfights who directed him to the end of the street to the Avenida Mexico were he found the place around the corner and half a block down. It was eight o'clock starting time for the fights.

He went in. Three-meter high filthy whitewashed walls surrounded the arena. An unpainted rotting plywood door to the street was the entrance and an opening at the back of the arena gave access to a black cobbled courtyard, an anti chamber of a grimy vacant motel. Two rooms lit in the courtyard were the filthy toilets. The arena's floor was dirt, tiered down to accommodate chairs—the cheap plastic white and red kind. The top level had bleachers four rows high. The circular fighting pit was ten-meters in diameter, floored with dark sand and enclosed by a whitewashed plywood hoarding forty-centimeters high. Two entrances on opposite sides of the hoarding, painted red and green, gave access to the pit. Opposite the entrances the judges and weight recorders sat with their raffle wheel of chance, weigh scales, score sheets and other bric-a-brac of their trade. Above this crude hole in the dirt a tattered black plastic canopy undulated in the breeze like some huge bat. Hung below the bat was a four by eight sheet of plywood with rows of fluorescent lights screwed and wired to it.

Near the entrance to the arena a makeshift kitchen was set up where corn was roasted on an oilcan barbeque. Large, stainless steel cooking pots boiled on a gas stove and gave off a delicious aroma. The cook was a young woman whom Jonathan recognized from a little restaurant she operated on the east side of the highway. A number of plastic chairs and tables were arranged and a gang of well-heeled men from Puerto Vallarta set up business to gamble the night away. An audience of young men gathered around them—they could not afford to play a hand.

Along the wall of the entrance were ticket-takers and vendors that charged an entrance fee of fifty pesos and sold beer and pop from ice chests. On the outer walls the rooster cages were laid out and men were busy preening and cooling the birds with water sprayed from their mouths. The birds were transferred from cardboard boxes to cages with cardboard on the bottom that covered the dirt. The cardboard prevented the birds from pecking up glass and foreign objects, which would cause stomach problems.

Men relaxed around the perimeter of the arena telling stories, drinking beer and Tequila. The roosters crowed to each other across the arena. The whole place was filthy and it crept up the whitewashed walls and Jonathan.

Poncho, short for Francisco, was a stocky English speaking Mexican from Ixtapa. He wore tailored jeans, a white shirt under a Jimmy Dean jacket, lizard skin cowboy boots, the expensive tooled kind, and a beige cowboy hat. He held himself well and had six helper-friends that milled about him—all were young. They giggled and laughed with the excitement of being there. The six preened, talked and soothed the roosters with spit and water. They held them with pride for in this country the rooster is a machismo expression for a young man. The ultimate show of masculinity for a young Mexican is to be on horse back with a cockerel under his arm—riding around town and showing off. Poncho is the lead cock with his group and his demeanor showed it.

Jonathan wanted to learn this game that was to be played; he walked over and introduced himself—they soon became friends. He watched what Poncho and the boys were doing as they babbled on and did their thing with the chickens. He couldn't believe he was in Mexico, in this filthy place, drinking beer, making friends with a head rooster and having such a good time.

The birds were ready in their cages and it was time for the events to begin—it did not happen for the next two hours. Not used to bad timing and a little drunk, Jonathan got ticked off and told the judges his displeasure. The judges gave him a blank look as though this had happened before—they would start on Mexican time.

Poncho, the boys and Jonathan sat in front row seats. Because they were poor farmer folk with very little money, Jonathan bought a case of twenty beers from a vendor—he passed them around to his new friends. With nothing to do they sat drinking beer and waited for the call for entries and the fights. The judges gave him the eye and Jonathan gave it right back. He was only afraid of the eye from old women.

Finally the place had a few hundred people in attendance and the tournament got underway. Poncho gave a running commentary to Jonathan what was going on. Two owners and their assistants entered the ring with a rooster each, presented them to the judges who weighed and registered the birds. Each must weight between two and two point five kilograms. The birds were let out on harnesses with tethers to prance about and the betters assessed their quality. Each owner or handler presented their charges close to the other, which made the birds angry. The handlers stepped back to the hoarding and released the roosters to the end of the tethers, which was short of contact for the birds. This encounter lasted a few seconds. The crowd moved forward in their seats and concentrated on each bird; how it strutted, its weight, how it presented its physique, how it charged, squawked, puffed up and how brave they believed it was. These are the qualities that are betted on and this is what the fights are about. There is nothing else; the roosters have no names, there are no heroes, there is no glory—only a bet. Roosters are not cuddly nor are they intelligent like bulls whose deaths cause more emotion.

Judges and owners came together to inspect the razors, which must be exactly one inch long or under. The weapons will be attached to the rooster's spurs. It is not uncommon for some unscrupulous handlers to switch blades after the inspection for longer deadlier spurs. The inspection done, the handlers cradled their roosters in their arms. The assistants attached the razor-knives to the rooster's legs and covered the weapons with tape.

A boy bought an older retired bird into the arena and each handler agitated the fighting birds by thrusting them at the old warrior. The fighting birds became angry, puffed up, squawked and attacked each other in a fury of wings and flying claws. The handlers were careful for if the birds struggle the handlers can get cut, not by the taped razors, but by the sharp claws of the birds.

A dozen men and women entered the ring and called for bets. The bets were taken and the ring emptied, leaving only a judge, the handlers and the roosters who were bought to the center of the ring. The razors were unsheathed, wiped with a lime to neutralize any poison or drugs and the handlers blew spit and water on the birds' heads, under the wings and anus to cool them. The roosters were released.

The two birds were furious with each other; the black puffed up its red collar and the gold flared its wings, both trying to look larger than their two-kilograms. They rushed at each other, claws extended, slashing as they went. The razor on the black slashed the neck and chest of the gold; it crippled the large pectoral muscles of the bird and cut the major arteries of the heart. It squawked, crouched and died and the black hovered over the body until the handler retrieved it. The black was wounded and flapped his wings frantically spraying blood over the handler and Jonathan. He washed the blood off his arm with some beer. The black was injured badly by the gold; it too had a deep incision down its chest and was given to the veterinarian for surgery.

A curious eight-year old girl and Jonathan, both eager to watch what the vet could do, went to his operating station against a filthy wall. The vet sat down to business; on his lap he cradled the bird on a cardboard sheet. The bird lay there and breathed heavily while the vet tore the feathers from his chest to expose the wound; it was long and deep and Jonathan could see the heart beating under a thin membrane. The little girl was fascinated by the open wound and asked questions of the vet who patiently pointed to different parts of the chicken's innards and explained what each was and used for. Her interest was intense and Jonathan thought that someday this young girl would grow up and be a veterinarian.

The brave rooster did not protest as the vet stuffed cotton batten into the huge wound to clean it. With a surgeon's needle he sewed together the large pectoral muscles and some other fleshy parts that Jonathan did not recognize that operate the bird's wings. The vet sewed him up, cleaned the wound with alcohol and gave the little guy a shot of antibiotics. He washed the blood from the bird's feathers and handed it to the delighted little girl who delivered the injured cock to its owners across the arena. A few minutes later the rooster was standing up in his cage pecking at corn and vitamin feed and looked ready to fight again.

"Will he survive?" Jonathan asked.

"Yes, I think he will if there is no infection. He should be retired from fighting; he is a weak bird now. He will probably end up in the pot before the week is out," the vet said. He wiped the blood off his hands and instruments.

A young boy raked the arena clean of blood and feathers.

Between the bouts, Poncho and Jonathan talked about chickens. He knew from his research many years ago when he was contracted to illustrate some roosters, chickens will eat anything and are cannibalistic.

"My uncle," Poncho said, "lived in a village east of the Vallarta airport. He lived alone in a hut on a small vegetable farm. He raised chickens and eggs for himself and the butcher's market. Each morning he would feed and water his chickens that he kept in an open pen behind his hut. The place was hidden from the road by lime trees. One morning he suffered a heart attack while feeding the chickens and died in the pen. Not many people visited my uncle. His body was hidden from the road and no one could see him. He was dead for three days before the local butcher came out to pick up some chickens and eggs. He found my uncle's body. The flesh was eaten off his head and hands and there were rats living in his stomach."

"Shit!" Jonathan said. He opened another beer, "Mexico can be a brutal, harsh and raw place, eh?"

Just before midnight Jonathan said goodbye to his new friends—Poncho and his buddies. He was getting sober and hungry so he stopped by the kitchen for a bowl of whatever was in the big stainless steel pot. The dark skinned woman with Maya features lifted the lid to show him the fare. Surprise! It was chicken soup and he ordered a big bowl. In went the ladle and up came the soup, claws and all; he sat down and had some of the best soup he had ever tasted. He gnawed on the claw but there was little meat. The beautiful woman and Jonathan laughed.

He left the filthy arena and the tournament with a smile as broad as Avenida Mexico. It was a fun time.

Bucerias was still celebrating so he made his way to the bandstand and beer stall. The church clock tower read it was a few minutes before midnight. The mariachi band blasted away and the lead singer sang on to a crowd of several hundred dancing cowboys; their women swaying under the amber glow of the town square's lights. The band and singer serenaded the moon and Quetzalcoatl. The church bells struck midnight and things started to happen.

Small sparks ran around and up the base of the Castillo—a spidery twenty-meter wooden structure. Sparks became larger, menacing, hissing and igniting gunpowder pinwheels. Three pinwheels exploded the Castillo into life throwing green, orange, white and red light into the crowd of eight thousand. Before finishing its set, the wheels sent a huge cloud of white sparks raining down on the heads of screaming delighted children. They held cardboard sheets over their heads so hair and clothes would not catch fire. The huge Castillo was on a stand imbedded into the cobbled street and rotated by ropes pulled by the pyro-technicians, who built the monster for the church. The pinwheels burnt out and diamond geometric shapes in all colours of the rainbow took over. A huge flower of fire appeared partway up the ancient-looking structure and it span in circles whistling and exploding in colours and then changed to bright white light. From the top of the Castillo a flaming wheel turned and shot off its base spinning into the air, riding on a comet tail of crystal white sparks, smoke and fire. The crowd gasped in awe.

The celebration of fire had been performed thousands of times over the years in Mexico and every night in Bucerias's town square during the Patron Saint Festival. The Banda band played a rocking dance number, heavy on drums, the music and dancers created a pagan atmosphere. They blasted and danced their right of passage. In front of the band was a withered toothless one-eyed old Sinatra who sang to some ghost of his memories.

Jonathan saw above the bandstand the spinning, flaming wheel as it hung in the air; it started down from the heavens raining fire. He was directly in its path. He moved a meter to his left. The flaming piece veered and landed an arms length away. The crowd scattered, screamed and laughed. Wide-eyed women clutched their babies and covered them from the falling debris and men took off their cowboy hats shaking off the gunpowder residue. A very drunk man collapsed beside Jonathan; he had looked up and lost his footing. He reached down and grabbed him by his shirt and lifted him to his feet. The moving, swaying mass of people would have trampled him. Fire, cordite powder, bits of wood and paper floated down and a reveler's hair caught on fire. A friend of the human torch rubbed it out with great laughter. Jonathan could smell him burning and was reminded of the times he had burned himself from exploding aerosol cans he threw into fires in his childhood.

A young alcoholic was rubbing the debris from his eyes; tears mixed with dirt—rolled down his face. He was filthy and ready to pass out. Jonathan helped him over to the steps of the bandstand and sat him below the crooning Sinatra. The alcoholic's day was finished and he slumped into sleep against the balustrade. Many in the crowd were worn out from the weeklong celebration. The smoke and stench of the gunpowder was exhilarating; the crowd roared its approval—the fireworks, laughter and noise increased.

With a roar, two hundred rockets shot out of the churchyard; they rose on shafts of orange sparks into the black sky and exploded in a deafening roar. Explosions were heard from the battle ground church yard and a few seconds later giant flowers of light lit up the sky and rained fire and smoke into the square. The noise was deafening; exploding fireworks, screaming joyous revelers, crying babies and the blasting band rattled the night.

The words Our Lady of Peace in fireworks lit up the church—the crowd roared its approval. The palm trees, souvenir stands, food carts, balloons, cowboy hats and silver paper toys around the square reflected the light through amber smoke and gave the scene an air of ancient ritual. Everything bounced, vibrated and swayed to the beat of the drums and the band's brass. The human mass, a sea of flesh and blood swayed and writhed to the rhythm of life.

Suddenly, at the base of the Castillo, panic raced through the crowd. People ran in all directions, some fell on the sidewalk and cobbled street; some, running to safety, trampled others. Out of the churchyard leapt a ferocious apparition—a bull of flames, sparks and fire. It whistled and hissed noisily chasing people down the street shooting rockets into the fleeing mass. It was paper, sticks and rockets with a cardboard cutout of a bull attached to its thin wooden frame. A young boy carried the apparition; he raced everyone's heart with his stunt.

High above the celebrating mass was the basket moon lying on her back in a bowl shape crescent with the star Quetzalcoatl just below and to the right. The ancient God shone his blessing on the crowd. A dozen air bags of red and white paper with cans of lighted fuel strung beneath them floated upward from the square into the night sky to create their own cosmology with the moon and ancient god. The clock tower above the church read twelve o'clock; it was midnight on the last day of the festival. The colours, smells and sounds of life's celebration filled the night on what was the last day of the Patron Saints Festival.

Cast Her to the Wind

After four months in Mexico Bank Robber was running low on cash. It was time to hit Jonathan up for a meal, which she did and blatantly said why. They always told the truth to each other, there was no point in lying about anything so far away from home. When people tell the truth to each other, they become very close and they did, which surprised her because she lived in a world where lies were commonplace. Sadly, thought Jonathan, Robber had to be far from home to learn that lesson.

He dressed the best he could with the little he had; beige pants with a hole that his wallet had made; over a white t-shirt he wore a blue tropical shirt. It all match in style, colour and decay. He felt adequately dressed for an occasion like fine dinner downtown. A freshly washed Bullet and Jonathan picked her up outside her apartment and they drove to old town Puerto Vallarta.

She went all out and dressed up for him. When he saw her under the lights of the highway, she was stunning and he thought, with some suspicion, that maybe there was a little more about tonight, or was it something that she felt it was time to do? She had on a very short yellow dress, low-cut hanging from shoulder ties; there was no need for panties or a bra, her body was firm, well developed and held itself in place. He recognized the dress from the first time they met. She wore nothing else but sandals and earrings. Her thick black hair was curled and cascaded over her shoulders. Just a little mascara and lip-gloss highlighted her tanned face. She looked the full grown mature woman she was, sensual beyond description.

He felt a bit inadequate; this beautiful woman should be with a man her own age. This situation would never happen at home, because she would be with a young man and never know him. They would not make eye contact if he passed her on the street. The age difference between lovers fades away in the tropical nights.

With sexual overtones, an Italian-American waiter looked her over. She looked particularly beautiful gliding into the restaurant. She noticed him looking, grasped Jonathan by the hand and quietly and politely said to the waiter, whom she knew, "Do I pick my daddies or what?"

Jonathan went red through his tan. "You can be such a bitch," he whispered to her and she smiled and giggled. He knew he looked like some rich old fart with his young trick but he quickly dismissed it. They sat at a table that overlooked a busy street mad with tourists, thin ones and fat ones, dressed in their garish best. Beautiful gay men walked hand in hand from the hotel zone and the Pink Chairs. The sounds of parties and good times came from doorways up and down the street filling the old town with warmth and life. Jonathan had spent many hours over the years in the clubs, restaurants and bars of Puerto Vallarta and with her at his side for dinner, he felt very much at home. The waiter came and they both agreed on a bottle of

Pinot Noir. He complimented her on how she looked and apologized for saying it but she was a work of art and he loved beautiful art. She squeezed his hand and they got into small talk.

"You have been going to the cock and bullfights lately."

"Yes, I do it all when I come to Mexico. Why?"

"Why don't you take me along?"

"I never thought you would go for that kind of entertainment. It's pretty brutal, you know, blood all over the place and sometimes on you. I get drunk at these affairs."

"Well, I want to go along sometime with you and get drunk. I want the experience—the full experience of Mexico. Okay?"

"Okay, you'll get it. I'll find some violent killing event for you. I was old fashioned and fatherly protecting you from harm—"

"Thanks babe," she leaned over the table and kissed him.

They continued their small talk for a time and she listened intently at what he said. She loved listening to him ramble. He again promised to arrange for a cock and bullfight and changed the subject. He wanted to know more about her relationship with her father. He thought it a dumb thing to do but he was morbidly curious.

"What made your father come after you, honey?" said Jonathan quietly, leaning over the table.

"I would rather not say right now. I have something in mind," she coyly said. Unusual, he thought she never avoids my questions.

"Oh," he quipped and her eyes flashed at him suspiciously and he dumbly said, "sorry, I was just digging; wanting to find out why he did it to you. I've known others who were raped by their parents, brothers and relations and—"

Bank Robber looked him straight in the eye and her black eyes dove into his brain. Quietly and gently she went into a tirade of anger and passion. It was so controlled nobody nearby would know the annoyance emanating from her. She grabbed his right hand and held on, "Look!" she said, "the fucking truth is, it was me Jonathan—it was not my father who started the affair. It became so strong I wanted him to divorce my mother and run away and marry me. How bizarre is that? I wanted his babies—my sisters and brothers. Dad was not to blame, it was I all along—I tore them apart. I love my dad as a daughter and love him big time and passionately as a lover. Mom and dad made a very strong offspring and they could not handle her. Dad is a handsome and beautiful man and my mom even more beautiful and an extremely intelligent woman. I love them both. Intimate and incestuous sex ripped us apart. I'm over here now, Jonathan, in Mexico with you and I'm wet and I want you like my father. I want to fuck you. I'm sorry to tell you this but there it is—I'm sorry but you asked for it! Please don't ask me to stand up because right now I have a wet spot on my nice yellow dress where my lovely ass is resting."

They both howled with laughter and Jonathan bent over, kissed her, said he was sorry for prying and he loved her when she was angry. The raging she had with others was not on him, her controlled anger and humor with him was delightful. The vast difference in their ages was shrinking. Careful, Jonathan told himself—you're falling into a Greek tragedy.

"Electra," he said.

"Huh?"

"Oh, nothing."

The waiter arrived and Robber ordered without looking at the menu, "We'll have the Greek salad each to start and I'll have the Pasta Alfredo and Jonathan will have a New York Steak well done with mushroom sauce. Thank you. Oh, and no salt on anything please. Thank you."

The meal was simple and delicious; they ordered another bottle of wine and strawberry ice cream for desert. She talked about her parents and the wonderful years in North Africa, school and travel in Europe. Her love for her parents was totally foreign to him and he realized how little he knew of families' intimate relationships. They finished; he paid the bill and led her out of the restaurant. They weaved their way through the mass of people on Olas Altas. They past a restaurant, which had a roaring party going on; it is the same party that goes on seven nights a week. They petted an old Mexican's burrow that customers ride into the place to have their pictures taken. They arrived at Bullet and he guided her into the passenger's seat and leaned over her to clamp her seat belt—she pulled his head to her breasts.

"Thanks for a great evening," he said and gently kissed her on the mouth.

"I'm sorry I tried to seduced you. Can we sleep together anyway? I'm lonely sometimes."

"Sure, honey." He took her home to his cottage and they both stripped; Jonathan put on a sweatshirt and pajama pants and she put on his boxer shorts and a t-shirt. They rolled up tight together and slept. They did not make love and they never would.

The cockfighting tournaments ended in Bucerias so Jonathan inquired about the nearest town that was holding an event to entertain his friend. There wasn't any except an illegal fight at El Tuito, just south of Puerto Vallarta over the mountains, an hour's drive away on the highway to Barra de Navidad. Since the fights were illegal, it was going to be difficult to find the place. His source, the boss at the fish market, suggested he inquire at the village local liquor and convenience store on the west side of the town square of El Tuito.

They set off on a Sunday afternoon. They went south through Puerto Vallarta, Mismaloya, Boca de Tamatlan and up onto the Cuale Mountain Range and through the jungle to the village of El Tuito. They found the liquor store on the square and asked the woman selling beer to two young Mexicans where they could find a cockfight that afternoon and evening. The proprietor did not know or understand a word he said but one of the young men overheard him. Not saying anything, he handed Jonathan a crude map of the countryside with a mark were he would find the local tournament. Jonathan thanked them and the young men walked to their expensive automobile and put the beer into freezer packs in the back seat. There, on the floor, was a big red and gold rooster prancing on a sheet of cardboard.

"These cowboys are on their way to a cockfight for sure," Jonathan said, and he gestured that he would follow them because he couldn't read the map anyway. Robber and he had only been to El Tuito once before and didn't know the village or its network of roads through the jungle that flowed down to the coast.

They followed the cowboys west to the edge of town. By a little country church was a small, green sign with painted white lettering that pointed towards a rough road to the coast and Yelapa; a road that is not on any official maps. After half an hour of following the cowboys with the occasional stop so Bullet and passengers could catch up, they pulled into a farm with a lavish hacienda, outbuildings and barns.

Chestnut racehorses pranced about a pasture. Fences and walls festooned with bougainvillea surrounded the property; the lawns were green and manicured. Tall Primavera trees dotted the landscape; their bright yellow flowers glowed in the sun. Dominating everything was a large white washed barn and dozens of cars, trucks and farm vehicles were parked in a nearby field. Horses were tethered to fences, their leather tooled saddles and bright blankets draped over posts. Men in cowboy hats, jeans and boots leaned against the fences and cars drinking and smoking, some deep in conversation, others laughing and joking. They parked beside their new friends who didn't speak a word of English but knew the word cockfight and what they wanted. Robber was excited and so was Jonathan.

Together they entered the barn with seating for several hundred people around an arena pit in the dirt floor. Three meters above them was a balcony with wooden railings that went around the perimeter of the barn. Cowboys and cowgirls leaned over the railings with small baskets on the ends of ropes to exchange betting money and chits with the hawkers below. Along one wall was a bar with well-stocked freezers of cold beer and boxes of taco chips, salsa and candy bars. A man cooked hot stew of some kind on a propane stove behind the bar. The fighting ring was well lit with flood lamps and a fancy green stained glass pool table light lit the bar. Tables were set up at the back and they spilled out the rear doors into the field beyond. These were for the owners and handlers of the birds. A local veterinarian wearing white pants and shirt with a black tie was present to sew up the mess that would inevitably come. This was a clean and posh operation,

Jonathan thought. There was no cover charge, the tournament was illegal; the interests were gambling and drinking.

"Maybe this is by invitation only." Jonathan wondered to Robber but no one challenged them for a fee. The audience was mostly men—prosperous and sassy cowboys from nearby farms and ranches. There were some women present, dressed much like the men, in cowboy gear, which he found unusual.

And then Jonathan noticed her, an old crone, the same one he saw the day he went to the market with Tim and Barbara. It was she and he could only see her face in the blackness way up in a corner of the balcony—she looked down at him like a turkey vulture on her perch.

"The bitch," he said.

"What?" Robber responded.

"Oh, nothing—just something silly." There was an evil up there among the rafters and it was too close. He dismissed it and thought himself an idiot for carrying on about naive hocus-pocus. His mind went back to the moment.

The place was nothing like the hole he was in at the Patron Saint's Festival—this was classy. They were in the countryside where little English was spoken—Robber did most of the talking. He was the only blonde in the barn besides the chickens. They were foreigners and stood out dramatically, so people asked who they were and made them welcome. He assumed, they wanted to talk to his partner; the woman attracts attention wherever she goes. At the bar he ordered a beer for himself and a Caesar for her. It was almost six o'clock; the tournament was to start—and it did. They took their seats and he described what was going on with the judges, knives, tethers, poison, the cooling of the chickens and the gambling. She listened intently then sent him to the bar for more beer and another Caesar. They both felt like they were on a first date—uncomfortable and a bit nervous. There was definitely a feeling of longing for each other; their relationship was becoming intense. They knew something sexual would definitely happen that night.

After round one she turned to him and said, "Since you won't make love to me, tell me about someone you have made love to."

"I don't talk about such things, honey. I've never felt right about that. Telling stories about sex is fine with me but not an actual experience; that, I have always kept private," he explained, "once I had a woman who told me in detail about her past boyfriends' prowess and I found it distasteful; I became jealous and hurt."

"Come on, this is Mexico—there must be someone you can tell me about," she pleaded, "don't be boring."

"Let me think—I can tell you about a disaster I had down here once if you promise not to laugh too hard," he said taking her hand.

"Okay—go on. Tell me," she said excited, squirming in her plastic seat.

As they waited for the next round he told his tale of love's disaster:

"It was in my early days as a tourist in Mexico ten or eleven years ago. One morning at a beach restaurant I met a woman from Eugene, Oregon. Don't ask me her name, because I can't remember it; let's call her the Good Doctor. She was having breakfast and writing in her diary. She looked so pretty and young that I had to make a comment. I asked her if she was writing about love lost or love found and as I said those words she wrote them in her diary and closed it. She invited me to her table. We talked about where we came from, who we were and where we were going—feeling each other out—getting to know each other. This twenty eight year old turned out to be a Naturopathic Physician with a degree in acupuncture of all things, so she was very interesting, intelligent, articulate and full of humor and wit. She was young like you Bank Robber—beautiful in her way but not as good looking as you."

"Thanks."

"Her legs just went on and on; that's what gave her height—her long legs. Her skin was white for down here in the sun; she was very conscious about protecting it and was always caressing it with sun block and lotions—"

"Get on with it Jonathan," Robber demanded.

"Okay, well, we got to know each other and by mid afternoon I was getting excited and working hard at a relationship with the hope it would blossom into great sex. She was hot, Robber, I could feel the heat radiating from her—her eyes and body language spoke it all. We promised to meet the next morning for breakfast and spend the day together on a boat trip to Yelapa—"

"Oh, you old dog, you."

"The next morning I ran to the restaurant from my hotel five blocks away, walking the last half a block to make sure I wasn't panting and looking to eager. She was there in short-shorts, a halter-top and sandals carrying a wicker beach bag. She was more attractive than the day before. We ate breakfast, went to the pier and boarded the boat.

"Now this boat holds about two hundred people and has an open bar so most passengers get pissed and we were no exception. At 10:30 in the morning we were into double tequila sunrises on the foredeck. We talked mostly about sex, she clinically, me romantically.

"Right into it, eh, Jonathan?" she quipped jealously with a Canadian accent.

"Well you wanted to hear a love story didn't you? What else does one talk about aboard a boat on a blue sea, a blazing sun overhead and the beautiful green jungles of Mexico rolling up the mountains, pelicans and frigate birds floating in the blue sky, a drink in hand to soften the brain and a set of legs three meters long wrapped around you? May I—please?"

"Yes Jonathan, sorry, please go on," she said smiling and squeezing his thigh. There was a look of jealousy in her eyes.

"Thank you," he kissed her cheek, "the boat stopped at Los Argos for half an hour so we could watch the divers and tourists snorkeling. We went on to Yulapa, the boat docked and we were told that it would leave at 3:30 p.m. We made ourselves comfortable at a beach restaurant for the afternoon—both quite drunk and horny. We decided to hire a fishing boat to take us further south, a few miles around the point to one of the remote fishing villages where we could be alone and do a little skinny dipping."

"And a little of you know what," she injected, feeling her Caesars.

"Sh," Jonathan ordered and he continued, "I sat on the bow and she decided to straddle me, she wrapped her long legs around my waist. The Mexican fisherman's eyes popped out of his head and rolled onto the deck. The little fishing boat rose and came crashing down over each swell that became higher and higher as we left the bay. Finally we went up one swell and came down the other side with a jolt. My back took the full force of her weight, bruising my spine and our mouths, which were on each other. The impact bruised her jaw. The pain in my lower back was terrific and I could hardly breathe. She screamed at the fisherman to turn around and take us back to the beach. I could barely get myself out of the boat but I mustered my strength and with the Good Doctor's help we made it to some canvas chairs where we could rest and drink beer for our pain. Her jaw hurt but she managed to laugh about it and with her great wit she made me laugh to. Time went by and the Good Doctor suddenly said, isn't that our boat? It was pulling out of the bay. We just waved it goodbye.

"Next to our canvas chairs were a couple of gay pilots from San Francisco. They were down for a little R and R. They were shacked up at the Pink Chairs Hotel. I used to stay there before it became an exclusively gay resort destination."

"Please will you concentrate on the subject," she said impatiently.

"Anyway, these were nice guys. We told them of our dilemma and assured them we were not worried and that we were castaways—someone would come for us in a couple of years—they offered to help. They had a car in Boca de Tamatlan and would be taking a water taxi there in the late afternoon. We could come along and they would drive us the rest of the way to Mismaloya and the Good Doctor's hotel. It was a hell of a ride, the Good Doctor and I hung on to each other like two wounded birds. I suffered the most in the bouncing water taxi, the pain shot across my lower back like fire from a gun barrel. She massaged my lower back and slipped her hand into my shorts once in awhile.

"Finally we made it to the hotel, to her room and what a place—marble everywhere for two hundred and fifty bucks a day. Quickly we stripped and eased ourselves into the marble shower and the hot soothing water. Our bodies ached but our blood was fired up and we made love, the pain of our wounds gone, erased by the heat and our passion for each other. Out of the shower we gently dried and oiled each other and on the porch overlooking the beach we settled into a rattan chesterfield. We made love again for the next hour. I lay on top of her and when I had finished—Jesus Christ I couldn't get up! I couldn't get off her. My back had seized up and I didn't know whether to laugh or cry. She began to laugh which ejected me from her and she rolled me off her body and I fell to the patio floor. I screamed in pain and she laughed some more. Since she was a big woman and strong, she lifted me by my arms to my feet and guided me to the bedroom. She rolled the covers off the bed and made a pile of pillows. She instructed me to lie on them with my ass in the air. By this time we were crying with pain and laughter. She massaged and kissed me all the way up and down my poor back, ass and legs promising to cure me since she was a doctor and could work the hand of God, which at this point is what I needed."

Bank Robber broke into hysterics.

"Now comes the fun part. She got up and went to the closet and from her travel bag she pulled out a leather pouch. She removed a plastic container from it and laid it on the bed table, opened it and removed a set of latex gloves, which she pulled over her long fingers. Christ! I thought here I am helplessly propped up with my ass in the air; a naked angel in latex gloves hovering over me. Out came another container from the pouch and this time it was scary—needles, dozens of them about eight centimeters long. Don't worry my love; I'll fix everything, she said. Just stay still because I'm still drunk and if I miss I will penetrate your heart. This is it right here by the way, she said, poking my ass.

"The Good Doctor pulled a small plastic bottle of sterilizer from the box and with a cotton swab from her cosmetic kit she sterilized each needle and gently rotated them into my back, ass and legs. After two-dozen needles were inserted she sat down on the floor beside the bed and looked at her victim—err—patient—giggling and smiling, with tears running down her cheek. We were drunk, exhausted and happy and I thought thank God for Mexico. Where else could one end up in such a bizarre situation, drunk and suffering a happy pain, propped up in an expensive hotel room looking like a porcupine and a naked beautiful woman nearby. I had no place to go. I thought I'm a lucky man!"

"Did you ever see each other again?" She kissed him and squeezed his hand.

"No honey," he said sadly, "we were too dangerous for each other, we parted, and the Good Doctor went home. We all go home eventually from this place."

Bank Robber reached into her short's pocket and pulled out a wrapped condom; looked him in the eye and without saying anything she slipped it into his shirt pocket. They both smiled and gently kissed not saying anything; they would just let nature happen.

More spectators and gamblers arrived and the arena was packed with Mexicans and chickens—it was the third round of the cockfights. Bets were in place and the chickens were readied for battle. Jonathan put two hundred pesos on a black with a red head. He bet on him because he strutted about like a good cockerel should; head up, bobbing and proud.

Behind them a shouting match began between a middle aged cowboy and a drunk on the opposite side of the arena. Jonathan had noticed them muttering at each other when he was waiting at the bar to be served. Both men were now visibly angry.

She quietly said, "They seem to be talking about someone beating someone else's brother, something like that—he says he will get the bastard who did it. He is very drunk and angry."

The drunk was familiar but Jonathan could not place him. Then he realized, "Christ! It's one of those guys that we met on the road to San Sebastian--the bastard with the scar on his mouth. He's dressed up today and not in his work clothes. I don't think he recognizes us. He's drunk now and was drunk then. There may be trouble here!"

"I think he's too drunk and that's good—he won't be any trouble for us—will he?" she whispered nervously.

The argument sounded like an old feud between the drunk and the cowboy. Now it had grown to the size of the arena. The audience laughed and shouted at them to shut up but they kept it up—irritating each other. One of the officials, a large fat man who seemed to know the drunk approached him. He ordered him to sit down, relax and enjoy the fights.

Suddenly, the drunken man reached under his shirt and pulled a gun from his belt—aimed and fired at the official. The bullet tore through the official's forehead and the back of his skull came away. His brains and skull parts exploded over the audience. He was dead before he fell to the ground. The other side of the argument that was behind them drew a pistol from his jacket pocket and returned fire.

The audience screamed and panicked—they moved in all directions. Some people ran through a plywood wall on the side of the barn. The tables with the chickens were overturned and the birds flew into the air squawking; panicked from the sight of the moving mass of frightened people. A man beside the drunkard fell forward dead from a shot in the face and another beside him slumped back in his chair, blood oozed from a hole in the left side of his chest. The drunkard fired a rapid succession of shots into the crowd and several people behind Bank Robber and Jonathan screamed as they went down. The cowboy returned a shot. It went through the drunkard's neck and he went down on his knees, terror in his bulging eyes. His mouth made swallowing movements and he vomited, his left hand held his neck as it gushed blood from a ruptured garroted artery. Before he dropped dead he fired off the last shot.

The last bullet tore through the chest and exited the back of a young cowboy that sat in front of Bank Robber, killing him instantly. The spinning bullet ricocheted off the patella of her knee and traveled up and under her ribs at the base of her sternum; it shattered her heart and lungs. She turned her head and looked with dead eyes at Jonathan, then just laid her head back; blood gurgled from her mouth and down her cheek as she exhaled her last breath. Life left her before she knew what had happened. There was not a chance for her to scream or say goodbye.

He caught her body in his arms and the chairs beneath them split apart—they crashed to the floor. His face crushed against hers and he held her close and tried to keep her spirit from leaving but it was gone. He looked up to the barn ceiling and through a large vent in the roof he could see the bright star of Quetzalcoatl in the darkening sky. He held her tightly and said goodbye and told her he loved her. From the balcony the woman in black stared blankly, no pity or sorrow was on her hollow face.

The barn was in chaos as screaming shouting people ran in every direction trying to take cover from the raging fight—it was too late. People were dead and many were wounded. A cowboy jumped from the balcony onto the gunman that was alive, his feet landed on the gunman's head and shoulders and drove him to the ground. There was a cracking noise of bones snapping. A number of the cowboys jumped on the gunman and beat him senseless as they wrestled the gun away. They tied him to a chair using their belts. Many were on their cell phones to the police.

Soon police trucks and ambulances roared into the compound and the police lined the spectators up and searched them for weapons. A sizable stack of knives and guns were loaded into a police truck. Jonathan did not move; he held Bank Robber close; his body was bloodied and shaking from shock. The police questioned everyone in the arena. The cowboy gunman and the sponsor of the illegal event were arrested and taken away, handcuffed and tied up in the back of a police trucks.

Incredibly, Commander Bernarda Perez that Jonathan met on the road to Alta Vista was on the scene and took care of them. Jonathan sensed the sympathy from the commander. It was written across his strong dark face.

"Mr. Owen, we meet again. This is bad—very bad. Let my men take her now. She will be taken to the morgue in Ixtapa. We have to perform an autopsy in this case. You understand?"

"I understand." Jonathan released her to police officers that placed her on a stretcher and carried her to an ambulance. "I will need to question you at headquarters in Ixtapa tomorrow. Please be there Mr. Owen." He reached into his breast pocket under his badge, "here is my card with information—does she have identification?"

"I think so," and he checked her shorts back pocket and pulled out her wallet, "here." And he gave the wallet to the commander.

"I'll be there tomorrow Commander. Please if you can, would you see the press doesn't get her name, or at least ask them not to print it?" he said tearfully.

"I will try—but may not happen. Now I think it best you go home. Will you be able to drive?"

"Yes, I think so.

"You know my name?"

"Yes, we take down the names of all who go to drug country. Dangerous place Mr. Owen. Be careful you may be next body I take to morgue. Now, please go home."

"Thank you officer." Jonathan drove home alone through the darkening jungle in disbelief of what had happened—in an instant life had changed. His beautiful friend was back there far from home, family and friends, alone and cold. He missed and loved her. His mind raced: Why did this happen to her and not him, after all he was turning sixty she was barely twenty-five? He had enjoyed so many good years; she was just beginning her life. He was numb by the time he got home. Regardless how he felt, he must take care of business—she would have wanted that.

At his cottage he gathered his strength, showered her blood off his body and put his bloodied shirt and shorts in the bathroom sink to soak. He found the condom she had slipped into his shirt and thought of what might have been and the love they would have shared. If only he had the power to turn everything back he thought and images of their future flashed before him—even marriage and babies.

He knew he must keep himself together and not fall apart. He concentrated and focused on what to do and immediately went to her apartment; woke the landlady, told her what had happened and explained he must get in touch with her family right away. The police and coroner would need her papers and contacts that were in her room and he would pack her belongings and take them with him. The landlady, visibly upset by the tragedy, showed him to her room and unlocked the door. She knew and trusted him and invited him downstairs to her apartment office to use her phone when he was ready.

He went through Bank Robber's closet, drawers, bags, and bundles and packed everything as he went. He could smell her. Each piece of clothing reminded him of their adventures. There were pictures of them on the beach, at the volcanoes, on the streets of Bucerias and Puerto Vallarta. There were pictures of others with her—those images hurt him. In the top drawer of a dresser he found her passport and diary with email addresses and phone numbers listed. He went downstairs to the landlady's office and phoned her mother who was in bed napping halfway around the world. It was the hardest part of all but he managed with grace and dignity in his voice to tell her he was a friend and what had happened.

There was uncontrollable sobbing on the other end of the line for several minutes. Her mother pulled herself together and they talked of arrangements that needed to be made. She would get in touch with Robber's father who was on business in France. She was frail, she said, not in good health and would not be able to manage the journey to Mexico. She would get Robber's father to fly from Paris to Puerto Vallarta on the next available plane. Jonathan gave her his email address and the phone number of the police in Puerto Vallarta and said goodbye.

For her belongings, he gave the landlady a receipt that he scribbled on a page out of her diary. He finished packing her things, put her diary in his shirt and passport in his pocket—he loaded her bags into Bullet. He would hand them over to her father when he arrived. Returning to her apartment he sat on her bed. He found one of his palm tree shirts beside the bed on the floor. He held it to his face. The musky smell of her youth drifted up through his nostrils; memories of Bank Robber came rushing back.

He did not cry for her. That night they would have made love even though he knew it would cause pain and longing. Their relationship never had the chance to go beyond friendship. No, he felt an overwhelming sadness for the young woman; she would never live a full life, meet a man, fall in love and have babies. Jonathan took back his shirt.

Two days later her father arrived from Paris and Jonathan met him briefly at the airport. Jonathan waited with a cardboard sign so they could identify each other. Her father was visibly shaken and sad as he entered the airport. Christ, he said to himself. This man is extremely good looking. This was not good for him, he felt very embarrassed and intimidated by Bank Robber's father's presence. After seeing him he felt he should be his limousine driver. Her father was actually beautiful, five eleven, black hair, black tailored suit with a gray t-shirt and black Italian shoes with no socks—tanned face and hands. His body was in good physical shape and filled his clothes in the right places. My God! Jonathan thought I'm looking at another form of her. He had only seen such men in Italy, which perhaps has the most beautiful people in the world, as far as he was concerned. Poor Bank Robber, she grew up worshiping and loving the wrong man but what a man—such presence, he thought.

They greeted each other, shook hands and expressed their sorrow. By the look on his face he was uneasy at meeting Jonathan. Her father had been her lover and he was just a white tourist in shorts, bad shirt and sandals. Jonathan handed him her few belongings, her passport and got him into a taxi to take him to a hotel that Jonathan had booked for him. He handed him the phone number of the police investigation team and directions to the coroner's office, where he could claim his daughter's body.

He was glad he didn't have to be with him long. He didn't want to explain his relationship nor did he want to become friends with him since dad and daughter were responsible for all the hurt in their lives. Or was that true? He pondered. She was a powerful woman; she had manipulated through her beauty and cunning, her bank, her mother, her father and him. He thought I loved her more than I realized! He completed his final duties for her and left the building at a run. Beautiful father would go through life not knowing if Jonathan was his daughter's lover.

On the beach at Ensencido Litigu a few weeks before the tragedy, Bank Robber told him she kept a diary of the things and events she experienced day by day. She wrote down the emotions she experienced and as their time together progressed, she wrote her intimate feelings for him. She wanted to read them to him but these were feelings that he did not want to know. He stole the diary.

Ensencido Litigu was gray the day he took a last walk across its sands. The surf was higher and more violent than usual; he had hoped for a sunny afternoon but it was not to be. He was not alone on the beach; he had the company of the turkey vultures, pelicans and frigate birds soaring overhead; the ghost crabs that scurried about, and the dark clouds over Punta de Mita.

It was a walk with the ghost of Bank Robber. In his heartbreak he felt her beside him—her hand in his. He had her diary. He would do one last thing for her on the beach she loved to visit and be in the sun and surf with him. The place were she let out her anger and sorrow but most of all a place were she and Jonathan rejoiced her youth. The years between them had slipped away.

They walked south toward the rocks where the pelicans fished. The wind was coming up going from the land to the sea; huge clouds moved towards them; becoming darker and menacing. Jonathan told her how sorry he was for not protecting her and that he never acted the loving partner that she wanted. She did not answer him.

He opened her diary and looked at the pages without reading them, every page was full—some with little drawings. Coasters and tickets from nightclubs, restaurants and tours were taped down; over them were scribbled stick figures, names and numbers in coloured pencil. He took each page and tore it from the book and each page he tore into fine bits. Like confetti, he threw them in the air and they rode the wind down the beach. Every page, every scrap of the diary he threw to the wind and by the time he was finished the gray cloud had arrived and it poured with rain. He did not mind—it was warm and wonderful and so was life. Soaking wet, he climbed the stairs to the parking lot and Bullet and drove from the beach and the ghost of Bank Robber. He looked into the rearview mirror and saw her through the rain, standing in her little yellow dress up to her knees in the surf. She waved to him and he knew he would see her now and again for the rest of his life. She would be there at the back of his eyes, giggling and looking over his shoulder.

There was so much that might have been for them but life takes turns and twists you cannot plan and to speculate would drive him mad with sorrow. All that was left were the sweet memories of Bank Robber, Silver Bullet and him. He would treasure the short time they had together and he would never return to the beach again. Driving home to Bucerias, he realized it was nearing the end of his time in Mexico and he would have to return to his life in Canada and prepare for a crime he had started.

Moving On

Rhonda's restaurant sits on the edge of a small resort hotel up against the beach of Bucerias. It was Jonathan's favorite place to spend a quiet day or watch the sunset. Umbrellas and lounge chairs are spread out along the beach, a welcome shade from the searing sun. The restaurant is made of palm frond thatching supported by ironwood poles; the floor is a mixture of red brick, gray concrete, yellow stones and black river rock. A yellow painted cement-walled kitchen and a white tiled bar sit to one side. Chandeliers of woven vine baskets hang from the rafters. Palm trees, wrapped with lights, grow through the roof. Apart from the kitchen there are no walls, the sea breeze gently blows through the restaurant cooling the afternoons. Two table cloths grace each table—one white overlaid with another of midnight blue, coloured with small subtle yellow and red designs. The chairs are wicker and wood, painted with yellow, green and red motifs. The architecture and design is minimalist, blending into the scene which is the clean uninterrupted beach lined with coconut palms that lean out to the sea and sky. They stretch down the kilometers of beach north and south eventually fading into a blue-gray mist.

The ocean is so bright from the sun it's blinding and in the afternoon Ehecatl, the God of wind, billows up giant white clouds deep in the south end of the bay. He gently blows across the bay agitating the water's surface into a billion, sparkling diamonds. The scene is so romantic your heart soars with joy for the good life and the luck of being in such a place.

Looking out onto the bay, he would scan the scene through his dark sunglasses. He absorbed the striking immense sea to sky beauty with its contrast of colours and textures. To the south in Nuevo Vallarta were the concrete gray, cream, pink and red roofed towers of the beach hotels. Further on is the airport and Marina. Deeper into the bay in the cluttered mass of reflected sunlight is the city of Puerto Vallarta with its tourist hotels, restaurants and Plaza de Toros. And in the heart of the city is the gallery where he first met Bank Robber. Silver Bullet's service center was just beyond the airport on Francisco Medina where she got her new radiator. Further south, over the bridge of the Rio Cuale, is old town were Jonathan vacationed in past years.

He remembered Mexico's brutal history and the fate of the innocent as Mexico, along with the rest of North and South America, marches west into the Pacific Ocean. Around him was a land of power and mystery, the birthplace of a great nation of people and gods. Volcanoes sleep nearby. For him, Rhonda's is in the center of all he had come to expect. It is a reflection of the heart and light of ancient and modern Mexico.

On his last evening he visited the Café Bucerias. He hugged his friends who were watching a soccer game, joking, laughing and pickled from beer and tequila. Wolf handed him a beer; he thanked him but he did not take it. The next few days would be long and dangerous and he needed his strength and wits. He had five thousand kilometers of highway to drive. He did not stay long at the café; it hurt knowing he may never see these friends again and they had become good pals. They looked at him with sadness in their eyes knowing he was leaving paradise—whatever that might be. He shook their hands, wished them well and left quickly—not looking back; memories of Bank Robber were welling up and about to drown him.

He walked the two blocks to the beach choking back tears of emotion and joy. His bare feet in the warm waters, he walked to Rhonda's to watch the sunset and reflect on all that had happened to him over the past months. His tanned feet now matched the colour of his sandals, his shorts were faded, his tropical shirt tied in a knot at the waist was still bright and cheerful and his hair was bleached blonde by the sun. His lean body was tanned and healthy. He was at peace with the world around him and had gained a greater understanding of his life, physically and spiritually. He was not a guest anymore in Mexico; he felt he was part of its landscape and spirit. The warmth of the people and gods were now inside him—the dust between his toes was his badge. Jonathan would always be here in spirit wherever he went in the world and he was going places—that he promised himself.

Mark, a waiter at Rhonda's, watched him come down the beach and opened a soda. When Jonathan sat in his usual place out on the beach, he handed the can of pop to him not saying a word. Jonathan picked his favorite opera, Madame Butterfly by Puccini on his portable player for his last sunset in Bucerias. The piece he picked is sung by Butterfly who is full of hope and longing in her vigil waiting for her husband to return from far away. High above him was the moon but Quetzalcoatl was still a faint light.

Jonathan looked to the north where two teenagers about fifteen years of age, a boy and girl trotted hand-in-hand down the beach from the Bucerias Malecón. They carried an inner tube, net basket and bucket. She was a girl yet a physically mature woman; walnut brown with full breasts, round buttocks and thighs; her hair tied high on her head and knotted with a red bandana. She looked so much like an Aztec princess—warrior-like. She wore red shorts and like young stylish girls of Mexico, the button above the zipper was left undone to reveal her naval adorned with a silver stud—a badge of her youth. She wore a tank top for the rest. The boy was not a man yet, skinny and lanky, he would soon become broad in the shoulders and muscular in body. His skin was walnut like hers. He wore shorts down to his knees, black with a bright yellow and red designs emblazoned across them. Both wore shell necklaces and anklets they had probably made for each other. Butterfly's voice soared over the scene.

Diving into the water near Jonathan they swam out beyond the surf into the sunset. For an hour they dived for oysters, laughing and giggling with joy, faces glowing in admiration of each other, two pals, buddies, partners, lovers, and spirits of Mexico. He thought how many times over the thousands of years had this ceremony been repeated in this bay? Life was eating up the years in such great joy. The sun was falling down on its way into the bay and a massive thunderhead filled up the sky and bent toward the sun in the south. The mountains were painted in pink, purple, gold and shades of blue. The hotels to the south gleamed as the sun slammed its rays onto the bright painted plaster and stucco. Butterfly finished her aria.

With their catch of oysters the couple came out of the water, the sun bathed them in light—it sparkled across their wet bodies. Down to business on the beach they shelled their catch and filled up their little bucket. As the massive red ball dove into the sea they stopped their work and watched the dying of the day—arms around each other. As the sun disappeared into the ocean they gently kissed and clapped their hands to celebrate the sun's time on earth and its departure for the night. Gathering their gear and small catch they left, jogging down the beach hand in hand, to the stairs. They climbed onto the town square and disappeared like the sun. They left the basket of the moon, Quetzalcoatl and Jonathan on that empty beach in the Place of the Divers on the Bahia de Banderas, Mexico. Their culture, youth and energy tore his heart out.

Two

A Dead Artist Can Make a Good Living

Canada Germany Portugal Spain

Gibraltar Morocco

Prologue

He used a large magnifying glass; he did not have a nose on which to place reading glasses. The faceless man read Carl Jung within the shadow of a King's monument. Above the man, in a niche, was a frieze of a naked soldier being trampled by an elephant. The meaning was lost in antiquity but it did not matter, he felt related to the battling mass.

He had read thousands of volumes in his sixty years; most of civilization's classic literature of the arts and science were stacked up to the ceiling in his apartment. Every few years he would donate the books to the library only to fill his rooms up again. He became wise and fluent in languages, knew the principals of engineering and could identify birds that migrated from the north to the Province of Algarve in the south. He had nothing else to do but read, he did not have friends; people could not stand the sight and smell of him.

It was time to go home. Groaning from pain and the weight of his labored life, he rose on his spindly legs, tucked his book in his shirt and from his jacket pocket took out his plastic cup with his identification card inside. He was well dressed in an all black suit, black shirt and polished banker shoes. He dusted himself off with a handkerchief. If nothing else, he was proud of his clothing.

He crept to the entrance of old town Lisbon and a huge triumphal arch. The avenue below ran to the main square of the old city. For fifty years he made the same journey—going home through the heart of old town. Before entering the arch he crossed a through street stopping only to let a yellow electric streetcar pass. The driver looked at him in disgust; the passengers looked on with incredulity. An old legless woman in a wheelchair claimed territory under the arch; she mocked the faceless man everyday, throwing him kisses. Down the road he mentally pulled himself, his breathing wheezing under the strain of his physical condition.

He came to a road that ran across the avenue and more yellow trolleys clanked and groaned by. Pedestrians on each side of him kept their distance as they waited for the light to turn green and those across the street to come the opposite direction made a passage for him and avoid contact. He stumbled through the oncoming crowd, plowing his way like a ship through the Tigris River. Faces stared and flowed left and right, only a few people reached out with a donation for his cup. He passed the beautiful neo-classic buildings of the old district. They rose like the walls of a canyon and reflected the sun's glow down onto cream mosaic tiles, emblazoned here and there with gothic crests.

The faceless man's only enemies were the young bullies that taunted him. A number of years ago he became very angry with one that bothered him for a week. He grabbed the bully by the hair and rubbed his face in his. The young man screamed and ran to his parents—they lodged a complaint. The police arrested and held the faceless man for a day while they investigated the incident. The local hospital told the parents and police no harm would come to the boy; the man's disfigurement was genetic and could not be transferred to anyone except by birth. He was released under the condition he control his anger.

On he went with his plastic cup and identification in his outstretched hand. In his other hand was a handkerchief to wipe away the weeping liquid from his eyes and mouth. Lately his eyes were becoming closed over by the invasive flesh; narrowing his peripheral vision. He would be blind soon and his only salvation from total isolation and a desperate future would be his breathing—it will kill him. He would, at times, become claustrophobic and experience waves of anxiety. His face was choking and smothering him to death. He had lived a long time with his condition and was not afraid of the inevitable; on the contrary, he felt lucky and thankful that he had come so far.

He looked up to the left and saw the elevator tower of the old town, a filigreed wrought iron structure that takes tourists and residents up to the Bairro where he lived. All his life he took the stairs up the hill to avoid confinement with people in the elevator. His affliction gave off an unpleasant odor; now crippled he had no choice. Each day was torture for him, crowded into an elevator with others. Sometimes people were polite, stood aside and he rode up alone. Tonight he would make one more round of the square before he took the dreadful beast into the sky.

The man stumbled into the square and looked up to the castle where his mother abandoned him after the war many years ago. He never knew his father or his mother. He remembered the two nights alone and afraid on the battlements, huddled under one of the black cannons, a letter of introduction and apology pinned to his thin jacket. The letter said nothing of where or when he was born. He cried for hours until he was found by one of the grounds keepers who took him in until the time his affliction took hold. He went from family to family, eventually into a home for the infirm; he escaped into the streets of Lisbon. His passed was something to forget but he could not, it haunted him all his life.

One thing he did manage to do, many years and heartaches later, was to forgive his mother. His reading about the ravages of war healed the wounds. The horrific crime to humanity that spread and touched every city, town and hamlet of Europe was greater than his affliction. His mother had suffered alone and helpless in those years and she surmised they would not have survived together. She made a heart wrenching decision. She set him free in the world to learn how to survive alone—he did.

In the twilight he reached the square and the giant granite pillar of Dom Pedro IV. The naked bronze women of the fountains sprayed water over reflection pools; in the distance was the classic building the Theater Maria II. Over and above the buildings he could see the façade of the Church of Sao Domingo glowing in amber floodlights. He visited the Church most days—it was his sanctuary. But God he did not believe in. All his life he had studied the religions of the world and even practiced meditation to overcome his guilt and physical pain. But he was stuck within a shell and could not get out to touch the gods that his fellow men around him loved. The priest had tried to help him find the peace that comes with spirituality, but alas, the priest failed.

The cathedral's interior was once a magnificent baroque structure; its Corinthian, Doric and Ionic columns lined the nave. Above them were crowns, pediments, friezes and adornments. In the distant past ignorant clergy and their flock chiseled all the beauty away to clean the cathedral and perhaps themselves of the trappings of wealth. They left broken columns of gray rock the entire length of the Church turning it into a cave. This is where he felt comfortable, for he to was once beautiful but now was ugly beyond description. They had both suffered together.

He made his way to the cafés that lined the square. A pedestrian light glowed red but he did not notice it. His eye's limited vision did not register the signal and he stepped into the cobbled street where a black limousine roared down on him. The driver saw him step out and the black beast came to a screeching halt. The driver screamed obscenities out the window but quickly stopped after seeing whom he almost killed. The faceless man shuffled up the sidewalk toward Jonathan Owen.

Jonathan's new world found him relaxing in a café with a cup of dark coffee and a British newspaper. On the edge of the sidewalk under a fig tree, a black man was entertaining everyone, playing a broken wooden plank—his guitar, he sang into a microphone—a bundle of sticks. Obviously desperate for money he used anything he could find to make a living. Or was he just plain nuts? He murdered an English rock song; oblivious to its meaning, emphasis was put on the wrong syllables. It was all very outrageous and comical and people donated to his efforts regardless. Jonathan hoped for his sake the money was not for his singing.

Suddenly a loud screeching of tires and shouting grabbed the café customer's and his attention. They all stared down the street, curious at what all the commotion was about. No one was hurt at the crosswalk; people went back to their meals and coffee. He glanced up from his paper for a second and an apparition caught his eye. Shuffling down the street toward the café was something with a strange shape where a head should be. People flowed around it, some looked away and others looked back at it in morbid curiosity. He was a well-dressed man holding out a plastic cup with an identification card sticking out of it. He could not believe what he was seeing, for the man had no face. There was not a nose, mouth, eyes or ears just a hanging mass of red, bloated, fleshy folds. Jonathan wanted to pull his eyes away but he could not. A few brave souls moved forward and put donations in his cup and he shook his head up and down in approval. The face, or whatever it was, jiggled like it was made of jelly and Jonathan feared if he shook it too much the fleshy mass held by ribbons of skin and fat would come away from the man's skull. His heart went out to this poor wretch and he got to his feet, reached in his pocket, pulled out a handful of euros, walked up to him and put them his cup. He touched his shoulder and searched with his eyes for the man's eyes and mouth but could only see liquid oozing from red bloated folds.

Jonathan was speechless and astonished that in this age there is no help for this man. We all have masks of some kind that hide our own private secrets. Was this hideous flesh his mask? And if it was, how big was his sorrow and how powerful was his strength to carry on with his life? The face thanked him for his kindness with a shake of his head; he then turned, shuffled down the street and disappeared into the crowd. He returned to his seat, looked about and noticed sad eyes and whispers.

He felt the faceless man's suffering—he too was now faceless—out in the world alone behind a mask of his own making and wondering if the journey he had started a few days ago was going to be worth it.

A Silent Crash on The West Toad River

The white and red striped floatplane sputtered and choked on the last fumes of gasoline from her empty fuel lines—she became ghostly quiet. All that could be heard was the faint sound of whooshing air passing over her body—a whisper of impending death. She started dropping gently from the sky in a level glide over the forested Boreal landscape of Northern British Columbia. From two thousand meters she would glide many kilometers quietly and unnoticed except by grizzlies and deer forging in the autumn sun. Their heads raised, they followed the strange bird floating across the sky and as it passed out of sight they went back to their business. The plane dropped over the upper reaches of the West Toad River. Mountains loomed on each side of a deep cut valley. A forest of pine trees and patches of grasslands came up at her. She touched the tips of the trees and they seemed to sense her presence; they reached up, tore her floats and wings away, and pulled her body into the thick undergrowth of the forest floor. Her pilot's cabin came to rest in a ravine and settled in a bed of pine needles and moss covered dead wood. Her appendages hid themselves in the forest and snow. The forest was dense and she soon disappeared into its darkness as the early fall snow from the surrounding trees powdered her remains.

The cockpit was smeared with blood and hair; a blood splattered windshield was smashed; artist's paints, brushes, canvases and easels were strewn about the plane and crash site. Bloody handprints covered the pilot's seatbelt and door handle. There were no passengers—Jonathan Owen had left by parachute at Moose Lake, eight minutes and twenty seconds earlier.

A short time before the crash Jonathan unwrapped a small cloth sack containing a plastic and steel syringe, plastic bottle, cotton batten and a small bottle of rubbing alcohol. He lined them up on his hotel room's desk and opened the containers. He rolled up his shirtsleeve and rubbed alcohol on the supine side of his lower arm, and tightened his fist to enlarge and expose blue veins. He drove the syringe needle into a bulging vain and let his fist relax. Gently pulling on the plunger, the syringe body turned deep red with blood. He pulled the needle from his arm and loaded his blood into the plastic bottle. He returned the syringe, cotton batten and rubbing alcohol to the small cloth sack and walked out to the back of the hotel and threw them in the dumpster. He returned to his room and packed his gear in a small pack that he wore on his chest and walked to the nearby airport. His plane was waiting, parked between two hangers out of site of probing eyes.

It was early morning and nobody was around to watch the curious goings-on as Jonathan unlocked the pilot's door. He took a latex glove from his pack, put it on his left hand and from the bottle of his blood, poured the contents on his glove making a pool in the palm. He rubbed blood on the door casing that would be near his head and with his right hand pulled a few strands of hair from his scalp and imbedded them in the smeared blood. He then threw some blood creating a spattering on the windshield. He pictured his body moving violently in the plane's cabin. During the crash his head would have hit the door casing to his left and then jerk right, splattering blood on the windshield. He removed the latex glove by turning it inside out and he put it in his pack. From the bottle of blood he dowsed his left hand and he grabbed the pilot's seat belt buckle and door handle leaving his fingerprints. He put the plastic bottle in his pack and wiped his hands on the grass beside the runway. From behind the pilot's seat he pulled out his parachute and put it on, boarded the little plane, turned on the ignition and felt her engine roar into action. After letting the engine warm up for a few minutes, he taxied to the end of the runway and took off south into the morning light and mist.

Jonathan secretly landed; he pulled his parachute release cord only three hundred meters from the ground and dropped unnoticed. He knew the area well; he had mapped the landscape for the government many years ago and slept in these mountains. From a map of existing and decommissioned mining and logging roads he chose a remote area, one that had not been used in many years. He had calculated his drop and landing well, even though he was bruised from the impact. It was a short walk to Silver Bullet; his Jeep was buried in thick brush, gassed up and supplied with full gas tanks—refills that would get him to his destination. Stowed in the back was his mountain bike, food and water—he would not have to stop and be noticed.

A week before and traveling at night, he drove Silver Bullet up the province to the West Toad River, hid her and made a six hour walkout. All was ready to take Jonathan out of the province of British Columbia and into Alberta. This would be Silver Bullet's last journey. Like Jonathan his Jeep must also disappear. He had stripped her of serial numbers, washed and scrubbed her of DNA. He was thorough with the cleaning for he had owned Silver Bullet for seventeen years and he was all over her.

The journey into the neighboring province was made dressed in latex gloves and white painter's coveralls. He traveled by night, camping each day of his two-day journey to Calgary, Alberta. Arriving on the outskirts, he drove up a deserted road that he had previously selected from a seismic access map. He came to a river and part of his life stopped for him. On a cliff over a deep pool he removed the Jeep's license plates, backpack and bike. He poured the remainder of gasoline that was left in the reserve fuel tanks over the body and interior of the jeep. He struck a match and threw it onto Bullet's driver's seat and she exploded in flame. He burned her and some traveling gear. Taking his time feeding the flames with logs making sure that no evidence of Jonathan could survive—she burned to a charred hulk. When he was satisfied his crime against his friend was done, he pushed her off the cliff. She dropped into a pool and sank unceremoniously. This was the hardest part of his journey into anonymity—he had destroyed Bullet—an old friend that had been faithful to him for so many years. They had traveled together through storms and sunshine across the landscapes of British Columbia, the United States and Mexico. His heart was broken, he could not believe what he had done and he choked; emotion rose up inside and tears flowed down his cheeks and for a time he could not breathe. It's a piece of metal, a car for Christ sake, he told himself.

It would be unlikely that anyone would find her and bother to investigate the remains but then that didn't matter to Jonathan. He put the license plates in his pack to be buried off the dirt road that he biked to Calgary.

He sat on the cliff and stared into the pool, reality reared itself—he was a criminal and there was no turning back—his adventurous scam was underway. He was dead to all that knew him except for one person whose loyalty was above reproach—his daughter, Annabelle.

Frank Willard and The Law

Frank Willard sat across from Jonathan, his huge body filled up the Union Club's leather chair and; is belly flowed over his belt and rested on his lap. His large head was balding and the last few hairs were white; his face was a bright pinky red tomato. His black suit and white shirt strained at the seams from carrying his bulbous body. The knot of his tie could not be seen for the fold of fat under his chin. His breathing, through puffed up pink lips was heavy and labored from the weight and years of eating, drinking and smoking. His hands were large swollen fleshy appendages; one wrapped itself around a scotch glass. Jonathan felt sad for his lifelong friend and lawyer and had in the past offered to help him get back into a reasonable physical shape. Frank refused his offer.

"So Jon, what's up? Why am I here with you today?" Frank wheezed, filling up his leather chair and taking a gulp of scotch.

"Well Frank, I need your advice on something," and he leaned forward so no one in the room could hear their conversation. "Whatever you and I talk about here—there is a professional confidentiality on your part—right?"

"That's correct—yes," Frank said with a suspicious frown.

"Good, so here it is," and Jonathan leaned closer. "If someone fakes their own death by, say a plane crash or a boat sinking, in order to make them famous and cause their art work to increase in value— or say the artist just wants to create a conceptual piece of art—a metaphor. Would the artist go to jail for doing such a thing and if he does go to jail how many years do you think he would get?"

"Now look here, Jon!" the lawyer bellowed as he sat forward and hushed to a whisper, "you're not planning some scam to sell your art are you? Jesus Christ Jonathan! You're always coming up with crazy and dangerous ideas! Of course you would get time, ten years maybe. You could get probation, a fine and have to pay back any search team that you caused to be sent on a chase. It would be expensive. Most likely you would be charged with mischief and fraud," he leaned back in his chair and rushed his scotch to his mouth. Frank leaned forward again and said, "Jon, if you are planning anything dramatic, I don't want to know about it and now that you have described to me some scam you're up to I can be implicated, so I will not defend you in a court of law if you are planning your own demise and a return from the dead.

"God, you could make a fortune," and Frank jiggled with laughter, "realistically the fine and penalties would be trivial compared to the cash flow from your art because you're damn good—shit—what am I saying? Don't drag me into this."

"Okay Frank, that's fine. You've told me all I need to know. Now let's talk about that crazy wife of yours and your mess of grandkids," he said changing the subject and beckoning a waiter for more drinks.

Check In

Annabelle's father always checked in every third day from remote places in the wilderness he was painting. He called her or a local airport would make the call. One day of grace was all that was needed before sending out the alarm that something was amiss. It was going into the end of day four so she made the call to the local Royal Canadian Mounted Police Detachment in Fort Nelson.

"Fort Nelson, RCMP Detachment, Constable Jack Garland, can I help you?"

"Yes this is Annabelle Owen from Vancouver. I would like to report a missing pilot."

"Yes Ms. Owen. Could I have some details, please?"

"My father has not called in at his usual check in time. I think he could be missing in your area. On the Toad River to be more precise."

"How is he traveling?"

"By single engine float plane. He would have filed a flight plan with the Fort Nelson airport I'm sure. Officer I'm really worried about him—please would you look for him? He is getting on in years and I don't know if he could survive out there in the cold. He always checks in—something must be wrong," she said with panic in her voice.

"When was he to check in with you?"

"Yesterday."

"And he always checked in you say?"

"Yes, always."

"What is your father's name?"

"Jonathan, Jonathan B. Owen."

"Thank you Ms. Owen we have enough to go on for the moment. I will check the airports and see where he last checked in out of, and go from there. Your phone number please and please stand by for the next twenty-four hours while we conduct an initial investigation," the Constable said, finalizing the conversation.

She gave him her cell and landline numbers, "Thank you officer, I will stand by."

Constable Jack Garland immediately called the Fort Nelson airport for Jonathan Owen's flight plan—it was faxed to the constable. They also knew he was missing. He recorded the date, time and information of the calls that came into the detachment. The constable established himself the contact of Canadian and International law enforcement in the investigation of the bizarre case that would unfold in the next year. The events would change the constable's life.

The constable put in a call to the Toad River airport: "Ted—Jack Garland here. Give me some details about this missing pilot and plane would you?"

"Yeah, sure," a gruff voice replied, "he flew out at first light up the Toad River to paint and sketch at Moose Lake and planned to continue on to the river's headwaters. It's all in the flight plan. Everything looks normal but something disturbs me; he neglected to top up with fuel at the airport, and you know pilots flying in the north always top-up whenever they get the chance. There's no record of any fuel transaction made with the local fuel guys. I've known Jonathan for years when he was doing work for the government around here and as an artist spending time flying the north. We've had many beers and great conversations over the years. He is an experienced pilot and has never been this neglectful. On the other hand he is getting older. I don't know, he may not be quick like he used to be—maybe he was not paying attention the day he flew out of here. Does that help you Jack?"

"Yes. I'll put this in my report to the accident investigation team, if there is one. Thanks Ted. See you on my rounds," Jack hung up the phone.

Not known at the time, Jonathan's plane went up the West Toad River not the Toad River; it would be recorded as an error in judgment after the search crews found the wreckage.

Jack Garland phoned Annabelle Owen in Vancouver after his initial investigation of the crash: "I have some news and I am afraid it's not good Annabelle. Your father is definitely missing and he has made a serious error in fueling and he may have been forced to land because of it. We have bought in a search and rescue helicopter and crew. It's now searching the Toad River Valley area. Let's hope we find him before the snows set in. Our men are on the case now, Annabelle, and we will try our best to find him."

"What do you think has happened constable?" she queried, "Oh God! My poor Dad!

"We don't know. It's too early to tell or speculate on anything except about the fuel business. That could be where the problem lies but we will see. The detachment will need personal information on your father and his background. Could you fax or email such information?"

"Eh—yes—yes of course."

"Are you okay Ms. Owen? Is there someone you can call for company?"

"Yes, I'm fine officer. Thank you. I have a friend I can call."

Annabelle agreed to email some digital photos of her father along with his biography. "Thank you constable for all your help and thank the team searching for my father will you? Please call me the minute you find something."

Jonathan's daughter hung up and smiled; phase one was complete, the snows would come soon and the plane would not be found until spring. As she opened a bottle of Pinot Noir, her father was riding his mountain bike into Calgary and to a local three star hotel near the Calgary International

Airport. It was time for him to be someone else.
Jonathan got up at first light and dressed in the traveling gear he bought especially for the occasion: light leather shoes, beige pants, wine t - shirt, a floppy Australian hat, that he hated, and a navy-blue light weight summer blazer. The night before he dyed his hair and his two-month old beard black to match his doctored passport, with black reading glasses that he bought for a few dollars he was unrecognizable. So he would not set off the metal detectors he stripped metal from his clothes and body and put the articles in his backpack. To enhance his disguise he tucked his left arm behind him and under his shirt and backpack; the airport cameras would be picking up an image of a one armed man. Why the one arm charade—he put it down as being dramatic—a troubling trait of his. He was now William Robert Martin, retired car salesman, born in Wales. Billy Bob Martin, the best damn car salesman on Vancouver's Broadway was catchy and amusing to him.

He put his room key on the bed and left the hotel early in the morning; he used the back stairs avoiding the hotel manager's office. In the back alley he checked for his bike by the dumpster where he purposely left it unlocked; it was gone. Down the block from the hotel he caught a bus to the Calgary airport and picked up his ticket to Frankfurt, Germany. He had purchased the ticket a month ago on the Internet, using a Visa card under his new name. After clearing customs and entering the loading area, he checked for security cameras and he saw there were none, or so he thought. Within the hour Jonathan was bound for Germany, France, Portugal, Spain and North African adventures— at least for a year or two.

The Nice Gentleman from America, Out for The Winter

Jonathan's plane landed at Frankfurt International Airport, he quickly moved through the mass of buildings to customs and immigration. His counterfeit Canadian passport was accepted and stamped with no questions asked. Jonathan left the airport quickly and taxied to the train station where he caught the next fast train to Garde Nord Station, Paris. On arrival he transferred to the metro line that took him across the city to Montparnasse Train Station and its southbound trains. He must get to the south of Europe and fast.

It was the middle of the week so he did not need train reservations to travel on to Irún on the French, Spanish border and on to the Portuguese border town of Vilar Formoso. He flew across the steel rails into his illusion. He relished the experience of rail travel in Europe, especially the sound of the sleek orange monsters and the sharp ring of steel against steel. He felt like he was riding in a radio, everything tight and finely tuned. If he stared out the windows at the landscape he had to look in the distance. Everything close and near was a blur and if he looked at the blur long enough it would make him sick.

The trains in Portugal were much slower and they had that familiar clickity-clack, clickity-clack sound as steel wheels met the spaces between the rails. The cars swayed and swung as they rounded curves and hills. His train pulled into Lisbon's station; in the terminal he stopped by the information booth and reserved a three star hotel room. His digs for two nights were in old town; it had been a hectic and intense journey from Frankfurt. The taxi driver was a maniac—Jonathan was at his hotel before he could buckle his seat belt.

His first night was terrible but he did manage to sleep. His internal clock had been thrown out of whack; he had been up for two days, only cat napping when he could but he soon adjusted. In the fine clothing shops along the Rua Augusta he purchased new clothes and threw his traveling gear away. He explored the local area, touring the castles, squares, monuments and shops and talked with many of the locals who to his surprise spoke English very well. The food in the outdoor cafes was delicious but the wine was too dry and harsh for his taste. In time he would find the right grape to savor.

He left for the south one morning by catamaran ferry and from the terminal in the town of Barreiro he caught the train to the Province of Algarve. The train trip was complicated or it was the language; he misinterpreted agents and conductors. He changed trains twice to get where he was going. The Algarve would be his base for his adventures where he could get lost among the tourists haven at Praia da Rocha in the city of

Portimão. It would take some time for anyone to find him down in the bottom edge of Europe.

Praia da Rocha is the tourist district of Portimão; its main street, Avenida Tomas Cabreira, runs a few kilometers east and west along the coast. The street is lined with high-rise apartments, hotels, bars, souvenir shops, supermarkets and hotels; it sit on a rise of sandstone cliffs stained with ochre earth; the beach below the cliffs is broad to the ocean. Scattered about are resort umbrellas and chaise lounges with comfortable padded coverings; bars nearby serve inexpensive drinks and food. He bought a mountain bike for long hard rides exploring towns, villages and Portuguese life.

The strip was starting to empty of customers as winter approached; only a few tourists were on the streets and in the bars. The police made a drive-by of the area about once a day, they were young and had no interest in him. He knew there were very few people in the tourist area; the huge high rises shone one or two lights when darkness fell—their parking lots were empty. He took a room and found himself a local coffee shop—come newsstand that supplied English and American papers. Most importantly he found a local pub where a blonde burly Welshman named Steve, whom everyone called Taffy, served good beer and laughs.

Jonathan's temporary home was a one-bedroom suit in a white and cream twelve-story apartment block over looking the ocean. A young couple with two children and Jonathan were the only tenants in the building. The tourist place did not draw attention to him; to his neighbors he was—that nice gentleman from America out for the winter.

A Dead Artist Can Make a Good Living

In Fort Nelson, British Columbia the call went out for volunteers to search for Jonathan Owen. The local media picked it up and sent stories on to the national and international press networks.

In Annabelle's computer system was an email package of introductions and links to images of his art ready to be sent to several hundred dealers, galleries and individual collectors. She bought up the package stored as a draft and pressed the icon on the tool bar—send. Within hours calls came in from the media requesting statements and more digital images of him and his work. She had everything ready for them and a warehouse of his work waiting for the calls from collectors and corporations. The orders came in fast and furious.

Jonathan's work was good but not widely known until his demise. The exhibits that Annabelle would arranged will drive his status into that of a Canadian icon and send the price of his art soaring. A year prior she hired the best photographer in the province to photograph her father and his works. With her writing skills she and her father created stories of his life that were true but embellished. By their calculations, if all the paintings and drawings in the warehouse sold over the next few years, they would make well over four million dollars—perhaps a dead artist can make a good living.

"Ms. Owen?"

"Yes."

"It's Constable Jack Garland from Fort Nelson. We don't have any news on your missing father. I'm sorry to say this, but we are assuming he is dead. It has been two weeks and his plane and body have not been found. The snow is heavy on the ground and the temperature is below zero. Chances of survival are slim and—"

"Oh poor Dad—" she whimpered and blew her nose.

"Since the first heavy snowfall of winter has now blanketed Northern British Columbia, we have called off the search until the spring. Until then Ms. Owen there is nothing we can do—everything is snowed in for the winter."

"Thanks for your effort, officer. I will miss my Dad—I will really miss him," she sobbed into the phone and blew her nose again, "please thank the search party for me, will you? I will call you in the spring after the melt when the search will continue, is that all right?"

"Of course, take care Ms. Owen and we will be in touch in the spring. In the meantime there will be a few bits of information we will require. I'll send that all in a letter."

It was time to make contact with Dad electronically at Rosie's Internet Cafe. Away from her office she bought up the Internet browser, typed in her email ID and password Big Hat and powderblue and connected to her email account. She typed in under To: indigohue, its extension and

Are you home? In the message window—she clicked the send button. It was nighttime in Portugal so she must wait for the reply to come the next day. She loved her father and was very worried that his latest adventure had gone bad and that he truly was missing and dead. But she stuck to the plan they had devised. He had tremendous power over her since he had bought her up and not her mother who only saw her daughter one weekend a month.

The next day at the café, Annabelle waited anxiously; the screen came up showing her email account. After a dozen spam mails rolled up the word she was waiting for shot off the screen—powderblue. He's alive! She screamed inside, quickly she double clicked on the closed envelope icon and opened the mail.

To: powderblue

Greetings my love. I'm safe and getting a great tan. I've taken up residence in a beach resort in the south of Portugal. It feels strange knowing I can't come home for some time. All went well—no hitches at all. The scariest part was the parachute jump, I didn't pull the cord until I was close to the ground so I landed hard and fell on my ass. I had blue and red bruises there for a couple of days. Burning Silver Bullet was heart breaking—I felt like a traitor to an old friend. I must be crazy to think sentimentally about a bucket of rusting bolts but I can't help it.

Give me the news of what's happening on your end. Cheers.

To: indigohue

Oh Dad, I've been scared to death that something might have really gone wrong with this hair brained scheme of yours. Ever since I was a little kid you have been scaring the hell out of me—and now this; jumping out of planes in the middle of nowhere; faking your own death to make money and dragging me into this crazy art scam. I'm not going to take any of the money from this Dad. I've given this some thought over the last few weeks—I make a good living honestly, and as we agreed, I know nothing of what is going on and pretend that you are really dead.

I've put five thousand in your new name checking account—you have forty thousand to play with. You're going to make a lot of money; orders are coming in for your work. I've sent clients your bio. and catalogue.

Remember to destroy all emails, temp files and backups. Shred all receipts, bills and paper trails—no postcards, letters or any other type of correspondence except Internet browser. Do not write or talk of the incident to anyone but me. I will write to you soon. Luv yu.

To: powderblue

Forty thousand will just be fine. I can live quite nicely for the next six months to a year here before I give our friends another shocker.

The weather is fantastic. I bet its raining there! Cheers.

To: indigohue

What do you mean? You just want forty thousand? You're going to make a fortune in the next while – so what's up now? A shock in six months to a year? Something you're not telling me? Jesus, Dad you're scaring me again!! Take care.

To: indigohue

Re. your wish. Ralph, my new boyfriend who you haven't met, and I held a memorial service for you at the cathedral and the place was packed – I didn't know you had so many friends. A bunch of your old girlfriends showed up, some even had tears in their eyes. Mary Jane was really upset and Maxine comforted her – two of your lovers hugging each other – Christ Dad! Betty was particularly beautiful and that bimbo that screwed your head up just sat and didn't show any emotion at all. It's amazing the bitch came; she sure didn't attend any of your shows. She was dressed in her usual black, looking the old crone that she is.

Mom showed up without Bob and she had been crying for a week mumbling – son of a bitch, son of a bitch. It upset Bob to no end. He can't understand that you were her first love and she will always love you as well as him. Jesus, you can make life hell even in death.

Charles Bothal, your biologist buddy, stood up and gave a wonderful eulogy praising you and your art and career; he even choked a few times. Then your old boss got up and said some things that were pretty dry corporate stuff. Some young girl that nobody knew, who looked Mexican and I can't remember her Spanish name, got up and made a speech in Spanish. I couldn't understand a word but the sincerity on her face showed us she was something special to you. Dad – she was so young – must have been in her mid twenties. There was a lot more going on down there in Mexico than you have let on!

Our neighbor from long ago, Mrs. Hobbs was there and mother was upset about that and has never forgiven you for the affair you had with her. She's old now Dad. I don't think you would like her much anymore – you like beautiful things – shallow bastard that you are. I think they would all come over there and kill you if they knew what was going on. The whole time after the service at the pub with some who attended I was choking from stopping the laughter building up inside of me. If I hear again, well he died doing what he loved. And he died with his boots on – I'll puke.

Your old friend and lawyer Frank Willard was there and he made some excuse to me that he did not want to get up and say anything. He kept looking at me strangely like he knows something. Does he Dad?

What a burden you have left me with – I can never tell the truth again. Luv yu.

What's the point Dad?

Jonathan moved from the tourist centre of Portimão and took up residence in the fishing village of Ferragudo. The days of sun and surf floated by for him in the tropical Algarve and spring soon came to the West Toad River in Northern British Columbia. Winter's snow melted fast under the rising sun. The forests and their secrets were revealed.

Sonny Kilshaw, an eighteen-year-old aboriginal from the Dene-Than Nation was out on his first hunt of the season. He walked along a logging road that ran beside the upper reaches of the West Toad River. He noticed something shiny a few hundred meters up a mountain's southeast slope. It was deep in the forest undergrowth. Unless it is human, nothing shines in the forest. He took off his backpack and laid it on a log with his rifle and climbed through the thick undergrowth. He came upon a white and red-stripped airplane wing with bold black call letters painted on it; a battered pontoon lay nearby. He followed the trail of debris and soon spotted the body of a plane resting in a shallow ravine. He climbed down through rotten moss covered logs and brush, and approached the pilot's partially opened door. He saw blood spattered everywhere but no body—no bones.

Lying outside the fuselage was a dark stained wooden box with a brass plaque on the lid—J. B. Owen was engraved on it. Sonny picked it up and opened it—paint tubes and brushes fell out. Suddenly he realized—this plane might be the one that went missing before the first snows last year. Sonny made a mental note of the call letters on the wreckage. Without touching anything else he left the crash site carrying the paint case to his hunting gear and walked back to his truck. Sonny called the Toad River airport manager and the RCMP on his CB radio.

Constable Jack Garland took the calls from Ted Maxwell from the Toad River Airport and Sonny. He immediately called the coroner's service office in Prince George, the Forensic Anthropologist Team in Surrey and the Transportation Safety Board (TSB) in Vancouver. The three services would be in Fort Nelson within a few hours and on their way to the crash site guided by Sonny. Jack contracted a local logging company to pull the plane out of the bush after the on site investigation and deliver the parts to the Toad River Airport. The investigation had begun that would vibrate its way around the world and a little village on the Mediterranean.

The coroner found only blood and hair. The Transportation Safety Board, photographed the plane's parts from dozens of angles, filled out crash site templates, wrote scenarios and took measurements. The technical group found the plane had enough fuel to take the pilot where he was going—but barely. The engine was intact and in working order at the time of the crash but the fuel lines were empty. Although sheered off and scattered by the crash, the wings, rudder and ailerons were found to be in working order. Only damage from the impact was evident. A check of the instrument panel found it in working order except for the throttle plungers that were in a closed position. The propeller was attached and in working order but bent from the impact. The maintenance book was up to date and documents in the book stated that the plane was registered to Jonathan B. Owen. There was a certificate of airworthiness taped to the instrument panel. The aircraft was not equipped with a flight recorder and the emergency locator was not operable—its internal battery was dead. There was no excessive baggage. This concluded the on site investigation and determined there was no civil or criminal liability. But the team did not rule out the crash may have been intentional.

The TSB classified the crash a Class 5 investigation, which was to record for possible safety analysis, statistical reporting and archival purposes. Samples were gathered of blood, hair and fingerprints from the windshield post, door handle and seat belt. The samples would be sent to the RCMP Forensic Laboratory in Vancouver for analysis and entered into the fingerprint and DNA databases.

The RCMP officer and Sonny watched the investigation from a distance.

"What do you think happened to the pilot, Sonny?"

"I think he was bashed up pretty bad, climbed out and took a deer trail into the bush. There are griz and black bear, wolverines, wolves and all kinds of meat eaters out here. He wouldn't have lived long after the first snow and the hungry critters around."

"Yes, I also think he would not have survive. It doesn't look good. Do you think we'll find him?"

"No, maybe some clothing but that would be it. Bodies are soon eaten and bones scattered out there."

"Yeah, I've collected a few bones from this country."

With little hope the coroner, volunteers and dogs searched the area for remains—the team found nothing. The dogs were no help since it was almost eight months since the accident.

At his office desk, Jack poured over the information and was satisfied with the team's findings. Evidence said the crashed plane was Jonathan Owen's and he did not survive—case closed. But the fuel, throttle plungers, flight plan and flying up the wrong river bothered Jack. Taking the West Toad River route Jack dismissed as an easy mistake to make. The landscape has hundreds of mountain, valleys and rivers that look alike. But the combined anomalies bothered him. The constable would keep the file open on this case; it just didn't sit right with him.

Annabelle received the call from the constable the evening the wreck was found: "Ms. Owen—Constable Jack Garland in Fort Nelson."

"Yes Sir."

"A hunter found your father's plane this morning. We identified it by its call letters and we found a paint box at the scene with your father's name engraved on the lid. The crash report says the plane fell out of the sky after a few minutes of flight up the West Toad River. His flight plan said the Toad River. We looked in the wrong place last year."

"Did you find his body?" she asked quietly and gently made sobbing sounds."

"No," Jack talked clearly and with no emotion, "your father's body has not been found. It has been surmised that he survived the crash only to wander off with a severe head or bodily injury and probably died miles from the crash site. I apologize for saying this but the animal life here is bountiful and—"

"Oh poor Dad, I hope he didn't suffer too much," she sobbed into the phone.

"Yes and I am sorry to say this but the Coroner and the Forensic Anthropologist believe as well as I, that his body would have been consumed by wildlife leaving no trace of him. We will still put a few more days in with the dogs but I am afraid the outcome does not look good. I have to ask this Ms. Owen for our records; did your father carry a life insurance policy?"

"He just had his Government insurance from when he retired, like all retirees, he kept his payments up. I believe it is for around—eighty thousand dollars. My brother and I are the beneficiaries."

"Where is your brother now Ms. Owen?"

"He is in Brazil working for Global Three Engineering on a portable sawmill factory. I am in touch with him about once a week. I can give you his email address."

"Thank you—yes please give it to me," and so she did. "Ms. Owen, the investigation is almost complete. We will package his belongings and send them on to you; we have your address. The coroner will send you a death certificate and the Safety Board will forward their report to you; these documents you will need for the insurance company.

"Oh, there is one more thing, to complete our investigation, we need a sample of your father's DNA. Would you happen to have one of his combs or brushes that may have some strands of hair or scalp tissue? We could make a match with the blood in the cockpit."

"I think I might have a brush or comb. I'll check in some of his boxes in my garage. I'll see what I can do."

"You have some of his possessions in your garage?"

"Yes, my dad was a bit of a vagabond; he scattered his stuff everywhere," she sobbed into the phone. Christ! She thought I must be careful with what I say.

"Thank you Ms. Owen. There will be an RCMP officer from the Surrey Detachment calling you in the next few days and he will pick up the items."

"Thank you Constable it is a relief to have closure, she sobbed, "goodbye."

"Thank you and goodbye Ms. Owen."

To: indigohue

Hey Dad. There is renewed interest in your art again since the discovery of your plane. The story goes that you were badly injured – bashed about the head. You wandered off into the northern wilderness to lose a fight with a pack of wolves and a bear that ate you. The story is in every paper and magazine in Canada and the United States – on every television news show. You're not only a tragedy Dad but also a romantic one. Stories and nonsense are coming out everyday; your case seems to have stirred some adventure in the public. I think the RCMP in Fort Nelson has closed your case but I'm not sure. So watch out and make sure you destroy these emails.

I have squirreled money away in safety deposit boxes all over town for you as well as keeping your phony bank accounts nice and tidy. So what are you going to do now Dad? Too bad you can't enjoy your fame – now you've got the cash to play with. I don't get what's going through your mind. What's the point Dad? I miss you. Luv yu.

Rick Thomas

Life in Ferragudo

To: powderblue

Hey honey. It may sound strange but I'm living in an attic – but what an attic! I'm really getting into this place. I'm in this little fishing village called Ferragudo, you would just love it and I'm doing a bit of art for fun. I do it behind closed doors since no one around here does any art; just me doing it draws attention to me – and that's not good. All is well honey – no worries. Love Dad.

João was old – in his mid seventies, and only went fishing when the urge came, which was most of the time. He had fished all day a few hundred meters off Praia da Rocha, five kilometers from his home in Ferragudo. His little sailing boat affectionately named Picasso bobbed in the gentle waters like it had done since he built her forty years ago. The sun was going down soon and it was time to make headway for shore. He turned the rudder of Picasso to northeast and set his little triangular sail to catch the following wind coming from the south west of the Atlantic, a breeze from the womb of a hurricane. Picasso took to the breeze and soon heeled to port and sailed past the breakwater that protects the estuary. Sailing to starboard he steered Picasso up to the quay of his little fishing village. Filomena his wife was waiting on the old stone quay for him to come home from the sea.

He dropped Picasso's sail after weaving with precision through the moored fishing boats. The vessel gently touched the stone quay at the stairs that gave fishermen access to their boats. He stowed his sail and made fast his running gear, unloaded his life jacket, fishing tackle, lunch box and two pails of fish. With lines from the bow and stern he disembarked and climbed up the stairs pulling his craft along the quay to a large iron ring cemented into the cobbled street – he made Picasso's lines fast. Filomena fetched up his gear from his boat and João fetched his pails of fish and with his old knife he cleaned his catch on the piled up fish traps stacked along the dock. He threw the fish guts to the swarm of seagulls that he has fed for many of their generations. Most of his catch he would give away to his friends in the town square who were as old as he but unable to fish anymore.

The large weathered hands of João were deft with his fish knife and he chatted to Filomena as he worked telling her about the weather, Picasso and the fish that did not get away. She gave him the football scores and the daily local gossip that she heard at the grocery store. Both stand no more than a meter and a half in height and were probably a few centimeters taller a few years ago. Their bodies had turned the colour and texture of the landscape around them – a sandstone colour, furrowed and worn. They still have their own teeth but they are long, some now at angles because of their changing anatomy. Their minds are alike and codependent on each other, a wonderful relationship, a bonding of the two. The couple need and use each other to make their way through life and cope with its bumps and bruises – relying on each other to pick up the other when they stumble. They are one.

João and Filomena were married in the Cathedral on the hill sixty years ago and spent their lives in the parish never roaming far, just once to Lisbon for the wedding of their only son, who is now a doctor in the city of Portimão across the estuary. Filomena wears black most of the time but does have variations in her dresses; some have white patterns of flowers, small and not too garish. João always wears his heavy black work pants with braces, black leather shoes and checkered shirts, which are always red or black. On his head he wears a brown and white tweed cap to protect his bald spot from the sun and the cold breeze of winter.

When João isn't fishing he sits with his friends outside their old boy's club in the square. His friends are as old as he and one is now crippled from a stroke and unable to talk. He and his friends keep their silent friend close and they will sit for hours sometimes not saying a word, at other times they will get into a passionate rage over women, politics, money, fishing and the price of horses. But most of the time the arguments are about football. Filomena would come out of her shop and tell them all to shut up, sit down and behave themselves and they do, to the chuckles of all in earshot. João and Filomena are very much in love and their bond is strong after years of hard work, wars and revolutions.

They managed to survive in their village home that João's ancestors, generation after generation, had passed on to them. Now the couple has a fear that their traditional home may leave their family since their only son is a modern Portuguese living in the big city with a successful medical practice. Their son told them that he would never sell the house that he was born in, up on the hill in the shadow of the Cathedral. They still worry—after all the smell of fishermen and their women was all their little home knew. Its tiny doorway into little rooms of whitewashed walls and worn floor tilling had embraced generations and experienced births, deaths, laughter and tears.

Each night they sit down under the portrait of the Virgin of Fatima at their small kitchen table for their dinner of fish and vegetables. Their little tabby cat crouches on the windowsill beside them. Shortly after darkness creeps over the village they curl up together under a blue flannel blanket and crisp white sheets; their heads sunk into broad pillows in a bed that João was born in over seventy-five years ago.

Jonathan watched João and Filomena, his landlords, from his chair at the restaurant on the quay. They like everyone he meets become part of his experience—his adventure. He admired them for their power to hold onto a life that is in danger of drifting into history and forgotten. Across the white bridge that separates the new from the old, the world is marching towards Ferragudo.

He drank his glass of red wine and looked across the estuary and its colorful fishing boats. Jonathan could see in the sunset the massive apartment blocks where he once lived on the Praia da Rocha, to the bright coloured condos of the Marina with their multimillion dollar yachts from around the world and further on, to the gleaming white buildings of Portimão proper.

An angry old woman in black with a stick ran past Jonathan chasing her dog that was as big as her. The dog's tongue was hanging out, his ears stood straight up and his eyes were open wide with delight at being chased around the quay. He had escaped from home for a brief moment and was enjoying himself while he could. João's friends, all nine of them, were supervising a frustrated young man who was putting up a sign over the square that advertised an up coming festival. Others were busy inspecting a fresh load of firewood in the back of a truck and were in deep discussion on the quality, quantity and price of the load. Fishing boats of all sizes were arriving home; green trawlers out in the estuary were swarmed with hundreds of seagulls. Smaller boats moored off the quay and the young fisherman pulled their nets ashore for cleaning and repairing.

João finished his chores and checked that Picasso was safe and with his free hand he took Filomena's and they walked between the little buildings, up the cobbled stairs and disappeared into the labyrinth of Ferragudo. The sun had set and Our Lady on the hill tolled the hour.

The restaurant was filling with customers for their evening dinner. The stars came out and candles were lit on the tables. On the other side of the estuary lights were turning into something brilliant, like strings of lights on a Christmas tree. On the edge of the quay was a modern stainless steel barbeque where fish and kabobs were cooked for the restaurant. A young man dark, short and stocky, very Portuguese was busy cooking the fresh catch of the day. Jonathan's waitress, a trim young girl in a revealing red top, tight white pants and an apron, flashed her eyes, smiled and laughed. Jonathan noticed she could not keep her big brown eyes off the busy cook and he could not keep his eyes off her. Just a matter of time, Jonathan thought these two would be together and what would be their future? Would they stay here in Ferragudo and be at peace with the world of old Portugal or seek their fortunes across the estuary? Perhaps if they are lucky they will fall in love; give their vows to Our Lady and become one like João and Filomena. And within a year on some sunny Ferragudo morning, the tops of the chimney stacks with their nesting storks will be abuzz.

To: indigohue

I worry all the time about you so be careful. Don't lose your focus and do something foolish like fall in love. You're on your own out there and survival means being on your own. You can't take anyone along on your journey – remember that. As usual, sales are going well, Mom is fine and the weather here is terrible, raining everyday now for thirty-five days. Some crazy who lives up on forty-first and Oak is building an Ark. It takes the edge off these dull gray days. Martin, my latest flame who sells shoes at Philbrooke Brothers – by the way, he is a Philbrooke, and I are thinking we may go to Mexico for a few weeks for some R and R. I am still under stress coping with what you're doing and the events unfolding in Fort Nelson. It's hard on me Dad. Luv yu.

To: powderblue

Sorry Honey for the stress, don't worry I will keep focused and be careful; and for falling in love – can any man prevent that from happening? I don't know. But I can tell you this, I do have a mistress and that's art and she keeps me busy and content. This is a beautiful place to be with my mistress. I am happy and relaxed for the time being but I am getting strong feelings that I may be on the run again soon. Go to Mexico with your shoe man, and may I suggest Bucerias just north of Puerto Vallarta. Have a good time and write me from wherever you are. Love Dad.

Tegwyn and Richard

A sunny day washed across Ferragudo, there was someone that Jonathan must see who works up on the hill in the wind and in site of a thundering ocean. She is from his country, Wales, and she is beautiful. He pushed Silver Jr., his bike, up the stairs towards the stark white washed walls of the cathedral tower. She was there waiting at the bar door, framed by bright red umbrellas over white tables that were waiting for customers. Her strawberry blonde hair fluttered in the breeze that caresses the hill. The long mass was tossed and clamped on top of her head like a helmet in the shape of a fighting bird. Wrap-around sunglasses covered her blue eyes above a big smile. Her arms were folded under her ample breasts, which were covered by a white sleeveless blouse; her legs were crossed in tight black pants. Painted nails and tanned feet were snuggled into black leather sandals. She leaned against the front door jam.

"Good morning Richard," Tegwyn Bevan said in a thick Welsh accent, her teeth flashed against her tanned face, "good to see you out on your bike. You all right then—coffee?"

"Thank you Tegs, yes I will," Jonathan said. He parked and locked Silver Jr. and leaned her against the concrete railing. "Beautiful day isn't it?"

"Looks very nice from here," she smiled and gestured him to come in. "The usual for you—milk?"

"Yes please," he moved very close behind her and she rubbed her firm, round bottom against him before entering the doorway.

He entered the bar with Tegwyn where Jane of New York, the owner, was busy doing the books in a small alcove off the bar. A little sign on her coffee table read Staff Only. Her long white hair flowed down over her shoulders that were covered by a thick, wine coloured sweater.

It was late in the year and inside the bar there was a chill; the sun had not made it through the windows. Jane was coming up to eighty and was feeling the chill of the bar deep in her old bones.

"Good morning Richard," she said cheerfully.

"Good morning Jane," Jonathan said, "and how are you this fabulous morning in the Algarve?"

"Fucking freezing!" she blurted out and they all laughed.

Jonathan sat at the bar and the three of them made small talk. Mostly their discussion was about the weather because that's what people talk about in the tropics when winter comes. Then this was not winter to him; these people had no idea what winter was or had forgotten; rain and snow, that's what he knew about winter and he was glad to be out of it.

He watched Tegwyn at the coffee machine as she operated the contraption; her arms held high, the muscles in her shoulders and back showed off her strength. She had never had children so her breasts below her out-stretched arms revealed themselves to be pointed like a teenager's; they were firm and they stirred Jonathan. He saw something he could not describe in this woman, she was so different from the women he had known. From the first time he laid eyes on her during one of his walkabouts up on the hill, he wanted her. The day he first passed by the bar he returned and dropped in for a diet pop and struck up small talk. She spoke to him full of smiles and curiosity, telling him in a few words and gestures volumes about herself and he liked her immediately and felt an instant bond with her—she was from his ancestral home. He felt a kind of kinship, if you will, with her and he said to himself that he would get to know this woman better.

This woman who was going through a tourist season of seven-day weeks, serving thousands of customers and along he comes—a possible match for her. What are the odds of that happening? He thought. She had not noticed anybody in all those thousands of tourists year after year, until he arrived on the scene. Tegwyn had not been with a man for a long time and had no intentions of being with another until her retirement in a couple of years. She was not sure if a relationship would ever happen for her again even though she said she would like to grow old with someone. She had become busy with her life like all singles do. A trap of work, laundry, vacuuming and shopping; basically busy doing nothing but the daily work for bread on the table. The daily grind can take your life away; you can wake up one morning and find yourself dead.

"So Tegs, do we have a date on Sunday?" Jonathan queried.

"Yes, I think so Richard, but I have some things to do first. My place is such a bloody mess, all my winter clothes are mixed up with my summer ones and they are in a big pile and I haven't hoovered in days. And the damn laundry—I just don't know if I have the time. My bits 'n' pieces must be done—"

"So honey, again, do we have a date on Sunday?"

"Yes, of course. Meet me down on the quay five and ten after ten in the a.m. and we can go for a walk on the beach but if it rains we will have to find something else to do."

"Say again."

"Sorry, make it fifteen minutes after ten tomorrow morning."

It poured with rain so they did find something else to do.

Tegwyn Bevan and Jonathan Owen, Richard Jones, to her, became friends and lovers. With the warm evening nights on the beach and the hot nights at home the time went by and they both became fond of each other. They made plans for the future whether it would happen or not—their plans gave grounding to their relationship. He wanted to move in with her but she was frightened of him and herself and, God knows what the neighbors would think! Unfortunately his big lie would embrace Tegwyn and break their hearts.

Tegwyn was born in the village of Cowbridge, Wales, one of the prettiest villages in the UK. She told him that nothing ever happens there, people are born, work six and seven day a week for nothing, marry, breed, drink too much like the Welsh do and die. She attended school as little as possible and was working by the time she was fifteen, married by eighteen to a man who was a laborer on building sites. After six weeks of marriage Tegwyn sat on their marriage bed as she did every night waiting for her man to come home from the pub. She said, this is hell and there is no future in this little room, in this little village with this little drunken man. So she packed her bags and with a few British pounds loaned from her Mum, she bolted to London. She worked at different basic jobs and enjoyed her youth in the fast city life of the late sixties and seventies. It was the time of Carnaby Street, the Beatles, mind-altering drugs, bell-bottom pants and giant hair. Her husband went home to his parents to live forever and she enjoyed the London scene until it deteriorated in the early seventies.

She followed the crowd of pop stars and celebrities to India and Thailand in search of their lost souls; with them she became engrossed in far eastern religions. They all left eventually, disillusioned, and returned to normal lives like we all do. Eventually she made it to Israel and worked on a Kibbutz where she was arrested and put in jail for not having a working visa. The Israeli government incarcerated her in a prison with murderers, drug runners and thieves and would not release her unless she told them who her parents were. They needed to extort money from them to pay their daughter's way back to the UK. She would not tell them since she loved her parents and did not want them to know she was in jail. After three months she became sick enough for it to be life threatening. The British Consulate stepped in and paid her way out of the country for fear she may die and they would have a scandal on their hands. They escorted a weak, sick girl to the airport in handcuffs and pushed her into the air.

Back in the UK she spent a few more years working in the pubs and clothing stores of London, getting depressed by the weather and changing culture. She knew her homeland was not the country where she wanted to spend the rest of her life. Tegs finally left for good; ending up in the fishing village of Ferragudo. She had come to the edge of her world, high up on the edge of a village and into a bar overlooking the Atlantic Ocean with Africa just over the horizon.

Her life became quiet and predictable; she met a few men and had relationships but in the end her partners treated her badly. She lives alone in a very organized life. Purposely she has kept herself busy and in a constant state of worry of what her Portuguese neighbors may think. This has furthered her isolation, causing her to live on the periphery of her community and not in it. Jonathan assured her that she was not Portuguese but Welsh and always will be and she need not worry what the Portuguese think—she will never be one of them. She knows the time has arrived for something new to come along and shake her life. She has come to the time where she can meet a Richard Jones, Jonathan Owen, William Robert Martin or Billy Bob Martin, the best damn car salesman.

Journey to The Edge of The World

Tegwyn had the day off. They wanted sex in the country but some ghosts would have their say about that. They picked up a rented vehicle from the vendor down the street from where he lives and drove out of Ferragudo north and west towards the village and battlements of Silves. The sky was clear and blue, the temperature semi tropical; it made a comfortable ride through villages with their simple blockhouses of white plaster. Old women in scarves and aprons leaned out their windows and chatted to passers by like hens in a coup; some waved and gave them toothless smiles as they drove by.

They drove through the rolling foothills to the village nestled in a valley in the upper reaches of the Rio Arade. The lush fertile land was blanketed with almond, orange and lemon groves. On the side of the river was the village its red sandstone castle and cathedral sat majestically atop the high ground. They drove across the modern motor bridge and parked by the business center and market.

Silves is old, nobody knows how old. Primitive people lived here when the Arade River's estuary came up from the ocean many kilometers away at the city of Portimão and Ferragudo. People prospered from the rich land but wars raged here on the hill over thousands of years. The river ran with blood many times. Today the estuary has silted up and the economy has moved toward tourism. Prosperity is evident by the new condominiums, homes and townhouses going up on the outskirts of the village. People come here now to experience the ghosts of the past—for the studious, the wonder of history.

They walked the narrow deserted Sunday cobbled streets. They made their way to the ramparts, cathedral and fortress. On the south facing side of the baroque cathedral is the Sun Door with marble steps where the town's poor beg. Among them was an old tanned woman dressed in black with her hand outstretched to Jonathan. Quickly his hand went in his pants and bought out a few euros for the old gypsy crone. She did not smile or thank him.

The midday sun was low in the winter sky. It shone a shaft of light into the cathedral, bathing the remaining parishioners of the morning service in light and warmth. They entered and not to disturb anyone, crept quietly across the sandstone floor and down the aisle to the main entrance. Emblazoned on a winter curtain of the main door was The Cross of The Order of Christ, symbol that led the Christian warriors and the Knights Templar into the last hand-to-hand battle to regain Christian sovereignty in Portugal. Red sandstone octagonal pillars supported a vaulted ceiling; down the nave on each side are Stations of the Cross and chapels. Light in the morning blasted through stained glass windows above the altar and down on a statue of Nossa Senhora cloaked in blue velvet fabric and gold filigree.

Jonathan looked down at the sandstone floor, polished by worshipers through the ages. Inscribed on a stone cover over a tomb were the words:

≤A

BARbOZA

XĄNTRÉ

Chisel carved, deep, thin and crude, the name rang through him like it was a piece of poetry—BARbOZA XANTRÉ. Who was this man, what did he do and why did he get a bed to spend eternity in this place? He asked an English speaking guard.

"Many characters are lost to antiquity," he said, "but he must have been somebody important to be buried here. I don't think he was a holy man—the engraving would have said so. He could have died in one of the many battles next door in the castle."

The simplicity of his name and grave conjured up what he may have done with his life long ago: sea captain, warrior, prophet, poet, engineer, or maybe he was just a plain soldier who performed a deed beyond mortal means. He could have been a rich farmer with the money to sneak in the back door. Jonathan dismissed the latter; his name was too beautiful to be insolent. The sun shone through the door and he studied his name. BARbOZA gets a daily ray of sunshine to warm the stone above his body.

At an altar in a side chapel, they lit candles for their families who were far away and missed. As they left the cathedral he stopped, ran back and lit one for BARbOZA.

Jonathan's head has been buried in art and history books for too many years; visions of terror and beauty come easy to him and those old malaria ghosts were starting to come into view—wisps of transparent gray clouds and images floated very near. They went next door to the Church of Mercy dodging the old crone. He looked back at the old woman—she became transparent. He was looking into the darkness of another universe—a hole the size of the earth. She was pulling him into nothing; into a place were nothing existed, not even time.

"Let's get outta' here." he said, "It's giving me the creeps." He took her hand.

"Me to—your hand is cold." Hurriedly they went their way—he was disturbed.

Next door they entered the little whitewashed Church of Mercy, a simple barrel-vaulted building. At the end of the nave was a floor to ceiling altar; it floated against the far wall. Its gold and wood frame shimmered against the stark white walls of the Church. He had read about the paintings; the large one in the center is the visitation of Christ; the others are masterpieces depict the Misericórdia.

He held onto Tegwyn and they crept in silence down the aisle to the altar, looked up at the vibrating oil paintings and wondered: how many thousands had bowed their heads here in reverence to a God that he was not certain he believed in. Lights and shadows flickered across the painting above them; it had come from the outside. Jonathan quickly turned to see the light source but there was nothing. Many experienced terror before this altar—why today? For what he felt at that moment he could have been burned by the inquisition on a pillar of fire in the courtyard outside—many had in years past. Quiet, he thought.

Time was moving fast for them; they left the church and climbed the cobbled roadway leading to the red sandstone battlements of the castle. They arrived at the main portal and its huge wooden doors; standing guard was a bronze statue of King Sancho the First. With the help of the Knights Templar he took the city from the Arabs for Christian domination. The King's metal statue was five-meters tall and he carried an unsheathed three-meter sword at the ready. Dressed in his armor of chain mail and sheets of steel the King weighs thousands of kilos. He looks to the south waiting for ships to come up the river carrying pirates, Phoenicians, Visigoths, Moors or whoever threatens to take his kingdom from him.

"This knight is made to his actual size and it was very difficult to keep him still to make the mold," Jonathan said straight faced and serious.

"Really Richard!" she said and after a pause she looked at him in puzzlement and reacted with, "you bastard!"

"Let's go in Tegs. I'm getting a weird feeling something is about to happen," he whispered, "boogey men are about. I can feel them all over me," and he held her hand tightly.

"Oh shut up!" Tegwyn commanded, tightening her hand on his.

They entered the castle by the tower gate, passed under the portcullis and through the thick doors. The doors were studded with steel bolts that would be a hindrance to axes attempting to chop through the heavy planking. Passing through another iron-gated portal they entered the eleven-sided fortress.

Suddenly Jonathan heard noises of clashing metal behind them. The gates of the castle slammed shut and the bells of the cathedral chimed. "Let's get up to the watchtower," he said—panic in his voice. They climbed a few stairs to the top of one of the watchtowers—suddenly arrows whizzed by their heads. He ducked but she did not—the arrows went through her head without touching her.

"Christ Tegs! Did you see that?"

"See what, Richard?" Tegwyn squeezed his hand.

"There were bloody arrows flying through your head!"

"No more joking. You're upsetting me."

Shadows of men in armor appeared along the walkways. A battle had begun. Drums and trumpets blasted in and out of the castle—heralding orders to charge. There were screams below as arrows of longbows and short vicious steel arrows of crossbows tore through armor and bodies. Ladders were put up against the castle walls; soldiers climbed them to be cut to pieces by the waiting defenders. A flood of invaders poured over the walls. Some suffered horrific burns from boiling oil and water poured from kettles swung out over the walls on davits. Others died from arrow crossfire from the embrasures and between the merlons of the battlements.

"Tegs, something is happening here! Can't you see it? The place is coming alive." He held her against a wall as an armored soldier ran by.

"Now, knock-it-off Richard, you're scaring me." She could see nothing—he was on his own, stuck somewhere in time and it was scaring the hell out of him. A group of knights in full armor soaked in sweat and blood ran down the parapet towards them. He tried to move, pulling Tegwyn with him but to no avail—there was no room. The ghosts ran through them; all he felt was a cold chill.

He turned to Tegwyn, "Bloody hell! Did you see that?"

"See what?" she said looking somewhat frightened, "are you okay Richard?"

"No, I'm not okay," and he hugged the wall and she squeezed his hand and held on to him, "but I will be fine soon—this will pass."

"What will pass?" she said now becoming concerned, "You're sweating terribly." He did not answer, he was fascinated and terrified at what was going on across the battlements and down in the castle compound.

There was chaos below, masses of peasants were busy organizing weapons, boiling hot oil and taking care of wounded soldiers. Makeshift leather tents were set up to protect them from falling arrows. The cries of the wounded and dying were terrible. Many people huddled against the castle walls crying and screaming in terror at the carnage. Their bowels opened in their fright. Soldiers and peasants wore different uniforms and costumes from many lands. It was if all the wars Silves had experienced over the thousands of years had come together in the same space and time. Kings and their entourages, cardinals and bishops, soldiers and peasants all armed and ready for the enemy to enter—who were they?

He looked down into the town and saw to his amazement—it was their own countrymen trying to breach the walls. All the good men and women were fighting each other in the name of God. Arrows flew into the compound and bodies fell with screams of agony. From the village below rotting dead farm animals and balls of fire pots and debris were catapulted from trebuchets and massive crossbows into the castle. Up over the ramparts and parapets they came—stinking, roaring and exploding, setting the wooden houses and people on fire. The bells of the cathedral rang on.

The ground trembled—a thundering noise came from the locked gates. They started to disintegrate; something very big and heavy pounded through from the rampart outside. With a great cracking noise the gate and portcullis came crashing down. King Sancho the First roared in, all five-meters of him, kicking broken bodies out of the way and waving his giant sword. Across his chest on white linen The Cross of The Order of Christ was painted in blood red. He smashed and crashed through dozens of soldiers who tried to take him down. Body parts flew through the air and soldiers screamed from their wounds, others ran in terror from the giant of the Knights Templar. He was so powerful he smashed the very rocks beneath his iron feet. Behind him galloped a fierce armored man leading a number of mounted knights. Their horses snorted, teeth gnashed, hooves stomped, and eyes blazed in terror and madness. Armor and linen bearing the coat-of-arms of the horses and men shone in the sunlight and red and white feathers atop their helmets swayed and fluttered in the breeze and from the majestic canter of their Belgian steeds. Running beside them were dozens of Irish wolfhounds, pit bulls, mastiffs and other vicious dogs, frothing at the mouth—full of rage—eager to join in. The leader of the dogs and mounted knights carried a flag on a metal staff with its base tucked into a holder on his stirrup. The flag displayed The Cross of The Order of Christ. It was Dom Peio Peres Correia, Master of the Order of Santiago.

Hundreds of Muslims and Christians descended on the knights and dogs but they were no match for the giant and the horsemen who cut them down. The dogs attacked in packs tearing at arms and legs. Jonathan watched in horror; an unarmed Arab and Knight fought on the ground with only their hands and teeth. They moaned in agony, they were both worn out. Their ears were torn off—their faces ripped to the bone. One would soon give in to the other who would beat him to death. He could do nothing but watch.

A Roman soldier in leather armor jumped down onto the walkway beside him and raised his sword above his head; it came down through Jonathan without touching him and cut the head off a young naked boy—one of the swarms coming up from the courtyard. The children ran naked in packs of ten to a dozen throughout the compound. The mates of the decapitated boy, ten of them, swarmed on the Roman soldier like insects and stabbed him to death—a hundred punctures within six seconds. They quickly moved off looking for their next victim.

The site was sickening and he looked away down into the village for relief and something awesome was taking place on the bridge. A huge cannon on a carriage with massive wheels that were taller than a man was being pulled up to the center of the bridge. Chocks were placed under its wheels; the barrel of the cannon was made level with the ground—aimed at Jonathan's rented vehicle. A wagon loaded with sacks of gunpowder and granite cannon balls was hauled up. The sacks of gunpowder were loaded into the cannon's mouth and rammed home and a ball of granite was loaded.

French crews set up an A frame over the cannon and made fast a block and tackle to a steel ring on top of the barrel. A commander had instruments, one a square like carpenters use; he placed in the cannon's mouth. On his orders the crew raised the barrel with the block and tackle while a man below drove wedges between the carriage and barrel. The cannon raised its ugly mouth from his rental car towards the castle. When the commander was satisfied with the cannons alignment he ordered his instruments removed, the frame unhooked and moved off. A soldier nearby gave him a flaming stick and he ordered everyone off the bridge—they all ran. When he was satisfied that everyone was clear, he placed the flame on the touchhole. Nothing happened--Jonathan thought--it's a dud. An explosion of smoke and flame came from the barrel and it took a second for the sound to reach the castle—it arrived like a clap of thunder. The granite ball rose into the sky and he could see its trajectory. It slammed into the watchtower they had just climbed down from. It struck it with such force the stones came away exposing another older tower inside. The castle shook from the impact and the tower collapsed taking the soldiers on the battlement with it down the hill in an avalanche. The granite ball went with them picking up speed and by the time it got to the village nothing could stop it. It tore its way through house after house, bounced over his car and into the river.

He turned back to the compound. A thickset man in leather armor ran over bodies and up the stone stairs to him and Tegwyn. He was Jonathan's height but weighed a great deal more; thick and strong in arms and legs; his hands large and callused from manual labor. His blonde matted hair flowed from his steel helmet and cascaded down his shoulders. His blue eyes blazed from their sockets, steel head and nose plate. His face was young, square and strong. He looked at Jonathan and he knew he was there. He had a Welsh longbow in his hand and stood straight and erect on the parapet and drew back his bow. Shutting his mind to the chaos around him, he took careful aim, taking his time—he let his arrow fly. Through the smoke and fire, across the bodies and debris the arrow found its mark in the right eye of the King who bellowed, screamed and staggered. The King went down, crushing men under his huge body. The ghosts started to fade, turning transparent. Jonathan could see the ground, the architecture of the castle and compound come back into view. Jonathan shouted to the bowman who was disappearing, "What is your name? Who are you?"

"BARbOZA XANTRÉ, a stone mason," he shouted and he disappeared into the sunlight.

"Jesus Christ, Richard you look pale—you're soaked with sweat. What's the matter? What are those words your shouting?" Tegwyn asked very concerned. She was beginning to think she was out with a madman. She was.

"I'm fine honey. I just need a coffee and a sandwich. I start seeing things when I'm hungry."

"Yes, well I feel like a little something myself. Let's have a coffee and croissant at that little place next door and then we can drive up to Monchique and have a proper lunch. Christ you're a bloody mystery to me sometimes."

They left the compound through the main portico and Jonathan looked up at the giant King—the King did not move.

After a snack Jonathan settled down. "Tegs, you know I read too much—I think. For years I have been studying art and history and reading about these ancient places and lately the past and my present reality get kinda' mixed up, if you know what I mean."

"No, I don't know what you mean."

"The past comes alive for me; I actually see ghost like things going on around me as clear as you and I sitting here. Tegwyn, how long was I out of it, when we were up on the parapets?"

"A minute I guess."

All that happened in one minute? Some minute, he thought. "I see ghosts a lot. All my life I have seen them. I believe they originate from my uncle who told me terrifying stories when I was young. Today there was something different; one of the ghosts recognized I was there and actually spoke to me. You know what that means don't you?"

"No, but you're going to tell me anyway."

"They say if you start hearing voices, you are going crazy."

"I don't think you're crazy Richard, maybe a little eccentric but not crazy. You function very well," and they both laughed.

"You know Tegs, in the end we all find out that nothing changes; nothing really improves and everything eventually goes back to the earth no matter what efforts we make to save our past: great castles crumble; paper and leather rot; armor, swords and guns rust; bodies turn to dust and memories fade.

"Enough said. Let's get out of here."

They drove up the mountains, which are more like foothills; mountains to Jonathan are the Coast Range and Rockies of British Columbia. The little villages of the Algarve are quaint and beautiful; their houses are painted pink, yellow and white; in the yards are pens of sheep, goats and the ever-present chickens scratching in the dirt. Lazy cats lay about on walls and dogs fuss about the doorways. Canopied pine and oak cork trees provide shade from the hot summer sun. The houses open directly onto the road that twists its way up to Monchique through forests and grasslands. They drove up to the highest point in the Province of Algarve; a windswept bald mountain with huge communication towers dotting its summit. Standing on a pile of boulders he looked east south and west and he realized how small Portugal is.

They continued on and stopped at a restaurant with an outdoor patio on a cliff overlooking the village of Meia Viana near Monchique. Below them and up the hillsides the land was a terraced orchard of cork, oranges, lemons, almonds and vegetables. The steps were excavated long ago, beyond memory, like everything here in Portugal.

They had a lunch of lamb chops, vegetables and drank a few glasses of local dry red wines. Stomachs taken care of, they drove to the turnoff to Marmalete to the east coast of Portugal and the city of Aljezur. They turned left toward the Cape St Vincent lighthouse and the edge of the world.

"We're here!" she shouted with excitement, "Twenty years I've wanted to come here. We're at the edge of the world!" She grabbed Jonathan and kissed him hard. "And it's with you my love," she gently whispered. They jumped from the car and ran to the edge of the two hundred foot cliff beside the lighthouse and ancient fortress. She kept him close for the hour they spent in that desolate place.

"Just out there, maybe a hundred kilometers is a giant waterfall," she said raising her arms and pointing towards America, "it drops into blackness. Nothing there but stars and floating coffin ships for those who dared to wander from home—for those who dared to go beyond the gates of Hercules." And she went silent savoring the moment; he kept quiet. "This is the edge of everything," she said quietly to herself. She turned to him and her eyes filled with tears. He held her close and looked out to sea.

They watched in awe, the sports fishermen on the edge of the cliffs with their lines out hundreds of feet from were they stood. The fall would be unforgiving. He turned away from them; his legs were turning to rubber. He knew dozens of fishermen are lost each year in their efforts to catch a few sardines.

"I live out there Tegs, far away in Canada," and he pointed northwest, he held her and kissed her hard.

"I love you for this Richard," she shouted over the roar of the ocean, wind and screaming seagulls. They stood out on the cliffs, holding each other from the wind that would take them a way if they let it.

They did not stay long. It was a long drive home to Ferragudo. He knew Tegwyn would visit the Cape again someday and perhaps with someone else. For him this would be the only time. There will be other places as moving and spectacular like this lonely place, and the crowded battlements and nightmares of Silves. He will see and experience these things often in the future, places of glory and wonder and he knows the spirit of Tegwyn and others will be with him on those adventures.

They arrived home just after dark and checked in the car. The weather turned bad and they were hungry.

"Dinner my love?" He queried.

"Bloody hell, yes, I'm starving and we only ate a few hours ago. But then I'm always hungry with you," she giggled, "you'll do right by me, Richard, if you take me to dinner at the local," she quipped in her lilting Welsh accent.

They hustled their way up the narrow streets between the stark white hard walls of the houses and apartments. Amber streetlights danced across wet cold cobbled streets and sidewalks. The lights twisted and dipped their way through the neighborhood. From far below a warm rain-filled wind came up from the ocean and pushed its way along the streets; bouncing off buildings; driving them onward. Shadows of people rose and disappeared below the steep streets, alleys, and dark doorways of cafes and homes. People appeared and disappeared into the cubistic space. A full moon came out between the fast moving gray and black clouds; Venus was snuggled alongside. A prowling ink black sedan, eyes piercing the dark scene, stalked the streets and disappeared silently down a narrow alleyway. They made their way together down the street to its end and the Portuguese Bar of Ferragudo where they would feed themselves. They could see it in the distance, lit from the glow of Victorian street lamps.

"Tea and off to bed," she said.

Nagging Questions

Frank Gillies from the Forensic Anthropologist Investigation Team concluded how Jonathan was injured. Everything fit but the smacking of his head on the roof post. It could only happen if the seat belt was slack, like when a body gradually and slowly moves forward, the belt will not catch. The crash was violent and would have held him back from hitting the post with his head and he knew Jonathan had the belt on because of the bloody fingerprints on the release button. Frank checked and double-checked the seat-belt operation and all was in order. He felt this was a major observation so he flagged it in his report and it was included in the growing information of the case.

There were also nagging questions for Constable Jack Garland: Why did this experienced pilot fly up the wrong river valley when he knew the country so well, having worked and painted it for years? Was it to hide the plane until the fall snows came, giving him almost a year to relocate and hide? Why did he file a false flight plan? Taking off without checking his fuel and running on his reserve tank? Why were the throttle plungers in an off position? If this is a hoax how will he make money from it? Does he have a partner? Too many question unanswered.

Jack read the reports over and over to find some answers. Something was wrong; the crash scenario did not fit into an accident category; there was just too much evidence of a hoax. Jack was not stupid; he was hired because he was a meticulous officer with patience and foresight. He would not sign any case closed without a complete investigation. This accident began to smell. He also had a nagging suspicion that Jonathan wanted Jack to pursue him for some strange reason. The constable phoned the coroner's office in Prince George and told them not to send on the death certificate to his daughter.

Jack had the three investigation teams come to the airport at great expense to reevaluate the wreck. The extra expense would be questionable but he would take the risk. He wanted the blood spattering and impact zones investigated above everything else. The reports came out exactly as before, he ordered the forensic team to look again at the scenario of the seat belt extension on impact. The team proved once again the pilot's head could not reach the bloody impact zone of the doorpost. The pilot seat belt was checked again for the umpteenth time and found it was in good working order. It was certain Jack would have to go further with this investigation—but where? He would have to make a case for an investigation with the Board of Inquiry whether he would be justified in investigating further and incurring more expenses. Proof must be presented that hardcore criminal intent was evident.

He lay in bed wide-awake, the bedroom was hot and close and there was a mosquito loose, buzzing by his ear every few minutes. The house was quiet, even the frogs in the nearby pond had settled down. The Garland's Red Setter, Brandy, was sleeping on the floor next to his wife Caroline. He never gets stepped on when sleeping on her side of the bed. The moon and Venus shone through the window and Caroline was deep in sleep and snoring. The boys were on a fishing trip with some pals and would be home in a couple of days. Everything was quiet and peaceful in Fort Nelson in northern British Columbia. But his brain was racing. For weeks he had dreams that woke him up of huge black lettering on the fuselage and wings of the West Toad River crash: canvases, paper, paints, brushes, sleeping bags, clothing, toothbrush, soap, broken windshields, popped rivets, angles, directions, wheels, doors and doors—

"Jesus Christ!" he sat up with a start, "I've got him!" he shouted waking up Caroline, "sorry honey." quickly he jumped out of bed shouting, "I've got him! I've got the bastard!"

He pulled on his jeans and shirt and slipped into his running shoes. He hugged his wife, kissing her hard, and patted a bewildered Brandy. He left the house, jumped in his truck and roared down his driveway onto the highway, squealing the truck's tires and gunned it to the detachment office just a few minutes away.

The night duty officer was startled when Jack crashed through the door and dashed into his office. He pulled five large accordion files of the West Toad River crash from a cabinet behind his desk. He pulled the photos taken by the forensic team and Transportation Safety Board, spreading them across his desk. Quickly he separated out the photos of the fuselage. The photos were taken before anyone touched the plane, photos of many angles and details. He first checked for the blood smears on the engine cowling in front of the broken windshield—there were none. The pilot did not exit from there and besides the exit hole was too small for someone to climb through. Only a few of Jonathan's art supplies went through the windshield. The passenger's door was up against a tree and could not be opened. Jack found a photo of the pilot's door. It was open about six centimeters and the window was intact. Jack looked closer and saw moss covered woody debris one quarter the way up the door.

"Jesus Christ!" Jack shouted, "Nobody, but nobody got out of that plane after it crashed. Nobody was in it when it crashed!" he shouted excitedly to the duty officer outside his office.

He quickly phoned the Transportation Safety Team leader Sid Wilson in Vancouver and got him out of bed.

"Sid?" he shouted into the phone.

"Yes, who's calling? It's three in the morning you know."

"Sid—it's Jack—Jack Garland—RCMP, Fort Nelson."

"Couldn't this wait until morning?" he said, irritated.

"No, I'm too excited and this just can't wait. Tell me Sid, did you do anything to the West Toad River crash aircraft before you took photos, like touch it in anyway?"

"Of course not. We don't touch anything until every detail is photographed. What's up?"

"Did you have to move anything before you entered the craft?"

There was a silence then a "hum—yes we did. Some logs were in the way of the door—do you think maybe he went through the window?" Sid questioned

"There was no blood on the engine cowling and there would have been, just like the blood all over the cockpit. He was bleeding badly. And anyway, the hole in the shattered windshield is too small to crawl through. There was no blood on the exterior of the plane. He was not in the plane Sid—when it went down—nobody was there!"

"My God, you've got something here. If you need backup affidavits or anything just call me, okay?"

"Thanks. I will. Now go back to sleep. It's early morning, eh."

"Thanks and good night!" Sid hung up the phone.

To: indigohue

Something is up Dad! I don't know what but the RCMP came to visit yesterday and asked me a number of questions about you. Like how experienced a flyer you were; were you broke before you went missing? How much was your pension? What was your health condition? Did I have any insurance out on you? I don't know if they were just fishing, scaring me or what.

I haven't used my office computer or phone for any connection with you and I am making sure I'm not followed to the Internet cafés, which I am changing constantly. I will only be in contact with you once a month. Take care and watch your back. Luv yu.

Jack and Annabelle Do Lunch

The crash was now a crime scene. The West Toad River airplane crash incident would involve Interpol and police forces the other side of the world. Jack Garland made his case to the RCMP Board of Inquiry in Ottawa that the Fort Nelson RCMP Detachment suspect a crime has been committed. The situation was unique and his investigation to establish proof of criminal behavior was validated with the evidence of the blocked airplane door, the seat belt operation and blood smear on the doorpost. What was missing was the motive. With a budget, and release from his regular duties, Jack was reassigned to chief investigator of the case.

Media attention was high and rising about this now famous artist eaten or lost in the bush of Northern British Columbia. The media got out of hand and information was leaked from the search party, investigation teams and the Toad River Airport personnel that the case was not closed. In fact it was being reinvestigated and new evidence of criminal behavior was released. Great effort would be undertaken to find him. The media went into a feeding frenzy, because of the lack of a motive for Jonathan to fake his own death. They could make up stories and speculate like the reporters of old western pulp fiction adventures.

Political intrigue swept down the halls of the Federal Government. Ministers were questioned and grilled by the media in the halls of Parliament and the Legislative. The opposition raised accountability and things got ugly. Jonathan was turning into an embarrassment; something he didn't anticipate but was a bonus for sales and the project. The public was eating this great Canadian outdoor adventure up. So the search for Jonathan Owen by the Royal Canadian Mounted Police officer Constable Jack Garland was underway and as the old saying says—The Mounties always get their man.
It was time for the RCMP to have a chat with Jonathan's daughter, "Ms. Owen?" Jack said into the phone.

"Yes," Annabelle replied.

"This is Constable Jack Garland."

Not hesitating: "Hello Constable. Can I help you?" She felt sweat come to her forehead.

"I'm in Vancouver for a few days. Could we have a talk this afternoon or tomorrow at your convenience? I would like to chat about your father and I need some background information for our investigation into his disappearance."

"Perhaps lunch or something?" she said casually.

"That would be most convenient Ms. Owen. How about today at the restaurant in the Hotel Madeira? It's near your office and walking distance from my hotel. Say about 1 p.m.?"

"Sure, that would be fine. Just let me check my calendar," and she created a brief pause, "I'll see you there in a couple of hours—at one then."

"Thank you Ms. Owen. Goodbye."

Annabelle put down the phone and took a deep breath. She knew eventually she would have to face this RCMP officer whom she had only talked to. She relaxed and had a coffee from the pot she always has brewing beside her desk. She would be careful with this man who was no fool—neither was she. She turned and looked at the huge red and blue Miró above her--swore at her father and concentrated on her luncheon date.

She walked casually into the high ceiling restaurant just inside the hotel entrance. A large, good-looking man stood at a booth half way down the cavern; he signaled her to come to him. Jack Garland impressed her; he was handsome and conservatively dressed in a black suit, white shirt and dark tie. His hair was full and black on a large head that had a jaw that looked like it could break a brick. He stood erect and formal. He held out his open wallet to show her his badge and politely said, "Just a formality Ms. Owen. Nice to meet you," and he shook her hand. His grasp was firm, formal and powerful which took her by surprise. Annabelle told herself to be careful, this fellow was silk smooth—a well trained police officer. This was business and nothing else. They sat down, she in the plush red and gold upholstered booth and he in a chair on the opposite side of the table. The booth was discretely picked out and no one was seated on either side. Annabelle surmised Jack had made arrangements with the restaurant for privacy. There was a man at the bar noticeably dressed like him, watching them through the mirror behind the bar. There was no effort to hide his presence; all was for intimidation, she told herself—put her on guard where she may make a mistake.

Jack gestured the waiter over. "Would you like a drink, Ms. Owen?"

"Just a diet soft drink would be fine. Thank you."

"Very well," Jack gave a nod to the waiter, "make that two diet soft drinks. Thank you." and he turned to Annabelle. "Well Ms. Owen, we finally meet after all these months of chatting on the phone."

"Yes and its good to meet you. I have been curious what an RCMP officer from the north looks like," they politely smiled at the comment.

"As you probably know I have been assigned the chief investigator of your father's case."

"Yes, I read about it."

"We believe he is still alive somewhere out there in the world," he looked for a reaction in her eyes but none came, "evidence collected at the crash site suggests this to be true." Annabelle was surprise at his direct honesty, "We don't know why he was motivated into faking his own death but I personally believe it was for money and ego. What do you think?"

She evaluated her thoughts. She knew he would throw out questions as bait. She better not address he faked his own death. "I really don't know what to say about it all. I have no idea why he would do such a bizarre thing."

"What about the insurance? Do you have any comments?"

"As you know, Dad only had eighty thousand in insurance, of which my brother and I are the beneficiaries. We both do well in our businesses and I can't see him doing himself in for such a trivial amount," she summed up, "this whole thing about Dad just baffles me as much as it does you." She could feel Jack's eyes concentrating on her body language.

"We know you market his art work and have power of attorney of his accounts, properties and executor of his will. Is that so?"

"Yes I'm all what you say, and since the accident I have put all money acquired through sales of his art into a trust account, until this controversy around his death is cleared up. How long have you been suspicious of me being involved with my father's alleged criminal activities officer?" She stared directly into his eyes; they demanded an answer."

"Well," a pause and he stared directly into her eyes, "we must explore all avenues Ms. Owen, and every possibility must be scrutinized. We have to absolve you and others of any involvement in his disappearance; if we don't, the case will become a jumbled mess of scenarios." The waiter returned with their diet soft drinks and their eyes went to ordering the lunch pasta special.

Jack changed tactics to the emotional side of the interview, "Would you tell me about your father Ms. Owen? What kind of a man is he?"

Tricky question, she thought present tense. He's on his game. "Well he was a Dad—my Dad and he loved my mother very much. He always worked hard and kept his health although up to the time he went missing he was having dizzy spells."

"Dizzy spells?" the constable queried leaning back in his chair.

"Yes, that is what he told me. They came on about a month before he went missing and for some reason he went into denial about them and didn't see his doctor. He told me once he had trouble years ago with malaria.

"Who is his doctor, I would like to call him."

"Dr. Warinka, he's in the book."

"So what happened with the malaria pills?"

"Hallucinations—he hallucinated." Jack took out his note pad and quickly wrote the doctor's name and a few words, "He didn't tell me anything else about it."

"Now what about you and your brother growing up?"

"Dad made sure that my brother and I got the best he could afford and made sure we attended university. He always wished he attended university but settled for Art College. No matter, he lived a good life because of his enthusiasm. He raised us when Mom ran off, he kept his loyalty to us, which was important to him and he never did remarry, just had girlfriends.

"Many girlfriends?"

"Yes, many, some for sex, others devoted friends, some hurt him but most made him happy. Art was his passion not women.

"He told me that he didn't go into the fine arts in a big way because he wanted to raise a family and work at a nine to five job. He wanted work without the stress of putting bread and butter on the table and relying on the unpredictable art market. He managed to incorporate art into his career. That's how he made his participation in boring and ordinary work tolerable."

"He doesn't sound adventurous. Please, tell me about your father's flying." He scribbled more notes.

"He started flying ten years ago when he purchased a plane he could afford. He took maintenance courses to make sure he knew how to service it. He could get to many places around the province in that thing and with his Jeep and mountain bike he went everywhere." Jack wrote in his notebook and Annabelle felt like the lunch was an interrogation, which it was.

"So he was quite conscious about safety?"

"When he flew he was disciplined and called in regularly when he was out in the wilderness. He would call the local airfields; they would call me and tell me that he was okay. He did have a fear that he may crash someday, that is why he made me power of attorney in case there was an accident. He didn't want my brother and me to go through any bureaucracy."

"The Jeep, where it now?"

"I really don't know," Annabelle said, and she gave him a puzzled look like she had not thought of it before. She lightened up the moment: "You know officer Garland it's a funny thing, the two of us sitting here in this restaurant. When my father was in Art College he lived a couple of hundred feet down the street on the corner in an old dilapidated Victorian house. That was forty years ago. For two years he ate macaroni and cheese smothered in ketchup and beans. Since those days he would not have that meal anywhere near him." They laughed.

"Wow! That's what my kids eat. Nothing changes."

The waiter returned with their order and they ate. Jack Garland went over the evidence pointing to her father's fake death, searching for a motive. Annabelle stayed calm and looked puzzled at the constable giving him the impression of trying to fathom what he was saying.

"How is your company doing financially Ms. Owen?"

"Very well, especially in the last five years with the new break in tax credits for culture contributions."

"Oh, tax credit? Could you give this ignorant cop a little insight into the art market?"

"Yes, sure, many large corporations are looking for art work for a write-off and long term investments. Some corporations have art collections worth hundreds of millions of dollars. They bought the works over the years putting out only a few thousand dollars and claiming the purchases as corporate expenses."

"Sounds hardly fair. Do you think your father's work has gone up in value since he has gone missing?"

"Certainly, this is a common occurrence for artists who are deceased. Vincent van Gogh only sold one painting in his lifetime, and that was to his brother, I believe. Now he is dead the highest price paid for one of his works recently topped the one hundred million dollar threshold."

"In Canada?" Jack said with surprise.

"No, definitely not in Canada—Asia, China, USA, the middle east, countries with vast individual wealth. Perhaps someday when you and I are gone and it's another world my Dad's art will be worth millions. Who knows—he was good."

She refers to him in the past tense; hm he thought no slip-ups yet. Perhaps she is telling the truth: "Are you making any money from his work now that he is gone— there is so much publicity about his death?"

"Yes, I just put it into the trust account like I told you. I don't know what I'll do with it. My father was a fan of art schools and often taught and demonstrated drawing and painting techniques at some of them. Perhaps that's where his money should go—to art schools. I make my profit on living artists, some who are extremely good and sought after by corporate investments as I said before," Annabelle said impatiently and she took a deep breath to calm her and not show any anxiety. Under the napkin on her lap her fingers twitched but soon stopped.

They finished their meal, had coffee and chatted about families. They talked about living in the north and made idle banter about her father and his art. She kept her guard up and kept Dad in the past. The constable was impressed by her candidness, control and view of the situation and believed she was telling the truth which she was—to the questions.

He straightened his back making himself larger, the skin of his brick breaking jaw became tight, and his eyes became wide and black. He watching her closely and bluntly said, "Did you have anything to do with your father's disappearance?"

His change frightened her but she would not show it. Pure intimidation she thought. She knew this question would come and she would keep it short with no explanation. "No, I didn't," she said calmly looking him straight in the eye.

He relaxed. "Thank you Ms. Owen you have cleared up a lot of issues for me. Perhaps we shall meet again someday. The lunch is on me."

"Thank you," Annabelle said with a smile; they rose from the table and she reached out and shook his hand.

He watched her walk out of the restaurant and wondered, is she as intelligent as her father? I think so, perhaps she knows nothing and then again she knows everything. Keep it open Jack—keep it open, he said to himself. What to do next was to find out where Jonathan Owen went. He walked over to the bar and he discussed his findings with his local partner. They would need a search warrant.

To: indigohue

Hey, Dad, the RCMP officer from Fort Nelson, whom I was dealing with for months, took me for lunch today. He asked questions and said you were missing from your crash site. He wasn't normal, he kept asking questions about you—I think he is on to you. You trained me well, he got nothing from me—but I think he is on to me too. Luv yu.

To: indigohue

Hey, Dad, the press is all over me like they have their own investigation team so I'm feeding them back to the RCMP. They know I'm handling your work and I have told them: Yes, your work has skyrocketed in price – best I tell the truth on that one. Besides it's making more money; the media is feeding the whole scam.

Re. your instructions: I have opened a trust fund for all future sales and this is working. It has diverted suspicion of me being in cahoots with you. They think, because you may be still alive, I would be making a bundle on your death. Little do they know the tidy sums tucked away. Luv yu.

Europe and Interpol

Saturday, the day of the week that Annabelle spends at home with her books, Constable Jack Garland and five RCMP officers from the Surrey Detachment called armed with a search warrant.

The massed at her doorway, "Good morning, Annabelle. Sorry to disturb you but we have some business to attend to," Jack gave her the warrant. She scanned it and handed it back to him.

"Very well officer have a look around but please don't break anything."

"We'll be careful." She showed them to her garage where she stored her father's belongings.

"Is this all there is Ms. Owen?"

"Yes, I sold his furniture and art supplies. These are his personal things. I haven't gone through them yet."

"And his paintings, drawings—where are they?"

"Warehoused, I will give you a catalogue of them if you like."

"Yes, please. Thanks." She went off to get her study to get the catalogue. The officers went out to the garage and found eleven boxes of papers and a laptop computer—they confiscated the lot.

To: indigohue

Hey Dad, listen up. They are on to you. They know you are alive and living somewhere out there in the world. They came with a search warrant and took all that remained of you. I don't know what they will find but they will find something; the RCMP officers aren't slouches. They know from evidence you did not go down with your plane and now they are looking for Silver Bullet and God knows what is in your stuff. I'm worried Dad, not for me but for you. You're a crazy old boomer you know that? All you old guys can't sit still, you have to be out there doing what us young ones are supposed to be doing.

Luv yu.

At the Vancouver crime lab the forensic team poured over the material for days and found Jonathan could be anywhere in the world, and in contact with dozens of people. They surmised he was not in Canada; the man knew the world too well to stay home, be noticed and get caught. But where to look puzzled Jack. By all accounts Jonathan was an adventurer and a mischief. It will be hard to nail down a motive. Would he commit a crime for the pure adventure of it? Some have in the past but they were lunatics and easily caught.

They searched through his possessions and came up with a jumble of possibilities; they needed to narrow the scope. One of the technical people was assigned the laptop and going through the files she found them typical of an artist—full of graphics and pictures. He looked in the deleted file folders but they had been cleaned out; bringing up the temp files, he found they were also gone. She would have to go deeper into the laptop files and she looked in the Internet browser's settings. This folder had not been touched for two years and Jonathan was not aware it existed since these files were not accessed through the browser but through the system's operation settings. There were hundreds of entries and dozens of countries Jonathan explored via the web: Mexico, Japan, England, Ireland, Spain, Portugal, Italy, Germany, Malaysia, the list went on. Jack told the technician to pull out the names of the countries in the last year and half and any links.

The technician came back with better: "Going through the files," she said, holding up a print out, "I came across a discount airline ticket purchase agent in the United States. This is it and this is the date he contacted them—August of last year."

Jack jumped up from his chair with excitement and hugged the technician, to her bewilderment, and ordered an officer: "Get me on the next plane to Omaha, Nebraska and to the ticket company's head office. Sorry about the hug officer." An officer was on the phone right away and asked permission of the company to investigate a certain transaction and the company was only too willing to cooperate and said they need not fly down—they would fax the information and in a few minutes it came in. Jack was a little embarrassed at going into the old style of doing things but he shrugged it off. The fax showed an order for a one-way ticket in the name of William Robert Martin—Calgary, Alberta to Frankfurt, Germany, flight number 9639 September 30.

"Christ," Jack said, as he read the print out, "that's only a couple of days from the missing person report filed by his daughter in Fort Nelson. We got him! Or at least we know where our man is and his new name." He stopped his enthusiasm over what was taking place in the lab and thought this is too easy, Jonathan must be smarter than this.

The ticket purchased in the United States to Germany was all the evidence Jack needed to get Interpol involved. The organization will not assist if the crime resides and stays within the boundaries of the home country. Jonathan's crime had crossed over the border into one of the membership of Interpol. He immediately informed his superiors in Ottawa of the situation and they requested the Attorney General to request assistance of Interpol at their head quarters in Lyon, France.

Jack was a tired RCMP officer at this point and hoped he could return to Fort Nelson, his wife, children and dog. He had done his job. He was glad this would now be in the hands of Ottawa, Interpol and the German police—however this was not to be.

At his hotel he was packing his luggage; there was a knock on the door. An officer from the Surrey Detachment handed him a letter, smiled and left. He opened it. Ottawa informed him his job performance was superior in his investigation of the case and he has been seconded to

Interpol's General Secretariat to carry the case through to trial. He is to go to Europe and work with Interpol and the German authorities and assist them to hunt down, arrest and extradite Jonathan Owen to Canada. Under no circumstances must he take action against the accused. The countries' law enforcement agencies must make the arrest and legal authorities carry out the extradition, Constable Jack Garland would take custody at the airport. He slumped on the bed; I don't know if I can do this, he said to an empty room.

This would be a challenge for Jack who is a homebody and reluctant to leave home where life is simple to a place of foreign languages, cultures and customs. For a man like Jack; Europe is a mystery and alien to him. He took the first flight home to his family to pack and say goodbye.
Constable Garland kissed his wife, kids, hugged his dog Brandy and boarded the daily flight from Fort Nelson to Vancouver. He boarded a flight to Heathrow Airport in the United Kingdom and on his arrival, transferred to a shuttle that flew him to the Charles de Gaulle Airport in Paris. Two Interpol officers and a customs-immigration officer met him at the door of the airplane. The constable showed them his passport, identification papers, RCMP badge and letter of introduction from the Attorney General of Canada. On confirmation, he was quickly hustled down the emergency stairs to the airport tarmac. An Interpol agent who had his flight and baggage information picked up his luggage. At a waiting helicopter an agents gave him a typed itinerary for the next few days. Jack and the agents boarded the helicopter and the Sikorskyi rose into the air and sped south on the last leg of his trip to the Interpol offices in Lyon. They landed in the space reserved for helicopters in the parking lot behind the impressive office complex.

Officer Henry Dubois, from Canada, was waiting for him and whisked him off in a black Mercedes Benz. "Have a good trip?" I'm Henry Dubois—I'm French Canadian. As you can tell by my accent; I'm not from France."

"Good to meet you Henry. Do you drink beer?" He shook his hand.

"Yes."

"Good, because I'm in need of one."

They arrived at a bed and breakfast nestled into the countryside. Not a sterile commercial lodging but a quaint, four hundred year old, oversized cottage. Needless to say Jack Garland was in culture shock and suffering from the long journey with no sleep and jet lag.

Henry, saw that he was comfortably settled in his hotel. They went to the bar and had a beer. Henry filled him in on what he knew about the case of J. Owen. He was surprised—Henry knew everything. Before he left, Henry said he would pick him up in twenty-four hours, giving Jack's biological clock time to adjust. Henry would act as Jack's assistant while staying in Lyon, traveling with him as his translation/communications officer. It was 8 p.m. when Jack undressed and climbed into bed—he was exhausted.

He awoke at 6 a.m. the following morning. He had slept almost ten hours and felt refreshed. After showering and dressing he went for breakfast in the cozy dining room of the cottage. There were four other travelers with him at breakfast and he felt quite at home in the comfortable surroundings. Interpol really knows how to treat their people, Jack thought. Make them comfortable through their period of adjustment. He went for a walk to fill in the time and take in the beautiful scenery and village. Henry picked him up at 3 p.m.

Henry Dubois, a third generation French Canadian, grew up on a vegetable farm on the outskirts of Montreal, Quebec forty-two years ago. Graduating from the local high school he went on to study law at Dalhousie University and on completion of his degree he studied Criminology at Simon Fraser University. Shortly after obtaining his second degree he joined the Royal Canadian Mounted Police and worked for nine years in the frozen North West Territories assisting the circuit judges. He loved the north and the Inuit people and with the circuit judges worked hard to bring compassion, justice and fairness to a people living on the edge of a frozen world in a difficult and near impossible life.

In the car on the way to headquarters: "How did you get here Henry?"

"Some years ago, I was ordered to arrest a criminal living in a town on the shores of James Bay and assist in his extradition to Amsterdam to stand trial for murder. I met a few Interpol agents and we became friends. They showed me around Holland and we drank a lot of beer. I like Europe, with its old world traditions and culture, it reminds me of home. I knew I would be comfortable here so I applied to be seconded to the Interpol Headquarters. I was accepted within a month. I think the boys helped me out."

"Are you married?"

"No, I've never found the time for it. This job keeps me busy—hopping around the country. I love it and don't want to give it up. Although I think they are going to send me home soon. My stay is almost up." Like Jack Garland he was a large and fit man but completely bald by choice; shaving his head to the quick.

Jack noticed a vicious scar on Henry's temple, "So what's with the scar on your head?"

"My badge of courage," he said with a broad grin, "a drunk who I was ordered to serve a warrant put it there. He came out of his cabin and threw an axe at me. It lodged in my skull—I went down in the snow. My partner pulled his gun and shot the guy dead. I remember lying very still and conscious while my partner radioed for help, the helicopter didn't arrive for seventy minutes—the longest minutes of my life. My partner held on to me and made me talk so I would not go unconscious. I was almost dead when we arrived at the clinic. The priest gave me the last rights but the doctors operated and saved my life."

"Jesus, some experience. How long did it take before going back to work?"

"It took me six months to recover. I was tested at a rehab hospital in Montreal, to see if I was capable of carrying out my duties. Hey, I was lucky there was no brain damage. It was a bitch of a struggle, but hell, I was not going on disability pension. I still have the axe; it's mounted in a glass box at home in Canada—it sits on the mantelpiece."

"You could have the scar removed you know."

"Hell no, the scar's my other badge." They both laughed.

"Getting back to going home. Do you think that will happen soon?"

"Yeah, when we wrap your case up. And that can take months." Henry said and Jack sighed.

They arrived at headquarter, command center for one hundred eighty one countries and their police forces. The rounded configuration of square blocks rose into the sky giving the Interpol offices a unifying presence—blocks of information pulled together to support the whole.

The two constables, in their dark suits, walked briskly to the security desk. They flashed their IDs, were given clearance and received their day passes on necklaces. They proceeded to the elevators across the blue imbedded Interpol emblem in the floor. Jack stopped for a moment to look at the impressive icon. The emblem, held on each side by olive branches, showed a globe containing the images of all the countries of the world.

The elevator took them to the General Secretariat, the coordinating mechanism that gives its members access to international databases of criminal information. On the sixth floor they entered a minimalist and comfortable meeting room.

Working on an international project like the pursuit of an alleged criminal takes timing—twenty-four hours a day, seven days a week with no stat. Holidays. Jack was introduced to representatives from the Secretary Generals Office, Office of Legal Affairs, Management and Budget Directorate and Information Technology Directorate. Their meeting would go into the night; some gave briefings and communication protocol for their departments. The alleged crime of Jonathan Owen was fraud so assistance would come from the Financial Crime unit, Jack and Henry's unit, who would coordinate the investigation and search for Jonathan. The Forensic Unit would gather, hold and disseminate information on Jonathan to law enforcement groups wherever the search may take them. Already they had built a database on Jonathan: fingerprints, DNA, pictures and biographies. The reports from Canada where included: Transportation Safety Board,

Forensic Anthropologist and Coroner. A Secretary General's representative would monitor the case, the processes and be the diplomatic contact between countries on behalf of the General.

One week earlier the Secretariat of Interpol had accepted an official request by Canada for assistance in the search for Jonathan Owen for the alleged crimes of fraud under Section 380 of the Criminal Code of Canada. The request briefly described the current theory about the case and a summary of the unproven allegations. All statements that may erroneously suggest that conclusions had been made of the guilt or innocents of Jonathan Owen were filtered out. The request was granted and the international wheels of justice started to turn.

"This is a bit overwhelming, Henry." Jack whispered.

"You'll get used to it. I'll be helping you."

"Thank you."

Interpol's Legal Affairs would be the arm dealing with the extradition papers, legal processes and arguments between countries. The Management and Budget Unit would direct the expenses and keep the accounts of the search and ultimately, bill the Government of Canada. The last group was the Disaster Victim Identification Unit who would deal with the body of Jonathan Owen if he were killed before or during capture. They would fill out the proper forms; register his death; make inquiries and report on the manner and circumstances of his death. Jonathan's body would be disposed of as requested by the nearest relative. Annabelle's name was written into the file. Documentation would be sent to appropriate government agencies of the countries involved and relatives on closure of the case. If need be, recovery of any properties, goods or money would have to come under a separate request.

An Interpol Red Notice, Type 1, sent a warrant that circulated worldwide to all members of the law enforcement agencies. Of particular importance was the country of Germany where Jonathan entered and which triggered the Interpol investigation.

For the most part they were educating Jack on protocol and when the meeting was over he felt like he was just an observer in the whole process. He felt out of his league with all the protocols he will have to adhere to, the people, the travel, strange countries and cultures. It was nothing like his little town in Northern British Columbia where he was comfortable and part of the culture. Henry assured him that all would go well and that he would be on the front line with regional officers and Europe's law enforcement agencies. There was a huge community of support behind him, officers, administrators and technicians from around the world. He would soon learn how to use them.

Henry reminded Jack: "You represent one of the most admired law enforcement establishments in the world." Jack went for dinner and a beer with Henry and taxied home to his hotel. It was morning in Canada when he phoned his wife.

"We're do we go from here, Henry?"

A picture of Silver Bullet was sent by Fort Nelson's Royal Canadian Mountain Police detachment to law enforcement agencies of British Columbia and Alberta. Within days a call came in that a farmer's son had found a burned out Jeep in his swimming hole on the Rosebud River near the town of Irricana, north of Calgary, Alberta. The burned hulk was reported to the local police and was of no concern but the notice had come out and it flagged the attention of the local police.

Jack emailed the local RCMP Detachment and ordered them to confiscate the wreckage and hold it for investigation. The RCMP Forensic Laboratory from Edmonton examined the Jeep and sent Jack a detailed report. The Jeep was a 1985 CJ7 and all registration numbers were filed off the body, engine and chassis; there were no license plates; it was deliberately set on fire; fuel residue was found throughout the burned hulk along with woody debris to fuel the fire. A paint sample of silver gray was taken from under the side mounted rearview mirror housings. There was no evidence of organic material. The fire, heat and water had cleaned the vehicle entirely.

"Where do we go from here, Henry? We know he is in Germany, or he touched down there and according to all the carrier records he never flew out of the country—he just disappeared."

"Why don't we go back to his Internet records of locations," Henry queried? "Maybe we will find some clue or link in them."

"Yeah, do some filtering. We have the complete record on disk along with something else we should look at—the airport tapes of his flight out of Calgary. We will pull him out by the process of elimination. We need a new picture of him as he looks today since there hasn't been a response from his daughter's pictures we distributed. He will disguise himself for the next few years to the time he thinks we will tire of running after him—we won't."

Jack plugged his laptop into the boardroom projector system and loaded the CD. He bought up the file containing the Internet browser addresses that Jonathan had queried in the past two years—there were hundreds of them. Meanwhile Henry rolled in a white board and set it up beside the boardroom table and plugged it into Jack's laptop. They could download the images and writing for their reports.

"Write down along the top of the white board the countries and the number of times queried. We can do the cities of the countries on down to towns."

Jack talked out the countries and Henry wrote them down on the white board. There were nine countries with many hits: United Kingdom 16, Thailand 4, Mexico 85, Portugal 76, France 22, Greece 15, Morocco 8, Spain 18 and Turkey 11.

"This looks interesting, Jack said, "Mexico we can eliminate because we know he visited there a year before his disappearance and we know he landed in Frankfurt, Germany."

"Do we have a record of him in Mexico?" Henry asked.

"None, they won't give us anything."

"Okay, Then the next possibility would be Portugal and look at the number spread against the others. It looks like he was really interested in Portugal. Let's run through the data again and look at what cities our man was looking at and the numbers."

They pulled out Portugal and its cities. The capital of Lisbon 6, Faro 8, Albufeira 15, Vila do Bispo 8, Alvor 2, Portimao 21, Cape St. Vincent 1, Quarteira 4.

"All these cities are coastal towns are in the State of Algarve except for Lisbon," commented Henry, "and we know our man loves the sunshine. Bet you ten bucks Canadian he is hanging out in Portimão or close by. I've been there, it's a resort town filled with strangers; anyone can move about unnoticed and hide among the masses."

"Then Portimão is a start. So now let's go to the Calgary airport data and see what we will see," Jack said as he loaded the departure lounge CD."

It took a few hours but it worked. Jack and Henry got to know the images milling about and popping up at the counter to ask questions, some reading others walking about and others looking up at the departure television monitor.

Suddenly Jack blurted out, "That's him; he is the only odd ball. See right there!" and Jack jumped up and pointed at the screen. "We have to go back a bit to the camera beside the departure monitor," Henry reversed the images, "yes, right there, the man with the floppy hat, black hair, sunglasses and beard. If that's not a disguise I don't know what is."

"But if you look closely he only has one arm."

"Bullshit," Jack blurted out, "it's just one of those stupid romantic games that he plays. The Goddamn guy thinks he's in an opera."

"He is an opera—Jack, eh," Henry laughed. "I'll download the image of his face. We can overlay it on the photo of Annabelle's and make a new composite of what he looks like today. I'll attach it to a Red Warrant Notice to be sent off to the Algarve region with particular emphasis on Portimão."

Jack got up out of his chair and started to pace the room and verbally collated what needed to be done and Henry scribbled in his notebook. "Right, so number one, let's make sure we emphasize to the police that the best places to post want adds for our man would be at the bus and train stations, post offices and Internet provider sites since these are the most used places in these tourist areas. They probably know this but we should tell them anyway. Also at art galleries, Jonathan is an artist and he won't be able to stay away from them. Number two, have our people contact the police in Lisbon and start a hotel search for him, he has to use his passport to get any accommodation in Lisbon. Number three; let's make sure the police don't use extreme force. His crime is soft; not a violent one he is unarmed, I'm sure. Is there anything else we need to do Henry?"

"Yeah, paper work with the Portuguese government and I will handle that. Perhaps we should send out the warrants first for distribution and wait a couple of days to see if the Lisbon police and public come up with anything. Our scenario looks promising but it still is a big assumption that he is in Portugal."

"Agreed," Jack stated. There was a pause in his thoughts and he continued, "I have been scared of the public relations department. I have been keeping my distance from them but I feel eyes are on me wherever I go in this building. What's been happening at that end? I'm completely in the dark?"

Henry sat close to him, "It's not too pretty, the world is against you and you are on the front page of newspapers everywhere. This is something the RCMP and Interpol do not like but my sources high up understand what is happening and that sometimes things can get out of hand through no fault of anyone. Unfortunately for you the media has singled you out the smelly guy, not the RCMP, not Interpol or the local police forces. They are buzzing around trying to find a piece of you to exploit.

"Fortunately for me, they don't know I exist. I've managed to keep the little bastards off me. You have on, the black hat and Jonathan is in the white hat out there on the run. Politically, you are both out there on your own. Help is all around you but you have to take all the responsibilities for this case right up to the time you hand him over to the courts."

"Some responsibility!" Jack announced.

"When you were assigned the responsibility of carrying out this case, collateral damage was expected. It is burdensome to your investigation but you have to work it through. You are under the jurisdiction of Canadian law. Stay within that jurisdiction you have been trained to do and no harm will come your way."

"Yes I'm very aware of my place in this case from the protocol meetings we've attended," Jack sighed.

Henry continued: "The press and public they love it and can't get enough. The British tabs are all over this. Politicians in Canada are keeping the story at arms length and not commenting to anyone, they are totally numb, perhaps scared of their constituents. It seems once in a while a bad man comes marching into the spotlight and he becomes a hero. We have seen it through history—Jonathan hasn't done anything wrong in the eyes of the people and thank God he hasn't harmed anyone. They see him an adventurer, some a hero with the audacity to risk everything to make us all look like fools. I don't believe he expected his charade to become big. He is making a statement about our society; no doubt that statement will come out when he's captured—and then it might not. This guy might just be crazy."

"Jesus, Henry, don't say that. He would be unpredictable and that would make it a real bitch to catch him. I agree with the rest of what you've said. We have spent a lot of money searching for him and he has put public lives in danger. I don't particularly like chasing this man but the AG says he broke the law. The AG has given us our orders and if we become the fools, so be it. We are going to catch this guy, Henry, and the court will make the decision on what to do—not us or the sympathetic public. Although I have a feeling the public may have a say. We will see. Goddamn it! I have a strong feeling about this old man. He's just laughing at the world and us. I can't sleep at night thinking about my wife, my kids and how they feel about their Dad. I can't make it matter—we are getting closer—closer." Jonathan stared back at them from the screen and there was silence in the room.

Three days had passed since the information went to Lisbon and Constables Jack Garland and Henry Dubois were becoming frustrated—no responses. Then a police officer translator from Lisbon GNR station was on the phone to Jack.

"Mr. Constable Garland?" the thick accent said

"Yes, can I help you," Jack replied.

"Yes Sir, we have posted you warrants, but did not get response since it many months that he have been here in Lisbon," Jack's shoulders slumped, "but our men on foot in the Baixa district, check registry of hotel on Rua Vitoria and you fugitive stay there beginning last October. His name and passport number on hotel registry, they match number and name you sent us. The hotel clerk could not see him from photo but again was some time ago. We will be expecting you in Lisbon Mr. Constable Garland?"

"Thank you—*obrigado* officer, I will be on the first plane I can get. I will check in with your office. Thanks again Officer"

"I will inform my Commander that you would be here soon. *Adieus*, Mr. Constable Garland."

Jack hung up the phone and ran down the hall to Henry's office and shouted through his open door, "I'm on my way; we just got a positive on a hotel search in Lisbon. I'm heading downstairs to admin to order a plane ticket. This is it; we're on the ground and running. I'll call you by the end of the day, please call dispatch and the team—and tell them I have left for Lisbon. Thanks buddy." and before Henry could say a word he was gone.

He taxied to his B and B and packed his small bag of field gear: toiletries, clothes, maps, laptop, CDs, a hand tape recorder, batteries and recharge, magnifying glass, notepad, pens, letters of introduction, warrants, badge, passport, RCMP credit card and communications notebook. He had two cell phones; one a backup, which he packed, the other he kept on his person. He usually packed his RCMP issue gun but that was not allowed where he was going. Pictures of his wife and children were put in a zip pouch on the side of his pack—there when he needed them.

He taxied to the airport—his plane ticket was ready. There would be a stopover in Barcelona to pick up and drop off passengers but he would still be in Portugal and at the Lisbon police station before nightfall.

On his arrival a car from the Polícia de Seguranca Pública headquarters was waiting for him, driven by the officer/translator who made the welcomed phone call. Jack wore his badge on his jacket so the driver could identify him from the other passengers.

"*Olá*, Mr. Constable Garland. I am the one who call you," and the Portuguese police officer extended his hand and shook Jack's waiting palm.

"*Obrigado* Sir, I didn't have time to get your name when we were on the phone. I was just too excited about the break in the case. I do apologize."

"It no problem Constable Garland. My name is Carmona Lopez," he said, "and will be your communicator in Lisbon. We go to my commanding officer now to be briefed in what you do here in Portugal and talk international protocol."

"By all means Carmona."

Jack got into the passengers seat of the police car and they roared off down the main avenue, blue lights flashed and sirens blared to the horror of Jack. He had been in chases before and was used to getting to the scene of a crime quickly but had experienced nothing like this. Finally they reached the police station and met with the detachment's Commander who briefed Jack and gave him identification papers, phone numbers and names of his contacts in the Algarve. Carmona did the translating. The contacts had been briefed by email a few hours earlier. As Jack had requested the police station had booked him into the same hotel that Jonathan had stayed in. He would now follow in Jonathan's footsteps. Carmona drove him to the hotel with the same speed, terror and noise.

Before finishing for the night he had dinner at a local restaurant and wandered around the Baixa neighborhood. He walked up the narrow medieval streets to the castle on the hill. He looked down on the city and wondered were Jonathan was at that moment. Had he been here, walking these cobbled ramparts and leaned against the giant black guns that pointed out to the harbor? What had he seen here and was he amazed like he was of the ancient fortifications and the view down into the city, the life going on there, so different from their own? Jack walked down the narrow amber lit streets to his hotel. He turned on his computer and reviewed his files on his fugitive then reviewed the paper work from the Portuguese police and Interpol. When he slept he dreamed he was running; chasing after a dark figure in the distance that was getting smaller and smaller; treading air like he was on an exercise machine, running on the spot getting nowhere—he woke in a cold sweat. It was morning.

He made a call, "Henry, its Jack, we now have Jonathan's passport numbers from the hotel that he stayed in. Call the Canadian and British High

Commission passport offices in Ottawa and have them send you William Robert Martin A.K.A. Billy Bob's passport applications and start an investigation into how Jonathan stole his identity." He gave Henry the passport number.

"I'll get on it right away. I will email you the results."

"Thanks Henry,"

He made ready for the day, packed, had a continental breakfast of a croissant, roll, butter, jam and coffee in the lounge next to the reception desk. He left the hotel with his baggage, walked down Rua Vitoria to Rua Augusta and headed south to the square and the docks. At the end of the road he past under the Arch de Triumph and below it was a strange site; an old woman in a wheelchair was laughing and shouting at a strange figure in black who had no face. Jack was shocked at the figure's appearance and paused for a few moments to stare. He caught himself in the rude act and looked away. He walked on his way across the square and down an avenue dodging cardboard boxes of sleeping people. He arrived at the ferry terminal; bought a ticket from the machine and caught the next ferry to Barreiro across the river. At the train station beside the dock he boarded a train southbound for the Province of Algarve.

The train rumbled and clicked and clacked, stopping to take on passengers along the way. The villages would be great hiding places for Jonathan but there would be very little for him to do and Jack thought no, he has lived on the ocean all his life and living in these places would drive him crazy. Old men gathered at coffee shops, a blank landscape, no bikes, a few cars, no excitement on the street, just people sitting around waiting—and for what? No—the man needs scenery. The train rumbled into the station at Portimão and he disembarked, a car and officer driver was waiting for him. They took him to the local GNR station. This time things were a little more relaxed and the driver who spoke only a few words of English drove quietly. At the station the driver showed Jack in and led him to the commanding officer.

"Constable Jack Garland, welcome to Portimão. I am Commanding Officer, Tó da Silva," he said with pride and in perfect English.

"Good to be here in such a beautiful city. I only wish I was here under different circumstances. You speak very good English Sir,"

"Yes," and with a giant grin, "when I was a boy I used to hustle the Brits and the likes of you Canadians for a living—when you're young you learn fast. I speak German, Dutch and Spanish also.

"Now, officer Garland you know the protocols. We have to make the arrest and incarcerate the alleged criminal and you have to just be patient and wait it out. You know if we catch your bastard citizen we will hand him over to you at the airport. We would like you to be an active member with the team though—on a temporal level you understand."

"Yes, I understand Sir,"

"You have a profile of him in your head that is needed here. Now I give you good news, Officer. Something is here for you to listen to," and the commander turned to a tape recorder on his desk. "This is a surprise. A call came in from Barcelona to the station. A woman who would not give her name reported on the whereabouts of Jonathan. The conversation is in English."

"Portimão, Polícia de Seguranca Pública."

"English please."

"Yes Madam."

"Is there someone there I can talk to about a wanted criminal?"

"Yes Madam you can talk to me if you chose. I am the duty officer and will report what you have to say immediately to my commanding officer. What is your name Madam and where are you?"

"I cannot give you my name. I'm in Barcelona with my husband. We have just moved here from Portimão. That's all I can say about that. What I want to tell you is that I was in the local post office here in Barcelona and there was an Interpol wanted poster for a man whose name is Jonathan Owen, A.K.A. William Robert Martin nickname Billy Bob. I knew him some time ago and we became close friends. I knew him from the Praia da Rocha district where we hung out at Taffy's bar with the Brits and Canadians. He was only around for a few months drawing pictures, riding his bike and drinking beer. I think he was in some bowling league for a while. Anyway he did talk about finding a fishing village nearby to live and start a new life. He didn't talk too much about his past. I know this all sounds vindictive of me turning him in like this but I am upset to find out he is a criminal on the run. Was it a violent crime, Officer?"

"No Madam it was not, he is alleged to have performed a fraudulent act in Canada. We only want to question him, confirm he is the wanted man and hold him for Canadian authorities who will extradite him back to Canada where he will face their court system."

"Oh, thank God. I thought he committed murder or robbed a bank. Well I hope I have been of some help to you. I can't say anymore. Goodbye officer and good luck."

"Thank you Madam – goodbye."

Commander Tó da Silva started in, "We know he is not on the Praia da Rocha from the call and we have just in the last hour interviewed the owner of Taffy's bar. He said he used to see him a lot out on his bike since Taffy is always training for a marathon and they would run into each other and chat. I don't mean that literally," they laughed. "Taffy has not seen him for months. I have sent two units out: one to Alvor, a fishing village to the west and one to Ferragudo across the Rio Arade estuary to the east. They are the two closest fishing villages. As an artist, your bastard citizen would like one of those places."

An officer came into the Commander's office and spoke in

Portuguese, both did not look too pleased about what was said and Jack felt his shoulders slump when he felt bad news was on the way.

The Commander turned to Jack and said, "Bad news, there was no evidence of a sighting by the Alvor unit. Now Ferragudo is a different story; people our officers talked to knew our man in the village but did not recognize him from the warrant poster. We can assume that he has changed his identity. Also he has left the area and we don't know when or to where. We know from the villagers where he lived and we have a search warrant—we should go there now, our unit is waiting." A surprised and shaken Constable Garland, the Commander and driver left the station for Ferragudo. This time the ride was at breakneck speed, blue lights flashed and sirens wailed.

The Run to Albufeira

Jonathan had been feeling uneasy for a week; he was pulling out of life's complacency in Ferragudo. Something was going to happen and he needed to be ready to run. The uneasiness was triggered a week before when he was strolling by the Cathedral on the hill and a withered old woman dressed in black stood in the cobbled street. She just stared at him. Her eyes washed over and through him and he felt some impending disaster.

Early one morning he rode his bike across the bridge to Portimão and shopped at the sports shop in the Super Shopping Center up by the Municipal Hall. He would need a new outfit, a disguise for when he would be on the run again. Rather than travel by the traditional and obvious train, bus or plane he would undertake, The Racing Bike Escape. Something he made up with pride, it was ridiculous but damn, they would not be looking for a bike racer. He tried on all colours of outfits that one sees bike racers wear and he chose a yellow and black shirt with unreadable names emblazoned on it, a red and yellow cap, spandex black shorts, red and white racing shoes, black racing gloves and wrap around sunglasses. He looked in the change room mirror and laughed at how ridiculous he looked but was surprised how convincing he would look to everyone else. Even if he was old, he fitted the biking community genre with his lean sleek tanned muscular body in the sporty outfit.

He bought a small backpack to match; all he could take with him was his personal papers and travel gear. For the weather, he picked a set of water and wind-proof pants and jacket, the type you could roll into a little ball, nothing to them. He also threw in a Mylar emergency blanket and a small first aid kit. With his outfit picked out, he purchased a new black and yellow bike, the racing type with the curved handlebars and racing tires. He accessorized it with a battery-powered nightlight, water bottle, air pump, security lock and a little tool kit that came with tube change equipment. He ordered everything to be wrapped and delivered to his home that day. By the time he got home his purchases had arrived and he put everything together, made everything ready in case he needed to leave in short notice. He destroyed all incriminating evidence; wrappings and receipts that may give away where and how he was leaving and traveling. He made himself scarce around the village, João and Filomena in the days ahead. Late one night during the time he let himself out, to chat with Tegwyn at his favorite hangout on the quay, the waiter called him to the phone.

"Billy Bob?" a scared quivering female voice spoke.

"Yes," Jonathan said.

"It's Judy. I have phoned every café and bar in Alvor and Ferragudo to find you. I had to describe you since I don't know what name you're going by. Christ I have done something bad Billy. I'm sorry but I was angry. I ratted on you. I saw your picture in the post office here in Barcelona and I thought you were a rapist or murderer or something like that and I panicked and—"

"What did you do Judy?"

"I called the police in Portimão. Christ I'm sorry Bill—"

"What did you tell them?"

"I told them I knew you and we had an affair—you hung out at Taffy's with me—you disappeared one day and would probably be living in a fishing village and—Oh Christ I'm sorry Billy," she hung up the phone.

"Ah!"

Jonathan paid his bill at the bar, made excuses to Tegwyn and kissed her goodbye. He immediately left for home, sat down on his bed and gathered his thoughts. He would have to leave now, leave everything behind except the very basics—stuff he put into his daypack. It was nighttime and he would have to peddle out of the village and travel all night. He went to the bathroom and shaved his beard off, washed and bleached the dye from his hair and cleaned the bowl of any signs. He dressed in his new disguise and within fifteen minutes he was out of his little adopted village. As he passed the bridge in front of the square two police cars came around the bend of the coast road in sight of the village—blue lights flashing. Up a side road that hugged a canal, Jonathan rode into the night and countryside.

He peddled north until he reached the National Highway N125 at the city of Lagoa and stayed on it east to outside of the fishing village of Albufeira. It was 2:30 a.m. when he left N125 to the N270 south and his destination. The road was peaceful, no one around, a full moon lit up the landscape, the temperature was warm and the humidity just right. On a winding stretch of road Jonathan noticed a car come alongside him going slow—the speed of his bike. Suddenly it pulled up beside him and turned sharply catching the handlebars of the bike. The bike twisted and its rear tire slammed against the car. Jonathan leaned against the back window and slid on his back onto the trunk and down onto the highway. His body skidded about ten feet on the asphalt before coming to a stop. The car kept going and Jonathan could hear it pick up speed. He was stunned and filled with rage; he felt the driver purposely tried to kill him and he thought for what reason? It was something he would never understand or ever know the reason.

He lay for a few seconds sprawled on the asphalt trying to make sense of what had happened, his body was hot and tingled up his left side and right hand; he could not feel his arms or legs so he could not make an assessment of the damage to his body. In just a few seconds, but what felt like minutes, the tingling subsided and he crab walked on his back off the road to the paved shoulder. Feeling came back and he moved his legs, feet, knees, hips; moving his joints all the way up to his head and there were no sharp pains, so he surmised nothing was broken but he could feel where he had been hurt. Slowly he got to his feet and walked around; he knew these few minutes were critical after an accident. Not moving the muscles would let them stiffen, so he started moving, picking up the bike and checking it for damage. There was none he could see in the moonlight. He adjusted his backpack and off he walked wondering and cursing his dilemma and what to do next. He was shaking from shock but this calmed down after awhile. There were orange orchards along the highway and he picked one several hectares in size—a good place to spend the night.

Deep in the orchard he found a tree with long grass growing under it where he could gather his mind and body together. He was exhausted and ached all over. He removed the nightlight from the handlebars. He stripped and with the light made an inspection starting at his left foot. There was no damage just some tingling; moving up his left leg there was nothing until he got to the left of his kneecap. It was first contact with the road—a bright red round oozing spot surrounded by blue purple skin. This will be a dandy bruise later, he whispered. Moving up his leg to his thigh was contact number two, another spot of road rash on the hipbone, but no signs of bruising. This was sore and he felt a deep ache there. The left side of the trunk of his body felt and looked fine and up into his neck and head were all right; no abrasions or aches—yet. His left arm he felt had sustained the most damage, part of the elbow was the third contact; a large scrape mark with dead skin rolled up beside it. The triceps, biceps, brachioradial, and extensors to the wrist and fingers ached badly and he had trouble flexing those muscles and when he rotated his hand there was shooting pains in his elbow. "Shit!" he said, "tennis elbow coming up and probably carpal tunnel syndrome in the wrist." He took a small mirror from his toiletry pack and leaned it on the tree and raising his arm above his head and inspected his armpit and back of his upper arm. He saw a bruise the length of his triceps and one in the center of his armpit were the upper chest muscles, inserts into the upper arm bone. These were bad and he knew within a few days these would stiffen. His left hand that had rolled under him as he slid on the asphalt was damaged on three knuckles and the index finger at one end. This was the only injury he bandaged since it came in contact with everything he touched. His right side was fine, no damage except some tingling in his right palm from slapping the asphalt when he tried righting himself. Taking a wet cloth from his pack he washed his wounds and with a tube of first aid ointment he applied cream to the road rash areas. Jonathan was not a doctor but the assessment of his own body and the damage was the best he could make. His knowledge of anatomy gave him a good idea of what muscles to keep moving and the exercises he needed to do.

He felt deeply sorry and angry with himself and the world; he painfully redressed himself under the orange tree in his windbreaker pants, riding cap and mylar—he made the best of it. Snuggling his head into his backpack and sucking on an orange, he contemplated for a while. What the hell was he doing at his age, bruised and hurt sleeping in an orange orchard in the Algarve, Portugal? The police all over Europe looking for him to capture and kick him back to Canada for a jail term. What the hell was it really all about? He smiled and answered himself—this IS what it's all about.

He drifted into a deep sleep. The many colours of dreamland rose up from the depths of Jonathan's psyche. Blue melted into red and then turned sunlight yellow and his girlfriend, Tula, from long ago was there with him looking the beautiful woman she was when she was young. They held hands and looked into each other's eyes and knew they would make love, but where? The taxi they were in could not take them anywhere since it did not have wheels and the woman in the front seat was keeping the driver occupied arguing about where he should take her first and Jonathan's friends kept getting in one back door of the taxi and going out the other. The taxi suddenly disappeared along with his girlfriend and he was left standing on a cobbled street. A statue of a Roman soldier fighting an elephant stood in the square nearby. Jonathan tried not to look at it and the big, green, bronze soldier took umbrage with him. He started to climb down the granite pedestal from where he was bolted, tearing the bolts out with a terrible noise. The elephant, getting much larger, followed behind. Jonathan panicked and started to run for a hotel entrance that was trimmed in blue neon lights but he could not get to the entrance. The door kept moving away from him. He could not move, his feet would not step one in front of the other and behind him was the soldier and elephant. Together and attached they were now huge, menacing and weighed so much they were crushing the cobble street with every step making horrific sounds. He could see in front of him a giant dark shadow and he was inside of it. Jonathan tried to lift his feet to take a step forward but it just wouldn't happen. His face started to boil into bubbles of flesh; he was becoming blind and was choking. An anxiety attack came over him and he felt he was dying—smothering to death. Someone shouted in his ear, Attention! Jonathan woke up and screamed No, no! It was all a bad dream and Jonathan knew that if he kept up this charade much longer it would drive him crazy.

It took awhile for him to calm down, he hurt and ached down his left side and he inspected himself with the bike light. He saw big purple and blue bruises down his left arm and leg—they were getting bigger by the hour. He tried to go back to sleep but could not—he ached so much. By sunrise he tried to make the best of the bad situation; using his bottled water he brushed his teeth and shaved. He wiped himself down with a wet cloth and rubbed body lotion on his hands, feet, elbows and face. It was a struggle but he managed it and decided he had better spend the day in the orchard hidden among the trees. In and out of sleep he spent the day and ate about two-dozen oranges, drank all his water and ate cereal bars and snacks. The following day he felt a little better but not much. After cleaning up and a breakfast of oranges, he exercised his limbs that were damaged; they felt much better when warmed up.

He rode towards Albufeira and from time to time he joined others dressed like him out for their ride through the countryside. He joined in the packs and looked like any of the ordinary bike folk peddling their local roads. Like fish, it was wise to stay with the school. He rode into Albufeira.

It was time for him to change his appearance; he purchased all new clothing in a small men's shop on the edge of old town. He bought new pants, belts, checkered shirts, socks, underwear, a deep green sweater and sunglasses. He purchased a cap, the type the Portuguese fishermen wear; it covered his face quite nicely when he bowed his head. Whenever he dressed he would now look like a fisherman. He changed into his new gear and gave all his racing gear and backpack to the clerk to throw out. Next door he bought a suitcase, wheeled it back to the clothing store and the clerk neatly packed his purchases. He paid for everything by debit card using one of his accounts. With his bike in one hand and case in the other he wheeled his way across the town square stopping to trade his expensive racing bike for a teenager's silver mountain bike. Now all evidence of what he looked like in the last forty-eight hours was gone. He went into the old district mansions to look for a suitable rental until he had to be on the move again.

To: powderblue

Honey I've had an accident – not to worry, I am fine, just a little road rash and some bruises. I will be just fine in a week or so. I'm just a little stiff at the moment. A car sideswiped my bike and the driver ran off.

I am now in the fishing village of Albufeira on the coast about the center of the Algarve, disguised as a fisherman. Talk to you soon. Love Dad.

To: indigohue

Christ Dad!! Be careful. Get rid of the bike, PLEASE!!

A Nest in Ferragudo

The police cars rounded the bend and Ferragudo came into view for the Portuguese police officers and Constable Jack Garland. Half way up the hill among the street and window lights could be seen flashing blue lights. The police drove across the narrow bridge to the village square. They advanced left and turned up a narrow street to the waiting officers standing outside a doorway of a medium size, two story white house with yellow trim. An old woman was nervously gesturing and speaking loudly in Portuguese. Two paparazzi were shooting away with their cameras. The commander ordered the police officers with them to spread out through the village with posters and do a door-to-door check.

"This is the landlady who lives downstairs from our man," Commander Tó da Silva commented to Jack, "and she is quite upset," the Commander listened and interpreted. "She says she knows nothing about Richard—he is a good man—pays his rent on time—is clean—can't believe," she says, "I have a criminal in my house."

"Richard?" Jack commented.

"Yes, that's his new name."

The Commander ordered the officers to turn off their car's blue emergency lights, ordered the paparazzi away from the scene and gestured to Jack, "Let's go inside. Here, I've bought some latex gloves, put them on. My men have already taken samples of finger prints and DNA but we should not contaminate the place until we have the results recorded and added to the file." Two police officers saluted the Commander as they approached the door. Jack put on his gloves. He could not breathe from the excitement he felt; he shook from goose bumps all over his body.

The polished deep green door set into the concrete was ajar, beyond its threshold a warm, amber light came down the short hallway. Jack entered, took a few steps to a bare concrete staircase, its treads worn down from years of shuffling feet. A locked door to the left was the service entrance from the owner's suite on the main floor. Jack looked up to a strange site, the wall on his left leveled off at four meters to an iron railing draped in a brightly coloured blanket festooned with Moorish designs. The wall to the right went up all the way to the ceiling ten more feet above the railing and on the ceiling was a flock of birds in flight painted shades of red, orange, blue, green and white, flying across an azure blue sky. They ascended the stairs; the room opened up they and saw the walls were covered with drawings of boats, buildings, nets, stones, animals, portraits, nudes and palm trees. Some were coloured in pencil, watercolour and acrylic paint, others crosshatched in ink that resembled lithography. There were drawings in graphite of nude women. The drawings were done in the style of the old masters—sepia colour. They were seated at a table or lying in bed—his table and his bed. Jack and the commander were now seeing

Jonathan Owen's real world. He was no longer on paper or inside a computer, he was now—here alive—and Jack could smell him and touch him. He would now get to know his adversary—or would he? He thought.

The room was lit by an overhead light with a glass ball shade. On each wall was a Moroccan ceramic sconce; a small light glowed inside that sent shafts of light across the walls and drawings. The walls that could be seen among the mass of drawings were light yellow to almost white and the framework around the windows, one to the back and one to the side in bays, were painted a light blue. The ceiling, where the birds flew, was azure blue and it was level from the bathroom and stairwell to midway across the room, then it sloped gently to the far wall to a meter and a half above the floor. The room was seven by seven meters in all.

The front wall above the street had French doors that opened in to reveal a wrought iron balcony that jutted out a few centimeters into the street. Ceramic flowerpots with geraniums and ivy were attached to the railing. A Moroccan carpet covered a polished fir floor and along the railing over the stairway up against the bright blanket was a heavy old wooden table that had been recently refinished. A modern office chair with deep green upholstery was nestled into it. A North African basket was under the table filled with magazines. A double bed, neatly made with an embroidered blue Spanish duvet and white sheets and pillowcases was up against a north-facing window. Its wrought iron headboard rose a meter above its pillows. Gracefully hung on it was Jonathan's bathrobe detailed with a flat Japanese design of black and white storks. His slippers lay neatly half under the duvet that came to just above the floor. At the end of the bed was a short wrought iron footboard and leaning against it and chained, was Jonathan's silver bike. On each side of his bed were small night tables, the same knobby style as his worktable, stacked with books on Portugal, the Algarve and art. There were other stacked books spilling onto the floor beside the tables. On one of the books his reading glasses waited for him.

Against the wall beside a bathroom door stood a wardrobe, a painted scene of a North African desert oasis—camels, sand dunes and palms trees covered its doors and draws. Inset in a bay window was a kitchen with a hotplate, sink and small fridge set into a horseshoe counter; a row of cupboards was to the right. Vegetables, sausages and bread hung in baskets from the ceiling. A cradle of Portuguese wines stood on the countertop beside a bright yellow ceramic bowl of bananas, apples, oranges and tomatoes.

A small, round, wrought iron glass-topped table with two cane chairs squatted beside the French doors. On the bare glass sat a large white vase with Marc Chagall lovers painted on it. A composition of flowers, vines, branches and tree blossoms rose above the vase's mouth. Two small, silver candleholders with half burned candles rested beside the vase. Drawings of the Algarve and Jonathan's life in the fishing village were everywhere—the walls were covered and strewn across the floor and furniture. It looked and felt to Jack his man had just up and left a few minutes ago—he had.

"He's probably on foot or has taxied to the bus or train station since his bike is still here," the Commander said.

"I don't know about that—my man is a tricky son of a bitch. We have to look at all the possibilities," Jack responded, "let's go through everything."

They started in the bathroom and the usual utensils were not there. Toothbrush, paste and shaving kit were missing. There was some black water spots on the floor so Jack requested one of the officers take a sample of it if they had not already.

"Look at this on the mirror," Jack commented and he pointed to a lipstick kiss among postage stamp drawings of a woman, "She kissed him even when she was not here. Whoever it was loved him a great deal."

They finished inspecting the bathroom and returned to the main room. The Commander opened the wardrobe and went through the clothes pockets: "There's scraps of paper with drawings on them, pencils and restaurant receipts—dinners for two," he opened a bank of drawers and found socks, underwear, shorts and belts, "nothing in the drawers of interest. Best we check the books next." They picked up each book, inspected it for notes and shook them; shopping lists and scraps of paper with drawings fell out. They were put with others on the dining table.

Jack got down on his hands and knees and scanned the entire floor. "Nothing under his bed, kitchen and wardrobe, Commander, the area is clean except for his slippers, some books and the baskets under the table."

Jonathan's large table by the railing, which he used as a desk, was covered in drawings, small pots of pencils, pens and graphite sticks. A tall black ebony statue of an African woman stood on one corner of the table. She was adorned with necklaces of shells and silver earrings hung from large holes in her earlobes.

"This s not a cheap piece bought off a street vendor, but purchased from a serious design store or perhaps picked up on a trip taken to North Africa," commented the Commander. Beside the African woman was a woven basket filled with brochures of local attractions, pamphlets on art shows and art postcards that would never be sent. A sketchpad lay on the chair; open to portraits of old men arguing and a man working on a boat. "Just two sketches in his drawing pad and they look unfinished."

The place was void of clues to where and how Jonathan fled but overwhelming of where he had been. Jack felt frustrated, as he looked around at all the art on the wall and the world this man had created. It was a world so different from the RCMP officer. All was ordinary in his world, the furniture he sat and ate off, the bed he slept in, the pictures his wife had put up on the walls of his home. He tried to remember them but couldn't.

Jack commented to the Commander, "You know Commander, I've arrested dozens of people in the past and each one I understood. My subject's world's and mine were from department stores, drab and predictable. This is a sophisticated little home, neat, tidy in its jumbled look; the furnishings feel very close and reflect the man who lived here. Each item was hand picked with care—money no object. Up there," Jack pointed, "the birds on the ceiling welcomed him in the morning. His women and their images were lovingly laid out on paper. He must have sweet memories and moments that he won't forget." Jack looked to the bathroom, "a kiss on the mirror greeted him each morning. The drawn fishing boats, old fishermen and their wives, nets and palm trees tell me the interest and love he had for this place—his village," he scanned the room, "the art, the room, the flowers, the whole place is warm. I am getting a new appreciation for Jonathan and I feel a little guilty about what I will have to do to this fugitive when I catch him. And I'm going to catch him Commander—there is not doubt in my mind about that."

"You will officer, you will," the Commander said.

Jack opened the French doors to the night sky and the lights of the narrow stairs to the quay and harbor below meandered up to him. He looked across the estuary and saw the lights of Portimão. He dialed Henry in Lyon on his cell phone.

"Henry, good evening. We found where he has been living but he is gone—God knows where or how. I think he has changed his disguise so we should redistribute our pictures showing him with and without his damn makeup. Add a new name for him— Richard Jones. Let's do our standard distribution plan throughout Southern Europe."

"Will do Jack. Anything else?"

"I need some professional help here, someone in the arts. I know nothing of what this guy is about. Something is strange here that I don't understand. It's his thinking I'm not used to. I need someone who thinks like him because he is complex or crazy, I need a connection. You know this sophisticated society we are operating in, Henry, and I don't. Would you get me someone and fly him out here please?"

"I think that would be a good idea. I will call the Pompidou Gallery in Paris and get someone out to you."

"The who—Gallery?"

"The Pompidou Gallery in Paris, it's perhaps one of the best galleries of modern art in the world. Their curators can describe and interpret modern works along with their psychological ramifications. They can help work up a profile of our man. I have taken art therapy courses in the past to understand how people think, act and how they can express themselves through art. Interpreting art can be very useful in the examination of the criminal psyche."

"I see, great, I will call you tomorrow. In the meantime I have to think this thing out. Good night Henry," Jack said. He glanced over the room in frustration.

"One moment, Jack, please. On another note: we have word on how he came to be called William Robert Martin. I have sent you an email of the details. Good night, Jack. Don't worry we'll get him. He can't run forever like we can."

Jack pocketed his phone and looked out the French doors into the night and the stars and whispered to himself. "I'll get you Jonathan, have a good night's sleep wherever you are because I'm on your tail and its going to hurt when I catch up and step on it."

At the police station in Portimão Jack checked his email from Henry.

To: garlandrcmp

Good morning Jack. I received faxes of William Robert Martin's passport applications from both offices in Ottawa. I forwarded them to the RCMP detachment in Surrey who worked with the Victoria City police and the BC Government's security office to investigate the identity of the man Jonathan Owen stole.

William Robert Martin died twenty-one years ago. If he had lived he would be the same age as Jonathan and he was the perfect candidate to be alive again for his project.

The team concluded the most convenient and safest way for Jonathan to steal a new identity would be through the Vital Statistics (VS) office in Victoria, British Columbia. He broke into the system. It was easy for him to do even with all the government's security. He was often the one to book meeting rooms for technical, scientific and administrative staff of his ministry where he worked, down the block from the VS office. He got to know and was friendly with everyone in the path he needed to take to get to the files.

He coned his way with the clerks to gain access to their computers; he hacked his way into their files when they were on lunch and coffee breaks. One was a receptionist that issued security cards that accessed stairwells, meeting rooms and file cabinets throughout the building; another had access to electronic files of Social Security Numbers and the status of individuals. Our Jonathan is a crafty bastard. He used his position and power to get his way. He used the magnetic cards issued to him for meetings he set up at the VS. The cards gave him access to the third floor where the information on the citizens of BC going back to 1890s and up to 1978 is stored. Some of the old records are thick binders full of details about people—dead and alive. Some who are deceased have death and birth certificates, citizenship papers, government oaths of allegiance, even passports that relatives have sent in. Records of everyone born or died in British Columbia after 1978 are gathered electronically. Information prior to 1978, only vital facts are entered into the database. This is important information for the passport offices to verify the existence of an applicant.

Jonathan had plenty of time to pick and choose whom he was going to be and William Robert Martin (Billy Bob) fit his profile. He collected from the hard files information that he needed for passports: a birth certificate certifying he was born in Caerphilly, Wales in 1944 (requirement for his UK and European Union passport), a document with William Robert Martin's signature and a Citizenship certificate issued in Victoria, BC dated 1963. In the electronic files Jonathan changed fields in the VS computer database about William Robert Martin. Jonathan Owen bought him back to life in the eyes of the British and Canadian Governments.

We checked Jonathan's Internet records and found he went on line to the Office of the British High Commission in Ottawa, Ontario and their passport application link. From the Government of Canada site he downloaded the same for a Canadian passport. He filled out all the information in William Robert Martin's name on both applications and forged Mr. Martin's signature from an application form for a government job. He did the same for the back of the passport photos. The certification on all documents for the passports was Jonathan's lawyer, Frank Willard.

The Surrey Office has been in touch with Mr. Willard and he has assured us he did not sign any such passport documents for the name of William Robert Martin. When Jonathan Owen was mentioned the lawyer was visibly upset. He knows Jonathan but does not know his whereabouts and denies any improprieties on his part in Jonathan's illegal behavior. It was noted by the investigating officer that Frank Willard acted suspiciously when interviewed. Perhaps something is there, Jack, I don't know. The Surrey Office will dig deeper into Mr. Willard's association with Jonathan Owen. I will keep you posted when more information comes forward. In the meantime the full report on the passports is now on line for your review.

Henry.

To: Henryrcmp

"Great work. We will need new warrants for his arrest on forgery, identity theft, passport violations etc. Our Attorney General will handle those charges, please give them a heads up. They will be waiting for him when we get him home. Thanks Henry.

Jack.

Photographic documentation was made of how the drawings were exhibited in Jonathan small home. The artwork was removed from the walls, packaged and confiscated by the government of Portugal. Commander Tó da Silva apologized to Jack; a command had come from Portugal's government in Lisbon, neither Jack nor the Commander wanted to understand. Jack requested the loan of the art for a morning and it was granted, it would be held back in Portimão for a few more days.

The curator of Conceptual and Performance Arts of the Pompidou Gallery was arriving from Paris. To assist the curator, in a local school auditorium, Jonathan's work was set up on display boards, positioned relatively to where Jonathan had placed them on his attic room walls. Spotlights were set up around the exhibit to give it the confines of a small room. Off to one side on the floor lay the colorful birds distributed in the pattern Jonathan had pasted them on the ceiling.

Doctor Jean-Claude Fernando arrived by police car from the Faro airport and was rushed to the auditorium where he was greeted by the Commander and Jack. A table with chairs, hot coffee and pastries were available to the small group.

"Welcome Doctor Fernando," Jack said, extending both his hands in greeting, "I hope you had a good flight. This is my Portuguese colleague Commander Tó da Silva," they extended greetings and the three became comfortable with each other.

"I'm delighted that the RCMP, Portuguese, Interpol and you called me to the Algarve. I've read my briefing notes, from Henry Dubois and you, Jack. I know daily what's going on with the case, as does the rest of the world. The coverage is astounding, and to be called up in the middle of the night to be here is exciting. Thank you constable for including me in your pursuit, my daughter and I are great fans of yours."

"Well thank you Sir," Jack did not know what the professor was talking about since Jack was not reading newspapers or watching any television. His only communication with the world was through his colleagues and it would stay that way until he apprehended William Robert, Billy Bob, and Richard Jones, the bastard citizen—Jonathan Owen, he said to himself.

The three of them sat at a table and discussed what had transpired over the months. Jean-Claude listened intently but could not keep his eyes from wandering over Jack's shoulder to the middle of the auditorium and the exhibit of Jonathan's work. Jack told him the official version of the plane crash, the investigation, the involvement of Interpol and the chase up to this place.

"Mr. Fernando I am not an educated man in the arts and the fugitive whom I'm pursuing is. In order to catch him, extradite him for trial in Canada and complete my report to the Attorney General, I need to know more about my fugitive's character. I need to understand his profile. Are there clues in his work of where he is and why is he doing what he is doing? Anything you can read into his work may help us."

"I understand your frustration Constable," the curator commented, "first off, let me say, there are no conventions in art. I will do my best to analyze this man."

"He produced the artwork over the last several months in the fishing village of Ferragudo. This work," Jack pointed to the center of the room, "was on the walls of his hideout and we have exhibited them in their original position the best we could. The bird cutouts on the floor where stuck to the ceiling of his room and we have laid them in the pattern we found them. On a table nearby are digital images of his paintings in the possession of his daughter in Canada. With this information perhaps you can give us some insight into the man's mind. So with that said, would you please examine our exhibition of his art work?"

"I would be delighted constable, I can't keep my eyes off it," Jean-Claude walked to the center of the auditorium. Jack and the Commander poured themselves a coffee and left to sit outside in the sunshine leaving the professor alone with Jonathan's ghosts.

Jack slumped onto a bench thinking and talking random thoughts while the Commander smoked. It was only a few minutes and the Commander received a call to return to his office on urgent business. He apologized to Jack and left immediately.

For an hour and a half, the professor studied and made notes of the work and when he was ready he asked the Commander, who had just returned from his office, and Jack to join him in the auditorium. The three stood among the works of Jonathan.

"I've looked over the sketches of boats, the village and the harbor. These are done like illustrations, popular in magazines and newspapers thirty years ago. He obviously did them for fun and to while away his time down on the quay. You see the wine and coffee stains on the paper? This is the same paper used as tablecloths by the restaurants. The drawings are very well done with their intricate crosshatching. His women on these," he held up a group of drawings, "depict the sexual connection of an artist and his model—not surprising. They are very sensual and done with the care and skill of a renaissance master; as a matter of fact he has studied the masters." He took one drawing of a portrait, "I see Rembrandt's chiaroscuro style in some," he pointed to the light and dark around the head, "the torso and heavy muscular structure of a Michelangelo in others." And on another drawing, "Here is a Modigliani and a plump Renoir. His anatomy is correct. You see this arm, the way it holds her up on the bed? The deltoid muscle is bulging were it should and the triceps muscle is contracted to show the tendons that connect it to the forearm. The sternocleidomastoid muscle of the neck," and the professor pointed to the area on his neck, "is distended showing just enough pressure on it to carry and rotate the head. The line work is classic in structure, where the body is farthest away from the center of her, like the curve at the top of her breasts, there is barely a line visible and where it moves towards her body into the shadow below her breast; the line is more pronounced.

The nude I'm particularly fond of, and it reveals the complex character of Jonathan, is this one here," pointing to the floor, "it was on the sloping wall to the right of his bed where he could see her when he woke each morning. The woman is sleeping; her left breast is exposed where the blanket has come away. Her expression is one of peace and safety; she looks comfortable where she is in his bed. From the shadowing he probably drew her one lazy afternoon when the sun came through the window. She must have meant a lot to him because I see such purposely delicate lines laid down that form her face and breast. Perhaps he loved her, I don't know."

Jack's mind drifted to his own wife thousands of kilometers away. He had seen her in the same position sleeping but never took notice, being the busy man that he is. Perhaps he needed to look at the world a bit closer."

"Commander, we must find this woman," Jack said.

The Commander replied, "Right Jack."

"Would you excuse us for a moment professor," and the Commander took Jack aside," that's what I was up to at the station a few minutes ago. My men have been snooping around asking questions about our man and we have traced our woman, the one in the sketches, to the bar that Jonathan frequented. She is a waitress there and her name is Tegwyn Bevan; she is Welsh and has lived in Ferragudo for many years working in the restaurant trade. Married once, many years ago, she has lived alone in the village all the time she has been in Portugal. She apparently is in shock about Jonathan—she knows him as Richard Jones and a Welshman. My men believe our man duped her and she is an innocent. We have not placed her in custody; she's not considered a flight risk. Ferragudo police are watching her. I think her heart is broken. Will you want to question her?"

"I'll go and see her at the bar were she works."

"No, I think maybe it would be best to phone her and make an appointment to see her at home or some other place. We should protect her privacy—don't you think? People here are very conscious about that sort of thing. I don't want us to impact her life more than we and Jonathan have."

"You're right. I'll call her at home. Do you have her number?"

"Yes and other details about her," and the commander handed him a slip of paper. They returned to the professor, "Sorry professor, please go on," Jack said as he folded and slipped the paper into his breast pocket.

The doctor continued: "There are some interesting sketches of abstract work: this one of the village takes the geometric shapes of the buildings down to basic shapes like Jean Miró, Pablo Picasso and George Braque would do. This is obviously a William da Kooning and I recognize her, she is the one in the bed. You have to be a master to pull that off, da Kooning's are violent scribbles and splashes of colour. The blocks of coloured pencil are Mark Rothko; the edge treatment gives it away. These exercises are good.

"The clouds of birds fascinate me, they are simple, and Matisse could not have done a better job. You see in the photo here how the flock is flying—but to where?" with his hands raised Jean-Claude gestured an arch above his head. "They move from above his bed towards the French doors and freedom. Is Jonathan hoping to fly away with them, get carried away from the catastrophe he has created or are they simply decoration? Who knows really what's inside his head. Some of the drawings are tight like lithography; other sketches are free form; the lines run and dance across the paper uninhibited. He knows no boundaries since his drawings drift off the page onto the next. He is not afraid, our man Jonathan. The colours in pencil along with some light watercolour washes are free spirited in their application, strokes without hesitation, no going back to correct. Mistakes are not mistakes—they are part of the composition.

Your man is not a complicated human being, not like Van Gough or Edvard Munch or any artists in the modern movements of today; in fact he can be quite ordinary, a very skilled academic and perhaps intellectual in foresight as you will see. His skills and techniques are very advanced and exceptional. I find him to be a balanced human being by his subject matter and the way it is illustrated. I don't see any remorse or brooding, naivety or egotistical exhibitionism. No psychopathic or sociopath behavior comes through; there is nothing dark about your man.

"All right gentlemen, this is where he gets smart or crazy. What you need to look at is outside the academic art. What is here is a mental exercise to him. It is all puttering and doodling, stuff that artists love to do when sketching and exploring the world around them. For artists this gives them joy and involvement in the world. In the modern world there is something else happening that our friend Jonathan knows and is creating. It is right here next to the women sleeping in his bed." He crouched to the floor and picked up a drawing. "This is a drawing to remind him daily of his focus, his purpose, his project and what a project. You see what it is? It's egocentric. He has cut dozens of strips of newspaper five-millimeters wide and pasted them at an angle of about eighty degrees top to bottom on the paper. These strips are taken from the news stories about him. Where each strip comes to and ends at the middle of the page, they form a silhouette of a man standing erect and naked. Gentlemen—this is Jonathan—the rain is the media. The media is creating Jonathan with its stories; he is not creating the stories. The act of the chase, the political ramifications, the struggle of forces around us, the stuff you, and now I, are involved in is his art. In his mind his art is not about his sketches it's about us. We are the art—the media and the world stage. I believe I am correct in stating that this is a profound performance and conceptual piece of work worthy of an exhibit on a global scale, and that is now happening. Nobody has done this before, faked his own death for art; he has sacrificed his livelihood, his family and freedom for the glory of an art piece. Governments and international organizations have no choice but to follow the charade he has created to its conclusion—pray there is one. The laws of our countries have ordered it, they have no choice, and his audience is the world stage. We are part of his mad performance. Profound, isn't it?"

The commander and Jack said nothing just gave the professor a blank stare.

"This man, I understand, was in marketing in the past and alluded to the works of Marshal McLuhan of Global Village fame. Well he has created the global village concept to its ultimate and I cannot help but admire him for that. One single person has created a piece of art on an enormous scale, literally worldwide. He is a true artist in every sense of its historical context. You are both part of it, perhaps the bottom lip of his portrait. The fact is, Jonathan is a genius or he is just plain crazy. You will find out when you capture him," the professor roared with laughter.

"You will need me as an expert witness in Canada after you capture him and he goes to trial. I am available and I hope you call. In the meantime I will write a report for you and your governments, they will be confidential of course. Thank you gentlemen for including me in this performance, I can't tell you how wonderful for the Pompidou Gallery this is."

Bewildered Jack looked to the Commander, "Oh fuck! I knew the bastard was taking me for a ride. Ever since I walked up and looked into the plane wreckage back at the West Toad River, I knew something was not right and that I would be dragged into something crazy." The Commander and Jack were baffled at what the professor had said and in their hearts they knew he was right. They looked at each other: "Wanna' get drunk?" Jack said.

"I think so." the Commander Laughed. They invited the professor to join them; he was pleased to accept the invitation.

The next day Jack was on the phone: "Henry? God I hurt. It's Jack, Henry. I have a hangover from my bloody-enlightening experience yesterday. Things are turning to crap and I don't understand it all. The professor is on a plane back to Paris. A report will be coming from him in the next few days. Did you manage to get the new posters out?"

"Yes, they are out there and because of all the publicity the countries are eager to distribute them. I have a feeling their selling them or distributing them as souvenirs. Did you know that in the United States a popular wanted program is advertising our man in America and he isn't even in that country? Wow, the media is promoting this thing globally. There is a bar in Vancouver advertising a happy hour drink called a Billy Bob with a Jack Chaser. Even your image is changing and the public is warming up to you now. They are starting to believe you are also a victim."

"Yeah, I know. I've just gone through a lesson on it. We are in some kind of cultural phenomenon or madness that we are going to have to deal with. We need to isolate ourselves from the media. Let's treat it like any normal pursuit and focus on the law. What do you think?" Jack commented.

"Exactly, and I think we should isolate ourselves from our own people since I think leaks and misinformation are coming from them. I have already been onto this, I talked to our Secretary and he has given orders to staff that we operate in complete isolation. The labs and operatives that we use will be coded. I will send you this information in about twenty four hours."

"So this is what I am assuming," Henry continued, "he skipped Ferragudo and nobody recognized both photos of him at the train stations, bus stations, galleries, etc. The police checked the fishing, freight and pleasure boats with no luck. Hitchhiking is a possibility, but in what direction? I think he has headed east somehow, towards Spain and Gibraltar since the east is an open window to the world for him. North is going home and west he runs into the Atlantic. East is the Mediterranean and the gateway to North Africa. What do you think?"

"Christ, I don't know. Maybe you're right, eh. I guess we should concentrate on the east. I'm going to interview his girl friend in Ferragudo and then I will be on the road to Spain. I will call you as I move along the coast. Hear from you soon, Henry. Goodbye."

"Good luck Jack."

He felt like quitting and going home to Canada where things would be familiar; he would curl up with his loving wife—safe and normal again. He had come to realize the vast size and scope of the world and the complicated cultures that he did not previously understand. He is small town, a man from a little city in a frozen north, an innocent on the edge of nowhere. Now people around the world are watching him. He gave no interviews and only a few times did the paparazzi catch him but he has become a household name and his image is in the tabloids of the world. He was having his fifteen minutes and even that he did not understand. He was overwhelmed with guilt and doubt.

He rented a car, packed his gear in the trunk and stopped by the Portimão GNR station to see the Commander and check on the arrangements for his chase. The GNRs in every town and hamlet across the Algarve and into Spain had been alerted. The Commander was at his desk on the phone with a very pleased look on his face and saying a lot of, thank you and well done. He hung up the phone.

"You won't believe this but we have had a stroke of good luck," the commander said with enthusiasm, "our officer whose beat is the City Shopping Center flashed Jonathan's picture around and a clerk in the sporting goods store recognized him. He has the inventory of what items Jonathan bought. It looks like our man is on a racing bike, dressed like a racer and has gear to camp along his way. I believe he is on his way to Spain."

"Thanks commander, I have one more stop to make before heading east; a talk with his old girlfriend in Ferragudo. I will be in touch."

The commander stood up and shook his hand, "good luck my

friend," and to Jack's surprise the commander hugged him and kissed him on both cheeks.

Tegwyn Bevan's Interview with The RCMP

Jack phoned: "Hello. Tegwyn Bevan?"

"This is she. Can I help you?" she said with a cheerful Welsh-accent.

"This is Jack Garland—I'm an officer with the Royal Canadian Mounted Police of the Fort Nelson Detachment of British Columbia, Canada," he said formally and politely "I would like to sit down and have a chat with you about a fugitive that Interpol and I are looking for here in Portugal. He is Jonathan Owen, alias Richard Jones, a man you knew a short time ago I believe."

"Oh, yes I suppose. Where would you like to meet?"

"On the quay in one of those outdoor restaurants about two o'clock this afternoon?"

"At two then. I will be wearing a white blouse and black pants. There are only a few restaurants so we won't miss each other."

Jack drove across the bridge Rua Infante dom Henryque and turned right on the river road to Ferragudo. He parked in the town square and walked the hundred yards to the restaurants; he passed each one until he saw a middle-aged woman in a white shirt and black pants. He walked up to her: "Ms. Bevan I presume?" Jack reached out and shook her hand, "thank you for coming."

"It's my pleasure Officer—coffee?"

"Yes, with milk please," and she beckoned the waiter over.

"Two Galãos. Por favor, Luis."

Jack Garland took a chair close to Tegwyn since he wanted to keep his conversation with her private and there were a few people gathered nearby. One in particular looked like a reporter that he had seen around the police station with the Paparazzi. He showed her his badge and Interpol identification card and she inspected both pieces: "You know why I am here don't you?"

"Yes, I think I do officer."

"I'm gathering information on your old acquaintance, Jonathan Owen, a man you know as Richard Jones. I have to talk to him. Any information about him would be of great."

"Certainly, anything you like, but I don't think I can be of much help. Jonathan Owen, you say? I rather like that name."

"How long did you know him and where did you meet?"

"I knew him for about six—seven weeks I guess. We met in the bar where I work up on the hill by the cathedral. He would drop in during the afternoons for a couple of beers and draw pictures on the table clothes. Right away he got to know me—a very outspoken man is our Richard.

"This is a personal question and you don't have to answer it if you don't want to. Are you the model for the portrait beside his bed?"

Tegwyn flushed a little pink around the neck. "I'd rather not answer that." Their drinks came and they paused in the conversation.

"Did Richard ever talk about his past—about family and such?"

"Sometimes he talked about his daughter and son. He told me about his art and his job before retirement—things like that."

She was no help in connecting her to any crime so he put forward another question to see if Annabelle was involved. "Did you ever see Richard use the Internet and were you with him when he did? Did he email anyone?"

"Yes, I was with him many times when he used the Internet. He tried to teach me how to use it but he was not successful. He never wrote anyone on email when I was with him. We just roamed around the world—the weather—art—"

"Did he ever look at the news links on the Internet?"

"Let me think—no he didn't but then he knew I was not interested in the news of the world—too much violence for me. I don't particularly like what is going on outside my little village. I never have and never will."

"Were you surprised when you found out who he was and what he had done?"

"Bloody hell! I certainly was and then, for a while, I found it all very exciting that I was part of some kind of international play."

"Do you love him?"

"Now, I don't know. Perhaps I loved him—I just can't say yet if I did. I need a little time to answer that. He has many qualities that women like and all my friends adored him. I'm angry and excited, both emotions, at this mess he has put me through—he is the adventurer we love and hate. The press won't leave me alone and everyone looks at me like I have a disease."

"I'm sure the bad feelings and speculations about you will pass and quickly. I have the same problem in dealing with this case—the press hates me," they both laughed. "Did he ever mention to you other countries or places like towns or cities he would like to live in or visit?"

"He loved Paris and thought it's the greatest city in the world. Someday, he said, he would like to live there on the Seine River near the Museum D' Orsay where he could be near his favorite paintings. He talked about the masters of painting, sculpture, literature, and historical events—a matter of fact he was quite eccentric about it."

"How do you mean—eccentric?"

"He said to me that ghosts would appear at times when he visited old and ancient places. Old people do that, he said, because someday they would be ghosts themselves. There were times he would act a bit strange when we were out in the country touring the villages and castles. He would look at things like paintings, the architecture of buildings and streets and seem to be lost in them. Sometimes he would talk about the Kings, knights and priests of old. The Master of Santiago—people like that. He would be afraid of old black dressed beggar women; he thought they were bad luck. You know, he would say—like a black cat crossing your path. He always gave them some change. That evil eye is taken care of he would say. I think he had a bad experience in Mexico or someplace a few years ago."

"Getting to places he may visit in the future—can you think of any? Did he hint at anyplace?"

"He talked about the Trans Siberian Railway from Moscow to Vladivostok; another place was North Africa, perhaps Egypt—yes he mentioned Egypt. I have never had the privilege of a camel spit at me, he would say. I remember those places, nothing else. He did not talk too much about his, extended vacations, as he called them."

"How did he get around Tegwyn?"

"Bicycle mostly, sometimes the bus—he did the fitness thing. Bicycles were good for the heart, he said. Once in awhile we rented cars from a local dealer for trips out in the country."

"You knew it would all end for both of you someday and he would move on. Do you think you will ever hear from him again?"

"I sure hope so. I would kick his ass and kiss him at the same time," they both laughed, "he could have at least said goodbye. I guess he was in a bit of a hurry."

"He was in a hurry. Please call me if he does get in touch with you?" and Jack handed her his Interpol communication card.

"I will if I can but you may have to catch him without my help. I guess I am like many out there in the world who want to see him get away for maybe just a bit longer. He is not a violent man officer and he doesn't carry a gun or knife, so please don't hurt him."

Jack stood up and laid down some euros on the table to pay for the coffee and said: "We won't hurt him and thank you. You have been a great help to us and perhaps someday we will meet again. Good luck."

"Thank you Officer," she shook his outstretched hand and he left.

She watched him walk away down the quay and when he was gone from sight a reporter quickly took Jack Garland's seat.

As he walked back to his car he got on his cell phone: "Henry. It's Jack. I have just interviewed Tegwyn Bevan and she wasn't much help. She is in the clear as far as I am concerned but keep monitoring her calls and I will see the Portimão and Ferragudo police keep watch on her. Our Jonathan may just get in touch with her again. Let's hope so."

"I'll get right on it. Where do you suspect he is now?"

"He's out of the country. I think we will find that he is in Spain but I am going to stay in Portugal for awhile and follow up on places he has been."

"Right, I'll get the paper work ready for Spain."

To: indigohue

Dad, be careful and stay out of danger. I hope everything is going well with you and you're healing from your accident. Did you get rid of the damn bike? I worry about you riding around in a foreign country at your age.

I have some sad news. A few days ago Frank Willard your lawyer was found dead in his library. He had a massive heart attack. He did not suffer – if that is any consolation. I know you were very close to him over the years and you drove him a bit crazy with your pranks. It didn't matter though; he told me once behind your back that he enjoyed his time with you and you were a good friend, perhaps the best he ever had in his life. Sorry Dad.

We opened the show last night and we had a sell-out – it was just fantastic. The who's-who of Vancouver was there. Congratulations. The media were hard on me with some very sticky questions but I handled them. They are slowly getting the idea that I am not in cahoots with you. You would have been proud of me. The RCMP came in plain clothes and I gave them permission to take pictures and make notes. They said it was the request of Jack Garland who is over there chasing you.

The space we rented for your show worked out very well, after cleaning and painting, it displayed your work beautifully. I love the space and I think I might continue with the gallery – we will see. The curator we hired from the University Art Gallery was great and she did a beautiful job telling your story. The huge blow up of your hideout in Ferragudo was a sensation with the guests and even that was sold. Since it was wallpapered to the gallery wall floor to ceiling we will have another one produced for the client.

We had line-ups down the block but they were all mostly curiosity folk out to see who you are and your crazy story. Most of the work was pre-sold to clients a few hours before opening. Perhaps to pre-sell was unfair but these clients have been good to me over the years and they pay top dollar.

I have put out a letter asking clients who have bought your work if they are still satisfied with their purchases since fraud charges have been issued against you. They can return their purchases if they so choose. I have offered a full refund since the sales were made under misrepresentation. I received many letters back saying they would keep the works since they have now gone up in value and are a good investment. Some expressed that the art now has an interesting history and is great to show off. Nothing has been returned – so far.

All proceeds from the show, after expenses, have been put into the trust fund as you instructed and I have boosted some of your secret expense accounts. Too bad Dad you can't spend it over there but then you never did care about material things anyway – just adventures. Well you certainly are having one now. What's the plan? What are you going to do? You know that Jack Garland will catch up with you sooner or later – don't you? Luv yu.

To: powderblue

Hey Annabelle: Poor Frank, I will miss him. I warned him about his smoking, drinking and his gross weight. I wish I could have helped him get a few more years on his life. Alas honey, I did try.

It's great to hear about our show and its success. Wow, and that's great about the photo of my home in Ferragudo. I did love that place. Life goes well here in Portugal but I am afraid my time is near and I will be arrested soon, can't say when, but I have strong feelings that Interpol is near by. So that said you won't hear from me for a while but keep writing and if I can get near to an Internet site where I am going I will be in contact with you. I can't tell you where I am off to but it is relatively safe and I won't be going anywhere until Jack the Brat shows up. Tegwyn, my girlfriend, is still back in Ferragudo and is probable beside herself because she knows by now who I really am and what I have done. She believed I was on an extended vacation. I think I love her honey – she is growing on me fast. It's all a bit of a dilemma for me right now, I am confused – don't worry about me – my wounds are healed – I am healthy and doing just fine. I still ride my bike a bit but it's painful to my upper arm and wrist so I'm very careful. Love Dad.

Albufeira

Outside the French doors and down on the cobble street there came clattering and banging—dustmen were doing their collections. The noise nagged at him for a few minutes before drifting up the street—he was able to fall back to sleep. He caught another hour when he heard the manager of the restaurant across the street arrange his café tables. Jonathan rushed over to the French doors excited about a new day in Albufeira. He threw back the curtains, opened the doors to the brightness of a new day.

Rising into the blue sky above the old villas across his street was St. Sebastião Church, its face a blaze of morning pink as the sun warmed its walls, pillars and tiled roof. On its pediment high above the street its iron cross took him into the morning sky. The wind vane Angel Gabriel on its bell tower pointed toward the sun heralding the day. The huge windows on the Church's face above the main doors took in the morning light and it shone down the nave far inside to the altar, bathing it in radiance and warmth.

Jonathan's street was waking up, a people-street with no vehicles. A street of cream and black cobblestones creating a linear web of crosshatching. The street is old, with three story Moorish and Manueline buildings on each side, some hundreds of years old with their original tiled roofs covered with lichen. Their street front faces are painted white and beige and have bare sandstone trim around window eyes, doors and corners, for some their faces are entirely covered with the makeup of painted ceramic tiles. All have French doors on the second and third floors with filigree wrought iron balconies. Shops, restaurants and businesses fill the main floors. Awnings that yawn open each morning shade their entrances.

He leaned over his little balcony railing and listened to soft jazz coming from a restaurant down the street—life unfolded below. Sandstone pots of flowers, green iron filigreed lampposts and small trees, here and there broke Albufeira's stark geometry. At the south end is a tunnel through a sandstone hill that leads to the beach. An old man emerged from its depths; he walked his little dog across the cobbles that still glistened from the night's dew. He was Portuguese, well dressed in his blue baggy pants, shirt, green sweater and cap.

Soon Portuguese families strolled down the road; husbands, wives, children, grandma and grandpa all arm in arm but separated into gender groups. Across the street the jewelry store owner's cat lay on the cobbles in the morning sun. The cat had been out hunting all night and could barely keep its eyes open; almost asleep, the feline stared into the morning. Not even the pigeons that pecked for food nearby could make her move. Her owner's shop is small, well lit and shines and sparkles like a jewel box should; filled with merchandise—the upscale type. The jeweler washed and mopped the street in front of her shop and cleaned the windows. A few shopkeepers rolled out their sandwich boards, souvenir, newspaper, postcard and clothing stands into the street, making ready for the first early morning customers. Jonathan heard a commotion downstairs as the Money Exchange, Pharmacy and clothing store woke up. A young man rushed below his balcony with a fifty-pound bag of potatoes on his shoulder and one bag in his hand. The boy will make several trips this morning. With great drama other merchants arrived with fish, vegetables, soft drinks, liquor and a host of other goods. Money and words were exchanged, deals argued and made.

His landlady came out of the building, looked up to Jonathan's balcony and shouted to him: "Have a good day, Richard!"

Jonathan shouted back: "Obrigado, you too sweetheart."

Charles, a British vagabond is the hawker for the restaurant across the street; he arrived on his motorbike and set himself up for the day's business of persuading customers into the establishment.

He looked up and shouted: "Good morning Richard," and Jonathan shouted a good morning to him. An unsuspecting family of British tourists walked by the restaurant and Charles went into action: "Good morning to you all. Best restaurant in town. Best full British breakfast is right here: double Danish bacon, eggs, sausages, toast, fried tomatoes and British beans and only four and twenty-five euro. And for you Sir, our best ale for only one and one half euro," the hype poured out of him in a thick British accent, his ruddy red face beamed under a white sailor's cap and his huge belly jiggled. The potential customers smiled and moved around his mass and down the street and when they got to the end, and after a great discussion, they returned and he showed them their seats. It works for Charles most of the time.

The beautiful Portuguese secretary who works in the building next to Jonathan's floated down the street dressed like a fashion model; she cannot see anyone except herself. She always wears black with a smash of colour like short red tartan skirts over black stockings and black boots; she looked like an over-aged and over-sexed private school girl. Charles looked up at Jonathan and gave a snooty high sign, poked his nose in the air and they both laugh.

Jonathan retired from the sights and sounds and showered, shaved and made himself ready for the day. He walked downstairs to the street below and weaved his way through the restaurants and shops to the tunnel and the beach beyond. Besides the restaurant and shop keepers there are only a few people up early and they are children on their way to school or shoppers at the bakery getting hot fresh loaves straight from the oven. The local street dogs are lonely. One, a big German Shepard, noticed him and stayed with him for his walk. The dog is not hungry; he just wants company and a pat on the head once in a while.

The morning light was beautiful on the tan coloured beach—the same colour as Jonathan—if he were naked he would disappear. The sun and weather was doing to him what it has done to the land. The sand is warm and the sea calm with just small waves. Sand and seashells are all he sees for kilometers across its expanse. It rolled up to cliffs that are topped off with pine trees. The cliffs are sandstone edifices stratified in layers of rock and shell—seabeds of long ago rising out of the land and being worn away by a new ocean, rain and wind. The exposed shells will return once again to the sea after millions of years of imprisonment in rock.

The beach is a nude beach so one comes across startling surprises and most of the time they are overly endowed German women, it is too early for most of them this morning. It does not matter how they appear to him, everyone is beautiful under the tropical sun. Among the early morning tanners, the locals cast their lines out to sea with long fishing poles. They sit on the beach on their five gallon white pails looking out to the Atlantic; avoiding the bulbous breasts around them. If they don't get a bite it doesn't matter—it's all Zen anyway. Some fishermen cast their lines from the high cliffs at Cape St. Vincent. A dozen fishermen are lost each year, swept out to sea after falling from the high cliffs—Zen taken too far.

Jonathan walked the three kilometers down to the end of the bay, turned and walked back. Albufeira was in full view bathed in morning sunlight, cliff faces turned into piles of whitewashed blocks of homes, churches and businesses. Buildings and their little narrow streets undulated and twisted over the hills. Built and rebuilt they buried fortresses and cities of the past.

The ghosts of Phoenicians, Romans, Visigoths and Moors wander the cobbled streets and man the battlements against the inevitable invaders. He could see the ghosts of sailing ships out in the bay; their longboats full of armed men pulling up onto the beach, drums banged, warriors shouted and citizens screamed. Fear of death and the exhilaration of battle filled the air. Cannon fire from the fortress on the hill, and shrapnel cut through men and wood. The Knights Templar, swords drawn and held high, rode down the beach on great white chargers to meet their enemy and history. Many times this happened over the thousands of years. Many soldiers and citizens died here.

Into the city he came across the ghost of Vicente de Santo António wandering the streets in his long brown robes, iron cross and rosary in hand. His priesthood robe blazed a brilliant orange and red fire. In his desperate search for heaven and salvation he looked for converts—his mission in life. The Patron Saint of Albufeira was born here and suffered martyrdom by fire in Japan four hundred years ago.

Today a tractor arrives on the beach below to filter the sand of debris, cleaning it for the tourists who are now the invaders of the ancient fortress. Their thousands are armed with blankets, plastic toys, drinks and food. Their steeds are plastic chairs and billowy towels, their armor—suntan lotion. Evidence of the modern world mantles the landscape high above the old town. The new housing, hotels and business architecture in stark white with red tiles roofs are in keeping with the old world. As time goes by no one visiting will notice where the new and old begins and ends.

Below the jumble of humanity and down on the beach, some fish boats are still drawn up to rest and be repaired by the diminutive, weatherworn fishermen. A young owner painted a fish boat lying on its side like a beached whale looking for its stomach to be scratched. Three men in suspenders, workpants and checkered shirts, topped with the ever-present caps, looked on—chatting and watching. They nodded their heads in agreement and a short distance from them six men argued about the work being done. This will go on all day, some men will join the group, and others will drift away to look for other discussions and other arguments. There is so much time here and filling it can become interesting.

He stepped off the beach onto the quay and walked through the old market where each morning fishermen display and sell their catch. It is bare now and used only for shade from the hot summer sun. Modern restaurants surround its iron posts and tilled pavilion roof. Tourists and lovers now use the wooden benches. Fishing boats currently moor in a new marina on the west side of town behind a breakwater; they no longer pull their boats up onto the beach and make a colorful scene.

A short distance from the market, Jonathan climbed the stone steps up the cliffs and battlements buried under the houses, churches and streets. At the top of the hill he dropped into the Archeological museum for a look at the old pieces of buildings, mosaics, pottery and artifacts, evidence of other civilizations that have been here before. Mounted on steel brackets are keystones, the stone that is at the center of an arch; animals and crosses are carved on their faces. Jonathan stroked one of the stones and he felt the hand of the forgotten artist who lovingly made the carving a thousand years ago. The stone carver is still alive in that rock.

He left the museum to the street that dropped rapidly to above the tunnel and his street. He took the stairs down the side of the canyon buildings. Charles is waiting for him and this morning he manages to shove breakfast at him. His dog left to go back to the beach with a pack of friends.

At home Jonathan unlocked Silver Jr., the mountain bike he traded for his racer in the Albufeira Square. It has been a while since he had ridden a bike with any vigor; it had taken some time for his bruises to heal and the stiffness in his left side to leave. He will take it quietly today. It felt good to be riding the narrow streets of the fishing villages of the Algarve—through the gardens, around the quays, past cathedrals and up into the business districts.

On his ride around, he checked who might be displaying wanted posters of him the local post office and police station—he did not find any. He watched the police walking about and noticed they were young and more interested in the local junkies. His landlady said there are not many police in Albufeira in the off season; the police in their mass only come south during the summer months and then they are there more for crowd and petty crime control. This was good news to him.

But it was time for him to move again, to somewhere less conspicuous and he searched the neighborhood above old town. He found an apartment complex on a square above the cliffs overlooking the marina. His new hideout was on the fifth floor—the roof of the apartment block. It housed a bedroom, kitchen, living room and bathroom. The entire rooftop above his rooms is a balcony accessed by a cement spiral staircase. At the entrance to the apartment is a small balcony with outdoor furniture where he can have his meals outside in the morning, noon, and evening sun.

He moved in and checked for escape routes; the best was over the rooftops and down onto the street Rua Dr. Sousa Silva. The last rooftop was five-meters from the ground so he fixed a rope on one of the many Moorish chimney pots, made it fast and coiled it behind the chimney ready for use. Wherever he went he wore a pouch on his belt containing his bogus passports, fifteen hundred euros, his wallet, bogus driver's license, debit cards, new reading glasses, bus and train schedules, a few band-aids and first aid ointment. When he went to bed he hung it on his bedpost. An outfit of fisherman's clothes was always on a chair near his bed. He cooked healthy meals, sketched, and rode his bike into the countryside—he now avoided downtown. He felt it was becoming too dangerous. He was beginning to feel paranoid.

He missed Tegwyn and knew Interpol and Jack Garland would have questioned her by now. The poor woman was probably going through hell being accused of collaborating with a criminal—he felt bad about it. He would let things cool for the next few weeks and make contact with her on her cell phone, which was not safe to do but she did not know how to use a computer and the Internet, which would be safe.

The sun heated up another day on the rooftop, a towel covered a white chaise lounge that squatted out on the red tile terrace, a cool drink, a book and brochures were at hand. It was an hour from sunset, the sun to the southwest was bright in a cloudless sky; it shone across the marina from where it just left Africa. Jonathan was reading about the almond blossom festival that is celebrated in the Province of Algarve every February. The pictures were beautiful of the white blossoms on the right hand page of his brochure but he felt something was wrong—someone was watching him. He dared not move with a start—just act normal. Without moving his head, just his eyes, he looked to his right beyond the brochure, level with the roof top terrace. Off in the distance in a park in front of a cemetery were three men—

two with binoculars. Both were watching him—a police car was parked nearby.

Panic raced his heart. Adrenalin pumped and Jonathan went into hot flashes of flight. He took fifteen seconds of deep breathing to calm down. He assessed the situation. Time to make a run for it. He slowly got up and took a drink of pop. He looked out over the marina keeping the observers in his peripheral vision. He gathered up his things; meandered down the spiral stairs to his apartment. He quickly got into his gear and attached his pouch to his belt. On the hill they could see his front door but not the bottom half and he knew this. He got on his hands and knees and crawled behind his rooftop lair to a large terrace. His escape route was masked from the spies. Over the terrace he went sliding down the terra cotta tiles to the flat roof above the street and his escape rope—he was careful. His body could not afford any more injuries. Gently he dropped onto the street, moved towards the cliffs and an open courtyard with benches. Between the cliff fencing and residences, was an alleyway going to the road below the cemetery. The road led down the other side of the hill from the cemetery to the marina. In the alleyway he picked up a plastic garbage bag outside one of the residence's back door and walked casually to a waiting dumpster on the side of the road. He talked to and petted a few of the dozen feral cats that live in the alley. He was in site of the spies up on the hill and from his peripheral vision he could see they noticed him but they turned away to their business since Jonathan in his cap, gray sweater and baggy pants looked like a Portuguese fisherman who lives near his work—the boats just below and behind the marina's breakwater. He moved down the road casually until he was around a curve and out of site. He made a mad dash down the hill for a kilometer and into the marina residence's courtyard.

He ran across the courtyard, past apartments and townhouses. Out the other side he ran to a restaurant and a few waiting taxis lined up at the front door. Jonathan leaned against a wall to catch his breath. Casually he walked up to the nearest cab. The driver let him into the front seat. He ordered him to take him to the Municipal Hall. The taxi headed north and caught the Ring Road to the Avenida dos Descobrimentos to the hall and let Jonathan off. He paid the driver and walked across the boulevard to a bus stop.

Tourists milled about waiting for their bus to Faro; they had spent the day shopping in Albufeira. Jonathan removed his cap, tied his sweater around his waist and quickly started a conversation with them. He soon looked like one of the group. Screaming down the Rua Dos Bombeiros Voluntarios behind Jonathan and his new friends came four police cars—blue lights flashed and sirens wailed. In the distance Jonathan could hear sirens wailing all over town. He could not help but smile as the blue, yellow and green EVA bus followed the police parade and turned towards his bus stop—Faro Express was written in lights above the driver. He had done his homework well; the police had been waiting for him at the bus depot on the edge of town and at the train station in Ferreiras. They forgot the Faro Express picked up passengers within the Albufeira city limits. Jonathan and the chatty tourists boarded the bus and they departed Albufeira and for some like Jonathan—never to return.

To: powderblue

Just a quick note honey: I'm on the run again, on my way east into Spain and I don't know where I will end up. Jack is on my ass and it was just luck I caught him watching me on my rooftop hide-a-way. I'm sure it must have been him. It is the first time he has seen me and I have seen him. He is getting too close and I fear the end is near. As usual I had to leave everything behind except my essentials. I will write when I can. Hate to sound so damn dramatic, Honey. Love Dad.

The Road to Gibraltar

Jonathan was on the run again. The bus took him to Faro, the capital of the Province of Algarve. He boarded a bus that went back to Albufeira and on to Tavira for a short stay before moving on to the Portuguese/Spanish boarder city of Vila Real de Santo António. Just outside of town at a service station before the border bridge that crosses the Rio Guadiana he picked up a ride with a young couple that were driving to Gibraltar. He left forever the Algarve, Portugal for Andalucía, Spain. He looked back and silently said his goodbyes to the Portuguese and the friends that he had made whom he may never see again—except one.

His new companions were a UK couple, newlyweds full of life and enthusiasm, touring Europe on their honeymoon. Pasty faced, badly dressed and chubby, they talked so rapidly and with such a thick accent Jonathan could barely understand them. He nodded his head in agreement and said, yes—yes—of course—yes. The couple had been on the road for fourteen days and wanted to go straight through Seville and down to Gibraltar where they could enter a world like their own at home. They longed for a good cup of tea and fish and chips smothered in vinegar with some mashed peas on the side. That was fine with him; he too missed the English and being able to communicate.

In Gibraltar he would know what was going on around him, up until now everything he overheard was in Portuguese. The English newspapers he read were very limited and he did not know if the local Portuguese papers were writing about him. He felt he had made it this far on pure luck.

Before Seville they crossed farmlands filled with oranges, olives, block architecture and tiled rooftops. Along the highway nearby ran power lines and the electric companies had placed platforms on top of the towers for the White Storks to nest, making out of a utilitarian structure, a picturesque, fairy tale across the landscape. In the distance on each side of the highway south of Seville, silhouettes of castles topped the hills surrounded by white villages, orchards and farms.

Deep in the south of Andalucía they drove the new highway that is known as the Route of the Bulls. Each side of the highway they saw Iberian Bulls foraging in grass meadows between forests of Cork trees. These are the magnificent, black fighting bulls that die in the bullrings of Aldaciras, Seville, Córdoba, Ronda and many other towns and cities across Spain. He noticed they were bigger than those in Mexico.

The highway wove through hills and granite-mountains and on the occasional hilltop were huge black silhouettes of metal bulls. These powerful images, some standing twenty-five meters high are symbolic of Spain's new democracy. Standing tall and proud, art on this scale and passion took Jonathan's heart away and it was his time to talk and he told the young couple about the art of Spain and the bullfights. He told them about:

Francesco Goya and his etchings and paintings of the horrors of war; the painter El Greco who immigrated to Spain from Greece, bringing with him his passion for Christ; of Velázquez and his Royal Court paintings, and of El Cordobés with his excitement and daring in the bullring. He rambled on with enthusiasm about battles between men against men and men against beasts. It took his mind of Jack Garland and his Interpol friends just a few hundred kilometers away. The couple was silent.

Granite mountains flattened out and industrial towns appeared as they made their way down to the coast to Cadiz and Algeciras. Suddenly before them, away in the distance, was the undisputed silhouette of The Rock. Gibraltar was a half hour away. Slowly The Rock's image cleared from the hazy, blue-gray of a distant mountain to the familiar green forests and towering white limestone cliffs. Jonathan thought it looked like a gigantic wounded hunchbacked Gulliver struggling to raise his head and body out of the ocean. His ancient body was riddled and suffocated by buildings, roads, tunnels, towers, battlements, gunpowder magazines and emplacements. The mass traveled up his spine, arms and legs, they pulled him down and held him in the sea—humanity was eating him. He looked worn and tired from his thousands of years of abuse. Jonathan was also feeling the weight of the world.

He asked the newlyweds to let him off outside the border gate so he could walk in alone. If customs and immigration recognize him from his British passport, it would be a disaster for all of them. It was rush hour; a line-up of tourists and workers crossing on foot both ways clogged the road to the airport runway. A British commuter plane was taking off. The access road into Gibraltar from Spain was closed since it shared space with the runway. Jonathan noticed those on foot just flashed their passports and were hustled through. He had no luggage with him and looked like a resident returning home and he passed through without a hitch.

Jonathan did a little thinking at this transition point between two countries. One thing was wrong; he was entering a closed space with no escape. Planning escape routes while living on The Rock would be essential.

He was weary of the chase. He noticed his hands sometimes shook—he was biting his nails from stress. It was almost a year since the plane crash on the West Toad River. His experiences on the road had been many and exciting if not damn dangerous. He had been alone most of the time, which he enjoyed—he did not need company. He had enough of that in his past life. On the road and being chased was exhilarating to him. The idea that someone was just down a street, behind a door, around a corner, looking, searching and waiting thrilled him. The end was near—they were close now. Would this be the place he thought? Would I be taken alive or would some officer panic and shoot me dead or would I get killed trying to escape again? He had always planned on being caught, but what if I don't get captured?

He thought about the prospects of being on the run for years to come, maybe the rest of his life. He was getting on in years. He was healthy again but is this the way he would want his old age to go? The bouts of madness he thought he had—would they come back? In the castle in Silves the soldier with the long bow talked back to him. That had never happened before. I must be very careful now, he muttered.

He walked out of the border administration building and down the street a few hundred feet to the bus stop where the blue bus number nine was waiting. He climbed aboard and paid his one-euro and the bus pulled out towards town. It crossed the airport runway, down a few streets and pulled into the bus stop at the Grand Casemates Gates. He disembarked and walked through the tunnel and into the Casemates Square—an old fortification. He had traveled for several hours and was hungry; he took a whicker chair at one of the many outdoor restaurants and ordered fish and chips and a beer.

He spent his first night on The Rock in one of the few hotels available. Old and musty, the hotel had seen better days; even the waiters were in need of a refit. The following day he looked around for long term accommodation. Perhaps the local marina that he saw when he arrived had something interesting. He walked down to the quay and talked to the marina office personnel and they told him to wander around and inquire. They said there is rental accommodation on board boats if he was willing to pay the price. Down one jetty a fifty-foot cruiser with the name Portage and Main, Manitoba, written on the transom, startled him. This name was an icon to him—the coldest, windiest junction in Canada.

"Ahoy aboard?" he shouted.

"Yes," a reply came from deep inside the cruiser, "can I help you?"

"I'm looking for accommodation. Do you have a berth for rent—say for a couple of weeks?"

A burly, blonde man pocked his head up out of the engine compartment and had a look at who was shouting at him, "Maybe—where're you from?" he growled.

"British Columbia, Canada,"

"Oh really, I was there once with my ex," he said wiping the grease from his hands as he rose out of the bowels of the cruiser. He walked down the gangplank to the dock, "where's your luggage?"

He had none but answered, "At my hotel,"

"I have one berth available at the moment and you can have it for three hundred pounds a month. I don't have any rules except keep yourself and your berth clean and don't get drunk and piss off the dock. Most male bodies found in the water in marinas have alcohol in their blood and their zippers are open," they both laughed, "now come aboard and I'll show you my home. My name is David Osborne, by the way, and you're?"

"Richard, Richard Jones," and they shook hands.

With David, Jonathan made his way down the gangplank at the transom; the cruiser was backed in and made fast by its aft, port and starboard lines. The galley and house cabin were large and roomy with a stereo, television, sofa, easy chairs, bookshelves, and dining bar with stools between the galley and lounge. On the bulkheads were the usual brass clocks and barometers, stairs led up and forward to the bridge and to the right of them more stairs led down to a passageway, cabins and storage facilities. The cruiser's hull was steel with a fiberglass upper structure; it's interior in mahogany paneling and trim. "Nicely laid out and clean." Jonathan said. He noticed the cruiser was well equipped with radar, gyrocompass, sonar, marine radio, first aid kit, flair gun and life jackets at the ready.

"There is one other fellow living on board, a Spaniard who comes to Gibraltar a few times a week from Seville to do business so you won't see much of him. I don't know what his business is and I don't ask and I suggest you don't ask either. Lots of foreigners come here to do international business because of the tax shelter and the confidentiality of the banks."

"I'm not on business, just and extended vacation."

"Last year I had a wealth businessman from Hamburg, Germany staying on board. Nicest person you could ever meet and he just disappeared one day, never to be seen again here or in Germany. As for me, I'm here a few days a week but most of the time I'm with my girlfriend in town. You have free run of the boat. I'll go over things with you later. Get your gear and cash and make yourself at home. Right now I got to get back to the engine, eh." He climbed down into the engine compartment and pressed a red button on the forward bulkhead and the engine roared to life. Jonathan made a mental note of the button.

He walked back to town and bought a backpack, toiletries and clothing suitable for living on a boat. This was perfect for him, a cruiser, his most of the time and could be used to escape if necessary. Jonathan had been to sea before and knew how to navigate—Morocco is twelve nautical miles due south. He was soon alone on board and he researched David's charts and plotted a course to North Africa, checked all the mooring, water and electric lines that they could be quickly let loose. He started up the engine using the engine compartment ignition button since he would not have a key for the bridge switch and checked all the engine gauges and running lights. He could sail the cruiser out of the harbor with no problem. At the library in the Mackintosh Center in town he researched the shipping rules of the Strait of Gibraltar and discovered there is no radar surveillance of shipping into the Mediterranean and at any one time there are at least three hundred fishing and commercial vessels working the waters. It would be easy to slip unnoticed out of the Bahia de Algeciras and cross to Tangiers.

A Call from Gibraltar

"Hello Tegs," Jonathan said softly into the phone.

"Richard—Jonathan where in the hell are you?" she yelled at him. He paused. She knew him as Richard. Oh crap, she knows everything now, "I'm out of the country—been out for a few days now."

"Well, you son of a bitch, you sure took me for one fuck of a ride didn't you? I've been in shock over this Richard—for Christ's sake!"

"Yes, I guess I did. All I can say is I never thought I would get involved with anyone on my project and then things happened I did not expect. I guess its all part of the project."

"What the hell are you talking about Jonathan or Richard or whoever you are? Project, you're telling me I was part of your project?"

"Unintentionally, yes, you are part of the project. Anyone in the last year or so who has been in contact with me or is chasing me is part of the project."

"Jesus Christ! The police were around and the ruckus you have caused in Ferragudo is really bad, everyone is talking about you and its not very nice things at that. Everyone looks at me with funny eyes wherever I go. You know this is a peaceful place and now it's swarming with the curious looky-loos, reporters and what look like shady people. Why did you do this here, Richard? Why did you pick our little place? We don't need the world banging at our door."

"Because it's beautiful and romantic and you're there that's why. You're the reason I stayed so long. The way people feel now will change in time and believe me if it weren't for you I would have moved on. I still love you Tegs and I miss you a lot. I never got to say goodbye and I feel terrible about that."

"And well you should. I still love you but I have accepted I will never see you again. I'm done, it's over."

"Have you met someone?"

"No! Bloody hell! I haven't moved on in that way—just emotionally. I was broken hearted that you lied to me about yourself and I am over that now. It was a terrible thing to do. I could not believe what the police told me; I felt I had entered a crazy world. I have never been treated like the way you treated me—not by anyone. You're such a sweet bastard and I never dreamed—"

"I'm sorry, Tegs, for everything and I don't know how I can make it up to you. I never meant to hurt you or anyone else. Perhaps I am going mad in my old age, I don't know."

"Mad? You're not mad and stop saying you're old—you're not. I think, and from what I have heard from the police, you have become overzealous in this game that you're playing—it's out of hand. They're going to catch you—you know that don't you? You will be back in Canada—in jail.

It's just a matter of time. I think you should give yourself up. Let it be over with."

"I can't do that no matter what, I have to take this to the end. I've come too far. Giving myself up would be cowardly of me. They must capture me and if they don't, well I will be gone forever. That's my plan, that's what I'm sticking to. I just hope I don't get shot in the process. That is the only fear I have."

"That is a possibility you know—of you ending this thing dead. So there is no persuading you to end this charade?"

"No, there is nothing anyone can do. The project must run its course. Do you want to still be a part of it, Tegs, and join me to the end?"

"Jesus! Do you know what you're asking? You're asking me to put myself in danger perhaps go to jail for conspiring with you, or getting shot. Now that would be crazy."

"Maybe I am crazy. What do you say? Join me. It will be an adventure of a lifetime for you.

"Look, this is impossible," Tegwyn said frustrated, "I have to go now. Take care of yourself and call me when you want or feel the need. I still love you regardless of the mess you are in. You have made me love you. You're truly a bastard. You know that?"

"Yes, yes I do know that and I love you."

"Goodbye Richard." She hung up

"Bye Tegs. I'll call you soon."

"Hey Jack," Henry said into his land line from Interpol head quarters in Lyon, "Henry here."

"Good afternoon Henry, what's up?"

"Jonathan has been in touch with Tegwyn but we were unable to trace where he phoned from but we know it was not from Portugal. We couldn't make a complete trace; but they are in contact and that is what we were hoping for."

"Damn, too bad about the trace."

"I will send you a transcript of their conversation via email. It wasn't much but it does confirm our suspicions that she knew nothing of his identity. One thing for sure, he will call her back. I sensed he wants her and that she's in love with him and he's in love with her. So I think we should just hang in there and wait for the call that will come soon. A woman is going to make him carry out the fatal mistake to end the chase. And she is like most woman, they hate rogues but love them the most."

"Do you think I should talk to her?" Jack queried.

"No, we don't know what she would do then. She may join sides with him or stop contact with him. She's our bait—she will go to him and we will get him for sure."

"Your right. Let's give this some time."

Mohamed

Mohamed was named Mohamed because he was the first male born in his family. Ragged and dirty with crooked rotted teeth and a deformed ear, he plied his trade as con man, tour guide and entrepreneur. Tourists entering North Africa via the Port of Tangier bought his services; his fees were whatever he could get. Jonathan came to know him the morning he left the fast ferry that bought him from Algeciras, Spain. He was among the dozens of guides and beggars that hounded him as he walked down the pier to the entrance to the Kasbah.

He was in Africa for a day or two to see if Morocco was worth coming to for an extended period of time and where he may end up living a good part of his life. What greeted him, he judged, was not good. Jonathan had planned if he was to be captured, it would eventually happen in North Africa. Bad idea, he concluded.

The Kasbah, an old ancient fort, squats on cliffs that hug the ocean on one side and the relatively recent city of Tangier on the other. On stonewalls, waiting for tourists, were a few dozen young Moroccans—ignorant and dangerous. They were like the monkeys of Gibraltar loafing about waiting for handouts and would snatch anything that was food or profit. Mohamed and Jonathan passed them and they acknowledge his guide with a smile and some giggles which aroused suspicion in him. They went up a road that ran between an old Jewish cemetery and fortifications built by the Romans two thousand years ago. Cemented on top of ancient stonewalls are white sheer windowless battlements of a fort of recent times. Stairs led up to a Moorish arch entrance, one of the few ways into the old place.

They entered a world that Jonathan had never dreamed existed. A Kasbah is in most cities in Morocco and they are not the romantic places of movies and love stories. This is a place of work and heartaches. A crowded place built over thousands of years that cannot support any more people. Shops, residences and archways choke its narrow passageways only a few meters wide, many turning into dark cave like tunnels. The passage ways are divided into neighborhoods selling gold, jewelry, rugs, copper kitchenware, clothing, silk, groceries, liquor, spices, aromatics, medical and naturopathic services—the list is endless. The smell of spices covers the stench. They passed sweatshops only a few meters square, enough room for two or three people to work. This was the place where products had come from that Jonathan had seen on shelves and racks in stores across his journey.

To Jonathan the Moroccans looked happy and content in what they were doing but around them in the huge population, lurked shadowy figures in full-length dresses with hoods—the hoods drawn over their heads. Not all are willing to work for a living and these shadows lazed around—

opportunists of any situation that may come up. Friends in Portugal and Gibraltar warned him that the Moroccans are thieves and cannot be trusted. His friends didn't know that Jonathan was no better.

Lies and Mythology are created here; Mohamed took him to a naturopath selling herbal remedies. Sex enhancement drugs are now part of our modern culture; the Moroccan merchant tried to convince Jonathan that most of his herbs were a good substitute for modern drugs and also as aphrodisiacs. His bottles that lined the shelves looked dangerous filled with items that could have been scraped off the street.

"No Mohamed—no let's move on," Jonathan said, "I'm not in the market for any of your friend's goods and please don't put me up against any of your other dealers, Okay?"

"Okay," Mohamed said and Jonathan knew he was not happy.

They chatted. "What are you doing here in my country Sir?"

"Well I was thinking I might come here and live for a while, maybe travel around North Africa. And you, Mohamed, what do you do besides being a tour guide?"

"I'm attending university studying the Koran; I want to be a priest calling my people from a minaret in some holy place. I have a wife and three children to feed," and then he gave Jonathan his price for the tour, which was outrageous, and Jonathan gave him a quarter of what he asked for—disgruntled he took it. He said: "Now, Sir, if you will excuse me I have to say my prayers and this is where I live," pointing down a dark passageway, "goodbye Sir," and he disappeared.

Yes, Mohamed, he thought the physical condition you're in, living in the Kasbah and married with kids. You're studying of the Koran in university? No, it doesn't fit. Poor Mohamed if you could only tell the truth, I'm just a poor Moroccan making a living, would all you had to say and life may change; you would get a good fee and a tip. How many millions like you are stuck in such a basic world of survival here in Morocco and the rest of the world? Sure, disappear and say your prayers.

In reality Mohamed had to get back to the dock since another ship was on its way in and he knew he was not going to get anything more out of Jonathan—for him or his vendor friends.

Jonathan was in the Kasbah—alone. Mohamed had abandoned him. Scary, he thought when he first realized it, but people were everywhere and they all looked busy and smiling so he went on his way for the next hour looking into shops at the goods for sale. He wondered if any one escapes the Kasbah and goes on to a better life. He did not think Mohamed had the looks or values to make it out; he would hustle for the rest of his life in this dark and dismal place. Perhaps he would even be murdered in the end, since he was a con man. Jonathan felt sorry for him.

He was deep in his thoughts and deeper into the Kasbah; he didn't know where he was. Every passageway was different and no recognizable landmark could be seen, not even where the direction of the sun shone. He knew he was in trouble and had lost Mohamed somewhere in the anthill, on his knees his head toward Mecca. He spent the next half hour like a rat in a burrow traveling the passageways, greeting the folks and dodging the shadows trying not to look lost, but he was and quickly felt panic about his situation. To gather his thoughts he sat down off one of the passageways on steps under an ancient Moorish arch that led into a mosque—he took some deep breaths and the chanting behind him soothed and calmed him. The Kasbah was claustrophobic and he had nightmares of not getting out of there before dark. He got up and kept walking kilometer after kilometer in circles.

Suddenly the passage emerged into a small square full of sunshine. About twenty boys were playing soccer and they stopped their game, they all looked at him. They knew he was lost in the anthill of their town. He asked them for directions back to the Avenue d'Espagne and the beach. One of the boys who spoke some English came forward and gestured Jonathan to come with him and the other little urchins decided to follow, pulled on by the smile on his new guide's face. This did not look good and he imagined being swarmed by the kids. He told them all to go away and was left with his guide in the square.

"They are kid Mafia," the boy said. He nodded his head in sad acknowledgement. The guide led him down a passageway a short distance, which led him to the Hotel Continental that is above the ferry terminal; there was no passageway down to it. He gave his guide three euros, which was a fortune for the boy, he ran back to his friends shouting his luck. By the end of the day he would not own those coins. He left the hotel keeping the fortress wall to the left and made his way down to the main gate and out of the Kasbah. That was interesting, he thought as he wiped the sweat from his brow and checked his underwear.

Back onto the beach avenue and out of the Kasbah; desperate characters offering drugs; women or boys greeted him. One of the most desperate approached, an American who spoke good English out of his horrible head and rotten teeth. They struck up a conversation and he told him he was from Oregon, USA; he ran away from home when he was in his teens to travel the world. An alcoholic and an addict, he ended up in Tangier. He was now in his forties but looked a tired seventy—a look of death on his face. He was so filth Jonathan could not tell what colour his clothes were; he stank of his own excrement. His gray hair was long and matted; his gray wispy beard—thin and straggly. His hands and beard were stained black with the tar from smoking; the skin of his face, hands and feet were dark brown from the dust, weather and sun. Thoughts of friends from years ago flashed through his mind.

Tangier and free open places like it around the world are the bottom end for many on the run from their past and if alcohol or drugs are involved these places are a haven—everything is cheap. Eventually the money runs out, shelter disappears, clothes become old, self esteem floats away and drugs destroy the body and soul. Life is relative—the worse your surroundings, the worse you become. People like the American live on the street and eat with the rats, becoming part of the dust cloud that floats down across the city. Jonathan wished him luck, said goodbye and before he turned away he gave him a twenty-dollar Canadian bill.

It was too late for Jonathan to catch the last ferry back to Spain so he booked into an old hotel—five dollars a night. The room was clean and on the forth floor. From shuttered French doors and a rusting wrought iron balcony it looked over the palm-treed boulevard and beach. On the main floor of the hotel across from the lobby was a restaurant; nicely appointed with flowers, table clothes, napkins and tall wine glasses. Old desert oasis paintings hung on the walls with one wall exclusively for the bar, which was a large, antique structure of Victorian design in wood with a marble countertop and art nouveau mirrors. Wicker stools surrounded the bar and one of them carried a large red-faced Brit who was very drunk. Jonathan wondered if it was legal to drink in Morocco.

The Brit, waiter and Jonathan were the only ones in the place that night and after his supper of lamb stew he joined the Brit at the bar and drank the best scotch at fifty cents a glass. He is not a hard liquor drinker, beer is fine for him but he was in Tangier—land of Crosby, Hope, Greenstreet, Lorie and Bogart. Before bed he stepped outside to the avenue bathed in the dim streetlights of the boulevard. It was dark but gently lit by a full moon with Venus near by. Jonathan watched dozens of shadows float across the boulevard and under the street lamps to huddle down for the night in doorways and passages. Others were going home to the Kasbah after a long day in the sweatshops. Someone in the distance in the rubble of buildings behind his hotel screamed. Jonathan slept well that night knowing that he didn't have to stay.

He ate a hardy breakfast in the morning of what appeared to be bacon and eggs. It was a beautiful sunny day so he walked the beach to think about this place in North Africa and to consider whether it fit with his project. Would he like it here? Would this be the place for him to end up? No, it would not—it was out of context, he thought. Life here for him in North Africa would run counter to the basic principles of his project—counter to his agenda. The people he met and talked to in Tangier are not people he would want to run to and fight alongside. They were demons in their own hell. This place is a place to visit and a lesson on how well those from the western world live. He had to be arrogant about this—he would find a more suitable place to be arrested—someplace with colour and flair. Perhaps his fate would end somewhere along the Route of the Caliphs—the highway between Cordova and Granada.

Jonathan left the beach for the ferry terminal and began the nightmare of getting his passport stamped to get out of the country. He was glad to get back to his boat in Marina Bay, Gibraltar, in sight of the white cliffs of Gulliver.

Tavira in The Shadow of God

Jack Garland had been wandering around the Algarve, driving from village to village when a message came in from Joaquim Bentaroza, the commander of the local GNR station in Tavira. Jonathan was spotted in the seaside city but had disappeared and there was a strange message left for Jack. And he thought this wisp of a man moves across Portugal with impunity. How did he do it?

"Joaquim? It's Jack Garland RCMP, Interpol."

"I have been waiting for your call."

"Maybe you could take me to some places in Tavira you think Jonathan Owen may have spent some time. What's this about a message."

"Yes, of course. Your man left a message at the art gallery, in the guest book. You'll see it when you get here. Are you nearby?

"Yeah, I'm near Tavira now, driving on the N125. Can we meet?"

"Yes. Take the posted turnoff and drive into the gorge to the river, cross the bridge, pass the bus station and drive to the square with the column monument. Park there and I will be at the café nearby. You won't be able to miss me. I'll be in uniform."

"Great, it will be about a half hour. See you soon," he hung up.

"Let's have a coffee, before we do our walkabout." and they sat down in an outdoor café on the town square. A waitress came: "Douce galáo, por favor," she took the order, "It's good to meet you constable, we have heard so much about you and your friend Jonathan over the last few months. Too bad he's not still here. I am very curious about what kind of a man he is."

"Well I'm going to get him and it will be soon—that's guaranteed. We are getting close. We almost had him about a week or so ago.

"You have quite a name. Very poetic," Jack commented.

"Yes, my family has been here forever, we go back before memory. I have been to grave sites and our name is on them from hundreds of years ago."

"It's different for us in Canada. Our history was left behind when our ancestors immigrated. The past was forgotten in just a couple of generations. I'd like to know where my family came from. I know it was somewhere in England. I'll find out someday." Coffee arrived along with a small sweet.

"So you want a bit of an insight into your man do you?" Joaquim said with excitement.

"Yeah, I'm beginning to understand his art now I want to know about his spiritual side. I want to know what he sees about himself in these historical places. Is he running, searching, on a pilgrimage or what? I need to understand what he has seen. I've never been to these kinds of places, my Church, when I was young, was a country shack of a place in rural Manitoba.

As for sacred art—I never knew that existed. What's he seeing? What is he looking for? Those are the things I want to know."

"I have studied my village all my life, so I know religion has always been the most powerful force after the army. Both of them were worthy of being feared since both could kill you quite quickly if you did not fit into their grand scheme. They excommunicated and ostracized people—people starved to death outside of the Church and military spheres. People run the state now, not the uniform or the cross. Thank God, with no pun intended," they both laughed."

"What are you going to show me," Jack queried.

"We are going on a journey, one that Jonathan I know has taken. Right now we are in the center of town and you can see over there on the other side of the war memorial—that is the city hall with the arcade arches. In the center of the building, up high, you can see it through the trees, is the crest of Tavira, an ancient fortress with a crown. Look to the right, Jack, down on the corner of the building. Do you see that head in the stone?"

"Yes."

"That's the knight, Paio Peres Correia, responsible for how everything is in Southern Portugal today. People say that's a portrait of him, but I don't know for sure."

"I've heard that name before, Jonathan's girlfriend told me about him," Jack commented with excitement.

"Good, you're going to hear more about him—let's go," Joaquim paid the bill and the two walked half a block up the square to the gates of Manuel the First.

"These stairs and gates will led us back in time. Your man has walked up here—we know that. Above us on the archway of the gate is the old King's crest of a crown and odd-looking spheres, which I believe, are navigation tools. Just ahead is the Misericórdia Church, very old, very ancient, built in the Renaissance back in the sixteenth century."

"The professor who analyzed Jonathan's art said that our man had studied the artists of the Renaissance."

"Sure, this is what artists study, the art that's in the churches, monasteries, government buildings and the rich estates. The art in these places existed because these were the only locations where there was enough money and power to create such things. Jonathan does not have to be a religious man to be in these places, just a lover of art. Above the great door on the Church here is Our Lady of Compassion and to her right and left are the apostles Peter and Paul. You do know who they were?"

"Yeah, there are a few things I do know eh? Say, do I hear music coming from inside?"

"You do. Let's slip around to the side door," Joaquim said. The door was open so they entered.

"Isn't that music from Broadway?" Jack queried.

"Yes, Summertime, from Porgy and Bess. This Church isn't used very much so it is rented out to a music instructor. That's him on the grand piano and those are his students." They sat in the pews for a few minutes and listened to a young boy strain away on an alto saxophone the notes of that endearing musical and it filled the Church. Jack looked around him and saw the interior of Renaissance architecture and art built and rebuilt over the centuries. The walls were covered with Baroque designs in white and blue tiles; the chancel's stage rose from cascading stairs to a high altar of gold filigree that receded into darkness and mystery. Against one wall in a niche was a large painting of Jesus Christ blessing followers. The painting was old but the colours of gold, blue and red shone brilliantly through the heavy varnish.

"You know, I always felt Bach or Beethoven more appropriate for a place like this with its classic brick-a-brack." Jack commented.

"Culture doesn't stop with age, it renews itself constantly. We're glad to see the place being used for educational programs. There are thirty-seven religious buildings in Tavira and most of them are locked except for the occasional funeral or special service. They have fantastic art in them—hidden away," Joaquim said sadly.

They listened for a while and Jack thought of Jonathan and how well he would fit into this place. The musical rendition was over and they quietly left the teacher and his students.

Joaquim continued his tour speech: "When we passed through those gates behind us we entered the ancient city of Tavira. Nobody knows how old this part of the city is; you will see pieces of the castle that enclosed the hill we are on. Most of the fortress is gone now, broken apart to use the stones for new buildings and street paving. Some of the walls are the foundations of others built in recent times. I'm talking about a seven hundred year span, mind you. At the top of this cobbled stairwell you can see a baroque palace, which is now a museum and art gallery. This is the place we know Jonathan visited. He attended an exhibition opening and talked at length with one of the curators and an art teacher. They told us he was friendly and very knowledgeable about Tavira and Portugal. We are nearing the top of the hill; you can see our oldest Church and perhaps one of the most sacred in Portugal—Santa Maria Castle Church." Two white towers, one for a bell the other for a clock, confronted them. The towers were trimmed in yellow and the roofs were lichen covered terra cotta tilling. "That's the castle just to the left across the courtyard," Joaquim added. "Stone Age Man probably stood here forty thousand years ago and we are still Stone Age Men. We are still throwing rocks. Anyway, Jonathan would have walked around to the front door of the Church past the stations of the sacred way," Joaquim pointed them out, "people still pray to these icons."

Jack reached out and stroked one of the plaques of sandstone and he sensed the tears of ages. "We have nothing like this at home—nothing like this at home," Jack said with emotion. He felt Jonathan and all his ghosts near him as he walked across the cobbled courtyard past the white washed-walls and balconies. Everything was in stone to last the ages and absolutely simple in design. He was starting to understand how simple can be best.

"Here we are, this is the entrance, Gothic in design but was Moorish at one time. There are important people buried here," They entered the massive Church and walked quietly down the aisle; people were on their knees praying in the dark brooding giant nave. A thin mentally challenge man sat at a table, his distorted face on an unusually large head bulged out another half a head size—he looked up at them. His eyes were huge and crossed—he dribbled down his filthy shirt. Dressed in rags and worn out shoes, he was selling postcards and Church trinkets. He grunted as they passed, a sound of displeasure at the intrusion of his space. The place belonged to him and God. Above them were the sculptures, trappings and decorations of the cult of Catholicism; dark gold, blue, red, chipped and cracked icons, dust of the ages encrusted on them. Carvings of Christ, Mother Mary, angels, cupids and apostles were everywhere. Great candelabras sat on coffin like altars and lighted candles were at different stations with donation boxes for those buying and lighting a candle in prayer for a loved one no longer with us.

Massive columns rose to a barrel ceiling festooned with stars. The main altar was a giant structure rising to the ceiling on Corinthian columns with capitals and friezes high above the Church's marble floor. The years of embellishments and weathering had made it ghastly, distorting it from the beauty it once was. Everywhere the paintings and sculptures told the story of the agony of a man and his people of long ago. The place was soaked with tears of grief not joy. Effigies of Christ, covered with blood from gaping wounds, and crying mothers were everywhere begging for forgiveness for a crime they did not commit.

In a dark niche of the church: "This is what I want you to see and your man would want to have seen." Joaquim whispered as they crept quietly among ghosts and bones, "This is the Chapel of Our Lady. There she is standing on a glass coffin. Inside is her crucified son. Do you see that soldier in armor carrying the white flag with the Red Cross?"

"Yeah," Jack whispered.

"Well, that's Paio Peres Correia—the Master of the Order of Santiago. We think that's his coffin he's standing on. Remember I pointed him out to you down on the square; he's the guy who changed this part of Portugal forever when he drove out the Moors. Through that archway Jack, to the right—do you see those seven red crosses next to each other on the wall?"

"Yeah, I see them," he whispered and squinted in the dim light.

"Those were some of Correia's knights. They were killed in the battle taking this place. That's were they're buried—in the walls," From behind them came a grunting from the keeper of God's place. "This is a sacred place," Joaquim whispered," let's get out of here."

"Yeah, please, let's get out of here," they walked hurriedly out of the cathedral back to the new world and into the blazing Algarve sun.

"It's a different world from what you're used to." Joaquim said as he led him to the steps of the Seven Knights Lane, "There are dozens of these places around Tavira— major cathedrals of art and history. These were the temples that ran the world for so many citizens. Today they fill up at Christmas, funerals, baptisms, religious events and curious tourists who come everyday. It's really not the celebration it used to be one hundred and fifty years ago and more."

"Amazing stuff, it must have cost a fortune back then to build these places and fill them with all that gold and art. I can see why Jonathan is interested in these places. The sheer grandeur is overwhelming and the history powerful and fascinating. You know, it all turns to dust eventually doesn't it?"

"Yes it does, and we go along with it," Joaquim said, "and for many, this place cost them their lives. I'm going to leave you here for you to wander back to the Palace Gallery. Look in the guest book, there is a message waiting for you."

"Oh, yes, the message," he said nervously.

"Yes, from Jonathan. I'll see you in an hour back at the coffee shop on the main square."

"I'll see you there." and Jack hurried across the cobbles and down the narrow street to the Palace Gallery.

A nervous and out of place RCMP Constable said, "Hello, I'm from out of town and here to see your fine gallery. Do I buy my ticket here?" He asked awkwardly of the beautiful receptionist. She fits into the place well; Jack thought how did I know that?

"Yes Sir, three euros please," she cheerfully said.

"By the way, do you have the guest book from the last two weeks? I would like to read some of it," he asked.

The receptionist smiled and handed him back his money: "You are Constable Garland aren't you?"

"Why yes. Have we met before because it's unlikely, I just arrived this morning and I—?

"Mr. Owen said that you would be by for a visit—he paid for your ticket. If you follow the stairs straight up from where you came in you will be in our main gallery. The guest book is in our offices. I will fetch it and bring it up to you."

"Thank you," Jack said a little bewildered.

He opened the floor to ceiling glass doors and walked up the cherry wood stairs past white on white walls of the stairwell to the large upper rooms with high ceilings. The gallery walls were matte white and the floor was planked with heavy wide boards, dowelled to the sub floor. There were no moldings on the windows—clean to the frames. White wooden shutters kept out the morning sun; now open to reveal the view of the river that cuts Tavira in half and the salt flats that extend to the Atlantic Ocean.

The ceiling was made of reed matting with exposed rafters woven into them. They held up the main roof structure shaped like a pyramid in each gallery. There were five rooms—five pyramids, the large one that he was in and four smaller. Each had a different style. The most startling ceiling was of pine planking. It randomly lay over the top of an old baroque painted artifact in deep gray and blue with deep red filigree—very old and weathered. After feeling the starkness of the place Jack concentrated on the paintings that were huge, averaging three by four meters. Jack slumped down on a lone black leather and chrome chair and studied the paintings. The receptionist came in with the guest book.

"Here you are, Sir. I have bookmarked the page of interest to you."

"Thank you," Jack said. She left; he opened the leather bound book and saw half way down the page a message to him:

Dear Jack,

Welcome. We have never met but someday we will and perhaps not long after your visit here in this beautiful space. I feel privileged to have you chasing me.

I have read many articles about you in the past few months and you appear to be a very dedicated family man and a good officer. The media did not say that in the beginning – did they? I wish you luck in the chase. It is coming to an end since I am tired and I am starting to blunder with some of my moves. You must be tired too. Nevertheless you are going to have to work to the very end. Enough said about that.

These are the places I come to, places like this all over the world. It is where I can find peace in these crazy times and you can find peace here to, if you have a little patience. You are an analytical man and don't have much time for the romance and the wonder of life, as I understand from reading between the lines about you. I empathize with you in what you are going through in this strange land and cultural confusion. Perhaps in the art you see before you and the architecture they rest in, you will find peace for a few moments away from the chase.

This palace is an old and ancient site. Let me explain: It was built hundreds of years ago and served many purposes and lay for years abandoned but held its high ground to eventually be captured by imaginative people who restored it to its former grandeur. The artists, architects and designers have been sensitive to the building's style, condition and location during its renovation. Its exterior is done in the baroque style with its fantastic twists and turns of moldings and plaster, all in contradiction to the modern simple white painted walls. The new ambiance given to the old structure is a salute to the past and present men and women who toiled at their crafts to help the old palace rise out of a violent history.

On the inside a minimalist world has been created, mixed and comfortable with the baroque extravagance of yesterday. The bare unpainted planked floors; the boarding and molding design of the ceilings are from yesterday. And for today between the old designs is nothing but blank white walls ready to hold the creations of artists lucky and worthy enough to hang their work here. It is a space of study and reflection, of contemplation and comfort. The windows look out onto Tavira which itself is art and the village comes fluttering in at you. The space lets us breathe with its openness and the ceilings float above, protecting us. Over all, what is here is what we humans are purposely capable of creating and it is like no other on this earth.

It is time for you to take a breather Jack Garland – sit for a while. To be here is to witness something great. Enjoy.

Jonathan Owen

Jack closed the guest book and gently laid it on the floor beside his chair and gave some thought to what arrogant Jonathan wrote. He looked up at the recent exhibit on the walls—paintings he did not understand. The focus on Jonathan that Jack had endured over the last few months would not let him believe in all this art. How many times over the years had he read about galleries paying good tax money on work like this? He thought I must give it a chance; I must have patience. Besides if I want to learn more about Jonathan I need to spend some time looking and wondering. Three quarters of an hour went by and then something happened.

The huge canvas he was looking at came to life. Its mass hung next to a window that looked out on North Tavira and the country forests and farms beyond. The huge conglomeration of lines and polygons started to make sense. Three quarters of the painting was a black oval and coming from the opposite side a one quarter green oval; not painted accurately, to Jack's mind. Two curved thick yellow lines were painted in heavy paint dissecting the ovals. They were painted on a field of lime green; there were splatter marks on the black. He knew they were splatters because he had seen such things in his investigations; like blood on windshields—that reminder made him smile. There were thinner lines over the black that countered the movement of the thick lines. Jack noticed the lines were not painted haphazardly over the black and green fields but the black fields were painted up to them creating an edge of fuzziness. Things were not layered; they were on the same plane—in their own space. The canvas was not square, at least he thought it so and he saw at the top and bottom of the painting the edges had wedges painted from left to right distorting the entire canvas field into an odd shape, not square anymore, now more like a rhomboid.

The entire painting was starting to dance for him and he looked out of the window to the fields beyond and saw the same thing, cultivated fields and forests, stone fences dividing the land and a lone tree out in the middle of a field. He understood what the painting was doing, simplifying the details of the world into just forms and the illusion of movement. Was it telling him that Jonathan moved and hid in the landscape—he wondered?

Jack jumped up and ran into the room with the fancy design on the ceiling and he noticed the new pine planking and the old baroque pieces were fitted together—neither one was holding the other. They weren't nailed together haphazardly, they were meticulously cut and fitted—they matched. It was a mix of the old and new and it felt comfortable to him. In the room he just came from was an interpretation of a country landscape and the real thing out the window—side by side. High on the ceiling was the old and new bound together in harmony. He thought to himself, what if they did the same thing next door in the cathedral: took out the old carpeting; painted the walls and ceiling a super white; polish the woodwork of the doors and windows; clean the art work and cut slits in the stone to let in the sunlight. A lighting system could be installed that would turn off and on when the sun shone in, and positioned to highlight the altars and figures and floodlight the whole place at night to make it glow. Bring in the new and help the old, what a difference that would make. I'm getting it Jonathan—I'm getting it and I'll get you.

A Call to Cardiff, Wales

Tegwyn was in the local pub with her sister and mom at home in Cardiff, Wales. They talked of her retirement a few years away. Perhaps the house in Wales would be available where she could live out her years. Her cell phone tried to ring itself out of her purse. She excused herself from the table and went outside to the cold and rain to answer the call in private.

"Hello," she sang into the phone. She huddled in the doorway out of the rain.

"Tegs my love. It's Jonathan."

"Bloody hell, Richard—everything all right then?"

"Yes everything is fine but I miss you something terrible."

"God, I miss you too. I think about you all the time. What are we to do? I'm not over you and I thought I was."

"Will you come and see me, Tegs?"

"I can't—for Christ's sake! I'm here in Cardiff with my Mom and sister. I leave for Portugal tomorrow. I only have a few days until I'm back at the bar."

"Tegs, it's perfect, eh? I'm in Gibraltar. Why not fly here from Cardiff. How about it? You can see me for a day or two and then we can go back to Portugal together. I could stay in a town a bus ride away—maybe in Silves with my ghost friends. Interpol would never expect that I would return to Portugal. What do you say? It would be wonderful for us to be together again. Even just for a little while, eh." He was surprised at what he was saying. It went against what he started out to do.

"I don't know, I—"

"Tegs I'll pay for the whole shot—everything. This would mean so much for the both of us."

"Aren't the police still looking for you?"

"I don't know. There are no notices up around here or in Spain. There's nothing on the news about the chase or me so I guess I'm dead news. Maybe they have given up. I don't know. I don't really care now; I'm tired of being on the run. I've aged two years in the last year. It's all been so mentally and physically exhausting. That's why I need you here, even for a few hours."

"Al right I'll fly out tonight on the next available plane. I must be mad for doing this, you bastard. My mom and sister are going to be furious. They want every last minute of me. You check from there what time the Cardiff run arrives, Okay?"

"Right—I love you."

"And I love you too Richard. Christ, what do you want me to call you?"

"Jonathan."

"Stay safe and you will see me soon. Bye love." The dark and cold of

Cardiff chilled her to the bone. She quickly went inside to her family.
The technician monitoring Tegwyn's cell phone rushed into Henry's office with a transcript of her conversation with Jonathan. Henry immediately phoned to Jack Garland somewhere on the road in Southern Portugal, "Jack. It's Henry."

"What's up?"

"Jonathan is in Gibraltar and is going to meet Tegwyn Bevan tonight when she arrives by plane from Cardiff, Wales. We have him now—he's made a slip in judgment—he is tired of running—we have him now!"

"Fabulous—finally—wow! It's a long time coming. I will get to Gibraltar. Alert the Gibraltar police force, fill them in on everything and get administration working on the extradition papers. Will you fly down?"

"There is no way I would miss this. Not even the Secretary can stop me from being there. Must run and get on this. See you in Gibraltar,"
Constable David Axeworthy of the Gibraltar Police Constabulary opened the urgent email from Interpol.

"Oh my God!" he shouted, "Sidney! Sidney, get in here and have a look at this!" Sidney rushed into the office from the front desk—the two duty officers read the message.

Constable Sidney Pritchard commented, "We're going to be busy tonight, better get in touch with the Chief Inspector."

"Right," and he dialed the home of the Chief who was about to sit down for dinner with his family and guests.

"Constable Axeworthy—It'd better be good young man," answered the Chief Inspector. He always knew who was calling him.

"Yes sir, you might say it is. An urgent message has come in from Interpol, Lyon, France and they say that Jonathan Owen is in Gib and will be meeting his girlfriend, Tegwyn Bevan in a few hours when she arrives by plane from Cardiff. We thought you had better know about this one Sir. We have not received any official paper work on this case. Should we carry on with an arrest anyway Sir?"

"I am sure the paper work is on its way as we speak. Obviously this has come as a surprise to them so we should co-operate the best we can regardless."

"Yes Sir."

"Right Officer, handle it efficiently as I know you will. May I suggest getting the Interpol notices out? I think there is one on the bulletin board—yes I'm sure of it."

"There is one Sir."

"Have copies made and distributed to the night duty immediately. Call them in from the field for a briefing and have them question the shops in Casemates Square, Main Street, Internet providers and especially the bus drivers on the four routes. I will call the Governor and have him call the

Spanish border and police forces; they will close the border until we have captured the man. No words to the media—this is imperative Officer."

"Yes Sir."

"Get your men to lock down the town. Alert army headquarters of the situation and get your police boats on the alert. Now I will get back to my meal, family and guests. Give me a call when the lady's plane lands and you have apprehended your man. Good luck, Officer."

"Thank you Chief. Enjoy your dinner. Good night Sir," and David looked at Sid for reassurance, "Right Sid, call everyone in and I'll make copies of our wanted man's mug."

The constabulary on night duty arrived at the station in Irish Town, picked up their copies of Jonathan's wanted poster and moved out across the city. In a quarter of an hour calls came into the station—Jonathan had been seen all over Gibraltar. The bus drivers recognized him from his trips around town and to the Spanish border. An Internet provider said he recently used their computers. A bar maid, at one of the restaurants in Casemates Square gave the best lead. She lives on a boat in the marina—Jonathan Owen is living on a cruiser on the first finger of the marina wharf.

"David, why hadn't we seen him before this?" Sidney queried.

"Because we weren't looking." Constable David Axeworthy radioed his men and ordered them to make their way to the Marina but not to enter the premises until he gave the order on his arrival. He ordered those with weapons to keep them holstered and no lights or sirens are to be used. No one was to talk to any media present on orders of the Chief Inspector.

"Let's go and get our man," they rushed to their vehicle parked on Cloister Ramp and roared down Fountain Road to Queensway Road and the Marina. By the time they arrived dozens of officers were milling about in great excitement—reporters and cameras all over them.

"Who are you going to call on that bull horn? It's Jonathan Owen, isn't it?" one reporter questioned, "Come on tell us, we have to do our job here," another said.

"All in due time. Have you fellows been monitoring us again?" asked the Constable.

"Of course, always."

"Sid, take charge of a dozen men and move them off to the entrance to the north marina apartment complex and the commercial area. I'll secure the parking lot here and the area south of the Marina. When you're ready, call me and I will give the signal to move onto the wharves to do the search. Remember, guns holstered there are too many people about and a misplaced shot could—"

"Right," Sidney acknowledged David's order, collected his men and moved off. The event was picked up by the media monitoring police broadcasts who in turn broadcast it to the world and into the cabin of the plane carrying Tegwyn from Cardiff. The Gibraltarian's heard the chase and capture might happen at the marina and airport; they flocked there by the hundreds to watch the drama unfold. Crowds of people lined both sides of the runway, a local television station's cameraman ran out to the edge of the tarmac to film Jonathan's flight of folly.

The little country of Gibraltar came to a standstill and strangely quiet; Constable David Axeworthy looked southwest into the night sky and saw the flashing lights of a plane descending, coming around The Rock for an easterly approach to the runway.

"It sounds like there's a spot of trouble down in Gibraltar," commented an English gentleman sitting next to Tegwyn, "that Canadian fellow, Jonathan something-or-other is about to be apprehended."

"What!" Tegwyn said, "How do you know that?"

"Right here on my portable radio. It seems the entire town has shut down and the border is closed. We are the only ones allowed in."

"God no, poor Jonathan!" she cried. She looked out her window and The Rock stared back at her.

Run for Your Life

Jonathan squeezed into the little shower on board his rented cruiser, sang a few bars of Land of Hope and Glory and gave himself a scrub and shave. Out of the shower he dried and rubbed down with body lotion, dressed in beige slacks, light brown sandals, white shirt and dark tie. He would look his best for Tegwyn who was arriving within the hour on the last flight of the day from Cardiff to Gibraltar. He would walk to the airport that is just a few minutes away. Happily he skipped across the gangplank and down the dock whistling. To the entrance of the marina he joyously went.

He stopped suddenly and all the hopes for the evening and days, maybe years to come came crashing down. Over the top of cars in the parking lot he saw the entrance to the marina—it was filled with police officers. Their white cars lined the street. "Ah shit!" he said to himself, "not now!" There were dozens of them dressed in their bobby helmets and glowing, lime green jackets. Quickly he ducked and hid behind the cars. Crouched, he made his way back to the dock and cruiser. He unplugged the electrical system, unscrewed the water line, let the lines go and scrambled aboard. He pulled aboard the gangplank and stowed it aft on the transom. He opened the engine compartment hatch and pushed the red starter button and the engine came to life. On the bridge he turned on the running lights and slowly pulled the cruiser out of the slip. Turning to port ninety degrees he ran the cruiser up the finger dock, turned to port again and steered her up the side of the airport runway towards the Bahia de Algeciras. In the distance beyond the cruise terminal and between the lights of moored freighters were flashing blue and blazing searchlights. His heart sank—the harbor police were also on to him.

He steered for the service jetty jutting out the south side of the airport's runway. He pulled up, turned off the engine and lights and climbed onto the jetty leaving the cruiser to drift. He crouched down on the side of the runway; lights came up everywhere. His heart pounded from fear that he would soon be killed or severely hurt. There was no place to hide; the landscape was flat and he was just a blip on the radar.

He ran onto the airport tarmac: "Run Jonathan, run!" he screamed. Looking back over his shoulder, searchlights from the police harbor cruisers were on him. They docked at the jetty and armed police poured onto the tarmac. Police were running like ants across the marina. A speaker from somewhere commanded him to halt and give himself up—he would not have anything to do with that. He ran knowing—this is the end—he knew it—he will fight to the finish—whatever that will be.

In the distance he could hear sirens but they were not for him. A plane was coming in to land; the airport and road were closed off. He ran east along the tarmac beside the white line that marks the runway boundary. He was soon beside the closed entrance of the road on the airport runway's south side; police and border officers ran out to meet him from both sides of the airport. He ran onto the center of the runway. The officers did not follow; they obeyed a command from the loud speakers.

Two bright lights shone in the distant sky making their way to the runway and him. He ran toward them with all his might and this was something for him—he hates to run. It was always punishment for him in school—5 laps Jonathan—2 laps Jonathan—6 laps Jonathan, Christ, he hated his gym teacher. He kept running and he could see on his right the gigantic white cliff face of The Rock. The mountain, Gulliver—his sleeping head lit by floodlights. Jonathan's body started to hurt; body acid burned his leg muscles and his lungs were raw from fighting for oxygen. The lights at the end of the runway became brighter. Someone chanted in his ear, run to the east, run to Mecca, another voice, best breakfast in town, only four and a half euros, and another, good morning Richard—coffee then? Jonathan's lungs felt like they were going to burst and he ran at full speed down the runway. He had never run like this before. His gym teacher would be proud, he thought. Meet me at five and twenty after said Tegwyn's voice out of nowhere. He was overwhelmed—tears flowed down his cheeks.

The lights coming down the runway were huge now and he could hear the roar of powerful engines in the distance. What are you going to do now Dad? He heard Annabelle whisper. Suddenly there was a calm silence in the air and his lungs did not hurt; he could not feel his legs but they pounded down on the tarmac. He felt strong—something kicked in and his body was finding new life. The lights were very close and things seemed to slow down. An image appeared ahead of him that he will surely run into but he did not care—he was at peace. It started out small and was between the floating lights. It became bigger and grew to an enormous size.

"Christ!" he screamed. The sound came on a deafening hell. It was the Master of Santiago and the seven knights in full amour on massive silver horses—bigger than elephants. On the knight's chests and horses' flanks were colours of battle—white linen emblazoned with The Cross of the Order of Christ billowed around them. The giants' waved their swords above their heads and screamed obscenities. The monstrous steeds galloped frantically down the runway; breath steamed from their nostrils and mouths of gnashing teeth. Their eyes shone red and amber—beacons from hell.

Jonathan was not frightened anymore, his body did not hurt and his limbs were in perfect motion; nothing in the world could stop him now—he ran and ran. The armored knights and horses glowed and shone in the expanding light around them. The Commander of the knights screamed, "JONATHAN!" The light was blinding but he kept his pace and faith.

With a scream, "ENOUGH!" he ran through the galloping knights and everything went black.

The New Gibraltar Hospital Psychiatric Ward

Jonathan could not feel his body nor open his eyes. He felt empty like he was floating, held up by a flock of birds in a black pool. Pains came to his head and face. First, a terrible headache on his forehead and then stabbing pains in his nose and the bones around his eyes. He knew he was awake and could feel hands in his. It all came back—the horrific moment of running down the Gibraltar Airport runway and seeing giants on horseback charging. He was in trouble and he knew it—his project was complete. He hurt, ached and was so tired. His eyes would not open. Gradually faint slivers of light came into view. Figures on each side of the bed appeared; he could see women. In the distance by a door, were two large shadows of men but they were too far away and out of focus. Slowly the two women came into his vision—one was Tegwyn the other Annabelle. All he could say was: "Hi," he was so tired.

Annabelle leaned forward and whispered: "You've been gone from us for twenty-six hours. It's okay now, Dad, you're safe. It's all over—no more ghosts and nightmares. I'm here. I'm going to take you home."

Tegwyn leaned over and kissed his bandaged cheek: "You hit the tarmac at a full run and broke your face up a bit; you gave yourself a concussion but the doctor says you will be up and about in a few days and able to go home. I was on the plane that almost hit you and if it weren't for your stamina at running you wouldn't have made it. You're okay now, get some sleep, Annabelle and I will see you in a while. I love you—think of me in dreamland."

Jonathan drifted off to join his ghosts—they were waiting.

Three

The Dust of Sayulita

Canada Mexico Switzerland Germany

Tula

Green sphagnum mattress
Sword fern and willow blanket
Like a wolf I slept

A wet morning dew
A red and gold rising sun
Slapped me in the face

I rise from my den
Stretch, yawn and rub my cold eyes
A new day is here

Charlie stamped his feet against the bitter cold morning and breathed a white cloud through the slit in his ski mask. A yellow school bus from the recruitment center rolled down the road from the highway and through the security gate of the military base. Something different from the usual routine was about to happen on the parade ground. Someone was on board the bus that would impact his life.

He waited with his men on the edge of the concrete parade ground. His new ragtag batch of recruits stumbled out and a sergeant bellowed orders to line up. Charlie smelled something musky like the strong scent animals give off in the early morning when their fir is damp. He sensed something like him was nearby. Ancestral genes responded in him and he rarely felt like he felt at that moment. When he was young in the forest or on the waterway of his home he sensed the presence of animals long before he saw them. A dark figure of something stood among his new batch of kids—a girl or is it a boy? It was young, dressed in hunter's gear, camouflage, heavy kaki green jacket, hunter's red cap and black work boots. It stood stiff and straight, its black hair, like crows' feathers, cascaded from under the cap and shone in the low morning sun. Its black marble eyes in shadow looked straight ahead and avoided any contact with him. It shook from the cold and fear, its face jerked and ticked with anger. Charlie saw something that was terrifying with this young thing and knew it was to be one of the fortunate to make it through his training.

Charlie approached it and whispered, "And who are you?"

"Tula Sir," the young girl whispered.

"Ah, so you must be a woman?" Charlie barked.

"Sort of Sir!" Tula barked.

Tula kept to herself during her training in boot camp and Charlie kept close surveillance on her to see when the appropriate time was to pull her from the pack for special training. She was different and minded her own business. He noticed her independence but also her team spirit and leadership qualities. He knew intuitively that she qualified for his Group and one morning when she kicked a fellow sapper in the backside for not pulling his weight—he pulled her out. Her training in the art of war and espionage began; training that would drive her into darkness and sorrow.

Tula felt safe at last in the army, a place that embraced and protected her. She felt affection for the ugly brute of a man, Charlie, and obeyed his orders and sometimes-personal suggestions without question. He was someone she trusted and she could handle his barking anger and did not cower as others did. It was not their choice of time and place, and on a field operation in Wainwright, Alberta they became lovers on a riverbank on a hot summer day. It was only once that they were together and that was enough. They knew they would part and have other lives. They did not want the agony of pining for each other and Tula knew in her heart this relationship with a man far older than her would not work and would become a tragedy. She had had enough of hard times in her life. Besides being too old he was ugly and mutilated and she told him so. They both laughed and knew they were now equal, if not by the hierarchy of the army but in fellowship. They vowed they would always be comrades and she could call him if she was in trouble or needed advice. It was something she would do in her dark future.

For three years Tula worked hard in the classroom and field. She was aware that her commanding officer was interested in her more than the other recruits. He made evaluations of her performance at bimonthly interviews and always marked them above average, never superior or outstanding, even if she demonstrated that she was. She traveled the world to learn from the experienced and best of the Canadian Forces. She traveled by her wits: hitch rides on helicopters, private jets, air transporters, fighter aircraft, ships and submarines to get to places. She slept on the road, hotels, barracks, tents and trucks—anything convenient. She came across fellow Special Forces troops and they traveled together until their orders changed; they wondered what it was all about. It was a long time for Tula to comprehend that she was on standby and may have to perform some duty anywhere in the world. She was there at the whim of the government to show the world that Canada has such a force to protect its sovereignty or destroy those who dare question it. She must learn how to get to places in conflict apart from the pack; learn to be her own force, resourceful and obedient, and learn how to become dangerous. But most of all she must learn how to defend herself and kill when ordered.

Charlie Richards, Tula's commander, gave the impression he was as wide as he was tall—a short, squat, Songhees, aboriginal man. He was ugly to some, beautiful to others. His huge body went up to a large domed head on a neck that was tree trunk wide. His right foot was clubbed but he did not limp noticeably, his legs were short and thick which held up a massive torso. When it came to his strength he was stronger than any man he met.

He grew up on the upper Gorge Water Way near the Tillicum Bridge in Victoria were his ancestors, the Kosampson People lived and fished. Charlie's playground was the waterway that cuts the city in half. On hot summer days Charlie and his buddies would swim and dive off the rocks for hours beneath the Bridge. It was dangerous; a large rock below the surface punctured boats and it could not be seen during the tide changes that foamed the rushing water. One day Charlie made a dive; he miscalculated and dove into the submerged rock; it cut open his chin and gave him a scar for life.

Charlie and his gang always left the bridge for home before dark, because the ghost of Camossung, a girl who was turned into the rock at the falls, would rise out of the water hungry for wayward boys. They new this to be true, because of what she had done to Charlie. When the season was right the gang of boys with old men would fish for herring and salmon from a wharf in the eddy below the bridge.

Charlie's life was stable and rewarding. Despite his physical attributes he was a dashing and commanding in uniform and received the respect of all who dealt with him. Over the years he instructed his students the skills of survival in the hostile climates of weather and dangerous people. Only a few that he taught, like Tula, could survive his rigorous courses.

Tula's military career terminated after her three-year contract. She learned everything Charlie could teach her and though she loved the army for the self-esteem and confidence that it gave her, she felt she needed to move on with her life. It was a time when people went exploring to find their ancestry; they went to Africa, Asia, China, India and Europe; she went to her ancestral home in Haiti. She found pieces of her family and in Port au Prince she met a white man that gave her children, a boy and a girl. They were light skinned, big-eyed, bright children and she adored them. She loved the father madly but briefly and when the children were strong enough to travel she left him.

The Haitian military investigated her—her military dossier scared them and they offered her work. The death squads of the Duvalier family, the Tonton Macoute with their atrocities were on the rampage. She knew if she got involved with them she would not survive. She became involved with the voodoo groups of the island and tried unsuccessfully to fit into Haitian society. She sensed she was being watched.

With no prospects of making a living and with the blessing of the military and her husband, she packed up her few things and children and moved to Puerto Vallarta, Mexico. She took a job with an international resort complex selling time-shares; she eventually became a top sales person and was paid in American dollars. It was a good life for a few years until Sub commander Marcos of the Zapatista Army in Chiapas came along and devastated the Paso—she found herself unemployed. Down for a while she began making and selling voodoo dolls on the street until she landed a job at the Bank of Jalisco. With what she saved she managed to rent and later buy a nice home in old town.

Life became good for Tula with money in the bank, and boy friends that wined and dined her. One was Jonathan Owen who was a favorite but they argued a great deal and he could not tolerate her promiscuous ways. She was never satisfied with men, something was always wrong; something better was nearby tanning on the beach. She had very few friends but the ones she did embrace she emailed regularly. Her list was international and one was her retired army friend and mentor—Charlie.

Tula and Jonathan

Blackened body of pirate
Muscle, blood and bone of slave
From this mud she came

"Hey, Jonathan!" came an excited voice from behind him. He turned and there was his old love and perhaps the only true love of the past twenty years. She came running to him full of smiles and joy, "so when did you get out of jail, old man?" she laughed grabbing him by the arm.

"Tula honey, so good to see you," he shouted above the din of the street.

"I've been following your story for the last few years," she kissed him on the cheek and hugged him, "my, you are quite the man."

"What the hell are you doing here in PV? I thought you and the kids moved back to Canada a long time ago," he said with surprise and happy to see her.

"No, I couldn't stand the bloody cold up there any more so I got out. I left my kids in a private school. They will get a far better education in Canada and they want to go to university and become lawyers of all things."

"You having lawyer kids, now that's a novelty. So conservative of them with you so right wing."

"I don't want them coming up the hard way like me. Other than that I don't know why anyone would want to stay in Canada in that cold, it's a mystery to me. Hey, even if I wasn't born here, I belong here in the tropics, Mexico or Haiti—in my ancient past. I'm still a fucking pirate you know."

Her body was scantly dressed in white shorts and red halter-top, her muscular legs, breasts, arms and shoulders were bronzed deeper than her ancestral colour. She was taller than him, about an inch; her legs were taut and shapely from jogging and working out hard at the gym. There was very little body fat on her, just clean cut developed muscle and he was startled by the clearness of her skin, which had not aged. A straw hat rested on her long black curly hair and sunglasses protected her eyes from the noon sun. She looked and smelled familiar and he felt she was a female version of him. Her anatomy was much like his but he was lighter skinned and thicker in muscle.

"Oh, so dramatic, you still look beautiful and just as bad," he said as he hugged her. The primitive smell of her shot up his nostrils and the feeling of her curls against his face made him close his eyes and let memories flash though his head. He felt her deep in his heart. He quickly held her away from him, faking that he wanted to look and talk to her face but really he did not want to let her go. "Cocktails or something? Please say yes, I've had enough of this today and I have to get out of the heat," he said with excitement.

"Would love it, you do look a bit done in from the sun. How about there?" and she pointed to a popular cantina with an outside wrought iron balcony above a jewelry shop, the place where Bank Robber and he laughed and drank together so long ago. They bundled up his equipment and trundled off. They entered the cantina, climbed the tiled staircase to the dining room and an Aztec hostess showed them to a table. They settled in on a shaded balcony overlooking the Malecón and the endless blue ocean beyond.

"What have you been up to honey?"

"Fighting with lovers as usual, breaking up and waiting for you to get out of jail and visit me again," she said putting on a sigh.

"Oh bullshit," he laughed out, "as for me with nothing to do behind those iron bars, I did think of you—and before that, during my disastrous adventures. Sometimes I wished you were there. You would have loved to watch me fuck up."

"Yeah and go down with you? No thank you. Faking your own death was quite an unbelievable thing to do but I wasn't surprised knowing how eccentric you are. You've been told you're an opera. But the breakdown; that worried me and many of your friends were also concerned."

"How do you know? Did any of them talk to you?"

"No, Annabelle wrote to me."

"Annabelle?"

"I know she doesn't like me but she is decent and wrote to me about what had happened to you and like a complete fool I went to your funeral."

"You what?" Jonathan laughed, "That was sweet of you." He leaned over the table and kissed her on the cheek.

"So you owe me fifteen hundred bucks Canadian—airfare and hotel."

"Well was it fun—an experience?"

"Christ no!" Tula said getting a little exasperated, "I was sad that you had died and I wanted to pay my respects. I was in love with you as were the many women sitting around me in tears. What really hurt was there wasn't a coffin. You never made it to your own funeral, you bastard!" They both laughed.

"The breakdown I didn't plan on. The whole event I orchestrated got out of hand and I couldn't cope with it. It was art, I tried something different, I took a risk and it was a hell of an experience honey. I kinda' loved it. Some say it was manic behavior but my doctor said it wasn't. It was exhaustion from the chase. I feel fine now and I'm not on any medication."

"That was bizarre, you chasing a plane down the runway. Jesus, when they broadcasted it on PV air, people were saying; who the hell is this nut case? You should have written or phoned or something, you should have gotten in touch with me," she said and diverted her attention to the waiter who arrived at their table, "dos Cuba Libre por favor, one with ice and the other without for my amigo—gracias," she remembered what he drank, "I would have been there for you. I would have flown up to the prison in Canada and visited you perhaps tormented you a bit," she giggled.

"Torment is the operative word. That you would have, that you would have," he dryly pointed out.

"What happened to your girlfriend—the one that got you captured in Gibraltar? I'm jealous of that bitch. That woman should have been me. Did you love her?"

"No, she is a good woman and she's not a bitch, she is still working in Portugal in the bar where we met. I was in love with her for a while but she would not leave the fishing village. As beautiful as she and village were, I had no desire to live there. I couldn't see myself sitting around in the square with all the old fishermen arguing politics and football, dressed in gumboots, baggy pants with suspenders over a checkered shirt and a cap on my head. No not me. The trial and my jail sentence put a final damper on that adventure and the possibility of working anything out with her. I do miss her though."

"Despite the fact that it looks like someone took an axe to your face; you're still a good looking man. Even after all the trouble and breakdown you have put yourself through you haven't changed much."

"Those are my Mother's lines. I see her face each morning when I look in the mirror."

"It was that damn ego of yours again wasn't it?" she said, becoming serious. It's all about you—right?"

"Yeah, you know me. I came out with a bundle of money through it all—so what the hell. It was an expensive investment of my soul but I don't care," he said, "look at me now, money in the bank, a contract to practice my art, a beautiful day in the tropics, and drinks with my favorite pirate." Suddenly Jonathan saw a little angel that he recognized dance across her face and kiss the corner of her mouth as she laughed. He had forgotten about them. "Where are you working—same place? Have you got somebody?"

"Yes, the bank took me back after my stay in Canada. They have been good to me so I may as well stick around for the duration. As for somebody, well, I can't find a handsome beautiful wealthy hunk good enough for me in PV," and she leaned forward smiling and looked deep into his eyes, "the man I love is crazy," she said and leaned back in her chair, "I will probable face the future alone, but I'll be all right; I have a stash in an off shore account for my old age."

"Why? Don't you trust the banks here?"

"I don't trust them because the government is too unstable and they are the ones who run the banks. The government could collapse at any moment and the peso would be worth nothing. Besides, banks are run by psychopaths."

"I guess it is financially dangerous here," and he changed the subject back to them, "Yeah, and I can't seem to find a beautiful voodoo witch like you that will put up with me, although I haven't looked too hard. You know, I guess we are victims of our modern age."

"Oh crap!" she blurted out as an angel raced across her face and quickly dashed beneath her curls, "it's our old age. We are now the old ones that we used to talk and laugh about. We aren't the victims—we are the ones in command. We are in charge of our own destiny—destined to go it alone. Look at the age of those who run the governments. The bastards were in school with us and they run our countries. We are no longer the victims!" she blasted out and he remembered the ferocious edge of hers.

"Okay, okay, you're right about that I guess," gesturing with raised hands for Tula to calm down. He changed the subject. "What about the voodoo stuff? Still making the dolls?"

"Yes and I've expanded the line with luck, money and love Wanga dolls. I manufacture about twenty styles now and have many women folk around PV producing for me. I don't need the money but it helps others make a bit of extra cash for their families. I keep the biz underground of course, and I have been able to ship dolls to New Orleans. When the time is right I'll drop my job and be well positioned to expand and sell worldwide. Some are very interesting and old in their magic."

"I still have that valentine doll you gave me years ago. I have always treasured it. I don't know why—it's so S and M," Jonathan laughed.

"Keep it; it's going to be worth a great deal someday, besides I did something special to it just for you."

"And what was that?"

"Something far too sexy," she said leaning towards him, "far too sexy."

"Yeah, I can imagine."

"You know I'm the PV Voodoo Queen now—got elected last year by my people in Haiti and PV. Were only a small group here in Mexico but we are growing."

"Jesus, really," Jonathan gasped, "you're the Queen? Cheers Tula!" they toasted the moment.

"Right honey—I'm the big one now—the big Maman of them all. My old teacher from Haiti, Sonja, spread the word across Mexico I was touched by the Loas. She always blessed me and watched over me since I was in Haiti when she first saw the angels, like you see them. I guess I have always loved you for that. You two are the only ones that call them angels and the strange thing is you have never met Sonja." She removed her sunglasses. Her skin colour bought out the white and black marble in her eyes. An I-can-kill-you look flashed at Jonathan.

Tula was born in Canada of Haitian parents but returned to her place of ancestry for a few years and then to Mexico. Jonathan had watched her age and she looked beautiful—older but beautiful. As a surprise to him, she had developed a tuft of gray hair above her forehead and a peppering around her ears. Her African slave and Spanish pirate ancestry shone from her—bronzed and beautiful. She is a proud and powerful woman, comfortable in her sexuality, making all the right moves with men. Her sensuality sucks them into her being. Once there, inside, they fall in love and she numbs them like a female spider numbs her lover. Their souls become part of her and she discards the husk. She had been frightening to him over the years and he loved her too much, leaving himself vulnerable to her every whim and her impossible expectations. Their relationship was off and on and in between sojourns, each found different partners but the relationships always ended unhappily—some disastrously. For them there are too many ghosts and dusty stuff to deal with.

They talked for an hour about adventures and Jonathan's disasters, which were many and bought on much laughter. Both looked warmly at each other and her eyes flashed over his body as though she was remembering moments of their past. He watched her eyes and where they went. Did I look all right? He thought Christ she's at it again; that look and control is still there. She cannot help using that—come here—body language. She is so sensuous, he thought and so much the woman that he wanted and so did most men that met her.

"What's your next disaster Jonathan?"

"Now that I have seen you again my imagination has been moved, so I guess the next disaster will include you. I do want to see you again."

"Wow, and we have just run into each other," she said leaning back in her chair to take in more of him, "that would be cool to be included in some of your madness as long as I don't get harmed and you pay the bills," she giggled.

"I will think about it more and put it in my head file," he said finishing his last gulp of rum and coke."

"So what's the job here that you're on?"

"I'm on a field trip. I'm doing some paintings for an airline company. They will hang my work in their corporate offices and place my graphics in their tourist information brochures. It's all a write-off for them. I'll paint them all bright and beautiful, like you."

"Thank you babe," she stroked his arm, "you can be so damn charming. Here comes the waiter. Do you want another drink?"

"Of course," he answered.

"Uno más, gracias," Tula ordered.

"How come you are allowed to travel, I thought criminals weren't allowed passports?"

"Artist, Tula, I'm an artist.

"Yeah, yeah, whatever you say."

"The Canadian Pardon Agency gave me a pardon which let me retrieve my passport. I applied for it as soon as I was sentenced and sent to jail."

"Jesus, you do get yourself in and out of interesting situations. Hey, maybe I can help and hang with you for a while. I should anyway to keep an eye on my peoples' heritage."

Oh Christ, he thought it's happening again: "Sure—what the hell—why not? By the way do you still write poetry?"

"You bet, every day I try to write something," and she reached into her purse and came out with a sheet of paper, "I do mostly Haiku now which are short and keep my attention," and she handed him the sheet:

Sayulita dust
A native ran from her home
Terror in her eyes

"That says much about you—another one of your tragedies?"

"Yes, but it's not a tragedy, I look at them as experiences," she said very seriously defending herself, "I will tell you about it sometime. Will you walk me home?" she said softly and with that sensuality that destroyed him in the past. An angel peeked at him out of the corner of her dark eyes and said: "I'm around the corner and a few blocks up."

"Of course—finished your drink?"

"Yeah," she said and she gulped it down.

"Right, let's go," they rose from the table and Jonathan paid the bill. As they walked they didn't say much, just savored their chance reunion. She helped carry some of his equipment; she put her arm around his and they walked up the street passed the cathedral and across Insurgentes Bridge into Old Town.

Near the neighborhood church was home, an old brick Spanish castle like edifice, beautiful and charming in its old age. He was surprised; the voodoo business must be good he thought. A round three story brick and white plaster tower behind a high black wrought iron fence dominated the villa. Large wood beams and posts held up a terra cotta roof and stained glass windows let in the light and kept her privacy in. Baroque swirls of iron curled across windows. Bougainvillea bushes grew up the walls and cascaded over the high iron fence and onto the boulevard trees in a fall of green leaves and bright red flowers. The yard was bricked with tropical ferns in large ceramic pots on each side of a heavy wood and steel front door.

They stopped at the wrought iron gate and she turned and hugged him. She held him tight as though they were long lost friends—which they were. "It's so good to see you again and to know you're safe. I missed you and cried when you died. You had a beautiful funeral you know. Will you call me? I'm in the book of the dead, it's the same number," she sounded sincere and Jonathan's mind fell into the cobbled street.

"I will, I don't need the phone book, I still have your number in my head. It won't leave," without saying another word she turned and unlocked the wrought iron door. He watched her walk across the brickyard and an angel flew out of her long, black curls and blew him a kiss.

He called her at work shortly after their reunion and she agreed to meet him for a drink. He knew of a cozy bar where they could have an intimate conversation and they could get drunk if they wanted. He picked her up at the wrought iron gate and in Silver Bullet and they drove out of town past the airport to Bucerias on the north shore of Bahia de Banderas. Tula looked particularly nice in her white cotton dress that hung off her breasts leaving her bronze shoulders bare, her hair billowed out and down her back and shoulders. Her long, black curls blew over her face as they rumbled along, so she held her hair back, her bare arms raised over her head. She could be her ancestral pirate on the bridge of her brigantine, full of fire, barking orders to her all male crew. A look of remembrance of happy times with Jonathan was written on her big smile and her flashing eyes.

The doors were off the Jeep and she giggled and cursed him for still having the truck and not having the doors on to protect her: "Jesus it's rough! When are you going to get rid of this thing and buy a real car like everyone else," she laughed, "I read that the Jeep was destroyed when you were on the run." she shouted over the roar of the engine and whining of the tires on the concrete blocks of the road.

"Yes, I burned and sank her in a river in Southern Alberta. My son bought her from the RCMP after they were finished with her. When I was in jail he had her restored by a friend of mine who builds hot rods for old guys who can now afford them. It was rebuilt at my expense, of course, and I'm not like everyone else. You know that," he shouted above the noise.

"I know and you wouldn't be you if Bullet were gone," they pulled off the highway onto the lateral road at Bucerias and slowed down to a rumbling roar, "I guess. You are different," she said and they parked a couple of blocks from the bar. They found a couple of stools after weaving their way through nooks and crannies of plaster, metal, glass and wicker. The jukebox played an old tune and couples were dancing. They were mostly tourists in a drunken euphoria of their annual short vacations. Men clung to the butts of their wives in desperation, rekindling a lost past and passion.

She lifted herself onto a high stool at the bar and sat erect looking with a naughty expression at Jonathan. It was their real first date in years although she would deny it. It wasn't a date for her; that would say too much about their relationship. He could feel her warmth and the smell of her from where he sat—within an inch.

"Buenos noches," the bartender said."

"Buenos noches," Tula replied, "dos cervezas por favor."

She turned and looked intensely at him, "I have something to say honey."

"Ah—is it something serious?"

"Maybe, I've just come out of a relationship with a man I was in love with and I'm still grieving so I'm hesitant to do anything with you except become friends," she said in a sad tone as she pulled a Cuban cigar from her purse and attempted to light it. Jonathan reached over and took the matchbox out of her hand and lit the cigar for her. The bartender arrived with the beer. "Gracias," she said.

"God, are you still smoking this shit?"

"Fuck you, Jonathan. Now listen, I gotta' say something to you. I'm on medication for depression. I'm not a well person anymore. Not like when you knew me years ago. My doctor told me it's not my fault."

"Oh really?" and his eyes opened wide, "when did this come about? I hadn't noticed anything unusual."

She took a deep breath and he knew she had some explaining to do to someone who cared about her, "I've been off and on pills. In the last three years. It's been hell; my life has always been hell for me. Relationships fizzle away to nothing. I end up quitting everything. I think I should warn you of that."

"I've always known that. I've never been stupid."

"It's time I tell you about my past, things that you don't know about me."

"Ah shit, honey. Do you really want to tell me?"

"Yes, I must! Hear me out—please."

"Go ahead then."

"My last relationship was with an abusive man full of Mexican machismo. I loved him and found out I was his mistress. You know how the Mexican men and woman can be? All women are married and all men are single."

"Yeah, I know."

"He drove what was left of my self esteem into the ground—into a fucking pit," anger and angels swept across her face, "I lost weight and I shook like a leaf in the wind all the time. It was terrible I even contemplated suicide. At one point I almost threw myself off the pier into the sea. My therapist, bless her, saved me from carrying it out."

"Was it that bad? You wouldn't have drowned you know. You are a good swimmer and—"

"I'm serious here, Jonathan!"

"Sorry, what did you do?"

"I killed him."

"Sure," He nervously giggled and repeated, "and what did you do?"

"Killed him and returned to my life," she calmly replied, "my mother drives me crazy too. I can never do anything right with her; she is one of those irritating perfectionists. Nothing is good enough and when something is good, it's—but this—but that. Whatever I did wasn't good enough. Jesus that was hard on me. BUT is the worst word in the universe. The woman calls me from Canada every day and always our conversation ends with some guilt trip. She once—"

"Did you kill her too?"

"No. The bitch is still with us. I wouldn't kill her; after all she is my mother."

"That makes me feel more comfortable. So you get into situations where you never win, where things never or can't complete themselves? Sure can be a shitty place to be—burnout, a place where there are no rewards for your efforts. You didn't actually kill this guy did you?"

"Yeah, I killed him and yes that's it, burnout."

"I guess I have been lucky all these years making things with paint, photos and sculpture. What about your voodoo doll business? Why are you telling me all this personal stuff and the kill shit and all?"

"The doll business will fail I know it. I can't tell you everything but I'm more than what you see. Years ago the only time you ever noticed me was in the gym and then I sensed it was only a sexual attraction. You didn't really see me."

"I'm sorry. You going to' kill me to?"

"No. I understand if no one looked at me, that *would* be a problem," she giggled, "treat me bad and I will kill you."

"I enjoy beauty—I'm an artist, free and single. It's what I do, it's my job to look at beautiful people and things in the world," they both laughed. Tula was his muse and nemesis. Now that is a good and a bad thing at the same time—an inspiration to create but an emotional burden. A paradox if you will. He was always the kid in the candy store with her—she looked and tasted so wonderful to him.

"So, I just want to be friends, okay?"

"Hmm. Being friends is okay, we can take our time at this," he responded but a wave of jealousy shot through him when he heard the word, love, directed to someone else when he for so many years was in love with her. Life can be cruel—people can be cruel he thought. She always bought a lecture out of him and he said, "We split apart about half a dozen times and I know what happens with you. Long-term relationships are not for you and perhaps never will be. You tend to focus on the negative—little things get blown out of proportion and you neglect to focus on all the good in your men—"

"I—"

Tula made a move to say something but Jonathan gently raised the palm of his hand and stopped her and continued with his lecture, "Making this date tonight is very risky for me since you will eventually blast me for my relationships with my women friends and my past. I will probably end up pining for you as you move on to the next guy and the next. Sad thing is you never trusted me and believed I was unfaithful which I never was," he wanted to stop lecturing but he couldn't stop, "one thing that I have learned on my journey is you never can change a person's belief system. Once a person believes in something: religion, cult, behavior, love and such; it is very difficult to deprogram them. We men are doomed having a relationship with you because of your beliefs. Your love for this past lover will soon pass like it did with all the others and me. You're a heartbreaker, baby."

"I know that, God damn it and I don't need a lecture. Life at our age can be difficult, I know. I've become such a damn perfectionist." He could detect a brief shock wave of anger come from her as she heard and recognized the truth, "Did you ever cheat on me?" she said calming down and blowing a smoke ring past his head.

"No honey, as I told you many times, never, you probable don't believe that and I can't do anything about it. Hey that's a nice smell coming from that cigar."

"It's expensive. Yeah, I don't believe you because you don't respect me."

"Damn it Tula! There are three things you have difficulty with: respect, trust and abandonment. You bring them up every time we get together. Respect, you overuse that word. Only crazies and comedians use it. It's all about you, if you don't get your way, if you are not the center of attention, you believe people don't have respect for you. Well we don't kiss your ass. Abandonment, no, nobody has abandoned you, you abandoned them, always moving on to new jobs, cities, and boyfriends; besides people come and go in our lives, their not abandoning each other. Trust is about your paranoia and low self esteem, you have difficulty trusting anyone. Then that is something you have to live and wrestle with. You have never trusted your boyfriends or me. I have never cheated on any girl friend in the last twenty years. Don't ask about before that, as life was very different and I was immature."

"And now you're crazy! Christ and another lecture." They both laughed and broke the icy moment between them.

"Yeah, I guess I am when it comes to you but I sure have fun. Do you think you're crazy Tula?"

"Perhaps, maybe that is why I have been alone all these years; searching for something. I'm tired of men but I still need them once in a while, for sex that is," she repeated her statement out of self defense, "I have thought about us and I am frightened, so I want to be just friends. Is that okay with you?"

"Sure," he said looking her lovely aging bronze body over and imagined what they had for each other long ago, "but I can't promise I won't try to win your heart again."

"All right I know you're a man and who you are. Let's change the subject," she smiled, "will you teach me to paint again? I've always wanted to learn more. Can we please try again; it was always incomplete what we did."

"We can do that and it can be at your convenience since I have all the time in the world for you. I'm going to do a painting where I'm staying, a big one and not for the contract—for me. You can work along side me. It will be fun. I still paint naked you know."

"Oh yeah, that's right and I remember were the paint splattered. You were so funny."

They drank more beer in the dim amber light of the bar; the angels danced across them both, their little night-lights shone from their wings like fireflies. They both were becoming drunk. He noticed a warm smell come from her—a sweet smell of sweat pulled from her by the heat of the moment and the hot night in Bucerias. It was so familiar and she surprised him, fore she thought the same. She placed her face on his shoulder and said how Jonathan smelled like Jonathan. Memories washed over them. They discussed all kinds of things like their children and relationships—hers and his. Sometimes she reached out and touched his hair and he wondered whether she was doing it or the angels. He felt enormous affection from her—she was master of her body language and sensuality.

It was all too soon for them to leave but Tula would be working early the next morning. They left into the night in Silver Bullet guided by the moon and Quetzalcoatl. They drove south, home to Old Town and he left her at her wrought iron gate. "I will call you." He hugged and kissed her. He wanted so much to sleep with her and he wondered if it would ever happen again for them. He watched her walk to her door and there was that naughty little angel again blowing him a kiss.

Destroy After Reading

He saw her two sides
The light of a thousand fires
The dark of black ashes

Tula was tired and happy after her time with Jonathan; she pulled herself up the spiral staircase. Following her to her bedroom were gothic shadows from the lights of a wrought iron chandelier that hung in the tower. Carlota, her maid, had pulled back the crisp white sheets of her bed. On a dresser by a window that overlooked the neighborhood her computer was on and flickered geometric shapes. She touched the mouse and a message sprang to life telling her she had email.

To: Tula

Good morning Tula. Please read carefully.

It is time for you to begin your work for me as an international assassin.

This is not a joke and your life depends on you reading further. Do not be surprised, the training you received in the Canadian Armed Forces has made you a prime candidate for international work; work that will make you a very good living. I have contracts with political and wealthy clients that conduct business with major international corporations and governments. Many employees and executives of these agencies vacation or have residences where you live in the Mexican state of Jalisco and the adjoining state of Nayarit. Some of these people come into conflict with strategic and operation functions of my clients and at times I must fulfill my contractual obligations by removing the conflicts.

Keep reading your life depends on it.

You are to be my operative in your part of Mexico. You have no say in this—no choice to reject my orders. Over the years you will make a great deal of money and my people will protect you. The organization has operatives in many locations around the world; each operates independently and alone. Most importantly they do not know each other and like you will not, and cannot know me; they do what they are told. To falter in their work or noncompliance means death. Again, you have no choice but to obey the orders you will receive from me. You will start your new job soon and don't be afraid; you are competent to carry out the tasks you will perform. Your dossier is formidable; you have the skill and mental strength to carry out your assignments.

And now your compensation: a retainer of fifty thousand American dollars has been deposited and every eight months another fifty thousand in a Swiss bank account. You will carry out the instructions in a timely manner and you will be paid handsomely over and above your retainer.

Your contact is the bank manager, Bank of West India, Zurich, Switzerland. You are to fly there as soon as possible to meet your contact and set up your accounts that are deposited under the guise of interest from a family trust fund. The deposits are pin money for you to live a good life in Mexico and in a style I expect my people to live. I suggest you keep your work at the bank; it makes a fine cover. My clients have investments in your bank and arrangements have been made for you to take extra time off when required. Your supervisor does not know the nature of your business and will not ask questions and neither will you.

Your assignments will come to you via email; an account is set up in your name:

Web email engine: Falstaff

User ID: Wiloh05

Password: Duglus

Your instructions will be a draft letter addressed to no one. Destroy after reading.

You need to take a deep breath now. This offer is nonnegotiable. You will carry out your assignment or forfeit your life. There is nowhere in the world you can run or hide.

It may be some time but I will be in touch. Welcome aboard.

Destroy this email, format your hard drive and reinstall your programs immediately.

To: CRSF

Attachment:

Charlie, I'm in trouble and this time it's big. I have received an email from someone who demands that I work for him or her as a killing machine. I thought it a hoax and then I checked on an account in my name in Switzerland and discovered it was no hoax – money, fifty thousand in my name awaits my arrival and signature to activate it.

I cannot see or touch this person and don't know where this person and organization is. They know all about me. As far as I know the person next to me in the coffee shop may be an agent. I feel helpless, there is nothing to grab onto. You taught me who the enemy is but this is different – I'm blind.

I retyped the original message before I destroyed it and reformatted my hard drive as instructed. Everything is attached. Please forward advice.

Tula

To: Tula

Before I retired I was briefed in Ottawa about the possibility that an organization that you are up against exists and that our highly skilled military people, like yourself, could be held hostage. It was a dreaded scenario at the time and now here it is.

Soldier, you have a tough decision to make, it is a do-or-die state of affairs for you. You can do exactly what this organization wants and survive or take your chances and disobey the orders and be killed. You have combat training that was the best we could give you so I know you can carry out any mission you are ordered to do and protect yourself. We must assume in the short term that this organization means business. If you go to the Mexican police they will not respond. They do not have the resources and you will be exposing yourself as a risk and get deported. If you decide to leave Mexico you will be followed, you cannot hide. If you commit a crime and come up before the courts in Mexico we will not be able to help you. There are so many ifs. It is your decision which way to go.

I still have friends in Ottawa, London, Berlin and Paris that I will talk to and perhaps get you into a protection program.

What is interesting is how they got your name, history and your location.

Go to Switzerland and keep in touch. Don't use your computer to talk to me, go to an Internet café.

Charlie.

First thing the next day at the bank Tula talked to her supervisor about taking a few days off to go out of town for personal reasons.

"Take all the time you need," said her supervisor, "I have received an order from the bank president to give you time off whenever you request it. I didn't know you had friends in high places."

"I don't!" Tula said.

She flew to Frankfurt, Germany that afternoon and was at her Swiss bank the following day. She was treated graciously and the manager had all the forms ready for her signature. The bank saw to it she had a five star hotel room for the night and arranged for a limousine to the airport the following day. It had been a whirlwind three days and she came out of it frightened, apprehensive, bewildered, rich and excited.

Your Death is My Pleasure

A hammer came down
Fire and gas and belching smoke
A life went its way

Draft

Good morning Tula

The client to be dispatched is Randall Harrison Comstock. Randall is a hit man who moves into companies and organizations tearing them apart, firing employees, ruining lives and reorganizing thousands of families. Randall has no remorse for what he does.

An example of his character: when he was a boy, he and his family, an upper New York State family, were on vacation at their Villa in Mexico City. He shot his maid in the face at point blank range with his father's pistol, for no reason but for, as he said, …the fun of it. An eyewitness confirmed this in the Mexican courts (some years later the witness was found murdered). With a payoff by his family to the local officials, he was found too young to be guilty of murder and was placed in his parents care. The family left Mexico City for America never to return. He has murdered others in his short thirty-one years but no one can prove it. He has bullied his way through life and the education institutions he has attended. A genius in mathematics, he graduated from Princeton with a Masters and applied his knowledge and vicious personality to the financial world.

What we know of his present location is that he is living in a gated community north of Puerto Vallarta near La Cruz Huanacaxtle.

Mr. Comstock is a dangerous man and may be difficult to dispatch. He may be armed and his movements are unpredictable. Be assured, you have greater powers and skills than your client.

On completion of your assignment please send me a draft of your accomplishments.

To: CRSF

Attached

I have just received my first order. What should I do Charlie?

Tula

To: Tula

You will have to make the decision yourself Tula. Whatever you choose, I will personally stand by you but our government won't help you if you commit murder in Mexico. You will be on your own. Our people here and in Europe are trying to track down the organization that is doing this to you. We think something will come to light soon in Germany. Good luck my friend.

Charlie

Randall was a tough character to keep track of. Tula had been working hard for the last two weeks chasing her victim and the hunt was running out of time. Soon she had to kill him before he left Mexico or she would loose her own life, she was getting frustrated and angry. Charlie was not moving fast enough on his research so she made the decision to follow through with the murder. She had no fear of her own death, inevitably that would come, the price of doing business in a dark world. The frustration and anger came from being unable to do ones job clean and quick with the full cooperation of ones victim. He was an elusive recluse operating out of a suitcase, Internet and telephone.

Day after day she waited patiently in her car eating pizza and beer outside of Randall's gated hotel. An uncomfortable way to do business but she had no choice, he came and went at all hours and was never anywhere private and alone. She did not challenge the security of the five-star establishment since it is a high security accommodation with alarm systems and private security police with dogs. He drove a rented black SUV when leaving the compound; several times she followed to end at cocktail parties in other inaccessible gated communities. There would be only one chance to get close enough to eliminate him and she made a weapon that could be operated in contact with her client. She carried it in her backpack at the ready. She checked and rechecked it several times a day since the weapon would have to operate only once and efficiently.

Her luck changed one evening when the SUV parked on the Malecón and Roger took to the street, joining the holidaying masses. The hunter pumped and ready for the kill, walked a few feet behind him up a narrow sidewalk. Her muscles were warm, supple and ready, feet and legs moved gracefully, her body weaved among the crowd, eyes focused on the back of the head of her victim. She transformed into the hunter she was trained to be and she suddenly felt a passion for what she was about to do. Her breathing became heavy, her breasts ached and she felt wet between her thighs. The angels hid in her hair, afraid to come out. She whispered, "Your death is my pleasure." The killer reached over her head and into her backpack.

Rick Thomas

Celebration for a Virgin

Blue, vermillion and gold
Barefoot, dark slave skin and halo
On her knees in prayer

A block up the street from the city square in Puerto Vallarta stands the cathedral to the Virgin Guadalupe, a towering edifice of red brick topped by a crown of wrought iron and patina green copper. The crown was adorned in red, green, and blue Christmas lights for the holidays. The cathedral's huge wooden doors were open to the devoted, gathered to pay homage to their patron saint and be blessed by the priest. They came from the city's neighborhoods and numerous villages of the valleys and foothills of the Sierra Madre. The priest in full regalia stood below the altar of blazing candles; his arms outstretched he looked down on his flock of thousands flowing across the nave, down the cathedral steps, across the cobbled street and into the city square. From all the neighborhoods they had come in parades led by beating drums and ferocious warriors of ancient ancestry. Characters of Mexico's vicious past led the groups of worshipers to the cathedral. The parades were a mix of pagan and Christian pageantry blurred into a religious fervor, a palette of colour, sound and passion. Thousands walked, danced and followed the warriors who were dressed in their finest, feathers, leathers and bells. The peasants and the wealthy displayed the Virgin on their chests, some carried baskets of offerings of fruit, vegetables, pastries and drink. They represented businesses, clubs, families, neighborhoods and schools. Hundreds carried candles in cups singing and rejoicing.

With each group that moved down the streets were flat deck trucks festooned with lights, paper cutouts and a young girl dressed in blue and gold; the traditional colours of the Virgin. A halo above her head glowed and kneeling in front of her, in prayer, was the poor peasant, Juan Diego, who introduced her to Mexico four hundred years ago.

The noise was deafening, the bells of the cathedral rang, drums, trumpets and cymbals crashed. Two blocks away on the Malecón thousands of tourists and families strolled beneath the palms strung with Christmas lights. Artisans from neighboring villages displayed their handicrafts of sewing, ceramics, jewelry and paintings. Bands played and above all the chaos was the roar of traffic. It was time for a party in Mexico just as big as the one last week and the one the week before.

Gently the metal barrel of the crude apparatus touched the hair and flesh at the base of the occipital bone where the skull links with the Atlas vertebra. Randall flinched as reacting to a fly or mosquito. His hand moved an inch from his side towards his head. The apparatus rammed a nail into the firing cap of a blank twenty-two long cartridge. Black gunpowder exploded into his head severing the Atlas from the skull and taking with it his spinal cord. The explosion moved into the occipital foramen, expanded and destroyed the Cerebellum. There was no need for a bullet; the expanding hot gasses were enough to kill him. His eyes bulged in realization that something drastic had happened; he did not feel any pain only emptiness. He had no time to cry out, swear or watch his past life, just bewilderment and the thought—not now—not here. Panic ran through his mind—my God a heart attack—a stroke. His communication with his body was instantly gone. His brain no longer felt a support system: heart, lungs, muscles, bones and bowels—nothing. All he felt and was a warm blackness; a hole was forming around him, an expanding black universe—he fell into it.

The killer grabbed him by the belt in the back and guided his collapsing body into a merchant's doorway, sat him down and pulled his legs up by his knees into a crouching position. Quickly she placed a straw hat she was wearing over her victim's head and pulled a half empty bottle of cheap liquor from her pack and placed it between his legs. Desperately he tried to raise his head to see his killer. Darkness and nothingness flooded his brain. "Some friends wish you a welcome rest," was quietly whispered into his ear and the last thing he saw was the worm at the bottom of the bottle.

No one in the dense crowd heard the muffled shot or noticed what had happened; fireworks and music were roaring down the Malecón and it would go on for most of the night. No one took notice of the sleeping drunk in the doorway.

Tula shivered with excitement at what she had done; this was the second murder of her life. She was surprised there was no remorse, just a feeling of power. She shook from the excitement and her clothes were soaked from sweat. She wasn't sure what this new-elated feeling was.

Carlota of Old Town

Blessed are the poor
Or so you say from your church
So little do you know

"Carlota my dear, ¿Como esta?" Tula said breathing heavily.

"Muy bien, Ms. Tula, you all right Ms, you look red and hot?"

"Si, Carlota, I'm fine. I've jogged from the Malecón and the festival. I see your wearing that new dress I gave you."

"Yes it's so pretty Ms. Tula. Thank you again."

"How is business tonight?"

"Slow, all the boys are at the festival, nobody around. Ms. Tula your hand is black. What happen?"

"Oh I tripped and fell down by the river while jogging. I lost my hat to," she moved her powder stained right hand behind her, "I'm sure your business will pick up soon; the parades are almost over."

"Mr. Owen is at your place. He is at the taco stand across the street from you're house. He is stuffing himself with shrimp."

"Good, I need that rascal. See you in the morning Carlota," She jogged down the cobbled street and into the dark.

"Adiós Ms. Tula," shouted Carlota and she assumed her position. Against a corner building she raised her right bare leg up against the white wall and leaned back. Hands felt the warm wall behind her and she thrust her breasts forward against her white blouse. Her black hair framed her dark face and fell down around her shoulders.

Carlota waited as she has waited for years on the corner of Francesco Modero and Insurgents for her clients. The streets were dark and empty in Old Town; a street light above her showed off who she was and why she was there. She could hear the drums of celebration and the peeling of the cathedral bells; they made her feel terribly alone. Her old mother was at home taking care of her two children. She would love to be with them on this night of celebration but if she and her family are to have a Christmas she must work tonight. Her children have no father, he ran off five years ago to another woman and he now has four children by her. He still lives in the neighborhood but does not give any support to his ex-wife and children; fore he doesn't acknowledge they exist. His education of grade three and his ignorance won't let him feel self esteem or respect for his family, just machismo, survival and greed. He is alcoholic now and pulling his hair out in frustration.

Tonight Carlota will work hard at her nighttime job. Her day job is house cleaning in the neighborhood and one of her clients is Tula. She will give herself to the local men who will be hyped up from the party and perhaps if she is lucky, a tourist client will pay extra. She also prays she will not be beaten.

The whorehouse where she and twenty others service their clients operates two blocks away behind a row of tropical plants that hides the entrance from the street and probing eyes. It's one large room with cots cordoned off by hanging blankets. A couple of old chesterfields are strewn around with a few low tables covered with beer bottles, cigarette packages and ashtrays. It is the home of an old gray fat man who lives in the back. He guards the entrance and surveys his property from a filthy yellow plastic chair out on the sidewalk where he sits and reads his paper and chats to regular customers about football, politics and the latest girls in his care. He sometimes negotiates a price but that is the girls' job, they know what to charge and it hasn't changed much over the years. There were high times before 9/11 but those times are gone and the old man will probably not live to see them come back. His legs are becoming gangrenous and mummified from some malady.

Carlota is one of his favorites as she treats her customers with care and doesn't steal from them or him. She often buys her customers beer from the bar across the street and sits and listens to their troubles about their wives, children, work and bosses. Sometimes the fat old man charges her cheap rent for her booth and cot but she is still chattel to him.

She demands her customers use condoms and she gets her medical check up regularly when the fat man's doctor brother comes to the whorehouse. Life is hard for Carlota but she has no choice. The alternative would be to run away like her husband and she probably would if it weren't for her children and old mother. Her days are long with cleaning and servicing the neighborhood.

Tula arrived home and shouted to Jonathan at the taco stand across the street, "Come in when you're finished eating old man." He waved, gave her the finger and nodded his head. He could not say anything as there were fat shrimp sticking out of his mouth. Tula ran in, up the stairs and got into the tub. She ran the water hot to wash the death and sweat from her body. She was relaxed and content with the night's work and excited that Jonathan was around.

Soon Jonathan came into the bathroom, leaned over and gave Tula a kiss and sat on the toilet, "My God woman, you are beautiful," he said as he looked over her body.

"Thanks, and what did you do tonight?"

"I hung out at a bar near the cathedral and watched the parades and felt a little lonely so I came over to see you. Carlota told me you were out jogging so I decided to have supper at the taco stand and wait for you. What have you been up to?"

She didn't answer, "I'm glad you waited. Take your clothes off and come on in." He obeyed.

Together in the tub they washed each other and Jonathan said, "When I first met Carlota I didn't know what her other business was, why did she become a prostitute and why is the whorehouse allowed?"

"Don't be naive. If the young don't leave this neighborhood when they have the chance, the chains of life hold them here forever. A few manage to go on to higher learning and some inherit local businesses but for most it is a life of toil and forever seeking ways to survive. Most of the people in the neighborhood are of a family that has lived here for generations. A few like Carlota fall out of the family and don't get support. They must make it on their own," Tula's eyes glowed, "just like me, I have to make it on my own. I'm not Mexican and have no relatives here. I'm on the outside to."

"But you live very well."

"Let me get between your legs and you can scrub my back." He obeyed. "I'm educated, not like the rest of the neighborhood. Most living here have little education and if they do its grade six, nine at the most. As for Carlota and the whorehouse they are part of Old Town like the hotels, bars, stores, markets and laundries. Here's a brush, scrub a little harder."

"But these people are whores and corrupt. Some are little girls who should be in school. They should not be doing what they do. Don't you think?"

"I don't judge the lives of others in their country; it's none of my business. If Carlota wants to clean house for me and screw the neighborhood for money that's her business," she shrugged her shoulders, "that's Mexico. We may be revolted by how they work and treat life but we should not voice our opinions. Indigenous life is snuggled here in the valley and up on the hill is the rich in their million dollar mansions, a stone's throw away, never the less, a million miles away. Little has changed over the years in this part of PV and what is here is repeated all over the world. That will never change—up on the hill life will change. Do you understand Jonathan?"

"Yeah, I guess. Time for you to scrub me," and she obeyed and they changed positions.

"I help Carlota—her family will not go hungry. Do you want me to tell you what happened to her last Christmas?"

"Yeah, do. Lie back on me." He lay back between her legs and she held him to her.

"For Christmas Carlota wanted to see that her children and mother would have a happy holiday, and with all the trimmings. Many families in the neighborhood will not celebrate Christmas; it's too expensive; they will treat it like another day. Not Carlota's little family, she wanted piñatas for the children and friends over for a good time. She worked long hours and into the night for several weeks putting money away in a ceramic jar on a shelf in her little kitchen. I gave her extra for her work around here. She counted her savings everyday and was excited about the coming holiday. She talked to me of nothing else. Saving for the future is not a common thing to do in Mexico—if you have a hundred pesos in your pocket today, spend it today. Tomorrow will take care of itself.

"The tourist season started, the hotels filled up, in the Zone and Nuevo Vallarta. The year was particularly good since storms had hit the Mexican Riviera resorts of Cozumel and Cañcun on the east coast, diverting tourist dollars to the west coast. Money was rolling in for the whorehouse. George, Alfonso, Chico, Poncho and Emilio; Carlota's regular customers—"

"I recognize some of the names from the bar. Careful with your nails honey, you're a strong woman," Jonathan said.

"Yeah, those are the boys. Anyway, they were making money and were generous with their tips. They were also making extra cash for their families, which eased the pressure on their lives. The old fat bastard was happy also, buying candy and giving a few pesos to the local kids. It looked like a good tourist season for us in the village.

"One night, it poured down rain so hard the streets turned into rivers. They didn't see the police come after midnight when the whorehouse was in full swing. Three white trucks flashing red and blue lights, followed by a bus, descended on the whorehouse. They were loaded with police in riot gear who shouted and cursed. Usually when the law busts the place the police are gentle and sympathetic but not that night. I guess they were all pissed because they were ordered out in the rain."

"Some of the boys at the bar told me about the raid and how upset they were."

"The officers rushed the unlocked dirty blue door, smashed it and everything in their way: cots, walls, doors and people. They knocked the corrugated steel off the roof so everything got soaking wet. Bloody and hurt from the swinging rifle butts and stomping jackboots, Carlota was dragged off; her body was scraped against the cement sidewalk, dragged through the water and mud and thrown into the bus. They treated her like a piece of meat. Ten of the twenty girls and the old fat man were taken away to the holding jail in Ixtapa to spend the night and appear in court the next day. The customers caught in the raid gave up their money and were sent naked into the rain clutching their clothes. Lucky for them one of the officer's brothers-in-law was a customer or everyone would be in jail. Put your head under and wet your hair. I'll shampoo it," he obeyed and came up sputtering.

"The young brother of the old fat man, the local doctor, was alerted. He rushed to the police station with his medical kit to treat the poor whorehouse crew. Others arrived with hot coffee and clean dry clothes. Early the following day Carlota's mother arrived with the money from the little ceramic jar; it took the entire savings to pay off the law. Okay, dunk your head under to rinse the soap out." He obeyed.

He raised his head out of the water and she rubbed in hair conditioner. "Why did the cops do the raid?" he sputtered.

"Control—intimidation or the old fat bastard had not paid his dues. Maybe a disgruntled customer demanded a raid. No one really knows in the end why things happen the way they do in Mexico."

"When did you hear about the raid?"

"Put your head under again and I'll rinse out the conditioner." he dunked his head, she rubbed the suds out, and he raised his head, "Not until late the next day. I would have been there in a flash to help the poor girls out if I had known."

"So what happened next?"

"After the fines, deals and payoffs were made, everyone returned to the whorehouse and their homes in the village. Some of the local customers and I discreetly helped the old man and his girls put the place back together. Within forty-eight hours they were back in business. We pooled pesos and sent beer and goodies to celebrate the opening."

"Were the girls hurt badly?"

"No, the few bruises on the girls and the old fat man soon healed and the pain was forgotten. The law pulled in its fangs."

"And Carlota's Christmas?"

"Yes, she had a Christmas party. Lots of relatives and friends arrived with gifts." They got out of the tub and toweled each other.

"So everything turned out all right then?"

"For a moment in her hard life, yes. For some in paradise, Christmas can be heartache. Now off to bed, Jonathan, it has been a long time for you and me." He obeyed.

Deep into the night Jonathan was twitching and snoring; Tula quietly got up and sat at her computer. She typed an email to the death squad:

Draft

Randall Harrison Comstock has been dispatched.

Finished, she opened a draw in her computer desk and took out a box of Cuban cigars and matches. She pulled a cigar from the box and drew it past her nostrils; she breathed in the sweet smell. She licked its length and with shears from the draw she snipped the end and rolled the stiff cigar in her mouth. She lit it and puffed clouds of smoke. The moon and Quetzalcoatl shone through the window and danced in the swirling blue gray smoke. She watched Jonathan peacefully asleep in her bed. She hoped she would not have to kill him.

The morning came to the Bahia da Banderas from the southeast over the Sierra Madre. Carlota and her family were asleep. Tula stirred and snuggled up to Jonathan. White uniformed street cleaners were out cleaning the Malecón of cups, bottles, and trash from the parade the night before.

A man sat in a store doorway; his head slumped forward and to the side, at rest against a door jam. His pants were wet from his urine and a bottle of liquor rested between his legs. A cleaner walked over to him, shouted to wake him up—the man did not move. The cleaner pulled on the man's shoulder; he fell forward onto the sidewalk taking the bottle with him. It rolled into the cobbled street, smashed and let loose its dead worm. Blood soaked the back of the man's shirt and at the base of his skull a three-centimeter powder blackened hole exposed itself to the morning light. The cleaner jumped back and screamed for his friends.

Christmas in Buenas Aires

Jolly round red rosy
Black booted balding and fat
He's big as the town

The little troop gathered at the foot of Francesco Madero and loaded bundles and bags of Christmas presents into cars and Tula's big red SUV, "Get in Jonathan my love; this is going to be a fun day," she said excitedly.

"I'm with you," and he climbed in beside her and two elves got in the back. Santa's caravan rattled and banged its way west to the Rio Cuale bridge, drove over it, through the river park, crossed under the highway, over a rise and down into Buenas Aires. Mountains and green jungle rose around them, horses were tethered to trees on the river bank and women and children washed clothes on the river rocks. Chickens, dogs and dust scattered and billowed in front of the cars as they drove deep into the village. The road became rougher and dustier as they neared their destination.

"The eyes of the jungle are on us," Tula said, "look at the black turkey vultures above the tree tops."

"Their down from Canada for the winter to keep the jungle clean," Jonathan said.

The troop stopped at a white plaster villa with red brick trim. Graceful wrought iron covered the windows and doors. Potted tropical plants and flowers were everywhere; a bougainvillea tree climbed up the side of the villa.

"Wow!" said Tula, "who owns this place?"

"This was once the restaurant of a gay couple who have opened a new club in town. Now they just live at the villa," said one of the elves from the back seat.

In front of the villa among palm trees on a concrete patio were sofas, chairs and tables the couple had assembled for the boss—Mrs. Claus. Everyone pilled out of their vehicles: Santa Claus, Mrs. Claus, her six elves, Jonathan and Tula. Mr. and Mrs. Claus and her elves were in full Christmas regalia. The gay couple fluttered out of the villa sipping champagne in oversized wine glasses. Fabric antlers adorned their heads and their makeup was outrages—red rouge, heavy mascara and bright red lipstick. One had a red nose. On their heads they wore fabric antlers and they had a few extras for anyone who was out of uniform. The troop became a walking talking cartoon.

Mrs. Claus immediately took charge and ordered everyone to do some duty or other. Mumbling and giggling the men did what they were told. Jonathan and Tula were assigned to organize the masses of kids. All was arranged, the toys laid out beside the sofas, the tables decked out with cookies and glasses of orange juice, a body was ordered to take count and an elf was assigned to ink stamp little hands to identify those who had received gifts. They found out, when it was too late, the ink was soluble. The children would lick the stamp off and return for another gift. One little urchin would lick her stamp off, change her clothes and redo her hairstyle. Tula caught her and gave her another cookie and drink for her effort but no present.

Word quickly spread across the village that Santa was in town and the children started coming. They came by the hundreds from their adobe homes along the river and from stairs down from the jungle. Many came in the arms of their mothers; older brothers and sisters dragged the young along; very few came with their fathers. Tula set to work organizing the lines of kids into boy, girl, toddler line and older kids line. That plan soon fell apart and Jonathan just fed them one by one to Mr. and Mrs. Claus who gave them the appropriate presents. The elves handled the gifts for Mrs. Claus and the helpers gave the children cookies and juice. Some children burst into tears from fright and would probably forever be afraid of clowns. Others their eyes bugged out huge brown and beautiful in awe at the sight of the toys. It was all a wonderful sight and Jonathan's cynicism dissolved.

"This is pretty amazing," he said to Tula and he snapped some pictures of a tiny girl getting her present from Santa.

"Yes, I love these people," She kissed and hugged Jonathan.

One pictures a sleepy Mexican village in the jungle--on the contrary, it was bedlam. Across the cobbled road up against the river was a chain link fenced area. A green and white farm truck arrived with huge black speakers, which were unloaded and set up in a portable tent. White plastic tables and chairs were arranged and a portable bar was put together. The local beer company truck arrived and unloaded dozens of cases of beer with promotional banners to string up around the place and make it look festive. Young people arrived dressed in white tight clothing; they pranced like peacocks ready to drink and dance. Music blasted across the village and up the valley. Nearby howls came out of a store where some boys watched a football game on four television sets—the volume at the max. A dusty beige burro tethered to a primavera tree bellowed its dissatisfaction; cowboys galloped down the road making thunder from steel shoes on cobbles. Manic hot rod buses without mufflers roared by, trucks of families laughed and sang, children shouted to each other to be heard above the din and so did the little Santa troop. And over it all the hot sun cooked Mr. and Mrs. Claus in their bright red Christmas suits.

"Hey Jonathan." Tula whispered, "Look what's coming down the street." A girl, no more than sixteen years old dressed in white walked towards the little troop, her tiny two-year old baby rested on her hip.

"My God," Jonathan whispered.

She and her babe were a startling sight. Their faces were brown round and flawless with huge brown eyes that looked in awe at the white folk from the north. Dress in a white dress, she and her baby were not used to these white folk in her garden—in her Eden. Their hair was the blackest that black could be. On mother it was pulled back tight and flowed down her back ponytail style with tiny white satin bows like snow attached randomly. Her baby's hair was held back from her face by a piece of fabric the same material as her yellow and white flowered dress. A white hibiscus flower was tucked into it and the shining black mass flowed down around her shoulders. Both mother and child were barefoot and the dust of the road had gently powdered mother's feet. For Tula and Jonathan the noise, people and jungle around them disappeared.

"Something tells me she has walked along way," Tula said and she moved her to the head of the line. No one protested; they made way for the mother and child.

"I'll take her straight to Mrs. Claus," Jonathan said. He reached his arms out and gently guided them forward. Mrs. Claus looked astonished at the sight of the two. Both baby and Mrs. Claus reached out for each other, one with little stubby brown hands the other with long white fingers, thin with age and strong in faith. Tula and Jonathan had to look away. For Mrs. Claus this innocence, this child was what Christmas was all about. The giving of the gift of love to the beautiful people of Mexico and if by chance this child carries with her this gift for the rest of her life then Mr. and Mrs. Claus's life long task was worth it.

"What went wrong?" Jonathan whispered.

"What do you mean?" Tula said holding him close.

"You and I, we are complicated misfits out in the world searching for peace, happiness, love and all those other clichés. Spoiled rotten by what we have, never satisfied, and always wanting and expecting more."

"I know but that's our life, that's what we are all about. We were bought up spoiled and we can't change it, we can't change the way we are," Tula said and she looked away up into the deep green jungle on the side of the mountains. Vultures circled in the thermals above the palms and a few cotton ball clouds hung dead still in a brilliant blue sky. She thought about the sins and the horrific crimes she had committed—committed so she could survive. Life's circumstances that she had no power over had bought her to this place. She could not see any hope for herself now; it would not be long and she will have to face punishment and die in a Mexican prison alone and afraid. With luck she would be killed during her capture. Her innocence was gone; it left many years ago on the grasslands and in the forests of British Columbia. If only she could return to the animals that she loved: the deer, rabbits, bobcats, quail and bears. She had to leave that garden of innocence, a garden that we all have experienced at one time in our lives, our own little Eden. She returned to that world once when she had her babies who used all her waking hours with feeding, scrubbing and loving. Back then nobody but her and her children existed; they were one until they grew up and left her.

Inevitably events dragged her from Eden into a violent world. Tears of loneliness filled her eyes.

The troop all felt the spirit of Christmas as they watched the young woman and her baby leave their company. They had bought to everyone perhaps the most treasured gift of all—innocence. The troop watched her walk back the way she came; her little girl clutched a stuffed camel. Her eyes never left Mrs. Claus—they disappeared around a curve and into the jungle.

"She had come along way," said one of the gay couple, "she has walked from her parent's farm several miles up the valley from Paso Ancho. This is the first year her little one has become aware of Santa Claus. Her mother probably remembers what it was like her first time. It was not long ago."

The children were stunning, all four hundred and seventy of them and Mrs. Claus had spent all year collecting toys and packaging them for this day. For years it has become her duty. Everyone today was beautiful in this Eden even if it was just for the day. The little urchins were beautiful that tried to get second gifts; beautiful was the bare-foot boy dressed in rags with a filthy face hiding behind a tree. He was terrified at the red suited giants that had come out of his mother's television set.

"Who are these two Tula?" Jonathan pointed to Santa and the Misses.

"Mr. and Mrs. Claus were in the church many years go. They met when doing missionary work in Africa. Disillusioned by church politics they left their calling for careers and families in the United States. Santa became a successful corporate executive in Chicago and she became a professor at a university in Arizona. Now they are in their seventies, their partners died years ago."

"Wow! So now they hang out in Mexico helping out."

"Yes and they have kept their faith all these years in their own special way. Each year they give their time and love to the children of this country." And Tula held on to Jonathan savoring the moment.

"I miss my kids."

"And I miss mine."

The sun had set over the Sierra Madre, darkness crept in, the children all had their gifts and gone home; someone had taken the poor burro away. The troop packed the remaining toys for another year and put the sofas back in the gay couple's villa. There were thanks all around and the troop left the little village to the roaring party and cowboys.

"Thanks honey," he hugged his lover and friend, "thanks for inviting me to experience this special day with such special people."

They drove into town, Tula parked in front of her home and they walked down Francesco Madero to La Playa de Los Muertos. The night air was warm and a feeling of goodwill was in their hearts. The full moon was high in the sky and the star Quetzalcoatl hung over Old Town. They lit the jungle on the sides of the valley in a deep blue.

"Funny, you know that star is usually below the moon but tonight it's over the valley," Jonathan said, "it's usually keeps the moon company."

It's the moon that has moved Jonathan, not the star."

"Yeah, I guess so." But he still wondered.

Music and laughter poured out of the bars, restaurants and hotels. The beach palms swayed in the gentle breeze. They took their sandals off their brown dusty feet and walked in the water now high on the beach. They thought silently to themselves of the day they had just experienced. They thought of the devoted missionaries and their good friends, the children of Old Town and the Madonna and her child's first Christmas.

He held her close to him and said, "I understand now that no one is poor and no one is rich. It's life above all else that matters, this is Mexico, it's Christmas and I love you."

Shopping can be Dangerous

Draft

Good morning Tula

There are two people to be dispatched:

Eva-Jane Cranston and husband Walter Franklin Cranston.

These clients will be easy for you; they are in their fifties and not physically fit. As you will see in your surveillance, they run predictable lives and are together most of the time.

The husband and wife team are New York investment brokers that specialize in investments in natural resource extraction; their portfolios represent billions of dollars. They hold people financially hostage and practice economic terrorism on corporations and their executives. Eva and Walter are in denial of their damaging practices and cannot be reasoned with.

You will have to dispatch both at the same time. Either one could do financial damage to corporations across the world if he or she escapes. They are loyal to themselves and not to each other, if either one is murdered or in an accident, the other would flee the area immediately.

They are registered at the Prince Oz Hotel, which has low security. Their room is easily accessible.

On completion of your assignment please send me a draft of your results.

Carlota hummed a child's song as she dusted the daily cobwebs from the chandelier in the tower. To her frustration a pesky little spider had been making it home for the last month. It was her last chore before finishing her cleaning. The front door opened and Tula walked in loaded down with packages. "Let me help with those things," Carlota said.

"No, that's fine," Tula, said, huffing and puffing. She went to the kitchen and placed her purchases in the pantry.

"I am finished with the house cleaning Ms. Tula," Carlota shouted from the hall. "Can I help you with anything else?"

"No, gracias Carlota, everything looks fine," she said as she quickly inspected the main floor, "you can leave now and go home to your family. Here is your wage for this week." She handed her a one hundred-peso note.

"Thank you Ms. Tula but you have already paid me, this is extra."

"I know but I'm in the mood and you do such an excellent job for me. How are the kids?"

"Very well, they are back in school again, such long holidays they give them. I never know when they are going to be called back." Carlota went to the kitchen and picked up her purse and sweater and came back to the tower and the front door, "adios, Ms. Tula."

"Adios Carlota," and Tula locked the front door behind her. She had been shopping all day at the farm suppliers and local hardware stores in Las Palmas. She successfully purchased all the ingredients she would need for her recipe. She unloaded the packages; an assortment of items that the normal household kitchens would not have. The day was hot and so was her kitchen. She went upstairs, got naked and returned to the kitchen. She put on her favorite apron that is covered in flowers of many colours and shapes. Humming and singing she organized everything on the counters and table to make a little item that Charlie showed her how to bake. She talked to herself:

"What are Walter and I having for dinner Tula?"

"Oh, a little something I cooked up that will blow your teeth out. The main course will just kill you."

She had to prepare the nitrate of soda that she purchased since it contained moisture. The one hundred percent dry stuff was not available. She placed the beads of soda in several baking dishes and baked them in the oven at two hundred degrees for fifteen minutes. When the baking was complete she ground the beads in her blender to powder. She placed the powder in a large bowl and put it aside.

She turned her attentions to a bag of briquettes and wrapped the chunks in an old towel; she pounded them to a powder using her meat-tenderizing hammer. She strained the dirty mass of charcoal through a baker's strainer and set aside the fine powder in a metal baking pan. She did the same with a brick of sulfur. In a large copper cauldron she mixed her ingredients in the following proportions:

6 parts sodium nitrate
2 parts powdered charcoal
1 part sulfur

She moistened the mix with water, stirred it until it stuck together and when she pinched it between her thumb and finger it took on the consistency of clay. Preheating the oven to two hundred degrees she placed the cauldron inside for thirty minutes that made the mixture absolutely dry. With her large granite spice mortar and pestle she ground the concoction until she had a slate-grey powder. At this point the powder could burn furiously—not explode, that would need the pressure of packaging.

"Ah, dinner is ready, now to set the table."

Among her purchases was a black four inch diameter steel drainage pipe coupler threaded at both ends; two feet in length with two end caps and sealant. At this stage she put on latex gloves and washed the pipe pieces thoroughly in the sink, and dried them off with a towel and hair dryer. She could not leave fingerprints inside or outside the pipe. She covered the threads on one end of the pipe with sealant and screwed on an end cap and tightened it by hand. The sealant dried rock hard in a few minutes.

With a wooden spoon she stirred her concoction and fed it into the pipe compressing each spoonful with a round wood dowel. Every few inches she pounded in a layer of newspaper, this created greater compression on the ingredients.

With an electric drill she drilled a hole, one-sixteenth in diameter in the other end cap. The drilling took thirty minutes with a carbon tip drill bit to get through the steel. She had to go slow; careful not to break the drill bit. She fed the wire of a number three blasting cap through the hole from the inside and taped the blasting cap to the inside of the pipe end cap. She attached the end cap; glued and sealed it and placed it aside to let the sealant dry.

"Dinner is almost ready my lovelies."

The next part was a mechanism to detonate the blasting cap. Keeping her gloves on, she took one of her empty cigar boxes, wiped it clean of fingerprints and taped a detonating plunger inside. She stole the detonator and blasting cap from a pyrotechnical company, one of the many up the Valle de Banderas that make fireworks for festivals. The handle to activate an electric charge was a simple eight-centimeter bar that needed just a half turn. Two terminals came out of the top of the unit that would be connected to the blasting cap when the time was right. Tula drilled two holes in the cigar box, one opposite each other. One would feed the electric charge from the unit to the blasting cap. The other would be access for a wire wrapped around the handle in such a way that when pulled the handle would turn generating electricity. The wire would be attached to an object that would move like a car door, hood or trunk. She attached the wiring except those running to the blasting caps. With utility tape she made the contents fast to the cigar box and taped the mechanism to the black pipe. She wrapped the pipe with several rolls of utility tape. She was finished and cleaned up and placed all remaining items in the garbage that would be picked up that night. The ugly black package with a red wire coming from one end sat on her kitchen table. It reminded her of Charlie.

"Oh, Charlie, you taught me well."

Pleased with herself, she sat on her kitchen stool and opened a bottle of red wine, lit a cigar, hummed a song from her childhood and wrote a Haiku:

For you a present
From a black knight of fury
Alas, I am Death

Eva was shopping all afternoon and was tired from carrying her bundles and boxes so she walked back to her car parked on 31 de Octubre. Reaching her rented black Mercedes Benz she laid her bundles down on the cobbled road and turned the key in the lock of the trunk but found it was unlocked. Raising the lid she looked inside and noticed something odd, a black round taped object with a red wire running from it to the trunk lid. She raised the lid up and leaned in for a better look and the wire attached to the object pulled out of it.

The bomb went off. So powerful was the blast it tore her upper body, head and arms apart and threw them in all directions, smashing into buildings and parked cars. The heat was so intense parts of her body were on fire. Her legs lay in a heap at the back of the car that became completely engulfed in flames. The burning gasoline from the car's tank engulfed the cars parked beside the bombed hulk, setting them on fire. No one else was hurt but the wreckage was substantial.

From her observation point two blocks from the blast she felt the shock wave; it flared her hair back from her head. "Fuck! Just a little too much spice in the soup. Where is that bastard husband anyway?"

Walter was not with her; he had stayed home on this particular shopping day—this was a set back. Quickly, the killer left the scene angry and full of rage. If word got back to the company that a mistake was made, she would be in big trouble. If Walter got away she would be dead within the next twenty-four hours. The mess must be made right and done now. Walter must be killed immediately before he finds out his wife has been murdered. He would leave Mexico and it would be months before he could be found and God knows what damage he could do.

The killer knew where to find him and within a few minutes was on the balcony of Walter's hotel room cutting through his neck with a picture wire garrote she quickly made from a picture hanging in the hall. This was a dangerous thing to do for many would see her come and go but time was of the essence and Walter could not be allowed to escape. The job completed Tula calmly left the hotel muttering, "You should have done it this way in the first place, stupid."

Draft

Eva-Jane Cranston and husband Walter Franklin Cranston have been dispatched.

48 Hours

The engine stalled, he tried the ignition—nothing—the battery was dead. What the hell to do now he thought. He got out and waved the traffic around him.

It was New Years Eve and in forty minutes Annabelle's plane was landing and with the traffic on the streets that would delay him he had just enough time to get to the airport. Cars were everywhere and no parking spaces were available. He spoke next to nothing of Spanish—what to do—what to do? Fortunately a white police pickup truck pulled up behind him and two dark Mexican officers with big smiles on their faces waved and shouted out the window, "Need help Gringo—dead battery?"

"Yeah, Si, dead battery," he said in a panic.

"We push you?"

"Si, por favor," They got out of the truck, Jonathan jumped into the Jeep, put it in second gear, foot on the clutch and when he got up to enough speed he let the clutch out. The engine kicked in and he was on his way. He waved a thank you out the window. He made it to the Pemex station on the highway to Mismaloya to fill up with gas but the damn car would not start again. The good guys at the station pushed the car to a parking space and he told them he had to be at the airport in half an hour to pick up his daughter; could he leave the car there for a couple of hours and would they install a new battery. They said that was fine with them and the car would be ready in an hour. One of the pump operators ordered a young boy helper to go out on the highway and hail a cab.

A black boat of a car drove up beside Jonathan, "Get in!" shouted the burly Mexican driver, "I hear you in trouble and need ride."

"Gracias Señor," he said and quickly opened the door and got into the front passenger seat beside the huge driver who took up half of the interior of the car—his breath, the rest. A cascade of black gray hair on a round brown head with an ear-to-ear smile filled with a keyboard of white ivories greeted Jonathan. His double unshaved chin rested on an acre of chest festooned with green and yellow parrots. Large black hairy chubby arms decorated with tattoos and gold bracelets ended in bear-paw hands decorated with diamond, silver and gold rings.

"Broken battery huh? Damn bitchin'," he bellowed and pulled the car up to the entrance of the Pemex station.

Through the open window Jonathan threw ten pesos to the boy sent to get him a taxi, "Gracias," he shouted.

The smiling boy caught the coin, "Gracias Señor."

"Yeah and what a hell of a time for it to go on me; my daughter's plane arrives in half an hour—one o'clock."

"No worry I get you there. We smash our way through," and with that said and a lull in the traffic on Insurgentes the car roared down the hill to turn on Venustiano Carranza and east to the tunnels under the highway, "You American?" he said and he floored the beast through the first tunnel that has a bend in it and Jonathan hung onto the door so as not to land in the driver's lap.

"No, Canadian from British Columbia." He looked around for a seat belt but there was none.

"Very nice place—never been there. My children have been there. One she go school there."

"You live in PV?" Jonathan asked. They reached the second tunnel that was full of exhaust fumes and so dark the driver turned his headlights on and swore something in Spanish to a slow car in front of them. Before the end of the tunnel he saw an opening in the other lane and pulled out to pass. Suddenly an oncoming truck appeared but moved over out of the way, its horn screamed dissatisfaction.

"See, they get out of my way when they see me coming—damn bitchin'. Si, I live on Francesco Madero, family been there many years."

"You have children Señor?" And the beast roared passed the PV graveyard filled with white marble stones and flowers.

"My family buried there and so will I soon. My children and their children and their children will visit me and bring me food and drink and I will live forever with them." and Jonathan mentally agreed that he would be there soon, "Your question—Si—five children and seven grandchildren. We all live together in family home. I want twenty more grandchildren and great grandchildren before I die. You can not have enough," he said, "they will take care of me." They reached the intersection where, Libramiento and Blvd. Francisco Medina Ascencio meet. The laughing Mexican gunned the engine through the intersection not taking notice of the yield sign and Jonathan heard the squeal of tires behind them. For the next fifteen minutes that it took to get to the airport parking lot, Jonathan hung on to the front seat and with the instinct of his ancestors, his toes held on to the carpet beneath his sandals.

"You must have a strong wife Señor."

"Wife dead long ago, now mistress live with me. She live now with me for fourteen years."

"Are you married to her?"

"She is mistress, nothing more."

"Oh," Jonathan changed the subject," so what do you do for a living?"

"Did—do nothing now except drive people to airport," and he broke into laughter, "when I was boy I was fisherman, never go to school but I sell my catch at the market place for good price. I learn arithmetic very fast to make fair deals with the restaurant owners. I grow up when they make big film here when only four thousand people live here. I carved coconut faces, strung beads and made palm tree sailing ships to sell to the tourists. As city got big I got street educated and worked for the resorts and the money from the north. Some Americans help me buy property. They were not allowed to buy property, I became their partners so in last twenty years I and American friends get rich and all my sons and daughters I send to school in America and Europe and now they get rich."

"So you still live in Emiliano Zapata?"

"Si, family home there. I cannot leave my family home. Now it is as big as a hotel and very fancy." He roared the engine and blasted the horn at a taxi in front of him and the driver moved his yellow cab into another lane. The taxi driver laughed and yelled something out the window at them and the burly Mexican honked the horn and waved madly, "my young brother."

"You like this old American car?"

"Si, it my bitchin' American gas eatin' pig. We have other cars in the family but they are poco. Other cars see me—they let me in traffic or they get out of way. My friends know me and the police know me and everyone stays out of my way. The police don't know I don't have driver's license. I have never had driver's license. Look at the cruise ships there full of money for my country," and he pointed to the marina, "the tourists will go to the bullfights and think badly of us."

"What about insurance?"

"No need in Mexico. You have accident they throw you in jail, insurance or no."

They chatted away about NAFTA, Presidents Fox, Bush and family. The burly man was good company even if he was a maniac behind the wheel. They finally reached the airport and Jonathan checked his pants to see if he had peed himself.

"How much do I owe you Señor?"

"Nothing Señor."

"Come now, everything has a price in Mexico."

"Okay, the price of gas," he said. He gave him one hundred pesos and the burly Mexican gave him fifty back. Love your family you will need them when you are old."

Jonathan stepped out of the car, "Adios and gracias to you and your bitchin' American pig." They both laughed, Jonathan closed the door and the black boat roared off. Jonathan forgot to ask him his name.

He thought he was late for the plane but he was not, the plane was thirty minutes overdue and Annabelle soon passed through the automatic glass doors at arrivals, full of smiles and hugs. She was so glad to get out of the north and its cold, rain and business. He was so glad to see his daughter from home, even if it was just for a couple of days.

"Dad, how are you, are you staying out of trouble, you haven't been stressed have you, because you know what that means—?"

"No, no babe, everything is fine. It's so good to see you," and he hugged and kissed her, picking her up off the floor, "here let me take your bags."

They prepaid a cab at the terminal that was exorbitant and the driver did not get a tip from Jonathan when they arrived at his place. The driver was pissed at him. This was not new to Annabelle and she said laughing, "Yup it's good to be back in Mexico."

Annabelle showered, dressed in her beach gear, and they went to Playa de Los Muertos for drinks and the sun. The night before a storm surge had taken out some of the beach and deposited it someplace else. Some of it was up on the sidewalks and had buried the plastic chairs of the restaurants. All was a mess in the morning but by the afternoon everything was back to normal which is all part of doing business on the beach. Annabelle was in the water of the Bahia de Banderas within the hour. Jonathan drank beer and watched the jungle, birds, palms, sand and water try to swallow everything and it did just that. A parachute man, a burly handsome Aztec with a black ponytail worked the crowd on the beach—they watched him perform. Four-meter waves thundered in and young boys tried to surf the impossible water.

"Okay, Dad, now tell me what you have been up to, and the truth, you hear?"

"I have been good honey, doing the contract, enjoying the beach, seeing a friend and just having fun."

"Friend—what friend?"

"Tula."

"Jesus! I knew it. I just knew it. You're back with her again. Will you never learn?" she reached out and held his hand, "she is not good for you—she never was and never will be."

"I can hope, can't I?"

"Not in this case—not in this case," she said with a sigh.

"I know that I'm a fool when it comes to her but what can I do? I still love her."

"I know. Will you promise me you won't act up and get into trouble again? If you do it will be the death of me. No more running down runways after planes, okay? I don't want to be coming back here and taking you home in an ambulance again."

"I promise I will behave Annabelle," and he gave her a peck on the cheek, "by the way, Tula is taking us to a New Year's party tonight."

"Oh Christ," Annabelle groaned.

They waved goodbye to the parachutist and walked towards home; they stopped at a store to look at the bone art of Day of the Dead. When

Annabelle was young they had come across a weird piece of work, a little box of sculptured skeletons. There was a skeleton doctor, a skeleton nurse and a skeleton woman in bed with her skeleton legs up giving birth to a skeleton baby. The dead giving birth to something already dead—how bizarre can you get, they thought. They wondered if it had any kind of Zen thing attached. Unfortunately they did not buy it at the time—they searched but did not find one like it.

They stopped by the Pemex station and picked up Silver Bullet and she was ready for them. He paid the bill and kissed bullet on the hood, which he usually does when she gets sick.

"Oh Dad," Annabelle groaned.

It was New Year's Eve and dark by the time they got themselves together, bought some Champagne and made a veggie plate for the party on the mountain. Tula walked over to Jonathan's place with a magnum of Champagne in hand. She let herself in.

"So good to see you again," Tula said with a forced smile as she handed the champagne to Annabelle.

"Good to see you Tula," she said with a forced smile as she took the magnum.

"Have a seat and I will get you a glass," and she went to the kitchen where Dad was preparing appetizers, "Jesus, she is beautiful, you weak minded old fool," she said in a whisper.

"Yeah I know, now you understand, Si?"

"Yeah Si," she poured the bubbly into a tall tulip glass and returned to the living room. He followed with the appetizers and bent down to a seated Tula and kissed her on both cheeks. Annabelle smiled; her father was so cosmopolitan in his greetings with women. The three had a polite conversation about art, Mexico and her Dad's health and welfare. And it became evident to the two adversaries that they both loved Jonathan the vagabond.

They taxied to Tula's friends George and Floss's condo on the mountain above Old Town for an hour of Champagne and small talk before going to the party higher on the jungle-covered mountain. George and Floss were very gracious, embraced his daughter and introduced her into the group.

After drinks and a great deal of fussing about, they continued up the mountain by taxi, six on board with booze and food. They arrived at a penthouse atop a new development of luxurious condos. They all felt a little uncomfortable, as the outside stairs leading to the penthouse were concrete cantilevered structures jutting out the side of the building. The road had taken them to the penthouse level; the concrete and steel structure cascaded down the crumbling mountain and jungle. A bunch of what-ifs crossed Jonathan's mind about earthquakes, rainstorms and slumping mountains.

All that was between them and a long drop to the jungle below was a low curved stainless steel railing.

"Hold on to me," giggled nervous Tula to Jonathan and he held on to the arms of her and Annabelle. They gingerly walked on the concrete cloud to the front door.

The two-story Penthouse was grand: wall to ceiling glass doors, marble everywhere, a kitchen with blood red cupboards against gleaming white walls and a terra cotta tilled covered deck supported by ironwood tree trunks and thick cedar beams. There were bright paintings of women and ceramics pots and spheres strategically spaced, the best of Mexican culture, all tastefully chosen. The furniture was from Morocco, heavy wicker with white cushions. The design was minimalist and geometric, neutral in colour and accented with shades of colours that can only be used in the tropics: tangerines, primavera yellows and lime greens.

The view was spectacular. The jungle dropped down the mountain to the south and La Playa de Los Muertos; the city of PV spread out, the cathedral bell tower lit in green, red and yellow lights for Christmas rose above the surrounding buildings. To the north was the Malecón stretching out to the hotel zone that curved into the distance to the Marina. Several cruise ships were docked and they were decked out with strings of lights. Far in the distance were Nuevo Vallarta, Bucerias, Cruz de Huanacaxtle and Punt de Mita. Overlooking everything and everywhere shone the moon and Quetzalcoatl. It struck wonderment in all of them and they got into the Champagne. Annabelle took pictures of everything and everyone and Tula got into the strawberries and chocolate dip.

An old woman in her seventies from New York, dignified in her gray hair, black turtle neck sweater and black and silver sequined pants sat graciously on a sofa of white cushions. Huge silver earrings hung from ears that loomed large and ponderous from a deep tanned, bony face, "Nice to meet you. I'm Mildred," the women said after Tula approached and introduced herself, "and where does that lovely body of yours reside?"

"Here in Mexico," she giggled, "This is my friend Jonathan."

"Hello Mildred," Jonathan said and the wicked woman *Of Human Bondage* flashed across his mind. They shook hands.

"Sit down you two," she said and they made themselves comfortable beside her, "New York is my town and I love sex but alas the men are getting old and sexless there, can't get it up anymore and when they do the moment it is far too brief." They laughed and admired the candor of the old woman. "There aren't too many active older men who want an old cat like me, they want the young ones. It's their natural calling, what they are born and die to do, but socially it pisses women off."

"Yeah, I'll say," Tula said and glanced at Jonathan who shrugged his shoulders.

"At seventy-seven I'm just getting started and I love men so much. Would you lend me your man Tula? I would return him undamaged."

"Oh, I—"

"Just kidding. You know there is nothing outside of New York City—just desert." She reminded Jonathan of a Georgia O'Keefe or a Gloria Guggenheim. They got to know the old lovely woman; they talked about men, art and the good life that is a stone's throw from Central Park.

They did not notice the clock ticking the time away except for their host and she gave each guest a plate with twelve grapes to eat at midnight. Twelve wishes, one for each month of the coming year. Suddenly in the distance beyond the jungle the sky exploded and the Bahia de Banderas lit up and glowed in the light of fireworks. Everyone moved onto the balcony. At first it was all the hotels that exploded their pyrotechnics, and then the Malecón erupted with hundreds of rockets that sent flowers of fire above the bay. In the distance they could hear thousands of people singing and yelling. Sounds of Mexican Banda bands of drums, tubas, trumpets and trombones rocked the night and above it all was the peeling of the bells of the cathedral and churches. The host's dog ran to the railing, raised his head, howled at the moon and Quetzalcoatl and pissed on the marble floor.

"No!" the host screamed and she grabbed the dog's head with her hands and scolded it giggling and kissing its forehead. Everyone howled with laughter, kissed and clicked their glasses of Champagne.

Jonathan's daughter turned to him, clicked his glass and said, "We have a good life Dad. Be careful with yourself this year and particularly with Tula. She has a magic about her that scares me. There are many who care that you are safe."

"I promise I'll stay out of harms way. We sure do have the good life," he said and gulped down the champagne, "I knew someday we would be in a place like this, happy with our lives. Fairy tales are true." and he kissed his daughter on both cheeks.

Tula next to him gently pulled him away from Annabelle to the other side of the room. His daughter smiled and was cautiously happy for her father and Tula; after all; Dad's an adult. She left them alone and joined a group of new friends.

Tula held his hand, pulled him close and kissed him gently. She whispered, "I love you." He hoped it was true. He had eaten six of his grapes because six wishes of his love for her were all he could think of—the rest he threw into the jungle.

New Years Day Jonathan and Annabelle slept in, rose and cleaned the apartment. They walked, talked and laughed their way to the beach and a restaurant for breakfast. The sun was high, the humidity just right and the temperature at thirty-four degrees Celsius—a fine New Years day in the tropics. Life is good.

"I'll have the pancakes, juice and coffee, por favor," Annabelle said to the waitress.

"And I'll have the American Breakfast: huevos sunny, hash browns, bacon, orange juice and whole grain toast, por favor. Oh, yes and coffee with cream and sugar."

"Si," the waitress said and she left for the kitchen in the back, banging through empty tables and chairs as she went. She returned shortly with their coffee and left. Father and daughter chatted about the party the night before until he noticed the waitress had not returned with the cream and sugar. She passed by the table and he gestured to her.

"Cream and sugar por favor."

"Si señor." and the waitress went about her business. She returned sometime later with the cream and sugar but the coffee was cold—they sipped it anyway. Twenty minutes later their meals arrived. Annabel's was right but Jonathan's—

"Excuse me," he gently said to the waitress, "these eggs are over-easy and there is no bacon." Without a word the waitress snatched up his plate and returned to the kitchen. Shortly she came back with his plate that now had four rashes of burned bacon, the hash browns and the same over easy eggs covered with a layer of green hot sauce.

"No, I can't eat eggs with that green stuff on it, that's why I ordered an American breakfast," he told the waitress who was now getting flustered and irritated at her gringo customer, "please redo the plate." The waitress took the plate banged her way through the tables and chairs to the bar and behind it out of site; she poured off the green liquid and returned his plate.

"Okay," he sighed in resignation, "now where is the toast?" she went back to the kitchen and returned with some artistically laid out cold thinly sliced, burned white bread in a basket covered with a tattered piece of fabric. She quickly laid it on the table and moved on. He waved to get her attention, "knives and forks por favor." She returned with knives and forks. He looked at his meal and it was cold and had a look about it like someone had already started eating it— he could not eat it—it was disturbed. Slowly over the course of negotiating to get breakfast he had slumped down in his chair, his shoulders rounded and his demeanor was one of rejection and victimization. In the meantime Annabelle had her pancakes, orange juice and coffee. She ate quickly; he paid the bill and left no tip. Annabelle reached in her purse, took out fifteen pesos and left them on the table when Dad was not looking.

Walking up the street to Tula's place Dad said, "You know, honey, I get about one out of three meals that I can eat and enjoy in Mexico."

"Yeah, that's about the same ratio back home when you were with Mom."

They arrived at Tula's and she was up and had cooked herself brunch. Jonathan poured himself a coffee and scrounged her last piece of toast and half a fried egg. He opened her kitchen cupboards and found some granola bars; one he quickly opened and ate.

"Let's go to Mismaloya and drink some beer on the beach," Tula said.

"Good idea," he said, "we can stuff ourselves on shrimp tacos, beef burritos, enchiladas, fajitas, maybe some of those yellow chickens and pork and—"

"Okay, Dad," Annabelle said.

"What have you two been up to?"

"He hasn't had breakfast."

They decided they would spend the day down in Mismaloya. "Since its New Years day and it is Mexico we may get drunk," Tula said, "so we should catch a bus. We can get one a couple of blocks down the road from here. The ride will be fun since *The Night of The Iguana* was filmed in Mismaloya and the characters in the story rode a bus to the fishing village, although the road wasn't there in those days."

The bus stop on Manual M. Diéguez filled up with tourists and Mexicans. They butted in front of the trio and took up all the seats on the bus. Once loaded to bursting the blue and white bus rattled and banged its way down the coastal road past beautiful homes nestled comfortably in the jungles of Altavista, Las Amapas and Conchas Chinas. The bus roared past golden beaches, gated communities and pink and terra cotta hotels that hung onto the land above crashing surf. The three islands of Los Arcos came into view. Thousands of seabirds flew above the white islands painted with their droppings. Dive and fish boats bobbed in the blue green waters nearby waiting for their tourist customers to emerge from visiting the sea life. People got on and off the bus at stops along the way—off to their jobs pampering and servicing the rich.

Soon the bus dropped down a steep hill into the Mismaloya estuary and turned right before the river bridge onto a dusty road that leads to a beach covered with tourists and Mexicans. They jumped from the bus and ran like kids to the beach and hotel that filled half of the estuary. Jonathan had spent the night there a few years ago and as ugly as the hotel is, it bought back sweet memories. The shacks of fishermen emerged out of the rich green jungle that is tying to take back the land. A rickety old suspension bridge of boards and cables gave access to the dilapidated beach restaurants on the other side of the river. The fishermen were pulling their boats up the river and under the bridge to docks at their crumbling homes.

In the hot sun beautiful Mexican children jumped off the bridge into the cool clear water of the river and splashed around. Friendly pelicans hung out with the children and scrounged off the fishermen. Booths of bright clothing, baskets and blankets stacked themselves up along the pathways to the beach.

"I feel sorry," Annabelle said as she shot pictures, "for kids back home, bundled up in their strollers getting fat and ugly. The kids here are slim, healthy and full of fun."

They picked a restaurant on the beach whose host was a hyped up Mexican who would not stop calling Jonathan macho man because of the two women with him. He was all over them babbling about men, Mexico, beach and sun. He pissed the girls and Jonathan off and they told him to settle down which he finally did.

"Mister, you got a sugar problem," Tula barked.

He realized they lived in PV or were frequent visitors. He ran around like a beach rat getting canvas lounge chairs and a couple of tables. The tide was coming in and it ran under their chairs and tables so they started to move everything and all hell broke loose. The strings of restaurants claim a piece of the beach. There is an imaginary line between the tables that the waiters demonstrate with hand gestures like string puppets marking out their territory. This is the Soda place, this is the Cola place and this is the Juice place and so on. They had just ordered food so they were ordered by the babbling waiters to stay put in Soda land.

There was a good-looking blonde woman in Cola land and Jonathan asked permission of their arrogant little waiter if he could talk to her. The waiter had to stop for a moment and think about that. He gave him a toothless grin and left to get their beer. A bunch of flea-infested dogs ran by and dove under a few tables each in a different pop land; they carried on like humans, bickering with each other for territory. Tula said, "Put this on your legs," and handed Annabelle a pesticide cream. Tula pulled her bikini from her purse and put it on under her dress like something magic then took her dress off and ran into the ocean. Annabelle changed into her bikini in the communal bathroom.

The sun was high and hot and they jabbered and drank the afternoon away and dove into the waves to cool off. They didn't get drunk, just into an altered state, one that can only be experienced on a hot day in Mexico. Annabelle and Dad got into a deep discussion about what will happen to Mismaloya in the future. Life is basic and raw here and you have to face it with a comedic eye

Dad said: "If it isn't drowned by the sea or on top of a mountain, monsters would again walk this land and the jungle would be a hundred times as big. If something of us does survive perhaps we will be as big as King Kong."

Tula joined in the conversations. The waves washed in, and along with the canvas lounges, tables and buckets of beer they slowly sank into the beach and became quiet. Jonathan looked with sleepy eyes into the distance along the rocks beside the sandy bay up to the pile where *The Night of The Iguana* was filmed. He swore he saw through the haze and heat, the ghosts of dead actors yelling and screaming at each other. He lay back and snored.

Monday morning came and Annabelle made ready to leave. Her male friend, Rick from Canada arrived from the airport. Father, daughter and Rick went for breakfast down on La Playa de Los Muertos and around noon, forty-eight hours from the time she arrived in Mexico, Annabelle and Rick left by taxi for the bus station. Jonathan waved goodbye and he knew the moon and Quetzalcoatl would watch over them.

Annabelle was now into her Mexican adventure and she and her friend would go north to Rincon de Guayabitos, San Blass and other towns and villages, exploring the country and watching in village markets for old original Huichol art that she loves. They will eventually arrive in Guadalajara and at its center, enter the huge orphanage. Walking into the silence of the great hall she will take a deep breath, look up and be awed at the terror and glory that is Mexico.

La Rosa y Azul Bar

Desperate eyes met
They knew what they had to do
Who would last the day?

Draft

Good afternoon Tula

There are three people to be dispatched.

The grandfather: Piero Vincente Pinturicchio, his son: Alonso (A.K.A. Bud) Vincente Pinturicchio and his son, John Vicente Pinturicchio.

These clients are old crime family, from New York and may have security guards on staff. Although their family is operating legal businesses now, they are still using strong-arm tactics on their employees and partners. They are jeopardizing their legitimate operations to the dissatisfaction of our organization. They have been warned of the consequences of their actions but continue their indiscretions. Members are constantly being threatened by the grandfather/father/son operation particularly the son who is an alcoholic and drug user. They are renting a Villa in Las Altavista, which may have security personnel but we are not sure of this; therefore, assume there is security.

They do not carry weapons and are not trained in self-defense. The son is physically fit but intoxicated most days.

On completion of your assignment please send me a draft of your results.

Sonny Ray was drunk and a little miffed that he could not play bullshit dice. He mumbled to himself as he hunched over in his usual seat at the regular's table. La Rosa y Azul Bar was packed with sports fans and they overflowed onto the street. The finals of American football were being played and sounds of laughter and cheers vibrated the place. Curious street dogs weaved among the legs of patrons and tables sniffing and eating anything that landed on the floor. In one corner the bar the owner's dog, Bustercrab, was curled up in deep sleep. Fat people, young and old, rich and poor, boozers and roustabouts, junkies and prostitutes, lovers and haters mixed together in the heat of the moment as a classic event in America was beamed by satellite into a warm friendly hole in the wall in Old Town. The smoke and smell of cigars, cigarettes, beer, nuts, hot dogs and popcorn filled the air with a blue gray haze. Ceiling fans turned and moved the haze from one side of the room and back again. Beer bottles came out of their boxes in a steady stream, eight hundred would be emptied into bellies that day along with dozens of hot dogs covered in Franklin's mustard, relish, onions and salsa. It is a sports bar that caters to Americans and Canadians; some are on a regular visit but the majority live and run businesses in PV. Some have dark backgrounds and can't go home to their countries.

Franklin worked the crowd selling his pickled cucumbers, relishes and plastic bags of chicken soup. He did quite well that day selling his entire stock. He is retired from business in the United States but can't help getting himself back into business again, "Pickling is my life," he would say.

Bobble head kids, as the customers called them, with wide smiles and huge brown eyes plied their trade of trinkets. Their little hands moved through pockets and table change. They must take home many pesos each night for their drugged family; if they don't they will be locked out to sleep on the sidewalk with the street dogs. The two children, nine and twelve are the sole supporters of the family and work seven days a week from eight in the morning until ten at night. They don't go to school and unfortunately through no fault of their own they are urchins and thieves. The two little ones may die someday in a Mexican prison. All they have is each other and when Jonathan sees them on the street or on the beach hawking their goods they are holding hands. They take comfort in each other and it helps them cope. The two have made it this far—somehow they will survive.

The American gladiators finished their game, looked exhausted, did their interviews and walked off screen into history. The bar slowly emptied, patrons tumbled into the street, some satisfied with the game they had just played and relived the great plays with each other. Others were disappointed at their favorite team's loss and it was because of the bad calls, of course, by the blind linemen and referee; calls that will soon be forgotten along with the game. The street dogs finished off the popcorn. Beatrice bought out the dice cups to Sonny Ray's delight and the gang of nine started in with a ten-peso bet. The bartenders and waitress cleaned up the place and everything was back to normal.

Mexican Elvis was in the corner with two American women, wooing them in his drunken state and getting nowhere but closer to the floor where he eventually landed. The old fat man in his chair across the street watched his prostitutes work the crowd; his stare pierced the wrought iron encased windows. Carlota came in and said, Buenos noches, to everyone and turned down their offer to join them. She was busy at the whorehouse and came over to pick up some beer and cigarettes for her customers. The old fat man sat in his yellow chair shaking his head at all the Americans and Canadians but remembered his youth as a football player playing for team PV many years ago.

Alex yelled to the bartender, "A round of beer here on me, por favor."

The regulars said in unison, "Keep your money."

Sonny Ray said, "Now wait a minute, Alex knows what he's doin'."

Alex and his wife Grace are from New York City and managed to make it to Mexico each year when they were poor. They became rich in the nineties investing in the .com phenomena and pulled out when they made their fortune. They could go to the best places in PV but the La Rosa y Azul was their home away from home and they would never give up their old friends. Alex always wears jeans and a motorcycle club black t-shirt and she is the queen of the second hand store. The only evidence of wealth on her is a big fat diamond on her finger that looks like costume jewelry but is the real thing.

Chris piped up, "Did anyone see that fucking great fire that was up on the hill by my place?"

"Yeah, I saw it," Jonathan said, "Christmas Eve wasn't it?"

"Yeah, a gas tank exploded in the house next door to me, blowin' bricks into the street and set the roof on fire. It took forever for the fire trucks to arrive. It was a really shitty thing to happen on Christmas Eve. Their families came and stripped the house of what was left and put on a party right there in the street, booze was passed around, someone made fish tacos and they all got back into the mood of Christmas. Strangest thing I ever saw."

"Yeah, there's always a festival goin' on here," Sonny said.

Tula arrived in her shorts, halter-top and running shoes. She had been out for a jog along the Malecón and dropped in to say hello to Jonathan. She knew where to find him when the football finals were on. She hugged and kissed him and rubbed sweat in his face from her arms and chest. The crowd at the table encouraged her to do more--everyone laughed at his expense.

"Ugh honey," he spat and wiped the sweat off with his sleeve.

"Hey, Tula!" Sonny Ray shouted, "take a seat and have a beer."

Tula scanned the table with her eyes and fixed her gaze on Bud. "Sorry I can't, got things to do," she panted and she was gone as quickly as she arrived. Jonathan noticed the glance at Bud and wondered if Tula was on the hunt for men again.

Chris leaned over to Jonathan, "What are you going to do about her?"

"Marry her, if I can."

"What?"

"Yeah, marry her. But I know it won't happen. She can't have a long-term relationship with me. For some reason it just doesn't work for us."

"Oh well," Chris said, "you still got us."

"Groan!"

"Twelve eights," Sonny Ray blurted and the player next to him called him on it, "Jesus Christ why do I play this game? By the way," and he leaned over to Jonathan, his breath gave him shivers, "I have an idea about languages that I have been working on for years. I think we can take light, colour and music and add it to our alphabet. We wouldn't need to prattle and carrying on as we do now. All would be simplified—"

"I think that was in a movie," Chris said overhearing, "how long have you been up there in the jungle Sonny Ray?"

Tina, the old crone went on to Alex next to her, "I loved that John Huston; he was such a renaissance man, treated me like a queen. John, the cast and I had great fun together. He bought many pieces of my pottery. Did I tell you about the pottery?"

"Yeah, a hundred times already," blurted Franklin on the opposite side of Alex and growing impatient with the old woman. When she got drunk she would go on about the days that John Huston lived in PV and the parties she used to attend with the cast and their gang from Hollywood. It was probably true; she had been in PV for fifty years or more and in those days everyone knew each other when PV was a small fishing village. People said that she had a love affair with the old director, but then so did many women. The man was charismatic and rich. Her memories of John Huston and a few friends are all she cares about. Now she spends her time in the bar on the edge of nowhere.

"Sorry," she said looking quite miffed at Alex but she knew he was getting drunk.

Jim Bob and Boston Betty sat in the back corner of the bar; they weren't welcome at the table since they had stolen from some of the patrons. Jim is a chronic liar and junkie, jumping at any opportunity, legal or illegal, to make a buck for his habits. He is still a good-looking man but that is changing rapidly as drugs and booze destroy his soul. Jim Bob uses the local prostitutes on a regular basis and pimps for them getting a kickback from the old fat man. Betty came down from Boston to live with Jim—they went through her savings in less than a month. She broke her lower plate and her two front teeth are missing. She hasn't replaced them since she is stoned most of the time and now can't afford to. In their sickness they are in love and co-dependent. A sad couple, they will soon disappear from the bar and finish life in the dust of Mexico. Boston Betty got up and went to the bathroom—Jim Bob went through her purse.

"Vamonos!" shouted Beatrice to two street dogs just inside the door, their tails wagged, tongues hung out and their big eyes tried to get the attention of the customers. "Vámonos!" she shouted again and they ran out and up the street to the next bar like a couple of naught street kids. The old fat man looked through the dark at the bar, keeping an eye on his girls.

"How are you Jonathan?" Paddy said as he took a seat next to him. He raised his hand to the bartender who understood what he wanted—rum and cola.

"What have you been up to Paddy?" asked Jonathan.

"Well, let me tell you. I got me two whores last night, not the neighborhood ones, the ones they sell to the tourists in the Hotel Zone. Prettiest girls you ever saw and only three hundred bucks for the two of them."

"Did you use a condom?"

"No, I hate going through that guilt trip the farmacia puts you through. You're looked at like you're the biggest sinner in the world when you order rubbers. There's too much religion in this country as far as I'm concerned."

"Jesus Paddy! Why do you do this stuff, you're getting on and that kind of partying is dangerous? These girls have all kinds of diseases and I hear that half of the whores in the city are pregnant. Beatrice told me ten out of the twenty girls across the street are pregnant."

"I don't give a shit anymore. I'm in my late sixties and I have had a hell of a good life playing baseball for New York and selling cars in Canada. The wife is gone, dead long ago from cancer and I still miss her. I was screwing my wife last night not the two girls," he said sadly. The waitress came with his rum and cola and he clicked Jonathan's beer with it.

"Cheers, Paddy, you dog," Jonathan said and he embraced his troubled friend.

"Sixteen sixes, no bloody way!" Sonny Ray shouted, "bullshit!" The players showed their dice and he counted, "one - four - two - three - zero - zero - three - four that makes seventeen—oh Christ, lost again!"

"Jonathan, what are you doing tomorrow?" Chris whispered, "I'm catering a big party up on the hill for Bud. Wanna' come along? The place is huge; Bud's paying fifteen hundred a day for it. He's entertaining former business partners his son ripped off."

"What? Ripped off? What are you talking about?"

"Yeah, he's trying to make amends for his son and if he doesn't his son will end up dead no matter where he is. He might still get snuffed. Anyway it will be fun, mirage pool, beautiful women, a fantastic view and my good food."

"Thanks Chris but I have to pass. I'm busy all day tomorrow."

"Is she beautiful?"

"Yeah."

"Well that's good."

"Ten pesos señor," said the bobble head boy as he put his arms around Jonathan's shoulder and shoved a roll of necklaces in his face. He quickly picked up his change from the table as he saw from the left of him the little hand of his sister moving towards it.

"Oh no, you little thieves—you dust of the earth—gracias," he said laughed and unwrapped himself from them. They moved off to find another victim and they did in Chris who was always a sucker when it came to the street kids.

"Good, finally I get one," shouted Sonny Ray.

Suddenly there was a crash at the back of the bar and Elvis was on the floor; his two women looked like they were about to join him. They were laughing hysterically. A few of the gang got up and helped him to his feet, straightened his clothing and helped him and his guitar to the door. Everyone shouted, "Good night Elvis," and one of the guys walked him the short distance home. The old fat man from his perch on the sidewalk waved, "Buenos noches Elvis."

"I'm not paying his bill," one of the women said, "me neither," slurred the other.

"Not to worry ladies," the bartender said, "he will be in tomorrow to pay it—he always does."

Chris invited the women over since they didn't look like they were finished for the night and there was room since Alex and Betty had gone home. They introduced themselves as Mildred and Fay of Ohio.

"Jesus," someone said, "who would call themselves Mildred?"

"I like my name," she said straightening her bra, "it was my Mother's and my Grandmother's name." Hm thought Jonathan, another Mildred.

"Jesus Christ, lost another dice!" came out of Sonny Ray.

"Uno más for everyone on me," shouted Franklin to the bartender.

"On behalf of everyone—Franklin, thank you," said Sonny Ray before anyone could intervene.

Two fat prostitutes sat near the door taking a break from business and Paddy was getting drunk and making eyes at them. It wasn't long before he left the table and took the girls across the street. Jonathan tried to stop him but Paddy was too drunk to listen, only his lost love and memories spoke to him.

Fay moved into his seat beside Jonathan to chat him up. She leaned close to him and said, "The basic sexual attraction I find in men is clean nails and a squared off haircut at the back of the neck. What do you think Mr. Jonathan?"

"Well the basic sexual attraction for women is a hard round ass on a man, a pump for their genitals, so anthropologists say," Jonathan said.

"Well I totally disagree I think it is about personal hygiene," she rebutted, "not someone's ass. That's disgusting what you think."

"Listen it's not about you, Fay, or me its basic biology, the stuff you read in books on the science. You're older now and don't remember what a nice male ass is like." and there came laughter from the table. Fay got up and moved back to her old seat beside Mildred.

James was watching one of the televisions and some American news channel was on and the president of the United States was making a speech to the nation. There were boos and guffaws from the table about what a bad president he was and Jim said, someone should take him out to the rose garden and string him up. Others joined in the chorus of put downs and obscenities of their leader, their president. They went on and on about America, the home they ran away from, the home of the brave. When it came to their home they were not happy people. He did not say anything to James or the rest at the table, it was their country and they would have to mend it—that is if they go home.

Suddenly Sonny Ray jumped to his feet and quickly put a chair by the window and went to the door. Standing outside in the dim streetlight was a little man in tattered white clothing, a worn out straw hat was on his white haired head. His face was like an aged golden brown cherub, accented with a handle bar white mustache. He was barefoot and his feet were filthy bags of leather. He had come by bus from El Tuito—he was the liquor man. A ragged kaki shoulder bag lay heavy on his arm and inside was a number of two liter bottles of alcohol that he had bought down from the mountains. The transparent liquid gold was organic stuff, very potent whose alcohol content varied with each batch that was made in the distilleries deep in the jungle. Too much and you go blind. Illegal booze of course but that was the fun of it and it was cheap. The old man was treated with great respect as he came a long way bearing gifts to the island of white folk. If Sonny Ray lost at the dice at least he could go home with a two-liter jug of the good earth. He showed the liquor man his seat and ordered him a beer.

Evening was coming and most of Jonathan's bar cronies had been at the Azul y Rosa for most of the afternoon, some were tired like him and the rest quite drunk. Alex and Betty had gone long ago. A Mexican came in and talked to Jim Bob and Boston Betty and they left in a hurry. Purdy was snoring across the street and Bud, who said nothing all night because of the worry about his wayward son, taxied home. Tina fell asleep in her chair and the bartender woke her up; she lifted her frail body and staggered home. She was more than tired; she was ready to leave this world. Franklin ran out of pickles and his mind and staggered out with Jim, each holding the other up. Sonny Ray led the old liquor man to the bus stop to catch the bus south to their homes in the jungle. Chris said good night and walked home relatively sober for such a day. Beatrice and the bartenders/waitresses prepared for the late night crowd. She turned down the lights and switched the TVs to the music channel. Bustercrab still lay in the corner curled up in deep sleep and Beatrice wondered if he was still alive so she called him. He raised his head with his eyes still closed only to quickly lay it back down again. The old fat man across the street watched the night fold and unfold as he did every night of the week and under his watchful eyes the prostitutes came and went doing business in the shadows of Old Town. Lonely dogs howled and chickens squawked in the distance.

Jonathan paid his bill and left a handsome tip for the hot dogs and extra entertainment. He left for home that was around the corner; tomorrow will be a long day with Tula.

Like Grandfather, Like Father, Like Son

Belching bawling bus
Black tires of the unholy
The devil in iron

John Pinturicchio got up from his table at the D and D bar by the pier on La Playa de Los Muertos and shouted, "Bloody good game—now pay up you guys!" and his two drinking buddies paid him a thousand pesos each, "Thanks, gentlemen it's a pleasure doin' business with yu'," he slurred and he staggered out of the bar onto the walkway.

John was very drunk and wanted to stay with the guys and drink but there was a good-looking older woman he wanted to see. Someone who had become a friend, someone he felt he needed in his life. He was twenty-eight and all his friends were gone, they didn't want to be around him anymore since he developed a serious drinking problem—he drank everyday. Near the bar was a Minisuper Store where he bought a six-pack of beer before staggering down the beach to the Boy on a Seahorse statue. He climbed the hundred steps to the highway and to where he was staying with his father and grandfather for a few weeks of R and R mixed in with business. It was an arduous climb up the stairs in his state but he had done it everyday for the last two weeks. He would run into her at the top of the stairs as he did most days.

He was puffing by the time he arrived at the highway: buses, taxis and cars streaked back and forth. Beside him were beautiful villas nestled into a jungle of palms, primavera and bougainvillea that climbed up walls and wrought iron fencing. Across the highway were multi million dollar condominium complexes scattered about the jungle. He and his family rented one of the more luxurious of the condos. They had money, old money, old Italian money, old Italian crime family money. The businesses around the world they invested in were legitimate now, not like the old days of his grandfather.

"Hi Tula," John said and he waved to her as she jogged up the highway towards him, "you sure look good."

"Hi, John, thanks," and she ran up to him and gave him a hug, "how was the game?"

"I won two hundred bucks, American."

"Good on you. Are you drunk?"

"Yeah, drunk everyday, even Sundays," he laughed and staggered and Tula caught him from falling.

"You got a beer for me? My jogging has made me really thirsty for one."

"Yup, got a six pack minus two right here," and he lifted the paper bag to show her.

"Hey, okay. Let's go up the road a bit and sit down and chat," she said. They walked up fifty yards to a steep cobbled road that went up into the neighborhood of Las Altavita. She had meticulously picked this spot. A high stonewall and narrow sidewalk came down the drive to within a meter of the highway. They sat down on the sidewalk, their backs rested against the wall and John opened a couple of beers.

"It sure is nice getting to know you Tula. I have no friends you know, they're all gone, there's just Gramps, Dad and me now," he blurted out as he did every time she talked to him. She was patient of the repetitiveness of a fried brain.

"Yes I know and that's too bad, I feel for you. We all need friends," Tula said and she looked at him but did not listen to what he had to say. This young virile man, she thought was such a waste—she concentrated on the traffic going by.

"I think I will have to change my life. Maybe go to AA or someplace that can help me."

"Yeah that would be good for you going to AA. There are many people here in the tropics with drinking problems; it comes with the good life." Too late you fool, she told herself.

She knew the sound of the yellow and white taxis, the smooth sound of the large American cars, but most of all the sound of the big murderous buses that geared down as they descended the hill to an average speed of forty kilometers an hour. Every five minutes one would roar in a white and blue blur past the stonewall. For the last three days she had ridden the buses past this spot from half a mile up to half a mile down the highway, jogging back up to ride the next one coming along. She got to know the gear changes and when the driver dropped down in gear to let the engine break the speed of the bus on the hill. She sat for many hours on the sidewalk were the stonewall meets the highway listening for the buses. She recorded in her mind the traveling time, speed and sounds of the machines before they became a blur. She was very familiar now with the landscape and her weapon—the giant PV killer buses.

"Buenos noches," an elderly woman shouted from across the street. She was loaded down with bags of groceries. Tula heard a gear change in the distance and in a few seconds a bus roared by.

"Buenos noches," Tula said waving and smiling. In a few minutes the next bus would come and if nobody was around on the next gear change she would make her move. Another person walked by with his dog and the bus blurred by. She would wait patiently for her moment.

"I know we have just met only a few days ago and I like you Tula, you're a beautiful woman. Do you think that we could become more than friends?"

"Oh John, I told you I'm old enough to be you mother; someday you will find someone. Your handsome, rich and your loneliness will end soon."

"Maybe you should meet my Dad then," they both laughed. No one was around—she heard a gear change.

"Stand up John I want to see how tall you are."

"Whatever you want." and she helped him to his feet and turned him to face the highway. She put her hands on his shoulder blades.

"You have a strong back John."

"Yeah I—"

Tula gave him a push and he took two large steps beyond the stonewall. He disappeared into a blue and white blur. The massive tubular bumper of the bus smashed into him and he fell beneath the huge front wheels that crushed most of the bones in his body and flattened his skull. The wheel kicked his remains up under the bus tearing it in half. The double axel rear wheels tore the body to pieces. "You are no longer lonely my friend," she said into the dark.

From her shorts pocket she pulled a pair of latex gloves, picked up her beer can and wiped her fingerprints off and put it in the bag with the rest and left it on the sidewalk. Quickly she ran up the road into Las Altavista and disappeared down a jungle trail.

It was a short distance along the jungle path to her next tasks—grandfather and son. The retaining wall around the condo's pool was ten feet above the path; she climbed up for a look and there was grandfather at his usual place at the edge of the pool in his wheel chair watching television. His back to her—Bud was not around. Further up the path was a construction site and the workman's tools lay in a heap: shovels, pickaxes, hammers, saws and crowbars. The killer had checked out the site in the last few days and decided what she needed—a double ended pickaxe; the type used for breaking hard ground. She threaded the handle through the belt on the back of her shorts. Returning to the retaining wall she climbed up the stones and onto the deck and like a bobcat moved across the deck pulling the pick from her belt as she went.

Grandfather's back was to her. She lifted the pick with it's double twenty-four inch spikes high over her head pointing her toes and stretching the muscles of her body to the maximum. With the pickaxe's weight, trajectory and her muscular force she drove it down through the top of the Italian, American criminal's head and out the bottom of his chin and into his chest where the sternum and clavicles meet in the triangle of the upper chest. There was a light squish as the pick instantly took the old man's life. Grotesquely the pick in his head stayed in a ridged position when the killer let go of the handle. Quickly she turned the wheelchair and pushed the old man into the pool. There was no blood on the deck, just a few drops of urine. She turned the TV off and pulled a short knife from her pocket and went hunting for Bud in the condo. She checked everywhere but he could not be found. He was still at the bar she thought so she would wait for him.

She heard sirens in the distance—she looked down through the jungle to the highway—lights shone everywhere and the sirens arrived. The killer crouched at the edge of the pool deck—waited—breathed heavily; her heart pounded and she trembled from the overwhelming excitement. Sweat ran down her chest, arms and legs, she felt triumphant like a Greek warrior—no, she thought like a Roman warrior. Jumping off the pool deck into the jungle, she lay in hiding all night, but Bud did not come home.

Bud's taxi drove up highway 200 from Old Town. It was a fun afternoon with the guys; he enjoyed the football finals. The taxi flew past the Pemex station and around the mountain road's curves. Suddenly there was a great commotion up the hill towards Altavista. Cars were strewn across the highway and a white Policia Municipal truck, flashing lights was parked next to a bus on the side of the road. Passengers were getting off; some were crying and some holding their mouths. He could see from the headlights and police flashlights blood on the bumper of the bus and blood and body parts scattered up the highway. The mess was unrecognizable but Bud knew from the clothing that it was his son and that he had been murdered. He was expecting it might happen, "The airport," he ordered the taxi driver, "now!"

Within the hour Bud was on a plane to the United States.

Draft

John Vicente Pinturicchio and Piero Vincente Pinturicchio have been dispatched, Alonso (AKA Bud) Vincente Pinturicchio escaped and is believed to be in New York.

Draft

This is not good news Tula.

Of Manacles and Madness and Other Horrible Things

"We have a task before us, babe, and it will take us most of the day to do it. I've got food and beer in the fridge; we don't have to go out for anything. We have Spanish music on the stereo and the of sounds from the street below," a deafening noise from a hot rod deep-throated bus boomed up from the street and one block down two musicians with oilcan drums broke into a Latin American number. Two green parrots chatted on an electric wire that ran up to Jonathan's terrace.

"Are you going to be naked doing the painting?" Tula asked with excitement.

"Not today, there are too many neighbors that can see us."

"Oh shoot! But you are going to boff me later?"

"Yes, Tula."

"Because I am attracted to your naked— "

"Tula, please let's do the business at hand."

"Just having fun, beautiful, just having fun."

"I saw something the other day that was disturbing; a woman was being taken away to prison or hospital, I don't know which, but she was in a terrible physical and mental state. We are going to paint her and we will have a statement about those who live on the edge of our society, those who can barely cope and those who are suffering in madness. We must tell the world about them. Understand?"

"Yeah. But I think people are aware of them."

"Maybe, but I think they are in denial. Let's stick it in their faces. Our canvas is big, three by four meter and standing a few meters from it your field of vision will be filled—an assault on the mind. So disturbing, vulgar and obscene the painting will be; people will remember it and perhaps carry the vision with them for a long time. So are you ready to do this?"

"So serious, aren't we? Yeah I'm ready, Tula said with confidence and perhaps a little annoyed at the question.

"Good. The canvas is thick and heavy and has been primed with a matte white acrylic. It's as tight as a drum. I have screwed it to two by fours and fixed them to the wall. This will be a painting created by attacking the canvas with materials. It is to have an edge to it, raw and violent. Think of the tension like that of a stretched elastic band, when it snaps it bites the fingers and hurts. We have to create the illusion of that tension across the landscape of the composition. If you touch it—it will bite back.

"Our palette of colours is on the table and it consists of the primaries with shades for each colour, about forty tubes plus bottles of gel to thicken the paint. If you think we need a certain colour here or there, we will add it in. Use paper, brushes, rags, knives and your body, whatever you feel will do the job for us. We can scrape the paint off with knives and sandpaper. Throw beer and food at it if you need to—stain it. It is important that you get angry at it, which is the only way it will be successful. We will keep pushing until it works, until it jumps out and bites us."

"What do we do first?" Tula whispered looking at the huge space to fill.

"We lay in some ground work. Pick some colours that express your anger and others that are comfortable to you." Tula got up and went to the table and picked up tubes of red, orange and yellow for anger and deep blues and greens for comfort, which were obvious choices. "Okay—for the next half hour I want you to rub those colours onto the canvas, don't make any patterns, just rub on the paint and I suggest doing it with a wet rag. Before it dries, scrape it with a palette knife. It will be messy and you will ruin your clothes so be aware of that."

"I wore these especially for today and I know they will be ruined and if I'm lucky ripped off me," Jonathan laughed and kissed her and sent her back to work. She started in by dipping a rag into a picture of water on the table and squirted vermillion on the rag, "Oh cool," she said approvingly, "beautiful colour."

"That's right, use more water," and she poured water on the red soaked rag, walked to the canvas and with both hands smashed the rag onto the surface and when she moved it, the rag made a huge stroke pattern like Japanese calligraphy. The impact sprayed and splattered dots and blobs, "that's it make it splatter, we want those splatter marks, now big swoops across the canvas," and she moved her body and arms across the expanse. It all looked familiar to her—red blood. She took a knife and quickly scraped the paint off some areas leaving streaked stains. "Now remember we tend to focus where our eyes are level, so bend down to take in the bottom half and raise your arms to do the top," she did and soon the canvas was splattered and streaked blood red as though a murder had been committed. The blood red was all over the floor and her. "The paint will dry in a few minute so in the meantime take the rag over to the sink and wash it and your hands." Tula cleaned up the artistic mess she was holding and smiled at the splatters down her halter-top and shorts.

"What about the paint on the floor?"

"Don't worry about that it comes off the tiling easily with hot water. It's plastic, acrylic and clean to work with. Now while it's drying squeeze some of the yellow colour you have chosen into one of the margarine tubs and add a bit of clear polymer emulsion from one of those plastic bottles. That's right now and lay the colour around the edges and across the middle of the canvas with a four inch brush." She did what she was told and he instructed her to move fast and not go back over areas she had painted, "the canvas edges are five-centimeters thick so when you get to them push the rags or brushes around the edge and that goes for the top and bottom of the canvas also. Good, now we have brush strokes, splatters and streaks all over the place. On the table is some thin tissue paper about forty-five by forty-five centimeters take them and paint one side with clear emulsion." She did by holding a tissue against the canvas and slopping the emulsion on. He helped her, "turn it over and paint the tissue to the canvas letting all the wrinkles stay and don't be careful about it. They did ten sheets of tissue. "Good excellent now let's let it dry for a bit." Jonathan opened two beer and they sat back in the rattan chairs, "Now we have a base to work with."

"It looks pretty good," Tula commented, "almost like it was finished."

"Yeah, if we were back in the sixties in New York and hanging out in the village we would stop here. Funny how we now accept an explosive mess like that," pointing his finger at the canvas, "back then people thought that children and elephants did this art.

"Now we will talk about what you have to get into what's next while everything is drying. Some women have a fear of becoming bag ladies when they are old. I heard it said once while watching a famous woman writer being interviewed. She feared her cerebral wiring would change and she would not be able to connect with anyone, not even her family. Her money would not be able to help her to cope with the simplest things like maintaining an apartment, keeping a bank account or shopping for food."

"I knew an actress once," Tula said, "It happened to her. She stopped her medication and was lost to society for several years until a friend saw her on the street and took her in. Her friend got her back on her medication and now she is with us again. To this day she doesn't remember those dark years."

"What do you think Tula? Are we going to paint madness today?"

"Yeah, I have thought of what might happen to me and I have heard bag lady comments come from friends of mine. It seems men don't have these fears like women. We are savers when it comes to the future, putting money away and investing—stuff like that. We end up with apartments and men end up with a room with the bathroom down the hall."

"Hell, I had that in art school and I was a young man," they laughed, "Now, what I saw the other day I want you to help me paint and comment on it while it unfolds. This may become disturbing. Is that okay?"

"I told you I can take it."

"The entire colour composition here," he said, pointing with a sweeping finger across the canvas, "we have to tone back and build the landscape for our narrative. On the palette put a large blob of titanium white and with a pallet knife mix in some burnt umber and a big blob of clear emulsion," she went to the table and mixed the colour, "take a large spatula and scrape the paint on. Don't worry about the scratches that will appear and the cuts in the tissue because that is what we want." They both worked together mixing and adding paint to the canvas and an edgy ground for the painting started shaping up. It took a good hour to do this and he took heavy sandpaper and rubbed it on the canvas edges exposing the red and yellow. He gave Tula a turn at it.

"What are we making?" she asked in bewilderment.

"A wall of atmosphere like the walls of this city; they all have bumps bruises, scratches, and years of layered paint and stuff just like life. There is a layer of dust across this city and we want to show that, a wall of colour and dust. Now take some more white and burnt umber and spread it out in smaller areas about a foot in size, and while still wet take a spatula and make scratches in it. Imagine a crazy woman trying to write a letter on paper with a thick black pencil. What would her writing be like? It certainly wouldn't be smooth and flowing. It would be sharp and stabbing—right? It would express her feelings about life and how it has treated her. Her mind would be racing with uncontrolled thoughts," soon Tula was writing on the canvas about her past, scratching it through the paint exposing her in red and yellow. She did this for another hour with Jonathan coaching her on, getting information out of her and laying it on the canvas. She spoke of her abusive friends, parents and incidents in her life that had bought her to where she is today but most of all her sexuality. When Tula got angry the word fuck can get out of control. She laid on the colour and scratched things like: No, I won't fucking go! Fuck off liar! And other remarks. When she had finished they rubbed paint over the writing that was in relief. The writing made a pattern of shapes from a distance but to decipher the notations you would need to be closer to the image.

"Time for a break," Jonathan said and he went to the kitchen and made ham sandwiches with lettuce, cheese, tomato and dressing. He made a plate of fruit and Franklin's pickles and put everything on a tray and returned to the terrace. Tula sat in her rattan chair drinking her beer staring at what she had done, getting up she would add another line, another scratch. She threw some beer at the painting and it dripped down the canvas. Jonathan had said to do it, so she did. From the kitchen Jonathan watched her. She was beautiful in her shorts and top splattered with paint. She reminded him of her daughter after getting into dad's paint box. But there was a look of concentration on Tula's face and an anxious demeanor about her. Her back was straight and she sat erect ready to pounce, she wanted to do more, this was a release of some sort for her; he could see it in her body language.

"We are ready to start including our subjects—a white pickup truck and a bus—they will fill half of the canvas area. I will start with a sketch of them," he picked up a thick graphite stick and with swift long movements of the arm he sliced in the outline of the truck, drawing in the perspective sight lines of ten feet above the street so the bed of the truck would be partially seen, quickly he sketched with coloured pencils, going over his lines, driving them into the paint. Two dark officers appeared in black baseball caps and riot gear, their automatic rifles held to their chest. They sat crossed legged and jackbooted, one on each side of the tailgate. Gold lettering of *Policia* could be seen across the back of one of them. Both officers looked dispassionately at their prisoner who is yet to appear. On the tailgate the lettering read Policia Municipial and the number PV42. The same was written on the cab door below the scribbling of the Puerto Vallarta's city crest. On top of the cab were blue and red lights that threw colour onto an object taking shape.

The object became a huge white bus with red and blue trim, leaning away from the pickup as though turning to go around it. It appeared to be traveling far too fast. Its front wheels were in a turning position, the right wheel strained from the weight and the left, closes to the viewer, rose from the street. It was one of the many stinking rattling monsters of the streets of PV; one of the big white and blue monsters that kill fifty people a year in the city. He drew it in a position three quarters on. In the windows he drew and painted distorted faces of passenger's gawking in disbelief into the back of the pickup. The buses destination, written in rainbow colours above the windshield was CENTRO, Emiliano Zapata. On the windshield Tula painted in white the names of stops for the bus Ixtapa, Agua Azul, Cruz Rosa and Las Palmas over a smiling white-toothed Mexican driver. A rosary and cross-hung from the rearview mirror. The massive front steel bumpers of angle and tube steel were almost the size of the pickup and looked menacing, ready to smash anything in its path. Thick black slashes were the tires that roared over cobblestones.

"Take a rag now and rub some black under the bus and truck for shadows, keep rubbing until the shadow is gray. That's it—good," he stood back at the painting a surveyed it, "These are our subjects and the last one we will paint is our prisoner in the back of the truck." Tula's mouth dropped and she could feel herself scream inside. Christ, does he know what I did yesterday?

"I don't want to see myself."

"It won't be you, don't worry."

With one-centimeter brushes they started into the details of the vehicles. For accuracy, they used a couple of photos of buses that Jonathan had taken, "we will paint the light falling on the objects and not the objects themselves and this will force us to drop some details and let parts drift into the landscape. This will obliterate some of the composition characteristics of negative and positive space. Understand?"

"I think so."

They worked for half an hour painting and drawing the bus and truck and he stopped the process. "Now throw water mixed with white and burnt ocher on the painting," she did what she was told, "rub it with a rag—that's right. Now using the edge of the spatula take some black and extend some of the edges of the vehicles into the background and don't try to be correct just slice into the painting," she started to do that and suddenly the vehicles became part of the terrible obscene dusty landscape. Black, red, yellow white scratches turned to scars and wounds and the rubbing of rags on the paint became bruises. The bus was straining to keep upright as it tore across the canvas leaning desperately out of the way of the pickup. The pickup moved in the opposite direction tearing the painting's composition in two.

"We must do the center now, the center of our attention, our statement. But first let's have a beer and settle down a bit." And he went to the kitchen.

This is exhausting, she said to herself. He got the beer, some potato chips and salsa dip and they relaxed for a while studying the painting. Each got up quietly when they felt the urge and made more marks and rubbings on the painting. The bus and truck vibrated and looked as if they would drive off the canvas, the bus off to their left and the truck into the canvas. There was a space in the back of the truck—waiting for something. They had a couple of more beers and were getting drunk.

"Rub the painting in one spot Tula with this heavy sand paper," he place a small dab of black paint on it and handed it to her, "imagine being crazy and worrying a part of your body or something by constantly rubbing it until it became raw, "soon a worry spot was worn into the paint in the bottom left quadrant of the painting, "Okay, now with this bottle with its narrow spout, draw some symbols, perhaps ancient like hieroglyphics or a Celtic symbol, draw them somewhere on the canvas, anywhere," she quickly drew the symbols for earth, water, air and fire near the police pickup truck, "wow, the four Greek elements of Empedocles—very good."

"Yeah, I do remember some of my high school history."

"Let them dry and rub a little ocher on them. When you come up with more symbols add them in; mathematic equations are also good especially those of biomechanics."

"Why the symbols?"

"Symbols of the forces of nature add to the mystery of the composition. Some mad people think in mathematical terms turning the world into one giant equation. One of my mad friends at home turns the world into the geometry of triangulation. He has triangles scratched into the walls of his apartment—right into the plaster. They are equations—engineering equations. An economist friend of mine told me they were real. The equations really meant something, mostly about stress points on bridge spans. Perhaps he relates those stress points to what is going on in his mind.

The drawings are quite neat actually; they remind me of the drawings done in the caves of Lascaux, France. Those ancient, mystical artifacts are not primitive works as they have been described but are highly sophisticated interpretations of animal life.

"It's working honey, its working," he stood up and with his graphite stick started drawing in his main subject, remembering his anatomy, "now this has to be good, correct and must convey a feeling that it works," he grumbled as he concentrated.

"What do you mean by works?"

"It is something that is difficult to describe but I'll try. Artists study the masters through the ages and when they do, over the years they come to understand, light, colour, line, shape and other elements of composition it takes to create a painting, a sculpture or an architectural element. The artist comes to an understanding or perhaps achieves enlightenment of what is correct; what has rightness. A good analogy is the human body. We are so familiar with it; we know when any piece of it is drawn or painted out of place, deformed or not right. After all it is we. We do not have to study the body to know if it works or not, our inner genes will tell us so and I'm talking about the visual form of the body. Our genes are trained to pick out the correct body form, especially for mating, in order to reproduce the correct body form. It is the same in art. When you become familiar with the great art of the world, subconsciously you work towards that end. With all the stuff the mind of artists have gathered they know when a piece of art works. Does that make sense?"

"I think so. I'll have to study and really think what you said since you're mad. Can we fuck now?"

"Later my dear, we are almost done."

Jonathan's poor naked woman sat cross-legged on the large spare tire her arms outstretched and handcuffed to the cab. A man's shirt, the arms tied around her neck draped down her torso covering her left breast but left her right exposed. He drew the lines over and over on top of each other. He mixed some paint of white and burnt umber with a touch of vermillion and painted the arms, legs, belly and breasts of the tormented woman. Her exposed nipple looked red, tender and sore. The face had to be spontaneous like the rage that was emanating from her. Eyes bulged out in madness and bewilderment. Her mouth was a toothless black and red hole that screamed obscenities. Her hair was long and ratty; a brown blonde tangled mess. Her armpits were unshaved and with dirt on her deeply tanned body, she looked filthy and diseased. Over and over he drew and painted her. With a few strokes of titanium white he highlighted the madwoman and parts of the vehicles, "You try a little, Tula."

She moved in with a small brush and painted a film of white around parts of the screaming body to separate her image from the iron monsters.

"Take this line brush and with some red lightly touch her left upper arm and wrist up from the cuffs to give the effect of scratches from fighting and bruises from the iron bracelets." She carefully made the wounds and he gently rubbed blue on parts of her body, bruising her. Suddenly she was alive, a tormented soul, lonely, wounded and helpless against a world that had rejected her. In her rage she flew off the canvas at Jonathan and Tula.

"I can't do this anymore; I'm drunk," she cried, "Oh Jesus! That's me in that truck. It's going to happen to me, I just know it! God I don't want to be mad someday. What did she do?" He held her hand. It had been six hours since they started and she was mentally exhausted.

"Who knows honey, she could have been running down a street naked, evicted from her apartment for not paying rent, a vagrant sleeping in the park, or screaming at people on the street. Maybe she was caught stealing food or stuff to keep herself alive—whatever, she needs help. She needs to be taken away for care of some kind and for her own protection. But most of all we don't want her around. She has come to a state in life where she is out of control and in harms way. She can't take life anymore and we can't take her. She has come to the end of her wits and it will be a long time until she gets them back and perhaps she won't be able to. We see these people everyday, muttering to themselves, sleeping in doorways, pushing carts, carrying old suitcases or walking, walking, walking."

He held on to drunken Tula and led her to his bed. She climbed in and he removed her clothes and with a damp warm face cloth he washed the paint from her face, arms and legs. He pulled the bed sheets up over her and kissed her good night. Tears rolled down her cheek and he gently kissed them away. His thoughts were of this woman who is so strong and yet overcome with emotion from creating just an image of what can come to all of us. We all walk a line between sanity and madness; just a little chemical imbalance, emotional trauma or injury can set us on a path of destruction and oblivion, or to a place where we cannot come back. From sleeping Tula's point of view—things were completely different.

"It's going to be all right honey. You did a fine piece of work today. Get some sleep." He closed the bedroom door and went out to their painting and opened another beer. He would scratch at the poor woman in the back of the truck for hours into the night. He got drunk and worked the paint, scratching and rubbing and when he knew he had finished he gave the entire painting several coats of high gloss polymer emulsion. He turned off the lights and climb into bed with sleeping Tula.

Close the Shutters, Lock the Doors

Brass band of thunder
Carried on the breath of Chac
Wrought ancient vengeance

"Look at that!" shouted Jonathan. They sat at her bedroom desk and watched an extraordinary event take place on her computer. A huge spiraling plum of white clouds hundreds of miles wide filled the web site of the United States Weather Bureau. Tula loved the excitement of catastrophic events; she had experienced many of them since she had lived some of her life in the Caribbean. She hugged and bit Jonathan on the shoulder.

On the monitor was illustrated and announcement:

"Above the Pacific Ocean the Moderate Resolution Imaging Spectroradiometer aboard NASA's Terrestrial Satellite has transmitted this image of a hurricane making its way north up the west coast of Mexico. An estimation of the size and intensity of the hurricane has been calculated to category five. Warnings have been sent to communities on the Pacific Coast and the government of Mexico that catastrophic events will take place in the area in the next twenty-four to seventy-two hours."

"We are in for a hell of a blow. Do you think we should get out of here and go up in the hills until it passes over?" Jonathan said.

"No let stay here and watch and see what happens," Tula whispered in his ear.

"You're a crazy woman."

"Perhaps."

At eight in the morning the Puerto Vallarta's Malecón was deserted except for patrolling military troops and civil defense authorities. The roads along the Bahia de Banderas were cordoned off by military trucks and heavily armed soldiers in battle dress.

Huge black and gray thunderclouds hung over the city. The ocean churned under the outer winds of the hurricane moving past the mouth of the Bahia. The eye was heading in a northeast direction. At its edge the wind raged at one hundred and sixty-five miles an hour and the winds hitting shore were blowing at one hundred and fifteen miles per hour. Rain fell sideways spiraling down from the north arms of the storm. Low pressure caused by the raging storm raised the ocean and as it passed the water fell and surged into the Bahia. Those still near the shore watched as the sea receded exposing the beach. There was not a bird in sight to feed on the floundering fish, they knew better and had headed inland, up into the jungle of the Sierra Madre to perch in trees and watch the event.

Ten thousand residences were ordered to evacuate hotels, condos, townhouses and homes. Thousands moved inland by taxis, buses, and cars or walked. Many did not heed the warning, stayed behind and suffered injury from flying debris.

Across the road from the abandoned Malecón a thick glass window exploded from the impact of a thrown street cobble. The glass left its frame and shattered into a million pieces on the sidewalk. Two men reached into the window and from the display they quickly filled their pockets with silver necklaces and rings. They climbed inside the shop and smashed through glass cases that held gold and diamond rings, scooping up as much booty as possible—filling a trashcan. A gun in his hand as a hammer, one of the thieves smashed a jewelry case; he cut himself and the blood rushed from a deep gash in his arm. Suddenly a shot was heard and the armed partner collapsed, clutched his leg and screamed in agony as a bullet tore through his thigh. Three federal police officers jumped through the window and grabbed the two thieves pulling them out of the store and up the street to safety.

The sea surged fifteen feet from its normal high tide. It thundered into the shore, bringing with it boulders, gravel and millions of yards of sand. The huge waves destroyed swimming pools, hotel lobbies, nightclubs and stores along the shore. Two storeowners who stayed behind to protect their merchandise were sent hurling through their establishment and out the back door with all their goods. Both were lucky and survived but with many scratches and bruises. Three times the water receded and three times it returned up the cobbled streets carrying boats, cars, carts, refrigerators and anything else not bolted down. Beach umbrellas and pieces of palapas sailed in the wind. Palm trees bent to the storm's rage and lost a few fronds but they did well since they are built to withstand nature's bad moods. A four star hotel was slammed by a giant wave that lifted the beach and drove it through the first four floors leaving a huge boulder in the hotel's lobby. The infrastructure of the hotel was terribly damaged—it would be closed for a year. The mile long Malecón structure was undermined of its gravel and sandy base and collapsed; the entire length of cement, brick and rock structure would have to be replaced. The waves made a horrific noise as they crashed into buildings and cars and it all ended in an eerie silence. No one was killed.

Jonathan pulled up the bed sheets and blankets around them. The storm pelted rain against the window—the electricity was off and a candle burned on the night table beside the bed. The computer, now on battery power, glowed on its desk. An old black and white poster of Emiliano Zapata stared down on them from the wall above the wrought iron headboard. He was a handsome killer in his day but he is long dead. Jonathan sensed Zapata's ghost nearby—his vicious eyes pierced through the lowlight, into his lover and him.

"We have known each other for years and I still don't know about your family. I do know that things were bad for you years ago. Tell me about them, honey," Jonathan said.

She looked at him for a minute and did not say anything—she calculated the risk: "I guess I can now. Life has changed for me lately and I don't care about the past anymore and who else cares anyway? It's not a good story," she said sadly and looked at him with fearful eyes that glistened in the candlelight, "I was raped and abused by my high school friends and no one came to help me, the teachers and my family thought I instigated the whole affair and ran away. It was gang rape, by a bunch of bad bastards."

"Didn't your dad stand up for you?"

"No my dad was crap. I only saw my father a few times and I don't remember those events for some reason. I know there is something there and I know it's horrendous—my mind blocks it out. My head won't see and deal with it; my memories of my childhood aren't there anymore. My doctor says it's something deep in my past that makes me explode with anger—we all understand that generalization. You've seen that anger before. Right?"

"Yeah, I remember," he said and gently kissed her.

"My family was all bad except my mother and one brother—dope growing, dealing, gambling and murder—none of them got caught. It was all about dope. It all centered on that crap and those fuckers who deal in it. They should be blown away, strung up by their thumbs and beaten to death! I get so fucking angry when—"

"Whoa—its okay—easy."

"You see?"

"Murder and your stories, are you sure they are not just your imagination? Come close—it's cold," He thought Tula was healthy and she could talk openly about her experiences. But there was a sharp edge to her and there may be others inside her head, and if there were; he would eventually see and feel those dark shadows. He knew the angels could come out charging in full armor to cut him to pieces.

She snuggled up to him and continued her story: "It was real, I was about eleven and I overheard my father on one of his rare visits home talking to one of his cronies at an automotive repair shop. They didn't know I was listening from the open window of my dad's car. I have never told this story before so please respect my confidentiality."

"I will," he snuggled to her as the wind howled outside. Suddenly a shutter protecting the window came loose and swung back against the building with a crash. Jonathan jumped out of bed and opened the window, grabbed the shutter and made it fast. He quickly returned to bed soaking wet. Tula howled with laughter and excitement and pulled him close to her, "go on with your story," he said shuddering.

"I love you babe when you take care of me. Oh you're wet and cold from the nasty storm. Now where was I? Yeah, I know. I heard my dad ask some big greasy filthy guy where he had stashed the body and he told my dad, it's in the mountains, Mark, it will never be found. That's all I know and heard and I've kept it a secret until now. Sometimes I try to think it's all a dream or nightmare that I had years ago but I can't. I know it was real. I hadn't lost my identity at that time."

"You lost your identity? Why didn't you tell me about this trauma before? What the hell else is inside you?" An updated image of the hurricane flashed across the computer screen, "looks like the storm has passed the Bahia," he commented.

She glanced at the screen and went on with her story: "I didn't tell you all this before, I didn't trust you then and I don't now. I just don't care anymore. Yes, I still don't know who I am. Anyway, my childhood was a terrible ordeal. The only happy times I had were on hunting trips with my mom and her friends. We went out to the mountain valley wilderness down into the Coast Mountain Range to the town of Bella Coola, which is at the end of a fiord that cuts deep into the mountains. Do you know where I'm talking about?"

"Sure do, I've been there a few times."

"I learned at a very early age about wilderness survival, guns and knives and how to use them to hunt and dress animals for the dinner table or the camp fire. Those times were beautiful because I learned from my mother about the birds, caribou, marmots, bears, beavers and all the lovely creatures and flowers of the forest. She knew much about them and always took her books on the flora and fauna of BC with her whenever we went out. I became very close with the forest and grassland wildlife. She even taught me about the weather systems and how to read the clouds and set up camp to weather the storms that came in from the north and west coast.

"When I could, I spent my time in the forest on long walks or riding my horse Mr. B across the grasslands, valleys and mountains. Mr. B. and I would sometimes be gone for days. At times I would sit still deep in the undergrowth and watch the creatures there. I would barely breathe. I would watch the little mice, voles, lizards, snakes, bobcats and deer going about their business. I longed to be one of them. The wilderness is my favorite place today, it's where I'm most comfortable and at peace. I can yell, cry and scream out there and no one will hear me. The forest never strikes back at me; it folds its arms around me. Out there I can be like the animals. I can hunt for food and find a safe place to bed down for the night away from those who hunt and kill in the dark. There was danger where I went but nothing like what was at home.

"In the wilderness hunting, dad didn't give a damn about anything of course—the corrupt bastard that he was. He wanted to kill everything in sight. He never saw the forest, grasslands and mountains like me. Luckily I was only with him a few times on our family hunting trips."

"Where is he now? Is he still alive?" Jonathan asked and he thought she doesn't need his help, just companionship. Or was he in her feline pride—a cub of a ferocious mother lion?

"Dead," she said with a big sigh and pushed herself up from Jonathan and leaned on her elbow against the pillow.

"Tell me the story," he said, kissing her breasts.

"Don't do that Jonathan. I can't concentrate. Do you want me again?"

"No, the story, tell me the story?" he said with excitement.

"Right, my dad and his two buddies, one the greasy bastard and the other I can't remember, went deer hunting outside of Anaheim Lake by Tweedsmuir Park on the edge of the Coast Mountains. They were quite high up on the edge of the tree line; up in the Engelmann Spruce-Subalpine Fir Zone where grizzlies hibernate in the winter."

"Wow, you know about zones?"

"I have seen some of the maps you made."

"Their ATVs were loaded down with bloody deer kills and for some stupid reason they decided to dress the deer out there in the wilderness and not bring the kills back to their motel where it would be safe to do the butchering. I have a feeling that my dad and his buddies had some weird ritualistic ceremony they liked to perform when they dressed their kills. Anyway, I don't want to get into that sickness. They had strung up a white tail deer to the limb of a tree and were skinning it, the blood and viscera dropped into a hole that they had dug below the carcass. Of course there was blood everywhere and on them and the smell drifted down the avalanche slopes and into the rivers to fishing grizzly bears. According to the investigation team what happened next was a mother grizzly and her two three-year old cubs charged into the camp killing my dad and his buddies. The coroner said they were naked at the time they were killed as their clothes were laying on their ATVs and there was no shredded and bloodied clothing at the site. All that was left of them was chewed crushed bones and ripped flesh scattered around the area. Two heads were missing; they were probably hauled away by coyotes or wolves. Other creatures had their fill after the bears had departed. DNA testing had to be done of the remains to separate them into partial bodies for burial. The white tails had barely been touched."

"Jesus, what happened to the bears?"

"A team of hunters and conservation officers tracked the bears by helicopter and found them a few miles away foraging for berries in an avalanche chute. Unfortunately the officers had to shoot the bear family since they had smelled and eaten human flesh. No one living in the area would be safe with that trio on the loose. It was a sad thing all around."

"When did they find your dad and his buddies?"

"About three days after my mother made the report—about four days after the killing. It's amazing what bears can eat—there was not much left of the three of them to bury. You know, thinking back on it now, none of the family cried at the funeral. I know I was relieved and I felt a wonderful sense of freedom after my father's death even though I only saw him a few times in my life. I left my family when I could. When I was strong enough I got the hell out of there."

"Where did you go, you must have been young?" The hurricane was moving on and the winds were light against the shutters.

"I was sixteen, big for my age and tough but lousy at concentrating on anything because of my fucked up family life. I completed junior high and read someplace that if I joined the army I could get my grade twelve and more, so I joined up and was stationed in Chilliwack, BC and Wainwright, Alberta. Within the three years of my contract, I got my grade twelve and an education in making firearms and Special Forces skills of all things. A real career move that was, where the hell was I going to use those skills?" and they roared with laughter.

"I can make rifles and handguns out of anything and produce gunpowder and explosives from stuff in the kitchen. I'm a crack-shot with a rifle and trained in Special Forces and the art of killing. I'm a woman of survival, babe, and perhaps crazy because of my past. Little does Canada know what they have let loose on the world. That's all I can tell you Jonathan. It's too dangerous to go any further."

"What do you mean, too dangerous?"

"No more questions. It's quiet now. Just make love to me again," she said softly and so he did.

The police dragged their looters to high ground. They waited on Av. Juárez for the storm to subside. Both thieves were treated for their wounds, handcuffed and put in the back of a white pickup truck along with a few other bandits. They were driven off east to the Ixtapa jail that was bursting. The troops and civil defense officers kept everyone away from the wreaked hotels, stores and homes until the owners could return to safely, remove their property and secure their businesses. The hurricane passed, traveled at eighteen miles an hour and made land fall at the fishing village of San Blass. It destroyed the little town and its small fishing fleet. It killed four people before exhausting itself in the Sierra Madre. By the time it reached Texas it was a small tropical storm.

Rick Thomas

A Wet Death in the Afternoon

Is my dress too short?
Is my eye makeup just right?
It's great to be gay

Draft

Good morning Tula

The client you are to dispatch is David M. Somerset.

David is a homosexual from a gay community in Chicago. His sexual preference is not an issue here; his financial investments on behalf of major international clients are. Evidence suggests David has been operating a very sophisticated inside trading and money laundering operation parallel to his legitimate occupation. He cannot be proven guilty of any wrongdoing and he knows that and has sheltered himself from prosecution. He now has immunity from the legal system.

Mr. Somerset has been openly confronted about his behavior but he feels he is above reproach. He suffers from an enormous ego or he has become manic, in either case he must be dispatched. He is physically fit with no martial arts training and does not carry a weapon.

He is vacationing at the Red Chairs Hotel and spends most of his time in the Romantic Zone of Old Town.

On completion of your assignment please send me a draft of your accomplishments.

Tula moved down the beach as she had done for the last five days weaving gently between brown tanned bodies. She moved with a purpose and focused on her objective to do one thing only—kill. No gray fuzzy thinking, just mental on off switches working. Her state of mind was that of an animal on the hunt practicing what she knows best—stealth and cunning. Each day between the hours of 10:00 and 13:30 she chose a different place for a few hours of observation. When her task was done the police would investigate patterns and behavior of customers in the restaurants and cafes. She could not afford to be remembered.

Today the spot would be on the north edge of the chaotic forest of gay bodies, chairs, umbrellas and palapas. The sun was rising and heating up the beach; she took a shaded place under a palapa with a single red and green canvas chair and a small round table. She aimed the position of her chair in line with a section of the gay community less than one hundred yards away. The waiter came by and she ordered a cup of fruit and a light cola. She reached into her beach bag and took out a paper back novel, opened it and leaned her head back to read. She did not read the book but rested her sun glassed eyes on a spot down the beach were a group of ten to twelve gay men spent their late morning and afternoon.

They were consistent these gentlemen from Chicago. At the beach they giggled and laughed in their feminine way and when the waiter came they ordered cocktails, beer and snacks and became very drunk. Not smashed but pleasantly smashed socially, talkatively, drunk. Jokes and cattiness were always present and rarely did they talk about the business in the marble halls of the windy city.

It was their habit to be organized since they all worked for powerful financial institutions. All were disciplined predictable individuals; something Tula counted on. They were very handsome men, lean and tanned in little tight bathing suits that revealed how well endowed they were. Some padded themselves to make up the shortcomings that nature had given them. They always arrived at their spot near the edge of the steep drop to the water at the south end of the beach. Fussing about, they gathered chairs and small round tables in a circle with spaces for blankets and towels if they wanted to lie down to snooze or pass out. All carried beach bags packed with lotions, reading material, small bottles of liquor, cigarettes, cigars, condoms and make up. Some had dresses and women's gear and if they got drunk, which were most days, in the late afternoon thing's got outrageous. The makeup would be laid on thick and heavy, and colourful dresses would be adorned. The cattiness and insults would hit a crescendo disturbing others around them. The waiters sometimes would have to disperse the gang. All would leave the beach hand in hand in laughter, some off to make love, others to drink at the roof top bar that put on games like Gay Bingo. By evening, after a siesta they would clean themselves up and fan out across PV to celebrate the remains of the day and the good life.

These were gentlemen of wealth from one of the most powerful and influential cities in America. Their yearly gathering at one of the most famous gay destinations in the world was a two-week vacation they all deserved. They had other destinations with family and friends but this was their gang and they had met on this beach for years. The boys fell in love each year and sometimes rekindled old loves and friendships. All went home in the end and left their stories in PV.

Tula concentrated on one of the group, David Somerset, perhaps the best looking stud on the beach. David was having his well-deserved vacation from his job. As every year his fun crowd was living in a hacienda on the hill that they rented and decorated with rainbow flags and Christmas lights. He had many Red Chair friends and lovers around him—all well positioned in American financial institutions. Some he did business with and they were sharing his vacation. One might say it was a busman's holiday of a powerful financial cartel.

Today, as everyday that Tula observed, David partied with the boys with their gay jokes and camaraderie and after a couple of hours the heat drove him and the boys into drowsiness and sleep. At 13:00 everyday, with no exception, she watched David dive into the surf for his mid day swim.

Always at the same time and to the same place, and no matter what colour danger flag was flying. He swam about one hundred yards off the beach and floated in the gentle swells.

She rose from her canvas chair and looked back at the hotels and up and down the beach surveying the scene. The sun was over the bay shining in from the west no one would see what would happen to David in the bright mid day sun.

A few days later on a Sunday when the beach was packed Tula made her move. She surveyed the scene; the weather was cloudless; the hot sun burned and everyone tanned. The brown pelican police soared in formation over the surf and high above them drifted the frigate birds, riding on the thermals coming up from the heated beach and concrete hotels.

The red flag was up warning swimmers of the vicious undertow but David knew how to swim in the bad waters off the beach. He had been swimming in it for many years and knew, like the Mexican children, how to use the undertow to his advantage. He took his daily swim every day before cocktails with the boys. Today was like any other.

Sometimes fish explored David's body when he floated out in the swells beyond the breakers and they tickled when they touched his legs and arms. On one occasion when he swam a mile out into the bay he was with the dolphins that rubbed against him, a thrill he would never forget. Playing with the wild dolphins can be risky since they can be rambunctious like overgrown dogs. A five hundred pound playmate can be hard to handle. Once was enough for David.

Today something rubbed against him; something large, it did not tickle; it was not smooth like a dolphin. For a moment David was startled and he righted himself from floating to treading water. He sensed something was wrong and it frightened him. In an instant he was pulled under. Something had grabbed him by the ankles. Holding his breath he looked down to see what it was and saw the hands of a scuba diver holding him. He bent his body and tried to reach down to the hands but his body started to turn. Crocodiles flashed through his mind and how they kill pray, they grab on and rotate their bodies drowning and ripping their victims apart. David turned and turned and could not break free from the hands. He was pulled deeper and at twenty feet he could no longer hold his breath. He let the air out with a scream that no one could hear, an instant later he inhaled the sea. He shouted to himself, this is how I'm to die—in this place, away from home, my family, my mother, my— It was only a few seconds and his mind, starved of oxygen, drifted into a drowning sleep. His limp body turned until it reached the sandy bottom where the hands let go of his ankles and pushed his chest against the bottom of the bay. The pressure forced any remaining air from his body. The killer rotated his body and David's white dead eyes stared back at her. Satisfied, the killer moved off along the sandy bottom, south, parallel to the beach to the rocky outcrop and Playa Conchas Chinas. No one missed David until the cocktail hour.

Draft

David M. Somerset has been dispatched.

Love Finds a Strange Place

Please keep your distance
Oh, woman how I love thee
You are just like me

Draft

Good morning Tula

Sorry, but we have clients back-to-back.

The client you are to dispatch is Gloria Riva Husband.

Gloria is a sexual deviant and predator, blackmailing a number of executives on boards of powerful international corporations. She has been warned of her behavior but we have not been able to deter her.

She is very fit and strong from weight training and jogging but has no offence or defense skills. Never the less, be cautious.

She is bisexual and very sociable.

She is vacationing at a rented condo in Conchas Chinas.

On completion of your assignment please send me a draft of your accomplishments.

"Good morning," Tula said to the beautiful woman jogging in the opposite direction on the Malecón.

"Good morning," the woman replied with a broad smile of gleaming teeth. After they passed each other they looked back and smiled. The next day was the same; they both said their good mornings, smiled and gave a little wave to each other. On the third day the beautiful woman was not around.

On the fourth day Tula jogged early and hung around hidden from view at the Taco stands at the fish market on the north end of the Malecón. She saw her beautiful woman jog by and she quickly jogged up behind her. "Good morning, I'm Tula."

Gloria looked a little surprised and gave her a big smile that conveyed a feeling of acceptance, "Hi, I'm Gloria, nice to meet you," and they awkwardly shook hands while still jogging, "been her long?"

"Yeah, very long, I live here."

"Oh, lucky you, I manage to come here a few months a year. My job demands I travel."

"I guess you get to see much of the world then."

"Sure do and that's the nice part of my job. The other is I have a variety of lovers," Gloria wisecracked and they both laughed. They slowed down at the bend in the Malecón by the lighthouse and sat down on a wrought iron bench.

"Where are you from?"

"British Columbia, Canada," she said.

"Me to, I live in Vancouver—fantastic place."

"I lived in central BC but my ancestors originally came from Haiti. They were slaves from Africa and pirates from Spain."

"Really? That's exciting as hell. That's why you're hair and skin are so beautiful," Gloria commented and she quickly scanned Tula's body.

Tula felt her eyes move across her and it stirred something inside she did not recognize. She talked about living in PV and her ancestry. Gloria told her of her dream of living in PV someday but for now she needed to work hard so she could live in style in the tropics. They were two healthy, fit, good-looking women and they knew it.

"What do you do for a living?" Gloria asked.

"I've done many things in my life but for the last several years I have been working in a bank as a loan officer. I will stay there for now, maybe forever. I make great money. And you?"

"International financial investments, I am a free agent and represent several organizations. It's tiring work with much traveling so I pump iron and jog, it keeps my energy up and I'll admit it; I like to look good on the beach."

"You know you look just like my ex," Tula said.

"Well if that's not a pick-up, I don't know what is."

"I'm sorry, I hope I didn't offend you. I don't know of any other way of introducing myself. I have to admit I have wanted to meet you this last week."

"That's okay. I have noticed you to and wanted to meet you. Oh let's cut to the chase, Tula. I'm gay and so are you, so perhaps we should get to know each other better."

"That would be nice. Maybe we could have dinner tonight?"

"Great idea, how about we meet at the arches around seven? I'll make a reservation at a restaurant on the river."

"All right at seven, see you," and Tula jogged off. Gloria watched her go and was excited about the prospect of being with a beautiful older woman and a slave/pirate to boot.

The hours could not go fast enough for Tula, she hummed and sang all afternoon. She went shopping in old town for something special to wear for her date; she had never done this before—dressed for a woman. She tried many dress styles and colours and settled on a simple dress that was a cream colour, low cut and short, it went perfect with her dark skin and black hair. She would not be able to wear underwear with it—she wasn't going to anyway. The built-in support for her breasts gave her cleavage justice. She picked out a matching pair of sandals; she could not wear heels that would make her too tall for Gloria. They were the same height in running shoes. She picked out a small handbag to match her dress, very plain with a Huichol design on one side and a long thin gold chain shoulder strap. Jewelry she had plenty of but tonight she would just wear her simple gold watch and one gold ring in her ear, a symbol of her pirate ancestry.

She rushed home with her stash of goodies, laid them out on her bed and got naked. She ran a hot bubble bath, poured herself a glass of Champagne and settled into the hot womb of the tub. She giggled to herself at what she was doing. She had never been with another woman sexually and was a bit baffled at what she was to do and how to act with this woman, her new friend and after tonight—her lover. She decided she would let Gloria take the lead, be the dominant one—the dominatrix. Christ, she thought these words have a whole new meaning for me now.

She watched herself in the closet mirrors, toweled and rubbed on lotion. She was pleased at what she saw. She turned to her side and thrust her bottom out and held her breasts up, she pouted—they drooped a bit. But she smiled, they reminded her of her children and the wonderful times they had when they were babies. She turned and faced the mirror; she put her right leg forward and pointed her toes. She could see the cut of her thigh muscles. For years they had been her powerful friends. They glistened from the shine left by the lotion. She flexed her arm muscles and they bulged with strength and power. She turned sideways and rotated her shoulders to expose her back, raised her arms and bent her left knee. Muscles rippled down her back, buttocks and legs. Her back, she felt was her best feature—broad and muscular.

Gently she let her new dress fall around her and she slipped into her sandals. She brushed her long curly black hair. Her gray hairs among the coal black mass gave her an air of dignity and intelligence that comes with age. From her jewelry box she pulled out her gold Rolex and a ring of gold for her right ear. She checked her nails and filed a rough edge on her left forefinger. Deftly with single strokes she laid clear polish on them and dried them with her hair dryer.

She giggled uncontrollably at the revelation that she was going to be with a woman. Juliet flashed across her mind, standing out on a balcony under a black tropical sky filled with stars. In her innocence she is waiting for her Juliet.

She did not need makeup tonight; her face was dark from the sun and her skin clear; her eyelashes were naturally long and her eyebrows as black as her hair. Perhaps, she thought a little transparent gloss to make her lips shine; she put a little on. With a large gulp of Champagne she turned and looked at her image in the closet mirrors and smiled. She was stunning and the sexiest thing she had ever seen.

Before leaving the house she checked her lips in a mirror in the hall below the chandelier and told the angels to stay back tonight. She floated over the new bridge and along the walkway to the arches. Gloria was waiting for her looking incredibly beautiful, a new kind of beauty now for

Tula and a beauty she had not experienced before. Gloria had dressed simple like Tula and they recognized it right away. They greeted each other like they were already lovers and the best of friends, they kissed each other on the lips and it was the first time Tula experienced the taste of a woman's tongue.

"My God you are stunning Gloria."

"Thank you my friend and you are amazingly gorgeous. I've made reservations at Castro's. I hope you don't mind."

"I love that place Gloria, well done. Let's go, I'm ravenous."

"Me to," and they walked back along the walkway to the bridge and down to the islands in the river to Castro's Restaurant. They chatted away like the little green parrots that huddle in twos on the electric wires off Jonathan's terrace.

The table Gloria reserved was ready, simply set with a white tablecloth, napkins and silver service. Two wine glasses, one small for red the other large for white were at each setting. In the center of the table was a glass bowl and in it floated red Bougainville flowers. Two candles lit up the table that sat overlooking the river. The table was set off from others for privacy and the chairs were arranged so they would be seated side-by-side. The host, a beautiful Mexican boy, seated the two and asked them what they would like to drink. Gloria took charge and ordered a bottle of Pinot Noir, which came right away. The waiter poured it out for Gloria to taste.

"Excellent," Gloria beamed. The waiter poured their drinks picked up the larger glasses and left the table. Gloria turned to Tula, "I'm nervous."

"I'm horny," Tula said and they both giggled like school children.

"To us, and to *our* Mexico," they raised and clicked their glasses. They chatted away about whom and what they were, about work, what they thought of men and what it was like to have a true female companion.

"Look!" Gloria said, pointing to a tree that stretched toward them from across the river.

"What?" Tula said straining to see something through the dark.

"There—about halfway up the tree on that big branch—see it?" Suddenly the big branch moved; on it was a meter long iguana with a fat green body with spikes running down its back and thick tail. The light from the restaurant reflected off one eye that glowed from its spiky head; its mouth opened to reveal red moist flesh and a fat pink tongue

"Wow, ferocious looking isn't he?" Tula said.

"Biggest one I've seen around here," and she squeezed Tula's hand, "He looks like my ex husband," said Gloria. They both laughed, "no that's mean. I take that back. He was a nice man, but he did this crazy thing with hair gel. He made spikes on his head that didn't suit him but he thought them cool and an *in* thing. I loved him and miss him."

"Where is he now?"

"He was killed in a logging accident in British Columbia."

"Oh, I'm so sorry Gloria."

"Thank you. He was the only man I have ever loved. I have never found another man I could love after him and then I found women. That's not to say I don't have boyfriends but I doubt I will ever love another man again." Tula moved towards Gloria and they gently kissed. The iguana rested its head on the tree branch and closed its eyes.

"Looks like our friend has settled down for the night," Tula said.

"Yeah, he's good company, isn't he?"

They agreed on something simple to eat and went through an appetizer of escargot in mushroom caps and a main course of Pasta Marinara with Caesar salad. Tula felt a strange sensation come over her; she was in love with this woman. She had never had such a friend like this and they had just met. Ridiculous, she thought. I have missed something warm and comfortable all these years. She felt as if they were two giggling sisters on vacation in paradise.

"Have you ever been married Tula?"

"Yes, once, a long time ago to a handsome blonde, blue eyed beauty. He was the sexiest man alive for me at the time. He loved me so much he wanted to keep me naked and pregnant forever. He gave me two light skinned children and then I bolted. I broke his heart. I took my two kids and got out of Haiti and I never saw him again. I hope he is happy with another woman and has a family; he was a family man you know, that's all he wanted, kids and a wife to take care of him. Sometimes I wonder where he is and what he looks like now."

"Why did you bolt? I'm sorry, I—"

"That's alright. I don't know the answer. It seems when I become attached to someone something tells me to pull away. I don't know if it is fear of commitment or fear of loosing my freedom. I don't know. The only ones I have kept close to all these years are my children but then they are me aren't they?"

"Would your man still be handsome and strong?" Gloria asked.

"I don't know, perhaps he will have gray hair like me, a paunch and wrinkles around the eyes. I don't want to see him. He is a beautiful image in my memories now," Tula drifted off and became quiet.

"Do you have a man now, Tula?" Gloria held the back of Tula's hand and bought her out of her daydream.

"Now I have a crazy man that I see once in awhile," she said perking up.

"Crazy?"

"Yeah, he's an artist and a criminal that I have known for years. Intellectual and all that and he teaches me about the mind and other ways of looking at the world. I like him very much but no matter how hard we try we can't get along with each other. It could be we are in love, I don't know. I do have other men once in awhile but this guy shows up and we start hanging together, bitchin', fightn' and lovin'.

"Tell me the criminal part."

"He faked his own death and got caught which he arranged. First it was to make money then it became an art project. Things got out of hand and he spent a little time under psychiatric care. I think he faked that one to."

"Hold on here a second Tula, he's not that nut who crashed his plane and ran away to Europe a few years ago? Why he's famous."

"Yeah, that's him. He used to talk of marriage all the time but he doesn't do that anymore."

"Do you think he has given up on you?"

"Maybe, but I know when I am old, and I'm old now, but when I'm very old he will be there, I know it. I can see him, shuffling down the hall in his tatty night gown and slippers, a bottle of cheap wine in one hand and two plastic glasses in the other, sneaking into my room at The Home," they both laughed out loud, "but you know, my door will be unlocked for him."

"That's sweet—what's his name?"

"Jonathan, Jonathan Owen."

"Of course, I remember him now."

"Hey, do you smoke Gloria?"

"Thank God no. Don't tell me you do?"

"Yes, once a week," and Tula reached into her purse and pulled out two Cuban cigars. Gloria laughed with delight and Tula lit them both with a candle and gave one to her friend. With a broad smile on his face, the attentive beautiful waiter rushed over to the table with an ashtray.

Dinner, another bottle of wine, ice cream dessert and the Cuban cigars were eventually over. The Iguana was snoring in the tree and Castro's was dark and empty but for them. Tula put her hand on Gloria's thigh and she felt the muscles of her woman and she could hardly breathe. Gloria looked into her eyes and said, "Let's go home, honey." They paid their bill and left Castro's holding hands.

They made love that night in Tula's bed. Lying in the arms of Gloria, she had never known such tenderness. Sex with women was new to her, she let Gloria do what she wanted and she was surprised how loving she was. Not like with men whose sex seemed violent and sometime down right abusive. She loved her men and making love to them but this was something different, something she knew she could do for the rest of her life. Perhaps becoming gay would bring her peace of mind. Friendship and companionship is what a woman could give her and that is what she felt she would need as she aged. Lying with Gloria was peaceful and a reprieve from her violent world and then she thought of what was to come in a day or two—she will have to murder her lover.

No matter where she was in the world Gloria went to the gym everyday: Paris, London, New York or Puerto Vallarta. It was part of her daily lifestyle like eating and sleeping—exercising must be done. She was a strong blonde blue eyed woman, five foot seven with a trim cut body that drew eyes to her when she took to the beach in her bikini. Her posture was straight and graceful and when she walked, a telltale duck walk was displayed when seen from behind—it gave away her ballet training.

Widowed and wealthy she operated her business from her hotel rooms around the world. She had a penthouse that she called home overlooking False Creek in Vancouver, British Columbia, but was there only in the summer months of the year. She liked to be on the road and have friends and lovers in many places. PV was one of the cities she loved most of all.

Each day at sunrise she would drive from her rented condo in Conchas Chinas to her favorite gym off the river. After her workout she would jog to the north end of the Malecón and back three times. The gym was quiet on this Monday morning; she had it all to herself. She was well into her exercise session and her muscles where pumped and beautiful as they strained to get out of her tight white shorts and halter-top. Sweat made her flawless tanned skin glow under the lights. She looked at her body in the wall-to-wall mirrors, flexed her arms and thigh muscles—she loved her image. Sex with her PV lover flashed across the mirror.

The girl from the reception desk put her head in the door of the gym and said, "Gloria, I'm going down the street to see my mother. She needs me at home for a few minutes. Watch the place, will you?"

Gloria nodded her head, "Sure, take your time, I'll be here for another hour at least." She prepared for her next exercise, bench press for her triceps and pectorals muscles. She liked this compound exercise; it made her feel powerful. She was a strong woman and loaded two large plates on the Olympic bar and mounted the bench lying flat on her back below the cradled weights. She raised her legs and crossed her ankles. Looking up she grasped the bar and prepared to lift it out of its cradle. A shadow loomed over her and said, "Let me help you with that."

"Tula," Gloria said with a smile, and in an instant Tula picked up the bar from the cradle and with a lunge drove it down on Gloria's throat. The sounds of squishing flesh, gurgling blood and the snap of the neck bones echoed in the empty gym—flesh and blood shot out of her mouth. As she died she looked straight into the eyes of her lover and killer. Her legs and hands lifelessly flopped to the floor. Tula left the bar across dead Gloria's neck.

She ran from the gym, tears streamed down her face. She ran up the river road and when she got to the bridge she dove into the water. She skinned her knees and elbows when she hit the submerged rocks. She went under in three feet of water, took a deep breath, came up, violently coughed and threw up. She screamed in agony. Onto the riverbank, she struggled, retched, sobbed and fell into the long grass.

The receptionist returned to the gym, she looked in the door, gasped and wet herself.

Tula lay on the riverbank for several minutes; she heard sirens in the distance. She pulled herself together and climbed onto the road and ran the few blocks home. Up the spiral staircase she pulled herself, ran a bath and got into the tub not bothering to undress. She ran cold water and lay there for the next three hours sobbing and shivering in loneliness and grief.

Carlota came in with groceries, which she put away in the kitchen. She went upstairs with bathing lotions and shampoos and found Tula in a terrible state. She shivered, whimpered, cried and whispered Gloria's name over and over. Carlota said nothing—just worked in silence. She undressed her, ran hot water from the shower and bathed her scrapes and bruises. She patted her down with towels and treated the wounds with first aid ointment then put light gauze bandages on the scraped knees and elbows. Carlota was silent in her work and holding Tula by the waist she led her to her bed and tucked her in. She went downstairs and made hot tea but when she returned to the bedroom with it Tula was sound asleep. Carlota called her old mother and told her she would be spending the night at Tula's.

Carlota stood in the bedroom doorway and realized her suspicions of Tula were right all along. There were too many connections between Tula and the murders in PV. News spread across the neighborhood of an accident at a local gym and with the recent deaths, speculation was rampant it was another murder. Carlota would not say anything; she too had her troubles and sins, and besides her employer had been good to her and her family. Carlota pulled Tula's reading chair to the bedside and made herself comfortable to watch over her lonely heartbroken friend.

Draft

Gloria Riva Husband has been dispatched, you filthy bastard.

A Voodoo Doll for Jonathan

Doll bones – white and clean
Of twigs and old cloth she made
A spirit catcher

Summer was on its way; the heat soared and drove the people of Puerto Vallarta indoors. Jonathan continued his contract painting and drawing the Mexican landscape and culture. He traveled up and down the coast, village to village, enjoying himself immensely. He was burned as brown as the locals and if it wasn't for his blonde hair and blue eyes he could have been born a citizen of Mexico. One thing he loved was being part of the country he was in, living among the people and their culture, Being There, was his way of adventure.

One morning as he prepared to go for breakfast there was a knock on his apartment door. He opened it and a large black woman filled the doorway. She was dressed in a bright yellow fabric; it covered her from neck to toe. A turban like cover of the same colour and fabric was wound around her head and spiraled another head size above her. Her huge black face with massive white and black bloodshot eyes stared at him. Her fat lips shone over giant white teeth. Large round silver earrings hung down to her shoulders. Her huge breasts heaved a silver chain that cascaded down her chest and rested in the dark cleavage. She was out of breath from climbing the stairs, "Mr. Owen?"

"Yes, can I help you?" He was dumbfounded, it was only in Africa had he seen such a preponderance of physic and colour in a woman.

"Ah good—maybe—may I talk to you? My name is Sonja and I Tula's Bon Dieu," she said in broken English. She breathed heavily and sounding concerned.

"Yes of course, come in—come in and sit down," the colourful mass moved into the room and he closed the door, he felt small in her presence. She evoked a feeling of royalty. He quickly removed some clothing from one of his leather armchair and the huge woman sat down. He sat down in a chair beside her. "Tula told me about you," he stammered, "we are the only ones who see the angels. It's nice to meet you Sonja," and he shook her thick hand. "What can I do for you?"

"Thank you Mr. Owen—your girlfriend, my precious Tula, talk of you and make me promise that if anything happen to her I was to call you whereva' you were in the world. Well some'ting has happened Mr. Owen—she has disappeared."

"Disappeared?"

"Yes, Mr. Owen. She gone and I don't know where. One week now she be gone and I am worried for her safety. Some'time she would disappear for a few days but never this long without tellin' Carlota or me. I feel it in me bones that some'ting very bad has happen."

"Well what can I do Sonja?" and he thought of the communicating he would have to do to help, "I don't know Spanish too well. Have you reported to the police that she is missing?" He got up and went to the kitchen and opened the fridge—.

"No," she called to him, "she not get along with policia and they may be the ones that have taken her. Some'ting is going on with her and the policia," she heard the rattling of glasses and the pouring of liguid, "I know it not about her doll business—we all have to make a little extra to survive and da government know that. There is some'ting else and I think it to do with the assassinations that have been happen."

He came back into the room and handed a glass of lemonade to her.

"Thank you."

He took his seat. "Assassinations, what do you mean? Do you think she is involved in all those murders I've been hearing and reading about? How could she be involved in those murders? I—"

"I know it hard to believe Mr. Owen but her past and military training, well—"

"No, impossible. Jesus, I hope you're not right." And the possibilities flashed through his mind. I can't rule it out he thought.

"Will you please look for her Mr. Owen?"

"I don't know—I—She is in my soul though and I guess I should try—it will have to be on my travels and doing my work. I hope to cover some local villages in the next few days. And—well—maybe I can work something out. Ask about her in the places I go. I can't promise anything Sonja."

"I know Mr. Owen, I know. If I was young and get around better I be out der now, looking for her. I go to her home and see if there are any signs to where she be. You come Mr. Owen?"

"Of course, Sonja, I'll come along."

They left his apartment and walked the few blocks to Tula's home. Sonja had her own house key. They entered and set about searching for clues of where she might have gone. Everything was in order, clean and tidy since Carlota had been through the place that morning. Nothing was out of place or unusual in the living room, dining room and kitchen. They climbed the spiral stairs to Tula's bedroom and her computer was still on which was unusual since when she goes away for some time she always turns it off. A screen saver of floating geometric figures glowed from the monitor and Jonathan moved the mouse. The screen saver went away to reveal an email addressed to her from a fellow named Charlie.

To: Tula

Get out now. We have word through our investigating office in Ottawa that you are on a hit list of some German organization and to be executed immediately. There are other operatives working in Jalisco and Nayarit and they have been ordered to kill you. Leave now and email me from another computer once you are out of there. Disguise yourself and trust no one.

Charlie.

"Christ, Sonja, she's in trouble and by the looks of it she may be the next victim of the assassin. This is a little too much for me; I'm not good dealing with crazy situations like this." He mentally took that statement back.

They knew she left in a hurry, but where? Jonathan went through a pile of papers beside her computer but found nothing. On her night table beside her bed were a number of maps and tourist books about Mexico. One book was open with a line through Sayulita.

"This is too obvious," Jonathan commented, "why would she tell anyone of her whereabouts?"

"No, Mr. Owen, it is a message to whoever is after her; like in days of old when enemies picked their ground for killing."

"You may be right Sonja. Damn it; if I go to Sayulita I will be putting my own life in danger."

"Please Mr. Owen you must find her," and she got excited, her white eyes bulged from their sockets, "we must make a doll, a voodoo doll for our Tula. You carry it close to you it will protect you and help you to find her. Come into garden and we will gather some sticks for her body."

Ridiculous, he thought, "Anything you say that will help."

They went out the back of Tula's home to an untouched part of the garden courtyard and collected branches that had fallen from the trees, small branches, about twelve-centimeters long and a two-centimeters thick. Each one was bleached white from the sun. "These are good," Sonja, said, "these are her bones, all delicate, smooth and white. Now let us go inside and find some flesh for her bones."

They went upstairs to the bedroom. In Tula's closet was her wardrobe mostly black, red, gold and with a few other colours. Sonja ripped a piece of material from a blouse. She then tore a strip from a beige dress and from a few pairs of lounge pants she pulled out the drawstrings. "There—this is good this is her flesh. Now the bathroom," she said, and they went through Tula's cabinet draws and from her hairbrushes pulled black curly hair with some gray strands. "Now we will go downstairs and sit in the kitchen and make our sacred doll."

They sat opposite each other at Tula's kitchen table and Tula's Bon Dieu started her ceremony, she chanted in some language that Jonathan did not understand. She tied the sticks together with the drawstrings and when she was done she magically made a white dress and halter-top from the fabrics. She bound it to the sticks with drawstrings. The black, red and gold material made a waistband with tails twice the length of the body. The hair from the brushes she pushed into the tight spaces formed by the sticks at the head of the doll. With black and red markers that she took from her purse she made some eyes and a mouth on the bone white sticks. One eye was marked open and happy the other in the shape of a star—anguish. At the other end of the doll she painted red toenails.

"Well that was a fast piece of art Sonja," he commented.

"No Mr. Owen, it is not art, it is a Loa our people use everyday to govern and help us with our lives. The dolls give lives meaning and make us look on what is important. These dolls are our deities, the spirits of God," she said as she finished and kissed the effigy. She chanted something, again Jonathan could not understand and then she drifted back to English. "Now we must go back to bedroom and find the essence of her," and they went up the spiral stairs to Tula's bedroom and Sonja pulled back the covers of her bedding and rubbed the little doll over the sheets. From a laundry basket in the corner of the bathroom Sonja reached in and pulled out some clothing and rubbed them on the doll. We must make our Tula come alive - make connection to her," she said as she handed him the doll. "You carry with you always Mr. Owen. It will help you find her on your journey. The doll and Tula will pull to each and come together when time is right."

Jonathan put the doll to his face and he could smell Tula and he felt her presence on him and through him and he said sadly, "Why should I help find her Sonja? She was always bad to me and her other men. Why should I care for this woman?"

"Tula will always mean something to Mr. Owen. You cannot run away from her. She is a part of you. Like me, you have seen the angels, the good ones and the bad ones that have ruled her life. We have an obligation, Mr. Owen, a bonding, to this woman and her little people with wings. She has cursed us like she has cursed others; her men live in silent desperation with her vibratin' and crashin' about in their heads. She tol' me once that you were the only one that would not put up with her bad side—that is why she feel you the strongest. You are the one who can help her in her bad time. And that is now Mr. Owen. Right this minute she is crying out, somewhere out der in Sayulita, from prison or grave. She needs you Mr. Owen."

"I don't think she is crying out for me, I think she is playing a deadly game. I will keep the doll with me until I find her but I cannot promise anything. And I will say it again, I don't speak Spanish well and know just a little of the country and it will be difficult to connect with people to help guide me to her," he said gently holding the doll as though he was holding Tula.

He felt so sad and afraid of what lay ahead of him and what he might find. He was still obligated to fulfill his contract that was almost complete. He could not afford to break the deal and be sued since the

Canadian Government who pardoned him for his sins of the past. Who knows what they will think of his involvement with an international assassination organization. If he screwed up he would never be able to travel outside of Canada again.

Back in the kitchen Sonja pulled two photographs of Tula from her purse and handed them to Jonathan. "Deez will help in your search," she said, "show them to everyone you see, they will recognize her—I know that. She is a beautiful woman and not easy to forget Mr. Owen."

He studied the photos and remembered his past with her and like Sonja said, the good and bad, and what he felt was sadness for this medusa of a woman who has to deal with so many demons.

The Dust of Sayulita

As I ran Charlie said,
"The other way, other way,"
So I did and won

The morning sun's rays hit the surf a hundred yards out in the bay and the brown bodies of young and restless surfers rode their first waves of the day. Tula watched them from her table in a hotel restaurant on the edge of the beach. Palm trees silently fluttered above her. Fishing boats had just been hauled out of the sea adding colour and culture to the scene. Fishermen were emptying them of their catch and equipment after a hard nights work. A smiling laughing fisherman ran up to the railing that surrounds the restaurant from the beach and hoisted up a roosterfish for her to see. It was a beautiful silver thing about a meter long with dorsal appendages flowing out of its neck and head. He offered it to her for a price. She shook her head, "No, gracias."

Sayulita is a seaside community filled with young people from the countries to the north. They are a Rastafarian, tanned, scruffy, smiling and happy tribe taking vacations of a year or two to live in a paradise of surf and sun. Some make a living working in the bars and restaurants while others make bead jewelry that they sell from tables set up wherever they can. All of them will eventually return to their homes in the north. But for now, for the short term, they are creating memories. A few older hippies have thriving businesses; they will not return home—they will become the dust of Sayulita.

When she comes to Sayulita, Tula's feet, like all the feet in the village are never clean, they are the colour of the dusty streets and where she starts and the dust ends, she and the rest don't know or care. At time she thinks perhaps she should stay here forever—disappear. She could go into an alternate state of mind through booze and drugs and become one with the jungle and its creatures. She could do it, become part of the beach, part of the dusty choked tribes that wander the streets barking, clucking or muttering incoherently. She could let her hair grow long and Rastafarian; be beautiful for some brown surfer boy for a few years until her age starts to swallow her in wrinkled leather and sagging muscle. Become ugly and be one with the dust. It's all just dreams from a brain roasted in the sun.

Every morning in a restaurant on the beach after breakfast and newspaper she takes a walk. At the north end of the beach is a hacienda on a cliff of black granite rocks that are streaked with white mica. Each morning the tide is up so the relentless ocean pounds the rocks trying to tear them down and inevitably it will. One morning there were a few more people on the beach than usual and Tula felt something was not normal or maybe it was. On top of a pile of beach pebbles was a twisted gray and brown piece of flesh and skin about three-meters long. She did not recognize what it was or what part of something it was. A man pointed up the beach to the rocks and she saw the rest of the carcass. A humpback whale had died. The whale had come to the end of her life and washed up on the beach during the night. She was huge; her fluke was two-meters across and her bloated body three meters thick. A crew of workers from the village arrived with a backhoe and prepared the beach to bury the great beast. One of the crew, an old wise looking Mexican who seemed to be in charge, said she was a female. There was no a sign of how she died or how long ago but he speculated she had been dead a week and judging from her size, she was old and her death was natural.

"Many whales die here," the wise man, said to Tula, "this is where they live most of their lives, here and in the north."

The crew dug a deep trench in the sand down to rock and dirt and with a chain around her fluke dragged her into her grave. They covered her up quickly as the stench was over powering and they all wanted to get away.

It was all unceremonious the way she was buried but Tula did see a few of the young Mexicans look back when they had finished the burial—a look of sadness on their faces.

"We see much death in our country," the wise man said, "it is so rich with life. The jungle and ocean are bursting with creatures. Our Gods are good at what they do."

Tula thought of Jonathan when she saw the great beast and how he loved nature and the journey that everything in the universe takes. A few years from now, from out of the south a hurricane will come upon this little bay; pound its shore and change its shape. With all its power it will expose the ghosts of the past and cleanse the good earth. The whale's bones will surface and her remains will be pulverized and ground by pebbles and stones. The rivers will flow down from the jungle into the streets and carry the dust and all that is in it to the sea. It won't take long and all will become the dust of Sayulita.

Tula had come to the village for a few days and did not tell anyone of her retreat. This trip to Sayulita was arranged and the rocks below the hacienda at the north end of the beach would be her focus this morning. Charlie had taught her about the hunt, she was strong like him and she would not run away. She knew what to do when hunted—become the hunter.

A little knife was nestled in its leather sheath that was sewn to the inside of her short's pocket. When pulled from the pocket the sheath would not come with it. The handle, three inches of black Bakelite, was knurled around its centre—a firm grip for the user. A blade, eight-centimeter two-sided stubby triangle made of Sheffield steel, was honed by her daily on a barber's strap. Tula used the knife as one of her kitchen utensils and was familiar with every movement she made with it and that was beyond just preparing food. Charlie had taught her other ways of using this deadly weapon. Her protection was near and ready.

Tula wore beige shorts and a black halter-top that just covered her breasts. All she had in her pockets were her knife and one hundred pesos to pay for her breakfast which was a hardy one this morning. She would need the energy in the coming hour. Her hair was pulled back and tied in a tight bun at the back of her head; she did not wear makeup or jewelry and was barefoot. Despite her age she was striking to look at, tanned, muscular and strong with an air of arrogance in the way she walked—proud and straight. Her head shook every few seconds since the angels were agitated and restless this morning. They darted in and out of her hair and behind her sunglasses, the large military type.

She scanned the beach and the beauty in front of her without moving her head just her eyes behind her sunglasses. She slightly turned her head and from her peripheral vision she could see her adversary. He had been following her for the last few days and had not made a move; perhaps he was wary of her. He was now getting daring and confident, having breakfast only thirty feet from her. Not too bright, she thought, and she sensed that this was the day one of them would die and she had prepared for it. Her body, mind and spirit were ready and primed.

"La cuenta, por favor," she gestured to the waiter who bought her bill which she paid with her single one hundred peso bill. She rose from her table and out of the corner of her eye she saw her hunter rise. He was a large man, very muscular and military looking with his shaved head and rawness in looks. His face was chiseled and lined; pockmarks scared his cheeks from bad acne in his youth. Tula estimated his age was approaching forty. She assessed his body and movements for what he had to do today. He was right handed and there was a bulge on his right thigh; long and thin—a weapon, perhaps a knife. In his surfer shorts and t-shirt he could not hide anything else. Tula sensed an arrogant demeanor about him. He assumed that he could do what he had to do without much effort. After all she was an old woman and all he needed to do was catch her alone and dispatch her by hand, breaking her neck or stabbing her to death.

Tula skipped lightly onto the beach looking left and right and smiled at the wonderful weather and the beauty of the scene. She showed confidence and a carefree air about herself to her adversary who followed behind her at what he thought was a safe distance. She glanced at him through her sun glassed peripheral vision every so often to make sure he was there. She skipped into the water a few times and picked up pebbles and tossed them out to sea as far as she could. The crashing waves and the cry of birds were all that could be heard.

There were no people at the end of the beach but some lonely dogs waiting for sunbathers to arrive to hang out with. It took twenty minutes to get there. The rocks she knew quite well for she had made love to Jonathan there in a crevice a few years ago. But now was not the time to think of Jonathan, it was time to concentrate on the business of killing. It was on the other side of a four-meter boulder, a hidden place; she was to lure her adversary to. A sliver of sand between boulders and the surf gave access to the grotto that Tula would use to end the charade of the last few days.

Suddenly she became focused on the moment. Her body shuddered, became fluid, then tightened like a rubber band; the angels stopped dancing on her face and hid themselves in the tight bun at the back of her head. She glanced over to the crude grave of the humpback whale and silently said a pray for the beast and herself. She could feel the ghost of the whale stir and she felt and concentrated her thoughts to make her as big and powerful as the beast. There was no one as strong and powerful as her and there was nothing stronger in the world than the beast. Together they were one. That's what Charlie taught her. You and I have lived with them and we are the strongest. Now, at this moment, you are the strongest and most powerful creature in the world. Nothing can harm you. She was ready.

Casually she made her way around the boulder and she could feel her adversary's presence a few feet behind. A turkey vulture was feeding on a carcass on top of the cliff above the boulder and below the hacienda porch. The ragged birds ugly featherless red head and neck dove in and out of the belly of a rotting dog. The stench was nauseating but she was so pumped with energy and focused she did not notice it. She looked to her left out to sea and in her vision he was there no more than a few meters away, she moved to the right, out of sight, behind the boulder and into the grotto. With a quick calculated move her right hand dove into her short's pocket and pulled her little knife from its sheath and at that moment he was standing in front of her with his knife, a big ugly hunter's tool. The turkey vulture squawked and took flight, which distracted her man for a fraction of a second, just enough to interrupt his concentration. He lunged at her awkwardly, thrusting the knife at her chest.

"An unfortunate move sir," she quietly said and smiled. With her left hand raised she grabbed his armed fist and calmly moved it towards her and to her right across the front of her body, missing her chest. He was now off balance and she moved her knife in her right hand under his outstretched arm and thrust it into his side cutting through his oblique muscles and intestines beneath. Letting go of his arm she held his torso with her left arm and hand and pulled him across the front of her. She moved across his back pulling the knife with her; like a butcher she neatly sliced his back muscles down to his spine and continued three quarter the way around his body almost cutting him in half. She pulled her knife from his body and as many dying people do, he screamed for his mother. Tula wrapped her arms around his torso pulling him to her and she gently led him the few feet to the water and said, "It's over—it's over."

The wound was so large most of the warm blood from his body gushed out soaking Tula's shorts, body and legs. He struggled and cried and she felt sorry for him and wished he was here to make love to her like Jonathan had. He was in misery and Tula knew he would be in agony for some time if she left him like this. He was on his knees, his hands clutching his back. She stood in front of him and took his head and placed it between her thighs. She drove the knife into the back of his neck and severed his spine. He no longer cried.

After searching him for identification, which there was none, she pulled him into the surf and washed herself. She sheathed her knife and put his knife in the same pocket. She pulled his carcass through the water past the rocky outcrops to a place hidden from the beach. Taking a five-kilogram rock from the shore she tucked it into his t-shirt and sank him in six feet of water. In the rich sea of Sayulita the sharks, fish, crabs, vultures and worms would eat away at him and in a few days some beachcomber may find what looks like a foot or hand and report it to the police. There would not be any evidence of a murderer or who he was. Just another unfortunate surfer or swimmer would be the gossip.

She said a silent thank you and goodbye to the humpback, left the scene and walked back up the beach diving in every so often for a short swim to wash away the death on her. She threw her adversaries knife as far out into the surf as she could. She felt so powerful she screamed with delight, startling a nearby beach dog. At her hotel room she changed into her black bikini and threw her soiled shorts, panties and halter-top in the garbage bin beside her surfboard. She was in the water in a few minutes paddling beside Robert, a young California friend.

"Hey Tula," he shouted with a big grin, "is it gonna' be a good day or what?"

"Yeah, Robert, it's gonna' be a good day. Race you out to the reef?"

Would-be-Knights on Horses

Wide brimmed dark and heavy
On the backs of wet horses
Lovers came for me

"Buenos tardes, Tula, how are you?" Jonathan said.

"Buenos tardes," she said as she came out of the water with Roger; her surfboard tucked under her arm. She was surprised to see him, "fine and you? Oh, this is Roger, a surfing buddy of mine."

"Nice to meet you Roger," Jonathan said extending his hand to Roger's which he shook vigorously.

"Nice to meet you," he said, showing a gleaming set of teeth against a deep tanned face framed in wet shaggy blonde hair, "I'll see you later Tula," he said, and kissed her on the cheek; he headed up the beach to join his friends.

"Good looking boy Tula."

"Yes, and he is just a boy, a very sweet one and a good friend. He is like a son to me. What are you doing here?"

"Sonja was worried about you and asked me to look for you and see if you're safe. She thought maybe you have been involved in the assassinations in PV. I thought that a bit bizarre but I looked for you anyway."

"Oh really, she thought that? Well that's silly. I'm not involved in any murders. You finally got to meet Sonja did you, good hearted woman isn't she?"

"She is a good woman."

"How did you find me?"

"You discreetly left a message on your night table that you were here. I just had to ask a few people to find you. It looks like you had set yourself up to be found. What's going on? Is everything all right with you?"

"Yes of course—perfectly all right.

"There was an email on your computer from a guy named Charlie. He said that you are in danger and should get out of town. What the hell is that about?"

"Nothing, everything has been taken care of."

"What do you mean, taken care of? Christ, what's going on?"

"You don't want to know what's going on!" her voice raised in anger. She clenched her fists and angels flew across her face. It's my business and I take care of things. What you read is old news."

"Well—"

"No more, Jonathan. Don't ask, okay!"

"Ah shit, Tula!"

"Let's change the subject. I'm here for a week of surfing and hiking. Are you going to stick around for a while?" suddenly she was calm, "It's fun here in Sayulita. It's my home away from home."

He was not going to argue with her, she was safe. "Yeah, I guess, I will eventually have to photograph the place for my contract so I might as well do it now. I have a room up at the hotel off the square. Do you want to meet this afternoon—in an hour or so?"

"Let's meet down here on the beach and go for a walk and have an early supper. I'm free when I'm here. You can have me for the next few days."

"Okay, in an hour."

"Fine, see you then," and she walked up the beach, her surfboard held on her head with its line still strapped to her ankle. Her body was wet and gleaming in the sun.

The hour went quickly and Jonathan almost ran to the beach, he was so excited. You old fool, he said to himself. What the hell are you doing now? You should have seen she was fine and said goodbye, gone back to PV, reported to Sonja and gone your own way. But no you had to be suckered again. The Goddamn pirate said I could have her for the next few days? What the hell did that mean?

Tula looked beautiful as she walked down the beach to him in a black dress with an intricate gold baroque design up the side. Her body had a luscious tan from the day's surfing and glowed from freshly applied body oil. Her hair was out and full and lay on her bare shoulders. She wore no jewelry and her sandals were in her hand. Angels darted from the corner of her mouth and into her black curls. She puffed on a cigar and looked arrogant as hell. "Let's walk," she said and Jonathan gestured towards the north end of the beach, "no the other way today."

"Darn, I made love to you there once. I wanted to stir up some old memories."

"We have never been together at La Playa de Los Muertos at the south end. It is beautiful and private in the evening. I want to be with you there. Wanna' puff," and she handed him the cigar."

"Damn this shit Tula, you shouldn't smoke," he took the cigar had a puff and handed it back to her,

"Fuck you, Jonathan."

"La Playa de Los Muertos? I thought there was only one and that's in PV?"

"No there are Beaches of the Dead all over the coasts of Mexico."

They wandered down the beach and he held her hand and she squeezed his in hers. Flashes of good times with him went through her mind and she wished that things were different. She enjoyed killing now. To be with him would put him in danger and she knew her future looked very precarious. There was not much left of it. She made up her mind to have him tonight and if all worked out, for the next day or two but that would have to be it. She was feeling very light headed and powerful since she had survived this day and must live each moment now to the full.

At the end of the beach they took the path up to the road that leads to a small expensive hotel resort whose yellow colour fit well with the green jungle that flowed down over it. Massive gnarled trees stretched their trunks and branches over the beach. From their huge appendages fishing boats were hung at the high tide mark. White caste iron tables and chairs where set up on a flagstone patio jutting out onto the rock-strewn beach; roosting perches for brown pelicans. Candles were lit even though it was not dark. They took some chairs at one of the tables beside a rock wall close to the beach. Jonathan gave Tula a seat that looked back on the village of Sayulita. He took a seat next to her. The sun was now at a deep angle and the brilliant light struck the buildings and palapas on the waterfront enhancing their colours. The palms waved gently above everything in deep green, highlighted here and there with lime green. Behind the village the jungle rose gently into the mountains of the Sierra Madre. The beach that stretched on and on was golden and the warm blue waters from the Pacific Ocean pounded it with strings of white waves.

The waiter came and gave them menus, "Buenos noches. May I bring you drinks? Si."

"Si," Jonathan said, "deuce Cubra Libre—one with no ice, por favor."

"Gracias," the waiter said and he left for the bar.

"The chicken fajitas are excellent here," Tula commented, "I'm going to have that—how about you?"

"The same, but I think I will have the beef."

"Good," she said and in the same breath, "so why are you really here in Sayulita?"

"Like I said, I was asked to check up on you. There are people including me who think you're in danger and you know how I feel about you."

"Yes I know how you feel about me but I can't let you into my life and I think that will all come clear soon. I don't need checking-on. You have no idea what you are dealing with." She thought of the man she murdered today; he was a trained killer and twice the size and strength of Jonathan.

"About the assassinations you mean?" This caught her off guard and she sat up straight.

"No, I don't know about any assassination," she replied and he knew that she was lying by the way she reacted to his question, but he still did not want to believe it, "you ask too many questions. Why do you do that? You don't respect my business."

"Like I have told you, I love you and care about you and that has nothing to do with respect of you or your business." The waiter came with their drinks and appetizers of chips and salsa and they ordered the chicken and beef fajitas.

"Let's change the subject. It always leads to trouble and disappointment when we talk of such things."

"Your right, shit I hate it when we get on each other. And I particularly hate it when you tell me to fuck myself. It's so crude," she giggled at that remark, "anyway I sold the painting that we did together to a dealer from San Francisco and I would like to share the proceeds with you."

"Congratulations! No, I don't want the money, I got my pay learning from you, just get me something little and nice, something personal that will remind me of you, and she pushed his sleeve up and kissed his bare shoulder. They talked about Jonathan's work and Tula showed great interest in what he was doing for the airline contract. They ate dinner and raved to each other about the meal even though it was messy and the grease dripped down their chins. They kissed a few times and squeezed each others hands and felt warm and wonderful as the sun went down and the lights came on around them and the village.

"We must go to the beach," Tula whispered, and she took his hand. He paid the bill with the other. They walked the short distance to a rutted dirt road past an estate guarded by a dog and her two little pups. Some guard dogs, the bitch and her pups with tongues hanging out ran up to them to be petted and loved. A huge golden rooster came out of the yard clucking and crowing its dissatisfaction at all the attention the dogs were getting.

The road, grooved deep with car tracks, rose over a small hill and down through a jungle and graveyard. It was quiet and eerie; the white painted tombs dimly glowed through the dark, thick jungle and ghostly palm trees climbed up into the stars around them. Plastic flower wreathes, still in their wrappings, covered many of the graves; the Virgin de Guadeloupe was everywhere in sculptures, tiles and effigies. A big black iguana scurried over the dead flowers of a tomb lid. They both grabbed each other and yelled in fright that turned into hysterical laughter. The road leveled and opened out off the jungle to an expanse of sand and white waves of little La Playa de Los Muertos. There were no cars and no one to be seen or heard except the crashing waves in the distance. Tula ran to the water took off her dress and flung aside her sandals. That was all she had on, a dress and sandals. Jonathan stripped down and ran into the surf after her. The waves crashed over them and they made love in the surf until the evening water became cool.

On the rocks nearby they sat and talked of their youth and of dreams for their old age that was centered on their health. They talked seriously, between cuddling and kissing, of maintaining the quality of life they now have. Like kids they showed each other their changing body parts. They laughed when they realized what they were doing as they had criticized friends in the past for having the same talks. They realized the fact they were ordinary aging folk. Well not quite, one was a killer the other an eccentric, maybe crazy artist. They made love again on the rocks and when they finished they went for a swim. They put their clothes on over their wet bodies and walked back over the hill, through the resort and across the beach to one of the bars near the town square.

A jazz trio caressed the smoky bar with sounds. Jonathan and Tula soon got into the beer drinking like they used to do and got drunk. Jonathan wanted to make love again and pulled her out of the bar and in the distance the sound of a Banda dance band blasted across the village. On weekend nights dances are held in the ballpark under blazing lights with a sixteen-piece Banda dance band that keeps everyone up well past midnight. The place rocks and the beer is cheap. Most customers get drunk and dance their butts off and Tula is no exception when she is at the park.

"We have to go Jonathan, we have to go," Tula said excitedly pulling on his arm.

"Yeah we should, I love that Mexican country western stuff." Holding hands and pulling each other along they stumbled and staggered to the ballpark. Chaos was everywhere with no direction laid out for anything: buses, cars, trucks, horses, dogs, kids and cowboys were strewn for a hundred yards up the road to the highway and all around the stadium.

They paid their fee at the hole in the adobe wall and entered the brightly lit stadium with a stage at one end. Banks of black speakers were stacked at each side of the stage to make enough noise to be heard kilometers away. Powerful lights lit up the band and flashing strobe lights flickered across the hundreds of dancers. Cowboy hats and tight jeans bobbed and rocked to the music.

"Come on!" Tula yelled, "let's dance," and she grabbed him and swayed and jostled him into a rhythm of a Mexican dance step, "I love you."

"And I love you babe," he slurred.

She kissed him many times and said she loved him over and over but he knew she didn't, she was just drunk. He led her over to the beer tent and he bought a couple of beers and they watched and listened to the band. Tula couldn't stop moving and she danced around him, gently she touched his thighs and taunted him. Cowboys were all over the field with their ladies who were dressed in the tightest clothes they could possibly get into. The cowboys were big broad shouldered handsome men in jeans; light embroidered shirts and broad white or beige cowboy hats. Polished belt buckles shone from their waists.

Three cowboys from the other side of the field walked towards them and Tula jumped into the arms of the biggest one. He smiled and shouted something above the din in Spanish. He hugged her and lifted her off the ground. They went to the dance area and left his two smiling buddies with Jonathan who sensed something was amiss. The two cowboys and Jonathan drank a few beers while Tula and the big cowboy danced on. Suddenly they stopped and she ran to Jonathan.

"I have to say good night."

"What?"

"I'm sorry but I have to say good night. These are my Mexican boy friends," and with that, the three cowboys said, "Adios," and they took Tula by the arm and led her out of the ballpark. Jonathan followed and watched them mount their horses and the big Mexican reached down behind her and lifted her by her crouch like a rag doll onto the back of his horse. Two frisky, tough boxer dogs fussed and weaved in and out of the horse's legs. The cowboys pulled their horses around and Tula looked at Jonathan with a look of contempt, an angel came out of the side of her mouth and gestured to him—pushed him away with little hands. The trio with their dogs and lover cantered off across the bridge and down the dimly lit Av. Revolucion into the dust and night. Jonathan cursed her and himself for having loved her. He went home to his hotel and found Tula's voodoo doll in his suitcase and he threw it out of his hotel window in frustration and anger.

Rick Thomas

California

"Whoa!" Jonathan yelled as he fell backwards off an orange box onto his back. A black pregnant bitch scurried out of the way. His first thought was for his beer which he held upright and didn't spill a drop, "that's what happens when you're in good shape; you're reaction time is immediate," he slurred, "saved the beer anyway."

A river with a broken bridge runs along the edge of Sayulita. A hole in the bridge exposes decaying concrete, twisted steel and the river below. The hole is partially covered with a steel plate that makes a tremendous clanging noise when cars and trucks drive over it. At one end of the bridge a kindly old man, California, works on his paintings. He has been there for years with his easels; paints, brushes and canvases creating paintings that hang in the best residences and hotels of Sayulita.

In the afternoons when the sun is high and unbearable Jonathan would visit his artist friend. Together they hide from the sun behind his black plastic sheet that hangs like a spider on sticks attached to the back of his easel. Jonathan would buy the beer; drink and tell lies about themselves and others, but based on truth since lies have to come from someplace. The old man would paint during their visit and stopped only to make a point and drink his beer. A black pregnant bitch made herself comfortable with a cautious eye on Jonathan and the paint covered brushes that quickly moved about the canvas above her.

California sits on a little canvas chair, a large stretched canvas looms in front of him and a pile of oil colours in squashed tubes lay on a small table beside him. Some are scattered around his feet and some stick out of his pockets. Chaos is all around him: hungry dogs bark and fuss, food venders yell, buses and taxis noisily come and go, kids laugh, babies cry, peddlers and hawkers con and beggars steal. Over the years they and the dust have been painted into his canvases.

The old man is a painting. A straw hat rests on his white hair and his beard frames a nut-brown leather face. Aged, brown, wise eyes glisten under heavy fleshy folds, held up by bushy gray eyebrows. His shirt and pants are green and his sandals, made by him, are of weather beaten cowhide. He takes care of his feet, washing them often in the river below the bridge and rubbing them with coconut oil. His hands are huge, brown and strong from years of hard work. He does not use rags to clean his brushes; he cleans them on the canvas and finishes the cleaning on his clothes. Often the brush touches his mouth during periods of contemplation of his work; consequently he has a beard of many colours. Always with a smile on his face with the flash of pure white dentures, he is a wonderful site to Jonathan.

His art is open and free, a riot of colour and texture out of control. Gray rocks become orange, blue and yellow in rivers of red, green and blue. Palm trees are balls of spikes rising above seas of flowers and jungle vegetation. Homes are blocks of bright colours toped off with huge palapas. Bird species that no one has seen before fly across the canvas, some leaving feathers behind to gently fall into the jungle of his work. Most of the time the sky is blue but sometimes the sky is red and orange; some days it is green the same as the jungle. It shrieks the glory of Mexico and life.

Jonathan's visits with California were usually brief but today Jonathan needed him as he was drunk and lonely for his Tula and he wanted to know more about his friend.

"Where were you born old man? Around here?"

"Si, here, I was born in Sayulita about seventy years ago down the road one kilometer. I don't know my age. My family was poor and one of oldest of families in the district. We grew tobacco and vegetables."

"I like your painting. Were did you learn to paint? In school?" he said loudly as though California could not hear him. And he made sweeping gestures in the air.

"I am not deaf amigo."

"Sorry I assumed you would understand me better if I spoke loud—stupid, eh? I think it's the beer talking."

"When I was poco boy I loved to draw things: animals, trees, people and village. I go to school for few years but don't remember much. I always looking out window and drawing plants of jungle and bright birds. My teacher white woman from USA. She volunteer teach me, brothers, sisters and local children. In those days some Mexicans in farms around here got education. The teacher told my Madre y Padre I waste time in school and be best if I work. I left school for fields and for forty years grew tobacco but always in my heart I want to be artist." He slashed a brush full of bright red down the river.

"Do you see red in the river? I don't."

"Lay your head on your shoulder and look at river," and he showed Jonathan how to look at the river on an angle.

"Your right old man there is red in the river when you look at it that way."

"I like the colour red anyway." And they both laughed and drank their beer.

"Are you married and have a family out on the farm?"

When I was about fifty I lost farm to bank and bandits who turned fields into a marijuana farm. Then I lost wife in car crash."

"I'm sorry."

"Not to cry, long time ago now."

"And children? Where are they?"

"Six childs—they live in Vallarta. They beg me to come and live in big city with them but I have nothing to do with that. I love my little pueblo of Sayulita and my life as artist."

"What are we painting today?"

"The palapa on red hotel at the beach," and he lifted a fresh canvas and placed it over the river painting on the easel.

"The hotel with the banana trees that fill the yard?"

"Si that one. I won't paint house just palapa and banana leaves. That is enough, more be too much. Not much needed, they know were it is. If painting sell to tourist then won't matter anyway. A place on wall in San Francisco it stand by self, no relation to Sayulita anymore."

"Whoa! "And Jonathan fell of his orange box again. The pregnant bitch jumped into the street and was almost run over by a passing taxi. Whistles and waves came from the back seat: "Viva California!"

He waved back and turned to Jonathan, "Drink more beer," he laughed, "it will help you to stay in your seat."

Jonathan wanted to make a comment about that but decided not to. He picked himself up and dusted himself off. He did not spill a drop, in that go round.

"What makes you paint old man?"

"Don't know. It's something I must do it's something I love. I surprised everyday what I do and I know nothing when I start out. It is all in here," and he pointed to his temple leaving a fingerprint of red oil, "all in here. Maybe the old Gods are there. I saw book once that had Maya paintings in it. They were all over this pyramid—this house. These were my ancestors, maybe they still inside me, make me paint this way. Then maybe I am crazy like that Van Go man mistress tell me about.

"You have a mistress? You never told me this before."

"Not come up. She good to me. Wash me with gasoline every night to get paint off—damn near blow me up once." They both laughed and Jonathan opened a couple more beers.

"What will you do in the future?"

"This is future. I am old; I paint, eat, make love and drink with my amigos," And he clicked his beer bottle with Jonathan's. "What you do in future?"

"Go home to Canada and finish my contract and look for something else to do. I think I may go to Thailand next winter."

"Where Thailand?"

"In the east or west depending on how you look at it, anyway it's below China and near India. Do you understand?"

"Yes I understand. But why go there when you have so much at home? You rico man, Jonathan."

"I am rich in a way I guess but rich is not everything. I am searching for some other meaning to life. It's not happiness; I know that since I am happy with my life, perhaps it's about enlightenment, something mysterious. I don't know. Maybe the search is an excuse to have fun. Sometimes I think I am in a radio play or an opera. I'm not the star, just the observer standing in the wings watching the story unfold."

"Hum... I do not understand. My life has always been here in the dust of Sayulita. This is where I am happy, on end of bridge in the dust, painting my jungle, river, village, dogs, horses and amigos."

"That's all you need and your love of your home shows in the paint that dances across your canvas. Someday you will be famous, California. People from all over Mexico—no the world, will be after your work. You will be a piece of the history of this great country," and Jonathan raised his beer, put it to his mouth and leaned back and fell off his box. Sputtering he got back up and sat down, "It's going to happen. You may not see it come since you will be dead but it will come."

"If I am dead then it does not matter, does it?"

"Yes it does matter—it does matter. It says that you were here."

California painted on, the sun burned, the village went to bed, the pregnant bitch snuggled up to California's feet and a tear rolled down a drunken Jonathan's cheek.

A Short Rope for a Long Fall

Jonathan stayed on in Sayulita for a few days and photographed the local scene, made friends with the residents and spent time on the beach tanning and body surfing. Some afternoons he would have a beer with California. He did not go to La Playa de Los Muertos. Tula was not around so he assumed she had gone home to PV and that was fine with him. He did not want to see her again.

After breakfast one morning he returned to his hotel. Outside the entrance, and in a mango tree was Tula's voodoo doll hanging from a branch. Jonathan ran face first into it. It startled him and he grabbed the doll and threw it into the street where a truck crushed it into the dust.

At the hotel reception desk there was an urgent message waiting for him from Carlota. He is needed in Old Town and Tula's home immediately. The receptionist said Carlota sounded extremely upset. Jonathan packed, checked out, jumped into Bullet and was on the road to PV within a few minutes. He floored the throttle down the winding highway and across the Bahia de Banderas. He muttered to himself, would he ever get rid of this woman—this pain in his ass?

He parked in front of Tula's wrought iron gate—it was open. He walked across the bricked front yard to the front door that led into the stairway tower. He tried the handle and it was unlocked, cautiously he entered. On the marble floor of the tower was a heap of rubble. It was the large chandelier and heavy chain that held it to the ceiling of the stairwell. The ceiling, plaster, concrete and tiles made a great heap in the vestibule. Out of the pile of rubble a lariat lay across a bloody leg. Jonathan froze and his heart sank. "No—no!" he cried out.

Carlota ran into the vestibule from the kitchen and rushed to him crying hysterically. "She is dead Mr. Owen, she is dead. I find her this morning when I come work. Oh Mr. Owen—what we do?" He could not say anything he was in shock that this could happen to the one he loved. Now she had really left him, sorrow turned to anger and guilt.

"If only she had stayed with me, she would be all right, living a peaceful content life. No she had to screw around with life, screw around with people and screw me every chance she could and now look at her?" he cried out and held onto Carlota, "Call the police Carlota, they must be told," he let her go. She went into the kitchen and called the Policia Municipal.

Within a few minute a dozen police cars and trucks arrived. They told Jonathan to stay in the house and not to come out of the kitchen. Carlota was questioned for half an hour in the living room, they knew her from the street and did not suspect any foul play or collusion with Tula in the murders of businessmen and women visiting PV. Jonathan, on the other hand, was her lover and was seen many times with her by the surveillance team that was tracking her.

A familiar officer walked into the kitchen: "Mr. Owen we meet again," said Commander Bernarda Perez, "it has been a few years since your young friend was killed at the cockfights." He sat at the opposite side of the kitchen table from Jonathan. He laid down an open file folder in front of him. His hand held a ballpoint pen, which constantly circled the name, Tula, typed at the top of a page.

"Yes Commander we meet again under trying circumstances. I tell you I don't know what happened here and I don't particularly want to know."

"Once more you are involved in someone's death. So you will know what took place here. Do not avoid it. This is not good Mr. Owen and once again you have to explain yourself. You knew the deceased well didn't you?" queried the Commander who's English had greatly improved.

"I knew her very well; we had been friends and lovers for years. It is no secret and I have nothing to hide," Jonathan said with confidence.

"Good," said the Commander, "you are an honest man Mr. Owen, I know that from when your partner died a few years ago. You were a big help to the police and her family. But having two women friends who have died violently and your crazy antics in Europe Mr. Owen? One has to wonder. Let us return to why we are here. You are here in Mexico on a contract photographing, painting and drawing, is that right?"

"Yes, how did you know that? Have you been following me?"

"We have been watching you and Tula for some time and we know a great deal about your recent visit to Vallarta. You seem to be off and on with Tula. Why is that? She was a beautiful woman."

"Honestly commander she could be a real bitch at times. I loved her dearly but we just did not get along. Arguing all the time and she had quite an edge to her. She would flare up and get angry at the smallest things."

"Do you know of the murders of foreign business people that have taken place recently in Vallarta?"

"Yes, I read about some of them in the English newspaper. I understand there has been a rash of them lately."

"Do you remember reading about the incident on the Malecón during the festival of the Virgin Guadalupe?" and the commander spread out on the kitchen table some photos of a body lying on a cobble street.

"Yes, I believe I did read about that murder."

"Tell me about it."

"A financial businessman from the United States was found the morning after the festival in a store doorway on the parade route. The article said he had been murdered. A cleaning man thought he was a drunk and when he touched him he fell into the street dead. That's about all I remember reading."

"How was he murdered Mr. Owen?"

"I don't know, nothing about how he died was written in the paper, only that he was murdered.

"Very well," the commander said and he looked to the officer standing at the kitchen door.

"A body was found on the rocks down by the Boy on a Seahorse statue at the south end of La Playa Los Muertos," and he spread out pictures of a body caught between some rocks," tell me what you know of this murder."

"I know nothing of this body commander. I only read the paper once a week."

"Fine," the commander stated, "we are not sure if this gentleman was murdered or not but we are assuming he was as he was in similar financial businesses as the others who have been murdered.

"The car bombing on 5th de Octubre, do you know anything about that murder?" and he spread out those pictures. They were ghastly and showed body parts smoldering from an explosion, a pair of legs with no body and other unrecognizable lumps of things on the cobbles and atop cars.

"Christ, these are horrible, I sure do remember this murder," Jonathan reacted sitting up in his chair and the commander gave his full attention to his every move, "I was down on the Cuale photographing a restaurant and I heard the explosion and later the ambulances and fire trucks. It was north off the Malecón, I did not go there as there were crowds already running to the scene. There was a hell of a mess I understand."

"Can you prove you were at the restaurant Mr. Owen?"

"Hm—I don't know—yes—yes I can. I was using my digital camera and all my shots, days and times are recorded in my camera and on my computer."

"Is your camera at home right now?"

"Yes it is."

"Very well. Will you excuse me for a moment?" the Commander said and he stood up and left the kitchen with the officer. Through the window in the kitchen door, Jonathan could see the Commander talking to the officer who was on a cell phone. The Commander came back into the kitchen. "We are checking your story Mr. Owen. Our officers are at your home this very moment and looking for your camera to verify your statement."

"I thought you were not allowed to do that without a warrant?" they both looked at each other and simultaneously said, "This is Mexico."

"Be patient with us for a few moments Mr. Owen," and the commander left the kitchen to see how the forensic team was doing uncovering the body.

It was not long before he returned. "It all checks out, you were nowhere near the bombing and you did not say anything about the other murders except what is public knowledge. Our surveillance team also verifies you at other locations during the murders and your email records do not show any collusion with Tula. Our little interview, Mr. Owen, is just a requirement of our investigation. Our forensic team has sifted through the wreckage carefully and we have determined how Tula died."

"And how did she die?"

"We believe she tied a rope to the chandelier and the other end around her neck. She jumped from the stairwell railing and the ceiling could not take the weight of her falling body and tore it loose. She suffered a broken neck on the first jolt and her skull was crushed when she and the chandelier hit the floor. Our surveillance team has made a visual verification and it is Tula. We think that she knew we were closing in on her. In our report we will make the determination that she had committed suicide rather than face the future of life in a Mexican prison.

"We are sorry about your loss. You are free to go and I do not want to see you again Mr. Owen. Please stay away from these kinds of women while you are still in Vallarta."

"I will, thank you Commander."

"The team is removing the body now and we have to clear the building," he shook Jonathan's hand.

Events moved fast, the body was bagged and removed and the house was locked and sealed with tape. Everyone left the scene leaving Carlota and Jonathan on the sidewalk. Both locked out of Tula's life. Carlota hugged Jonathan for the last time and went home to her babies and old mother. Jonathan sat in the gutter still suffering the shock of his loss.

Across the street from Tula's home was Jonathan's favorite taco stand. A large dark ugly man was consuming many shrimp tacos and soda. He watched with others the police come and go, and Tula leaving her home for the last time. The Commander left the scene but before he got into his white pickup truck he glanced over to the taco stand and stared at the dark ugly man.

Jonathan sat in the dust of the sidewalk. The ugly man scratched a large scar on his jaw and smiled. He left the Taco stand and walked down the street to the La Parroquia de Santa Cruz. He made the sign of a cross as he passed the entrance. He hailed a cab and went to his hotel on the Av. México.

Jonathan quickly made the decision to leave Mexico—right now! He got up and went the few blocks to his apartment and packed Bullet. He drove down Insurgentes, through downtown PV heading north to the border two days away. Highway 200 passes the airport and as he drove passed the east end of the runway, a plane was taking off for Toronto, Canada.

"Thanks for taking care of the assassin. I'm so tired."

"She was like you, a victim of a group we can't identify. It was too bad all of this had to happen. This has happened to others. You are not alone."

"Where am I going, Charlie? What's going to happen to me now?"

"Home to Canada first for decompression and then on to Germany for a few years at a Canadian Armed Forces base and then you will be assigned to different outposts around the world. You're going to be given an administrative assistant position and will spend the rest of your days as a clerk. There won't be any retirement and the work won't be glamorous or with a future but you will live and be safe. Relatively it will be a good life, a new name, a job and most of all isolation from the world that is now too dangerous for you and you to dangerous for it. You won't ever see me again nor anyone else from your past."

"What about my kids Charlie, what about them?"

"Your children will be informed in the next day or so that you are dead. Ashes will be sent to them.

"Oh God." Tula whispered, "How do I get out of this?" She looked out of the window. Far below was the Bahia de Banderas. Charlie gently squeezed her hand; he looked at the open napkin on her lap and written on it was:

The present I give
For life you will never see
Just a memory

Viva Mexico!

Home the vagabond
The dust of Sayulita
Behind and away

People who come to Mexico take something home with them to remind them of their brief stay in paradise. Over the remaining years of their lives these artifacts pop up in basements, attics, garages, draws or from under beds. They all bring back sweet memories. We all have to take something home with us from wherever we are and that's what Jonathan did. He loved Mexico, its people and culture and in his heart he knew he would not be back this way again. He had his photos, drawings and paintings that he produced for his contract but he needed something special to remind him years from now of his Tula, the woman he once loved in the heat and dust of Sayulita. Highway 200 passes the seaside village; the last place he saw her, the last place he made love to her and the last place she humiliated him. He would take something from the little fishing village.

There is a store near the square that sells little metal boxes with pictures of Frida Kahlo on the lids. Tula researched and studied the lives of female heroes of the past and she was always fond of Frida as she was so brave—a special hero of the world of women. She and the painter had shed many tears in their lives. Tula had suffered mind-numbing abuse as a child and Frida had suffered years from an injury inflicted when she was young; a steel rod was driven through her body during a bus accident in Mexico City. Frida painted her way out of her agony to become and internationally recognized artist; one of the great artists of the twenty first century.

Jonathan bought one of the little boxes and with it drove Bullet along the road parallel to the beach, over the hill, through the graveyard and onto La Playa de Los Muertos. The sky was clear and blue; the sand was washed clean. For the next hour he sat on the rocks at the north end of the beach and sifted through the piles of broken shells and thought of his Tula and the colours and shapes she would love. There were white ones with brilliant red, blue and pink markings, little beige clams, tinny brown conches, and white jagged coral. He added two round rocks; a black and a white and when the box was filled; from his drawing pad he tore out some sketches of Sayulita, folded them and tucked them under the lid.

He thought long and hard about his Tula and he did not and would not believe she was an assassin. How could she be—he loved her? Right or wrong he would leave it at that. Tula would always be to him the brave courageous woman who went through life with angels dancing across her face and through her hair; a woman with children to bring up alone. He thought of the humiliation she put him through and of her other men who probably had suffered. Was all she did, done out of self-defense or revenge for what life had dealt her? It all did not matter to Jonathan anymore—she was gone.

He closed the lid and tied it with string. He packed the little box away in Bullet, packed the memories, packed the memorial to Tula away. He would never open it again. As he drove back to Sayulita Bullet picked up speed and the dust built up behind him. For Jonathan the excitement of going home was overpowering. To be going home out of the chaos of Mexico. To be free like in his youth was a joy to experience again. He raced Bullet down the main street past the square and the church, the outdoor restaurants, half finished buildings and out of the chaos. California saw his Jeep coming in a great cloud and he got up off his chair knocking it over; his paint tubes on the little table fell into the dust and his canvas flew off its easel. The black spider plastic sheet came away and out behind him. The old painter picked up his beer and raised it to the brilliant blue sky. The sun hit his forehead, his white hair and beard shone and his paint-splattered clothes turned him into the painting that he is. Silver Bullet roared onto the bridge and hit the steel plate over the hole with a bang. The Jeep left the ground and came down on the other side. California waved his beer. Jonathan laughed and waved back.

The old man shouted, **"Viva Mexico!"**

Silver Bullet roared full throttle and fishtailed as it passed dogs, chickens, cowboys and horses. Jonathan covered them with dust.

Four
The Monkey With a Golden Arm
Thailand Laos Union of Myanmar Cambodia

The mahout, near death, straddled his weary elephant's neck. They made their way across one of the busiest bridges in Bangkok. The mahout was delirious from malaria—his American father came into his vision in the arms of Lord Buddha and his mother in the arms of a pirate. Stabbing pains rushed through his body and he craved water but he had none. He trembled—this life was ending. The elephant moved toward the road his mahout survived on many years ago; a place where he knew Buddha would find him—Khaosan Road.

The elephant crashed through the boulevard bushes by the National Art Gallery and lumbered down the back alley to the service gates. The gargantuan beast smashed through the gates; once inside the mahout shouted a command and the elephant dropped to his knees. The mahout slid from his neck and into a pond; the elephant ate trees limbs and tore up the flowerbeds. The mahout cried and violently threw up fluid and blood. The elephant lay down beside his old friend and caressed him with his trunk, fore he sensed something was wrong but did not have the intelligence to do anything but keep him company. It is what elephants do.

A gallery guard discovered the two and called the police. The mahout panicked when he saw the guard and climbed on the elephant's neck and gave the command to stand and move out fast, which the huge beast obeyed. The elephant ran down the alley as if going into battle like his ancestors did long ago. He ran passed the Wat Chanasonkhram, crossed Samsen Road and into Khaosan Road. Market vendors were busy setting up their stalls when the elephant came upon them. They panicked and scattered; cars came to a halt to let the raging beast pass. People rushed out of temple and stores; the tourist and traffic police ran after the beast.

Delirious, the mahout saw fuzzy images of bodies running out of the way of his elephant that was confused. The commands coming from his master's feet and hook did not make sense and the elephant did not know what to do but charge. Finally the commands came to *halt* and *kneel*, he obeyed and the mahout slid off his neck to the pavement—the elephant rose. A motorcycle came around the corner from Tanao Road and ran into the mahout. He fell to the ground, blood and bile rushed from his mouth; his eyes stared at his elephant but he could not see him. The mahout was dead.

Khaosan Road, the Center of The Universe

Two blocks from Jonathan's hotel his limousine swerved and screamed past the wreckage of an overturned car and a battered truck. A man was standing inside the car, his head sticking out of the driver's window; he made a jester to a man from the other wreck to help him get out. His driver laughed—it's fate to him, something that in time, Jonathan will understand.

At one o'clock in the morning Bangkok had welcomed him at the new space age airport terminal, Suvarnabhumi. His limo came to a halt in front of his hotel; the driver quickly unloaded him and his luggage and drove away. Bloodshot eyes and boozy looks came his way from patrons in the hotel's bar restaurant that spilled onto the road. Jonathan made his way past them to the receptionist's desk. They did not have his reservation on file, no surprise, so he showed them a copy that he had made in Canada. He had the wrong hotel; his was around the corner—the Bangkok Inn. He made his way down the block past portable kitchens boiling and frying foods that he did not recognize. He past woks of cooked grease that smelled wretched; past young white men sleeping a bad night off, past prostitutes and their pimps who offered their services to him—he turned the corner.

A welcome noise came from the party madness of Khaosan Road. Thousands were still out on the garbage littered universe. They were dressed in black; makeup ran down their faces, spiked hair and tattoos spoke of rage. Young women's faces with blank looks in their eyes pleaded, will someone *please* take me home. The glassy look in their eyes showed that most were drunk or high on drugs. Jonathan's first thought was what had he come to, his second—keep your cool you've been here before in other places far away.

Suddenly it struck him—it's Halloween and there is a party going on. Fireworks cracked like gunfire down the filthy road and smoke and flashes came from the bars and restaurants. Exhausted and hallucinatory from the flight of twenty-four hours, he made his way passed shouting and laughing people. Some gave him high-fives. Some tried to talk but couldn't.

Half way down the kilometer block road Jonathan found his hotel, which surprised him since it was a wooden two-story structure with a blackened galvanized tin roof. Actually it turned out to be a building of shops with closed garage door fronts; an alley in its center led to his hotel and a labyrinth of passages leading off into the recesses of the neighborhood. Jonathan made his way down a broken tiled walkway to his hotel. He passed a bar filled with dark people; they looked exhausted from a night of partying—they stared at him, which is a habit here that Jonathan would get used to. Two rats, the size of small puppies, led the way jumping and diving through the litter of stinking food encrusted foam plates and plastic bottles. He thought they were hallucinations but they were not. They were so big they had cuteness about them and he thought perhaps they would make great pets. They escorted him down the alley, busy in their night duties and Jonathan ducked into his hotel. He checked in and went to his room, washed the stink from his body and changed his cloths. Exhausted or not he was going to join the party; besides, it was daytime for him and he felt some energy and excitement coming on. He looked in the mirror, Christ, what the hell, you're in Bangkok!

Next door was Khao Sarn; a bar with no front wall and no doors since it never sleeps. It flowed onto the road with music, furniture, booze, food and people. The bar was filled with young men searching for women, older men searching for their youth and Thai women searching for their dreams. The metro waiters and waitresses all wore yellow shirts with the emblem of the king on the chest. They are metro these people, never going outside the city, living in a world somewhere in between reality and fantasy. Who shall I love today—a man or a woman? At one thirty in the morning the bar was still packed with partygoers so he made himself at home and ordered rum and coke since only hard drinks are served after one in the morning.

It wasn't long before Jonathan made friends with a young Aussie, a middle aged German and their Thai girlfriends. Both men were drinking themselves sober and were exhausted. Their women were pretty but the German was very unhappy; he had a wife and two children at home in Hamburg, which were nagging at him. He missed them and fooling with the two Thai girls made him feel guilty as hell. The Aussie—he was single and didn't give a damn.

"What's your name?" one of the girls asked.

"Jonathan—Jonathan Owen," he replied with a smile.

"Are you married Jonatin?"

"No but I have a woman friend back home," Jonathan said. He lied

"No problem. I make you forget."

"Now that would be a problem. Where are you from?"

"My family farm near Chiang Mai."

"Why are you in Bangkok and not working on the farm?"

"It's between growing seasons, so I came to make money for my family and my child. I have a mother and father who take care of my girl and I have four brothers, two sisters and grandparents also on the farm. You come with me Jonatin, I make you happy."

"I can't, no I just can't be with you."

"To bad Jonatin," she said, "you know what we looking for don't you?"

"Yeah I do," Jonathan said.

The other Thai girl who was drunk. Her long day had taken its toll, "We want to get outta' here, outta' our country. Work too hard here and we get nowhere. I not be like Mother. Bus her ass all her life."

Across the room Jonathan could see the same story being exchanged by dozens of farangs and girls. It is a Bangkok ritual that has been going on for hundreds of years on this hunting ground of Khaosan Road and all the other roads, streets and highways of Thailand. In Asian countries many are looking for a passport to a dream.

The German, Aussie and Jonathan talked for hours about their travels to different parts of the world and compared experiences and laughs. They were vagabonds like him but they had to return home soon. The women got bored and left them for other prospects, which made the German more comfortable. He promised himself to leave the women alone for the remainder of his stay.

Suddenly there was a great commotion of cheering and laughing out on the road and then a terrible silence. Many in the bar and the twenty metro waiters rushed to the sidewalk. Jonathan was curious, as is his nature, so he made his way to the scene unfolding out on the street. There was a dying white man lying in the road, blood was coming from his mouth, nose and ears, it pooled beneath his head. His eyes were open and looked at nothing; his body twitched and shook.

"What happened?" Jonathan asked his waiter.

"The man was arguing with his friend who got up and hit him many times and ran away."

Soon a swarm of paramedics surrounded the dying man. They made an effort to stop the bleeding, gave him oxygen and got him onto a stretcher and into an ambulance. They tore down Khaosan Road, lights flashed and sirens blared. Five medics rode on the rear bumper of the ambulance—four motorcycles followed. Two police officers came and questioned those who witnessed the beating.

Someplace in the world a Mother of a family will get the news that her son is dead or brain damaged. He is out there alone and she will have to come and get him. And somewhere someone's son is being sought for attempted murder or perhaps murder. A night for two friends had become a life changing experience for both. Their lives and those of their families will never be the same.

Jonathan helped his metro waiter to a seat as his dark skin became pale. The customers returned to their seats, drinks and conversations, quickly the event faded. A few metro waiters washed the blood from the sidewalk and road.

The sun started to make itself known across the tattered buildings, signs and billboards; cleanup women appeared in their gumboots, blue uniforms and large straw hats. They swept the place clean of the party garbage, filling their wicker baskets. Shop owners came out with hoses and brushes and washed the sidewalks and street in front of their stores. Three wheel motor taxis, Tuk-tuks, arrived and lined up along the sidewalks. Metal carts packed with clothing and merchandise filled the road. Short, smiling Karin women from the Northern Provinces strolled about in costume selling silver jewelry and trinkets to the gathering crowds. They made croaking frog noises by rubbing sticks on hollow wooden frog carvings. Food stalls were raised that cooked pork, beef, chicken, vegetables, rice and noodles in wonderful spicy sauces.

As the day crowds gathered Thais prayed, made offerings and lit joss sticks to house spirits at the many shrines in the shops and stalls. Between the stalls sat the beggars; crippled and deformed they waited with dignity for money given by the tourists and food from the venders. Every third beggar was a child who belonged to a syndicate of rented and stolen children from neighboring countries. Never the less—a happy bunch.

Bony, smoking, brown uniformed, sun glassed, silver helmeted police officers patrolled the road and when they dismounted their little motorbikes they strutted like roosters. Only a few monks in their saffron robes made an appearance and they were very careful not to come too close to women. Jonathan wondered about the meaning of enlightenment. Over everything, Thailand's red, white and blue flags fluttered and beside them flew the yellow royal flag with the emblem of the king emblazoned at its center. Khaosan Road will get so crowded by midday the police will block off both ends. They only let through motorbikes and vehicles carrying goods or doing legitimate business with shops and vendors.

His new friends went home to their hotels and Jonathan stayed for a last rum and coke, it was only six at night in his time. He watched the road unfold into a giant market place whose customers were from around the world.

Young people with backpacks made their appearance. They gathered in groups eventually to be led away by tour guides and bus drivers; others walked and talked their way in and out of booths, bars and restaurants, tasting and smelling their new world. The white folk were returning or leaving for adventures in this strange land. They being strange themselves in their camouflaged shorts, t-shirts, tattoos, and body piercing. They were all young and beautiful and Jonathan felt—good for them. This was their adventure, coming before they entered a world of mediocrity back in their homeland and for some disappointment when they won't realize their youthful expectations. He had seen this before. They will do their best in their short time away from home to create memories that will last them into their old age when they will do it again. He knows this to be true. He was in Bangkok or an in-between place; the road vibrated with life. There are a few centers in the universe where the likes of him gather for a short time and this was one of them. How will he get into the dance of this land? Like always and for everyone arriving in Bangkok—he will learn.

Jonathan sobered up but he was exhausted by the time he paid his bar bill and tipped his metro waiter, he had had a long twenty-four hours. He walked to the alley that led to his hotel and the two rats were waiting for him. The woman bartender from the dark place ran after them with a broom to her breakfast customers' delight and probably to the delight of the rats. She would never catch them. The heavy air and atmosphere of this new place was lightening up for him and he was becoming comfortable. He climbed the stairs to his room, undressed and fell into bed that felt so good. In the distance he could hear the tuk-tuks whining up and down the road, people laughing and strange birds singing. Jonathan drifted away and all around him the sun and Buddha blessed another day on Khaosan Road.

For a few days Jonathan stayed around the hotel, slept and ate mild food; he let his biology adjust to the time and culture change. Soon he was out seeing the sites, visiting the museums, temples and galleries. He took the ferry up and down the river, stopping at different stations to see the temple architecture.

He did not know what he was going to do in Thailand, all he knew was he had to get away from the winter of home, memories of Tula and have some time for himself. He loved being out in the world alone but he was hardly alone with five million people nearby. He decided to rent a motorbike; the most convenient way to get about in Thailand and he was getting used to the city and the crush of its people. In the morning, when traffic on Khaosan Road and the neighborhood was light, he would get on his rented motorbike and ride. Off he would go down the narrow streets into places that got him lost. It didn't matter he always found his way back to Khaosan Road.

One morning he was out in the west of the city driving back to his hotel. It was a beautiful morning clear and crisp and the pollution of the cars, tuk-tuks and motorbikes had not filled the air yet. He was confident now with his handling of the bike and was driving up to the speed of other drivers. Returning home he drove down Tanao Road and turned onto Khaosan Road.

Suddenly there was an elephant in his path with his mahout standing in front of him. Jonathan tried to swerve out of the way but drove into the mahout. He did not hit him hard but the poor man went down and did not move. Jonathan dropped his bike and knelt down and held the mahout's head that was covered in water and blood. He could see his yellow eyes were open and he was dead. A huge trunk came down in front of Jonathan and caressed the mahout's head. He looked up and into the amber eyes of the elephant. Jonathan slowly rose to his feet and gently backed away. Immediately police surrounded the elephant that they had been chasing and a crowd gathered.

"You killed my brother!" an angry man shouted as he approached

Jonathan, "what you do now mister?" The confused elephant turned and started to move down the road, everyone got out of the way and so did the police. An officer took out his gun but another told him to put it away. Killing an elephant on Khaosan Road would be a crime against a sacred animal of Thailand and unforgivable. The officer knew the elephant and his mahout.

"Follow the elephant," the officer commanded Jonathan, "you now have some business to take care of." Jonathan picked up his motorbike and put it on the side of the road and followed the elephant, the mahout's brother and the police.

The huge beast crashed its way down the market, knocked over clothing stands, jewelry cases and overturned food carts. People laughed, screamed and cheered from the sidewalks, restaurants and bars. The big gray beast turned onto Samsen Road and down to the main thoroughfare of Chaofa. He crossed it, stopping the morning rush hour traffic. The elephant headed for the Field of Kings and there he stopped to pull down tree limbs and proceeded to eat. The mass and Jonathan surrounded the elephant and a dozens police surrounded Jonathan. An officer started to write out a ticket.

"Now wait a minute, what's this?"

"You now own the elephant, you killed his mahout. Someone must take responsibility," the officer said, "may I see your passport please?" Jonathan reached into his back pocket and pulled out his passport and handed it to the officer.

"Yes, that's right." the mahout's brother said, "You must take responsibility for Thunder Mountain."

"Thunder who?" Jonathan said bewildered.

"Thunder Mountain, that's his name and now he is yours but after you pay the Department for Domestic Animals for his ownership."

"I can't own an elephant. What am I going to do with it? I just got here. I'm not a citizen of your country."

"If you don't take responsibility," the officer said, "you will go to jail. The mahout was very sick, we know, but we will still have to arrest you for his death if you don't take over his responsibilities. And since the elephant no longer has an owner we will have to put it down. It is up to you Mr. Owen."

"Now that's blackmail—"

"Not in this country, this is fate," the brother said, "this is your karma and if you don't be careful you will come back as a worm when you die."

"Yeah, well I don't believe in that stuff." The elephant kept eating the trees even after the brother told him to stop.

"Tag Two," an officer said, "do you have your truck and food near by?

"Yes, it's just the other side of the bridge—"

"Tag Two," Jonathan said, "what kind of name is that? You people know each other?"

"Yes, Thunder Mountain has been operating in Bangkok for many years and we made a living on the streets. Everyone knew us," Tag Two said.

"Get in Tag Two," the officer command and gestured him to a waiting police car with its light flashing, "let's get your truck over here with some food for the elephant or he is going to wreck the place and Mr. Owen will have to pay more damages."

"More damages?" Jonathan said, "Quick, Tag Two or whatever your name is, get the damn truck over here."

They got into the police car and drove off and over the bridge. Police officers huddled around Jonathan and the elephant; some dispersed the crowd that had followed them to the field. Jonathan and the elephant, his elephant now, would be going nowhere until Tag Two and the officer got back. Jonathan took out the business card of the company that he rented the motorbike from and gave it to one of the officers and told him to call the company to pick up the bike. The officer did and after asked him where he was staying and Jonathan told him. The police officer walked some distance away and made another call.

The elephant defecated on the Field of Kings and the street sweepers came along and cleaned it up; they put out their hands for Jonathan to pay them. Jonathan looked around to the officers for help and there was none. He reached in his pocket and pulled out one hundred baht.

Soon Tag Two returned in his truck with the police car behind. It was a cattle transport, capable of carrying an elephant. Above the drivers cab was a sheet of plywood bolted to the roof and on it was tied a cage; inside was a huge gold python curled up asleep. On top of his cage was another cage with half a dozen chickens and a red black and gold rooster, it stuck its head between the bars and squawked a racket. The back of the truck was open and tied to a metal railing, were dozens of bundles of sugar cane, corn stalks and palm fronds. Attached to one side of the truck were hooks for a shovel and a number of burlap crap sacks. Tag Two drove up onto the field and everyone cheered except Jonathan. This whole fiasco was an event. Thunder walked to the truck, put his trunk in the back and pulled out his sugar cane and proceeded to eat. A taxi arrived and to Jonathan's astonishment the driver had delivered his luggage from his hotel.

"Two hundred baht," the taxi driver said. Jonathan looked around to blank eyes on everyone and he paid the taxi driver.

"Why is my luggage here?"

"You will need it when you leave," an officer said.

"But I am not leaving," Jonathan said.

"Yes you are," Tag Two said, "you are coming with me and bringing your elephant to where we live. Mr. Owen you must take care of the elephant now he is your responsibility, it is what Buddha wants. It is your destiny, your fate. Now you will need to pay the commanding officer the money for the elephant's registration transfer of ownership."

"You are required to have a valid Registration Certificate for Thunder Mountain. This document is a legally requirement and in your possession when you are with the elephant, particularly when traveling around Bangkok. An officer at anytime may ask to see it," the commander said.

"Possession—travel around Bangkok? And how much will that be?"

"Three hundred thousand baht," the commander said smiling.

"What! That's about ten thousand Canadian. I don't have that kind of money on me."

"It is fine we will stop at Siam Bank on your way home and you can make a transfer, he gave Jonathan the account name to put the money into and it read taxi license.

"Taxi license!" Jonathan yelled, "I now have an elephant taxi?"

"That is correct," the commander said with a big smile, "as long as Thunder Mountain has a chair on his back, he is a taxi," and he pointed up to the metal chair strapped to the elephant.

Jonathan felt frustrated; he was being railroaded into some kind of scam but he was in a foreign culture, so different from his own and he had no choice but to go along with it. If he didn't he could very well end his days in a Bangkok lockup for negligence in the cause of a citizen's death.

"Okay Tag Two or whatever your name is. What now?"

"We go to the bank then home; the police will escort us across the bridge."

Tag Two opened up the back of the truck and pulled out steel gangway from below the deck. Tag Two shouted a command and the huge elephant went up the groaning gangway only too willingly since there was delicious food on board. Tag Two stored the gangway and closed the back gates to the truck and locked them. Jonathan got into the passenger's seat of the truck with the excited commanding officer shouting orders to his men. The taxi driver threw Jonathan's luggage into the back among the sugar cane. Two police cars, with lights flashing, pulled in front of the truck and moved off. Police officers, on foot, stopped the flow of traffic and the parade began to cheers, hoots and horns. The group made its way to the bridge and the other side where the procession pulled into the parking lot of the Bank of Siam where a massive portrait of His Majesty the King looked down on them.

Jonathan and the commander went inside the bank and met with the manager and money was transfer from his bank in Canada to the Bank of

Siam. Jonathan did not flinch at the cost but the principle of it made him furious.

"Congratulations Mr. Owen," the commander said, "you are now a taxi driver in Bangkok. You will find the fuel will cost a little more than a motor vehicle."

"Oh really," Jonathan said sarcastically, his hands on his hips in an aggressive stance, "how much more?"

"That depends where you buy Thunder's food; you see he eats about two hundred kilos a day."

Jonathan dropped his arms and shoulders in resignation, "Oh Christ, now that's going to cost a fortune. Where am I going to get the food?"

"Tag Two will show you, he is your partner now. You will need him and the transport truck. Don't worry Mr. Owen, Buddha will take care of everything and if not, you have money in the bank. That always takes care of problems in Thailand. Here is your receipt," and he handed a number of document to him in Thai, "we will deliver a license, transfer papers and registration certificate for the elephant to you when it is ready. Always keep a copy of the certificate with you. The numbers on it corresponds with Thunder Mountain's microchip in his left ear. Thank you for your cooperation."

"Where will you find us?"

"We know where you are going."

"What about Tag Two's dead brother, where will he be buried?"

"Tag won't be buried, we don't bury people in Thailand, no room, he died of malaria and his body is being burned as we talk. Good luck," a look of compassion came across the commanders face, "remember Mr. Owen, I am your friend in Bangkok, and if you need anything call me. We all love Thunder Mountain here on Khaosan Road, he is a sacred animal." The commander gave him his card, bought his hands up in prayer and did a *wei* and so did a reluctant Jonathan.

They left the bank, Jonathan got into the truck with Tag Two and with Thunder in the back and the snake and chickens above they slowly moved onto the highway and drove out of Bangkok to the countryside of the South Central Plains.

After an hour and neighborhood after neighborhood of homes, shopping centers and industrial sites, the landscape started to change. At first the communities became farms with cattle grazing in fields and then hundreds of thousands of acres on each side of the road were planted in rice. The ponds spread out across the land, their monotony broken by tall royal palms that stood out alone against the sky. They passed by a hamlet, noble cows and their herd women stopped their business to watch them go by. The cows were beautiful animals, some brown, some white, huge and skinny with enormous brown eyes. Their skin hung on them like draped dresses, cut and stitched by designers. The women looked with concerned eyes at Jonathan in the truck—where was Tag? They were covered from head to toe with only their eyes showing, nothing religious, just protection from the sun and dust.

They drove off the highway and onto a lateral road. Tag Two slowed the cattle truck to a crawl as laughing and giggling families came out of their homes to throw sugar cane into the back of the truck for Thunder who always appreciated a little something when it was given. Tag Two would chatter away with them for he and Thunder knew everyone along the route home. In the shade of fig trees Jonathan could make out the shapes of tank sized black buffaloes, the old laborers of the rice fields. They stopped their feeding and stood motionless to watch the elephant pass. The view became majestic like an old woodblock print and Jonathan started to feel good about the day even though he had accidentally killed someone and was now responsible for taking care of an elephant that had cost him a fortune and he was sure to get a lecture from his daughter about how irresponsible he is. God, my daughter and son he thought. I forgot about my daughter. He had not called her since he had arrived in Thailand and she would be worried about him. His son was in South America; they only wrote once a month; plenty of time to fill him in.

"We must get to an Internet café fast," he said, "I must call my daughter, and I'm getting hungry."

"We are in the middle of farms. There is a fast food place up ahead in the next shopping center. We will see if there is an internet café there," Tag Two said.

"When will that be?"

"In about fifteen minutes."

"Good," Jonathan sighed. Soon they were in a modern shopping center with a fast food outlet, gas station, stores and office buildings.

"Let's stop and get some burgers," Tag Two said and the truck moved into a drive-through burger stop and a take out sign. Tag Two ordered two super burgers, onion rings and a large cola.

"What do you want Mr. Owen?"

"I'll have a super burger with fries and a strawberry milkshake please."

"Right," Tag Two said and he placed his order into the menu sign that connected him with the waitress by microphone and speaker. Thunder, with his trunk over the side of the truck, fidgeted with it and tried to pull the thing out of the ground but Tag Two shouted at him to stop and he did. They drove up to the service window.

The service girl asked, "Where is Tag, he is not with you today?"

"No, Tag is dead; there was an accident in Bangkok."

"Oh," the service girl said and she put her hands to her forehead and bowed to Tag Two and said a short prayer. Tag Two bowed back and she fought off Thunder's trunk that he pushed into the window to smell her. Customers and the fast food store staff rushed to the windows to stare out at the spectacle. The elephant gang left the service window with their order and parked in the customer's parking lot.

"This snake above my head," Jonathan asked, "what's his story?"

"That's Naga, he is a friend of mine and one of the family; he makes money off the tourists. They love to be photographed with him around their necks."

"And the chickens?"

"Naga's dinner of course."

"Of course."

"Not the rooster of course."

"Of course not."

They finished their lunch and Jonathan got out of the truck and washed the windshield with water from a spray bottle and a sponge. Tag Two made a walk around of the truck to check for leaking oil and that everything was fastened down. Finished, Jonathan put away the cleanup equipment and garbage and went looking for an Internet café. He found one.

To, Annabelle

Sorry I haven't written you sooner. I am safe and healthy and in Bangkok. I do have a couple of problems though, I was in an accident and ran into a very sick man and he died of complications. It was an accident and everything is sorted out with the police but I had to take over the responsibility of his elephant, which I now own. I don't know what to do about him yet but I will keep you informed as events change. I am on the road north of Bangkok with the elephant and a mahout. I will email when I can. Stay well.

Dad.

Home Camp and Family

Two hours northeast of Bangkok the elephant gang drove down a steep grade off the main road through a forest canopy and sugar cane fields to a clearing on a riverbank. They had arrived at Home Camp. Two young Burmese women and their Mother silently shuffled about the place cleaning with brooms. They stopped their work and sadly greeted them; bowing their heads, their hands held to their faces in prayer. The sad news of Tag had arrived at Home Camp ahead of them. But strangely enough, smiles would soon be on the faces of everyone.

Tag Two jumped out of the truck, "Hello my family," he shouted and bowed a greeting, "we are home. I see by your looks you know the news of Tag. Tomorrow we will talk of it. This is Jonatin Owen; he is Thunder Mountain's new owner and our partner," and everyone bowed to Jonathan who got out of the truck and bowed back. The three women untied and took down the cages of Naga and the chickens and placed them on a bamboo platform beside the pavilion. They opened the chicken cage and the chickens and rooster dashed out and pecked at grain that one of the girls threw on the concrete pad. They were primitive animals, small lean bodies atop relatively huge yellow legs and claws; their heads were small and shaped like cutting tools. If they are not from dinosaurs I don't know what is, thought Jonathan. Naga stirred, his eyes bulged open and the black slit of an iris grew wide. Hmm, we must be home; dinner is on the loose, Naga thought. The three women took Naga and laid him out in the pavilion.

Tag Two opened the back of the truck, pulled out the gangway and ordered Thunder Mountain out and the elephant obeyed. He commanded the elephant to its knees and he unhitched the tourist chair that was still strapped to his huge back. "Mr. Owen, give us a hand will you," and Jonathan helped him lift the chair, harness and blankets from Thunder Mountain and placed them on a bamboo table under the elephant's shelter.

Tag Two commanded the elephant to stand and he guided it to the pad and pulled a chain that was shackled to the pad and shackled it to one of the elephants back legs, "The chain is just long enough to let Thunder Mountain to his shelter or the pavilion where he can stick his trunk in—just a little," he said to Jonathan, "this makes him feel at home and one of the family; any longer and he would be in the pavilion trying to take a seat at the table and wreck the place."

"The paddock running down the trees beside the river and sugar cane field, what lives in that?" Jonathan queried.

"Thunder Mountain's friend—you will meet him soon. Please make yourself at home Mr. Owen. The twins will give you anything you like."

"All I want right now is a shower, a cup of tea and some rest."

"Very well," Tag Two said and he gave instructions in Thai to the girls to get a towel, soap, shampoo, and to make a special tea and prepare a bed for Jonathan. They moved off quietly.

Tag Two was busy with Thunder Mountain so Jonathan looked around at his new home. The roof was a steep blue metal structure for the monsoon seasons' torrential downpours. On the riverside of the house thrusting out over the bank was a pavilion, the home's outdoor living and dining room. A few hammocks hung between the bamboo support posts. The pavilion was furnished with wicker chairs, chesterfields and a large teak dining room table that could seat eight. In the house was a kitchen that was open to the pavilion; stainless steel pots, pans and baskets of food hung from the ceiling. Smoke and steam billowed from a wok on a large commercial gas stove. Off to one side was a toilet room with a shower and hot and cold running water. There were two bedrooms with fans to cool the heat of the night. Mosquito netting hung from hooks above the beds—a room within a room. Behind the house were three bungalows with porches and a barn like building behind them. Through its open doors Jonathan could see a pickup truck, washing and drying machines and some farm machinery.

Down by the river two large fig trees shaded the pavilion—Home Camp's sacred trees. Wrapped around their trunks were yellow, green and red materials. On one tree was an altar of gifts and orchids, offerings to the spirits that protect the camp. On the edge of elephant's concrete pad was a tall structure with a thatched roof—Thunder Mountain's garage. Close to it was a paddock that ran down the edge of the property. A cool breeze blew up from the river and the seasonal shedding of the trees sent golden leaves cascading onto its surface and Home Camp.

The River Kwai flows past Home Camp's bungalow, flowing from the mountains and the Burmese/Thailand border in the north, bubbling and eddying its way to Bangkok and the Gulf of Thailand. It carries in its flow the materials that built the mountains and valleys of Thailand and of life itself. Jonathan watched the setting sun from the pavilion; a huge red ball of fire went down across the river and into the forest covered mountains. Smoke rose from the valleys where farmers were doing their seasonal burning; the smoke fractured the sunlight to one end of the spectrum. The sun shone a brilliant blood red; a red that Jonathan had never seen before. He will find out soon it shines over a bridge thirty miles away that spans the river. It shines a Samurai Red over a shrine to immense suffering.

Across the river the vegetation was like a painting from Constable. Huge deciduous trees towered over the river's banks with breaks revealing lime green cane and cornfields beyond. A fisherman stood on the edge of the bank casting his line. Above him, in the distance, towered palm trees and bamboo, the only signs that this is a tropical place. Birds or monkeys argued in the trees, from their noise Jonathan could not tell what they were. Large black and yellow Butterflies fluttered about and giant beetles buzzed. A Kingfisher dove into the river. Red ants ran about, their venom toxic to the body. He noticed they were everywhere and he knows they will eventually eat the place.

Jonathan showered and there was a fresh towel and robe ready for him on a hook beside the door; a girl shyly showed him his bedroom. She did not look at him, just kept her eyes to the floor and giggled. His luggage was already unpacked and his clothes hung in Tag's closet. Jonathan saw the girls' Mother quickly scurry down the hall and out the back of the house with Tag's clothing. He came out to the pavilion to Tag Two "it doesn't seem to bother them much that Tag has died, does it?"

"No, it doesn't bother them since Tag was not a Thai and neither are they, like me Tag was nobody, a non person here in Thailand without a country; besides, he is still around but as something else."

"What do you mean—something else?"

"Tag is around, a reincarnation, in the spirit of something else. Perhaps as one of those fish out there in the river," Tag Two said and he pointed to the river where a few fish were jumping for food, "or perhaps that butterfly you see there," and a yellow and black butterfly flew through the pavilion, "he will be among us many times before he reaches Nirvana. Tag had good karma; he will make it soon," he sighed. "Make yourself at home Mr. Owen."

Jonathan sat in a large wicker chair padded with buffalo hide cushions and the girl who took it on herself to take care of him bought him tea.

"This is Girl One," Tag Two said. She bowed to him and Jonathan stood up and bowed to her, "this is Girl One's twin sister Girl Two and this is Mother," she had just entered the pavilion. Everyone bowed and smiled and the women slipped silently away to do their chores.

"They live here in Home Camp?" Jonathan asked.

"Yes, they live in the bungalows and share the pavilion and farm with us, keep the place clean, do the laundry and cook the meals. This is our home. We go out and work with Thunder Mountain and Naga and bring home our earnings. I deliver cattle when not working in Bangkok. We all work in the field in the off-season, which is most of the year. For you Mr. Owen, this may be a hard life but we are lucky and better off than most.

"This is a very lovely and expensive piece of land. It must be expensive to run."

"We are in need of little. Tag and I bought this forty acres long ago with money sent to us from America, we don't know who sent it but it started our business."

"And the women, where are they from?"

"They are from Burma; they were starving when they arrived. They escaped from a farm in the north were they were slave labor. They landed at the pavilion very hungry and desperate. Tag and I were desperate once so we understood and took them in. That was nine years ago. We are all family here in the pavilion on the river and share what we have and make."

"The river, isn't it the famous river of Siam?"

"Yes it is. About thirty miles up the river in 1957 Americans made a movie, *The Bridge on the River Kwai.*"

"Yes, I know about it. It was from my generation and I remember the movie well. Thousands of allied troops and Asian laborers were forced to build the Burma/Siam Railway.

"Yes, the Japanese, who followed Samurai philosophy at that time, despised those who did the disgrace of surrender so they treated the labor prisoners as if they had given up their human rights. Thousands died of cholera, malaria, malnutrition and abuse; most are buried in the cemetery at Kanchanaburi."

"You will have to take me there someday. Many of those soldiers died the year I was born; some were friends of my Mother and Father. I'd like to visit the bridge sometime."

"You may not like that, it's a tourist trap now, broken and run down—vendors and hawkers everywhere. You can walk across it but before you do you must pass through a gauntlet of souvenir shops, tour busses and clicking cameras.

"Thunder Mountain—where did you get him?"

"It is time for your tea and then off to bed Mr. Owen, all in due time about our great Thunder Mountain. I will tell you about him another day." He got up and left to take care of the big elephant that was looking a little agitated, perhaps jealous of Jonathan. Girl One graciously placed a silver tray on a side table and poured tea from a china pot into a teacup.

"You like milk and sugar, Mr. Owen?"

"Yes, a little of each thank you," he said and Girl One put a little of both in the cup.

"Your bed is ready when you are," she said and she slipped silently away to the kitchen. Jonathan drank his tea and went to his room for a much-needed sleep; it was still early evening but it had been a long day and life changing for him. His bed was waiting for him the sheets folded back; the mosquito net was in place and the fan rotated. He felt a little strange as he slipped between the sheets; his mind drifted into his new world; a strange place that he must come to understand and be part of. He shut his eyes and images appeared.

Burmese women, the keepers of an ancient pavilion, were frozen forever in time and a two-dimensional space. They watered baskets of orchids that hung from the perimeter beams. In silence they worked, their faces covered in a white powder to protect them from the sun. A huge tree was flattened against a meandering river; it sprinkled gold leaves upon its surface. Those that landed by the pavilion in the grass and tangled roots of the tree were brushed away by the willow broom of a ground's keeper. The keepers' work is never finished, for the scene is forever, always the same—no yesterday, no today, no tomorrow. Jonathan saw himself sitting legs crossed in a lotus position on a straw mat woven from palm fronds in a pavilion that had no perspective. The posts, beams and roof veered off in an isometric projection, for here in this land; the perspective of vanishing points has not been invented yet. Perhaps Buddha does not allow it here, only he can be perfect. Jonathan could only see in one direction in all others the world disappeared into a void—into *nothingness.* He is in the void where the pronouns of *I, me, us, they, them, those* etc. do not exist. An Asian elephant and his mahout stand guard beside the pavilion on the edge of the river. They watch the meandering swirls of water carrying islands of vegetation down to the sea. Above the dream is a massive red orb and below the pavilion a huge snake. The landscape turned to gold; painted on high gloss, black resin, teak, and three panel screens.

The day and the heat had been too much for Jonathan; he drifted away into dreams of other wonders he will see.

Jonathan's eyes opened and he could see through the mosquito netting a clock on a night table. It read ten-thirty, the morning light shone through the open window above his head. He jumped out of bed, fighting the netting as he went. He felt embarrassed that he had slept in, after all, this is a working farm and there are chores to be done. Quickly he showered and shaved, put his robe on and went out to the pavilion. There was no one to be seen except for Naga whose huge golden body laid the length of the pavilion, a chicken was half way down his throat. Suddenly Girl One appeared out of nowhere; a mug of hot coffee in her hand that she passed to him; her eyes glued to the floor.

"Good morning," she said quietly and gave a little bow.

"Good morning, Girl one," Jonathan yawned, "I am sorry that I slept in. There must be things for me to do around here."

"All is done Mr. Owen. Mother and Tag Two are at the market and Girl Two is bathing Thunder Mountain."

"Please call me Jonathan, okay."

"Okay, Mr. Jonatin."

"Oh—okay—where is Girl Two and Thunder?"

"Look out to the river," she said, so he stepped over Naga and moved towards the riverside of the pavilion and twenty feet out was Thunder Mountain up to his neck and Girl Two with a long handled scrubbing brush stood on his back. The elephant took water into its trunk and raising it in the air and behind him; he hosed down Girl Two and his broad back that she scrubbed vigorously. Girl Two's hair was tied up into a bun on top of her head; she had rolled-up her baggy white Thai pants and was bare breasted.

"Oh nice, very nice," Jonathan laughed and he turned to Girl One who was behind the kitchen counter with her head down busy making something. She was not smiling and he felt there might be some jealousy about Girl Two, "how about some breakfast, I'm famished Girl One?" he said clapping and rubbing his hands together.

"Yes Mr. Jonatin, would you like bacon and eggs with toast?" She perked up now that she was the center of attention.

"Yeah, please—you cook American breakfast?"

"Yes, the Tag men are half American."

"So what will Tag Two have me do today when he returns from the market?"

"Nothing today, it is a day of rest. Elephant training is tomorrow; you must learn how to work with Thunder Mountain. You will be returning to Bangkok in a few days to make money for Home Camp."

"Will I be able to learn about Thunder Mountain?" he said as he walked over to the kitchen counter and took a stool.

"You will learn slowly over the years Mr. Jonatin, Thunder Mountain must get to know you and love you. If not, he will kill you and if he loves you too much he will kill you with affection. You will find a place in between."

"I see, well that's good to know and especially about the years," I must think about that, he thought.

"So what about Naga and what do I need to know about him?"

"He sleeps all the time, eats once a week and has his bath everyday. Keep him away from small children. He tried to eat one once."

"Tell me, is this a dangerous job I'm going to do."

"Yes it is, these are wild animals no matter how much love we give them, they are dangerous."

"You sound wise Girl One and speak English well."

"The Tag men, my Mother and Buddha are good teachers. English is the language of commerce."

The pickup truck from the barn arrived from the market and Tag Two and Mother got out and reached in the back. Tag Two beckoned to Jonathan to come and help with the groceries, which he did. Mother and Girl One packed the goods into the cupboards, refrigerator and deep freeze.

"Did you have a nice sleep Mr. Owen," Tag Two said.

"I did, would you please call me Jonathan."

"Right Jonatin," and Thunder Mountain and Girl Two came up the riverbank and he could see by the eyes of the elephant that he had missed Tag Two even if it was for a short while. He quickly put out his trunk to wrap around Tag Two's arm and the mahout hugged the huge beast. Girl Two giggled and laughed and slid down off the elephant's neck and Girl One threw her a shirt that she put on. She shackled the elephant to the concrete.

"I am making Mr. Jonatin brunch. Would you all like some?" Girl One said. A resounding agreement came from everyone, "Girl Two, come and help please," and the twins left for the kitchen. Tag Two took a towel from the railing and went to the river and soaked it. He came back to the pavilion and wiped down Naga who was now asleep with a lump halfway down his body. Thunder Mountain stood by the pavilion trying to reach anybody with his trunk and under his huge belly ran half a dozen chickens. The big rooster, who seemed like he was counting his flock, scratched and fussed about; agitated that one of his hens was missing.

In the pavilion' "We eat together Mr. Owen," Tag Two said and he pulled a chair back from the head of the table, "this was Tag's chair—it is now yours," Tag Two took the other end of the table. The two girls and Mother bought out plates of eggs bacon, bread, butter, jam, juice, condiments, fruit and a large bowl of chopped sugar cane. An enamel pot of coffee was the last thing to fill the table. The girls sat next to each other and across from Mother who said a prayer in Thai to someone, Buddha perhaps, Jonathan could not tell.

"So Mr. Jonatin," Mother said to Jonathan's exasperation, "tomorrow you learn about the elephant but today we all rest," and she reached in the sugar cane bowl and took out a handful of succulent shoots. Thunder Mountain's trunk was right behind her—waiting.

"So I understand," he said and he looked around at his new family, the snake, the chickens, the rooster, the elephant, the twins, Tag Two and Mother. Deep in his heart he prayed to his own God that he was worthy of them.

Three Meters up in the Saddle

"Put these on Jonatin," Tag Two said and he handed him a pair of baggy blue three quarter length pants and a light blue shirt with three quarter length sleeves, "these are comfortable to ride in and they won't bunch up." He went to his room and put them on and slipped into his sandals and returned to the concrete pad, Thunder Mountain, Tag Two and Girl Two.

"You look wonderful," Girl Two said with a giggle, "here put this on," and she handed him a broad brimmed straw hat with a leather band. He felt like a plantation owner when he put it on.

"Perfect," Girl Two said.

"Bare feet Jonatin," Tag Two said, "the elephant must feel your bare feet if you are to become one with him." He removed his sandals and threw them in the pavilion. "Maintaining control over Thunder Mountain is essential, talk to him in simple sentences and command him with a forceful voice so he understands. This will prevent you or anyone else around you from being harmed. Remember you will be working together in the busy market places and streets of Bangkok. Approach him always from the side gently talking to him so he can see and hear you coming and won't be startled when you come out of his blind spot. Anyone approaching he will put his trunk out to touch and smell them."

Jonathan walked up to Thunder Mountain's left side, "Hey Thunder, have you had your breakfast?"

"That's right, now let him smell you," and the elephant put forward his trunk and touched Jonathan's arm and Tag Two pointed to his chain. "His chain is strong and polished so nothing can wear his skin. But it must be checked twice a day to make sure there is no chaffing. We change it to other legs each week. The U-bolt has a string wrapped around its bolt to prevent it from unscrewing. He knows how to unscrew these things and he can't if the string is in place. Attached to the U-bold is three meters of chain that is attached by another U-bolt to the steel ring imbedded in the concrete pad," and he pointed this out and picked up the chain, "you will notice in the middle is a swivel to prevent the chain becoming twisted and tangled. The length restricts him to going down to the river for a drink, to his shelter or to the railing of the pavilion but not in it. If he is not chained he will run away to the forest or worse end up in another farm field and wreck the crops. Don't ever park the truck or leave anything near him. He will take it apart bolt by bolt. Elephants like to be busy doing something.

"The are only a few tools, this is a hook which is your most important tool." and he handed Jonathan a half meter shaft with a point at one end and a menacing looking hook coming off the side. "It is used to pull the elephant around and not to be used with force as it will puncture the skin and we don't want that. Don't hit the elephant with it either. He won't know what you are doing or what the punishment is for. He is never to be punished just coxed along. Patience is essential when working with him because sometimes he will not do what he is told or will take his own time. He has had a violent past and it took many years to make him gentle and gain our trust. He has become more accommodating in his old age.

"Then you have the chains which I showed you. When traveling we take the chains with us and drape them over Thunder's neck," and he demonstrated by unhooking the chains, thunder bowed down to receive them. Other things like hobbles and ear tethers we leave at home since we haven't needed to use them for years. He knows about forty commands in Thai and English which makes it easy for you."

"This is your short knife Jonatin," Girl Two said and she handed him a sheathed forty-centimeter knife on a belt, "put it on. It is used for cutting up his food so he can properly digest it. Often when elephants eat large leaves, like palm fronds, they become impacted in their intestines, which can be a great discomfort and sometimes can kill the elephant. The knife is also used for other things like trimming gear that you make or cutting the neck rope if anything happens and you have to free yourself from his neck." Jonathan put the belt on.

"Show him the medicine chest." Tag Two said.

She went over to the pavilion and dragged a metal chest from the crawl space and opened it. "In here we have eye drops, pain-relief ointments, oral pain relievers, tincture of iodine, insect powder, povidone-iodine, hydrogen peroxide, alcohol inflammation-reducing medicines and antibiotic ointments. There are scissors, bandages, cotton batten, tape, pliers and other things needed for sores, infections and injuries. We watch any injuries closely and if something looks bad we call the vet. Watch out when you are on the road for glass and other harmful things he may cut his feet on or worse eat sharp objects. Sometimes elephants will eat plastic and human garbage that can give elephant serious intestinal problems. Check his dung everyday to see there are no worms, the food has been properly digested and that it is healthy looking.

"What is healthy looking dung?" Jonathan queried.

"You'll get to know," Girl Two said laughing. "You will be shoveling a lot of it. I also check it everyday when he is home. There is a manual here in the medicine box and it is a good idea if you read it as soon as possible. It tells you things that you cannot see or may not notice when checking out Thunder Mountain. There is also a manual on the training of mahouts."

"Girl Two washes Thunder everyday in the river and I encourage you to join in. You can also use the hose." And he reached in the crawl space and bought out a two-inch thick hose. He pulled it out onto the concrete and threw a switch in a junction box on the side of the pavilion that turned on a water pump, "We wash the elephant and the concrete at least twice a day. There is a scrub brush, bucket and a ten-liter bottle of antiseptic solution under the pavilion. Instructions are on the label for the right amount to mix with water. It does not take much so use it sparingly. There is a wheelbarrow and shovel by the tree to clean up his dung that you dump down the way on the edge of the field. We plow it into the soil and there is a family in town that comes and collects some of it to make paper. We get a small royalty. They label the paper, *Thunder Mountain Paper*."

"Okay Jonatin unshackle him," Tag Two commanded, "it's time to climb aboard. Remember he understands simple English commands. "Stand by the elephant and say, *down* and do it with force in your voice."

"*Down!*" Jonathan said and Thunder Mountain went down bending at his front knees.

"Now holding his ear with your left hand, your right hand on his shoulder, put your left foot on his knee and bring your right leg up over his neck," Tag Two said and Jonathan did what he was told and was on the elephants neck, "now say *hey-up!*"

"*Hey-up!*" Jonathan said and Thunder Mountain rose. He was so shocked he almost fell off. This giant animal was doing what he asked of it.

"The rope around his neck, see it?"

"Yes."

"Put your feet under it. It may be awkward at first but you will get used to it. Now with your bare toes and with both feet kick him behind the ears and say *Hey-ah!*"

"*Hey-ah!*" Jonathan said and Thunder Mountain moved forward.

"That's it. We will follow you around the farm. We are going off to the right so with your left foot nudge his ear and with the right heel nudge his shoulder," Jonathan did what he was told and the elephant moved off to the right, "You reverse the movements when turning left, understand."

"Yes, this is fantastic. I'm actually steering an elephant!"

"Now we use the unromantic word *whoa* to stop him. With your heels tap his shoulders and say *whoa!*"

"*Whoa!*" Jonathan said and the elephant stopped."

"Tap him again and say, *back!*

"*Back!*" Jonathan said tapping his shoulders with his heels and Thunder Mountain backed up.

"Say good boy, good boy."

"Good boy, good boy. What do we do know?"

"We spend a few hours riding around the farm and let Thunder Mountain get to know you. Now remember to be firm because he will want to do as he pleases. When he wants to crap he stops and nothing can make him move so be patient. He is always eating and on the lookout for food so you may find yourself in the bush and having to back him up. Remember you are up about three meters off the ground and will be in places where there is electrical wiring, bridges and overhanging tree branches, be careful and always look for danger around you especially on the ground. Elephants become stressed when they sense danger since they are so big and weight so much they are constantly checking their surroundings. They are in fear of their safety so they must not be put in dangerous situations."

For the next couple of hours Jonathan rode Thunder Mountain around the farm, getting on and off and at times crashing through the bush. Tag Two used the hook to gently pull Thunder Mountain in line. Jonathan sensed the elephant was having fun with him. They returned to the pavilion, He stood on the elephants back and Girl Two handed up the running hose and he washed down Thunder Mountain. It was his first day of training and he felt proud of what he had accomplished. Tag Two and Girl Two clapped and bowed to Jonathan and Thunder Mountain.

Jonathan came out of a cold shower, dried off, put his robe on and entered the pavilion, "Christ that was a long day, my poor crouch muscles ache from Thunder's neck. It's going to be hard getting used to that, I'll be bowlegged like a Chilcotin cow rancher in no time," sighed Jonathan as he gently lowered himself into one of the pavilions wicker chairs, "I think I'll just go to bed without supper tonight, I'm too tired to eat."

Girl One shuffled up to him and gently said, "Would you like a nice cup of tea while I prepare your bed, Mr. Jonatin?"

"Yeah, that would be nice, thank you," he replied. Girl One went off to the kitchen and Jonathan lay back in the comfortable chair and watched the river. He may feel some ache in his muscles but it was a good ache not the sharp pain of injury. He felt an enormous satisfaction at what he had achieved today. Just to the left of his vision beyond the railing, Thunder Mountain was dancing with his front legs and waving his trunk. Jonathan swore there was a naughty look in his eye. Girl One came back with the tea tray. "Thank you," he said and she took the tray and laid it on the mat on the edge of the pavilion overlooking the river.

"This is where you sit for your tea now, Mr. Jonatin."

Jonathan got up from the whicker chair and sat cross-legged beside Girl One who placed the tea tray in front of him.

"This is where you will learn to meditate and relax when you are here at Home Camp. It is peaceful here overlooking the river, is it not?"

"Yes it is, very peaceful."

For half an hour they sat silently, she watched him watching the river. She was going to talk to him about meditation but hesitated because she saw in his eyes and the way he studied the river he was in meditation.

He finished his tea and attempted to get up off the mat. "Ouch!" he cried, "I'm totally stiff," and he grabbed at his right thigh.

"Let me help you," she said and she put his arm around her shoulder, helped him off the mat and led him to his bedroom.

"Ha, ha," Tag Two laughed as he entered the pavilion, "you are tired and sore from the day. This is good; with a good night's rest you will be even better tomorrow. Good night."

"Good night," he groaned back and he and Girl One staggered off to bed.

She had pulled back the crisp clean sheets for him and tucked the mosquito net ends under the mattress. The fan was on quarter power and blew air gently across the room, the netting swayed in the breeze. Girl Two pulled back the netting and helped Jonathan out of his robe. He did not care that she could see him naked; he was too tired and sore. He lay back and closed his eyes and he could feel Girl One's gentle hands on his thighs, legs and feet. She softly hummed a Thai song about the moon and flowers that only come out at night. Jonathan drifted away up a river of dreams to forests and wetlands, places where crabs live in trees and gibbons swing from the treetops. A gold Buddha sits in a cave with bats all around and monks chant all day.

It was morning and Jonathan stirred awake, it was still dark but a faint light blue horizon told it would be light soon. In his drowsiness he thought he saw dark skin pass by the mosquito netting around his bed. He snuggled into the sheets for a few more moments before breakfast. Maybe he can go back and catch a few moments; but he knows he can't.

"Hey Jonatin, time to get up," Girl Two said the other side of the mosquito net.

"What time is it?"

"Five-thirty."

"Don't you know I'm retired?"

"Not anymore, Jonatin. Now get up, I have made fresh coffee and toasted some bagels. See you in the kitchen in fifteen minutes."

"I'll be there," Jonathan sighed. He got up showered, shaved and went to the kitchen. Where are Tag Two, Mother and Girl One?"

"Tag Two can't be with us today; he has to meet with the villagers about the next crop they will be planting at Home Camp and Mother and my sister are in town. So you're with me today. Take that look off your face and don't worry; I have lived with this elephant since I was little."

"No, I'm not worried. I know you know what you're doing. What will it be today?"

"Much the same as yesterday, we ride around the farm and talk about elephants. We keep it simple. We slow down; become one with the earth and the elephant. And I will tell you all about fashion," she said. He groaned and they both laughed.

They finished their coffee and bagel and cleaned up the dishes. Girl Two picked up the hook, knife and a small waist purse on a belt hanging on a post at the entrance to the pavilion. Out in his shelter Thunder Mountain was snoozing, his back legs crossed in a relaxed and comical position.

Jonathan walked up to him from his side.

"Good morning my huge feathered friend, you slept well I see and so did I," he turned to Girl Two, "he doesn't understand does he?"

"No but he can tell whether what you say is friendly or not. Remember he is very intelligent and sometimes I think he understands more than we think."

The elephant reached out to him and he took his trunk in his hand, moved toward him and touched the elephant with his body.

"Walk around and inspect him like you would a car. Look for any scratches and abrasions."

Jonathan walked around him. "He's clean."

"Okay, put your belt on."

Jonathan put his belt on, "Something new here—this pouch?"

"A place to carry your copy of the Registration Certificate, permit to operate in Bangkok, travel papers, ID card, money, cell phone, and taxi license," she laughed.

"What's so funny?"

"Nothing Jonatin, there are a number of maps in there of the markets and roads where you will work with him. These are important as the hazards are marked. Things like low electrical wiring, gratings in the road and sidewalks that could be dangerous if they collapsed. There are local police stations marked out and places to dump Thunder Mountain's dung. Let's move on. With the hook go from leg to leg, tap just below the knee and Thunder will lift his foot so you can inspect it. Run your hand over the sole to feel for glass, metal or other stuff that may be there." He went foot to foot and the beast cooperated with him.

"Everything is fine."

"Good, do an inspection twice a day at Home Camp and in Bangkok or often as possible. Undo the chain and get on him."

Jonathan undid the U-bolt at his ankle and coiled it on the concrete pad. "*Down!*" he commanded and the elephant lowered his head. He climbed aboard. "*Hey-up!* That's right my fine hugeness," and the elephant rose to his feet and lifted his trunk to smell Jonathan. He positioned his feet under the manila rope around Thunder's neck.

Below him Girl Two giggled. "Let's go."

"*Hey-ah!*" he said sternly and he drove his toes behind the elephant's ears. They moved off down the road and into the fields. Jonathan practiced getting on and off and learning new commands like lying down, sitting and trumpeting. He used the knife to cut banana leaves and other plants that Girl Two picked out.

"It is best that we cut some of the food for him because he may destroy the whole thing like a new banana plant—rip it out of the ground. Some of the plants are medicinal like high in vitamins and minerals that the elephant needs. We don't want to completely destroy them; we want to come back to them at another time. You will learn to recognize these plants in time. We will take many walks with Thunder Mountain to do this."

"Sustainable munching," Jonathan, said.

"What?"

"Nothing, I just remembered something from my past. Can I ask you something?"

"Yeah, sure."

"What do you want to do with yourself Girl One?"

"Become a stylist."

"I think I have heard of them, what do they do?"

"They dress people: clothing, makeup and hair—that kind of thing. People who are rich like celebrities have stylists. They also work in television and the service industry. Like if you build a hotel, Jonatin, you would hire me to design the style of the place. I wouldn't actually do the design of staff clothing and look of the place. I would be the one managing the look or the branding as we say."

"I think you would do well at that."

"Maybe, I don't know. In the meantime I have Home Camp and family to take care of, especially this big loveable brute here. How can I leave him?" and she patted the elephant on the leg and Jonathan thought soon he will leave you.

"It is time to head home, the sun is high and it is getting hot. It has been a good morning."

They arrived back at the pavilion and Jonathan dismounted.

"Now for the fun," she said with delight in her voice.

"What fun?" he said and before he knew it Girl Two took off her shirt and pants. She was now in just her panties and laughing. She ran to the river and dove in and Thunder Mountain followed. She climbed up on his broad back.

"There is a long handle brush under the pavilion. Bring it out to me."

He found it, "Okay, but I'm keeping my clothes on." He walked into the river and the elephant hosed him full in the face. Girl Two roared with laughter and he thought well when your learning you can become the butt of jokes. They scrubbed, played and bonded with Thunder Mountain and eventually came up the riverbank to the concrete pad. Girl Two put her shirt on.

"Why do you take your shirt off when bathing with Mountain, I thought Thais were shy."

"I'm not Thai, remember, I'm Burmese. I have done it since I was little when I didn't have breasts. It just feels natural to me to be mostly naked when I'm in the river with Thunder Mountain. He doesn't mind, do you?"

"No of course not and don't get me wrong. I like free spirits, I'm one myself."

"So Girl One tells me."

"Oh really."

"Now we have to clean up the compound. Here is the shovel, there is the dung heap and I'll get the hose."

The morning training over Girl Two took to a hammock in the pavilion and Jonathan went out to a shaded hammock that was hooked to the sacred fig tree and the paddock gatepost—just out of reach of the elephant. Mother and Girl One arrived made tea and came out to his hammock with a mug of ice tea to cool him.

"Here is a nice cool drink for Mr. Jonatin, yes?" Girl One said.

"Yes, thank you," he said and because he was so thirsty and tired he gulped the tea down and gave the mug back to her. She bowed and returned to the house and her nap.

Home Camp was in bed for the afternoon. His training was hard work and the elephant, Girl Two and he had been at it since six that morning.

In his sleep he drifted down a river past temples, villages, cities, forests and farms, palm trees, pavilions, boathouses and their bright coloured fishing boats. He floated in a gold inlay canoe with a red hull piloted by a Thai woman in gold robes. She guided the craft with a long tiller handle from the stern. Her fingernails were ten-centimeters long; her face powdered white, her cheeks were rose red under huge black eyes. There was no white in her eyes just wet black—a shinning marble black. On her head was a gold *chedi* crown that shot up to a point. She not only looked at Jonathan but the entire world; she was the world and he felt it. She was a mythological creature from a land that he knew so little about, she shone in the sunlight and he felt safe. The river flowed into the sea and the current took them out across a bay to an island of white and dark green cliffs. It was more like a ship than an island, a giant ship on a blue green sea, an intense blue sky above. The island was made of limestone with caves that were formed a million years ago when the island was underwater, now they were open to the gentle currents that took his boat inside one of them. Bright coloured stalactites hung from the ceiling dripping water that rained on him. The boat's presence stirred the bats and they flew down from the ceiling to greet him. Jonathan looked to his pilot and she smiled; her black eyes became bigger until they were the caves. Jonathan was no longer in a boat but floating on the water. The cave roof opened and sunlight came down in a shaft to sparkle the water into blue and white diamonds.

Suddenly a black shadow rose from the water in front of him, a huge brass shining ring attached. It became bigger and bigger until it filled the cave. Below it was black flesh. It rose higher out of the water and licked Jonathan across the face, tasting him like animals do before they eat. The appendage was wet and he could not get away. The cave disappeared and he was in sunlight again but the landscape was different. There was a large bulbous thing as big as his head in front of him with a brass ring through it and attached to it was a rope.

"Jesus Christ!" Jonathan yelled in terror and he fell out of the hammock, stood up and backed into the hammock and stretched it as far as it would go. He wiped a wet slim from his face with his hands. In front of him was a tank, he first thought, but as he became fully awake it took on the shape of a buffalo. A beast about half the size of Thunder Mountain, its massive black horns that came out of a huge head were five feet across. They looked like ancient Samurai swords, poised and read to cut him to bits. Its eyes black as anything Jonathan had ever seen stared at him its huge black tongue licked the air. Coming out of his nose was a brass ring with a rope attached and at the end of the rope was a little Gandhi man; a skinny, brown, bald, speckled, orange robed monk with a huge mouth of rotten teeth. On the other side of the tank was Thunder Mountain; his trunk draped over the tanks huge black horn. There was a smile in his amber eyes, the usual smile that showed he was up to some mischief.

"Welcome home Monk!" Tag Two shouted from the pavilion. Mother and the twins were beside him with their hands together bowing to Monk and his buffalo. Monk bowed to everyone including the animals even the chickens and the fussing rooster who were underfoot. Monk opened the gate to the paddock and the huge tank on ebony black hooves went in. The monk unhitched the rope from the brass ring and the beast snorted in satisfaction and put its head over the railing to be hugged by the monk.

Thunder Mountain did his usual dance with his front legs with a look on his face for Jonathan that smirked—you're mine now.

The training went on for the next few days and then Tag Two said, "Your training is finished at Home Camp and I think Thunder Mountain likes and trusts you—that's good. Elephants that have too many mahouts in their lifetime can come to kill or cause injury. I don't think we have to be afraid of that now." He and Jonathan lounged in the wicker chairs in the pavilion enjoying a cool beer in the afternoon. White mosquito netting had been unfurled around the perimeter of the pavilion and he felt like he was in a Greek temple.

"Tomorrow we will leave for Bangkok, you are ready to work the streets and Thunder Mountain can make his contribution to our family," Tag Two said.

"I'm a little scared about becoming a mahout on an elephant on the streets of Bangkok. Do you think I'm ready for such a thing?"

"You are ready, he is just an animal and he likes you and when you're firm with him he will do what you command and besides he knows his way around in the city. He enjoys being with you and trusts you.

"Okay, on another thing, when are you going to tell me about you and your brother?"

"What do you want to know?"

"Where did you get your names, Tag and Tag Two? Does Tag mean something in Thai other than what I think it is in English?"

"We came to be called that when we were left at the orphanage in Bangkok. We were dropped there by the American navy after they picked us up off the coast of Cambodia shortly after the war."

"Christ, you were one of the boat people?"

"Yeah, we were almost dead when they found us along with ten others—some young and some old. We were in an open boat floating in the China Sea; we had nothing left. My mother was raped in front of us and taken by pirates along with other women and all our possessions. We were left abandoned to die. Weeks later most of the people had died in the boat and were eaten by the survivors including us. We were too little to know what we were eating; an old man made sure that we would survive, he said, tell the story—tell the story, over and over again. We did not know until years later what he was talking about. Eventually we did tell the story to writers and one time on Bangkok television. Anyway, an American patrol boat picked us up and dropped us off at an orphanage in Bangkok. They tagged us, pinned a sheet of information about us on our shirts. We were too frightened to speak and tell our names. The Americans just wrote Tag on one and Tag 2 on the other. We went after them for years about our past but could get nothing out of the Thai or the American Consulates, eventually we gave up."

"Were you and Tag brothers?"

"No we had different mothers. We remember that, and when they were taken we hung on to each other—we were terrified and alone. When we grew up we found out who we were really were."

"And who were you?"

"Bui Doui, The Dust of Life, American and Vietnamese. Our fathers were soldiers in the United States Army. There are thousands of us all over Asia and many still feel we are out of place but I accept our place in history and Tag and I were proud of who we were. I am still proud."

"I have heard about you. Do you know who your father is?"

"No but someone out there in America knew who we were since we received money when we were old enough to buy this place."

"Was it hard growing up?"

"No it wasn't, we were well loved at the orphanage and we grew up on the streets of Bangkok, mostly on Khaosan Road among the merchants and people who come and go from Thailand, especially the tourists. They were and still are good to us. Tag and I knew long ago the tourist market was where we should work and do business. So we learned American

English, the language of commerce. Tag and I made it our first language and Thai our second. It has worked well for us."

"So Girl One tells me."

"When we were old enough we used to night watch for the hotels and in the day we slept under the receptions' desks. Part of the day we sold merchandise that we bought from the wholesale district behind China Town. We also worked in wholesale for a while but that was chaos and backbreaking work. We had no expenses so we saved our money. Some of our friends were the rats that came out at night on Khaosan Road."

"Yes, I have met them."

"Then out of nowhere came the money from America, it came through the orphanage. They would not tell us from whom it came, perhaps they didn't know either."

"Another beer?" Mother said from the kitchen.

"Yes please," Jonathan said to her and returned to Tag Two, "and then you bought the farm."

"Yes, we could not think of anything else but owning some land, not a store or hotel on Khaosan Road. Tag and I always talked of land and during the little time we had off from work we would take a bus out to the country and dream of owning a plot of land to grow vegetables. We could have easily bought a business in Bangkok but we found this place and fell in love with it. The work was hard at first and we lived in a lean-to home while we built this house. It was slow going; it took us three years to finish it."

"When did Thunder Mountain join you?"

"He came along in the early nineties when Tag saved him from the slaughter house. He needed a new job so we bought him and he earns his keep with us during the few tourist months of the year in Bangkok. Sometimes we even use him to plow the fields."

"You know in some parts of the world people frown upon what you do with the elephants in the cities."

"I know but Thunder Mountain has spent all his life with people and is a working animal. The Non Government Agencies want to regulate the ownership and use of elephants, if they get legislation past that will be the end of the Asian elephant in Thailand."

"What do you mean—end?"

"There will be more restrictions, regulations, licensing etc. Right now elephants are under the Domestic Animal Act and everyone has the right to own an elephant like cats, dogs, chickens and cows. All our elephants would end up on reserves, which are vulnerable to poachers, NGOs and government agencies. Let's face it the reserves are under pressure. In Africa the elephants on reserves are now being culled because there are too many for the small space allotted to them and yet the NGOs call them an endangered species. Sometimes the perception through ignorance to do the righteous thing can cause damage, heartache and death. Elephants will survive in this country if farmers like us use them on the farms and in the cities and adopt them into the human family like other domestic animals."

"Some NGOs want the elephants out of the hands of people no matter what the cost."

"Only the rich can afford conservation, the average family in Asia is not rich. The NGOs are rich, live far away and have groups behind them who know nothing about elephants and conservation."

"What's the answer?"

"The Domestic Animal Act should incorporate a department like the SPCA to inspect and possibly run a school where elephant owners and mahouts would be required to attend. The school should be free, small and portable so it can travel around the country. Elephants are not hard to keep it is an attitude towards the handling and the care of elephants that needs to be worked on.

"If we put Thunder Mountain out on a game farm or reserve he will die of loneliness and perhaps be poached for his tusks, as small as they are. Land is disappearing fast and there is pressure on the reserves. The Asian elephant, like in the past, must be adopted into the family and treated with care, love and respect. "

"What is his story?" and he pointed to a fuzzy gray mass, Thunder Mountain, on the other side of the mosquito net. His trunk, the netting draped over it, was inside the pavilion exploring.

"It is a long one and I will tell it to you since you have to know it and you are his mahout. You are a part of his history now and a very important part. Tag and I were told his story by his former owners whom we promised to keep it true until Thunder Mountain's death which is close"

"His death is close?" he cried, thinking of his investment.

"Yes, he is old, in his seventies and elephants die usually in their sixties when the last of six sets of teeth crumble and there isn't another set to take their place. Thunder is on his last set of teeth and the veterinarian says they are almost worn out. Without his teeth to chew the two hundred kilos of food he needs each day, he will deteriorate very fast."

"Oh Christ," he said disheartened, and he wasn't thinking of his investment anymore but a gentle beast that he was becoming to love.

"Let's go out and sit in the shade of his shelter," Tag Two said, and they walked out of the pavilion to the concrete pad. The big elephant followed them and stood under his shelter. They sat below his head and crossed their legs. Tag Two wrapped his arms around the inquisitive trunk and began the story. The elephant groaned his satisfaction.

"It is believed that about seventy years ago Thunder Mountain was born in the mountains in Northern Thailand near the village of Doi Mae Salong. His herd, of about twenty, lived in the Teak forests near the border of

Myanmar that was then called Burma. His home was among the hill tribes who respected the elephant as something sacred and part of the land since they looked like the rocks in the river. An Akha hill tribe opium farmer and his wife witnessed his birth one very terrible night. They had fled to higher ground because of flash floods that threatened the plateau and their home. It was a regular event for them during the monsoon seasons. The storm witnessed the birth also and expressed its approval with great crashing of thunder, lightening and rain. This was a good omen to the farmer who was uneducated and ignorant. Events that happened on the land and in the air were things that governed his life. The farmer believed that he was sent there by the storm to witness the birth. And so in his way, the little elephant belonged to him and when it grew up he would take him to work on the farm.

"He waited three years, keeping an eye on the little elephant and was amazed at how fast and big the creature grew. The day came and with a few other mahouts and their elephants they set out to take him. They went into the mountains, killed the mother, and took the three year old from the herd—"

"What a terrible thing to do," Jonathan interrupted.

"You must remember this is a different culture time and place. Don't judge them, you must still respect their hard way of life—their way of survival."

"Sorry, please go on."

"The little elephant grew very fast and was loved and cherished by the hill family. He was left to himself to come and go as he pleased but the only rule was to stay out of the poppy fields. The elephant's destiny was soon made clear when the farmer's old elephant died and the little one took over his chores. He worked the fields with the farmer and his wife and delivered the crop of opium to the village below the farm for transport out of the country. The family did not know where the opium went and did not much care as they were hard working hill people who could not read or write and no news ever came from the outside world. It was a good life; the farmer and his wife raised three boys over the next twenty years. Thunder Mountain was treated as one of the family.

"Life was peaceful and the family prospered, then the Kuomintang; Chinese Nationalist Army came into the area. They had fled China after being defeated by Mao Zedong. The Thai military let them stay under the condition that they would suppress communism that was infiltrating the hill tribe villages. Before long the KMT were acting autonomously and were allowed to tax and control the opium trade of the area. The warlord Kun Sa, a brutal man, controlled the hills and everything in them and so the area became a very dangerous place.

"Eventually the family was accused of selling part of their crop without paying taxes, whether this was true or not we don't know, but an example was to be made. Anyway the warlord's underlings, who were a savage and cruel bunch, one night broke into the farmer's home and hacked the family to death, all of them: Mother, Father and the three boys. One of the boys had taken a wife and she and her unborn child died in the massacre. The warlords burned the bodies in the farmhouse, raked the area clean and planted poppies over the site. They even cultivated the trail that led to their home. Nothing was left of the family except Thunder Mountain; he was spared since he could be sold, which he was to a lumber company down on the edge of the forested mountains near the plains and rice fields.

"Thunder Mountain worked the forest and the lumber yards for many years up to the time of 1989 when all logging was banned in Thailand. According to government figures, seventy six percent of the elephants in captivity were made unemployed. He once again was pressed into an illegal operation—the illegal logging of teak. His mahout, who was a very bad and impatient young man, beat him. If you look at his head you can see the scaring of the hook," Tag Two stood up and pointed to the scars on the elephant's trunk and head," he sat down, "they worked the forest for many years. One day Thunder Mountain came out of the forest alone and went straight to his enclosure, there was blood coming from gashes on his head where he had been beaten by the hook. He bobbed back and forth frightened and anxious; his eyes ran with tears. The other mahouts suspected what had happened for they knew what his mahout was like. They went into the forest and found him; most of the bones in his body were crushed. They all knew it was Thunder Mountain who killed him and they knew it would be very difficult to retrain him not kill again. They decided to put him down.

"Well wouldn't you now it; Tag came along looking around the district for a good cattle truck that we could use here in the village doing deliveries for the farmers. To sum up—Tag bought the elephant, a decision which I totally disagreed with since he was a killer and too huge for us to keep. We were barely scrapping by ourselves and now with two hundred fifty kilos of food a day for the elephant—well that was a bit too much. But we came to love Thunder Mountain, he came to love us and so did the village and farmers around here. We live in a lush and productive area; we found it not expensive to come up with the food for him.

"It wasn't long before he was making a living for himself on the streets of Bangkok. He loves his job in the markets, he is among people that he loves to smell—you will see. Since he was a baby he has always lived with people and treats them as though they were elephants." Thunder Mountain groaned as Tag Two hugged his trunk.

"So the name, Thunder Mountain, it has been carried down to each owner all these years?"

"Yes, if you look behind his ears there are tattoos in Chinese calligraphy; his left ear spells Thunder, the right one spells Mountain. Who put them there—we don't know. We have always taken it to mean his name. So, Jonatin, treat him well and he won't kill you."

Jonathan looked Thunder Mountain in the eye and he saw not only a gentle beast but also a powerful intelligent animal capable of throwing him across the farm. He knew he would have to make friends with this elephant not just be his mahout. He reached out to touch the elephant and the elephant touched him back.

"It is time for bed for me. I see Girl One is making tea for you before your bedtime," they both got up and walked into the pavilion, "good night, Jonatin."

"Good night Tag Two," Jonathan said and he took his place on the mat at the front of the pavilion, a breeze blew up from the river and with the fans above him the air was cool and clean. Girl One had raised some of the mosquito netting so they could see out. He looked over to his big gray elephant out on the concrete slab dancing away. His amber eyes were on Jonathan and his trunk caressed the pavilion railing. Girl One came with a tray of tea and some English cookies and sat down beside him. She did not say a word and neither did Jonathan. He drank his tea.

A Large Beer for Me and A Bucket of Water for My Elephant

Jonathan could not get out of the place fast enough—the stench of strange food was too much for him. Incense burned from alters throughout the market, lit to cover the smell or a prayer to the deities. He wondered if he could ever get used to it. Tons of shrimp, crabs, squid, lobsters, crayfish, oysters and a hundred other varieties of fish were stacked up on ice and in huge plastic pails. Some like the frogs, eels and tiny crabs were still alive in plastic tubs. Pigs, cattle and what looked like skinned horses and dogs hung from meat hooks—their blood dripping onto a filthy floor. Dried and fried insects: larva, ants, grasshoppers and other creatures were wrapped in cones of newspapers to be eaten like candy. The heat was unbearable in the day market—there was no air-conditioning.

A respite to the stench came from flower stalls filled with orchids, cut flowers and jasmine offerings. The Thais love their flowers and when the vendor was not looking Thunder Mountain grabbed a few on the way out. It was one of his tricks and if he got caught Jonathan ended up paying. Buyers bargained for the meat and produce bought to the cavernous hall and much of it would be cooked at the adjoining night market out on the street. Dogs ran about the place, smelling this, licking that and Jonathan thought of how disgusted he has become of these stray creatures.

The Bangkok day market was just closing down and the night market was being set up on an adjacent road. Young pirates, entrepreneurs and the local restaurants set up their stalls and kitchens to do their night business. Around them were the day shops in colonial styled buildings that are covered with huge advertising banners; their brightly colored signs, twenty-five meters high, screamed out from the buildings. Unless it is an official or religious building, architecture has disappeared in the new inner city; people live and move in a giant graphic of huge laughing faces, text copy, cigarette packages and soft drink bottles. At the center of the market, on the corner of two busy streets, was a huge portrait of the King in his gold robes. He is eighty now and still a handsome figure of a man. His image is displayed on a purple background with the letters of the Siam Commercial Bank emblazoned across the bottom. Guards at the entrance keep the market from encroaching too close to the King.

At night the buildings become super graphics; the dirt, grease and grime of the street disappears into fantastic images. Below the billboards, lights come on in the hundreds of booths and portable restaurants that spring out of nowhere. Ludicrous signs: Bang Hard Kok Café, Lazy Daze, Nervana Pub and La Crappa beckon customers. Fire and smoke belched out over the crowds of thousands and the noise of the night industry was underway. Vegetables, fish and meat were cooked in woks along the road and each cook made fire explode from their pans, impressing and enticing customers to buy their fare. Smoke, grease, steam and light gave an eerie, choking atmosphere to the air.

Jonathan sat atop Thunder Mountain and surveyed the scene. People gave way to the Mountain some bowed in wai to the great beast. Jonathan was reminded that elephants are sacred here and command respect.

From restaurant televisions flashed the image of The President of the United States giving a speech at Shanghai University. He was in Asia for the Asia-Pacific Economic Cooperation Conference. America has come to the emerging Asian elephant, but tonight nobody takes notice or cares—there is business to be done—goods and services to be sold.

"Ladyboy," Jonathan shouted to his favorite cook, "what's good tonight?"

"Deep fried vegetables, rice, shrimp and special tonight—frog's legs," shouted ladyboy through the smoke from his wok. Fire belched into the air as the ingredients were smothered with oil, spices and sauces.

"Fantastic, gimme' the works," and he dropped his stainless steel canteen down to ladyboy who took out a one hundred baht note for the meal and he/she loaded it with his dinner with a plastic fork and a face cloth sealed in plastic. Ladyboy closed the lid and threw the container and a can of pop up to Jonathan and bowed, "Thanks buddy," he shouted and Thunder Mountain reached over to ladyboy to smell him. Ladyboy kissed his outstretched trunk.

White tourists looked on in awe; the mahout, his elephant and the street market were overwhelming to them. Children ran under Thunder Mountain with delight, some swung on his huge trunk. He was used to little children and Jonathan always notice how calm and still the giant became when children were nearby. Like all elephants, he senses the fragility of things and never places a foot without knowing what is under it.

Throughout Asia this scene is repeated many times each night as another much bigger Asian elephant marches into the future. Stores around Jonathan carried the goods of a modern society, a metro society very different from the west. All the goods are made here in Asia: computers, radios, DVDs, small appliances, televisions and cameras fill store windows and booths of the market. India clothing stores with the names of: Versace, Armani, Next, Boss and Laurent were everywhere, bogus of course, along with watches with designer tags. The usual rip off Rolex is always present and people buy them up for ten dollars a watch. They may last a few years and no one cares except The President of the United States and the European moguls who are trying to get a handle on piracy. They will never stop the elephant; he is just too big and on the move. Jonathan read in the Bangkok English paper that the elephant left a few days ago on a freighter, the largest in the world, on its maiden voyage to the United Kingdom. Her cargo of

Asian goods is destined for the markets of London, Bristol, Liverpool, Dublin, Glasgow and Cardiff. The UK has voiced its dismay of the coming of the elephant for it feels it should be producing the goods. Labor costs are too high in the west where as in the east the labor force is cheap and abundant—in the billions.

The western world hounded Asia to release its chains of communism and isolationism—well the chains are off the elephant and the west is scared. China is now the largest computer and small appliance producer in the world and world banks are now in operation. Cambodia is about to drill off its pirate infested sea for oil. They have been warned of what comes with the wealth of oil but they will not listen. They listen to the elephant that has become bigger than the threat of terrorism that had gripped the world. Global focus is changing.

Jonathan finished his meal above the crowd. He noticed The President of the United States was still talking and it was about the relationships that will be forged between the Americas and Asians. He looked down and into a bookstore: books, magazines and newspapers spilled out onto the street. Some had English across their covers but most were huge fashion and gossip trash magazines displaying the look that all young Asians want to have, round eyes and light skin. He could see where the metro kids and ladyboys come from. Gender and race confusion is now apart of life in Asia.

The President of the United States finished his speech and BBC World did an analysis. Jonathan did not watch, as like the Thais, politics and economics are boring, the comics, fashion magazines and text messages on hundreds of millions cell phones are more interesting. The elephant is relentless and cannot be stopped.

Jonathan and his elephant moved out from under a blue tarp and into the street. It had started to rain, umbrellas came out and blue and green tarps were strung up everywhere. Jonathan pulled a red patio umbrella from under the tourist chair and put the handle end into a metal tube attached the chair. A battery pack tucked under the seat lit up little Christmas lights that he had attached to the umbrella. He switched on the red taillights and headlights attached to the chair. If they are to operate on the streets of Bangkok they must obey the traffic rules. The elephant and his mahout were quite a site coming down the road in their lights and those of the advertising graphics; the blue gray steam and smoke belching from the portable kitchens around them and the pouring rain.

The rain was brief, the umbrellas and tarps came down and the air became humid and hot. Thousands of motorbikes buzzed about like so many insects, their engines are made in China and their bodies are made in Thailand. Some carry a family or friends of up to five, all hanging on to each other laughing and giggling. The traffic police at the end of the market tried to control the motorbikes but it was useless, thousands of them will do as they please; besides the Thais are polite, no one gets hurt and the night market traffic was slowed to a crawl. Thais were on cell phones or plugged into tiny recorders and young girls picked at their faces with sharp instruments, others solicited customers to their massage beds or booths to buy ripped off fashions. Thunder Mountain gently moved his mass, commanding a pathway through the crowd.

For three days a street dog met Jonathan and the elephant at the entrance to the night market and each day it would bark and harass them. There was a look of irritation on the street vendor's faces and some of them chased the pest but could not catch him. The young Thai dog was a brat and a vagabond; there was no collar or marking on the pest, so as far as Jonathan was concerned, the mongrel's life span was limited. Jonathan and the elephant had had enough, there was a growl coming from deep down in the elephant's throat, something like indigestion. He ordered the elephant down and he dismounted. He put his hand out to the barking dog so it could smell and befriend him; then he could introduce him to the elephant. The dog would have nothing to do with him but backed off a distance and kept up the tired at the elephant. "Very well," he said, "you asked for it. Any day now you're gonna' get it."

Later on in the week they picked up an English couple for a ride around the night market. They were young with white tattooed skin and both had bright red and green hair. They wore t-shirts with Manchester United written across the chests; their shorts were camouflaged with many pockets and zippers. Their look screamed backpackers.

They came upon the rouge dog, "Hang on," he told his young couple, "there is going to be a fight here between an elephant and a dog. Guess who is going to win?"

"We are," the young man shouted and his lady laughed.

Jonathan gave the order to Thunder Mountain to pick up and when the wretched dog got close enough, like lightning the elephant made his move grasping the dog under his back legs with his trunk. Thunder picked up the dog and threw him through the air and he landed ten meters away, bouncing off a blue tarp over a booth that sold t-shirts. The young owner screamed as she and her customers rushed out. The dog landed on a table of an outdoor restaurant: dishes, glasses, bottles and food flew in all directions to the horror of the dining customers but to the delight of the vendors. There was great cheering and laughter as the dog ran down the street yelping from fright.

"Good show," Jonathan's passengers shouted.

"I used to like dogs and I had one for many years," but in my travels and seeing how they live in other countries I have come to dislike the creatures. I remembered a few mongrels from my travels in Thailand and the legendary white women who get involved with some of the wretched ones."

"What do you mean, legendary white women?" the female passenger said.

"Well nothing against you or white women but in this country the tourists befriend stray injured dogs and it is mostly white women who care for them. To back me up just ask any of the local SPCA. I'm a bit of a storyteller and I have a true story about some dogs that live on Ko Tao in the Gulf of Thailand. Want to hear it?"

"Well—," and her companion cut her off.

"Buggaration! I'd love to hear it. Carry on my great white mahout," the red headed freckled white passenger said with a jovial laugh.

"Okay, listen up," Jonathan moved sidesaddle on Thunder Mountain's head and began his story. He let Thunder wander—he knew where he was going.

"Rama, from a market place nearby, came jogging down the beach to the seaside resort, head held high and cocky, scanning the territory of the beach dog tribe. He was tough and mean, qualities he required to hold his ground, the males sulked away at the sight of him and hid in the forest.

"He was of a short breed with a large wide head connected to a barrel shaped muscular torso, his legs, short and thick, ending in large padded feet with tough black claws, excellent for digging and scrapping. His colour was black with some beige markings on his head neck and legs. His eyes were huge, dark and menacing. He came to the beach a couple of times a month to get into a fight or steal some females to take back to the market where, at any one time, he had several pregnant. He saw an enemy in everyone and that made him who he was, an alpha male—ruler of his own kind.

"Oh Christ," the woman said with a sigh, "you guys and your male stuff."

"Quiet darling," the man said and held onto his companion's hand.

"On this visit he saw a young dog, thin and frail, sitting and staring at nothing. Rama noticed his impertinence of not disappearing into the forest at the sight of his presence. He charged the little runt, grabbed his pelvis in his jaws and shook him vigorously. The little dog howled and screamed in pain, as he knew he was about to die. Two female dogs came to the pup's rescue and distracted Rama and like all animals were intoxicated by the strength of the male and size of his presence. He forgot the little dog that lay crippled and in agony and began playing with the females eventually persuading one of them to leave with him back to the market.

"The injured dog lay near death. He stayed motionless for several hours and when night came he pulled his injured body up the beach and under the pavilion of the bar, Karma." "Karma, that's reincarnation, isn't it?" the Englishman queried.

"Yeah that's right," Jonathan said, "for three days the dog lay in pain under the pavilion not eating, drinking or moving. He was close to death when a young English woman, who sunbathed nearby, noticed his distorted shape under the pavilion and investigated. She crawled on her hands and knees under the floorboards of the bar to comfort the wretched creature. She went to the local SPCA who said they knew about the dog; if the animal was a threat to the human population they would take care of it or if she requested that the animal be put down, they would do it for a fee. Otherwise nature would take its course. She started a program of feeding the young crippled dog. Each day she crawled under the bar with food and water and in her motherly compassion bought the little animal back to health. Eventually the dog hobbled out of his enclosure and into the sun and arms of its surrogate mother. Unfortunately the new mother ended her vacation and the little dog was alone again, unprotected, crippled and deformed, something the other beach dogs hated. Torapee's short life of terror continued.

"Torapee, what kind of a name is that?" the English woman asked.

"It is a character from a mythological story that the Thais believe took place many years ago. I haven't read it completely but I use the characters names to tell my stories. It feels appropriate in this place.

"Torapee was a skinny sick wretched little beast and the runt of the litter. He was blonde and white but for his black snout. Oversized pointed ears finished off his cute cuddly head and his eyes that were big round and dark had a look of sorrow in them. To the eyes of a human and at a distance he was a good-looking youngster but close up his ribs and backbones protruded from his emaciated body and his pelvis was deformed from Rama's attack. A darting head and ears listened for fleas as they roamed his body and when he heard them he attacked himself with snarling teeth, especially at the base of his tail where the insects gathered moisture from his anus."

"Now that's disgusting!" the English woman said squirming in her seat.

"Be quiet honey, let the mahout tell the story."

"Careful now people! Duck under the wiring coming up." The couple crouched in the chair as the elephant moved under a mass of wires that crossed the road.

And Jonathan went on with the story: "Most of the day the pup would spend sleeping in a sand hole. He vaguely remembered a human once who took care of him but that was in his short passed and now he was skinny and near death again. He stayed cool and quiet so the other dogs of his pack, including his mother Palee and his father Torapa, would not notice him. Torapee was no threat at this state in his life, the pack had established territories to scrounge—he was only a shadow to them.

"A German tourist came to the beach and unfortunately prolonged the inevitability for the dog; she took pity on Torapee. The compassionate woman fed the skinny wretch and within a few days he somewhat improved. He looked healthier with a little more meat on his bones and his coat had a luster to it. He showed more confidence in his gait and demeanor as he jogged and hobbled down the beach with his head and ears held high. For him his brief passed was forgotten. Food and affection was now coming his way, as the female humans could not resist the temptation of mothering the creature. The woman felt confident about the health of Torapee and kept feeding and petting the animal. She was not aware of what was happening in the hierarchy of the dog pack. Each of the dogs watched more intensely Torapee and the affection of the surrogate mother, petting, cuddling and feeding him. Their rage was building.

"Now I must tell you that on beaches in the tropics dogs are wild for most of their lives. They live paw to mouth and are very territorial imperative in their behavior to their own kind and relatives. They live by strict rules of survival designed by the natural environment. The dog was of no threat to the pack when he was sick and dying, and he was of no threat to their food source or the surrogate parent tourists that they had so skillful nurtured.

"Things start to get a little mean and unfair in the story. Do you want me to go on?"

"Yes mahout, go on. Don't worry honey it's only a true story," he giggled and hugged his wife. She took a cigarette from her purse, lit it and puffed ferociously. She gave her husband a menacing look.

"Torapee, acting perky and healthy romped down the beach early one morning in anticipation of visits by his surrogate parent. Two alpha males with Palee decided they had had enough of all the attention the pup was getting. Palee was getting furious that Torapee had not found his own food resources and territory. They surrounded him, each attacking a leg, biting and ripping him. Palee did the most damage; opening a wound in Torapee's right rear leg below his deformed pelvis. He screamed in pain and the German woman intervened in the mayhem but the damage was done. The attackers backed off and Torapee limped away injured, terrified and put in his place. He would be a victim of murder in the pack if his presence continued. You see there can only be a few dogs that can survive on the beach. If there is compassionate human interference of the pack's natural processes, life will be out of balance. These dogs are caught in a juvenile state; some say humans can be that way to."

"How bloody true that is," the Englishman said.

"But we can't leave them out there to suffer," the English woman intervened.

"Honey you would end up with half the dogs in Thailand if you had your way." Another menacing look to the husband.

"The women eventually left the pack and Torapee, whom they were now responsible for, and returned to their homes halfway around the world. They abandoned the dog to its terrifying existence. Before leaving they left messages for those vacationing after them to show some compassion for the little creature."

The Englishman leaned toward Jonathan and said, "Now, what about Rama?"

"When Rama returned to the market with his new female who was not welcome in the pack--a fight broke out. Rama bit them all and put them in their places and went about getting his new female pregnant. The market was a frightening place to the new bitch and after becoming pregnant she returned to the beach to get away from the harassment of Rama.

"This is something you both should remember. In the market there are ugly creatures that Rama and his pack leave alone since they have a dangerous scent about them. These outcasts have lost all their fur through disease; their black skin is covered with sores. Where they live is where the human population comes to buy its food everyday, vendors spread vegetables out on the concrete where these animals lounge and sleep. Customers in the outdoor restaurants pet these mongrels and then eat their food with their fingers."

"This is why I told you not to bite your nails here in the tropics honey. You can get sick from it," the Englishman scolded.

"Quiet," the English woman said.

"I'll digress a bit here. In the market lived a man creature that squatted and begged on a concrete patio; his face, hands and feet were rotting away from leprosy or some other unholy thing. The dogs stayed away from him but there was rage in their eyes and one night, when their fear was at its highest, the dogs turned into a raging pack and tore him to pieces. The dogs identified with him he was just another animal competing for food."

"What did the Thais do?" the English woman sighed.

"They picked up a couple of the dogs and put them down. The dogs just might have been the reincarnation of the local bad boys paying for *clinging* and *grasping*; becoming *I* and *mine* or they could be the diseases that make the dogs the wretches that they are. Maybe they are flukes in the dogs' livers, destined to live forever—asexual—cleaving for eternity."

"What a terrible thought. What happened to the little dog?" the Englishman asked.

"Eventually he died of his wounds. I hate these thoughts but I accept them fore this is beautiful Thailand and all around us life is thriving and dying under a tropical sun and the philosophy of a god. And here we are back were we started an hour ago."

Jonathan ordered Thunder Mountain down and he helped his English couple to the ground.

"One hell of a story, mahout, you should become a writer."

"Maybe some day, right now I'm having too much fun."

"What's the bill?"

"Eight hundred for the ride and two hundred for the story," Jonathan said with a laugh," no, just eight hundred, the story is free."

"Like hell, here's twelve hundred. It's been an experience." The couple said goodbye and disappeared into the crowd.

"Hey mahout," a German shouted from the sidewalk, "how much for a ride?"

"Well now…."

After another tour it was time to get out of the chaos, so Jonathan and Thunder Mountain made their way out of the night market, taking command of the street they had to cross. The heat and humidity had made Jonathan thirsty for a cold beer and he knew Thunder Mountain would be thirsty to, so they went into the bar district a few blocks away. The bars lay dim and mysterious along each side of the narrow streets. Shadows of white men and their Thai women moved about among neon signs, red Christmas lights and the shaded lights of pool tables. Out of the darkness Thai women called and white men fell off their chairs and stools at the sight of an elephant coming down the narrow dark street. Jonathan commanded the elephant to stop and go down. Jonathan dismounted and ducked into one of the clubs and took a seat at a bar with a Thai woman bartender whose smile filled up the place.

"A large beer and a bucket of water for my elephant please."

"What you say you crazy bas—," and she saw the bottom half of Thunder Mountain outside, "yes—yes—ry-away," and she yelled to a waitress to fetch water. Jonathan put the bucket on the street for the elephant and he sucked it up in a few seconds. The Thai girl, giggling and laughing, kept the buckets coming; finally the big elephant's thirst was quenched. Thai girls were everywhere and they did their best to solicit Jonathan but he was a no-taker and they eventually left him alone. A beer before taking Thunder Mountain to Home Camp and bed was all he wanted. The road was very dark at night; there were no street lamps just the light of the establishments that spilled out onto the road. Moonlight shone on the upper parts of the buildings. Tourists were everywhere and motorbikes drove back and forth, their lights flashing across the bar. The air smelt heavy of Thai women and the grease of cooking meat and vegetables. The smell of Thunder Mountain added to the aromatic ambiance.

Next to the bar a cook prepared noodles, sprouts and chicken on a kitchen attached to his motorcycle. He was making dinner for three metro Thai customers seated across the narrow road at a plastic table with plastic chairs. Thunder Mountain stuck his trunk into the cook's grocery bag and stole a head of lettuce and the cook protested. Jonathan bought the rest of his groceries for the elephant, as it was the end of the day for the cook anyway.

One of the cook's customers across the road was a ladyboy from one of the many nightclubs. He sat sidesaddle in his black and gold silk dress on his silver, black and red stripped motorbike. He talked on his cell phone; his long black straight hair flowed down across his shoulders and silicon breasts. On his head he wore a gold crown in the shape of a chedi and his makeup was bold and heavy for the lights of the nightclub where he performs in the Ramakien. He was a beautiful looking piece of art—he was Sita, the wife of King Rama. His two partners, young, well dressed in black pants, and white dress shirts, sat discussing business and going over columns of figures. Light poured out onto the trio from a tiny shop full of pharmaceutical products, electronic parts, CDs, computer games and toys that hung from the ceiling in plastic wrappings. The cook walked over to them and gave them their steaming hot meals in foam trays with plastic forks. They stood, paid their bill and bowed thanks to him.

Jonathan had had enough of the night, he paid his bill and went out of the bar and onto the road, commanded Thunder to kneel, he mounted the elephant and slowly moved down the dark street but before they turned the corner he stopped the elephant and looked back at the trio. They were still there eating and doing their business in the shadows; the only light was from the shop and portable kitchen. Above them was the moon; it shone its light on a huge graphic of a laughing Thai girl and boy having a cigarette high above the little store. He saw the shadow of an elephant; his mahout, with many heads and arms straddled the tusker's neck and high in a chair on the elephant's back were arguing businessmen. Jonathan and Thunder Mountain quickly left into the darkness to the cattle truck and Home Camp.

Mother, the Twins and Camping Monk Style

Mother was just over two meters tall in her sandals; straight black hair fell to her waist. Her skin was clear and clean as though she had been born yesterday. She was dark, very dark as the peasants are that come from Northeastern Myanmar. Her face was round with a mouthful of teeth that gave her a severe overbite; her eyes were like black marbles. The left eye would look at you while she talked, and the right would drift off to somewhere else. She did not have her unusual attributes repaired when she was young; the peasant life in Myanmar did not allow for such things, you lived with what you were born with; besides, only Lord Buddha is perfect. She was always barefoot; consequently, her feet were beautifully formed, the soles as tough as bull's leather. Supported by a high arch of muscle her stubby toes were her raw contact with the earth. Her hands were large and hard and like her feet her palms were tough—a workingwoman's hands. Her legs were well formed; they held up a shapely muscular torso with modest sized breasts now drooping from age and babies. Her personality was that of a tough worker from the farms, a strong sense of family, religion and duty to her twins.

Her young life was hard working twelve hours a day, seven days a week, all year long in the rice paddies. The only times she had off were religious holidays and those were few. When she was fourteen she did have a twenty-four hour reprieve when she gave birth to the twins at work and then she strapped them to her back and finished her shift. The father, a boy of sixteen, ran away and joined the army. He used a false name when signing up and disappeared into the anonymous mass of the military. She briefly searched for him but she never saw him again.

When the twins were eight and strong enough to travel, the three of them left Myanmar one night and crossed the mountains into the valleys of Thailand. There they were picked up by a Thai farmer and put to work. The situation was worse than in Myanmar, the farm manager raped her. She and the twins left down the Mae Nam Khwae Yai in an old leaky dugout canoe. They were on the water for days only daring to come ashore to forage vegetable from the farms and fish drying on racks along the riverbank. The food they stole was not enough to sustain them so they ate rats, mice and insects that they caught in the rice paddies and cane fields. By the time they reached Tag and Tag Two on the river at Home Camp the three were in a desperate condition from hunger, exhaustion, insect bites and fear of their lives. It was Tag who saw them drifting down the river, he swam out to them and guided the boat to shore. Life would be very different for them from then on—the owners of the camp were also refugees.

"Tell me, mother, why are your children called Girl One and Girl

Two?" Jonathan asked her from across the dinner table. The two girls sat in silence as the story unfolded.

"That's what Tag called them when he rescued us and the names stuck. I didn't protest, we were scared, I thought we would become slaves again. When we calmed down I didn't want to call the twins their names from the past. I don't want that time to exist anymore. We have a new life now at Home Camp and *I* and *mine* do not exist for us."

"For twins they are quite different from each other, not physically but in their personality," Tag Two said.

"Oh yes, Girl Two was born in the night and Girl One was born during full moon rise, she did not want to come out with Girl Two, she waited until the glow of the moon. Girl Two is excitable—how do you say it—precocious? She is always getting into trouble because she thinks that the world belongs to her. She does not practice the Dharma." Girl Two giggled from across the table and Girl One smiled.

"What does she do that's troubling?"

"One incident," mother said, and Girl Two was about to say something but mother raised her hand to stop her protest, "and I will only tell you of this one incident. She and Thunder Mountain are very good friends, as you know, and both are mischievous. In your world they are called kindred spirits. He is always excited when she is around since he has fun with her swimming and bathing together. She and the elephant used to sneak off in the middle of the night when everyone else was asleep."

"Oh no—not that, Mother—"

"Be quiet now please," Mother demanded and she went on with the story, "one night the police arrived at Home Camp with a complaint that the elephant was on the loose trampling the vegetable patches near town. We all piled into the truck and went out looking for them and yes there they were just down the road at the pig farm taunting the pigs and waking up the neighborhood. Three of the pregnant female pigs gave premature birth. Some of the babies died, which we had to make right with the farmer. Girl Two was stoned on Thai weed and Thunder Mountain was drunk on whiskey that she had given him. She could have been killed," Girl Two rolled her eyes, "after all the elephant weighs tons and when he goes on a rampage he smashes everything."

"Wow—drunk driving an elephant, "everyone laughed, "What's the fine for that, so what did you do for punishment?"

"Nothing," Girl One interjected, "Buddha served the punishment. Thunder Mountain had a bad hangover the next day and bawled for hours. Girl Two watched Thunder Mountain suffer. That was punishment enough for her."

Girl Two sadly looked at Jonathan, "You see Buddha has his ways. He is the only one that gives out punishment at Home Camp."

"So, Mother, what is Girl One like?"

"Girl One is quiet and mysterious, this is frightening for what she says is always true or will come true. She is very smart and has educated herself by reading everything in sight. Sometimes I have caught her speaking to Buddha."

"Really?" Jonathan said and he looked at Girl One. She smiled and shrugged her shoulders.

"Now Mother," Girl One said, "don't frighten Mr. Jonatin with our ghost stories," and turned to him, "we are a very superstitious people."

"She used to disappear for the day, so one day I followed her down the road leading to the western village from Home Camp. There was a path that goes off into the forest to a clearing where there was a huge wild buffalo grazing. She stood in front of him staring and whispering in another language that I have never heard before or since. The buffalo did nothing but stared at her and then he talked in the language she used. That was it for me, I ran home, I could not watch and hear anymore. The buffalo, Mr. Jonatin, is the one in the coral. She bought him home one day with old Monk. Buffalo is a gentle beast but I am terrified of him. Girl one often talks to him when she is putting out offerings to the deities, he never keeps his eyes off her."

"We all talk to the animals, Mr. Jonatin. Don't we?" Girl One said.

"Yes, I guess we do, I've talk to them in the past but they have never talked back to me."

"I think Mother saw him munching grass," Girl One said.

"So Mother, Monk, where is he from?"

"We don't know and we don't ask him; he is not from any monastery around here. He arrives and visits us three, sometimes four times a week. We give him alms for merit and he takes the buffalo for a walk around the farm or off to the forest. Sometime Girl One goes along; it is all part of family life now, since it has gone on for so many years.

"By the way," Tag Two interjected, "Mother and the twins think you and the Monk should go camping this weekend. Not far just out to the edge at the end of the farm to the Bodhi tree. I think it would be a good idea. You both should get to know each other."

"Yes," Mother said, "I have arranged it. Now I must excuse myself, the monkey men are coming."

"What?"

"The monkey men, they come with their monkeys to take down the mature coconuts from the palm trees around Home Camp. You don't want a coconut to fall on your head do you? They can kill you if they fall from so far up the trees." They all got up from the table, cleared away the lunch dishes and cleaned up the pavilion.

Jonathan watched Mother walk to the entrance to Home Camp; a pickup truck arrived. It had a large cage on the back to hold the coconuts and on top of it sat five monkeys. The men jumped out of the truck and the monkeys, tethered to their handlers immediately ran up the palm trunks and poked at the coconuts. They picked out the ones that were mature and proceeded to twist them off the trees. There was a baby monkey with them but he watched the operation from the ground—learning the job he will spend his life doing. For several hours the monkeys jumped from palm to palm, twisting and pulling at the coconuts, having fun on the job. Jonathan had seen men doing this job in Mexico but never monkeys. My God, he thought everyday I see and learn something new.

Monk and Jonathan strolled along the utility road of Home Camp; they were in no hurry. Buffalo and Thunder Mountain casually followed behind; they never let their two human companions keep any distance from them. They were always on their heels. Soon they came upon the huge Bodhi tree at the far end of the Home Camp where they would spend the night. Mother persuaded both of them that they should take the animals camping. A ridiculous idea to Jonathan and he liked it.

The Bodhi tree is old and ancient, made up of many trunks fused together as one. Around its mother trunk were wrapped yellow, green and red fabric, and leaning against it were bamboo and wooden poles. Some were wrapped in yellow ribbon, gold and silver foil. These supporting sticks were spiritual gifts given by the village to aid the sacred tree to hold up its massive branches. From vines hanging down from its canopy, Monk and Jonathan hung mosquito nets. They unloaded their gear off buffaloes back and stored their sleeping bags and mattresses inside. They hobbled Thunder Mountain and buffalo and went into the forest to collect firewood.

The surrounding forest and farm disappeared into the night; apart from his shinning eyes, buffalo disappeared to. Thunder Mountain shone gray, his forehead glowed pinky red and his amber eyes sparkled in the firelight. Mother had stuffed Jonathan's backpack with food and refreshments and warned Jonathan not to eat in front of Monk since he is forbidden to eat in the afternoon and evening. She packed a bowl of rice and vegetables that Monk could have in the morning.

The fire flooded red and orange on the huge tree, buffalo, elephant, little Monk and little Jonathan—a magical sight. Buffalo watched Monk and snorted his satisfaction that he was with his friend. Thunder Mountain watched Jonathan, curled his trunk and danced on his front feet, he stopped often to rest and cross his back legs. A natural thing to do for an elephant but Jonathan swears he learned it from humans. Jonathan looked around him and never in his wildest dreams did he ever think he would be in such a strange situation—in Thailand, with the beasts and the Monk.

"You know, Monk; I'm really sorry Tag died but if he hadn't I wouldn't be here experiencing this." The Monk sat upright on his mat and looked intensely at Jonathan.

"It is not your fault Jonathan that Tag died by your hand, there were other forces at work, forces shaped by Tag's life and his desires. They led him to the place of his ending, you just happened to be there."

"I know but I still feel badly about it. Taking someone's life is a sin in my world."

"It is an act which we are to avoid in my world to; it is one of the precepts of Lord Buddha. You are a victim as much as Tag was. Let's say things evened out because of circumstances. Perhaps both of you were on the same path; the path of Dukkha."

Monk's voice became a monotone like a chant, "You see, it all comes down to a brief sentence; the very heart of Buddha's teachings, *Nothing whatsoever should be clung to;* therefore, everything that is *I* and *mine* is Dukkha. As time goes on in Home Camp you will come to understand this, as the family is a good teacher of Buddha. You will notice that they are equal with each other and spend their days taking care of the family and the animals. They know it is not about them individually and that they will not last forever and will eventually die just as Tag died. Lord Buddha compassionately has warned us all, *Brethren, it is natural for all conditioned things to decay and cease. Be delighted in working for your own deliverance.*" The firelight danced across Monk's Gandhi-like face, his all knowing expression and toothless smile. Jonathan looked at the two beasts looming up behind him glowing in amber light like a Caravaggio painting and the world became very spiritual and isolated like they were the only ones left on the planet.

"Tell me, in your version, why is it Tag, Tag Two, Mother, Girl One and Girl Two don't have names like everyone else?"

"Like you Jonathan, they are from far away, from another life they have chosen to forget. In Buddhism there is no past, birth or death, so whatever was is no longer and does not need a name. They are in the moment, today and impermanent. They act as one."

"Ah yes, Mother told me a bit about that and it is familiar to me; I used to call it, *Being There*, many years ago when I managed people. I would always tell my staff to forget the past, even what they did when they got up that morning. *Now* was the time to focus, *now* at that moment in the task at hand, that way the mind is clear and unobstructed. With some discipline on their part some did achieve a state of mind where they excelled in their work."

"That's right they did not bring Dukkha to the work place, worries about themselves and what they own. Emptiness is in the Buddha teachings and emptiness is the state of being as you described. It does not mean the act of existing or a bowl with nothing in it but an attitude and action of the mind. Emptiness is the absence of self. Emptiness is Dhamma. This is a great simplification of the teachings but you get the idea."

"Where are you from Monk?"

"I am from the Hmong people who live in the hills of Northern Thailand and Laos. I left there long ago, so long ago I can not remember when."

"You must be very old. Pardon my intrusion but how old are you?"

"I don't know how old I am or what my name was since I entered the monastery as a novice when I was very young. I was told my family was killed in the opium wars."

"You mean at the time when Thunder Mountain lived up there?"

"No long before the elephant was born; it was in the days when the French were in Laos. I don't remember my family, just that there were many children. But then it does not matter, does it?"

"Then you must be close to one hundred years old."

"Yes and sometimes I feel it," Monk said and they both laughed, "especially in the morning when I get up."

"Why do you live in the forest?"

"When I was a novice I wasn't a very good one. I broke the precepts about not eating between noon and morning of the next day; I snuck food into my cell at night. I loved playing football, which was not allowed. After school I was caught many times on the football pitch with the village children. One thing about me that the abbot noticed was my way with animals; they were always around me and gathered at my cell door. Chickens, dogs, cats, rabbits, birds; they were there. When I grew up and was about twenty I had to make a choice whether I was to go back to my village or become a monk. I chose to be a monk. My abbot took me aside and told me I was as mischievous as the animals and that I should work with them so he told me to go to the forest and do it. So I did."

"That's it—you just did?"

"Yes and the abbot was right, my life in the forest has been a wonderful experience for the last eighty-or-so years."

"And what is your life now Jonathan?"

"So different from what it was, this land and its people they are so remote from my way of life. But I will do my part for Home Camp. I feel it is the right thing to do and I have nothing else to do now anyway."

"I think you will do fine here and life will change for you since there are forces at work around you and the teachings of Lord Buddha are here when you are ready for them."

Buffalo moved his right front hoof, clawing at the ground—a warning something was wrong; Thunder Mountain swayed from side to side and hummed, uncomfortable with the night. Jonathan looked at Monk who was unconcerned.

"Something is spooking them, don't you think?" and a deep-throated growl came from the black forest, a growl from all directions. It was something big and frightening.

"Excuse me Jonathan I will be back in a few minutes," and Monk rose from his mat and walked into the dark, "whatever happens stay here by the fire."

Don't worry I will." The animals became more agitated and there was another growl.

"That's it!" Jonathan said, "*Up* Thunder and Jonathan climbed up on Thunder Mountain's knee and onto his back, "there," and he gave a big sigh, "we will wait it out from here."

It was three quarters of an hour before Monk came out of the dark of the forest. He laugh at the sight of his friends huddled together around the fire under the huge Bodhi tree.

"Everything is all right; you can come down now Jonathan."

He dismounted, patted the two beasts that were now calm, came back to the fire and sat down with Monk.

"What the hell was that Monk, it scared the Jesus out of me?"

"Hum," Monk said smiling, "more room for Buddha."

"No really, whatever it was sounded really big and ferocious."

"Not so big, not so ferocious," Monk said casually, "it was a tiger friend."

"A tiger friend, what do you mean?"

"A tiger that I have known for many years. I think he likes me because of my robe; it is the same colour as him. He comes down from the mountains to see me now and again. I think he worries about me since I am so old."

"Is he gone now?" Jonathan said glancing around him.

"Yes he is gone back to the mountains. See how calm buffalo and Thunder Mountain are? I'm sorry he scared you."

"I don't know if I want to know anything more about you Monk, you're too scary. Its time for bed," Jonathan got up and grabbed every scrap of wood they had collected and put it on the fire. Sparks flew into the night and the forest.

I Have Been Here Before

Friday night came and the Bangkok working week was over. Tag Two had loaded the truck ready to leave for Home Camp, if they left now they would be at home by midnight for a few days off. They always traveled to Home Camp at night when the air was cooler. Thunder Mountain, Naga, rooster and the chickens minus one had done well over the last five days making many thousands of baht for the family bank account.

Tag Two was worried about Thunder Mountain and Jonathan as they were unusually late but before he could get on his cell phone to them they came lumbering down the alley. Jonathan dismounted and directed Thunder Mountain into the truck. Tag Two locked the truck's gates, "I've packed everything—let's go home." Thunder Mountain happily snacked on the cane shoots stacked up around him. Naga was asleep as always; the rooster and his clutch clucked away happily.

With a big moon shining in the west they entered the compound of Home Camp and everyone helped with unloading the truck and taking care of the animals and when they were done they went to bed for a well deserved sleep. Jonathan's transition into his new life was a success and he could not believe it. How on earth could a man like him fall into such a place in life? Was it luck or good marketing? He thought, put yourself in the right place and good things can happen.

The next morning everyone was up early and it was the day after the workweek that is always a day of rest for all.

At breakfast Jonathan asked Tag Two, "Would you mind if I drove over to Kanchanaburi to visit the War Cemetery?"

"Of course not," Mother intervened, "perhaps Tag Two could go with you."

"I think maybe Jonatin would like to go alone," Tag Two said, "I will drive him and leave him there for a while. I want to pick up a few things in town anyway. Does anyone want to come for the ride?" Tag Two said looking around the table.

"I would like to come," Girl Two said bubbling over with enthusiasm, I need some new shorts and make up, and some hand lotion and maybe some of that new toe nail polish, and—"

"Yes, okay," Tag Two said.

Girl One looked down disappointed that her sister would jump in before she had the chance to be polite about asking to go.

"How about you Girl One, why not come along and save the sales girls from your sister," Jonathan said and everyone laughed.

They finished their breakfast and cleaned up the dishes. Mother saw them off in the pickup. Thunder Mountain had a look of concern that they were leaving without him and it showed in his dance and eyes. Mother, always in the know, diverted him with a stick of sugar cane. Thunder

Mountain is very easily bought off.

They drove to Kanchanaburi and Tag Two pulled the camper over to the side of the highway, "I'll do some shopping; I want to look at some new cell phones for us. I'll pick you up in and hour, okay, Jonatin?"

"Yeah that will be fine. An hour will be enough time to pay my respects," he said and he jumped out of the camper.

"See you later," Girl Two shouted from the window and from behind her Jonathan could see Girl One gently wave and smile.

He walked into the pavilion gateway of the War Cemetery of Kanchanaburi. The pavilion was a simple marble structure; dignified in its classic design, brass plaques told the story of those buried there. After the war a different army went out into the forest; a compassionate army, they exhumed the remains of all those who died building the Siam/Burma railway and bought them to the War Cemetery to be interned.

It was morning and the air was cool, the sky a brilliant blue and there were only a few dozen people about. The place was carpeted with a perfect lawn; grave markers were lined up neatly like good soldiers on parade and small bushes of flowers grew between them. The soldier's names, rank and an inscription of poetry or script from the Bible were etched into brass plaques. Spread out over a dozen acres of land was buried thousands of soldiers. No soldier stood out from any other; all where the same; all equal in death. On some of the markers medals and poppies had been left, perhaps by a relative or some thankful person. Several Thai gardeners in large straw hats tended the plots. They were hunched over in their endless work; one man was watering the flowers and the impeccable green lawn.

Jonathan wandered aimlessly for the scene was over whelming; friends of his family were here. All these soldiers never did go home; this place is their home, forever among their comrades, among their brothers in arms. Two visitors moved passed him quietly, parents he supposed of the three young boys with them. They did not say much just read the names off on those placards, markers above quiet old bones. He spent some time reading the names and wondered about the dates. He made his way to the far end of the cemetery, to the last row near the corner. Below a fig tree that reached over a bordering hedge into the cemetery from the adjoining street and in the only shade in the cemetery—he looked for what might be familiar.

Glyn Evans

Private

Kings Own Rifles

In the arms of God

He wondered about this young soldier. Something was familiar about the inscription, although he had never known anyone with these names. Perhaps when his father and mother were alive they had mentioned this name. He wondered—he could not keep his eyes off the placard—he could not move—he became rooted to the ground.

The cemetery faded from view and Jonathan found himself among naked men on a dirt mound that stretched for miles in either direction through a hot steaming forest. The men moved hunched over: walking skeletons, bandaged hands and feet, tell-tail lumps of ringworm and other parasites living in their legs. Sores blistered across their yellow, wax-skinned bodies. Their hair was mostly gone from their heads, fallen out from malnutrition or cut away with dull knives to rid them of lice. Their eyes, dark and cavernous, were sunken into their skulls. Some wore a string with a piece of leather in the front and back, enough to gain some dignity. Jonathan knew that these thousands were the prisoners, now the slaves who built the railway of death. But they did not look like the characters in the movie that he remembered from so long ago—of course not, he thought. In the nineteen fifties Hollywood would not have depicted the real thing, but more of a romantic story of the time and place. This was not romantic thought Jonathan, no—not at all.

Down the track he could see the front of a huge black steam engine, a red sun painted on its boilerplate. It belched steam up and around the horde of men working with it to build its tracks to take the war machine into the heart of Burma. Its noise and steaming breath commanded life and death of all this humanity. In the end it would take them all and spend eternity rotting in a shed; its rust picked at by tourists.

The wretched laborers toiled at their work, slowly plodding away, carrying baskets of crushed rock in an endless line from a quarry dug into a hillside. Others unloaded timber and steel from the train while still others dug with shovels and picks. Some men carried water buckets and the worker skeletons gulped the tepid water from bamboo ladles. There were no guards or soldiers around; the men governed their work themselves. They could not escape, there was nowhere to go; the surrounding forest with its animals, insects and diseases would kill them in a few days.

Jonathan walked down the mound passed the slaves and came upon a clearing in the forest. Lean-tos made from bamboo and palm fronds, and bamboo cots were set up for shelter and sleeping. Latrines and showers on bamboo platforms were off to one side. Lines of men stood urinating and some were taking showers with the help of other men pouring buckets of water into a suspended bucket with holes in the bottom.

On a hill covered in palm and banana trees, Jonathan saw two naked men digging a trench among crosses. On the crosses were shingles of bamboo with the names of those interned. They would have their own bamboo shingles soon, markers for after the war when the army would come back for them. The two exhausted men sweated under the hot sun but they needed to do their job with haste; there was someone waiting nearby to die.

Near the graveyard was a lean-to with several bamboo cots and on one laid a naked man and as Jonathan approached he could not tell if the emaciated man was dead or alive. There was no muscle structure on him at all just yellow waxy skin over protruding bone. Ants had discovered his condition and were beginning to collect and crawl on him. Jonathan could see his skull through his skin and his nose was hooked and black in death like an old Egyptian mummy. Open sores covered his body and the ends of his limbs, his hands and feet were black with the onset of gangrene. His white belly below his ribs pulsed from his heartbeat. He was near the end of his life. Jonathan stood above him; the soldier turned his head and with eyes yellow and sunken he looked at him. His mouth, a dark blue cavern with white mucus around the lips, gapped open and a rattling of breath came forth. The hole tried to say something but it could not. Jonathan was the last man the young soldier saw.

It had seemed like an hour that he was among those ghastly slaves and their engine but it was not, within a few seconds his eyes once again focused on the placard.

Glyn Evans

Kings Own Rifles

In the arms of God

Disturbed, Jonathan took a shivering breath, moved away from that now familiar name, and walked back to the pavilion. On his way over the billiard table green lawn he paused and in respect bowed to those attending the interned. "My parents and I thank you," he said. To his relief he saw Tag Two parked out on the main road and he quickly got in the passenger's seat. He wanted to get away from the place; he wanted to be at Home Camp and the life there. He looked into the back seat and into the black eyes of Girl One, "I need a drink of your ice tea."

"You look pale, Jonatin. Is everything all right?" Tag Two said, concerned as he pulled the pickup onto the highway.

"Yes, everything is fine. I have discovered something about myself."

"And what is that?" Girl One asked.

"I have been here before."

His Thailand, His Bangkok, His love

"Did you pick up the twins order Jonatin?" Tag Two asked over his new cell phone.

"Yes; besides, the usual papers and mags, I managed to pick up a *New York Times*, weekend edition and a *Financial Post* for Girl One. They were the last on the rack at the market."

"And for Girl Two, what did you get her?"

"The usual: lipstick, five shades of her favorite colour, whitening, eyebrow pencils, two shampoos and conditioner, body lotion, pumas stone, sponges, cotton batten, two—"

"Yeah, that's fine Jonatin."

"—magazines of beautiful babes, boys, makeup, music; that entire Asian surface stuff. There seems to be more of these trash mags coming out every week. I picked up those ladyboy CDs for her. She's going to put us in the poor house. Did mother want anything?"

"Yeah, she wants some yellow ribbon, width nine if you can find some. She needs a dozen meters."

"What's she going to use the ribbon for?"

"She ties jasmine and flowers together for offerings."

"Okay, I'll pic—there was silence from Jonathan's cell phone. Tag Two looked to the sky above Bangkok and flashes came from different parts of the city.

"Jonatin, are you there. The sky just lit up and I heard explosions from across the river. People are panicking around here. Wait—," there was a pause, "Jonatin, are you all right? We just heard that a bomb exploded on Khaosan Road."

"Yeah—Thunder and I are fine but there is chaos here. I'm about half a block from the explosion and heading there. Thunder is handling just fine it doesn't seem to bother him. People are running everywhere—I'm at the blast scene—and it's a mess! There is smoking and broken debris strewn across the street and sidewalks—there is no fire but I can smell exploded material and burnt flesh. At the side of the road there is a clearing that is black with some uprooted pieces of sidewalk scattered about. We're heading over there—ah shit! I think I see what were an arm and a leg—they're covered in black soot and blood—It's the blast center—I'll talk to you in a few minutes," and Jonathan hung up the line.

Shouting came from across the road, "Quick, help me pull this fucking thing off these people!" a police officer screamed, his face blackened from soot and blood.

"It won't move, they are welded together!" another officer shouted.

Jonathan saw a shattered ice cream wagon; its small refrigerator blown apart, the motorbike attached to it was crushed into another motorbike. It was a police vehicle and both where heaped up on each other and on their sides. Under the carts were two bodies, a police officer and a vendor who ran a portable kitchen. He could only see legs and they moved. Whoever was under the mess was still alive. A large Thai man, a merchant from the street, ran up to the cart and tried to lift it with the officer and another man but the tangled mass was too heavy.

"Move out of the way!" Jonathan shouted and with sharp jabs of his feet he commanded Thunder over to the cart. As if he knew what to do the elephant wrapped his trunk around the handlebars of one of the bikes and lifted it into the air like it was a toy. It landed a few feet away and burst into flames from a leaking fuel line.

"*Back!*" Jonathan shouted and Thunder Mountain backed away from the wreckage and fire. The Thai man and the officer rushed over and dragged the injured away from the flaming mess. They were badly hurt with blast burns and broken arms and legs—the officer's right hand was gone. They were alive and conscious and moaned in pain and shock. A police officer ran up to the wreckage and doused the flames with a fire extinguisher.

A backpacker with a broken beer bottle in his hand stared in shock at the scene--his face was covered with blood. Two people took him by the arms and sat him down on the sidewalk.

"Oh no!" a woman screamed. She appeared to be the backpacker's girlfriend or wife. She knelt on the sidewalk beside him and put here arms around his neck and sobbed.

Jonathan backed Thunder off as police cars and running officers came down the road with their emergency vehicle's lights flashing and sirens blaring. The side of one of the buildings of the blast site caught on fire and merchants from the stores came out with buckets of water, one with a hose, and managed to put out the blaze. People were scattered about on the road screaming in pain, others not injured were crying. One man screamed obscenities to the black sky that he had had enough. His Thailand—his Bangkok—his love had been assaulted.

Jonathan speed dialed Tag Two, "I'm all right, the police and ambulances have arrived an—" a thunderous blast was heard.

"What's that—are you all right?" Tag Two yelled. At the end of the block came a bright flash, flames and smoke. Debris and bodies flew through the air and smashed into booths and windows. With a deafening roar the side of a building collapsed into the road burying taxis, carts and people.

"Christ, another bomb has gone off! I felt the shock wave and heat of that one. It was much bigger than the last!" Jonathan screamed into the phone.

A huge electrical transformer came crashing to the ground bring hundreds of electrical cables with it. Live wires arced a brilliant blinding blue up and down the road as signs flashed on and off turning Khaosan Road into a flickering blue smoking hell. People panicked and ran, some fell and were trampled by others—a stream of bodies ran around Thunder Mountain. The big elephant did not move but held his ground. Jonathan felt him rise tall; he raised his trunk and trumpeted a terrifying blast. His huge silhouette and raised trunk against the blue flashing lights and sparks was the cry of agony for Thailand and his diminishing race.

"Here are some pictures," Jonathan said and he aimed his cell phone to the street—shot half a dozen and sent them to Tag Two.

"Jonathan, this is awful, get out of there!" Tag Two yelled into the phone, "there may be more bombs to go off."

"There is no place to go while these people are panicking. Thunder is fine so we will wait a few minutes while things settle down. He just let out one hell of a trumpeting blast."

A group of people ran into a portable kitchen spilling hot cooking oil on them—they caught fire from the gas flames of the kitchen. They were ablaze and screamed in pain as they ran. People grabbed clothing off the merchant's racks and wrapped the victims, smothering the flames but they were badly scorched. The scene turned to slow motion—the street became a flickering strobe light from the electrical arcing. Soon the street was empty of those alive and those who were hurt but able to make it out. The injured and dead were everywhere from the bombs force, burning debris and the trampling.

Thunder Mountain stood in the middle of it like a tank on a battlefield. A handful of police, ambulance attendance, and Jonathan riding the elephant, were the only ones left standing on the road—shadows in a haze of blue gray smoke. The smoke, fire, police and elephant where the image of today's terrorist battle zone, the big elephant still playing its part as it did in ancient times.

"My God!" Jonathan said into his phone, "You read about it, see it on TV, but never believe that you would ever be in it."

The commander of the police force for Banglampho ran up to Thunder Mountain and Jonathan. "Did you see anything unusual before the blasts, Jonathan?" he shouted.

"No, there was nothing unusual commander. Hell, I doubt I would recognize anything unusual on Khaosan Road."

"Best you two move out, Jonathan," the commander ordered, "move over to the Field of Kings or best move tonight to Home Camp. There are more bombs going off around the city and there may be more bombs around here ready to go off. I can't believe this is happening."

"All right!" Jonathan shouted down from the elephant, "let's go Thunder. Good luck commander." He gave the foot commands to turn and the elephant responded and walked out of the smoke and fire weaving its way past the dead and injured scattered down the road. The huge crowd at the end of the street parted to let them through.

Tag Two called him. "Jonatin, we are going home tonight and now. Mother called and she and the twins are worried about us so let's go home. Make your way over the bridge and I will see you on the other side. There is no way I can get over there to pick you up. It will take most of the night to get out of Bangkok."

As Tag Two predicted, it took most of the night to get to Home Camp. The police and military had set up roadblocks to question everyone. Thunder Mountain munched on palm fronds the entire journey, acting like nothing had happened. Jonathan recounted the story over and over again to Tag Two's insistence and as the sky became light they entered the compound—the twins, Mother, buffalo and Monk were waiting. Except for buffalo, they all bowed to each other, and everyone hugged in relief—tears were in everyone's eyes. Everybody felt like hugging Monk and so did the monk but everyone just bowed in respect. The animals were first to be taken care of and Jonathan told Girl Two how brave Thunder was and she hugged her best friend and all helped take the chair and blankets of his huge back. Girl Two led him to the river for a bath and the care that only she could give. Naga was let out of his cage onto the pavilion floor and given a massage with a warm wet towel by mother's capable hands. Tag Two unloaded the truck and let the chickens loose and rooster went about in a fuss counting his clutch. Girl One fed the chickens and started breakfast for everyone. The community of Home Camp was grateful that day to be alive in their troubled Thailand. For the next few nights Girl Two slept in a hammock under a mosquito net beside Thunder Mountain's shelter.

The day off was quiet and peaceful; the family went off to do whatever they do to amuse themselves in town, the outbuildings, and on the farm. Buffalo was in his coral, his huge head resting on a post, his eyes closed in sleep. Monk had left with his alms bowl of rice and vegetables. Thunder Mountain, chained to his concrete pad, danced and ate palm fronds. He was content, washed and massaged—always with an eye on Jonathan. The chickens fussed around his feet. Jonathan and Girl One sat in lotus on the mat overlooking the river. Naga, sensing Girl One's warm body nearby, moved his tired bulk over to her and laid his head on her lap and quickly went to sleep.

"Oh wise one, what do you make of all this mess going on?" Jonathan asked Girl One who giggled at the comment.

"Well it may be the separatist insurgence from the south," Girl One said and she became very thoughtful and serious, "but maybe not. The insurgent's, from the southern provinces modes operandi is quite different; they don't use the same explosives and detonation mechanisms. But there may be evidence that we don't know about yet." Jonathan had not seen this side of her before and was surprised at her knowledge of the bombings as they had only taken place in the last eighteen hours. "The military bureaucrats don't give us much information. As for Al Qheda, they would not be so clumsy with their targets, only a small number died. Their terror takes in more victims and targets Americans when bombing in foreign countries. The deaths in Bangkok were Thai although there were many backpackers injured.

Acting Prime Minister General Surayud Chulanont is blaming politicians who are loosing power and dismissing it as the work of a counter coup d'etat. I think it could be the Thaksin Shinawatra sympathizers, an opposing faction against the military rule, but they are not acting under orders by Mr. Shinawatra. Corrupt as he might be he is the democratic leader of Thailand and should be back here to defend himself against charges being bought. People want a democratic government now; Mr. Shinawatra back in or some new person elected. Perhaps there is a fear that if the military becomes too entrenched there may never be a democratic government again in Thailand."

"What about the military in power since the coup, won't their ranks become corrupt? Corruption is endemic to this nation," Jonathan said.

"That is a big problem, if they become corrupt now they can never give up power because the incoming government would prosecute them. Kinda' Catch 22 don't you think?"

"Yeah, maybe your right, I guess we will know who did the bombings in the next few days."

"We may never know who did it. This is all very damaging and puts the writing of our new constitution in jeopardy."

"How do you know so much? Is it the magic about you that Mother tells about?"

"No magic, I read and the TV is on all day and when I see or hear something important going on, I pay attention. I watched the TV all night worried about our family in Bangkok and on their way home."

"I will get you an ice tea, yes?"

"Yes please, thanks."

Monk and the Mekong

"I have an important announcement to make," Jonathan said quietly and the family stopped eating their dessert. The family looked at him attentively, "Monk has asked me to take him home to his village in Northern Laos on the Mekong River. He says he is near his end and he would like it to be where he believes he was born."

Girl One got up from the table and left the pavilion for her room, the rest of the family fell silent. They knew that this was coming but they were still shocked by its suddenness and the announcement coming from Jonathan.

"Why you Jonatin?" Mother asked, breaking the terrible silence.

"I don't know. I asked him why not Tag Two or you or the twins. He just said I want you to take me home. That was all."

"I think Monk made a good choice, Jonatin is strong and knowledgeable and if anyone can get him home, he can. I approve," Tag Two said, "does everyone else?" All at the table agreed and he turned to Jonathan, "I think you should talk to Girl One. Monk and she are friends."

"Right, I'll do that now," and he left the table and went to her bungalow where she sat in a corner staring at the floor. She was not crying but looked sad. He sat in a wicker chair beside her.

"Why does he have to go?" she said softly, knowing full well the answer but needed to be told.

"Because he is old and tired of his long life. He believes he has done enough here and should move on. Do you approve that I take him home?"

"Of course, Tag Two was never close to him and we are women and not allowed in his life. You are the one closest to him, except maybe buffalo," she said lightening up the moment.

"And that damn tiger out there," Jonathan said and they both laughed.

"You know about him?"

"I sure do, he scared the crap out of me. I never saw him but I heard him."

"I saw him once and he was twice the size of Monk but was a lamb in his arms. He has such a way with animals and people. I will miss him so much."

"Are you all right then?"

"Yes, I need a little time alone. Thank you for coming to see me Jonatin. Tell everyone I'm okay," she said softly and he went back to the family.

One bright Saturday afternoon Jonathan, Monk and Tag Two left in the pickup truck down the dirt road between the sugar cane fields. On the concrete pad stood Thunder Mountain wondering why he was not invited.

Buffalo stretched his neck towards the truck and moaned. Mother, Girl One and Girl Two were on their knees heads bowed, hands clasped in prayer. Monk left Home Camp for the last time.

Monk had never flown in a plane before and as far as he was concerned it was impossible for anything that big to fly so high; therefore he would not believe they existed. Trains were fine as they were on a track and would go where they were pointed.

Tag Two drove them to the Bangkok Train Station to catch the six p.m. night train to Chaing Mai where they would arrive at six the following morning. Tag Two was sad seeing the old man leave, Monk meant a great deal to the family even though he and Monk were not close. He never had time enough for him; it was all he could do to keep Home Camp together. They took their seats in car fourteen and talked to Tag Two through the open window but the conversation and goodbyes were short. The train soon pulled away from the platform leaving Tag Two alone, his hands in prayer watching a treasured piece of the family leave forever. There is no permanence, he whispered and his eyes filled with tears.

Monk had the lower berth and Jonathan had the upper; they slept well that night as the train rumbled north to the end of the line. In the morning the conductor came by with coffee and a light breakfast of rice and vegetables. Mother had put together a package of cake, cookies and pie for them so they ate that to. All would have to be eaten before noon. From the Chaing Mai Train Station they took a tuk-tuk to the Northern Bus Station and caught, within the hour, the bus to Chaing Khong on the Mekong River and the border of Laos.

"Wow!" Jonathan said as he looked out the window of the bus, "the landscape has exploded in green."

"Yes, the monsoon season is beginning, "Monk said, "soon it will rain everyday for months. It renews the land and feeds the animals and people. This is where I spent the seasons of my youth."

"You were around here?"

"Of course, my people are Hmong; we are everywhere in this part of Thailand. We would travel here to work the rice fields and vegetable farms, pick bananas and harvest the opium in the hills that you can see in the distance."

"You harvested opium?"

"Yes everyone did. There were no laws and boundaries in this land in those days. The land was tribal, full of nomadic people. There was no electricity, roads, cars, airplanes or funny motorbikes. Dirt roads, with water buffalo pulling huge wooden carts, were the ways we traveled. The Mekong River was our home and highway most of the year. The river was our life; we did not know where it started or where it ended. Until I joined the monastery I thought it went on to the edge of the universe."

"Life must have been very hard for your family?"

"A hard life is relative. By the standards of the time life was good. We ate well and maintained our health. The weak died young and the short time they were with us was celebrated for they were going on to their next life. Nothing is permanent. The part of life that had an impact on me was seeing the cruelty of the warlords, the men who owned the poppy plantations. The French, English, Dutch, Chinese, to name a few, who came for the opium and the money they could make. They were a mean lot, those people. They murdered and made slaves of people—my people, the Hmong."

"Is that why you became a monk?"

"Yes, it is all about clinging and grasping. That is what causes badness, Dukkha—greed and selfishness. Those people who used others for their own gain were the worst of the lot. There was no protection from these people, they did what they wanted."

"Time repeats itself Monk, now its energy—oil."

"Yes, we have learned nothing. Look over there to the mountains in the northeast," and Monk pointed out the window, "that is where Thunder Mountain was born and raised. Those mountains are the border between Myanmar and Thailand, the route that the opium traders use to this day. That is were all his ancestors came from, there and along the Mekong."

After many hours of dropping off and picking up passengers the bus finally reached the river town of Chaing Khong and at the market station a rusting tuk-tuk made from many brands of motorbikes took them to a guest house overlooking the Mekong and the town of Huay Xai across the river in Laos.

The guesthouse was a three story teak building that had aged to a rich deep red-brown hue. Its inside was a sprawling lobby, kitchen, dining, lounging area and balconies. At the entrance to the house were chained monkeys who were high strung nervous little creatures.

"Poor little guys," Jonathan said, "they should be in the forest playing and fighting or working somehow for the family here. Not chained up, bored with nothing to do. Oh well, this is not my country."

"It is your country and it isn't. It belongs to everyone and no one. These little creatures know no boundaries, political or economical and neither should you. Do you understand?" Monk said.

"No I don't."

"You will, you will."

They entered the guesthouse. Shutters opened out to view the river and let the light and mosquitoes in. The floors were made of two inch by two foot red teak planking. Across its polished wood walls were broken framed photos, old and yellowed, of the owner and her family. Their youthful faces were slowly decaying and it bought home the word that Jonathan has heard so much in Thailand—impermanent. The old woman proprietor had aged but had a youthful smile and exuberance about her; she fluttered about the place like a butterfly. She wanted to cook for them but they declined and she was embarrassed when she realized why.

They registered and Jonathan rented one of the motorbikes in the courtyard. He wanted to take a drive in the morning to visit someone he had read about. They both went to their rooms and checked their papers: passports, photocopies, visa applications, extra visa photos and cash fees; everything was in order for the next day. Monk and Jonathan settled in for the night. Jonathan read and thought about Mother's cooking. Monk went to bed early; he was tired and not just from travel.

Jonathan was up and in the Mekong River for a swim and shave at six thirty a.m. The sun was not up yet over the mountains across the river in Laos but it was light and the sky a deep blue. He did not wake Monk; he let him sleep in. Quickly Jonathan dressed and was on his rented motorbike by seven; there was someone important he had to see. He drove down the main road that took him out of the village and into the country to a hill with temples whose gold architecture towered over the forest. He passed under an ornate Gate of Harmony, drove onto the grounds and parked his motorbike under a Bodhi tree that was festooned with coloured ribbons. A monk, in his small temple, was sitting in lotus next to his Buddha statues, bowls, joss sticks, rings of jasmine and the other paraphernalia of his religion. Jonathan greeted him with *wai,* bought a few joss sticks and hurried past him to the stairs leading up to his destination.

Each side of the stairs had a temple; one was for a reclining Buddha the other for a large fat jovial Buddha. In both temples there were many smaller statues along with offerings of flowers and food. Walls and pillars were stucco and decorated with monsters and pretty people painted in gold and primary colours. Coming down the stairs was the monster snake Naga, huge gaudy and powerful, his many heads spitting plaster tongues and mosaic fire. Jonathan took his sandals off and climbed the seventy purple-tiled stairs and when he reached the top he looked up and there was the man he had come to see—Big Buddha, the man who was formally known as Prince Siddhartha Gautama.

He was covered in gold leaf and the morning sun from the east had come over the mountains of Laos hitting him full force, all thirty-eight feet of him —and that is when he is sitting down. His hands were in the Bhumisparsa mudra (attitudes), the right hand and fingers pointing to the earth and the left hand resting in his lap. A grid-like sphere of a sun radiated behind him festooned with red jewels and strange umbrella decorations. Below him were standing Buddha in mudra vitarkaha, dhyana and abhaya.

On a semi-circle platform of red tiles was a joss bowl with offerings of water, fruit, soft drinks and other objects. Surrounding Big Buddha was a quadrangle building open on all sides with large brass bells hung every few feet. Everything was lit up in the morning sunlight as Big Buddha watched the rising fireball in the east.

Jonathan walked to the altar and from a candle in a glass holder he lit the sticks and said a little prayer for Monk and spent a few minutes in thought.

In the past few weeks before coming here with Monk Jonathan read two books the first was the principals of Buddhism written by a philosopher and monk from Southern Thailand. What Jonathan read and tried to understand was the essential points of Buddhist teachings. Dhamma is the ultimate truth; the truth of nature; the duty of all that lives, the teachings of the Buddha. All other is Dukkha; the suffering or imperfection of everything clung to as *I* and *mine*. The heart of Buddhist teaching is—*Nothing whatsoever should be clung to.* Nirvana is the ultimate; if not it is karma and one repeats the cycle of life and its misery. To achieve Nirvana without the suffering of karma, one must understand the world is Dhamma and all things are Dhamma; all things are emptiness; therefore, Dhamma is emptiness.

The other book he read, by an English physics professor, was what we know now about the make up of the universe. His world is not empty, on the contrary, it is full of stuff and he is searching for more stuff to put in it and he thinks he has it in the name of Dark Matter. He talks about the content of the atom to the content of the universe and beyond and of a creator who just might be there with not much to do. Jonathan understood a tremendous amount of what he talked about but of course there were passages beyond him. The professor and his colleagues see a place filled with stuff, galaxies, white dwarfs, strings of atoms, protons, neutrons, quarks and stuff we cannot see but the results of their presence is seen. He talks about the forces that hold the universe, us and beyond together, the glue that binds us: weak force, strong force, electromagnetism and gravity. They put us in a spaceship to fly to the event horizon of a Black Hole and turn us into strings of fettuccine when we enter its violent singularity. They talk about the Big Bang and what was once a speck of nothing to become the mass of the universe that is out there today—flying away from us in a red shift of light. Perhaps it will stop and come back on in and we will remember the future and relive the past.

The professor and his colleagues from around the world have dreams of a grand theory, which is the combination of all the theories postulated by geniuses of the past and future. Their thoughts and theories will be pulled together giving us the truth about the universe and our place in it. They will announce it someday and it will be in a great hall at a prestigious university with the media and academic elite of the world present. And when they do make that speech the voice of The Creator will come back at them and say, enough professors, enough!

Buddha speaks of another emptiness; an emptiness of Dukkha and not tangible things like what the professor and his colleagues dream about. But Buddha still says to achieve emptiness you need to eliminate the past and future—life is in the moment. To look at the universe and the way it is, the past must exist. Oh what a jumble! Perhaps I will never get the hang of it, Jonathan thought.

He said his goodbyes to his new friend, Big Buddha. Jonathan looked up at him and the sunrise was hitting him full force. To see the light from a rising sun hit a huge wall of gold is quite a sight.

Down the stairs he went and into his sandals and onto his motorbike; Jonathan drove back to the guesthouse and Monk.

And Jonathan thought in his own way about big Buddha, for someone who has no pronouns and has nothing; he sure is a big guy in this land.

Jonathan had to wake Monk and the old man was still very tired; there was an ashen look of fear on his face. Monk had little time left—death is always recognizable when it is near. They had breakfast in the dining room but Monk only ate a few mouthfuls of rice and a glass of water. They said goodbye to the old innkeeper and her monkeys and made their way by tuk-tuk to Thailand immigration and the beach where long tail boats waited to take travelers across the Mekong River. The landing was very muddy from the rain the night before so Jonathan carried the little luggage they had to the boat and went back for Monk whom he carried across the muck and sat him in the middle seat. The boat roared over the Mekong in a few minutes and they checked in with Laos's immigration and customs which all went well. For some reason the border officers did not charge Monk an entrance fee.

"We have been expecting you," the officer said to Jonathan's surprise.

"You were expecting the Monk and me?"

"Yes, a call came in from Bangkok last night to say that everything will run smoothly for the two of you. The village also knows you are coming and they will meet you on the river bank."

"Well I'll be—who was it that called?"

"Someone very official, that is all we know and that is all we want to know," he said with a serious look on his face, "there are tuk-tuks up the street to take you to the slow boats. Would you like one of my men to get you one?"

"Yes please, Monk is very tired. Thank you." The officer gestured to a fellow officer and he ran up to the main road and ordered a tuk-tuk to the immigration office.

Jonathan helped Monk into the back seat; loaded their few possessions and climbed aboard.

"To the slow boat pier, please," Jonathan, said, and they left up the river road one kilometer to the pier. They were in time for the next boat south to Luang Panang, it was packed and when the crew saw the old monk they quickly ordered the mass of backpackers to open up a floor space at the front of the boat near the captain. Jonathan noticed two novice monks that bowed to Monk as he passed. The long boat with its one hundred passengers was soon underway. Jonathan felt nervous as Monk looked terrible. The captain looked at him and nodded to Jonathan that he understood what was inevitable.

In their own little space at the front of the boat they settled themselves sitting cross-legged on a grass mat, their backs rested against the bulkhead. They could watch the meandering river, its banks and people, through the cabin door. For a while the landscape of Thailand was in view and then only Laos. A few hours later they neared Monk's ancestral home.

"Are you all right Monk? Are you comfortable?" Jonathan asked.

"No—I'm not all right and I'm not comfortable but that will pass soon," replied Monk, "it's not about me Jonathan, it's all about the land and the people, the Hmong. Think about them now," and he pointed to a group of children and their mothers on the riverbank. A herd of black water buffalo was in the water and the children were throwing buckets of water on them. The giant beasts relished in the attention of the children—their family. Cows stood on the beach nearby; their big brown eyes looked out to the boat. Further up the bank was a herd of black and brown goats; their kids leaped, kicked and danced across the embankment.

Around a bend was the people's village that was high on the riverbank. It was made of the earth; everything was fashioned from bamboo, grass, palm fronds, tree trunks and mud. Time had stopped for these people or they were in another time, Jonathan could not make up his mind which. In a doorway a mother held her suckling child to her breast while she stitched figures on a sheet of blue fabric.

"What is she stitching Monk?"

"Figures of her family and her life; figures of her chopping wood, tending her crop of vegetables, cooking and feeding her family and live stock and flowing through it will be the Mekong River. The simple basic things of life, the things in life she knows best and the things she only or wants to know about."

"What will she do with it?" Jonathan persisted.

"Every few months she will pack up what she has stitched and sewn and with her husband and baby they will set out with others to the night market in Luang Pabrang. There she will sell her needlework to tourists for a shamefully low price and with the money she will make from her months of work she will buy clothes for her family and materials to run her home. She is proud of her heritage and dresses in the costumes of her people. Ironically in patterned silk fashioned in a style any Parisian couture would be proud of."

"And how would you know about that?"

"Girl Two."

"Oh yeah—Girl Two, so how are you feeling—all right?"

"I'm tired. I hope we get there soon. I should not think that way but I don't want to be a burden on anyone."

"You're not a burden Monk." And they both fell silent for a few minutes as they watched the green tropical forest drift by.

And then Monk said in a whispering voice, "Promise me something Jonathan."

"Yes, what is it?"

"On your way home will you go to Angkor Wat in Cambodia where my friends died many years ago and say a prayer for them? It is not far out of your way."

"I will Monk, I promise," Jonathan said. It was not what he had planned and Home Camp is expecting him home in the next day or two, "you had friends that died at Angkor Wat?"

"Yes many, some committed suicide at the start of the war. They poured gasoline on their bodies and lit themselves on fire to protest the conflict."

"I remember that. I saw what they did on the news many years ago. It is still a vivid memory for me. It was terrible."

"Then the Khmer Rouge came and two million died at their hands for their belief in Buddhism or for having any intellectual knowledge. They killed everybody, doctors, lawyers, teachers, engineers and priests of all religions: Buddhist, Christians, Muslims and Jews. No one was spared; the remaining population was reduced to slavery."

"How did you manage to survive?"

"They fired on us at the Wat so we fled into the forest to Angkor Thom and The Bayon, and hid there among the giant faces. A number of us gathered up the children of the villages surrounding Siam Reap and took them across the plains of Cambodia and into the Thai refugee camps. Many died on the way but many survived."

"Amazing, does anyone at Home Camp know about this past you have?"

"No, I have not told anyone about it until now."

"Why are you telling me this?"

"Because you are a mister-know-it-all but don't know enough," Monk said and they both laughed, "I believe you will do some good for this earth. You're a leader, cocky and arrogant. If those qualities are directed to the right end you will be of great help to those around you. And I mean the *big around*."

"Well thanks Monk. You talk as though I was Buddhist, which I'm not. Sometimes I'm even blasphemous about Buddha."

"Buddha doesn't care. All he cares about is that you become, wise, moral and caring of all living things."

"All this talk of religion; I am so much in the dark about it all. How do you find spirituality Monk?"

"Start with your death and work backwards," he said and his eyes looked very tired.

The captain leaned down to them and said, "We will arrive at your village in about one and half hours."

"Thanks captain," and he held Monk's hand.

From where Jonathan sat on the deck he could see the Mekong's current flowing by and heard its gentle water lapping at the hull. A blue smoky mist, from the slash and burn that goes on at this time of the year, painted the forest. Banks of sand and dirt came into view covered in vegetable plots and between them were paths leading up to a village of huts. Makeshift shelters and fences of bamboo and reed were erected here and there, temporary to shade the working families from the hot afternoon sun. Families in colourful clothes and straw hats were hoeing and working the soil. Out of rocky outcrops bamboo poles held fishing nets jutting out into the flow of the river and half naked men, short brown and strong, were working the nets from their canoes. Nothing in the scene could place it in time.

It was then that Jonathan noticed what Monk was talking about. This *is* Thunder Mountain's place. He was all around them coming out of the water. The rocks were the elephants—colour and texture. They were gray wrinkled and weathered like the legs, backs, bellies and heads of those beautiful beasts. The rocks walked out of the water and up the sandy banks. This was definitely his place here in this part of the world and up there in the forest was enough food to feed the thousands in his herd. Here on the Mekong, the world's tenth largest river, life has been sustained for hundreds of millions of people and elephants during the millions of years of its existence.

"Now I know what you meant about Thunder Mountain, this is home I can see him everywhere. In the boulders and rocks, same colour, same texture even the same size," Jonathan said and squeezed Monks hand.

"Soon the monsoon will be here and the waters will rise taking away the farms and cleaning the river's banks, towns and cities. I remember my family and a time of the year when it was a rush to get the crop in and the huts to high ground before the waters rose. Nothing gets in its way when it's on the move, not even the dams planned for the future can stop it for it must go down to the sea. There is no permanence," Monk said in a quiet labored breath. And then he said something in an ancient language and ended it "...Lord Buddha."

"This place is so beautiful Monk isn't it?" and he turned to Monk for his response but there would not be one coming and there never would be. His eyes were closed and he sat in lotus, his left hand lay on his lap, the other in Jonathan's hand, "Goodbye old man," Jonathan said in a whisper and he called the Captain.

The captain turned from the wheel and looked back to the monk and nodded his head. He dialed a number on his cell phone. He spoke for a few minutes and said to Jonathan. "They will be waiting for you."

"Thank you captain," Jonathan said and he turned to Monk, "you will be home soon."

In a short time the passengers knew the monk had died and they became respectfully silent, the only sound was the chugging of the engine and the sound of the Mekong River against the boat's hull. The two novice monks that Jonathan saw earlier came to the forward deck and kneeled before Monk and quietly chanted. The boat made a turn in the river and came in sight of a village—Monk's home.

On a boulder like the back of Thunder Mountain were eight monks. Their bright orange robes shone in the sun. The monks stood erect and quiet, ready to take care of their own. The boat pulled up, bow first and a crewman jumped ashore with a line and jammed it into a crag in the rock that held the boat firm. Silently, as if in a trance, six of the monks came aboard and with an orange robe rapped Monk. Lifting him in their arms they carried him ashore and Jonathan followed. He stood on the rock and one older monk raised his hand in a restraint position to stop him from going further. He said nothing just smiled and raised his hands in prayer. Jonathan raised his hands and smiled back. There was nothing to say, nothing more to do, Monk had moved on and his brethren would take care of him. In an orange robed procession the monks turned toward the bamboo village and forest. They walked up the beach with their precious cargo on their shoulders and disappeared between the huts to a temple on a hill, its golden chedi pointing to the sky. The passengers stood in silence and those who had cameras photographed the event. Jonathan thought, as he climbed back on board, how would they explain all this when they returned to their homes on the other side of the world? He hoped they would tell the story to friends and loved ones with dignity. The crewman let the boat go and it continued its mission to Pak Bang for the night.

"Captain, I need some privacy to make a phone call. Can I go up on the roof?"

"Of course," the captain said and he pulled a hatch open above the foredeck.

Jonathan climbed on the roof and called Home Camp and Mother answered.

"Hello Mother, its Jonathan."

"Hello is everything going well? Is Monk home?"

"Yes he is home but he died a half hour before we reached the village. It's a shame he didn't make it all the way."

"Don't worry, he made it home."

"Yes, I guess he did. He went peacefully, Mother, no pain, he just went to sleep here on the deck of the boat. When we reached his village the monks were on shore to take him home. We didn't exchange words—nothing—they took him and disappeared. Will you please tell everyone that Monk is safe?"

"Yes I will," a sad voice said.

"He made me promise him I would go on a journey to Angkor Wat in Cambodia, so I will be gone for an extra couple of days. I'll call when I am on the way home, okay?"

"That's fine, we can manage here. Be sure to keep in touch."

"Goodbye Mother."

"Goodbye, and you take care of yourself."

Jonathan put away his phone, stayed on the roof and gazed down the Mekong River. The sun was setting behind him and it threw pink, purple and amber light across the rocks, beaches and forest. It was beautiful and peaceful and he felt the exhilaration of life inside him. Pink rocks, pink elephants, and what will this country show me next he thought. He looked west into the sun and saw above the blue smoky hills a huge red/orange Samurai Sun. "What are you showing me?" he said to the flaming ball, "Is it what you will show me tomorrow?"

The next day the slow boat made its landing at the old capital of Laos, Luang Prabang and Jonathan took a room at a guest house on the Nam River, a tributary of the Mekong. In the old capital he went to the theater to see the Royal Ballet Company perform one of the stories from the Ramakien; the story when Hanuman, ordered by Rama, goes to the underworld to rescue Rama's wife Sita from the demon king.

At the National Art Gallery he saw the needlework of the Hmong conceptualized by a group of young modern artists. There was in the exhibition something Monk had described to him. A young woman who lived with a Hmong family, created through their style of needlework, the story a tribal woman's life. Across a bed sheet was stitched the life of the matriarch's labor: cutting wood, plowing the fields, feeding the animals, burning the dead and giving birth. The figures flowed a weaving gold line down the fabric—the Mekong River.

That evening in the night market on the street in front of the gallery there were dozens of Hmong who had come to sell their weaving and needlework. There, on a grass mat, was a little woman and her baby. She sat quietly among her wares of stitched fabric. Among the pieces was a square tablecloth of her needlework done just like Monk had described and what he had seen in the Gallery.

He picked up the work and looked at it closely, "How long did this take you to do?" he asked.

"With a few others—six months," she whispered, her hands in *wei*—she was in awe of white people. She gestured six fingers so he could understand her few words of English.

"How much for this one?" and he picked one up that had a rust coloured background with black figures wearing bright coloured aprons and performing village tasks. The surround was stitched in layers of deep wine, gray and white borders.

"Eight hundred bhat," she said apologetically.

That hurt him, "Only eight hundred? That's twenty four dollars Canadian," he said in astonishment. This would be stealing from this woman at that price and he handed her fifteen hundred. Holding her child in her lap she deeply bowed to him. He walked home to his guesthouse to pack it away in his bag. It would be a treasure for Mother's dining room table for special occasions and a reminder of Home Camp's dear Monk.

Jonathan started to sketch the countryside, temples and markets and he noticed the difference in Laos from Thailand. Laos had lost much of its culture during the Vietnamese and American occupations in the nineteen seventies and would take many years, if ever, to bring its glory back. The country is poor and situated between four other powerful unstable nations. For it to do business or partnerships with one upsets one or more of the others. Its people are pushed and pulled between ideologies and economies. A no win situation for poor native populations like the Hmong. Around Luang Prabang there still lingers the trappings of violence. Rusting and peeling revolutionary posters are still on display and school children in uniform with wooden rifles march in the schoolyard. The school band made up of drums that beat out a rhythm reminiscent of armies marching to war, drive the little armies.

He took a bus from Luang Prabang across mountains through primitive villages and pockets of armed soldiers or rebels; he did not know what they were. They kept their distance; on board his bus were young men with their AK 47s in view of everyone. They were about seventeen or eighteen years of age, dark with fear in their eyes. When the bus arrived in Vientiene Jonathan asked who they were and what they were doing on his bus but his answers were a shrug and a negative nod of the head.

Vientiene was not much to get excited about: karma temples, the meandering Mekong River and a few markets filled with terrible smells of rotting fish and vegetables. The noticeable culture shift for Jonathan was the old fortune-tellers and medicine sellers on the edge of the day market. Always busy rambling on to whomever would come up with a few kip.

Some sold herbs and medicines made from endangered species. He wanted to report them to the World Wildlife Fund but decided not to—people are hungry in Laos. He sketched the decaying French Colonial mansions and the colourful tuk-tuks.

The road to Siem Reap and his destination in Cambodia, the temples at Angkor, was too dangerous at the time to travel by bus. His hotel manager told him a tourist bus was attacked six months earlier by rebel Khmer Rouge still operating in Northern Cambodia. Fifteen people on board the bus were killed and two foreign tourists on bicycles went down with them. The bikers were just passing by when the attack on the bus occurred.

Jonathan took the plane; Russian built and sturdy as a tank. He wondered on take-off whether it would get off the ground, so with the ancient magic around him, he willed it into the sky.

Angkor Wat and Beyond

"Are those bullet holes in the pillars?" Jonathan asked his tuk-tuk driver.

"Yes," Sambo said, "the Khmer Rouge shot the place up from across the moat for fun when they used the grounds as an ammunition dump. At the elephant gate you can see where their trucks scraped the carvings away from the walls."

"Angkor Wat has taken a beating over the centuries. Are there any UXOs still around?" he asked as he studied the massive structure.

"No, the mines and bombs are gone, the fields and buildings have been swept by metal detectors over the last fifteen years. We haven't blown any tourists up for a long time," he laughed, "I will leave you here now and will pick you up at the causeway entrance at three thirty this afternoon. Make sure you drink plenty of water; it's hot in there."

"Thanks." And Jonathan set out across the causeway over a moat to explore the complex.

Surrounding the Wat, the moat or the univérse, is a quarter of a kilometer wide. The causeway runs across it to the complex entrance, which is just a small doorway in a large gate structure covered in decaying effigies of mythological creatures and characters of the ancient Ramayana. Hallways run each side of the main gate to elephant gates that were actually for the beasts to get into the complex. Beyond lies a space of hundreds of hectares that were for gardens, ponds and wooden homes for kings, noble people, shaman, support labor and monks. Across another causeway for another quarter of a kilometer lies the main complex, a huge heap of rock with towers thrusting to the sky. From a distance the rock pile is a blur of gray and black stone but as he approached it details came into view. Every nook, cranny and protruding structure was covered in carvings, most indistinguishable now since a thousand years of rain, lichen and mold had eaten away at the sandstone. Its majesty still comes forth and he wondered at the power that the man, Suryavarman II, had over his people to accomplish such a feat in a mere forty years. He thought they must have loved him as a living God; together they worked for the Lord Buddha whom in Asia the people can't seem to do enough for.

The causeways and platforms leading up to the temples are lined with balustrades of Naga with his five, seven and many more heads. On lintels and walls are carvings of priests, dancers, demons, heroes, elephants, monkeys, kings and gods. Fighting, laughing, dreaming and loving ghosts of creatures from long ago cover everything. The complex has had its time in history and now is just a record of what went on but never the less, a lesson on what greatness the human spirit can accomplish. Thousand of tourists slowly dwindled off to their tour busses and left Jonathan with a few others to explore the inner buildings in the roaring heat. Most of the structures are accessed by stairways that are almost vertical and why they were made so dangerous no one knows and Jonathan found it an ordeal climbing them but he was rewarded with the view of the complex from the top of a mythical world.

Inside one of the enclosed compounds that looked like an ancient swimming pool were statues of Buddha standing in the restraint position as though to say, this place has had enough, leave it in peace. Buddhist statues were draped in gold robes and protected by gold umbrellas. Jonathan looked on as the temple's pilgrims prayed and lit joss sticks. He thought of Monk and what he might have been like huddled here with his brothers wondering about their fate with the Khmer Rouge at the gate. He could almost see them escaping at night through the dense forest to a few kilometers away and the temple of The Bayon and refuge under the many huge faces of deities.

A very old, shaved head Buddhist nun dressed in white sat on a mat below a large Buddha. Jonathan knelt down beside her and she gave him a handful of joss sticks. He placed them between his hands in a prayer position and she lit them for him. He did not know what to say so from his heart he looked up at the image of Monk's God and whispered, "I come with greetings from my friend Monk. If you, Buddha or the deities of this place are near and if his brothers can hear me. He is now among you. May your journey through your many lives find you peace."

He sat down on the edge of the pavilion and sketched the crumbling, decaying walls and corridors of inside Angkor Wat.

Sambo picked him up in mid afternoon and drove him to the temple of Ta Prohm. It was magnificent in its splendor of a long slow battle with nature—a battle it cannot win. Giant silk cotton and strangling fig trees were cleaving it apart; thrusting their giant root systems between the blocks of sandstone. Monks, living dangerously, hold their ceremonies in the decaying buildings. Jonathan sat down in the rubble in the west gallery of the second enclosure and sketched the huge silk cotton tree roots cascading over the roof of the stone passageways—a favorite spot for tour photos and Hollywood movies.

Finishing the basics of a sketch he made his way to the south wall of the third enclosure and sketched a strangling fig with its long tentacle roots patiently tearing apart the main wall. If the archeologists don't cut it down it won't be long until the tree wins out. He thought the archeologists have a dilemma on their hands. The trees are magnificent in their size, colour and shape; their roots have the characteristics of elephant trunks. They have become part of the architecture of the temple and have the right to be there. To destroy them would be taking a piece of the soul of the temple. He made his way out of the crumbling Ta Prohm and Sambo was waiting for him. Jonathan was in awe at what he had seen and that Monk was right; there is no permanence and everything is in decay. Sambo drove him the seven kilometers home. Tomorrow was The Bayon.

Jonathan rose early, showered and shaved and killed whatever mosquitoes were buzzing about his room. He has spent time on his journeys killing the blood sucking insects and he hates it when he catches them, bashing their bodies against the wall and knowing the smear of blood is his.

Sambo and Jonathan met in the hotel lobby and in twenty minutes they drove past the causeway of Angkor Wat and two kilometers down an arrow straight road. In the distance a gray and black portal came into view—the gate of Angkor Thom. A huge benevolent stone face looked down on them. The edifice was on the other side of a causeway that was lined with dozens of giant soldiers restraining seven headed Nagas of the Ramayana. The gods used the Naga as a rope to turn the mountain atop a turtle where Vishnu lives. They stir the Sea of Milk. Before the causeway were buses, tuk-tuks and taxis that parked wherever they could. Dozens of black elephants were at the gate carrying their cargo of people to the temple and an adventure that they would not forget.

Sambo dropped him off, He walked over to the crowd of elephants and they were giants like Thunder Mountain, but these elephants were black not gray; they had a look of majesty and a demeanor about them—proud and arrogant. They carried kings at one time. Four of the elephants reached out to him with their trunks to smell him; the smell of Thunder Mountain was in his clothing. They swayed their heads back and forth and danced on their front feet. They were agitated; their mahouts quizzically looked at Jonathan. He paid his fee and from the loading platform climbed aboard one of the huge beasts. It was good to be in the saddle again. Like in a parade they set out for the gate and he felt the majesty of the place of mythical creatures and gods.

Once through the gate the elephant walked off the road and onto a dirt path that weaved its way through a forest of silk cotton and fig trees. They passed a green algae filled pool; a playground to a tribe of screaming chattering monkeys. Suddenly through the forest he could see a mass of black, gray and white rock. Stone faces on pinnacles rose out of the mass; the same face as on the gate, but dozens of them and Jonathan stared back in wonder. It was heart moving for him; he felt the presence of an ancient race calling to him from a thousand years ago. Shouting out to him like Oxymandias did for the poet Shelley years ago in the deserts of Egypt. How on earth could people build such a place? What force drove them to build this and what is it for? He did not know the answers and from what he had read, no one else knows. The peoples of the future will be asking the same about some of the art and architecture his generation has built. To Jonathan it was a wonderful piece of art, a conceptual piece, a magnificent performance, which is enough sacred ground for him.

He dismounted his elephant at the entrance to The Bayon; he took his time before entering and to think about Monk and his time here—thirty-five years ago. He was an old man even then, in orange robes huddled with others, terrified for their lives and the children in their charge. Jonathan's heart was pounding with excitement from the overpowering majesty of the place.

He made his way up the broken causeway. The Nagas at the end of the balustrades looked at him from their lichen covered and worn eyes. Walk carefully; you are on sacred ground they seemed to say. Under a lintel covered in mythical figures of the Ramayana he passed through stone doorways and into a courtyard, through another door he could see steep stairs—he climbed them. He was now on top of the cloud of carved rock among the stone faces; there were dozens surrounding him, their eyes were open but looked closed, their faces serene in meditation. Perhaps, Jonathan thought this is a place of meditation—a place for deep thinking and then maybe of nothing. The faces spoke from within but he did not know what they were saying—someday, he thought.

Set inside the center structure was small rooms big enough for an altar and two people for prayer and meditation. In one sat an old monk with joss sticks. Jonathan bought a few and the monk lit them. He held them between his palms and the old monk tied a string around his right wrist, prayed a few words and sprinkled some water on him. The string was made of over thirty strands, each representing a deity. They would protect him on his journey.

Something was on the wall behind the monk that startled Jonathan. Scratched into its moldy black surface he could discern gaunt figures with a crowd of tiny ones following them. They looked to be monks and children and one of the monks had a large cat on a rope. Could it be, he wondered, could it be my Monk and the children. No, can't be, too much of a coincidence. He strained to look at the image and the monk noticed and moved aside and with a gesture of his hand across the image he said, "It is something once upon a time when a brother and friends took the children from this place and fled to Thailand never to return."

"He has returned monk, he has returned," and he backed away from the little chapel and the monk. They both gave a knowing smile.

Jonathan spent a few days at Angkor; he would be needed back at Home Camp soon. Sambo picked him up from his hotel at noon. "It's the last day on your temple park ticket. Which temple today?"

"Back to Uncle Tom, please, I want to sketch the elephant terrace."

"Do you want me to drop you off at the gate so you can pick up an elephant?" said Sambo, struggling to put on his helmet over his huge Cambodian head. He opened a beer and gave it to Jonathan.

"Yes, I love riding those beasts," he said excitedly and he climbed into the tuk-tuk and away they roared towards Angkor Thom in Sambo's one hundred and fifty cc. taxi contraption.

Sambo took another route to get to the temples and it passed through a small village in a forest surrounded by rice paddies. Small houses made of bamboo and rattan stood on stilts; animals and people were abundant. The village folk were busy preparing to begin the planting of the rice for the next growing season. The tuk-tuk passed a clutch of houses with children playing in the yard with some dogs and scratching chickens. The youngster's grandparents sat half asleep on the porch. The men of the household were working on a tri-tractor making it ready to plow the rice fields. A young boy lay on his huge black water buffalo watching the men do their work. The buffalo took no notice of the scene; he went about his business of eating the remaining grass growing around the hamlet.

It was all a pleasant and tranquil scene but Jonathan noticed something different; something he had never seen before or even imagined could exist. A young woman was sitting on a bench, feeding rice and vegetables to a middle aged woman sitting with her. Suddenly the older woman got up. and ran but fell to her knees. Jonathan noticed, to his astonishment, she was chained to a tree; shackled at the ankles like an elephant or buffalo. Sambo kept driving and they soon passed the village and arrived at the gate to the temple.

"What the hell was that?"

"What?"

"That woman back there was chained to a tree."

"Yes."

"Well, what for?"

"She is sick in the head and there is no place for her to go. There are no hospitals in Cambodia that can take care of her so she lives with her family, mother, father, brothers, sisters, aunts and uncles. They all take care of her. She is chained to the tree so she won't run away and get hurt or lost."

"Christ in my country that would be a story on the cover of every newspaper across the country. We just lock them up out of sight or drug them and send them out on the street to die of loneliness and abuse."

"That is too bad," Sambo said sadly.

"Your country maybe poor but it has a soul. Every day I see something astonishing. I will see you about three-thirty, okay?"

"Yeah, meet me at number twenty-two restaurant," Sambo said, "eight dollars today?"

"No Sambo, six dollars that's what we agreed on yesterday."

"Oh, all right," he mumbled through his mask and quickly drove away.

Jonathan paid his fee, mounted an elephant and entered Angkor Thom. He dismounted at The Bayon and walked to the elephant terrace; a short distance passed the restaurants and children selling guidebooks. They surrounded him and jabbered away about the deals they had on books and trinkets in bags and bundles that they carried and dragged. He gave them an emphatic *no* and that he would see them later. He walked across a rope lying on the ground—a boundary line the children cannot cross.

The wall had been rebuilt some years ago from a broken heap; rebuilt by archeologist the best they could with the technology they had at the time. Dozens of stone elephants ran, walked, trumpeted and fought across the expanse and along with them soldiers, mahouts and animals. The sun was hot and blasting down on the wall and the only shade was from a stairway structure of carved elephants and garuda monsters that led up to the terrace. Jonathan took refuge in the shadow of a stone elephant and sketched the closest images to him. It took about half and hour; he had to move fast as the heat was tremendous coming off the stone effigies. Exhausted and soaking wet he quickly closed his sketch pad, put it in his backpack, got out of there and back to the outdoor restaurants. The children were waiting for him.

Jonathan took a table at twenty-two which is nothing but a tent with plastic chairs and tables, a make shift stove at the back and some ice coolers out front. The husband of the owner lay sleeping in a hammock strung between two palm trees behind the restaurant. Jonathan ordered a red soda and a large beer from his wife, a toothy middle-aged woman, full of smiles and goodwill. The children, moneymakers extraordinaire, were all over him.

"You buy my guide book mista'."

"No thanks, I have one."

"You need another. You don't have dis one."

"Postcards, one, two, three, fie, sax...."

"You buy my water sir. The best, I make it myself."

"Capital of United States, Washingdon; capital of France, Pari, capital of Canada Oottawa...."

"Show me what you draw."

They gathered around him hungry for knowledge, so he took out his sketchpad from his pack and opened it to the elephant terrace. They all oh and awed and he began to sketch in the details with a drafting pen.

They had watched and pestered him before and the ragtag group and he had somewhat become friends. He told them to be quiet for the next hour while he did some finishing on the drawing and have his soda and beer. The five little urchins did what they were told and stayed to watch him with the biggest dark eyes he could ever imagine.

One tiny one, no more than six, in a spotless white dress and bow in her black hair knelt on the table in front of him, practically on top of the sketchpad. She had a runny nose and snorted every so often. The owner of the restaurant would come by to drag her back from him and wipe her nose.

"Your daughter?" Jonathan inquired.

"No but she is family just the same."

The drawing started to take shape and little eyes were glued to it; the children chuckled, laughed and yapped to each other. A couple left to harass new customers since that was their job. For some time, about two or three beers, Jonathan sketched and an image came into view that talked to him. The weathered and black stained elephant he had drawn became more clearly defined; the trunk thrust forward and curled. His enormous back was arched up to take on the burden of life. The belly was not complete so the re-builders had placed a small effigy of Buddha in the vacant space. On the elephant's back danced or leaped a character from the Ramayana. It could have been a soldier ready for battle. Above the elephant and all around were placed blocks of stones with incomplete and broken carvings of cats, dogs, plants, monkeys and beasts that had become strange looking through weather and time. Above were cornice stones and running across them were leaf designs. On the terrace were benches of large stone slabs for the audience to sit and watch the elephants that fought there a thousand years ago.

What he sketched created a narrative of the elephant in time; the drawing metaphorically spoke of the past and present. The elephant, huge and powerful, held the people of Asian on its back along with all other living things. The stones were Asia itself and above them the benches for those today who are watching the new economic elephant walk across the world. He is very powerful and many are scared that he is on the move. He is the shock of the future, a leader of a shift in power. Everything is piled high on the Asian elephant—the beast with Buddha in its belly and heart.

"What things are you showing me Monk?" Jonathan whispered and the children looked at him quizzically.

A young man, a tuk-tuk driver, came and sat beside him, he had been watching from another table.

"Excuse me please," he said apologetically, "I see you come this last week to the temples to draw. I like to draw and maybe become artist some day. I do not know how to draw," and he gestured with his hands something he could not say—perspective.

Jonathan was well into the sketch for that day and there is always plenty of time in the hot afternoons in the tropics to teach so he said, "You want to know perspective?" and Jonathan gestured with his hands and eyes its meaning the best he could.

"Yes, yes," the young driver said with excitement.

"You want another one mister," runny nose said pointing to his beer.

"Yes please," he said and she ran off to get him one.

"Watch and listen," Jonathan said to the young man. He turned to a blank page in the sketch book and drew a line across the center from left to right, "this is called the horizon," he gestured, then he drew a line for the center of vision top to bottom of the page. He pointed to where the two lines crossed, "that's the vanishing point." he made a flat hand at eye level and gestured out an imaginary line towards the Bayon temple, "that's the horizon. Do you understand?"

"Yes."

"Here's your beer mister," runny nose said and climbed back up on the table pushing the other children aside.

"The point where the two lines intersect," and Jonathan pointed to the intersection, "is directly in front of you and all lines you draw going away from you go to that point. Understand?" He drew lines to the vanishing point in the center and to other vanishing points along the horizon.

"Yes I understand," he said giggling with excitement and the children's faces were concentrated on the drawing and him. Jonathan picked up a square napkin container and held it up eye level to the boy, "Can you see the top or bottom of the box?"

"No"

He moved the box up above his level of vision, "Now can you see the bottom?"

"Yes."

Jonathan moved the box down below his level of vision, "Now can you see the top?"

"Yes."

"You do for me?" runny nose pleaded, so he repeated the exercise for her.

Returning to the young man he said, "Now I will draw the terraces of the temple with the giant heads so watch carefully how the temple is drawn, "and he drew in the base terrace below the horizon then the middle one at the horizon and the upper terrace above the horizon. On the upper terrace Jonathan drew monoliths as a guide to drawing the head structures. He drew the lines of all objects part way to two vanishing points that he marked at each edge of the paper. All lines that were the forward edge of the objects were drawn heavier than the rest.

"I see the temple, yes that is what I want to know," his eyes bugged out of his head and he laughed at the revelation of his discovery and understanding of perspective. Meanwhile runny nose had a pad of paper and pen and was imitating what Jonathan was doing. He turned his drawing over and she turned hers.

He said to the young man, "Now we will draw one of the heads." Again he divided the page into quadrants and placed a monolith structure in the center, "we must imagine this box to be ten meters high and your eyes, your horizon, is at the five meter level. Understand that?" Jonathan gestured with his hands to their faces and the sketch.

"Yes."

Inside the box he sketched a form of a face of the temple. "I am going to use you for the face," he said looking closely at the form of his Cambodian face. He sketched it straight on. The boy's bulbous lips, wide nose, wide jaw and forehead came into view on the paper. He quickly sketched in lines of a decaying chedi or crown on his head that came down to cover his ears. On the right and left of the image he drew him again in profile. Quickly he slit up the image into blocks as though each chunk of his face and head was carved individually. Jonathan crowned the structure of decaying stones with a many head Naga—broken in decay.

"Let's pretend the light is coming from the right of the picture," and he shaded the left profile head structure and shaded features of the left side of the face that looked toward them.

The young boy looked at the sketch and was clearly agitated by what he saw. The other children looked nervous to.

Jonathan looked him in the eye and said, "It's you isn't it?"

He said something in Cambodian and little runny nose's eyes came up from her sketch paper to Jonathan looking for an answer.

"This make me scared," he said.

"It's you," Jonathan said and pointed to the temple.

"Yes, I did not know. I never thought about that. No one tell me of this.

"Your ancestors built this place a thousand years ago. Like you they also took people around from temple to temple long ago but on elephants and carts pulled by buffalo and cattle. This place belongs to all of you. Feel your face and all its features; they are carved in stone on The Bayon." They looked at each other; felt their faces and looked at the drawing. Astonishingly they did not know about their link to the past. They had never been told; never been taught their history. They thought they were from someplace else. Jonathan felt helpless at this point. How do these children feel about themselves? They have become disenfranchised through war and communism, slaves of dictators and bureaucrats. Jonathan felt for them and about freedom being such a precious thing.

"Here," he said and ripped the page from his sketchbook and handed it to the young man. He looked at it and touched his face and looked over to the temple.

"Thank you," he said and he quickly left the table and ran through the dust across the compound to the temple. He ran down the causeway and through a gateway to the inside. The children and Jonathan watched as he disappeared into the massive jumble of gray and black rock.

The only one not watching was little runny nose who was busy drawing and he noticed there was maturity about what she was doing. She was frantic and intense; her little nose running and snorting; tongue sticking out the side of her mouth—determined to learn. The owner came over and wiped her nose for her. Jonathan took runny nose's paper and her pen and put them in her bag and opened his pad to the elephant terrace. He gave her his pen and taught her how to use it, straight up and down with strokes of the hand and not the fingers. She understood right away what to do and practiced with him before Sambo arrived. She looked disappointed at Sambo; she was having so much fun, the fun that art is supposed to give.

"Keep the pen little one," He said and closed his sketchbook. The owner came over and he paid his bill.

"Little runny nose ripped a page from her pad and drew a hibiscus flower on it and wrote something in Cambodian which of course he could not read and will never have translated. He folded it and put it in a compartment in his wallet where it will be forever.

He said goodbye to the owner and the children as he left number twenty-two. He felt sad since he has said goodbye to so many people over the years of his travels—people and friends he may never see again across many very different countries and cultures. He hoped that he will return, especially to this magic place of Angkor with its stones, gods and elephants. He felt Monk close by and he whispered, "I kept my promise old man."

In the tuk-tuk Sambo and Jonathan, beer in hand, kicked up dust as they climbed onto the road surrounding The Bayon, he looked up at the noble faces across the upper terrace in search of the young man. He could not see him but he knew he was up there somewhere looking at himself and wondering.

It was time to get back to Home Camp in Thailand. Jonathan had kept his promise to Monk and in death Monk had guided him. The dirt road to the boarder of Thailand from Siem Reap was long and rough. He, along with five other people, had ordered VIP bus tickets to find out there was no VIP bus until they arrived at the border five hours away by taxi. They traveled through the killing fields across the rice paddies of Cambodia. He did not say much on the trip; he just looked out the window and imagined Monk and his group along with hundreds of thousands of refugees fleeing their homeland. He imagined Sambo and his family fleeing and the struggle for him to grow up far from home. But he knows that the human race is a resilient bunch and he has faith that it can rise above adversity. Not so the elephant, he thought. He will have to think about that.

"May I have your attention everyone," Mother commanded. And everyone stopped eating his or her dessert to listen, "I have some wonderful news and I have waited to tell you until now that Jonatin is home from Cambodia," she pulled out a letter that was tucked in her apron and opened it. She looked at everyone at the same time with her eyes, "in short, Thunder Mountain is the oldest elephant in the neighborhood of Kanchanaburi. He has been invited to lead the parade in the flower festival in two weeks. Who would like to be the mahout?" There was fast-talking and excitement at the table.

"The letter came to you Mother, this is your project, and you make the decision," Tag Two said.

"Very well, I have been thinking about it and I want to elect Thunder Mountain's best friend, Girl Two, to ride him."

"Perfect," Girl One said, "she deserves it with all the work she puts in for him."

"Well what do you think Girl Two? Will you do it?" Mother asked.

"Will I do it? Try and hold me back."

"Can I paint Thunder?" Jonathan asked.

"Yeah that would be a good idea," Tag Two said.

"I'll help Jonatin?" Girl One asked.

"This is starting to sound like a Judy and Mickey production—"

"Huh," Mother said.

"When is the event?"

"Two weeks this Saturday," Mother said.

The weeks went fast as Home Camp was busy with the village farmers, delivering cattle and taking Thunder Mountain into town. Everyone got up at six that Saturday morning full of excitement of the hours ahead, the parade would start at ten thirty. Jonathan had designed the painting of Thunder Mountain in his head and cut templates to make the job go fast and clean. Mother and Girl Two had been busy with her costume and they would not tell anyone about it.

"I'll be riding on a cloud!"

"This is how we do it, one person holds the template against the skin and the other paints the pattern. Don't use much paint, just a little at a time. That way there won't be any drips under the template," Jonathan instructed. Girl One held the paper template against the leg of Thunder Mountain and Tag Two dappled the paint on gently with a two-centimeter brush. They soon got the hang of it and the first image was done on the elephant that was enjoying all the attention.

"Is that right Jonathan?" Tag Two asked as he finished and Girl One removed the template.

"Yeah, yeah, perfect," Jonathan said. On the elephants leg emerged a baroque design from The Bayon temple in Angkor Thom—charcoal black swirls and leaves, "now we do the same all over his body making sure the design flows from bottom to top not on its side. The design should look like it is growing up out of the ground—the spirit of the earth or something like that."

"Oh, Jonatin," Girl One laughed and hugged him.

They worked for an hour on the black design; Jonathan making sure that it was not overdone. They had hobbled Thunder Mountain and chained him to his shelter post so he would not move when a ladder leaned against him to get at his back. "Coverage with the matte black paint should not exceed fifty percent of his skin or the design will be too busy," Jonathan said. When the black was done they started on a leaf template; these were fig leaves about twice the size of the actual leaf. There were three designs, flat, three quarters on and to the side. Most of the leaves were to be painted head on. He told his painters where to place the templates and dappled on gold paint. Suddenly Thunder Mountain turned into a magical beast from the underworld; his black spirit rose up out of the ground to meet the light of gold falling from the sky. Mother came out of the pavilion with Girl Two in shock.

"Das incredible!" she said.

Girl Two started to cry, "My Lord Buddha, I'll be riding on a cloud," and she hugged Jonathan, Girl One and Tag Two."

"Your make up is beautiful—great job Mother," Tag Two said.

"Well I just followed her instructions."

"Are you ready Girl? Are we all ready? I'm nervous as hell," Tag Two said.

"Yes, yes," everyone shouted.

"Let's load Thunder into the truck. Mother and Girl Two, you're going in the pickup, right?" said Jonathan

"Girl Two doesn't want us hanging around, she wants us all to go half way up the parade route and watch her from there. Is that okay with everyone?" Mother said.

All responded, "Yeah."

"After we drop her and Thunder off at the parade start we will leave. How about we watch the parade from across the street at that new department store?"

"Sounds good," Jonathan, said, "What are you going to be Girl Two?"

"You'll see."

"Let's roll everyone," Jonathan shouted. Thunder Mountain danced, his eyes shone and his trunk reached out and touched everyone. He was excited as everyone else but didn't actually know why.

They dropped Thunder Mountain and Girl Two off and drove the cattle truck and pickup to the their place on the parade route. The family was nervous when they arrived at the viewing spot in front of the department store.

"I need a beer," Jonathan said. How about you guys?"

"I'll have one thanks," Tag Two said.

"Me to," Girl One said.

"Not me," Mother said, "I'll pee myself. I'm just too excited."

He went into the store to the food counter, bought three large beers and returned to the sidewalk. The street was filled with people and band music could be heard in the distance—the parade had started. The family laughed, clicked bottles, joked and was excited and proud that Thunder Mountain and Girl One would lead the parade. Jonathan strained his eyes down the street and in the distance he saw an elephant gliding down the centerline followed by a herd of other elephants; their mahouts brightly dress in gold and silk. People were throwing flowers in front of the lead elephant—Thunder Mountain. Jonathan could hear clapping and cheering. The family looked at each other, as Thais don't usually express themselves that way. It was soon apparent why the celebration.

Thunder Mountain gracefully walked down the street, an apparition from the depths of mythology; he truly looked like a god resplendent in gold leaves from heaven. Atop his neck sat Sita, the most beautiful woman in the world, wife of Rama and captive of Tosakan the demon of the underworld who was pursued by Hanuman the giant white ape. There she sat alone, up there on top of a swirling cosmos. On her head was a pointed gold chedi crown covered in jewels and glass that cascaded down over her ears. Gold epaulets jutted out from her shoulders like wings. A gold belt around her waist held gold chaps over her thighs; her pants were green silk and on her feet were pointed slippers encrusted with jewels. Jewels and gold rope were draped over her and a large one draped down to a huge tassel below Thunder Mountain's head. She wore finger extensions on both hands, the right one held a golden bow. Her thumb held the weapon against her palm letting her other finger flay out. The end of the bow rested on her right thigh so her arm and nails were extended out to the crowd. Her left hand rested curled on her hip, her elbow out to the side. Her face was serene, beautiful and radiant with an arrogance of majesty. She sat tall on Thunder Mountain and she was bare breasted.

"Oh my Lord Buddha," Mother whispered, "she never told me," and tears ran down her cheek.

"Well done Mother," Jonathan whispered, "well done." The family held on to each other as Thunder Mountain and Girl Two went by. Her head slowly turned to look at her family; she winked and gave a little smile. They could not speak just shed tears of joy.

The crowd went crazy cheering and hooting and throwing flowers. She passed and her consort of a dozen elephants followed.

Girl One said, "My sister has style."

Perhaps a Butterfly

Home camp's family sat down and ate Sunday dinner. Mother and the twins had worked the afternoon cooking roast beef, potatoes, Yorkshire pudding, vegetables and baking fruit pies for dessert. Jonathan loved Sunday dinner at Home Camp since it took him, for a brief moment, back to his home in Canada and his children. After cleaning up and washing the dishes the family retired to different parts of the house and pavilion. Tag Two asked Jonathan to join him on the mat overlooking the river; he got a couple of beers from the refrigerator and opened them. They both sat down and crossed their legs. Off to the side of the pavilion they could see Girl Two leading Thunder Mountain down the bank to the river.

"I have something to show you," Tag Two said and he laid a handkerchief on the matting, "I don't want you to be upset at this but I found these on the floor of the truck. There is something we must face." And he opened up the handkerchief to reveal some large chips of stained white porcelain.

"So what have we here?" Jonathan said picking up a piece and inspecting it closely," then he realized what it was, "Oh Christ, I think I know."

"They're chips of Thunder Mountain's molars," Tag Two said sadly.

"I've been dreading this day. I knew it was coming. He is on his last set of teeth, isn't he?"

"Yes, I'm afraid. I've called the vet and he'll be here first thing tomorrow. It does not look good. Thunder is nearing the end of his life as we expected."

"You know, in the last week or so I've felt him change. He doesn't seem responsive like he used to be; he's a bit slow and sluggish."

"I've checked on his food consumption and it's down a great deal from what he needs. If his teeth are gone, he will go fast and I'm expecting the worst. I don't want him to suffer so we will intervene. Do you agree?"

"Yes, of course. Oh, Tag Two, how sad this will be for the family," he sighed sadly, "they have gone through so much just a short time ago with the loss of Monk. Have you told Mother and the twins?"

"Yes, I've told them and they are sad but taking it very well. Life and death is different for them, they have started the celebration," Tag Two said and he rose, "I have things to do. Will you be okay?"

"Yes, I'll be fine, thanks my friend."

He looked out onto the river and Thunder Mountain lay almost submerged with Girl Two standing on his back scrubbing him down and jabbering at him about some badly dressed celebrity that she had been reading about. He raised his huge trunk full of water and sprayed her and she laughed with satisfaction. Thunder Mountain seemed to wink at him and Jonathan had never felt so sad in his life.

"The molars are almost gone and there are no new ones coming in behind for support. There is blood on the gums where he is chewing his food. I'm afraid he is suffering," the Doctor said, "Thunder Mountain will last maybe a week at the most and it will be a week of pain for him. What would you like me to do?"

Girl Two ran sobbing to her room and the rest of the family stood firm in the pavilion looking out to their friend and family member.

Tag Two, with courage as always said, "I think you should intervene and end Thunder Mountain's suffering, Doctor. Do you agree everyone?" and they all nodded their heads in agreement. "This must be unanimous, Mother, will you please go and tell Girl Two what we have agreed upon and if she agrees."

"I'll be right back," Mother said and she went in search of Girl Two. No one moved or said anything until she returned which was only a few minutes, "she agrees that Thunder Mountain does not suffer anymore and there should be intervention."

"Very well," Tag Two said, "it should be done as soon as possible."

"I will go to the clinic and get the necessary equipment, it should be done today," the Doctor said and he left Home Camp immediately.

"He should be buried at the end of the cane field within sight of us, don't you think?" Girl One said. Everyone nodded their heads in agreement as they could not speak. Jonathan and Tag Two went off to the field and picked out a sight and Tag Two got on his cell phone to a neighbor to come in the late afternoon with his back hoe and Mother went to her trunk where she keeps important things.

It was late afternoon when the Doctor returned and by that time the villagers had heard about the coming death of the elephant and had gathered on the roadway at the entrance to Home Camp. The neighbor waited there with his backhoe. Sirens were heard in the distance and the commander from Khaosan Road arrived in sadness.

"Hello commander," Jonathan said. He bowed and shook his hand.

"I have known Thunder Mountain for many years and consider him my friend. I owe him and you for what you did the night of the bombings in Bangkok. Forgive me, may I join you?"

"Of course."

Jonathan unshackled Thunder Mountain from the cement pad. Mother, Tag Two with Naga over his shoulders, the commander, Girl One, Girl Two; all held the neck rope and guided him down the path alongside the cane field. They guided him to the spot Jonathan and Tag Two had picked for the elephant's ending of this life and the beginning of the next—Lord Buddha willing. Black buffalo watched from his coral.

The family carried lit candles, joss and offerings and when they reached Thunder Mountain's patch of land, Tag Two ordered him to his knees. He obeyed without hesitation for he was tired. The family kneeled on each side of him, Mother at his head who prayed and sprinkled water on everyone. She opened a tissue paper bag and pulled out two small faded and torn blankets and laid them across Thunder Mountain's back and said in a strong and serious voice, "I was wrapped in these blankets when I was a child. My babes were wrapped in these when we came to a new life in this country. We came across the mountains from Burma; these blankets kept my babies warm on the journey. Now they will take our friend on his journey to his next life."

Everyone sat within sight of Thunder Mountain's amber eyes, which looked tired and without the spark of mischief and life that was there such a short time ago. Tag Two nodded to the Doctor who moved close with a large syringe and placed the needle in a blood vessel just above the calligraphy of Thunder. The huge beast did not flinch or move and his eyes stayed open as the life drained from his body. It did not take long and once again a loved one was torn from Jonathan's heart. The commander with Mother took the twins by the hand and left for the pavilion. Jonathan and Tag Two thanked the Doctor. Jonathan took Naga from Tag Two and they left for the pavilion. Tag Two stayed on and called the neighbor to come with his backhoe. The neighbors, friends and villagers arrived with food, drink and fireworks to celebrate Thunder Mountain's life.

Within an hours there was a large dirt mound at the edge of the cane field; a mound that would in time disappear; a mound under bright stars and a Samurai Sun; a mound that holds a friend that would eventually be forgotten as the larger Asian elephant marches over him; a mound that holds an elephant of Thailand that with Lord Buddha's blessing will become another living thing as equally beautiful—perhaps a butterfly.

For Sale, One Big Elephant

The Home Camp family sat around the dining room table looking despondent. It had been a week since Thunder Mountain died and everyone was still grieving even if they knew it was the elephant's time and he had gone to a better place. Tag Two was not grieving anymore; he had been busy.

"I have something to say, so please listen and don't comment unless it is a positive thought," Tag Two said. He looked around the table and everyone nodded in agreement, "This morning I called my friend who is part owner of an elephant trekking camp on the island of Phuket. He told me of an old mahout who worked on a palm oil and rubber plantation. The plantation owner, an aging woman with two sons, bought him and his elephant many years ago. The old mahout is now in an old folk's home since he cannot take care of himself and his elephant, his mind is gone and he doesn't know his name or if he has an elephant. The two sons do not want the responsibility of the animal. My friend was offered the elephant but his business cannot handle another one, so the elephant is up for sale.

"How much?" Jonathan asked excitedly.

"Unfortunately, Rat, that's his name, is up for five hundred thousand baht, which is too much for us unless we mortgage or take a loan on the Home Camp. Getting into debt is not what we want but this place will just be a working farm without an elephant. It will not be the same; we have lost part of the soul of this place. Is there any positive suggestions?"

"Buy the elephant," Girl Two whimpered.

"You miss Thunder Mountain, don't you?" Mother said, and she reached out for her daughter.

"Yes he was my best friend." Girl One put her arm around Girl Two and looked to Jonathan to make the next move, as she knew he would. He looked at her and he knew he had to make a tough decision.

This decision was all too big for the Home Camp except for Jonathan, who figured in his head it was about sixteen thousand dollars, Canadian. He had a stash of cash squirreled away from his, *fake my death*, scam and sixteen K was just spit in his many offshore bank accounts. The financial decision was easy for him but he would be committing himself to something he did not know if he cared to get involved. He was looking for an opportunity to leave and this was it. He had filled his part of the karma bargain; he had bought Thunder Mountain after accidentally killing Tag and he took the elephant to the end of his days. Why should he pay more?

But there was something more here he thought, something beyond money. These people were refugees and in a way so was he. He did not particularly want to go home, life there was not what he wanted anymore. His family was well off and comfortable and could always visit him in

Thailand or he could get on a plane at anytime and return for a few weeks back to his sanitized British Colonial homeland.

Jonathan stood up and with authority said, "Tag Two, please call your friend and have a veterinarian do a full medical check up of the elephant and send us a report. Let's make sure it's complete: herpes, foot rot, teeth, estimate of age, everything. If we find it looks good we will make an offer to the owner of four hundred fifty thousand. I everything checks out on the med report we will send him twenty-thousand as a deposit on the elephant, the remainder to be paid on possession by you and me." Buddha was doing some work here and it felt good to him. Girl One gave him a knowing smile and Girl Two broke into a hysterical crying fit. Jonathan rolled his eyes at Mother and the family.

"Don't look at me like that, you know I'm a rich man," he said and they said nothing but just stared at him in bewilderment, "well, Tag Two?"

"Yes, of course Jonatin, I'll get on it right away," Tag Two said and quickly left the table.

"Girl one would you make me some tea? I'll take it in my usual place. Thank you."

"Yes Mr. Jonatin."

Mother rose from the table and was about to speak and Jonathan raised his hand to stop her.

"Nothing is to be said, let's make our family ready for our new member," and Jonathan left for the front of the pavilion to wait for his tea.

"What made you do it Jonatin?" Girl One asked as she placed the tray of tea in front of him and took her usual place beside him," you could easily have run away from us. You are not obliged to do anything for the family."

"Oh yes I am, there are forces operating in Home Camp that are overpowering. I don't know what it is but something good is about to happen and I'm not going to miss it," Girl Two poured his tea and Jonathan drank it, "Phuket, where is that exactly?"

"It's about eleven hours by car to the south, down near the southern provinces."

"It was bashed around by the tsunami a few years ago wasn't it?"

"Yes, many lost their lives, some their homes forever. We sent food and money down there. All the damaged beach towns have been rebuilt now and have become very wealthy with new hotels, restaurants and resorts. There was a second tsunami," Girl One said, "a tsunami no one talks about, perhaps it is out of shame or the gathering of Karma."

"Oh," he said, "tell me about it."

"The first tsunami took away the village's homes, boats and killed the families that had lived near the water for centuries. Hundreds of those families were related: mothers, fathers, grandfathers, grandmothers, grandchildren, cousins, aunts—all together living close by. Their property was in their families for generations but no records existed. The right of ownership was a matter of living on the land; no one questioned what belonged to whom.

The tsunami came and destroyed them. When the survivors came back they had no place to go, the administration took over ownership of the land and without the land they did not qualify for disaster funding. Money came in from around the world and it disappeared. No one, but a few know were it went. Families were ripped apart, some totally destroyed, those who where left had to fend for themselves with nothing, no family, property or help. Many committed suicide, others drifted away to the fields as laborers or to the city to work the streets in the sex trade, bars, tourist trade and other low paying jobs. It has been very tragic what has happened."

"Can't anybody do anything? Like finding out where the disaster funds went, establish some kind of ownership or grant system for the land?"

"There are people trying but Thailand is corrupt, it is a way of life here. It is the way it has always been."

"Well that's fatalistic, don't you think?"

"Yes it is, and that is the way it will be."

They talked into the night and he told her of his past and the crime he committed and got caught. He told her about Bank Robber, Tegwyn, Tula, adventures and his life. They laughed at some of his disasters.

"I have a copy of the Ramakien that I have read just a little. I'm very interested in the story but I don't understand the Asian way of looking at the world. I've told a few stories to people using some of the names of the characters. We don't have such powerful outrageous stories in the west. Maybe about the western God, Jesus, but his story is mild compared to Asia's. Tell me about it would you?"

"The Ramakien is a story of Gods and Demons—good against evil. It was written in India in Sanskrit two thousand years ago. Many years ago our warrior King Rama translated the Indian story of the Ramayana into Thai and called it Ramakien. The story title means, in honor of Rama, the hero of the story. All our Kings are called Rama and our present King Bhumibol is Rama the ninth, a direct descendant of Rama the first. His Majesty and his family are our living heroes here in The Kingdom of Thailand. Monsters, ghosts and magic are everywhere. You know about these things don't you Jonatin? You have experienced these things in the past."

"Yes I do, they're hallucinations, I think. Funny enough I enjoy them and they're not harmful to me. How do you know this?"

"I visit the library, read magazines and newspapers and use the Internet. I read about you."

"The size of the world has changed in the past few years, much like the size of your gods and giants. Please go on."

"The story touches everything in Thai culture, passion and life. The story is very real to the Thai people and many believe it happened. When I read it, I believe—I want to believe."

"You, the articulate logical woman that you are—believes in fairytales?"

"Yes, it is a story of love and the conquest of evil. You have to use your imagination when reading it for the time of past, present and future is all one time and the size of the gods, giants and humans are all one size, be they mountains or monkeys. The weapons they use to kill each other are powerful and they change to outdo each other. It is the story of heroes and villains, Shiva, the god of all gods, giants and men, Narayana, Shiva's warrior assistant, Sita the most beautiful woman in the world—"

"Yes, our wonderful Girl Two," Jonathan said.

"—Mongkut and Lob the sons of Sita, Rama the heir to the throne, Hanuman the giant white monkey and Adula the enemy of Sita. There are dozens of characters and thousands of monkeys, all flying in the sky, stretching over seas and rivers, and living in the deep ocean and the many layers of heaven. They all live and fight in a splendid battle for the good of mankind."

With the day of important decisions, the warm breeze coming up from the river and Girl One's tea and gentle voice. Jonathan felt himself drifting, "I'm very tired, I must go to bed. Would you come and tuck me in?"

"Yes, your bed is ready for you," and she helped him to his feet and led him to his bed; tucked the sheets in around him and secured the ends of the mosquito net between the mattresses.

"Good night Mr. Jonatin. You will have sweet dreams."

"Good night, thanks for the tea," and he slipped rapidly into a dream.

Sita and Adula

Jonathan floated above Khao Wang, celestial city of the mountain, on the edge of Phetchaburi. His skin turned green, fangs rose out of his mouth, his nose flared, his eyes bulged and became enormous, a gold chedi settled on his head and a gold jacket belt and silk pants painted their way around his body. Diamonds, rubies and emeralds sparkled all over him. A fierce glowing sword grew out of his right hand. He looked down upon the mountain and market below.

Sita slept under a worn out blanket on a bamboo platform in her hovel at the back of the market. The beauty of her youth was long gone. She is sixty-one, alone, a husband left many years ago for a younger woman. Her children are grown and live with their families in Bangkok in a new life westernized by the big elephant of Asian commerce. The elephant in its march forward in Asia's pursuit of prosperity can be brutal if you are in its way.

Jonathan watched Adula as she crept from stall to stall looking for scraps left behind from the day before; sometimes she made a good haul of rice, peanuts, cake, vegetables, dried fish, pork and beef. Just before daylight she worked and carried her treasures to the second floor rooftop where her babies lay waiting and shivering in fear. Cousin Hanuman kept guard over them.

The morning arrived but the market would not see it for a few hours since its pile of buildings lay in the shadow of the mountain. The traffic increased as the light grew brighter and there was clanging and rattling of iron doors and gates along the building as it yawned awake. Metal and wooden wagons were pushed out of the black mouths of the stores and onto the sidewalk. The market is in black decay; wiring is fraying and hangs dangerously above the booths. The smell signals the place is dangerous.

Sita opened the iron gates of her store and rolled out her wagons. Today was Sunday and the town would be one giant market with the merchants and farmers coming from the countryside to sell their goods. There would be too many merchants, which would cut the profit back to a normal day. She stacked baskets of fruits and vegetables around the wagon making everything look presentable and enticing to her few customers. The vendor suppliers arrived with: vegetables, baked goods of pies, buns, cookies and bread freshly baked that morning. She stacked those made yesterday in front of those made today. These were the only perishables that she sold; her goods were mostly dried and wrapped in clear plastic so they would last a few days.

Above the goods and very quiet, Adula hid in the rafters with twenty of her tribe. They waited patiently for their moment. Suddenly Adula jumped down and quickly snatched a bag of cookies. Sita had left her booth to pay the vendor at his parked truck on the highway. She turned and saw

Adula and dashed after her with a bamboo stick. Adula and the band of twenty jumped screaming to the electric wires and the rooftops as Sita pummeled the tin roof and wires making an awful crashing noise. Shaken and relieved Adula made it to her babies, she quickly tore open the package of cookies and she, Mongkut, Lob and Hanuman grabbed as many of the morsels they could in their little black hands and mouths. Rama, a big fierce red assed male, was right there baring his teeth screaming at them to back off. The big male grabbed the rest of the cookies. Jonathan swung his sword but it went right through Rama—not touching him.

Sita took out her slingshot and bag of round stones from the draw of her food cart. Adula could see the deadly weapon from the rooftop and moved out of sight. The pebbles from below had taken some of her children and relatives over the years. She had a few bruises herself from the weapon. Adula, with her brood on her nipples, jumped the three meters to the trees on the mountain and made their way to the entrance of the mountain's temple grounds. There her babies swam in a pool and swung on vines hanging down from the forest.

Adula will fight most of the day with the rest of the tribe for food thrown to them by the giant tribe and see that her children are not killed by their iron monsters. She will teach them how to climb electrical poles and trees and to cross the highway by wire to the park.

Today at the Sunday market there will be many slingshots about. Adula pulled her babies from the pool and took her family up the mountain to the temples to eat berries. It was still dangerous there but she knew the big males would be at the market and not bother her and her babies. Jonathan flew up with them.

He flew up the mountain to the temples built by the King of Siam, Rama IV, a King who had the power of life and death over everybody and anything that walked grew and swam. He flew around the conglomeration of European, Chinese, Japanese and Thai architecture. At the centre of the mountain rose a tall white chedi that contains an artifact of Lord Buddha—he hovered nearby. He looked down into the trees that bare beautiful fragrant white and yellow flowers. They lined the temples grand processions. He watched the king's entourage of wives, concubines, maids, servants and others gliding about the place.

Jonathan flew down to the forest and watched Adula climbing over the crumbling limestone rocks and through the trees and bushes; Mongkut clinging to her back and Lob was at her breast. She passed over the caves and hiding places of her tribe where her kind called home for centuries. She was soon in sight of the giant white chedi and Lord Buddha. She had been here many times on the back of her mother when she was a baby. But today for some reason, deep inside her, she sensed that the great white spike in the sky was very important. She was not like other monkeys of her tribe; she was physically different with a left arm that shone a golden colour. She sensed she had walked here before but as something else and it frightened her. In her primitive thinking she connected this feeling with the tribe with sticks and terrible weapons that worked in the market below and the same tribe that floated on the pathways above. She stood upright imitating them; the thought was fleeting and soon disappeared.

She could not see Jonathan floating above her. She made herself and her babies comfortable among the trees and bushes. There were no other monkeys or giants around so she let her babies have the run of the place. Mongkut and Lob swung through the trees taking turns chasing each other and ate the red berries from the bushes. They spent several hours at peace there but it was dangerous—Adula was constantly on the alert.

Suddenly there was the sound of a whiz and a thud as something hit the tree branch above Adula's head. She cried out to Mongkut and Lob, another wiz and thud and Mongkut jumped on her back. She saw Lob twenty meters away and she scrambled towards him; there was a wiz and thud as something hit Lob's head and the little creature went down into the bushes. Adula scrambled after him and found him limp. She picked him up and ran through the trees to halfway down the mountain—Jonathan followed. Mongkut clung to her neck in terror—he felt the fear of his mother. For the next hour Adula petted and cuddled Lob but he did not respond to her motherly commands. In her mind Lob disappeared and the body was another inanimate object to her. She laid Lob's body draped over a boulder and left with her surviving child holding fast to her back.
Jonathan was sitting beside two boys.

"Hey, did you see that—I got it. There's another," the young Thai boy said. He lifted his Thai weed to his mouth for another drag and freed his hands to work his murderous slingshot and steel ball bearing.

"Yeah," his friend said laughing, "nice shot."

Jonathan woke in a sweat. It was morning.

Rat and Hanuman

At breakfast, Tag Two gave a report: "Arrangements have been made to have the elephant examined by a vet. It will take about a week for the blood work report to come through. He thinks the offer we've made will be accepted. When and if we are ready, my friend has offered his cattle truck to move our elephant to Surat Thani. Once there we can transport the elephant to Bangkok by train.

"Great work Tag Two," Jonathan said, "let's meet later and plan our journey. Our family will be complete again soon. Girl One and I have a marketing plan I would like to discuss with you. And Mother, I believe you have some old elephant parade gear?"

"Yes, Tag bought it in Bangkok years ago. I have it stored away in a trunk under my bed. I will get it out and make it ready if you like. Where will we use it?"

"I'll tell you when I have the plan formulated in my head. This elephant is not going to arrive in Bangkok unnoticed."

"There is one more thing," Tag Two said.

"Isn't there always," Jonathan commented, "and what is it?"

"Well it seems the elephant has had a friend for the last six years. Now he is gentle; he was raised from and infant after his mother was killed."

"What ever it is, we all have to make a decision here, not just me. This is our home not mine," Jonathan said.

"It's an ape."

"An ape, you don't mean something big like a gorilla?" Mother said. It will make one hell of a mess of the pavilion and require feeding and—"

"No, no, Hanuman is a gentle gibbon. She craps in the forest and keeps herself spotless. She has never been behind bars. She has lived on the estate since she was a baby. She sleeps on the elephant's back every night. My friend can vouch for her since he has a similar situation at his trekking camp; a gibbon there comes and goes as he pleases. The old woman said they come as a pair. Now," said Tag Two, "it is up to you all. Do we take in the gibbon or leave it abandoned to die in the forest, without friends, alone, afraid—"

"Agreed, agreed!" everybody shouted with laughter.

At the dinner table a week later Tag Two was late from his errands. He arrived in the pickup truck screeching to a stop on the concrete pad. He jumped out of the rig with papers in hand and a huge smile on his face. Everyone was eating but stopped as Tag Two sat down.

"Good news everyone!" he shouted, out of breath from his excitement, "the fax of the medical report from the veterinarian gives Rat a clean bill of health. He is fit and healthy." Everyone cheered and hugged each other.

"Now what about the price?" Mother said.

"We will know soon. My friend is on his way to the estate at this very minute with the offer.

"Anything else on the report," Girl One said.

"He does recommend that Rat's tusks should be cut back since they can be dangerous and could hurt someone unintentionally."

"No operation on him please," Girl Two pleaded. Everyone agreed that Rat should keep his tusks.

"About the monkey—ape, Hungman?" Jonathan inquired.

"Hanuman," Girl One said.

"Has he been checked out?"

"Yeah, my friend made the decision to also have him looked at and he is healthy. The vet bill for the ape will be added."

"Why do I already know that?" Jonathan mumbled.

"What's that?"

"Oh nothing," Jonathan sighed, "Mother, do you have a large bottle of whiskey?"

"But of course," and she went to the kitchen and bought out the whiskey, Girl One bought out glasses for all and Girl Two fetched cubed ice from the fridge. Mother poured a healthy glass for everyone and they sat in the pavilion and waited for the call that would give continuity to their lives.

Tag Two's phone rang and he answered.

"Yes...yes...yes," Mother was wringing her hands, "of course... yes... yes," girl one and two had their hands together in prayer, "okay...yes... of course. You mean Rat is ours?" everyone cheered and hugged each other. Tag Two went out onto the concrete patio to continue the call and be heard. With his foot he gently shuffled the chain that held Thunder Mountain for so many years and as he made arrangements with his friend about bringing Rat and Hanuman to Home Camp, tears rolled down his cheek. His home that he and Tag had fought for would soon be complete again.

Tag Two would take care of the operation's details and he wanted to call it The Rat project. Jonathan took care of the financial structure of the operation and the task was easy; take out a bank draft from one of his accounts in Switzerland via his friends at the bank where he purchased his taxi license. He used a character reference from his friendly commander on Khaosan Road. He contacted the Provincial Livestock Department and acquired the transport permits and faxed the department the logistics of the transfer and shipment of Rat—he lied. Lastly he called Tag Two's friend to send on the registration certificate for Rat to the department and a copy to him. For freight charges, food, water, train and flight tickets and incidentals—he withdrew fifty thousand baht.

Jonathan had difficulty with the word, Rat. "No, we can't call it the

Rat project. I have something international in mind for Home Camp and an elephant with that name would not be appropriate."

"International, what does that mean?" Girl Two queried.

"Girl One and I have been working on a plan that will make the future secure. It will be controversial but then all successful projects are controversial. We haven't finished the plan and will not do it without everyone's approval."

"Tell us the plan as it is up to now," Mother said. Jonathan and Girl One agreed it was time to tell the family so they went over everything they had dreamed up to date but warned everyone that timing was of the essence and changes would happen up to the last minute. Everyone agreed on the plan even though they thought it a bit ambitious and illegal.

Tag Two made all the arrangements with his friend at the trekking operation in Phuket. The elephant and ape would be transported by their cattle truck to the Surat Thani rail yard were Tag Two arranged for a cattle car to be waiting on a rail spur at the main passenger station. Jonathan insisted that they travel by passenger train and pull the cattle car all the way to Bangkok. The elephant and ape would disembark at Hua Lampong Station. A little show, a little drama wouldn't hurt he insisted. After all the streets of Bangkok will be where the elephant would earn his keep. He called his friend the commander to help make arrangements with officials in Surat Thani and for an escort to their cattle truck that would be parked about a kilometer from the Hua Lampong train station.

With the blessing of the family, Tag Two and Jonathan left Home Camp by taxi to Suvarnabhumi Airport and boarded a flight to Phuket. There they were picked up by Tag Two's friend and whisked off to the elephant trekking camp. To their surprise their elephant, Rat, was waiting for them and up on his head was the sleeping white ape, Hanuman, his arms hanging down over Rat's ears. All they could do was laugh with joy.

"Oh my God," said Jonathan, "he is beautiful. I was not expecting this, he is huge and those tusks well—"

"He looks so dangerous Jonatin, those tusks well—"

"All the better to eat you with," Jonathan said.

"Huh?" Tag Two said.

"Look at the pink on his ears and the beautiful star on his forehead. Wow he is gorgeous," and Rat reached out his huge trunk to taste and smell his new owners. They were both stunned and silenced by the awesome majesty of Rat the Elephant. The old lady from the estate was there and graciously greeted them, she was relieved to see that Rat was going to a good home, even if he was going to work for a living. The first order of business was Jonathan handing over an envelope with the bank draft and registration transfer papers to the old lady. She quickly checked everything to see that all was in order, signed the papers, smiled and bowed her thanks to Jonathan.

Before leaving she said goodbye and bowed in *wei* to her old elephant friend and the sleeping ape.

Jonathan, Tag Two and the crew of the trekking camp immediately made plans for the journey north but they decided that the two must spend at least a week with Rat and Hanuman at the camp to get to know each other and understand the commands Rat knew and how to use them without anyone getting injured. Jonathan spent the next few days feeding, washing, talking, and loving Rat the Elephant.

With all the respect for elephants Jonathan cannot get an image out of his mind of a large leather trunk, the ones you find in attics and basements, the type fathers and grandfathers would have used many years ago when they visited this land. One elephant he noticed in the compound, the oldest of fifty-nine years, looked like he was wearing baggy pants. Folds of skin hung down his legs to gather at his feet, his temples were sunken and he was wrinkly all over. The old elephant gave him a good idea of what is inevitable, what he and his friends will become in the years ahead. Baggy Pants will live another ten years, maybe a little more—he is on his last set of teeth like Thunder Mountain. Funny, he thought elephant ages like humans, some show it, some don't. Such is life here in the forest of wild animals. It is the way of Buddha—perhaps years from now he will see Baggy Pants again, but as something else.

It became time for Jonathan to go solo with Rat—a little trek up the mountain. Jonathan climbed up on Rat's huge neck but the elephant was not going anywhere until he was ready, which he was after eating a few palm fronds and to pick up some veggies for the trek. Rat, from the beginning, had made it clear through his actions that theirs' would be a partnership not a master/slave relationship. He would stop for food without notice, holding it with his trunk and tusks. His huge molars crushed the fronds like humans would chew a piece of celery; the munching noise vibrated through his body. Everything Rat needs and does is multiplied many times; like Thunder Mountain he eats enormous amount of vegetation a day and drinks liters of water.

On Jonathan's prodding they walked gently and steadily up the mountain trail. Cautiously he stepped with his tree trunk legs and feet. Studying the landscape, he placed his front foot down on the trail and when he lifted it he placed his back foot exactly where the front foot had stepped. So his worries were about two feet and not four. He knows his great weight and size—he must be careful. Jonathan poked him on the back of his ears to speed him up and concentrate on the trail and not on the food. Rat took his munching time. Upward they climbed; butterflies flew around them, birds made a racket in the trees and squirrels ran ahead of them up into the trees. Reaching a pinnacle on a cliff face they stopped for a rest and he was awed by the landscape around him. To the north was a view of palms and forest that swept down to the sea and small hidden plantation villages. To the south, down a valley, was a golden Chinese temple, its standing golden Buddha shone brilliantly in the sun. The temple was the only structures in view, as the forest covered everything.

Suddenly there was a screaming and crashing going on down the hill and it came swinging up the vines and branches. It was coming after Rat and Jonathan. It was Hanuman chattering and screaming his dissatisfaction that they had left without him. Rat snorted a greeting and Hanuman jumped down from the limb of a tree and snuggled up to the back of Jonathan.

"Sorry my little friend," Jonathan said and Hanuman took his hand and kissed it.

The morning was clear and beautiful for a ride high on Rat. The rains of a typhoon that had passed over the valley in the last few days were gone. The storm had bought the forest to life after months of brutal hot weather. The high palms, green and lush in their majesty, fluttered in the breeze.

Rat didn't much care about the weather, the landscape, the people or the temple; there is always plenty of food, a bath in the swamp and now Jonathan and Tag Two to take care of him. He is the landscape and it has been that way forever.

Jonathan wondered what Rat had seen in his life and what he will see, since like Thunder Mountain he will now walk through the country side of Home Camp and the streets of Bangkok with tourists on his back. It doesn't matter, it is a good life, he still has a job that pays his rent and will always be taken care of by a loving mahout. He is one of the holy and sacred entities of Asia—then things as big as him can't be anything but holy and sacred.

Jonathan, Rat and Hanuman came down the mountain and back to the camp where the resident elephants were munching away on sugar cane and palm fronds. Some were eating pineapple plants and to tenderize them they smashed the husks against their legs and posts of their enclosures. In their all blue outfits, the mahouts were standing on the elephants' backs washing them down with water hoses and brushes. They giggled and laughed as they worked. Their happiness reminded him of Girl Two and Thunder Mountain and the enjoyment they had together in the river. It made him feel homesick. He could tell their working environment and relationships were in harmony with each other; the elephants, calm and cooperative, something corporate CEOs should look into.

Making one hell of a fuss, a three-year old standing two meters tall, was chained by one leg to the center of the coral. He wanted to join everyone in the outdoor kitchen. His young mahout about twelve years of age, fed, washed and hugged him. The two will spend their lives together. He fed the baby a batch of bananas and the little giant lifted his trunk and trumpeted a youthful blast of joy.

The next day Jonathan, Rat and Hanuman set out for the Chinese temple up the forest valley road. They climbed the access road to the temple passing under the gate of harmony and into the complex's main square. Visiting tourists stared in awe to see an elephant enter the sacred ground of Buddha and with Rat's majesty he had a right to be there. This is his land and this is were he lives and thrives along side Lord Buddha.

The temple consisted of four large buildings of pagoda style architecture; sweeping tiled roof tops capped with gold dragons snorted fire and hell. A fat gold Buddha seated on a huge black rock laughed a greeting. Jonathan dismounted Rat and barefoot he entered the temple. More dragons wrapped themselves around posts spitting fire; their huge claws grabbed the pillars, and some were reaching out for him. Sculptured and painted water was plastered below, reminiscent of the paintings of the Sung Dynasty. In their red blue and gold bodies the dragons leapt out of the sea. Huge lanterns hung from the ceiling and dominating it all was Buddha in all his shapes, sizes and gestures. The colour of everything was basic and bright: red, white, blue, yellow and accented with gold—gold everywhere. He looked back to the square; Rat unchained stood his ground watching him patiently and so did Hanuman, arms outstretched across Rat's head.

Jonathan came out and climbed a stairway to a small chapel where an old woman was fussing about. Out front, on the porch, was a large bronze bowl that held burning joss sticks. Cryptic symbols and languages decorated its girth and wrapped around it was bright cloth and jasmine wreaths. In the chapel he came across a moneybox and boxes of joss sticks beside it. He made a donation and took three sticks, lit them and placed them in the bowl to burn. There are many gods in this world living in many houses; he tries to recognize them all.

He left the temple and checked on Rat who was enjoying the attention of some tourist. Suddenly a woman screamed as Rat tried to stick his trunk up her dress to smell her. She jumped back and her husband roared with laughter. Rat made a little dance with his front feet and curled his trunk. Hanuman had jumped off Rat's back and was chasing a temple dog around the compound. The dog was yapping and barking with delight, they seemed to know each other. A monk stood by looking a little miffed because Rat had crapped in the compound. And I'm going to have to live with these two, Jonathan thought.

He walked up the mountain to another edifice, the one that towers over the complex. He climbed the red stairs with white cement handrails. A thirty foot gold Buddha, standing tall and in peace, was looking out over the valley below and all of Thailand off to the east.

It was beautiful and peaceful in the forest with a bright clear sky overhead. Looking down over the green landscape with its different culture and people buried into it, he thought I am a stranger here; it is not my place and never will be; our cultures and beliefs are so different. People here live in harmony day to day—tomorrow will take care of itself and the past is gone. They have Lord Buddha, the King and the Nation—each one is revered.

Jonathan stood at the foot of the gold Buddha and looked down the valley. Up to the right and among a forest of palms he saw a large boulder move. It was Baggy Pants with his mahout and tourists on board. What a great day, he thought as he went to save the tourists from Rat the Elephant and Hanuman, the Great Ape.

Night Train to Bangkok

"Careful Jonathan," Tag Two said, "if he gets you up against the hording he'll crush you. Stay under his belly. He weighs a good many tons."

"If he takes a piss now, I'll drown. I think I have him hitched. Give me a hand to get out of here," and Jonathan reached up and his partner helped him up to the top of the hoarding, "He's held fast and won't hit the side of the carriage and if he wants to relax he can ease his weight down on the cargo straps. He's also fast forward and aft. He's going nowhere."

"I'll load the food up to you and just pile it up around him. I'll take the first three hour watch," Tag Two said and he jumped down from the cattle car to the ground and handed sugar cane, corn stalks and palm fronds up to Jonathan who made them fast with rope to the hoarding surrounding the huge elephant. After loading the food they stored a number of ten-litter plastic bottles of water and a galvanized tub at the front of the cattle car. A plastic lounge chair with cushions and a shovel to clean the elephant dung over the side were the last things to load. Everything was placed in front of the elephant but just out of reach of his roving, playful trunk.

The passenger train arrived and pulled up alongside the spur line and Tag Two gave the engineer the signal that all was ready. Passengers hung out the window with smiles and cheers for the two men; one straddled an elephant with an ape on his head; the other, a white man, rode the hoarding of the cattle car. At the stationmaster's command the train backed up with a shudder and thump onto the spur to the cattle car; a yardman hooked it to the train. Tag Two signaled the conductor who signaled the engineer and the night train to Bangkok was underway.

Jonathan hugged the elephant, which was quite calm to their surprise, "Good boy—good boy. I'm going inside, see you soon Tag Two," he said and climbed over the front hoarding to the deck of the restaurant car. He went inside and down its aisle to the next car, a second-class passenger coach. He took the seat that was reserved for him and Tag Two and relaxed for the next three hours.

The heat was intense on board the train, it was not the latest model, all the windows of the train were open and fans in the ceiling swayed back and forth. The seats were hard and the décor was somewhat industrial; lime green and steel gray Government Issue. Four people could sit to a booth and he sat beside an old nut-brown woman with no teeth who did not acknowledge he existed. Perhaps she had had a man like him many years ago or maybe she was just tired from the hard work Thailand demands of its people. Opposite him were two Thais who looked like cherubs, a short round, roly-poly, smiling, giggling father and son. Mother took a seat in the next booth down. The boy could not keep his eyes off Jonathan; he probably had never seen a blonde haired blue eyed person from the west before and he was with the elephant out the back of the train. He was a cute little man and dressed like his father in three quarter length pants and a t-shirt with an alligator on the upper chest. Squat running shoes were on his chubby feet. Dad was something else again; he had a huge mouth of shinning white teeth, all of different sizes and going in different directions. They were so large his teeth force him into a constant smile. The two loved each other and hugged constantly.

Across the aisle were two young wives with their babies and sleeping husbands. The women chatted away and breastfed their hungry children. A teenage boy was in a booth behind them and he held a black, red and gold rooster in his arms. The bird's head was under the boy's shirt and was calm and serene; held by his master who was taking him to the chicken fights. The proud rooster maybe food in the pot before the night is over.

Vendors came down the aisle every few minutes with food and drink in pails and baskets. Buckets of ice carried, tea, juice, pop and beer. Some baskets were filled with clear packages of cut apples, eggplants, beets, cucumbers, carrots, pumpkin, sugar cane and onions, all skillfully carved to resemble flowers. With the flowers came *nam phrik*, a pork and chili dip. Bags of newspaper packages of cooked rice, noodles, vegetables, pork, chicken and beef gave off aromas of chili and curry—all around Jonathan were happy Thais. Baskets of candy and pastries found their way to his booth as the cherubs were buying up everything.

"You own elephant mister?" a woman vendor said to Jonathan. She had a tray of chicken and rice dinners in foam packages for sale.

"Yes I do," Jonathan said.

"Where you take it?"

"To our farm outside of Bangkok, to where he will live a good life."

"Very nice, I love elephant, everyone love elephant. You take good care," and she handed him a dinner. Jonathan reached for his wallet, "No, no pay, you good man to take care of elephant. You let me touch elephant later? Be my first time to touch thing that is close to Lord Buddha."

"Yes of course you can, maybe in an hour and after you have finished with your selling. What's your name?"

"My name Toy, what yours?"

"My name is Jonathan."

"Jonatin, very good, that be nice, I see you soon. I hurry now, got lot of customers," and off she went singing praises of her merchandise.

The train swayed, bobbed, clicked and clacked its way down the track that was straight and true as it pierced the landscape kilometer after kilometer. Hundred of thousands of hectares on each side of the track were planted in rice. The ponds spread out across the land, their monotony broken by tall royal palms that stood out alone. About every quarter of an hour the train would rumble by a hamlet and noble cows and their herd women would stop their business to watch the train rumble by. The cows are beautiful animals, huge and skinny with enormous brown eyes. In the shade of fig trees Jonathan could make out the shapes of tank sized black buffaloes, the old laborers of the rice fields.

Wats and religious complexes loomed over trees and houses and dominated the villages and cities. Huge multiple gabled roofs of red and gold flew on white pillars; *cho fa* tassels of the air thrust spines into the sky from the peaks of the temple rooftops. They are the fierce birds of Hindu mythology. Tall spiked gold leafed chedi thrust into the blue throughout the complexes, structures that hold pieces of Sidhartha—the man who became Buddha. Everywhere gold leaf and bright colours paint the delicate architecture of the temples. Among the trees in the grounds was the Bodhi tree; the tree that Buddha sat beneath in his attempt to achieve enlightenment. Floating in walking meditation in all their grandeur were bald monks in their orange robes. After many life times of reincarnation they will gain enough merit to end the cycle of karma and achieve Nirvana. He thought of Monk and the conversations they had.

The train stopped to let passengers on and off and Jonathan's cherub family bought more little newspaper packages of food and boxes of juice from vendors on the platform. The mother protests but it was no good, she could not help her little family from getting bigger and filling up the train. The woman next to him said nothing and the babies in the next booth were being well fed on mothers' milk. For a brief moment the chicken got loose and to everyone's delight the young boy chased him down the aisle.

Everything sweated and swayed and the sweet smell of bodies and spicy food hung in the air. The fans and open windows did nothing to make things comfortable. Jonathan smelled his wet shirt—he smelled okay. The two mothers fanned their sleeping children and leaned against their sleeping husbands. His rotund family snored but soon woke and summoned a passing vendor for a few packages of fruit, barbequed beef on sticks and packages of rice. They were filling up the train, eating their way to the north of Thailand.

Jonathan's three-hour watch was to begin so he left his chubby friends and made his way to the cattle car.

"Everything going well Tag Two?"

"Yes, I'm amazed how well he's doing. He has no fear at all in him and seems very comfortable. Watch out for his water drinking, he is mischievous and sprays water everywhere. Give him a bit at a time and not enough to play with; see you in a few hours. By the way he has just crapped and it's your shift" Tag Two jumped over the hoarding laughing and disappeared into the train.

He shoveled the dung over the side and few minutes late he heard, "Jonatin— Mr. Jonatin. Are you there?

"Climb up the hoarding Toy," and she did, dropping down on the other side to him and the elephant. She stood there in disbelief at the huge beast in front of her with a sleeping ape stretched out on its huge head. The elephant reached out to her and she backed up, screamed and put her arms around Jonathan. Hanuman woke up but did not move.

"It's all right Toy, he smells you to see who you are."

"But his nose is hard, cold and wet," she cried.

"Of course it is and so is yours," and they laughed. She reached out and touched his trunk.

"He is so tough and hairy. I did not know elephants are hairy." "A few months ago I didn't know they were hairy either, in fact I didn't know anything about elephants. All I knew was they had big ears and feet."

"Oh his eyes they are like my Mother's—amber," She moved to the elephant and without fear walked between his two huge tusks and put her arms and cheek on his trunk. The chattering of the train's wheels echoed up from the tracks. The light from the open door of the restaurant car shone through the wooden hoarding of the cattle car onto Toy and Rat, melting their bodies together in bands of dark and light. Jonathan felt the bonding between them; two beings of the landscape and culture of Thailand; two beings—children of Lord Buddha. Jonathan felt something was happening to him, but it was not about him, things or places anymore, there was something else coming into his life; something he could not stop and he welcomed it. She held onto Rat for the longest time and the beast did not move. Jonathan leaned against the hoarding and watched as the two of them gently swayed with the movement of the train, she said something in Thai, softly in a whisper and ended it in "...Lord Buddha," She moved away from the elephant and as she turned to him a band of light coming through the hoarding made her deep black eyes sparkle, "I must get back to work now Mr. Jonatin. Thank you very much," and she *wei-ed* to him, "a peasant girl like me from the north and the rice fields does not get near such things. I touched my heart tonight." and she climbed over the hoarding and into the train.

Jonathan got on the phone to Girl One who was waiting for his call and order, "Hi Girl One, I have some changes to be made." and he spent the next few minutes describing them and when he was finished he gave the order to initiate the global media release to the Kingdom of Thailand.

The train rolled into a small village station and Jonathan heard a commotion from his train car, he looked down the side of the cars and there was his rotund family reaching out the window, a vendor handed them some newspaper packages and chopsticks as the train pulled away. The scolding wife was pulling her son away from the window. A giant toothy grin smiled back at him and a chubby hand waved before it disappeared into the window.

Three hours had gone by for Jonathan, the elephant and the ape.

They had a snooze, something to eat and drink and Jonathan still had about fifty pounds of elephant dung to take care of—he shoveled it overboard. Tag Two had not arrived for his watch so he climbed over the hoarding and into the train to find him fast asleep. The fat family and old woman were gone and Tag Two took up the whole booth and snored to everyone's amusement. "Wake up," Jonathan said giving his partner a nudge. Tag Two awoke with a snort.

"How's everything?" said a bewildered Tag Two, rubbing his eyes.

"Buddha and his buddy are waiting to be watered. Your watch has begun."

"Buddha?"

"Yeah, Buddha, that's his new name, there is no way he can have that other name. Rat means something else in other languages and not suitable for an elephant who will be carrying foreign passengers around."

"So it's Buddha then. I guess it's all right, they name boats after him."

The e-mail went out to the media across Thailand. The title was: BUDDHA WILL ARRIVE ON THE NIGHT TRAIN TO BANGKOK followed by time, place and the signature, HOME CAMP. It was late at night but he knew he would stir up curiosity among reporters and journalists—and it did. Many got on the phone to Thailand Rail and inquired what was going on and it slipped out that the passenger train was pulling a cattle car—something not allowed. That was the reason for the late release. Whatever was on board was not supposed to be there. This looked to some that the story might be fun and of human interest and relief from the bad news of the last year.

The night train to Bangkok pulled into Hua Lampong Station on track number four and at the end of the platform was the cattle car. Jonathan jumped from the passenger car and ran down to the waiting elephant and opened the side gate of the hoarding. The sun was up and the sky was a pinkish haze, the lights from the station shone into the car and there stood Buddha, in all his majesty. A red and gold silk sash lay across his back and hung down dripping gold tassels that almost touched the ground and on side of the sash were figures from the Ramakien—Rama and Sita. Across Buddha's forehead was draped a headpiece of the same red and gold fabric with the embroidery of Naga. On each tusk was wrapped a garland of tassels. Anklets, with gold tassels, were wrapped about his huge feet. Tag Two beamed at his creation and hugged Jonathan. Sitting on Buddha's back was Hanuman with a yellow kerchief around his neck. Jonathan was in awe; Mother had done such a fine job with her sewing skills. Jonathan and Tag Two were dressed in their mahout blues and barefoot. They both put on yellow kerchiefs.

Gently Tag Two led Buddha out of the cattle car and onto the platform and the disembarking passengers cheered, clapped and bowed at the sight of a resplendent elephant in the train station. Buddha crouched and Jonathan climbed up onto his neck, Hanuman frightened of all the people and the huge station snuggled up to Jonathan's back. Tag Two, holding onto a gold braided rope tied around Buddha's neck, gently led Buddha down the platform—the press and television arrived full of smiles and laughter at the great site and fun.

To Jonathan's relief the entourage squeezed through the station doors and into the morning sunlight. Police officers were everywhere with their motorbikes and cars, the commander, smiling for the cameras, was waiting for them on the side of the road and he would personally escort them to the waiting cattle truck a kilometer away.

"Hey mahout!" shouted a reporter, "environmentalists want you and your elephants off the streets of Bangkok—"

"Yeah I know and back in the forest. How long do you think this elephant with those tusks would last out there?"

"It is still exploitation, is it not?" shouted another.

"Buddha is a working elephant and a domestic animal, a product of your country. He represents the giant elephant that is Asia emerging onto the world." Jonathan was surprised at that statement. Not bad, he thought. Buddha moved down the road encouraged by Tag Two and escorted by a couple of dozen police officers. Along the side of the road were hundreds of children dressed in school uniforms. They had heard on Thai radio that Buddha was coming to town so they arrived before school opening to cheer him.

"You say you will use the elephant, Buddha, as a teaching instrument. What do you intend to do?" a reporter asked, scribbling notes.

"In the off season, when we won't be working in Bangkok, we will take Buddha and his friend Hanuman, the ape, to the schools where the children will be able to touch and ride him. Many children never get to experience such a thing. Hopefully they will become the champions for the Asian elephants in the future."

"Why are you doing all this, is it about the money you will make from this beast?" a man shouted from behind a television camera.

"How did you manage to get Buddha here by passenger train?" asked another, "did you pay someone off?" Jonathan glanced at the commander who also heard the question and they smiled at each other.

"Are you the mahout who rode the elephant on Khaosan Road during the bombings?"

Jonathan avoided the questions, "To touch an elephant is to touch your heart. That is what this is about. Those children there," and he swept his hand across the scene of hundreds of children, "it's about them and Buddha the elephant not us. They are the future and the future of this elephant. Both must get to know each other if they are to live together. There will be a few billion more people born in Asia in the next ten or more years. Unfortunately wild animal habitat will disappear. Those species who survive will be the ones living in harmony with us on farms and cities across Asia."

By now Hanuman was getting used to all the attention and stood up on the elephants back, raised his spindly arms and waved back and forth, the children waved back and cheered. They were in sight of the Home Camp cattle truck and there was Buddha and Hanuman's new family, Mother, Girl One, Girl Two, Naga and the chickens. A stalk of bananas was hung on the hoarding. The women waved and Jonathan could see giant smiles on their faces and they all bowed to the new members of their family. He felt the pride of his family wash up the street to him and Tag Two. They had worked hard for this moment. For Jonathan a ghost image of Thunder Mountain rose up around the cattle truck and the remembrance of happy times flooded over him. He was breathless from the emotion of the moment and he wished that naughty beast were here today. No, Jonathan thought he is here, he is all around us and so is Tag.

"Are you saying you can save the Asian elephant from extinction?" a reporter shouted as he scrambling out of the path of Buddha.

No, but we will try."

"Jonathan—Jonathan Owen—Rube Waterton, Global Media Association—GMA," Oh Christ, he thought someone knows me. He turned and saw a blonde English woman, her camera came up to her face and three shots were taken in rapid succession. She smiled a knowing smile and Jonathan gave her a knowing smile back, she had obviously done a little research on this rogue, Jonathan B. Owen. They were at the truck and Buddha climbed the gangway and reached out his trunk to his new family to smell them and they reached out to him. Jonathan jumped off Buddha onto the hoarding and down to the deck of the cattle truck and hugged everyone. He climbed over the hoarding and jumped down onto the street.

"Are you going to spoil the day, Ms?" he whispered to her.

Rube Waterton looked over to the children. "Of course not, you have come along way Jonathan. This time I think it has been a good journey. What do you want to say to the world?"

He paused to think for a moment. He looked at the cattle truck and his Asian family. This tribe of refugees without names just labels, bundles of life shipped to Thailand—oh how he loved them. How will they survive against the bigger elephant? They will survive like the billions before them and the billions that will come after them. How will he, Jonathan Owen come out in the end and is it anything to worry about? It all doesn't matter for nothing is permanent. He looked at the cattle trucks door and on it was painted the words Home Camp and above the name were three butterflies painted gray, yellow and orange. He looked up to the hoarding and Girl One gave him a huge smile.

With a glint of mischief in his eye he turned to the crowd of reporters and said, "If you're ever in Bangkok and you see an old white mahout and his ape riding an elephant—climb aboard. Listen closely and he will tell you stories you won't believe.

Five

The Seven Stones

Mexico Guatemala Belize Cuba

Naked, starved and near death he and dragged himself onto the dock in Santiago de Cuba harbor. He looked around at his new world; he shook and urinated from fear – terror was in his eyes. He did not know where he was or whom all the strange people were who had come to meet the ship. They wore odd clothes and talked a strange language, but he knew they were doing business that involved him and the three hundred slaves that were with him. He vomited from fear and the stench of naked bodies covered with excrement. They cried from their ordeal and the loss of loved ones during their terrible three-week journey from Sierra Leon, Africa. There were no dead on board; he and other slaves had thrown the bodies overboard the day before. He did not mind the chore – he could see the sun and breathe the fresh sea air for a few minutes.

The master of the deck barked an order and the three hundred were led away to holding pens. Groups of ten were bought out onto a platform for inspection of their teeth, hands, feet, genitals, and injuries. Finely dressed gentlemen and others with whips looked them over. Some were black like him. Women screamed and cried for their men and babies that were torn from them. Some thought they were being sold as food like common cattle.

A bargain was struck and his new owner gave him a Christian name, Joseph, which was written next to his African tribal name in the owner's roster. He was shackled and shoved into the back of a horse drawn wagon. The wagon clattered down the street, across Santiago de Cuba and into the country of his new world. Within him were special things that he would give to his new home: music, art, religion and the most special of all – the genetics of his race.

Santiago de Cuba
A.m. May 7, 1782.

Isla Mujeres, Mexico (today)

He had done what she had instructed him to do. This better be good, he said to himself. Jonathan paid the taxi driver, slung his bags over his shoulder, crossed the cobbled street and entered the casa. He had spent the last twenty-four hours on trains, planes and boats getting to the Island from Home Camp in Bangkok.

"My name is Christmas," the young Maya said with a milky voice, "and you are Mr. Owen?"

"Yes I am, Jonathan Owen, please call me Jonathan."

"Fine, this way please," and Christmas led him to his reserved apartment in a building fronting the village's main street. Through a window in the caretaker's quarters came a huge smile on the chubby face of a young man who quickly disappeared. "That's Ismael." Christmas said, "He is my wife."

Christmas was a Maya between thirty-five and forty with black straight greasy hair; a large hooked nose that sloped down from a laid back forehead and below thick black eyebrows where large white eyes with deep black pupils. A mouth full of bright teeth shone from deep reddish purple lips. His body was lean and dark skinned—no fat just lean muscles. He was slick, mean and shifty looking to Jonathan.

"You have all the conveniences: stove, fridge, bathroom with daily fresh towels and sheets. You have a double bed and air con. Will you need a woman?"

"No, but I'll think about that."

"Anything you require, I'm in the main block across from your apartment. Here are your keys." He threw them on the bed.

Jonathan put his suitcase and backpack on the bed and quickly came to the reason why he was there. "When did you last hear from her?"

"Yesterday, she asked when you would arrive and I told her today."

"I see. Did you actually see her?"

"No, she has always emailed me. I do not know her, what she looks like and I don't know how she knows me. I receive money in an email pay system and instructions on what to do. From here on I don't think she will be in contact with me again since you are now on the island. You are someone she wants here for some reason. She has paid your rent for the month and you are instructed to enjoy yourself; she will contact you soon. There is a list on your table of restaurants, bars and coffee shops where she has accounts. Is she rich?"

"No, she isn't rich. Why do you ask?"

"Someone should pay for extra services. Don't you think?"

"I don't know Christmas. I won't be paying for any, if that is what you're asking. All I know is the apartment is paid for. Right?"

"Yes it is," Christmas, said, "she sounds very scary, is she?"

"Damn right--damn right."

"I will see you later. Enjoy your stay," and he left the apartment.

Instructed to enjoy myself? She is such a bitch; he chuckled.

Isla Mujeres is off the northeast coast of the Yucatan Peninsula, Mexico, an island of the state of Quintana Roo, seven kilometers long and about a half-kilometer wide and in some places just a few hundred meters. It is packed with people who are mostly fishing families: decedents of Maya, Spanish conquistadors, African slaves and pirates. In recent years a great number of entrepreneurs from around the world have settled on the island to try their luck in the booming tourist industry of Cancun that is a twenty-minute ferry ride away. In the morning thousands of tourists arrive by ferry to enjoy the food, drink and beaches. The sunburned happy lot all leave by late afternoon and the island goes back to the Mexican, Maya and people like Jonathan.

Devil winds out of Africa explode out of the southeast and batter the island; very few structures get finished on this windy place and most everything is in some state of decay. The coast on the Caribbean Sea is rocky with crumbling limestone cliffs; small bays are filled with shells and coral and the waters are teaming with animal life, it makes for the best scuba diving in the world. Plants and trees hug the ground wherever they can find a foothold; they are stunted because of the constant winds that blow across the craggy rock and nutrient poor soil. Iguanas take advantage of the sun baked rocky coast to heat up their bodies.

His days on the island start out with getting up late, cleaning up and taking a taxi to town from his casa on Salina Grande. Sounds boring for someone in the tropics but the day would unfold as it does everyday on Jonathan travels and something new, awesome or terrifying will come his way. Out on the road life usually turns out a head shaker for him.

"How much to town?" Jonathan asked the taxi driver.

"Twenty pesos," replied a bored over weight islander.

"Christ," Jonathan said, as he got into the cab, "last night it was ten and the other day—twenty five. Why is it I get ripped off by you guys everywhere I go in the world?"

"It is the way," the driver said, local people get a special rate and you white folk get another special rate."

"So I have noticed—centro, por favor."

He had coffee and a double seeded bagel with cream cheese at his favorite café on Ave. Matamoros. After he had his chat about nothing with the shop owner he made his way to the Café on North Beach where he took a lounge chair under a white umbrella. The morning sun was intense by then and everything sweated and slept. Offshore, a hundred yards out in light greenish blue water, the shadows of manta rays glided back and forth. He went out to them but could only get within twenty feet; they shied away to the deep blue depths a short distance from their shallow feeding grounds.

On shore a diet cola was waiting, from his smiling waiter.

"Buenos dias, señor Jonathan," he said with a broad smile of healthy white teeth. He had acclimatized into island life nicely in the last few days. If you get into a routine eventually the service staff knows you. Jonathan relaxed the best he could in the intense heat and humidity, and took in the spectacular view across the Bahia de Isla Mujeres.

In the distance on the flat expanse of the Yucatan peninsula huge clouds formed many miles inland, perhaps at Chechen Itza he surmised, a place where terrible gods live—a place in ancient times of sacrifice and death. He would be going there very soon; his time on the island was running out. She would be calling him.

In the meantime it was time for work, work that he usually does on his travels. In his own style he draws and records what he sees and keeps in contact through email with his families. He feels he has to keep busy; he has worked all his life and cannot stop just because of retirement. He set himself up at a table under the huge palapa of the restaurant, turned on his laptop and tapped into the wireless service. He wrote to his families in Canada and Thailand.

The night before at his casa he had started something different from the usual art in his sketchbook, something exciting for him. He pulled the sketchbook from his daypack and tuned to the page where he had started a drawing of the head and features of her as he remembered them. He ordered coffee with cream and in the next few hours would draw his disturbing friend and former lover. Today he would make her the female version of one of the most beloved, fearsome and violent gods of old Yucatan.

Jonathan tangled and matted her hair like he had seen on mad people he has encountered muttering and wandering the streets of big cities. The mass was tied together with cords, strings and threads. Beads, amulets, soul catchers and other objects spiritual to her were scattered in her hair. The tangled mass surrounded a huge black-eyed face, primitive in looks like some young male Maya warrior. This came about after the drawing progressed and he illustrated her anatomy of large firm breasts, wide pelvis, long thighs and thin waist.

Her lying position was leaning back, her upper body held up on her elbows, her head looking left to her audience and her legs drawn up with feet flat on stone ground. In her hands, shattered from defensive wounds from hand-to-hand combat, she held a sacrificial bowl. Held on her belly it contained several human hearts. Not sacrificial hearts but the emblematic hearts of her passed lovers. He was creating Señorita Chac, the female version of Chac. One of the gods stone alters called Chacmool sits at the top of the staircase of the Temple of The Warriors at Chechen Itza. Chac is the rain god of the ancient Maya and responsible for the murder of thousands, perhaps millions of Maya. The Maya's religion, as many of the religions of the world, performed murder in the name of a god. The Maya called theirs' sacrifice.

He wanted her to be made of stone like her disgusting relative at Chichen Itza. To achieve this he drew pebbles and bits of rock over her body but he got into shading her anatomy too well and these added textures and blemishes made her look like she had many diseases and wounds. That was all right though; it all kind of made sense to him.

Time was passing and Jonathan looked up from Señorita Chac and out to sea he noticed the clouds had reached the coast of the Yucatan and were about to embark across the bay to the restaurant. One leading cloud in particular was huge blossoming like some atomic explosion or erupting volcano, below it and across the horizon was a deep gray and violent black hole of rain. Lightning flashed up the cloud column—it was still too distant to hear thunder.

The drawing of Señorita Chac was now really coming to life under Jonathan's drafting pen and the waiters were getting excited at what she was becoming and they recognized immediately who she was.

She had company—three graces. He thought if Venus could have three caretakers then his Señorita Chac could have some. These creatures were unlike Botticelli's women dancing gracefully among flowers. They were ugly little things flying to her from some awful assignment. There were weapons in their hands and on a spike was the heart of a human. One was so powerful she had two right hands. They were returning from their dirty work to nest in Señorita Chac's hair. They would fly out and dance on her face whenever they pleased. These are the creatures that dwell in her and make her do the things that she does—so he believes.

"Jonathan, you bad man, you bring Chac to Café," said his waiter pointing out to the approaching chaos—they both laughed.

Señorita Chac was becoming more evil looking with her diseased body and slashes of scars from ancient battles etched into her skin. Her black eyes looked through her tangled mass of hair into his heart. The smile of her large lips reflected more of her madness and contempt for him. He couldn't have been more pleased at what was going on. It is easy to do a portrait of someone but to illustrate a personality—that is difficult.

Suddenly the waiters left the restaurant for the beach, closed the umbrellas and told the customers to come under the protection of the palapa. They all gathered at the tables and ordered lunch. It looked like it was all arranged. Jonathan watched a wall of black water out in the bay on its way to the cafe; the sea boiled and violently shook the pleasure crafts anchored offshore. Normally small swells come to the beach but now they were two-meter giants—the sun ran away. A crashing boom and a flash exploded a few hundred yards out. He felt Chac had come to see him and five hundred years ago, he probably would have been right. The pages of Jonathan's sketchbook rattled and flipped closed, his pen box top snapped shut sending pens and pencils to the floor, napkins flew off the table. He closed his sketchbook picked up his pens and reorganized the table. The wind blew, the waiters became serious and customers murmured.

Oh hell, he thought am I going to have to pay for tampering with the gods? A deafening roar and blinding flash of orange told him Chac was right over the palapa. Suddenly the god was gone; the sun came back, the sea became quiet and the boats bobbed gently.

He looked out across the bay and deep in the Yucatan he could see half a dozen giant warriors swelling into the sky. Gently he opened his sketchbook—she was still there. Jonathan's waiter smiled at him, he smiled back and ordered a margarita.

Jonathan made one last check of his email and to his astonishment he had a special message. How appropriate he thought.

To: Jonathan B. Owen

Hello Jonathan darling,

You must have had the shock of your life hearing I was still alive? Well I am and still the woman that you have always known. I have been in touch with Annabelle. I did online business with her to get details about you and your email address. I must say you have quite a life in Bangkok.

I apologize for what happened in PV but I had to keep you out of everything. If you had known about my work in Mexico you would have been killed. I will not go into details of what went down those many months ago. We will get into that when we meet, and I do want to see you and I know you want to see me. You have come all this way from Thailand my dear friend.

They (and, they, will be kept unknown to you) put me away for the last year; shipped me around the world doing clerical work. A real shitty time of being anonymous – being a-nobody for the rest of my life. I escaped from them in Germany, and now I am free and thinking about the future. They have seized my bank accounts and I can't work anywhere as they will find me and take me back or kill me so I have called on you my dear lover to help me with something I must do. I must make some money that will do me the rest of my life. Christmas has been my buffer in case you are being watched and your email monitored. I know much about him and he knows nothing about me and that will be best for him. Be careful, your life has been monitored in the past, as you well know. Stay unnoticed my love; I will be following you to see if you are being followed. Do not look for me. You will not see me.

You like adventure so we will have one. I know you and you will not be able to resist what I have in mind and known for so many years. It will be dangerous. Do not reply to this email.

Love you,

Tula

Jonathan read the email over and over tying to make sense of it and why he was putting up with this woman. He ordered another drink and asked himself: Christ, why am I here reading this crap from a crazy woman? I have a good life now with my family in Bangkok. I don't need the money, what with my fixed pension and a stash of money in banks around the world. I'm in need of nothing. I have the best of friend, family and Buddha, my elephant that loves me. The big elephant and I am the Kings of Khaosan Road. My Thai family is the dearest bunch of people one could ever know and over us all is the big Buddha himself with all his simplicity. My kids are doing well in their businesses and yet here I am on an island in the Caribbean in contact with a pirate/slave/witch/bitch who can only bring harm my way. The waiter returned with his drink.

"I need a shrink," he said in frustration.

"And here it is Mr. Jonathan, your shrink,"

"Yeah," he said with a sigh.

Midnight arguments started erupting at the casa. One-night things got out of hand; he could not sleep for all the shouting crying and beatings that were taking place in Christmas's apartment. He pulled on his underwear and walked across the courtyard and banged on the superintendent's door.

"Christmas—Christmas! What's going on?" The crying and shouting stopped and the door opened. Christmas stood there in his underwear sweat ran down his chest, his hair flared out in all directions and his eyes bulged from his head.

"We are playing a game and she is loosing. Good night Mr. Owen." And he slammed the door shut. Jonathan raised his fist to bang the door again but thought what the hell, and went back to his apartment. But something worked as there was no crying and shouting again, at least while he was in earshot.

A week went by and Jonathan noticed he was loosing money from his wallet. He decided to test what was going on with his two caretaker friends. He put five one hundred pesos notes in his wallet and left it on his night table. When Ismael came to change his sheets Jonathan said, I'll go for a walk while you do your business. He walked along the shoreline for twenty minutes and returned to the casa. Ismael had finished making up the room and had left. Jonathan checked his wallet that was still on the night table. A one hundred peso note was missing. Immediately Jonathan banged on Christmas's door.

"Christmas!" he yelled and Christmas opened the door, "Ismael has been stealing from me," Jonathan said angrily. Ismael peeked over Christmas's shoulder, Christmas turned to look at him and then back to Jonathan. They both shrugged their shoulders and Christmas closed the door.

"Well you son-of-a-bitch!" Jonathan said to the closed door and went to his apartment. He sent a reply to Tula on the email he was told not to.

Hey babe,

I have to send you this note because I'm moving. Your little friend and his lover are thieves and stealing my money. I confronted them about it and they just don't care. I fear they will just keep taking my things. I have bought a few valuables with me and I don't want to loose them, and hell, it's the principle of the whole thing.

I am moving to Valladolid. You'll find me around the town square or you can instruct me where to stay. Sorry love but I can no longer tolerate those little bastards.

Love JO

Jonathan sat on a high stool at the bar nursing his beer thinking of his family and the animals at Home Camp in Thailand. He missed them. The sun was setting in the west off North Beach and the flat landscape of the Yucatan could be seen in the distance; a place he would be leave for in the morning. The blonde drunk woman at the bar that was chatting him up decided to move on when there was no response from him. A large dark fat man with a scar down his jaw took her place on the stool. Jonathan had noticed him earlier waiting his turn to talk to him. A feeling of dread swept over him.

"Here on vacation?" the fat man queried.

"Nnn—Yes I am, just a couple of weeks in the sun," Jonathan said cautiously, "and you?"

"The same, but I find the heat difficult for a fat guy like me," and they both laughed, "My name is Charlie," and he stuck out his hand for Jonathan to shake.

"Nice meeting you Charlie—I'm Jonathan,"

"So what do you do for a living?"

"I'm a mahout."

"A what?"

"A mahout, the guy you see in pictures riding on the neck of an elephant. Actually I'm retired and I sort of fell into this new job in Bangkok."

"Oh really," Charlie said, "some job." The non-believer look was on his face.

"Really," Jonathan said and he reached into his back pocket, pulled out his wallet, rummage through it and took out a picture of him on his elephant Buddha in a market in Bangkok, "men usually carry pictures of their women with them, me, I carry a picture of my elephant. I miss him."

"Well isn't that interesting," Charlie said a bit baffled. They spent the next hour talking about the care, feeding and training of elephants; something Jonathan loved to do. The subject soon got around to women and he felt he must be careful. Charlie's questions where becoming personal and probing.

"Do you have a woman?"

"My past is full of them since I've been on the move for years. But—no—not anymore. At one time I did love someone, in Mexico but that seems a million years away."

"What happed to her?" A critical question thought Jonathan.

"She committed suicide one day and I left Mexico for what I thought was for good."

"I'm sorry to hear of your loss. And now you're back?" Another critical question.

"Yeah, I needed a break from Thailand and the last year of work, it's an eighteen hour day with an elephant you know. I've never worked so hard in my life."

"I understand," Charlie, said, "well it's best I be off, I've an early morning fishing charter tomorrow. Good night Jonathan, it's been nice talking to you," and he rose and shook his hand, "you have a good life my friend."

"Good night Charlie. Maybe we will see each other again."

"No doubt, it's a small island," and he left the bar. He watched him walk away. He noticed Charlie had a slight limp and he thought he knows me and he was fishing with me tonight.

Cantina

Charlie leaned against an algae covered wall at the top of the road; he was damp from a short shower that had swept over Valladolid. Hunched over, he had a good view of the cantina where Jonathan drank and did his art. He could see up and down the main street where she might appear. In an instant the world stopped, a feeling of dread closed in and he felt her deadly presence behind him. He held his breath. His defenses were down – no time.

"Hey, it's so good to— " He could not say anything more. A knife blade cut into his throat. He dropped to his knees; he could not move but to slightly turn his head and see her one last time. She bent down and kissed him on the lips.

"Goodbye Charlie," she whispered.

He dropped to the sidewalk; she removed the knife and stepped over him. In the darkness his head lay awkwardly on the sidewalk; life oozed out of him in a black stream of blood and urine that flowed into the gutter. He watched her casually move down the street and disappear around a corner. His last thoughts were of his youth; swimming and fishing with his friends on the waterway where he grew up. Death can be lonely away from home.

In Valladolid, a colonial town the capital of Yucatan, Jonathan found a comfortable room over looking the town square. One morning he caught the 9:30 a.m. bus to the most famous temple ruins of Maya Mexico, Chechen Itza. The site is now one of the seven modern wonders of the world. Why, Jonathan asked—it's nothing but a place of death and evil.

His bus pulled up to the impressive edifice, the main entrance to the complex of the temple park. He went to the ticket center and above the booth was a poster plastered to the concrete. It was in Spanish and he could only make out a few words but with the photo they were enough—Luciano Pavoratti was dead. Jonathan's world lags a few days behind and he did not know that this great artist had come to his end. And on a poster nearby there was something else he did not know; the opera star had performed at Chichen Itza in 1997. His thoughts went out to the great opera star, he had a good run at life and he admired him for that and of course his incredible voice—a gift to the world.

He bought his entrance ticket and a guard attached an orange band to his wrist. He entered another world, eight hundred years ago. Jonathan's weird madness stepped in. His doctors have called it madness and he blames the gift on too many drugs when he was a young man discovering his talents in art school—and then there were the malaria pills a few years ago—then maybe it was..."

At 11:30 a.m. out in the great courtyard the heat was in the forties—Jonathan was sweating terribly. Will we white guys ever get used to this tropical heat, he said to himself. Around him were the Maya; they had come for the ceremonies to witness the sacrifices to be made to the coming season and Chac the rain God, who for today's ceremony is the most important of all the deities. He gives life to all in the forest but at a terrible cost.

Glistening in the sun, the white pyramid with its bloodied masked priests and entourage, stood above them. The crowd could only see what was at the edge of the platform at the top—almost at the level with the gods. There was some shuffling going on and then horrible screams were heard, the crowd at the base of the pyramid, cheered in celebration. Bamboo and leather drums beat and conches moaned out their cries.

"Did we score, did we win?" Jonathan said to a Maya standing next to him who was dressed in another man's flayed skin. No! He saw a head roll down the steep stairs and a body after it. They reach the bottom and the body was torn apart by a number of blood soaked warriors and distributed among the crowd.

Nearby in a courtyard a bound man was bought forward to stand on a stone platform so all could see and jeer him. His hysterical accuser was shouting at him. He was an adulteress and his accuser wanted retribution. The accuser's wife stood nearby in terror for her fate was next, if her husband wished, she would be stoned to death. The judge, a civil servant dressed in feathers and wearing a hideous mask offered options to the accuser; let him go free with his sins forgiven or take his life. The accuser wanted his life. The judge ordered his assistants to open the adulterer's navel and remove his intestines. They did this quickly and then sewed him up with leather thongs and released him to the crowd in the square where he would undergo and agonizing death. The accuser, with the shock of the event on his face, led his hysterical wife away.

On a platform, above the thatched roof of the Plaza of Warriors, crouched Chacmool. He or it was covered in blood with human hearts stacked on its belly. The hearts will be taken from Chac to be burned—every few hours fresh ones will arrive. This gathering and sacrificing of human hearts would go on for days throughout the complex of Chechen Itza.

Meanwhile on the edge of the square, in a huge stone courtyard, thousands were gathered to watch a ball game. Notables were in attendance to watch teams from villages compete. The game went on for hours in the heat of the Yucatan sun and when it ended the score was calculated and the losing team's captain was bought forward and condemned to death. He was taken outside the court and placed on a pedestal next to a stone rack of skulls. There he was tortured and beheaded; his head was skewered on a pike pole and planted with hundreds of other heads on the platform. Jonathan thought—talk about your ultimate looser. The body was carved up and given out to the villagers for the much needed protein. His femurs were ripped out of his legs and given to a priest for some other bizarre ceremony and his heart was sent up the steps to Chacmool. Jonathan had been told in the past that the winner was the one murdered but this was not believable to him.

The sacrifices, judgments, games and debauchery went on for the next several days. Thousands died at the hands of deranged priests and bullies and eventually, except for a few priests and hangers-on, the Maya went home leaving this awful place empty until the next planting season. They went home to their villages—many never to return.

Jonathan bought his thoughts to eight hundred years later. The blood and bones of the misfortunate are gone back to the earth from whence they came and only the decaying buildings remain. No one worships cruel gods here anymore.

The sun has set, the lights come on and all the temples glow in their ghostly limestone white. Another stage is set but this one is different. Drums and conches are not heard but string, percussion and wind instruments of a modern orchestra rise from a stage and into a sound system that fills the complex and surrounding forest with the music of Puccini. Luciano Pavarotti's voice floats above all the ghosts that have come and gone. He sings the aria from Turandot, Nessun Dorma (No One Sleeps). It is the story of a man who will not die tomorrow because a beautiful vicious princess cannot guess his name—it is Love. The aria ends: All alba vinerò! At daybreak, I shall conquer. Jonathan wonders how many thousands over the years, in this place, wished they had known something that would have let them conquer their tomorrow. It was profound and he thought of *her*. Will *she* conquer her tomorrow?

In his school years he was told that the Maya, Aztec, Toltec, Olmec and other nations in Central America disappeared. Not so, he found them alive and living a good life all over the country. His cantina across the square from his hotel was filled with them. He wandered into the place the first day he arrived and became friends with the patron Maya and Méstizos and spent many happy hours drinking beer and drawing their impressive faces, ghosts and demons. They didn't say much to each other since he does not speak Spanish or Maya and they do not speak English. They got along with sign and pigeon English that became comical. At first they did not know what he was up to and why he did not go to the bar on the corner of the square where the few white folk frequent—they saw his drawings, understood and welcomed him. The beer he bought them also helped.

Once a colonial residence the cantina is a simple place, minimalists in design. It became a simple restaurant/bar, emptied of decoration except for its tiled mauve floor and antique three-meter doors disguised under layers of brown paint splattered with white. They have an extra set of swinging bar doors so when the place is open patrons cannot be seen from the street—kind of a Wild West look. Stepping out of the place one can easily be killed; the doors lead directly onto a busy street. The exterior is a simple square concrete plastered block painted dull beige; ancient paint shows through the chips, peelings, scrapes and weathering. In simple black block lettering is, The Bar painted above the door with the brand beer logo painted in red script.

The interior walls are whitewashed concrete with a wainscoting of bright red toped off with a gold four inch strip. The brand beer logo is written on two walls in the same red and gold. A large mirror hangs behind a plain tiled bar. Shelves run down one wall for a few hard liquor bottles and a TV on a stand high in a corner is hooked to a DVD player that plays endless Mexican pop video. The electrical wiring is stapled to the walls—a highway for ants and insects. Heavy metal tables with arborite tops and plastic chairs are strewn and stacked about the place. The backroom is for overflow traffic and the storage of beer cases stacked on pallets dozens high to the ceiling. At the end of this room is the men's toilet. The women's is permanently closed since no women come here, but they are welcome—this is a workingman's bar. There is a small kitchen with a barbecue made from the rim of a truck wheel. A dozen fluorescent tubes light the place.

The Maya patrons are small to medium in size, dark skinned, black hair, large hawk like noses and tilted back foreheads. A beautifying trait the Maya practiced in ancient times was to tie boards to babies' foreheads to force the growth of the skull's frontal bone to grow flat. They are an amazing likeness to their ancestors; very handsome and strong although now the majority of them tend to be overweight since eating in the modern world is less than a problem as it used to be. Their protein is trucked in—no one eats their relatives anymore.

They play dice with a leather-covered cup that they pound the bar with and release five ivories and the harder they hit the bar the better their odds of winning. The looser does not loose his head these days but goes home to his wife and kids penniless. What could be worse?

There is another patron, Méstizos. They are big men, two hundred pounds or more, and tall, hovering around six feet. Five hundred years ago their ancestors came to this place from Spain and other countries from the Mediterranean. They have large mustaches where the Maya do not; the Maya pick the hair from their faces with tweezers. Facial hair is ugly to them.

The patrons work at the usual jobs: government work as security police, civil servants, real estate agents, sales people and small business owners. Their wives are in the square dressed in their white and embroidered dresses making a fortune selling their crafts to the tourists who are bussed in each day. Their women have enormous power; they run the family businesses and keep the books. The indigena are doing well in Valladolid.

The Bar and its characters inspired Jonathan to draw the past and present mingled together in a blur: a time past of warriors and brutal gods; and a present time of love, liveliness and camaraderie. They are all there:

warriors, priests, civic workers, gamblers, comrades, terrestrial monsters, and the sun that is trying to get in the door to join the party. With other spirits, Chac that terrible rain god, are in the jaws of a terrestrial monster under the bar waiting to rise again. And he wondered, after all he has seen in the world—has anything changed?

Jonathan finished the drawing. He was becoming tired of the Maya sitting and drinking his beer, even though he was not paying for it. *She* had seen to that. Where the hell is she he thought it seems I have been chasing her forever. He closed his sketchbook and said adios to the locals and waved a good night to the bar owner and stepped through the swinging doors onto the street. A thundershower had recently passed over and the cobbles shone from the lights of streetlamps. Half a block up a road to his left he saw a police car and an ambulance parked—their blue, white and red lights were flashing. Some shadows were bent over a body lying on the sidewalk and a man was pulling a stretcher from the ambulance. Jonathan watched for a moment then continued on to his hotel.

He walked to his room and opened the door to find a note on the floor. It read:

Take the eight forty-five bus to Merida tomorrow and check in to the Fountain Hotel. I promise I will meet you at the Governor's Palace on the square. Read about the paintings you will see. Do not worry; although you cannot see me, I am with you wherever you go. I have finished the necessary business before we are to meet. Thanks for your patience my love.

Tula

My love? He thought it sounds like she has been up to something. She always plays that innocent cutesy stuff when she has been up to no good—like a guilty child. It gives me the creeps to think she is near by, just behind the door or around the corner. He quickly opened the curtains. No one was there. He laughed and went to bed.

At the bus station the next morning Jonathan did not notice the poster on the stations bulletin board. Christmas and his male wife Ismael were missing.

By The Feet of The Peasants

Jonathan took a taxi from the Merida bus terminal to the Fountain Hotel and checked in. She had not told him when to meet only where; he knew she was somewhere close by and watching. He did not bother looking for her because she is a former army intelligence officer and knows how to stay hidden and stalk. He would play the waiting game by being the tourist and visit the sites, museums and restaurants. He would go to the Governor's Palace on his own time. I must have some control he thought.

One afternoon he visited the Museum of Yucatan There is a placard at the start of the historic exhibit that reads:

When the conquistadors came to the Americas five hundred years ago they met the Maya people. As legend has it the Spaniards asked the indigena, what is the name of this land. Historians and anthropologists believe there were three similar replies:

YUK AK KATAN

"I don't understand your language."

UH YU UTHAN

"Listen how they talk."

CI U THAN

"I don't understand."

He wrote it all down in his sketchbook. He found it comical, because it is similar to how his country was named.

He had spent time in museums around the world studying the people that he lives with and he read that the Yucatan used to be one of the richest areas in the western hemisphere—this is where rope came from. Just a simple item but up to a hundred years ago the world was held together with this stuff—sisal or henequen. The only places you see it now is on packages going through the mail. It's the stuff you bind a parcel with after you wrap it with brown paper. There is another obscure place; the only rope left on a sailing boat—the leading edge of the mainsail or the luff.

Merida and its people made a fortune supplying rope to the world for clothing, rigging ships and wrapping material. Technology put an end to the industry and Merida collapsed into obscurity. The opulent colonial mansions are now offices, museums or abandoned and crumbling. The inner courtyards of the mansions that used to hold wonderful garden parties are now parking lots. Times move on—today the Merida and the Yucatan is now prosperous with a tourist industry and a real estate market. The Route of the Maya is a big tourist attraction.

Jonathan found this trivia by poking around in the museums of old Merida. He noticed many modern artists use sisal in sculptures and fabric art, making a political statement or using it as a metaphor of a lost world of wealth. But most importantly the recognition of the abject poverty and abuse the peasant Maya went through harvesting this product for their masters.

He went hunting through dozens of noisy fabric and craft stores in downtown Merida for sisal. He found some of the beige rope but it was part of the wholesale packaging stock and not for sale. Finally he found a Maya hammock maker who had sisal rope but in large bundles. He explained through sign language that he was an artist and needed only about one-meter of the stuff.

"CI U THAN" (I don't understand). The shop owner said. Then in broken English—"you have to buy the whole thing," and he held up a bolt of the stuff to him.

"No," Jonathan said frustrated, "one-meter and he held out his arms. Over the owner's shoulder on a shelf was a small bundle, the size of his fist. He grabbed it, "¿Cuanto cuesta esto?"

"Five pesos," he said with a smile knowing it was worth nothing but he noticed Jonathan's frustration and that he needed the stuff for some obscure reason.

"Trato!" he blurted out, gave him the cash and left.

He went to a restaurant bar across the square from the Governor's Palace and spent the next three hours sketching the piece of sisal. It was a Saturday afternoon and hundreds of young people where in costume performing their traditional dances to a twenty-piece orchestra set up under the arches of the municipal building. Through the crowd around him he felt eyes creeping up his back, watching from out in the square or from windows and balconies of the colonial buildings. He scanned the bell towers of the cathedral. He thought he saw a figure up there. She was here—now—out there. He searched the crowd—looked closely at the dancers. He could feel her presence. He scanned carefully. It was unnerving he could not sketch anymore—it was time. He closed his sketchbook and put it and the sisal in his daypack. He paid his bill and left the restaurant. He walked through the crowd and across the square to the Governor's Palace.

The federal guards in their blue and gold uniforms looked at Jonathan suspiciously as he stepped through the portals of the old colonial building. They guarded the government house that has held power over this part of Mexico for five hundred years.

There are twenty-seven paintings in the Palace that tell the history of the state of Yucatan. The curators had labeled them murals but they were not; they were free standing paintings on boards and hung on the walls. They were huge in size, averaging four by eight meters. The paintings around the street level courtyard illustrated Maya pre and post conquest; the pre conquest hung to his left and opposite this giant painting on the other side of the courtyard was the post conquest; a painting of the Maya being defeated by the Spanish conquistadors—death, chains and fire was the theme. The other two walls of the courtyard and on the upper balcony were giant portraits of those, the good and the bad, who built and contributed to what Yucatan is today. He followed her instructions and read the inscriptions. He sensed he was being set up or being educated before he was to meet her. God babe, he whispered, how theatrical can you get?

Jonathan climbed the marble stairwell to the upper balcony; massive paintings glared at him of the cosmology of the Maya. Warriors rose out of the dark where a jaguar stalked—he is the god of night, his amber coat smoldered in the black. Nearby was the Maya in the light, in their peaceful everyday work, some carving stone and painting their temples. All the figures were massive and majestic, bigger than life—the Maya as a nation was painted here not just individuals. The masterpieces are painted in the fashion as the Sistine Chapel, huge and powerful: a nation, a force, a religion and a god—that is what the artist, Fernando Castro Pacheco wanted officials and visitors to see. The message, like all monumental art in Mexico, is people must not forget where they came from and how hard life was for those before them who toiled in the soil. It's the old saying—to forget is to repeat.

She wanted him in this place for a reason, it certainly wasn't for the art; this was not to her taste—or was it. He did not know this woman anymore. He walked around the upper balcony looking and reading about the events in the history of the Maya and the colonists. He felt her presence and he smelled her. He came upon the entrance to a large hall, the hall of mirrors in Versailles he thought. Huge paintings hung between the grand windows that overlooked the square. Filigree and moldings finished the walls and ceiling. Huge chandeliers hung down the centre. The paintings, like those in the courtyard were monochromatic, washes of colour, the figures subtly outlined; a soft version of Raul Dufy; a little bit stronger than a Botticheli. The figures, whose anatomy was classic and perfect, filled the canvases. The horizon lines in the compositions were at the level of the feet of the figures; implying the conquistadors, peasants, officials and martyrs were giants and the observers—ants. The nation at that time became what it was on the tough working feet of its people—the Maya. All very dramatic, thought Jonathan, as he walked by each painting and read the placards. He was at one end of the hall studying the anatomy of a crouching peasant trying to lift a sack of sisal on his back and as the placard said—miserly Jewish businessmen looked on. Hmm, he thought such were the times. When will political correctness destroy that painting, he thought.

He looked down to the far end of the hall and below the largest painting in the palace he saw a figure of a woman in a too-small-for-her, shoulder less cream dress. She was looking up at a painting: her legs apart, head thrown back, black curls hung down her back, hands rested on her hips and a daypack hung from a shoulder. An unlit cigar was between the fingers of her right hand.

Oh Christ—it's her—the body—the cigar—it's her! Jesus—she still looks beautiful and I haven't even seen her face yet. He smiled—his heart pounded. He whispered I came five thousand miles for this, let's get it over with, and he slowly walked down the room. He could hear the orchestra outside in the square playing a Mexican folk tune. The characters from the past: slaves, peasant, conquistadors, governors and monks looked down on him and silently warned him that danger was ahead. He could feel them turning their heads, their hushed voices murmuring, no—Jonathan—no. He walked to the rhythm of the music and the clicking of the dancers' shoes on the cobblestone street. Suddenly he was standing beside her.

She did not look at him. She kept her eyes on the painting but she knew he was there. "What do you think of this painting? The man is stretched out on a wooden cross. Those bastards around him with the hot iron rods are about to quarter his body. This happened about two hundred years ago, out there in the square where you hear music and dancing. He died in front of his friends, the Maya and the governor. They murdered him because he tried to help the poor and forgotten," she turned and faced him, "Well, Jonathan, I will be poor and forgotten if what I have planned does not work," and an angel danced on the corner of her mouth.

He could not help himself, he grabbed her around the waist and drew her near and kissed her hard on the lips. She did not resist, "you beautiful bitch, Tula," he said laughing. She held him tight.

"I missed you when you died old man," she whispered.

He whispered back "And I missed you when you died old girl.
They walked out of the palace and around the corner to the Parque Hidalgo.

On the way they chatted like old friends and lovers do after not seeing each other for some time. They talked mostly about their health and established that they were okay. And then: "You have some explaining to do, Tula. I thought you were dead. You have thrown my world out of whack and—"

"I will explain everything to you later but first let's talk of the business at hand. Now listen to me for a few minutes please," and she led him by the hand to a concrete bench and they both sat down. She held up her hands to stop him from going on.

"Okay, this is nice and private. I'll make this quick and simple and please don't butt in: My Grandpa was not a very bright young man but one hell of a survivor. He worked as a fisherman on the Caribbean Sea but sometimes would do labor when the fishing was no good and he made stonemasonry as his other trade—," he started to say something and she put her hand delicately on his lips, "—he lived on Isla Mujeres for a few years; those were the days when there were just small villages and no tourists; the Hotels of Cancun had not been thought of yet. This was in the '50s, it was after the war and nobody traveled much; the world was busy raising families. My Grandpa worked for the Isla Mujeres Municipality repairing roads and old stuff the island people felt needed preserving. There was always stories of buried treasure in my family—"

"Oh Christ Tula—buried treasure?"

"Yes, my Grandpa knows where a horde of gold is—"

"Now, please—"

"It's under seven stones among the bones of my Grandpa's co-workers whom he murdered. I know that sounds bad but you see he had to murder them to keep the secret—"

Jonathan butted in, "Yeah sure, that's a lot of bull—don't tell me I've come five thousand miles to dig for buried treasure? Jesus Christ, Tula—"

"Now just a minute Jonathan. Remember my family goes back hundreds of years in the history of the Caribbean as pirates, slaves and before that Caribe Indigena. If any people were to be involved in gold and murder it would be my family."

"I don't know Tula," he said calmed down, "many people have been wrapped up in treasure hunting, lost their lives or their fortunes in the pursuit of gold doubloons. The murders—where do they come in? If I get involved in any more deaths I'll be sent back to Canada and never be allowed to leave. Worse still, we could end up in jail in Mexico and not share the same cell. Your just too crazy for words."

"No we won't. I'll see to that." she said holding his hand, "Let me go on: Grandpa said he and three others were sent to do repairs on one of the historical sights on the Island. They discovered a large cache of gold. This was a horde stolen by the Spanish hundreds of years ago—melted down, stored and was waiting for shipment to Spain. This batch never made it to the boat and was buried in a place that Grandpa said was safe high ground. He was a rough man in those days and saw an opportunity to be rich but his three fellow masons wanted to turn in the cache for a reward. He knew there would be no reward; the government would just grab the loot. He murdered the three men right then and there and buried them with the cache. He did a masonry job over top of them. Marking the site with seven stones."

"This all sounds like some fantasy story from my childhood or a B movie."

"And where do you think those childhood stories come from? Right here in the Caribbean, under our noses—on the Isla Mujeres. There are riches buried there, I know it. I have been living with this all my life and I knew it would not be until Grandpa's old age I would find out where it is all stashed—under seven stones. He promised he would tell someone in the family before he died. I am the only one left in the family in this part of the world except for that fucking uncle Christmas.

"Christmas! He's a relative of yours?"

"Yes and now very far removed."

"What does that mean?"

"Later."

"There's going to be a bunch of explaining to do on your part—

later."

"Now are you going to help me get rich or not? This is it, my last chance, if this doesn't come through I'll be telling fortunes in the market—an old woman throwing bones. The places you've been my love, you know what I mean."

Jonathan sat silently; he thought of all the places in the world he had been and seen the old who have been cast away, left behind as the modern world rushes on. God knows, he thought back, I have been hexed by a few of them. There was nothing left for Tula but hope in a fantastic story told by an old man. He was mesmerized by her beauty and ready to agree on anything. In his weakness and stupidity he said, "Let's go back to my hotel and bed and think about it."

"Good. On the way I will explain how we must find Grandpa." She got him. With a sigh she quickly pulled a cigar and lighter from her backpack, lighted it, stuffed it in her mouth and grabbed Jonathan's hand.

"You don't know where he is?"

"Well sort of," clenching the cigar in her teeth and talking out the side of her mouth, "we have to travel to San Christóbal de Las Casas and see his friend who is almost dead in a Dominican Monastery. He knows where Grandpa is." she dragged him from the concrete bench and hailed a taxi.

"Bizarre," he said, shaking his head, "bizarre."

San Christóbal de Las Casas

The filthy Maya boy crashed into their table; Jonathan caught his coffee before it toppled into the street. The little guy was dressed in a filthy red check shirt and black pants stuffed into far-too-big-for-him bright red rubber boots. They were split down the sides and about to fall off his feet. Jonathan could not tell what age he was; he was so skinny and small, he thought eight, ten or fifteen—maybe. From a dirty face he looked at Jonathan and Tula with half closed vacant eyes. He muttered something.

"Go!" Tula said sternly.

"He looks a little stoned," Jonathan said and he reached in his pocket for a handful of pesos. "Here." The boy grabbed the pesos and shoved them in his pants without a thank you. They watched him stagger across the street to an American fast food service.

"The place won't sell him anything you know, even if he did have enough pesos. He is just a filthy little street urchin who lives with the dogs. He will try stealing first," Tula commented in a matter-of-fact manner. Jonathan hated her cavalier non-caring attitude. He noticed it was getting worse as she got older.

"You need your kids," he said.

She said nothing but gave him a vacant stare. At the glass doors of the restaurant the boy cautiously peeked in.

"No gods." muttered Jonathan.

"What'd you say?"

"Oh nothing. Something I read on a bathroom wall—"

"Now when we get to the monastery, I want—"

"He is going to go in Tula and grab something—watch." The boy ran in and out a moment later with the goods; a waitress followed shaking her fist and shouting at him. Jonathan wanted to scream out a congratulatory hurrah, but he didn't.

"Will you pay attention, this is importa—"

"Ha!" Jonathan shouted, "The little guy scored! He's got a cup of something and a half eaten hamburger." He turned his attention back to Tula. "Sorry."

"Right. Now when we get to the monastery I will go in but I want you to slip quietly away for a while. Does that sit right with you?"

"Yeah, there is graffiti around here I want to photograph. So yeah, that will be fine. I have something to do. He turned his attention to the boy.

"Hey Tula, he's sitting in the gutter and scoffing down his burger and pop. Christ is he hungry—poor kid."

"Yeah," said Tula not looking. And she went on about what she was going to ask her Grandpa's dying friend. Jonathan could not keep his eyes off the boy.

"Oh my God, Jonathan said, "he just threw the cup and burger wrapper in the gutter and is now pissing on them." The boy finished, got up and staggered down the street towards Barrio de Mexicanos.

"Like I said, street dog," Tula said dryly and glanced over to the little urchin who melted into the crowd of Maya indigena.

"Let's go," Tula said and they both got up, Jonathan put some pesos on the table and they walked up the street in the direction the little boy had taken. It was not long until they reached a yellow and orange monastery attached to an immense cathedral. They walked up the cobbled pathway to the entrance where a group of nuns stood silently.

"Ms. Tula?" questioned one of the nuns reaching out to shake her hand, "we have been expecting you and you are on time."

"Yes, and this is my friend Jonathan," Tula said and she then turned her attention to the nuns, "is he still conscious?"

"Yes, but barely," the nun commented.

"May I see him now?"

"Of course, there is little time left for him."

"I will see you in about an hour, Jonathan, okay?" she said turning to him and dismissed him with a peck on the cheek.

"Okay—In an hour then." he nodded a goodbye to the nuns and walked into the barrio.

Across the city of San Christóbal de Las Casas is graffiti, not just graffiti that he was accustomed to. This is the real stuff he thought, graffiti that has statements and messages in them: LIBERTAD A LOS PRESOS POLITICOS! PRSENTACION CON VIDA DE LOS DESAPARECIDOS! And INFORMATE, ORGANIZATE Y LUCHA. These are the words he saw of a desperate people who want and deserve to be saved from poverty and abuse. He remembered January 1, 1994, when the indigena organized and started a revolution. The little band of revolutionaries shocked the world and the world applauded their gutsy move. They ruined the economy of Mexico but it soon recovered. A little woman named Roselia stopped a military army and turned them away from entering her pueblo. Such is the power of the righteous.

Among the graffiti lettering were small iconography stenciled on the brightly painted concrete and stucco walls of the administration and business buildings, small delicate images, typing paper in size, but they screamed for justice. A man with a nightstick beating a kneeling man was one—has nothing changed. He had seen this image before but more elaborate on temple stones carved a thousand years ago.

He had never seen graffiti with such power before and it was more than just a kid's ego tagging. He took photos and was soon all over the barrio clicking away and getting strange and concerned looks from the locals. He was soon moving deeper into the Barrio de Mexicanos. He walked up Av. Gral. Utrilla back to the cathedral he could see rising above the treetops—

Templo de la Caridad. He arrived at the square and it was full of tents of the indigena who had set up shops to sell their crafts. Mostly they were women dressed in their traditional costume of black skirts with silk blouses elaborately embroidered with flowers and animals. Their hair was tied back from their dark faces that emphasized their fierce white and black eyes. Pictures he had seen in books and magazines showed these women to be the fierce masked warriors that stood by their men and often led revolutionary skirmishes, standing up to the military, fists out, arms extended, carrying their children on their backs into battle. And in the battle there is a terrible sadness—the adversaries are related. They indigena have been here thousands of years and the colonists have been here for the last five hundred years—nobody is going away.

He felt awed to be in this place full of tiny women sitting on their blankets weaving and embroidering their goods. Their fierce eyes on him—these were the mothers of this land. Some breast-fed their babies while other babies slept on their mothers' backs under blankets, safe and warm for the first few years of their lives. Eventually they would be let loose to fight for their place in this valley. And Jonathan thought of Tula; she was also let loose upon the land. She suddenly reminded him of the little boy and these people. We are all just trying the best we know how, to make our way in the world. Even the Dominican monks who are now gone had to make their way in this land—translated they are the Dogs of God.

The five hundred year old cathedral squatted like a giant on the hill and Jonathan could feel her scream in agony. She had given everything to her people. She was now one of them and not the gilded lady she was once during her golden colonial days so many years ago. Her flock squats at her door. Young, old, broken, bruised and shattered hands reach out for a peso or two from those who make it to this place.

At the threshold Jonathan gave out ten dollars in pesos and went through the thick wooden, five hundred year old armed doors. The place had become no more than a cave; indigena, small, cold and shivering had set up shops inside the dark cavern. Besides its massive architecture, there was not much left of the old cathedral but the altar was still intact and below it on hands and knees a group of indigena prayed for their salvation.

He could not find any church candles for sale but he found a piece of a small birthday cake candle on the floor. He lit it from a candle on the altar and placed his beside it. Jonathan said a few words to the Gods of his travels and made his way out of there into the sun now warming the land on the edge of the barrio. Overhead rockets roared skyward, exploded and he laughed—the Mexicans love their fireworks.

On the side of the cathedral where the red and black spray-painted words: EZLN—EL FUEGO Y LA PALABRA. He photographed this scrawl, a masterpiece in content and composition hurriedly written. He moved on down the road and the crowd got thicker, the dark faces and eyes around him watched his every move. They looked with curiosity and awe of the rich man from the north—not many blonde white folk come here. A shaman and his pet boa constrictors, selling snake oil, displayed their works to an enthralled crowed gathered around them. Jonathan took a side street up to another square with a church and photographed the images scrawled on the concrete walls. The narrow streets were a labyrinth and reminded him of the cobbled streets of his childhood—suddenly opening up at the crest of a hill to reveal an old city below.

He made his way past businesses crowded with people and goods. Six women took up a parking space between some cars. Around them were black garbage bags full of black, brown and beige sheep and goat's wool for sale. Their faces hands and legs were the colour of their goods—the colour of the earth. Suddenly, without a warning, he was among thirty or so indigena women carrying tied up chickens hanging on their arms. The freaked out birds were kept alive for their customers who where bargaining a price for their family's dinner they would have tonight or tomorrow or the next day after that. Or maybe they were being sold as breeding stock. If they were to be eaten, that was very ingenious Jonathan thought why kill the beast until it is time to eat. He then remembered his mother so many years ago just after the Second World War plucking chickens on the back porch.

He was now in the Mercado Municipal of the Barrio de Mexicanos, a thriving place full of noise, sights and smells just like home in Bangkok. Hundreds of indigena were going through the place doing their daily business buying goods or selling whatever they found in the fields and forests of the valley. Dozens stood quietly in a line over their products of fruits, vegetables, firewood, tools and car parts. Jonathan walked past them and into a huge cavern of a building. He had been here before but on the back of his huge elephant friend, Buddha. A wave of homesickness swept over him and he felt sad to be so far away from his Bangkok family.

Small booths were packed with goods and people shouted out the quality of their products and haggled for the best price. This was a market of fresh perishable goods where people come to shop daily. And fresh it was for on a tile-covered bench five meters long where six pigs' heads with their noses pointed to the sky. They were rooting in the mud that morning. The rest of them: hearts, livers, feet and flesh were spread out along the rest of the slab. Down one of the aisles at a boiling kitchen, strips of them had been made into huge chunks of pork rind. Everything looked ghastly under the effigy of the Virgin Guadalupe dressed in pink crepe paper above the door. Numerous healthy dogs ran about underfoot looking for scraps that manage to find their way to the floor. This is shopping in the third world; it may seem shocking to see at first but then you realize its just different packaging. Jonathan remembered getting used to all of this. Suddenly rockets filled the air outside, exploding hundreds of feet above the barrio. He wondered what they were celebrating; the cacophony of sounds and sights were overwhelming.

He made his way out of the market and went further into the barrio and along a noisy street of stalls of clothing, shoes, hardware, building materials and everything else one could think of. Among them were video and music stands with not one legitimate recording of a movie or song for sale. Just like home in Thailand he thought. An indigena was selling bottled homemade liquor out of a wheelbarrow and by the look on his face he had drunk too much of his own product.

Jonathan soon came to the junction where the main street, Utrilla, joins Calzada Lazaro Cardenas that he took to walk back to the Cathedral and monastery. The square on the hill was packed with people and business was going well since the tour buses had arrived. The indigena women were all over the tourists with their doll effigies of the revolution, their bead necklaces and bracelets and their traditional embroidery work. Suddenly the drive gathered his pack and they all got back in their buses and left. Jonathan felt something strange going on; the fireworks of rockets and the indigena on the street were increasing—the market was packing up early.

Under the colonial arches of the monastery Tula was waiting for him. "Well I found Grandpa but your not going to like it and there is something else."

"Oh," Jonathan sighed, "now what?" Dozens of rockets exploding hundreds of feet in the sky around the city signaled from the barrios that something was about to happen.

"We have to get back to our hotel right away and get our stuff. We have to be out of here within the next hour. The fucking devil is on his way!"

"What do you mean?" Jonathan said, bewildered.

"Revolution, that's what I mean. The indigena are on their way into the city from the hills. They are armed, dangerous, hyped and fed up. Nothing has changed since '94 and they're pissed as hell."

Quickly they moved down Insugentes. The indigena were everywhere waving flags, pitchforks and machetes. Mostly they were women, a few had their babies on their backs. Some of the men were on horseback galloping ahead of the mass, their horses frothing at the mouth. Everyone was masked either with a scarf or black ski mask.

"Stay near me Jonathan," Tula commanded and she pulled a long knife from her shoulder bag.

"What the hell is that?" Jonathan yelled at her.

"Something I always keep handy—now watch around you. We are white and may be just as bad as soldiers or authority in the eyes of these people."

"Where are the police?" Jonathan said.

"Gone home to their families where they should be. It looks like everyone is heading in the same direction; probably to the main square in front of the cathedral downtown."

"That's a few blocks from where we live. Jesus, look at the explosions in the sky." The sky filled with gray white smoke as dozens of rockets exploded above them.

"That looks like some kind of signal, Tula said, the four horsemen are on their way." In the distance behind them in the direction of the incoming highway from Palenque, gunfire could be heard.

"Move, Jonathan, move!" He did, at a run, carried along in the mass of black indigena who where now thick around them. Tula reached up and grabbed an arm holding a machete that was on the way to Jonathan's head, "away bitch!" Tula yelled, and she brandished her long knife in the face of a fierce indigena woman. The little woman retreated; she sensed Tula was not someone to deal with. Others seeing the encounter backed away from them and turned their attention to where they were going.

"Thanks," Jonathan said.

"Your welcome, now keep close!"

They passed the town square that was filled with people; flags waved, guns went off and young men on rooftops lit rockets that streaked into the sky exploding in a deafening roar. The gazebo in the center of the square was on fire and people were throwing furniture, books; anything they could pick up to throw onto the blaze. On the wrought iron benches around the square, masked men stood screaming at the crowd, working them into a mad mob. People yelled and screamed and some cried; the revolution they had been waiting for was underway. The monster they were creating was now galloping and nothing could stop it. They would indiscriminately kill anything that was different; anything they could direct their rage on. Jealousy and hatred boiled over and anyone white, rich or had the look of authority was thrown onto the blazing gazebo.

Two men came after them with machetes. Tula stabbed and sliced one up through the mouth the other up through his arm pit and across his throat. They ran up Real de Guadalupe to Old Town and their hotel. The receptionist, a young woman, screamed and cried in fear at the site of Tula with her hands soaked in blood. Jonathan went around the counter and grabbed their room key; they rushed upstairs to the next floor and their room. Tula washed quickly, pulled a tourist guide map from her backpack and laid it out on the bed.

"I can sense where they are," and she drew a half circle over the city, "the indigena are here," and she arched a line around the town square, "and the military, will be coming from the main highway—here—into San Christóbal from the south from their main military headquarters. You remember them when we came in by bus? It looked like a paper fortress—

silly looking."

"Yeah, I remember."

"We need to move to the Barrio de Cuztitali the same way we came from but in a more westerly direction." she made broad sweeping strokes across the map, "we can get to the far side of the barrio by going through Barrio de Guadalupe which is near by." Cannon fire and military gunfire exploded in the distance from the south where Tula said the military would come.

"Let's go!" She ordered. They left most of their possessions behind and just took essentials in their packs.

The indigena were now in their thousands, pouring into the city. A private security guard burst through the door of the hotel and in his panic, shot dead the receptionist. They had just left their room and Tula saw what happened below them. She jumped like a mad cat over the railing from the second floor balcony onto the guard. To the astonishment of Jonathan, she slit his throat with one slash of her knife.

"Get down here quick!" She screamed at him and he ran down the stairs. By the time he got to her she had stripped him of his weapons and slipped into his webbing. He wasn't dead and he rocked his bloody head back and forth, his eyes bulged out and he gasped for breath, "Fucker dirtied me up with blood again. Here," she said, "take this and use it when needed." she handed him the guards handgun and a pouch of ammunition clips.

"I don't know how to use this thing." The guard stopped moving.

"Just point it at the fuckers and pull the trigger! Get with it or you will die! Understand?"

"I understand," and with that said, he mentally caught up with her, "okay, which way?"

She pointing in a north direction with the guard's automatic rifle, "That way, but first stay here," and she ran up stairs back to the room and came running back down with a white bed sheet. "We must show everyone we are neutral," she tore the sheet into strips, one she tied to the barrel of her rifle and another to the mussel of Jonathan's pistol, "now hold your gun up at all times. Hopefully they will respect our bloodied white flag and not kill us. Do not hesitate for a split second to use your pistol—understand?"

"Yeah. I—"

She kissed him, "Let's go—stay by me."

A river of humanity, black with colours of red and white, poured down the street and flowed around them. The indigena respected their flag of neutrality but the fierce look on Tula's face was enough to put them off anyway. The noise was earth shattering; the military was firing into the square a few blocks away and rockets, by the hundreds, rose from every hamlet, village and barrio across the valley. Hell had arrived in San Christóbal.

Quickly they moved up the street several blocks to the square in front of the church Guadalupe. A tide of indigena was running passed it. A masked man dressed in black and brown leather and riding a frothing black stallion galloped towards them. Tula was moving passed a crowd and did not see the rider thundering down on her. He raised his machete above his head to cut her down. Jonathan shot the horse in the chest. It screamed and his front legs collapsed. The rider lunged forward and came down onto the cobbled street smashing his facial bones, rendering him unconscious. Tula turned and saw what Jonathan had done—she shot the rider through in the head. The indigena screamed and moved around them.

"For effect—thanks." Tula said to Jonathan's astonishment, "let's move behind the church." The rider was not dead, he tried to get up and Tula shot him in the forehead. They ran up the road that swung to the side and rear of the church and the crowd was now just a few stragglers. They went into the barrio and the square. There were dozens of white taxis parked with a few drivers milling about feverishly talking among themselves and on cell phones.

"I'll be damned," Jonathan, said, "the drivers are pretty smart to get out of harms way." He looked back at the city; black smoke rose from its center and rockets were exploding across the sky; gunfire came from everywhere. Tula grabbed a man nearby who looked like a driver.

"Give me the keys to your car!" she screamed at him and held the automatic to his face.

"Where will you drive it too?" he stuttered in fear.

"Guatemala."

"That will cost you at leased two thousand pesos," the terrified driver blurted out and he handed her his keys and pointed to his car.

"Oh fuck, these guys never give up." Jonathan laughed.

"Send me the bill," she said, "get in, Jonathan. "Here you drive," and she threw him the car keys. They got in; he started the car and checked the fuel gauge.

"Three quarters full," he said, "enough to go a long way in this foreign job."

Tula laid her guide map on the dashboard and soon figured out a back road out of San Christóbal in the direction of the Mexican/Guatemala border.

"Okay let's get out of here, in that direction," she pointed to the hill in the south west, "when you drive, don't stop for anything. I'll ride shotgun," she rolled down all the windows and reached over him and rolled down his, kissing him in the process.

"Sex and violence are the same to you aren't they?"

"You know that already."

"Yeah."

"Now remember, don't stop for anything. I'll do the killing," and she took his gun and ammunition clip and laid them on the dashboard. Her automatic she held outside the passenger window in plain sight of anyone they approached. Jonathan put the taxi in gear and away they went throwing dust up as they left the burning city of San Christóbal de Las Casas.

They drove for hours through villages and farms on the back roads of Chiapas and saw very few people or police and no military since most had run to the hills or to the city of San Christóbal. They stopped at a country store and stocked up on water, soft drinks, cigars and junk food. They drove across a flat expanse of farms and soon they could see the distant volcanic mountains of Guatemala.

"This will be interesting," she said, "I don't know how we will get in."

"Up until this morning people have been trying to get out. Let's just get onto the highway to the border city of Cuachtémoc and hope for the best. If all goes bad we can abandon the car and walk in," he said. "What do you think?"

"Yeah, okay," she said lighting a cigar. They drove onto the highway and in a short time they were behind a long line of indigena pulling carts and carrying their possessions moving towards the border crossing. The crowd moved aside for the car and cigar smoking, gun-totting Tula who screamed obscenities at them. In sight of the border she pulled in her rifle and took the pistol and ammunition clips off the dashboard and put them under the front seat but handy if she needed them quickly. They drove into the chaos of the border town. People were in groups talking excitedly, some had portable radios and cell phones to their ears, others in bars were watching on television sets, the drama of revolution unfold.

Ahead was a black and yellow stripped crossing gate that was up. Two bewildered guards were questioning people in cars ahead of them and they waved them through. It was their turn.

"What is your business in Guatemala?" the guard asked.

"We are tourists and got caught up in the mess in Chiapas," Jonathan said, "we thought it best if we came to Guatemala. Will there be a military blockade ahead?"

"Not yet, but there will be by tonight. Go ahead," the guard said, "and get new license plates for your taxi as soon as possible." he waved and winked them on.

Soon they were cruising down highway 190 and the only vehicles they saw were military on their way to the border.

"Now where to?" Jonathan said, exasperated.

"We drive to Belize City."

"That's a days drive."

"Yeah, after Guatemala City we go north. There is only one highway so we won't get lost."

"So why me Tula?" Jonathan said after an hour on the road in Guatemala's Sierra Madras.

"What do you mean—why me?" Tula said and she stroked his thigh.

"I'm not used to this kind of stuff."

"And what kind of stuff is that?"

"You know: murder, escaping, violence, lying, that kind of stuff."

"Not now."

"Yes now, while I'm still alive. What is with you? I have never met anyone like you."

"Very well. In Germany, on the base where I was working, I thought about death. It's near for me. So near I can taste it. If it happens I don't want to be alone, that's why I called you to go on this journey with me. I'll be rich or dead, one or the other."

"You decided to take me with you?" he said with anger in his voice, "Don't you care about my life?" Tula squeezed his thigh. "You have pulled me into one hell of a mess and maybe implicated me in murder. Have you?"

"No, so far you're not implicated. I just don't want to be alone when I die."

"Don't you think that is acting selfish?"

"I am selfish and more than that," Tula whispered and she leaned over and pecked him on the cheek, "a military psychiatrist told me that in Germany."

"Selfish and what else?"

"Can't tell you but it took him a whole year and a battery of tests to find out. I do what I want and get what I need, I steal, lie and murder with no remorse. I just don't care anymore. Remember I said I would explain why I do the things I do? It all comes from my past abuse—my fucking family. They are the angels, the ones only you and my voodoo master can see. The army gave me the skills and tools to assist my behavior, and bring out the hell in me. Anyway, that's what my shrink told me. The company I worked for kidnapped me mentally because they knew I would commit murder and do most anything to protect or benefit myself. And dig this; the army through my retired staff sergeant supplied the information about me to the killing company."

"How many people have you murdered?"

"I have never kept count but maybe the number is in the twenties."

"Jesus Christ! I'm riding with a serial killer! I'm in love with a serial killer!"

"I won't kill you babe," she said as she laid her head on his shoulder, "I still need you."

They drove through Guatemala City and north to the Rio Dulce near the Guatemala/Belize border. They gave their taxi and weapons to a kindly village elder in exchange for getting them a private plane out of a jungle airport to Belize City. Tula kept the weapons on her and handed them to old man out the door of the plane at the last moment before take off. He was kindly and old but could not be trusted—this is dope country. Tula figured all this out; her obsession about the gold at the end of her rainbow drove her on.

Outside of Belize city the pilot touched down on a country road where they picked up a chicken bus. At the city's bright red bus terminal taxi drivers and beggars where all over them—Jonathan took command. He picked a driver and bargained a price for the short ride to the Regent Street Hotel where they were given a clean room with a nice veranda-overlooking Haulover Creek.

"Do you believe this place?" full of beggars and thieves; and abandoned people," Jonathan said, "all blacks, the god damn Brits just up and left this place."

"Yeah, did you see the junkies down the street?"

"Nice to know there is a seven foot tall black security guard outside with a big stick," he laughed, "so what do we do from here?"

"We rest, get a good nights sleep and take a cab south tomorrow. I'm going out to get some cigars. I'll be back shortly."

"You're not going without me."

"Now don't start getting protective with me."

"You?" Hell! I'm thinking about me alone in this place. There are pirates here!" they both laughed.

"Okay, let's go," and they went into the streets of Belize to find cigars and fight off the remnants of British rule. Down Regent Street, no more than an alley, they walked with an air that they owned the place and they both said hello to the huge guard who smiled generously back. Within a short distance was a group of drunken and drugged men leaning against a filthy white pickup truck.

"Good day Madam—Sir. Care for a nip?"

"Thank you, no," Jonathan replied. One in the group said something in Creole and they all had a toothless drunken laugh. An uneasy feeling swept over Tula and Jonathan and they swiftly moved on down the greasy street lined with plastic bottles, wrappers and trays.

"What the hell was that?" Tula said.

"They are just having a little fun at our expense. I had a flashback there for a moment."

They arrived at the swing bridge that crosses Haulover Creek where a kitchen of sorts stood with a line of people waiting to buy food at a cage door. The little building was fenced in to stop any snatch and dash thieves from stealing the daily fare.

"Well that sure tells you a lot about this place. Have you noticed there are no white people here?" he said.

"I've noticed. They went home long ago. Let's move on."

A crippled weather beaten old man came across the bridge toward them with the saddest look in his eyes. Jonathan reached in his pocket, pulled out some pesos and gave them to him. "Sorry, pesos are all I have," the leathery old man nodded a thank you.

"Now that is disgusting," Tula said and she pointed to the Creek bank on the other side of the Swing Bridge, "look at that man, he is crapping in the creek in plain view. This is the center of town for Christ sake. Why do they let him do such a disgusting thing? Look, now he's washing his ass."

"I don't know but the only cops I can see around here are for traffic control. My God, there are drunks and dopers everywhere. And look at the bridge; it has been painted recently and right over the rust. They are so poor here they can't do a proper job of fixing things. Look around, all the buildings are in advanced decay."

Across the street on the other side of the bridge was the marine terminal where a group of tourists from a cruise ship arrived. Their eyes were wide open in disbelief at what they were seeing. Their guide, a short stocky strong man, was lecturing them to stay near him at all times and not to stare. Nearby a large group of black men dressed like some LA gang or black basketball team helped people with their bags into the ferry terminal that would take them out to the cays.

Tula and Jonathan walked up Queen Street where people littered the sidewalk; some sat half naked starring into space a hat on the ground for alms, others lay asleep in filth, their bodies trembling from drugs or alcohol. The clothing of the destitute was rags, the colour of the earth and dust of the street. A school bus, painted sliver and red for local service drove by slowly; a woman went from window to window shouting, my babies need food, please! They kept walking and arrived across the street from the Queen Street Police Station and the destitution got worse.

"You know what?" he said, "They are all lying here in the protection of the Police Station. They probably feel safe here."

"I suppose so," she said, "There are many muggings and murders that happen in these fucked up cities, you can die for a few pennies."

Jonathan heard the sounds of his own language, English, that he had not heard for some time, except from Tula. He did not like it; in this place it was the sound of desperation, anger and frustration.

"Well there is a light here I guess," and Jonathan pointed down a street to a group of children playing in a schoolyard, "hope is not lost here just on hold for a while."

"Hey, there's a tobacconist," Tula cried. They moved swiftly the half a block to it and went in the open front door. They into a cage and on the other side of the heavy wire grid was the tobacconist; his merchandise of boxes of cigars and cigarettes lined the shop and out of reach.

"What a place," Tula commented. "Well let's see what they have and she inspected the shelves from the cage they were in, "there, and she pointed to a shelf of boxes with cigar labels attached. I'll have six Cohibas and a box of Vegas Robainas please. The clerk tallied her bill and handed it to her. She rummaged in her backpack for money and paid the clerk through the opening in the cage, "feels like I'm in jail again." The clerk wrapped her purchased and pushed it through the opening.

"You were in jail?" Jonathan said as they walked out of the cage.

"Yeah, military jail—just in a holding pen."

"I see. I won't ask for more."

"Thanks." They left the shop and hurried back to the hotel verbally fighting off the beggars, con artists and thieves.

"I am not going out tonight," he said, "the night clerk said he would go next door and get us food and drink."

"Chicken shit," Tula said, and she leaned back in a comfortable verandah chair and puffed on a Cohiba.

"That must be it," Tula cried. A decaying colonial mansion squatted on stilts in a cane field half a kilometer off the highway.

"It looks like something from my youth—haunted. What's it sitting on?" Jonathan said not expecting an answer.

"These old estates where built on concrete stilts years ago so they were up out of the lake that form in these lowlands during the rains," the taxi driver said, "very efficient for the masters but the slaves on the property were always flooded out."

The taxi pulled up the driveway to the mansion that rose above them three stories; its whitewash pealed away revealed silver gray sun bleached siding. Its roof was red rusting corrugated metal with two dormers; boarded over windows looked blindly down on them. The two livable floors of the house rested on a maze of concrete pylons. Verandas were on both floors but the second floor's had rotted, disappearing long ago. The coverings of floor joists and siding had dropped away exposing the bones of the house. Black mold cascaded down everything from the dampness and humidity that is Belize's climate. Shuttered windows still had their wrought iron security bars in place and the old wooden doors where open to let the air and light in. A web of plumbing pipes, electrical wiring, and mechanical superstructure hung from below the first floor like some horrific spider's nest. In the open space were stored old cars, boats and rotting building material. A big black cistern was among them with numerous pipes running into it and up the side of the house to the roof where they gathered rainwater. An old dog with tired eyes looked at them through some renegade sugar cane growing among the wreckage. In his youth he would have bounded out barking in protest that someone was on his land but he, like the rest of the place, was old and tired. He lay his head down and went to sleep.

"Certainly needs a paint job," Jonathan said getting out of the taxi with Tula.

"Pick us up in an hour will you driver?" Tula said as she paid him through his window.

"Very well mam," The driver turned the taxi around and drove back to the highway.

"From the ginger bread veranda of the first floor came a voice, "Miss Tula?"

"Yeah, that's me," she shouted up, "are you Dorothy? This is my friend Jonathan Owen," who shouted up hi and waved.

"Come on up, " and she pointed to a flight of rotting stairs beside the house. Gingerly they climbed the treads to where the big black woman waited for them," It is so good to meet you Tula, I was so surprised when I got you phone call," she said with a huge sincere smile, "over the years your Grandpa had spoken about you and your family. He misses his son, he hasn't heard from him for many years."

"He doesn't know he is dead?"

"No he doesn't," Dorothy said surprised, "nobody wrote us about that. Best not to tell the old man, at his age it doesn't matter anymore. Does it?"

"No, I guess it doesn't."

Dorothy led them into the old house which was full of colonial memories: wainscoting, plank flooring, floral wallpaper up to picture rails and built in wall cabinets whose contents were long gone back to Europe with the white family that left Belize in the early '80s. Set in a bay window was an old worn out padded chair with an old worn-out man staring out on cane fields stretching to the horizon. Dorothy pulled two wooden chairs from against a wall where they had been resting for years, and placed them on each side of the old man's chair.

"She is here old man." Dorothy said gently and lovingly stroking his head, "Tula is here to see you. She has come along way just for you," and she turned to Tula, "I will leave you two with him now and come back later with some tea. Speak up, he is hard of hearing and don't be surprised if he falls asleep on you."

"Thank you Dorothy," Tula said and she and Jonathan sat down on the chairs. Tula bent over the old man and stroked his head, "he is so old Jonathan. He's eighty but looks a hundred."

"What kind of a life have you lived Grandpa? Dad is old also and can't travel anymore but he sends his love." The old man looked up at her with open white wet eyes. Tula took the old man's hand in hers. His fingers were long and boney with bulging purple veins running through them; the skin was a deep brown tissue paper. Tula spoke of their family in Canada and she told him many lies about her life. Grandpa looked at her blankly, Jonathan sensed he did not care or believe anything anymore. Suddenly angels ran across his dark wrinkled mouth and Jonathan knew that he was really her Grandpa. Tula bent over him and kissed them.

"Seven stones," he whispered, "seven stones," he repeated.

"Seven stones?" and she looked at Jonathan, "You see, I told you, seven stones. All my life seven stones have been there." And she turned to her Grandpa, "where are they?"

"The clay people—the land of the clay women," he whispered.

"What clay women?"

"The clay women on the island in the north of Quintana Roo, maybe?" Jonathan said. But then I think you know that and that is why you sent me there first. The old man looked at him with wide eyes, "yes, that's it—Isla Mujeres."

"That's right," Tula said with excitement. Her eyes became brighter and focused, "somewhere on that island there are seven stones and under them is a vast wealth. So this confirms what I have known all along. This is why we've come her. Now we just have to find the seven stones." Tula bent over him with tears in her eyes. She pulled her chair close to him and Jonathan saw angels dance across her face and into her hair. They looked at him menacingly from between her curls. She was overcome with emotion or the confirmation of knowing where a treasure lay hidden. Jonathan took the scene with caution and fear.

Dorothy came into the room with a china tea set on a tray that she carried on a small table. They all sat in the bay window and had tea and cookies. Dorothy and Tula fed Grandpa and chatted like relatives. Jonathan and Grandpa stared out the window onto the acres of green cane fields. The scene reminded him of Thailand and his elephant and the good times together harvesting sugar cane. And then he thought of the slaves who lived and died here, ostracized from the human race. And who knows what Grandpa was thinking, perhaps the gold horde he left behind. The horde he had killed for and now age prevented him from possessing it. Buddha rushed by his thoughts and the principal Dharma of all *there must be no clinging and grasping.* He thought about his age and the time that will come when he to will come to the point of no return when he will not be capable of redemption or returning to what once was. The old man closed his eyes and laid his head on his chest.

"The old man has gone to sleep," Dorothy said and she stroked his head, "it is time for me to tell you about him and you."

"Really," Tula said, "is there something I should know?"

"Yes, you see there is a history you are not aware of since you were in Haiti and Canada a good part of your life. Actually this place here is your heritage, here in Belize, Honduras and the island of Roatán. You see you are Garifuna."

"What's that?"

"Garifuna are a people who came to this land more than two hundred years ago. We are the descendants of African slaves and Caribe Indians. Most lived on the island of St. Vincent when the British rounded us up after a slave uprising, put us on ships and abandoned us on Roatán Island. We survived: built villages, raised families and fished—created our own community and culture. Eventually we left the island for the mainland and islands all over the Caribbean. Your part of the family went to Haiti but most set up communities in Honduras, Belize, Guatemala, and Nicaragua. The famous ones are thirty-six Garifuna communities in Honduras," a look of wonder and shock came over Tula's face, "we celebrate April twelve, the date we arrived in 1797. The old man and I went to the anniversary parties for years and danced for days. We are black people but your part of the family became fair since they intermingled over the years with the whites from Europe and the many pirates that roamed the Caribbean. The old man left your father in Haiti and I think he regrets that. As soon as he could your father moved you and the family to Canada. The old man never saw his family again."

"What happened to my grandmother?"

"She died of cholera when she was very young. The old man never talks about her, I think he loved her very much since for thirty-five years he would not marry me."

"You have been taking care of him for all these years?" Tula said.

"Yes," she said sadly, "the old man and I lived up and down the coast doing work on the islands just like his Grandpa. When I was young, he was my lover and best friend and we fished and roamed the Caribbean together, but I was too young and now he is too old."

Jonathan notice her eyes fill with tears and he imagined her out on the tropical sea, young and bare breasted hauling in the fishing lines, her man working beside her.

"The money to take care of him; where does that come from?"

"This estate, we own it, paid for it with gold the old man found. The sugar cane," and she pointed out of the window, "is grown by an international company who pays us to grow it. We are in need of nothing."

"The gold Grandpa found; did he take it all?"

"No, just a little. He told me, many years ago, that there is a huge cache of it up on one of the islands off Quintana Roo. The island of women he said. But there are dozens of stories of pirate treasure in the Caribbean." Tula glanced at Jonathan noting confirmation, "he used to talk about us going back and getting more but time ran out for us."

"Thank you for taking care of him, Dorothy. I will keep in touch in the future."

"If you can, if you can," Dorothy said, but there was a tone to her voice that said, please don't make a promise you cannot keep. They got up and walked to the door, leaving the old man to his dreams. Out on the road the taxi was waiting for Tula and Jonathan. They left the plantation and drove north to Belize City. Tula looked back and saw Dorothy waving from the veranda, she burst into tears. She knew she would never see the old man again.

And through her tears she shouted, "I'm rich, I'm rich!"

The Ruins of Tulum

The collectivo bus dropped Tula and Jonathan off on a sand dune overlooking the Caribbean Sea; surf thundered across a reef onto a bleached white shore; huge clouds, many miles to the east, marched to the south across a giant sky. Gentle hills of sand rolled into the flat jungle landscape. In the distance on a rise were the ruins of the ancient city of Tulum. They checked in at reception of a cabana resort and unloaded their gear in a little rustic shack that sat on a sand dune. A couple of beach dogs used it for shade in the day.

Jonathan was exhausted from the murder and mayhem of their journey across Mexico, Guatemala and Belize. Soon they would be busy with the bizarre treasure hunt and he wondered whether he could take anymore of Tula's rampant lifestyle.

Their home for a few days stood on stilts with walls of poles plastered in unfinished gray stucco. A high steep thatched roof kept out the weather; fishnets held it in place since the rain and wind could get ferocious coming from the sea, raising the thatch and flooding the little home. It had a wooden door and the only window was small in a corner above a double bed that had a lacy mosquito net floating above it. There was no ceiling, the interior rose into the rafters exposing the underside of the thatching where fireflies and geckos lived. The furniture was the double bed and a small rough wood table with two matching primitive chairs—everything was raw unpainted wood. The interior design was Mexican minimalist—a quiet, beautiful, architectural accident. Showers and toilets were communal and located behind a restaurant pavilion that was not in operation since the owners had broken some archeological bylaw. They were given two candles and two bed sheets.

"Hmm, romantic," Tula commented sarcastically, "the least you could have done was get us a place with indoor plumbing."

"Now that's not the idea of a retreat," he said as he made the bed and spread out the mosquito net, tucking it under the mattress edge, "this is a *real* retreat—a place were we can get away from it all."

"A place where you can seduce me," she whispered gently.

"Yeah, now you've got the idea."

Beside the compound of cabanas and across the fishermen's sand access road to the beach was a restaurant bar where they could feast on Mexican fare, beer and international company. That evening they ate steak and lobster, drank a bottle of the best wine the house had to offer, walked on the beach and talked about their lives. The tropical night came fast and a full moon was out, bright and beautiful in the eastern sky. Hung gently just below it was Quetzalcoatl. They sat on the stairs of their cabana.

"We are so different, yet so much the same," he said squeezing her hand in his, "our timing is bad and we live in so differ—"

Tula reached out her hand and touched his lips with her fingers, "I know, I know and it hurts me to think that we can't last. It's all too dangerous for you."

"I want you to come back to Thailand with me."

"Let's get this thing over with first and then we can talk. I just can't get emotional at this time."

"It's that damn gold! Promise me we will talk about us after we get it."

"I promise. Now sit between my legs and tell me about the ruins up the beach."

He moved down a step and leaned back against her. He pointed to a few faint lights in the distance. "Tulum was a city and seaport occupied by the Maya up to the time the Spanish arrived. Like many ruins up and down the coast they had lighthouses that guided the fishermen ashore between the breaks in the reef. Tulum has one of those breaks off shore. It's a walled community for protection from pirates that where here even before the whites came and—"

"My ancestors."

"—plundered villages and cities on this coast is not a new thing. No one lives there anymore; just dozens of very big healthy iguanas that look rather pissed at all the tourists that go through their home. They have lived in the ruins for thousands years, living and dying among the white stones. The archeological and parks people are busy fucking their habitat up with new pathways, stairs, electrical wiring—that sort of stuff. The way humans are; it will be abandoned again and archeologist of the future won't know what the hell was going on. The iguanas will know because they have always lived there. It still is a beautiful place; regardless, and I always feel the ghosts of those ancient people flowing through me whenever I'm there.

"You were here before?"

"Yeah, many years ago," he said.

"Are you like me—looking for something, perhaps peace of mind?"

"No, I'm at peace as I told you that along time ago."

"I remember."

"I find the world and ruins like Tulum fascinating and I must see as much of the ancient arts as I can. I have a good life; I'm in awe of it and that I should be so lucky. My daughter and son are doing well, so I don't have to worry about them, my new family in Thailand keeps me busy and everyday I experience something different and exciting. I don't want to understand everything I see and experience in life; that would be too much; I just want to live it. You are part of what is life for me—hell I will never understand you. My Thai family was upset that I would leave them and my responsibilities to come and help you. But you called, and it was a terrible shock to know you were still alive, so here I am in a place and time that is dangerous and foolish. I don't' care, I just don't care. What about you babe?"

"I'm a criminal," she said casually, "all my life has been a fight to survive. Unlike you I have been in the wrong place at the wrong time. I've had to kill to survive; events and circumstances demanded it. And if I didn't kill I would and will be killed. It's been a dogs life."

"I know. Often in life we have no choice about were we are going or who with." And Jonathan remembered all the times he had seen animals in markets, city streets and towns across the world trying their best to survive—to eat or be eaten.

"You really do love me. Don't you?"

"Yeah, Tula, I do love you."

"Hey—remember that night on the Beach of The Dead in Sayulita."

"Of course."

"Let's go for that swim again," she said. And so they did.

The candles lit their little cabana but the walls flew away into the blackness of it's interior; the mosquito net hung like a giant butterflies cocoon; everything looked comfortable and romantic but the atmosphere had changed considerably from its daytime brother—the air felt alive. From the light of a single bulb out in the compound, amber shafts shone through the small wood shuttered window and the night-lights from the restaurant crept under the floor creating glowing lines between the boards. Jonathan closed the little window, blew out the candles and in the blackness Tula and he climbed into bed under the white mosquito netting. His eyes adjusted to the night and the little light that came up from the floor shone through the netting. The air did not move and the temperature was in the mid thirties.

Nighttime passed and Jonathan slept briefly, Tula fell into a deep sleep and snored peacefully. Jonathan did not know how long he was out but he woke in a panic, his head was filled with the anxiety of impending death. He was suffocating—his nasal passages were filled with fluid. The blackness was crushing him—the cabana was crushing him. He moved the net aside and got out of bed and took a long deep breath. He quietly moved to the door and opened it to let the moon give him some sort of orientation of what was up and down. He sat down on the stairs at the door and thought Christ am I going crazy, has the time come for me to grasp senility, had my time arrived? He could now see the walls and thatching of their cabana. He breathed heavily and sat quietly and waited for reality to return and the anxiety to leave. He thought of other things, his love for Tula, his elephant and his art. Reality returned and his thoughts drifted to normal. He lit the candles so he could see the thatching more clearly. The candles would burn while he slept; he believed the subdued light through his eyelids would keep life sensible for him.

With the window open and the candles lit he snuggled up to Tula's back and he drifted into sleep. He was soon awake, the candles and light in the compound were out but a new light was in the cabana. The floorboards seemed to be further apart and light was emanating from below. he jumped out of bed and things on the floor became normal but he woke up Tula.

"What's the matter? Are you okay?"

"No, something is wrong, I'm having terrible nightmares." He looked up and fireflies jumped around the rafters, their shining abdomens glowed like stars. Beautiful, he thought but he was still scared—the cabana was crushing him and his anxiety was becoming worse.

"I'll be fine, you go back to sleep. I will just sit out on the stairs for a bit." And for the next hour he stared out into the blackness—the moon and Quetzalcoatl had left him to the terror of the night. Only the distant constellations kept him company.

He returned to sleeping Tula and the net but he was not sure if he was asleep or not, the floorboards opened up even further. He was sitting on the edge of a floating bed, the mosquito net resting over his head; Tula was in a deep sleep behind him. This is bad, he thought, I will I have to go into town and see a doctor or worse go home to Thailand—my head in a basket, muttering incoherently. Suddenly something dark appeared between the spaces in the floor planking. Shadows were moving below, some had traces of colour: red, orange, blue and green, but they were mostly black. They flowed like they were liquid; the light became blue as it came up from the floor and in through the window.

"Jesus!" Jonathan screamed and woke up Tula. He ran out of the door onto the cool sand of the dune, a naked Tula ran after him. The only light was from the constellations that shone brightly over the beach and sea. He ran to the water's edge, lights shone and sparkled on the breaking surf like the fireflies from the rafters. A few hundred yards out where the surf was breaking on the coral reef, lights formed above the waves. They glowed dull amber and moved rapidly back and forth, crossing each other. The lights in the surf continued to sparkle blue and red accented with silver white forms. They were fish—Jonathan hoped so. Tula grabbed him from behind and sat him down on the sand. She held him tightly to her.

"It's okay—it's fine," she said gently, "I'm here—it will pass."

"Oh Jesus! It's scaring the hell out of me. Am I going mad again like I did in Spain, or is it an age thing?"

"It doesn't matter. Just sit quietly for a while. I'm here with you. She laid her face on the nape of his neck, kissed him and held on."

Jonathan looked down the beach to the ruins of Tulum and the Castillo on the cliff glowed a fluorescent white; black shadows danced across its walls. Further down the coast the ancient lighthouse of the ruins glowed orange. A fire was burning in its doors and windows, set to guide the way home for its ancient gods and fishermen who where out tonight somewhere wandering in the new world—perhaps to raise a little hell.

"Can you see that?" and he pointed down to the ruins, "they're on fire!" He turned to look up at their cabana. Tula hung on to his back.

Then he knew he was going mad. Coming up over the sand dunes from their cabana was an army of shadows led by two giant Iguanas. The lizards stopped, looked at them and huge fleshy tongues came out of their scaly spiked heads and licked the air.

"Christ, they tasted us!"

"Who, Jonathan, who tasted us?"

"The iguanas!" he shouted. The dark army about thirty meters long and ten meters wide moved silently in a tight pack, flashes of colour shone from them and black shadows of weapons and flags swayed above the crowd. They seemed to ride to the rhythm of the sea swells and the sound of the crashing surf. At first he thought they were coming for them but the commanders, the iguanas, turned toward the ruins and led the crazy army down the beach. The fires of the ancient lighthouse glowed, the lights of an ancient Maya fishing fleet drifted back and forth beyond the reef and from the crashing surf the fish winked at everything. The stars glowed above them and their little cabana sat silently high on the dune. They got up from the sand and walked up the beach to it and climbed under the netting and into bed.

Jonathan slept well in Tula's arms and the early morning light that shone through the window and the open door brought them gently back to this world. Jonathan wondered; had all that happened during the night. Perhaps I am going mad, he thought but dismissed it. He lay with Tula quietly and they told each other of their love.

"Sorry about last night honey," he said sheepishly, "I don't know what happened."

"It okay, it was the cabana, netting, the heat and no fan. That's what happens when you go cheap," she chuckled, "time for a swim, we stink." They jumped out of bed, put their swimming gear on, he grabbed his razor and they ran to the beach. The water was cold and refreshing and the shaving was rough as it always is without soap.

Jonathan looked up to the sand dune and their little cabana and suddenly the world stopped. "Tula—look," coming out from under the building between the stilts was a trench two meters wide; it came down the beach and turned in the direction of the ruins of Tulum. On each side of the trench were depressions made from some giant animals.

"Oh Christ—what's going to happen tonight?" she said.

A Ship of Stones, Gold and Bones

Jonathan and Tula stayed on the beach at Tulum for a few days and got used to cabana life. He overcame his fears and she became closer to him and even had those wonderful thoughts of living in paradise together forever, but it was fleeting. Unfortunately reality struck and there was business to be done.

They moved into a small apartment in the town area of Isla Mujeres using the names of Mr. and Mrs. Smallwood from Eton, Nebraska down for sun and sex. He rented a golf cart and they drove out to Mundaca's estate, a park about three quarters north up the island where Tula believed the seven stones and treasure might be. For days they searched the place for stones but with no luck. They abandoned the search; the security and grounds staff became suspicious. They probably were not but Jonathan and Tula where in a high state of paranoia by this time.

They sat dejected in the hotel bar, "Where's the stash?" she said very frustrated—angels danced all over her, "That old bastard lied to me!" she gulped down her Cubra Libra and puffed on her cigar.

"You know your Grandpa never said the gold was at Mundaca's estate, you have, assumed it is there. Maybe he worked other places on the island? Let's take our time and poke around a bit," he suggested calmly and he reached across the table and took her hand, "if we can't find anything you can always come home and live with me and my elephant, and monkey, and buffalo, and the refugees, and—"

"Stop it!" she shouted and laughter and tears where all over her face.

The next day on the hotels wireless Internet connection he bought up the satellite imagery of Isla Mujeres on his rented laptop. They scanned the island looking for possible sites where the treasure might be buried.

They went out and checked locations: the turtle farm, the beaches in the north, around the salt lakes in the middle of the island and all the inlets on the west. The east side had eroded over the years; if gold was buried there, it would be long gone by now. They had no luck anywhere they searched.

"Hey," he said as they were driving back to their hotel from one of their field trips, "what about out on the end point at that old Maya ruin; Ichtel—Ishell—or something or other?"

"Ixchel—yeah—maybe. Tomorrow we can check it out. Hey, I think you're starting to believe—Mr. Smallwood from Eton, Nebraska."

Punta Sur was the last place on the island they could think of that Grandpa might have worked as a mason many years ago. The hurricanes of the past had mostly destroyed the Maya temple that once sat majestically on the point. They drove there and paid their entry fee into the park.

"Oh hell," Tula said in disgust as they walked down to the end point of the island, "only one building is left and there isn't much of that either; just a platform with three walls of rock. Damn, how disappointing." The walls were half of their original height and the east wall was gone.

"Let's not be in too much of a rush here. We will look around." Jonathan climbed up onto the floor of the old ruin; he reached down and helped Tula up; she then climbed up onto the remains of the old temple wall. She stood looking out to sea to the south then north up the eight-kilometer stretch of the island. There was a terrible dejected look on her face for she was facing the unknown; all prospects for her future were dashed. It was just too difficult; structures had changed on the island over the years because of the ongoing decay and erosion of the buildings and the island itself. Everything was built of limestone, the victim of the harsh climate of hot temperatures, changing humidity and storms.

"God damn that old man!" she shouted, "that bastard, that bastard!" she repeated, "going to his grave and leaving his family wondering. The family promised me I would be rich someday. And damn the weather of this god-forsaken place!" she shouted to the sky and shook her fist in the air.

Jonathan laughed, "Gone with the wind," he shouted. He reached up and took her hand, "it was just too good to be true, it's an old story around these parts. There will always be stories of buried treasure and pirates. They will always be just stories. You can come to Thailand and live with me; I'll take care of you in the years to come. No one will ever find you or bother you and you can learn to love me again," finally he had her, she had no place to go, nowhere to run.

She looked down at Jonathan with a look of contempt. "I don't clean up elephant shit. Don't you realize this was my last hope? What do I do now? I have no—" suddenly she stopped talking and her mouth dropped open, "Look where you're standing!" She pointed down to his feet. She could hardly breathe.

He looked down, "It can't be!" he said in amazement.

"It is!" she screamed with excitement. She jumped down from the wall and held on to him.

He was standing on a dark gray stone, in front of him were two lighter coloured stones and a third long stone pointing west. He looked behind him and saw another stone and off it at ninety degrees to each other where two long stones, one facing south the other northeast. "It's them; the seven stones of my Grandpa. I recognize the three-pointed star. This is the place—this is the place!" she shouted and she jumped up and down like a child.

"Incredible," he said, dumbfounded that all along this treasure hunt nonsense was true and not some fantasy made up by a crazed woman. Along with the moment came the dread that he had lost her. He got down on his knees to feel the stones and she knelt beside him. Together they ran their hands over the stones. There was a pattern to them that was purposely laid out, laid out back in the '50s when Tula's Grandpa and three men repaired the old temple after hurricane Gilbert had torn it apart. The mortar between the stones looked new. The gray stone that Jonathan had stood on was cracked around its perimeter where it joined the mortar and would easily pry loose.

"The old man worked here long ago and I bet there are bones and gold just a couple of centimeters away. What the hell are we going to do," she said realizing the dilemma, "this is a public park we can't just go ahead and dig these stones up."

"Your right about that. We are going to have to give this some thought. I'll take pictures," and he opened his camera pouch attached to his belt, pulled out his digital camera and took several pictures of the stones at different angles and from atop the broken wall. Tula glowed with excitement and angels danced across her face; she moved her body in and out of every shot. They discussed and made mental notes of the position of the temple and the condition of the platform and walls.

At the hotel that night Jonathan and Tula made a dinner of chicken fajita and drank several bottles of red wine. They got very drunk and discussed wild plans for digging up the treasure that they imagined would be under the seven stones. They talked on about gold doubloons; Maya jewel encrusted statues, necklaces, bracelets and amulets of enormous value on today's market. On the computer, they looked up the going price of gold; one once was worth USD eight hundred dollars.

"If we take just one hundred pounds at the going rate," and he made the calculations on the computer, "that would make it—one million two hundred eighty thousand dollars."

"More than a million bucks!" she shouted and laughed, "If there is more down there we can come back in a few years and grab another million."

"Or two," Jonathan sighed who was having second thought about this bizarre situation.

"You don't sound enthusiastic about this, my dear," she said in a serious tone.

"I am thinking about Thailand and Buddha," he said, "This all goes against what I have become."

"And what is that?"

"Buddhist, I guess. I am starting to realize that I may be religious."

"Well get over it, Jonathan."

They made love and after Jonathan went to sleep. Tula sat naked in front of the laptop going over the digital pictures of the stones and making notes of what to do when the time came to dig—and that was a worry. She smoked a Cuban cigar as she did her plotting and imagined how much she and Jonathan could actually carry out—gold is heavy. What was most important was when would they be able to dig the stuff up? There are always tourists coming and going from the site, it's a major attraction on the island with souvenir shops, bars, restaurants and wedding facilities. There are maintenance crews and security people everywhere all day and night.

The weather—maybe the weather she thought. There must be some kind of storm out there about to come ashore; it is the hurricane season after all. She went on the Internet and to the American Weather Bureau. She bought up the forecasting page and behold there was a storm brewing out in the Atlantic and may make landfall in Haiti and Jamaica in about a week. Then its direction was not predictable, she could only hope it would come her way. All she knew was that it is the only time, during a storm, when the park would be empty with every one at home except maybe a watchman on the site. She jumped up from the computer, put her cigar out and climbed on the bed with Jonathan. "Wake up old man," she said pinching him on the thigh, "wake up."

"Christ Tula," he groaned rubbing his eyes, "what time is it?"

"She looked over to the computer, "two thirty-eight. I've figured out how we are going to do it."

"Do what?"

"The treasure—get the treasure."

"Tell me in the morning."

"No, now! We are going to get it during a hurricane, one that is on the way and will be here in about a week. I'm going to stay up and figure this out and make out a shopping list."

"Oh Jesus," he moaned, and he buried his head in a pillow.

A week went by and the reality of the hurricane was now on the island and the Yucatan peoples' minds. It was huge and on it's way to making landfall in the south. Jonathan and Tula went shopping at a suburban shopping center in Cancun. Tula had spent many hours putting together her shopping list: boots, lights, tents, ropes, an iron rod to smash the rocks, climbers fittings, plastic sheets, snack food and fast mix mortar to repair the breaks around the stones after they had taken the loot. He was amazed at her ingenuity. She picked out new clothes for him as their journey had started to turn his to rags. She thought of everything as though it was a military campaign and to her way of thinking it was.

"Where do you come up with all this stuff?" he asked.

"The army, remember, I was in the friggin' Canadian Army," she laughed. She would dress for the part in black leather boots, tight waterproof pants, black leather bomber jacket, black motorcycle jock's bandana and fingerless gloves. At home she modeled the outfit for him and all he could do was laugh and hug her for her enthusiasm.

The computer was on the weather channel twenty-four hours a day and Tula monitored the storm as it entered the Caribbean Sea whose warm water generated it into a hurricane. It soon went from a tropical storm to a category three and was one thousand kilometers wide. The predicted landfall would be in the south of Quintana Roo at Chetumal, by then it would strengthen to a category five but would suddenly collapse in strength when it encountered the severe temperature change between land and sea. Its outer arms would slap Isla Mujeres with winds two hundred fifty to three hundred kilometers and hour. That would be scary enough to send everybody packing from the park.

"Look," and she pointed at the screen, "the winds along these outer arms are the ones that will hit us, which is perfect. The walls of the ruin, even it they are small, will give us some protection. I figure we will spend about twenty hours out there."

"Twenty hours?" he said, "That's one hell of a long time bundled up together in a tent."

"Yeah," and she gave him a broad smile and gently squeezed his hand, "remember PV a couple of years ago?" He could only smile back.

At mid afternoon, the day of the storm's arrival, Tula and Jonathan dressed in their treasure hunting gear and packed their tools into their rented golf cart and drove south toward the park on Punta Sur, Isla Mujeres. Both were quiet for the trip, this was going to be dangerous and they knew it. But that was what their lives were all about—danger and risk. She looked at him and thought of their past. He was the only man she ever trusted and she had strange feelings of regrets deep in her for not loving him more like any decent woman would. But then, she told herself, I'm not a decent woman and I need him.

"This is crazy. You know that don't you?" he said quietly.

"Yes, I know it is," and she put her hand on his thigh. They soon reached the outskirts of the park and pulled into the wreckage of a construction site a half a kilometer away from the entrance. They put on their backpacks loaded with their supplies and like a couple of soldiers moved off to their destination. The sky was a deep gray, the wind was coming up and nobody was around. The staff had gone home to their families to ride out the storm and pray for their survival.

To his surprise a guard, the only one on site, greeted them at the entrance. He shook Jonathan's hand and gave him a huge grin. He quickly left and went inside the souvenir shop but before closing the door he gave them a thumbs-up and a broad grin.

"What the hell was that about?" he asked.

"I gave him a hundred bucks a couple of days ago to leave us alone out there. He thinks you are my kinky husband who likes to make love in unusual circumstances and places. Which you do."

"Did the Canadian Army teach you that too?"

"Yup."

"Look at that!" he said, "The last glow of sunlight is on Ixchel." A stream of light came out of the thunderclouds and briefly lit the end of the island in a celestial glow.

"It's so beautiful, isn't it?" she commented and hugged his arm, "What does gold sound like rolling around in your pocket?"

"Rich."

"The so called, calm before the storm," he quipped about the scene before them, "have a good look at it. It just may be the last of this world we see." he held back to take in the incredible view, Tula moved down the pathway to the temple. In the distant south he saw an astonishing site; thunderclouds like mountains, massive columns of them were marching onto the Yucatan; conquistadors and their priests in long black robes. The soldiers gleamed in the last of the sunlight and exploded up and down with flashes of lightning riddling their bodies. A distant sound of crackling and rumbling rode to the temple on screaming winds. The sea, rising under the low air pressure, was a boiling black mass crossed with white caps whose peaks turned to mist as the wind sheared them off. The blackness and the wind were changing and becoming more violent with every minute—he hurried to the temple and Tula.

On the temple platform they unloaded their gear. Tula tied a rope around the south wall and attached their tent and lifelines to it with mountain climber's rigging. They lashed their backpacks to the ropes and she tied her long black curls back and up with a bandana like the Mayan warriors used to do, knotting it tightly. The winds picked up furiously and he looked over the wall to see the ocean rise. It threw waves up and over the temple. She had done her homework; the walls were protecting them and they were dry in their gear. He looked at her and she was beautiful and excited. Fear shot through him and he grabbed her and kissed her hard.

"What was that!" she shouted over the storm.

"I love you and this could be our last time together!" he shouted back. She held on to him burying her face in his neck.

She pulled away, "Time to open up your Maya god," she screamed over the howling wind and she stood over the seven stones with a steel pike pole, raised it over her head and drove it down between the stones. Water flew off her clothing, her eyes where huge and white with black centers, muscles bulged from her thighs and arms and angels danced all over her face. Her hair whipped around above her head. The winds roared and water flew up and over the temple and her. He had never seen her this way before and he knew then and there, she was the killer, the murderer—the assassin of Puerto Vallarta. She had to be, she was so ferocious in her work.

Suddenly the gray stone she had been concentrating on collapsed about six inches. She stopped her hammering and stood over the hole and breathed heavily. Jonathan, on his hands and knees reached into the depression, turned the stone on its side and pulled it out. The hole was dark and she quickly pulled the camper light from her backpack and tuned it on. She stood over him and the seven stones holding the lantern while he reached down to a bed of sand. He sifted through it with his fingers. They eventually stuck on something. He pulled the object out of the pit. It was a human vertebra.

"Jesus!" he said, "a friend of your Grandpa?"

"Yes, he buried his partners with the treasure."

"Wow, this *is* becoming a fairy tale," he laughed out nervously.

"Come on, dig deeper!" she yelled above the wind. He clawed his way through the sand and pulled out more bones and a partial skull. He threw the bones into the boiling sea that had risen to just a few feet below the platform. They were now on an island, just them and the temple above the boiling ocean, lightning riddled the black sky.

"Wait a minute!" he shouted above the roar, "there is something different here. I can feel something round—its heavy for its size—there's a bunch of them." He pulled them up out of the pit and into the light of Tula's lantern. They were clean and shining.

"Gold!" Tula screamed, "gold—for Christ sake I'm rich!"

"It is!" and he handed some of the pieces to her. He rolled one in his hands: it was ten cm. across and one cm thick. Hallmarks that he could not read were stamped on one side, other than that there was no other marking to indicate age or place.

"These are gold slugs!" he shouted over the roar of the wind and sea. He rubbed the wet sand away and bought more out onto the platform, "before shipping the gold home to Spain the conquistadors melted down the Maya and Aztec's statues and jewelry into convenient sized slugs for shipment. These never made it to Spain. There is a legend that a smelter was on this island constructed by Cortez to prepare the loot he and his men had stolen!"

"How do you know that?" she queried, screaming.

"I read it on the internet!" he screamed back, and they both laughed, "The gold has waited here for centuries for your Grandpa and now us. I'll be damned—I'll be damned," he whispered to himself as he studied the twenty thousand dollar slug in his hand.

"Okay, let's dig this stuff out of here!" he said and gestured to her to help out. And she got down on her knees, set down her lantern and both hands dug into the pit, "now remember honey we have to carry this stuff in our backpacks so let's just take enough out that we can handle." They pulled the gold out in handfuls along with more bones that they threw into the sea. Soon the platform was covered in gold and she was laughing hysterically, which disturbed him. What if she is like Grandpa. Would I be walking out of here alive tomorrow or joining Grandpa's buddies below.

They cleaned the sand off the gold and packed them in their

backpacks. Tula's was three quarters full.

"Okay!" he shouted, "Put the backpack on and see if you can walk with it." She lifted it up onto the wall and slipped into the back straps and cinched up the waistband. She stood up slowly and staggered. "That's about it. That's all you can carry out of here."

"More, I want more!" she shouted.

"Don't get greedy Tula. This is all you can carry!"

"Shit—well—okay then." And she set the backpack onto the wall and got out of the straps.

He took a hold of her. "There's about three quarters of a million dollars in your pack and the same in mine. It's all yours. You're rich now."

"Aren't you taking any?"

"No, I'm already rich, I have my Thailand and an elephant to clean up after," they laughed and hugged each other, "we better get out of this weather, it's getting worse. Let's hope the water is at its peak and the winds don't become stronger. It will be tomorrow before we can walk out of here."

They attached their packs to the ropes and took out plastic containers of the ingredients to make a mortar to cement the gray stone back in place. No one must know they had been there. She mixed the concoction and he gathered stones from the base of the temple, that was not underwater, to hold the gray stone up in place. The repair was done and they placed a sheet of plastic held by rocks over the seven stones and mortar to give it a chance to cure overnight. They threw gear and equipment that they would not need into the sea and climbed into their tent cocoon to eat cereal bars, drink some cold coffee and wait for morning. They knew there was a danger that the storm could get bigger and kill them. It had already killed the watchman; the lighthouse, souvenir shop, restaurant and bar had all disappeared long ago—washed out to sea.

They were on a ship made of stone under the command of the Maya god, Ixchel. Booming above them thundered Chac the crooked nosed god of rain. Old Spain's conquistadors and inquisition priests in long black robes walked across the deck. Maya warriors, blood red from battle, screamed in the rigging; black slaves below decks rattled steel chains; pirates brandishing cutlasses and firing canons and muskets where all around them. Tula and Jonathan were on board that mad ship, on a black violent Caribbean sea—two very rich passengers with no place to go.

A Two Thousand Horses Chariot

Tula and Jonathan got back to the hotel without being stopped by the military or the police; there were only a few islanders out on the streets as the winds were still blowing strong. They passed the military base's back gate and saw soldiers loading trucks with emergency supply packages. Navy personnel were bringing their gunboats back that they had moored out in the bay rather than have them bashed to pieces against the concrete dock. Beyond them, on a spit, many pleasure craft were wrecked on the rocks some had sunk in the shallows.

They unloaded their remaining gear and the backpacks of gold and Jonathan returned the golf cart to the safety of the owner's garage. When he got back to the hotel he found Tula lounging on the bed naked on a layer of gold slugs, smoking a cigar and giggling with delight. Another dramatic moment.

"We made it honey," she said, "what a trip that was." He said nothing and moved her and the gold off the bed, pulled back the sheets, stripped and got into bed.

"Good night, honey. Sorry, I'm just too tired." he said. She climbed in behind him.

Jonathan went out into the neighborhood to help wherever he could to clean up the town. Some buildings had been completely destroyed while others their roofs, awnings and outdoor furniture had disappeared, taken across the island and out to sea. Most of the palm trees survived but some were shredded to pieces. Only two deaths and one missing were reported and they were two drunks who drowned under a boat on the beach and the night watchman from the historic park. The ferries had been docked in a protected area north of Cancun throughout the storm and were in twenty-four hour operation when it was safe, supplies and goods arrived hourly. The bakery and super-mini next to the hotel were up and running. It only took a few days for things to get back to normal. The island people are tough; they are people of the sea and used to Chac raising hell in one of his bad moods.

While Jonathan was helping out the island people, Tula was busy laundering the gold on the mainland. Some trips she was missing for several days but Jonathan did not worry about her and didn't particularly want to know what she was up to. He knew her power and street smarts. Making dangerous deals, death and murder were cousins of hers. She finished her business and they became the vacationing couple again, going to the beach, eating and drinking in the best restaurants and bars. They became known to the locals and treated to the best service. Rumors flew across the island about them and Tula started to worry.

"Someone is following us," she said one day when they were taking the sun on North Beach.

"What do you mean?" he said from his lounge chair at the water's edge.

"We are being followed, I have seen him for the last three days."

"Who and how can you be certain?" "Someone I recognize. I'm scanning all the time. It's what I do. Sorry babe but I'm an animal. It's the way I have been bought up," she looked over to him from her lounge chair and said, "I will be gone for a couple of days."

"What?" he said in surprise but it was too late for an answer she grabbed her beach bag and was gone. he swore, Jesus Christ, my life is crazy. He looked out towards the mainland the afternoon thunderclouds where building. Chac would soon be upon him.

"Ten thousand," Karlos, the fisherman, said as he sat on a metal pail repairing his fishing net, "ten thousand for the run."

"Five thousand," Tula said.

"Eight," Karlos said.

"Done," and she shook his out stretched hand, "instructions?"

"Be on the dock tonight at eleven p.m. She will be here with her boat and don't be early or late. Be careful, she is armed and will kill you if she becomes suspicious."

"My kind of woman," Tula said," and they both laughed, "Who is she anyway?"

"Nightrider, that is all we know. We don't know where she comes from and we have never seen her in the daylight. She has messengers, bankers and fishermen like me who takes care of her business. I am the contact for the Cancun area. Actually we are the ones who take the risks. She is like a black ghost."

"She trusts you with all this money?"

"More to the point, do we trust her? She has killed messengers in the past for cheating her."

"The money please and your name," Karlos said.

"Tula. And how do I know I can trust you?"

"You don't."

Tula studied his weathered face and his corrupt watery dark eyes; she knew she had to trust him. He was the only contact in Cancun with the notorious Nightrider, the woman that would get her into Cuba—illegally. There was no other way. The legal way was just too risky, she could not trust her passport and the chance of being caught transporting a huge amount of money—the odds were against her. She reached in her short's pocket and pulled out a fat bundle of American one hundred dollar bills. She handed the wad to him.

"Is this the right amount?" Karlos queried.

"Sure is, I figured it would be eight thousand so I had the bundle ready."

"Man, you are a shrewd bitch."

"Well thank you Karlos," Tula quipped, "I'll be here at eleven. Adios." She left the dock and walked to the highway and hailed a taxi: "Take me to a five star on the strip."

In her room overlooking the beach and Isla Mujeres she showered and from room service ordered a steak dinner, chocolate dessert and a pot of tea. After eating she went to bed for a five hour sleep. She awoke and it was dark, the lights of Isla Mujeres shone in the distance and melancholy swept over her—she longed for Jonathan. Quickly she dismissed him and prepared for her journey. She dressed in the outfit she wore to dig up the treasure: black weatherproof pants and shirt, and added other items, a sheathed short knife that she strapped to her right ankle under her pants and attached a barber's razor on a chain around her neck. She tucked that into her shirt. With a black silk scarf she tied her hair up in a bun and out of the way. In the garbage pail in the bathroom she dumped her other clothing, cosmetics and sundry items except for a thin feather light flowery frock, which she neatly folded and placed in her backpacks side pocket. She would leave her wheeled luggage behind. Her backpack contained cash, almost one million American Dollars in large bills. A water bottle was strapped to the side. In her shirt pockets were half a dozen quality Cuban cigars in waterproof tubes, a lighter and small flashlight was on a key chain attached to her belt. In her pant pocket she had five hundred dollars in Cuban Convertible pesos. She was ready for her run to Cuba with Nightrider.

"Wow," Tula whispered as she walked down the dock in the dark puffing on a cigar. At the end of the dock was an eight-meter, black fiberglass speedboat with no markings. It was pointing out to sea and she could see a dull glow of instrument lights in the open cockpit, its engines throbbed a deep rumble. A small radar scanner turned on a metal bar above the cockpit.

Standing on the dock by the speedboat was a huge black woman dressed like Tula in black waterproof gear; strapped across her large breasts was an Oozie gun. On a black webbed belt was a holstered pistol with cartridges, a ten centimeter sheathed knife and a small zipper bag.

"Tula?" she barked and leveled her Oozie at her.

"Yes," Tula answered confidently.

"Welcome—get in." Nightrider let a mid ship line go and they both boarded the magnificent machine, "stow your gear behind the pilot seat," she ordered.

"You have style nightrider," Tula said taking off her backpack and laying it behind the seat. She handed Nightrider a cigar, "everything fast and on time."

"Jesus woman, how did you know I smoke this Cuban shit?"

"I figured you did. Many of our kind do."

"Ha—ha—thanks, so Tula honey, we will be traveling for several hours so make yourself comfortable. In the backseats are life jackets if bad stuff happens, but it don't make no difference anyway, the damn ocean is full of sharks. There are fire extinguishers, first aid kit and flair guns under the front seat. In the bow there is a head and a bunk if you need to lie down. If you throw up, do it over the side. Got that?"

"Okay," Tula said laying down her pack and looking the boat over. Nightrider took the wheel, checked the gauges and scanned around the boat with a powerful flashlight. The black machine slowly moved away from the dock and the bow swung north to the stars and the black sea.

"Take the seat beside me," and she did what she was told, "here we go into the night." Nightrider pulled two throttle controls back steadily and slowly and the engines burst to life, the bow came up and after half a kilometer, slowly moved down into a plane position; the power and speed increased. Nightrider switched all the lights off and put the radar on standby. Before Tula knew it she was thrown back in her seat and the cool night air rushed passed her. She breathed deeply and felt safe, relaxed and alive in the care of black Nightrider and her powerful machine. They flew; riding high across the black water and soon Cancun, Isla Mujeres, Quintana Roo, Belize, Grandpa and Jonathan were far behind her.

"Honey," Nightrider said after a few minutes, "you wanna' tell me about it?"

"What do you mean?"

"You runnin' from life, police or man?"

"All three, all three—"

"Good for you, all three is bad shit."

"You like this business, Nightrider?"

"You bet, it's good and dangerous and I make huge money, I even get to kill people sometimes."

"Who do you get to kill?"

"My competition and those who want my boat and business. My customers are pretty good. I only kill a few of them," and they both laughed, "You kill anybody?"

"Yes."

"Tell me?"

The first was a lover who treated me bad. Then after that one it was easy. Once I was hostage to a cleaning organization based in Germany. I didn't like that, I didn't know who or where they were from. I didn't know if the people I assassinated deserved to die. I had no choice in the matter. I like to have choices if I kill or not."

"You tough lady. You have man now or is he back there?"

"Back there."

"Nice man?"

"Yes."

"Okay, I shut up," Nightrider said and Tula laughed.

Hours went by and they became friends. They had much in common and shared their stories about their ancestry, men, killing and life's adventures. Tula did not talk about her latest adventure. She did not want to lead Nightrider into the valley of temptation. One of them would loose her life.

Talk turned to Tula's journey, "I need to know how to get to Africa by freighter with a captain who will not ask questions. Can you help me?"

"Ah, this is good, I thought you wanted to live in that rat hole Cuba. It won't be long until every one there lives in caves. You sure you want go to Africa?"

"Yes, I want to go to Africa. Where will we be landing on Cuba?"

"On the south side of the island—Ensenada de la Broa. There is a little bay I know where I drop you off. My friend and partner meet you and drive you to Havana. From there you take a bus to Santiago de Cuba. That is the place you need to go. Many freighters are there that sail to Africa."

"Do I pay your partner?"

"No, you bought Nightrider's complete tour package. I have a brother in Santiago de Cuba who works as security guard. He knows many people and ships coming and going. Before we arrive I will give you his email but you be very careful since the Cubans are a bunch of Commy bastards and spy on people. When you mail him just write *I am a friend of your sister*. He will email you where to meet him. I don't want my brother caught or anything bad to happen. If anything happens to my brother I will come and kill you. Understand?"

"I understand," and she looked at the big woman who smiled back at her, "will I be able to get a freighter?"

"You sound like a smart lady. I think you can talk a captain into giving you a ride."

"Remember to be very quiet in Cuba, do not talk to anyone you don't have to. Keep to yourself, stay in hotels not casas. Those people want to know your every move. They may report you to the Ministry of Interior for not having a visa."

Tula looked down at the Oozie strapped across Nightrider's chest and noticed the safety was off and the barrel was pointed at her. This woman was no amateur.

Across the blackness of the Caribbean Sea to the distant lights of Cuba the two pirates flew in their two thousand horsepower chariot.

He did not hear from her for three days and then he found a large envelope under her pillow. He sat down, opened it and read the note that was attached to fifty American one thousand dollar bills.

Dear Jonathan,

I'm sorry but I must move on. My life is too dangerous and you may get hurt or dead being near me; I live in a world you can never be part of. I am going somewhere and you cannot follow. The man who was following us no longer exists and there is a possibility that Interpol is following me. My old organization just won't give up trying to get me. If Interpol talks to you, say yes that you DID know me but have not seen me for the last week. Say we met by chance in Merida and decided to travel as old friends; that will be believable. Be sure to see their identification badges or papers. You know about them, they grabbed you once so all the more reason you are clear of me. I know you do not want any of the treasure but take the fifty thousand I have left you and return to your family in Thailand. Buy some bushels of sugar cane for that elephant buddy of yours. I love you and always will and maybe someday, we may meet again. There is always hope. Burn this note after reading. Goodbye my love. Tula.

"Bullshit!" Jonathan shouted and tore up the note, "Enough!" He picked up his sketchbook and ran to the islands ferry terminal. The only image he had was the drawing of her as Chac; she would not allow any photos taken of her. The photos he took of her at the temple only showed her body not her face. On the ferry he showed the crew his drawing and he found one man who remembered her.

"Yes, I remember her. She had a backpack and a small bag on wheels. She was on the ferry yesterday." the deckhand said, "Beautiful woman."

"Gracias." Jonathan said. It was a tortuous for him, half an hour of thinking about her. Thinking not of her safety but of the woman he loves and on the run from her terrible passed. He thought how lonely she must be without her family and identity. Every one, but a few in the world, knew she was dead. He thought about characters he once read in books when he was a young boy in school. She was now someone without a country—persona non-gratis. She was a paradox to him—exciting, dangerous and sad all wrapped up in a beautiful package. He was experienced in life to know that love can be that way.

He ran up the dock showing Tula's picture to every one and the ferry ticket agent said, "Yes, I saw her."

"Did you notice where she went?"

"She did not go to the bus or taxi stand, she went to the fishing dock by the ferry terminal." And she pointed towards a cement dock piled with gear and lined with fishing boats.

"Gracias." He knew this would be easy as Tula is a striking looking woman and noticeable. She passes by you and you take a second look. She said to him once, it is difficult to disguise yourself when you are beautiful and have a big ego. He ran to the dock and things became more complicated.

"Si senior, I saw her. She left last night on a very fast boat," said a fisherman working on his nets, "Karlos told me he had a passenger for Cuba.

Karlos is a bad man, he is always breaking the law by setting up people with a very dangerous person who takes passengers to Cuba; some do not make it with her. She is an evil woman. I would fear for your friend's safety."

"I would fear for the captain's safety," he said, "gracias senior," and Jonathan left the bewildered fisherman and walked to the end of the dock. He looked out to sea, northeast towards Cuba, you crazy bitch, he said to the breeze coming off the Caribbean Sea. I will find you. You're not dead this time.

When he got back to the island and the travel agent at the ferry terminal, he booked a flight to Havana. He took a taxi to North Beach and the bar that Tula and he spent many happy hours; pointed a lounge chair in the direction of Cuba, and laid back to think about his next move. He would find her but would not know what to do if he does catch up with her. He told himself to play it the best he can and hope. He felt like running away, he loathed being in love with her.

"Good afternoon," came a voice out of a shadow that moved over him, "my name is Conrad Dillinger. I'm with Interpol, the international police. Could I have a few moments of your time?" It did not matter if he said yes or no, the stranger pulled up a lounge chair and sat down.

"Sure." Jonathan said, "May I see some identification?" Christ, she said they would talk to me. A badge was thrust in his face and behind it sat a very big middle-aged man in black pants, white shirt and tie. He held his jacket over his arm and was sweating profusely. Another white guy in the tropics that does not know how to dress.

"My credentials Mr. Owen."

"You know me?"

"Yes, I do. Jack Garland sends his regards."

"Oh, really," Jonathan replied trying not to look surprised. He remembered his old foe from the Royal Canadian Mounted Police, "and how is good old Jack?"

"Working in Europe and loving it. He said if it wasn't for you he would still be in Northern British Columbia in a boring life. He thanks you for the change."

"Well, that's nice. What can I do for you Conrad?"

"You have a strange knack for trouble; it follows you around like a yapping street dog, Mr. Owen. Mexico, Europe, Asia, Yucatan," and he emphasized the Yucatan, "we have been following you in Mexico. There are a number of murders that have popped up over the last few weeks along the path you have been traveling. We know you are not involved, as we can't place you at the sites and times of the murders. All we know is that you have a ghost that follows you around."

"A ghost!" he laughed, "what do you mean?"

"Tula is her name," an international fugitive. We cannot connect her to the murders at the moment but we would like to talk to her and return her to the International Military Protection Program from where she escaped. You have connected in the past a few times and we know that you are lovers. Do you know where she is?"

"International Military Protection Program? What the hell is that?"

"It is a program for military personal who have gone astray. The program is not for her protection but for the protection of the public. She needs constant care and supervision because of her psychological profile—psychopath. If she does not get the care she commits murder and mayhem. She is very dangerous—her training and her past have made her that way. Our countries our responsible for these people."

"And what countries are those?"

"The free world. Now, can you tell us where she is?" Jonathan thought I should turn her in now. There is no cure for her—not for a psychopath.

"No, she ran away. I don't know where she went."

"Any ideas Mr. Owen?"

"Maybe San Christóbal de Las Casas, we went there after we ran into each other in Merida. She said she liked the place and the little revolutionary women. Now that the latest revolution has settled down, I can see her going back."

"Ran into each other?" Conrad said sarcastically.

"Yes, I was wandering around Mexico on vacation and I ran into her in Merida."

"You ran into her before in PV a while back also. Didn't you?"

"Yes, It's a small world Conrad. We struck up an affair again but she is wild and secretive. I don't know what the hell she is up to most of the time. I had no idea that she had escaped from some protection program."

"I repeat, Mr. Owen, she is a very dangerous and we must stop her. You are also in danger. Surely you must know that?"

"Well—yes—I guess I do but—"

"You know I could have those two men sitting at the bar arrest you as an accomplice in murder Mr. Owen." Jonathan turned to the look at the bar and two Mexican police officers were sitting on high stools drinking sodas. They wore black uniforms with gold lettering on the arms and backs of their shirts. He recognized their type; they could hold him forever or have him disappear.

"I know, but you have nothing on me and if you did you would have me in custody by now. I know you cannot do it yourself—International Law—right?"

"Right," officer Dillinger said, "Just see that you stick around for a few days. If you see her or she makes contact with you call me at this number," and he handed him his business card with Interpol's international address on the front and a local phone number on the back. Nice talking to you Mr. Owen. We will talk again. Bye for now."

"Give my regards to Jack the next time you talk to him." Conrad got up and left for the bar and the two Mexican police officers. Jonathan lay back, relaxed and took several deep breaths. He knew he was in the clear and Interpol was playing with him. Scaring him into doing something rash. Damn it! He said to himself, and tomorrow I fly out of here. Then on the other hand these guys don't operate in Cuba. He was afraid and knew he had to get out of Mexico. He could cancel Cuba and go back home to Thailand. No, he thought, onward after Tula.

Havana – A Cuban Tale

From the balcony of his penthouse suite, eight stories above the street, Jonathan saw decaying Havana. Somewhere in that huge gray mass was an old man in a red tracksuit—also in decay.

Penthouse is an exotic word for where Jonathan would stay to start his search for Tula. It was a small cinder block house seven flights up on the roof of an old rotting art deco mansion on the edge of the Vedado district. Vedado was, before the revolution, a beautiful and rich neighborhood of Havana, home to mobsters and movie stars. His new home was a casa particulare, a private guesthouse classification, run by a family of four who rent out two bedrooms to travelers like Jonathan. The old mansion has eight families in residence where, before the ugly little man in the red suit took over, was a single-family residence with staff help living on the estate. Now in their small apartment adults sleep on the chesterfield in a tiny living/kitchen room. Their Down syndrome child and grandfather sleep in a small shack set up in the back that has bunk beds that fill the entire space. Grandfather suffers from a stroke. He and the child have not been down on the street in years.

No Cuban is allowed to stay at the casa and besides they cannot afford it. Jonathan paid his rent in Cuban Convertible Pesos, money on a par one to one with the American Dollar, twenty-four times that of a doctor's salary. The money the family charges their guests is taxed at two hundred dollars a month for each room, and that is whether they rent the rooms or not. In the off-season there are no renters so times get tough. The Special Times as the old bastard in the tracksuit calls them.

"What do you do beside running the casa?" Jonathan asked of his landlord, Francisco.

"Nothing, I take care of the casa and family. It is all I am allowed to do; I would make too much money if I had a job. That would anger my neighbors and they would bad mouth me to the authorities. My family income is very controlled. He," Francisco stroked his chin, "makes sure of that. They inspect us weekly, sometimes daily. There are spies in the neighborhood, some live in this building. They watch everything. We can not go above their level."

"And what level is that?" Jonathan asked.

"Whatever they make up at the time. We all must bow to the revolution and to those who carry the red banner forward."

"This morning I was in line to do some banking, and a young man standing behind me was questioned by a security officer. The boy shook with fear and did not take his eyes from the floor. What was that about?"

"The fear the old man in the red tracksuit has created is enormous, even from a thousand kilometers from his hospital bed people whisper his name. His army, like the security officer you saw, and the people themselves are the new guard. They harass and intimidate."

"Where can I get a newspaper? I'd like to read what's going on in Cuba."

There are no newspapers except Grandma, our state toilet paper, no magazines, comic books or novels but those published by the government and they are all about the revolution—nothing else. Internal information about Cuba is propaganda and news from the outside world comes from television sets that bring Mexico and Miami into our homes. You can watch CNN out of Miami on our TV if you like or the latest soap operas. They play constantly distorting the outside world but they are a way out for the bored populace. The people do not know the truth.

Francisco was on a roll: "No Cuban is allowed to travel; only foreigners have the freedom to move around. Even the currency has a double standard, the peso for the populace and the peso for the foreigners, which is pushed on us making our peso practically worthless. These standards upset many Cubans and me. That is why I am not a party member or a communist. I hate what happens here."

"But you were born in the revolution how do you know what is going on outside?"

"I read books and magazines that have been left here by tourists and I have a disguised TV dish on the roof to pick up American television and radio. I have a computer and email to contact the world. I search for the truth constantly. It is dangerous but I can not help exploring the world."

"I know what you mean."

"Quiet, he's coming," Francisco whispered.

A journalist from Greece, Martin, who rents the bedroom beside Jonathan's walked onto the roof deck. He is a devout communist who used to write but does not anymore, as he said, I have become imbedded in the socialist ideology, it takes all of me. He has taught Jonathan a few things about communism and how unbending an ideology it is.

"Hey, Martin. Did you have a good time today out in the city?" Jonathan asked and shook his hand.

"No, not really. It's a bit painful to walk around Havana and see what has happened to this beautiful city over the last fifty years. I think sometimes my chosen system has failed but then sacrifices must be made. It's all bourgeois decadence anyway, isn't it? I have just come from around the corner and the University of Havana. There is a coffee shop near the entrance where our great leaders used to meet after they liberated Cuba. I felt their presence in that sacred place. After a coffee there I went up on the hill behind us to the Habana Libra that our great army liberated from the decadent Hiltons. The hotel was the first headquarters of the victorious liberation front. I like the stories of the old mobsters from America: Myer Lansky, Lucky Luciano, Santo Trafficante, and the Cuban president himself—

Fulgencio Batista. I could hear Frank Sinatra belting out a song in the lobby bar and laughing it up with his rat pack. Those criminals are gone now."

"Well sounds like you had quite a day," Jonathan said in a sarcastic tone. His thoughts of the hotel were very different: relatively speaking, it has the best restaurant food in town and is a jewel of '50s architecture; clean lines of glass, steel, mosaic and marble that stands impressively at the top of a hill. Tall enough to create its own climate; a constant breeze caresses its base—very pleasant on hot days. He imagined the chaos for the family when the old mongrel in the red tracksuit took it over six months after construction was finished. He felt angry at the communist Greek robber baron's cavalier attitude but did not say anything. The Greek had a belief that had been brainwashed into him over the years that could never be change. Jonathan knows this last communist bastion, Cuba, will collapse economically and will have to introduce a free market economy. The Hilton's will, someday, walk into their great hotel's expansive lobby and rightfully claim their property.

"Have you ever read this kind of literature?" and Jonathan handed the Greek an international colourful tour guide of Cuba that he bought the day he left Mexico. The Greek opened it and read a few lines.

"No, this is all lies," he quickly handed it back and took out his dull green picture-less revolution manifesto to read. His head in the book, he went to his room. He acted like he was punishing himself for dropping his guard.

Jonathan was starting to understand the word revolution. The people live in a revolution. He always thought a revolution was a verb, an action that lasts briefly. *Off with their heads and be done with it!* The Revolution in Cuba is a noun, a thing that is ongoing, a thing forever pushing and shoving the populace down and under control. There is complete control of their lives, much like the slaves of old and their pay is relatively the same—no, worse. Revolution is spying, telling, arresting, jailing, disappearing and murdering. Revolution is controlling the masses and the work done. The workers must exist anonymously with no thought for the individual—a mass of one for the common good. Revolution is no advancement of financial security and little reward for outstanding work.

The poor people of the island have lived in a shocking state for fifty years and many look tired from living in constant terror and participating in the revolution. There is no incentive to work or study, and Jonathan heard that prostitution and student apathy are on the rise. To speak of the old lizard in the red tracksuit is to court danger, for anything said could be rationalized as subversive and trials are without lawyers. When speaking of the old man, his name is never said; people stroke their chins as though they had his beard. Jonathan could be on a plane back to Mexico in a few minutes if he is not careful. He avoided the name Fidel Castro when speaking—it frightened them.

The family went inside to make dinner—the Greek was in his cell. Jonathan turned his attention to the huge mass of Havana spread out before him, stretching for kilometers south to the harbor and fortresses. Havana looked tired from the five hundred years of her existence. The revolution has beaten her up badly and neglected her needs; only improvements and maintenance were done to the country's towns and villages at the start of the revolution, as the impoverished farmers were more desperate for help. Rumor has it, among the Cubans, that the old hog in the red tracksuit never liked Havana anyway.

The city's thousands of colonial mansions had been confiscated by government forces in 1959. Thousands of people came into the city from the country with hopes in their hearts for the new society, a new society that promised all would benefit. Where one family and servants occupied a home, now dozens of people are crammed into little apartments. The beautiful mansions soon went into decay and neglect. Most of the property and business owners where not welcome anymore, they did not fit in with the new socialist ideology so they were forced to leave to Europe, South America or the United States. They could not take anything with them, only their lives. Some stayed on but were no longer landlords and business owners. Today they live poor and old with dozens of their kind in faded crumbling palaces, and all eventually and inevitably will go the way of the old crone in the red tracksuit.

In a restaurant in old Havana a bartender told him, the majority of citizens must have some way to make extra cash to get by so they become active in the underground economy or involved in the tourist industry where they can collect convertible pesos and American dollars. Jonathan noticed a few markets around the city where crafts and art are sold; products made at home. Ordinary citizens are loyal to the revolution but are forced into breaking the law trying to put food on the table. Signage across the city indicated those who do not play by the rules are subject to horrendous fines, can loose their homes, be imprisoned or do hard labor in the country. Activity in a clandestine political party could result in trial and execution by a firing squad.

Francesco set Jonathan's supper out on the outdoor patio and sat down with him. He drank a coffee and they resumed their conversation.

"When the old man in the red tracksuit moves on, change will happen and perhaps there will be a new democracy like that of the Soviet Union and China. An open market economy for the betterment of the people who truly are the government," Jonathan preached to his landlord who had little understanding of what he was talking about.

Francisco responded, "The people of Cuba are beautiful. There are thousands of accomplished educated musicians here; their unique

Cuban/African music resonates throughout Havana. A man may take his trumpet and in the park will play some beautiful rendition of a Miles Davis or Sachmo tune."

"Yeah, sometimes I hear the musicians when I walk around the neighborhood," Jonathan remarked.

"Education and health care are the two and perhaps the only areas that the revolution has truly done an amazing job, Francisco said, "but then I have only the poorest countries to compare us to."

"It's all very well to have free medical, but if there are no medicines and adequate facilities, what's the point?" said Jonathan.

"Yes but take our women, they are healthy and the most beautiful in the world, especially the mulatta with their round prominent rumps that exude a rhythmic biomechanical phenomenon that rises from deep within their African/Caribe genes," responded Francesco with a look of passion in his Latin eyes.

"Hey, good English, Francisco," Jonathan laughed.

"Thanks. I have been practicing. Young men and women all over Cuba strut and sway when walking. They exude sex with pride, a Cuban trait that has no equal in the world. After the takeover the armed forces had a terrible time teaching the new young women recruits how to march in a serious military fashion.

And with a strange sadness in his voice he said, "All is not bad, the children in the streets and school grounds are filled with excitement and laughter, they play with whatever they find: an old tennis ball to catch, a plastic water bottle for a football or a metal hoop to chase. They are friendly and courteous and one needs to feel afraid among the crowds or late at night when walking home. The Habaneras are making the best out of what they have and bravely stretch the rules when needed."

Jonathan finished his dinner and looked out over the city and down into the bare street with its old American automobiles with Russian engines belting out blue gray exhaust. The people have never been free in their history, he thought, and that is going back five hundred years to the cannibalistic Caribe Indians. Someone has always been around to beat them up and keep them in their place. "I will not judge this country," he said to his landlord, "what the Cubans do is none of my business. All I can say is I will return to Havana again someday when the little old fucker in the red tracksuit has joined his fellow revolutionaries in hell and the sun rises on a new Havana."

"Whoa, that's dramatic Jonathan," Francisco said, "and we shall be business partners." They laughed, hugged and shook hands.

After exploring the immediate neighborhood he set out into the bleak landscape of Havana—the hunt for Tula was on. With a copy of his drawing of her in his pocket he walked along the malecón towards the center of town, and old Havana. He observed the awesome landscape and thought that It must have been breathtaking a hundred years go. The former mansions and hotels were fantastic. Their classic pillars of Doric, Corinthian and Ionic orders supporting sculptured lintels and cast iron grilled balconies flowed down the wide expanse of the malecón. He imagined the porticoes giving shade to those out for a walk or for families and friends to sit in cool comfort. Restaurants and bars once lined the wide street accented with potted palms and exotic plants. Their customers and guests came from all over the world for this was once *The Destination* to come to for the holidays. Caged birds of all colours and sizes would have made sweet sounds against the crashing surf beyond the breakwater wall across the street.

Reality came back to him; all is gone now of that glorious time and the buildings are crumbling—some already dust. Architectural art has always been a favorite subject for him and he is aware of a building's personality and these old girls were crying out to be saved. He noticed some were being worked on, but the task is overwhelming, there are just too many. He saw dozens of workers with wheelbarrows, trowels, picks and shovels but the majority was sitting around. Lounging inspectors in uniforms lazily watched over everything.

Suddenly where the Avenue of the Presidents meets the malecón he saw a remarkable structure that took him awhile to figure out what it was. Two hundred gray steel flagpoles thirty meters high stood on a concrete platform. Huge black flags with white stars flapped a deafening noise. He stood in the forest and realized it was the backdrop for a stage that rises between concrete bunkers. A black metal grid structure on four steel towers carried lighting into place. The other side of the stage was a concrete wasteland for an audience of a million chanting souls. Above the barren ground were metal arches and beyond were towers topped off with weird green abstract sculptures. Placards on their concrete bases had inscriptions of names of the heroes of the revolution. The design of the area reminded him of a Mussolini nightmare from prewar Italy. It was built with the idea of a grandiose entrance for dignitaries. He found out later he was wrong on everything; the flags snubbed and blocked the building behind that displayed a huge electronic billboard. The building housed the United States Office of Interest. There were many guards around and he wanted to question them but he kept his mouth shut.

On his journey, street after street, he saw the terrible shame of a misguided government, thousands of beautiful old mansions going down. They hide now in the mist of pollution; clouds of white and blue smoke smothered the streets. Most of the time he could not see down the adjoining streets off the malecón. Smog came from old American autos, Russian peoples cars and Belgian buses. The American autos have been rebuilt many times over, gas replaced with diesel; their bodies repaired like paper mache cartoons. Jonathan flagged down a '58 Chev to ride the rest of the way to old town. In broken English the driver told him about his American Pig. The tank was his pride and joy.

He was dropped off in old Havana and the Chev's engine roared a slow speed down the main street in a cloud of blue smoke. He looked around. Havana and its people were frozen in time; January 1959, ever since that date very little maintenance and care has been given to Havana but this area had been designated a world heritage site so the Cubans generals had to maintain it.

There is another group of people here; one Cubans and tourists rarely get to see. A plain-clothed officer redirected Jonathan across the street. There was a gathering outside of a palatial building that had no sign indicating what it was. About twenty male and female exquisitely dressed Cuban whites were having a discussion on the sidewalk; their limousines had just dropped them off. Suddenly Jonathan found himself staring like every one else at the sight not sure what to make of it. In his fading traveling clothes he felt part of the decaying streetscape of people and buildings and thought what would be his place if he lived here, a citizen of Cuba, a citizen of the Revolution? No thanks he whispered, I have a bigger limo—elephant Buddha.

Jonathan walked down the main street of the square in front of the Capitol and all was the same; gray edifices with their old colours of yellow, blue and mint green, straining from under dirt and filth to emerge again into the tropical sun. He arrived at the train stations—there were two of them. He spent the next hour showing his picture of Tula to ticket takers, security people and anyone who looked like they worked in the stations. No one recognized her. He left and made his way back to the Capitolio and hailed a Caddy that took him out to the bus station near the monument to José Martí on the Plaza of Revolution. He showed the picture to every one and nobody recognized her and he thought maybe the toilet caretaker and the old woman recognized her.

"Do you know where she was going? What bus did you see her catch?"

"She left from that station," and the old woman pointed to an area by the driver's offices, "I remember her because she was very nice and gave me a big tip."

"Gracias," he said and he gave her a few CUPs. He went to the driver's offices and showed Tula's picture around and one driver said he put her bags in the luggage compartment of a bus a few days ago.

"I noticed her, she is a beautiful woman," he said, "your wife?"

"No, thank God, just someone I love. Where was the bus going?"

"Spoken like a Cuban," he laughed, "Santiago de Cuba."

Now he knew that he was on the trail of Tula and was excited about the chase ahead. He was relived she had come to Havana, he would have never been able to track her had she not come to a major city. He hailed a taxi and returned to his Casa. On the way thoughts ran though his head as he scanned the crumbling city: Why am I chasing her. This is crazy. I should just go home to Thailand and forget about her and this place. It was all a good adventure in Mexico and I know she will be all right and secure in her old age. I will not run into her as a market witch and be hexed. She is a millionaire. How the hell was she going to keep that kind of money in a communist country where there is no way of keeping anything secret. She is up to something and he felt himself being drawn into the intrigue.

The taxi drove up to the old deco building, his home, and there was a great commotion out on the sidewalk. The neighborhood was out, milling about and chattering like chickens. A look of fear was in their eyes, wide open, white with black centers.

Furniture and bags of clothing were being thrown into a military truck by a group of men in uniforms. They were coming out of his casa.

"Shall I drive by?" the taxi driver said nervously.

"No pull up," and he reached in his pocket for his fare, paid it and got out of the cab, which quickly drove off.

"What's going on?" he asked one of the soldiers.

He shrugged his shoulders, "No English!"

A large full breasted, middle-aged woman in a green uniform walked up to him. She carried a two-way radio and a clipboard. Official looking badges and epaulets adorned her uniform. Across her left breast was a badge with lettering—Ministry of The Interior.

"The traitors have been taken away," she said with authority.

"Who has been taken away?" Jonathan demanded and looked at her straight in the eye, "and what do you mean by traitors?"

"The traitor family that you lived with," the woman said, "they have lost their house and possessions. They have been taken away to the country to work."

"Why?" Jonathan asked in astonishment.

"Francesco had been attending antirevolutionary meetings around the corner at the very place our heroes had their meetings fifty years ago. The traitor will be put on trial tonight with the leaders of the bandit party. They will be found guilty and executed tomorrow morning or sent to a rehabilitation center."

"What?" Jonathan shouted, "You bitch! Where are the wife, boy and grandfather?"

"Don't worry about them. They have been taken to the country to work on the farms. No harm will come to them and no one will know where they are going. He is to be forgotten; all records of him will be destroyed. He will no longer exist or existed."

"And where in the country is the family?"

"Not even I know that. I am just here to clean out the apartment and make it ready for the new workers."

"So I will not see them again?"

"That's right, there is to be no contact with their past and their future is not to be talked about."

"Who snitched on them?"

"No more discussion Mr. Owen."

"You know my name?"

"Of course, we know every one. Now no more discussion, your possessions have been packed and are on the stairs just inside the front door. Your tour books have been confiscated; the revolution cannot have that kind of bourgeois literature loose in Cuba. Please, be on your way."

There was nothing he could do, he had no recourse but to pick up his bags, hail a taxi and return to the bus station. He would get the next bus west to Santiago de Cuba, fifteen hours away. As the taxi drove away he looked back through the rear window and saw the Greek talking to the head woman.

The Flight Across The Universe To Santiago de Cuba

In a drunken rage, the huge black man raised his machete above his head and rushed at James. The blade came down and James raised his left arm. It sliced through muscles, tendons, nerves and bones. Again the blade came down and did the same terrible damage to his left leg. The attacker's friends stopped the carnage and they ran from the scene leaving him to bleed to death. He didn't and today the raging man, who happened to be a doctor in the hospital where he was taken, is now in a Cuban prison for thirty years. This incident and other prompted the Ministry of the Interior to write laws that any attack on a tourist by a Cuban the sentence can be death. For James his sentence is worse, he no longer has the use of his left hand and has no feeling in his lower left leg and foot. He will walk with a cane, in pain for the rest of his life—the trauma has aged him.

Jonathan met James when he boarded the bus in the city of Trinidad and they immediately became friends; they shared a seat to Santiago de Cuba. They talked at great length about themselves and their adventurous lives. Jonathan had never before felt so comfortable with someone that he would know for such a short time.

James is a pleasant man, well read and articulate in his speech. He was born and raised in the UK by a wealthy family of royal heritage and position in British society. His life is one of adventure: traveling the world, working when he needed, but mostly exploring and enjoying what the world has to offer. He is in his sixties and married to a very young Cuban woman who has stayed by his side through his ordeal.

They talked of many things: the monarchy; the impending downfall of Cuba's government; cattle ranching in Australia and Canada; Shakespeare, Byron, Burns and the beautiful women they have known and loved. Jonathan could see that he was once a handsome young man, and with his personality and knowledge he walked through life as king of his domain until that fateful day he wandered into a place that would change him forever.

"So why are you really in Cuba, Jonathan, I detect you have business here and not just on vacation?"

"You're right," and he assessed the moment, "I guess I can trust you. Can you handle this?"

"Hey, I can handle anything now."

"I'm chasing a psychopathic woman with whom I was running, hiding and loving, across Mexico, Guatemal and Belize in pursuit of a treasure of gold doubloons. We killed a few people to get to the treasure and managed to dig it up from under seven stones in a temple on an island during a hurricane. We dug up a million dollars of Aztec/Maya treasure.

The treasure was melted down, by some of Hernan Cortez's cronies, into Spanish doubloons. My bitch took off to Cuba with the goods and I'm chasing her, not for the money, because mind you, I don't need or even want the money. I have a good home with refuges in Thailand and an elephant and monkey that make me a living on the streets of Bangkok. I don't want to loose them so I must be careful. I can't get into trouble because I will get deported back to Canada and end up in jail again. It took me three years to get a pardon for the commotion I caused in Portugal, Spain and Gibraltar. This time they could put me away for good. Oh yes, I'm chasing her because I love her.

"So, there you have it. Foolish, don't you think?" They both had a hardy laugh over Jonathan's ranting of his mixed up life.

"You are kidding me, aren't you?"

"No, it's all true. I'm jinxed or hexed—or whatever."

"Your crazy all right but then you're not the type to walk away from adventure, are you?" James reached into his backpack and pulled out a bottle of red Cuban wine, crackers, cheese, knife and two cups, one paper the other plastic.

"No, I'm not. I'm in love with her and I have to carry this thing through to the end."

"Admirable, my boy, admirable," James said laughing. He patted Jonathan's arm, "paper or plastic?" They talked, drank wine and nibbled for an hour in the darkness of the bus. It was getting late, the bus driver turned down the lights and James drifted into sleep. The world went quiet but for the hiss of the air conditioner and steady distant rumble of the engine.

Jonathan watched the black landscape go by; his universe that he traveled in by bus, train, plane and boat. The more he learned about his universe the less he knew. His life was traveling across it and he knew he would never reach the other side—a place unattainable, mystifying—a soft terror of the inevitable. The rewards of the journey were all he sought, not what was at the end. He saw a flicker of ghosts and bones on the horizon.

The sliver of the moon was high and hung below it was Quetzalcoatl. Star towns went by and milky streams of thoughts of the past few years drifted over the rooftops. Images glowed beyond the window: his elephants, Thunder Mountain and Buddha; his refugee family in Thailand that he longed for, and the faces of his son and daughter—all together as one family in Home Camp Bangkok. A shadow moved across the rooftops.

He saw his friends and lovers from over the years of his life on the road and the beauty of the people in the towns, cities and hamlets he witnessed. Their cultures he treasured most of all and he worried that they could get lost in the giant global village. His universe rolled by and he saw monks, priests and preachers, and images of temples to Buddha, Mohammed, Christ and Deities. The shadow leaped from the rooftops to palms and back again.

Quetzalcoatl winked at him and he knew that the feathered serpent would come home some day from his thousand-year exile. Jonathan needed to be home, but he did not know when the universe out there beyond the bus window would let him—perhaps in 2012 when the world ends.

James gently snored.

He saw a figure waiting on the edge of the highway; backpack on and holding the handle of luggage on wheels. Behind him in the window of a café Bank Robber watched him. He is far from his destination waiting for a wandering taxi that will take him to a guesthouse and rest. He smiled at the memories.

The night bus past a bar and he saw Jonathan in Chiang Mai, he was reaching behind him and grabbing the trunk of a five hundred kilo baby elephant that was trying to get his attention. Black silhouettes of palm trees floated by and he saw monkeys harvesting the ripe coconuts. At the bottom of one palm he saw a woman chained to the trunk. It was a time in Cambodian that he learned not to jump to conclusions. He could see her face reflected in the bus window. He looked past sleeping James but no one was there.

Out of the universe the mountain of Gibraltar loomed. He saw a man chasing a monkey; the creature had stolen his bottle of soda. The door to a bar went by and Tegwyn was leaning against the jam. She stared from the universe to his window with a vacant look. His heart went out to her for she had fallen in love with a madman. Above her leaped the shadow across the rooftops and now it was on feet and knuckles.

The bus rumbled past a church and through the open door he saw a hunched and broken caretaker leading a man behind an altar. On the wall was painted seven red crosses. He could see a hand touch the wall before the church disappeared. Childhood stories told to him by his uncle rattled in his head.

Hungry eyes looked at him and he remembered a cafe in Havana. He waved the person in—a mulatta woman sat down at his table. You are hungry? He asked. Yes, she said. He told his waiter to feed her and gave him money. Hungry eyes disappeared into the black universe. The shadow monkey raced the bus.

Monk with Buffalo and Girl One waved to him from the shoulder of the dusty highway. Oh, how he missed them for their wise simple and loving way—the way of Lord Buddha. He recalled the journey to take Monk home to die in his village on the Mekong and the promise to journey to the temples of Angkor and the monks and children who are still out there looking for a home. Am I one of those children, he thought with no god, no teacher?

Through the passing villages the dark monkey bounded across the rooftops. Suddenly he stopped and stood on his legs. In the glow of a street lamp Jonathan saw a golden arm of the monkey reach into the black. Oh my God, he thought that's me. He laid down his plastic wine cup and drifted into sleep and the long night's journey to Tula and Santiago de Cuba. Angels danced across the window.

Rick Thomas

Fifty Years Plus a Day

... Do the Sierra Maestra rebels not want free elections, a democratic regime, a constitutional government? It is because they deprived us of those rights that we have fought since March 10. We are here because we want them more than anyone else. To demonstrate it, there are our fighters dead in the mountains and our comrades murdered in the streets or secluded in prison dungeons. We are fighting for the beautiful ideal of a free, democratic, and just Cuba. What we do not do is to agree with the lies, farces, and compromises of the dictatorship.
We want elections, but with one condition: truly free, democratic, and impartial elections. Fidel Castro's Sierra Maestra Manifesto (July 12, 1957)

James and Jonathan took a small round table at the end of the bar on the terrace of the Casa Grande Hotel, Santiago de Cuba. They looked out over the main square of the city.

"I will tell you the story of what happened here," James said. He gestured to the waiter for two Cubra Libras and began his tale: "Fifty years yesterday, at the start of the New Year, January 2, 1959 Fidel Castro and his men came down from the Sierra Maestra. Batista had fled the country the day before to Haiti and left Cuba to a rag tag army to rebuild it as one man saw fit. Castro, dressed in his green army fatigues and cap with star, gave his victory speech on that blue balcony," and James pointed with his good hand to the town hall, "tens of thousands arrived to hear him; they filled the square below; this terrace of the Casa Grand Hotel, the pedestal of the cathedral and the windows and balconies of all the buildings you see. They had come to hear their new leader speak of his promise of a democratic election to be held within the year of Batista's downfall—a promise he had made by radio two years before. They had followed and supported him on the premise that they would finally be free from the torment inflicted on them for the last five hundred years—the door to democracy was open. He made his speech and left by tank on a five-day triumphal march to Havana. His partner, Che Guevara, had taken the city and was preparing his blood bath of executions of thousands of Batista followers and anti-revolutionists. There would be no democracy—another lie and nightmare had begun for the Cuban people."

"So this is where it all began?" Jonathan said as he looked out over the square. It was all very sad.

"Yes, and here we are, fifty years plus a day, we sit with our drinks in a snack bar that was once the elegant terrace lounge. The corner of the old wood bar must have been a favorite of writers and artists many years ago," there were flies and dirty dishes now residing there, "the shelves are now barren except for a few bottles of Havana Rum," The waiters looked at the two travelers with disdain, they were just another couple of gringo customers to serve.

"Notice how the waiters avoid eye contact so they can put off serving us as long as possible—a government induced laziness," said James in disgust. In his past he was used to good service and gave good service, "no one is in charge of them; no one is in charge or manages anymore," he went on, "the service, as everything else in Cuba, is flat, tired, worn out, filthy and mediocre. The worker's wages have been the same for years—ten pesos a month. If they are lucky to work in the tourist industry, they make a little more; if not they must break or bend the law to survive.

"The people of Cuba gave themselves over to a government that has made them criminals. It is a desperate situation and many are tired and bitter. No one talks of the past and the speech that was made on the balcony that is within earshot of where we drink our rum from cheap glasses. Life is now in a trance for the Cubans. No one cares anymore, there is no incentive to work hard or work at all since they cannot move their lives up, down, ahead or sideways. The old ideology of sacrifice for the good of all is tired and worn out. Most in the bar and out in the square today were not alive when Castro gave his speech."

"You are very passionate about this country. Why don't you leave it and go back to England?"

"I can't, I'm married to this country. Despite its pitiful condition, there is a romance here. There is a way about the place you just can't put your finger on. When I hear the drums beat and see the Cubans dance in the rhythm and frenzy that they bought here hundreds of years ago, I feel rooted to this place." They watched the square and the people coming and going.

"No one is in a rush," James said, "there is no place to go." Jonathan noticed a quite calm about the place, a state of neutrality, no one standing out in the crowd—everyone the same. "Look down the street," James said, and Jonathan saw a group of a hundred or more people crowded around a local bakery door, "they will spend hours waiting to buy a loaf of bread and then line up again at some other vendor. Most Cubans' days are spent waiting for something, mostly food and basic necessities."

A bell from the cathedral clanged a pitiful four o'clock. "You hear that? The cathedral's big bells now lay silently along its wall. They were taken out of the belfry towers long ago. No more lovely banging of the bells." Church and state looked dumbly at each other across the square.

On the street below beggars were everywhere; some carried plastic containers for leftovers. One filthy man wandered by, on a sack he carried over his shoulder where three cockroaches chasing each other.

"This morning I did some banking at an exorbitant interest rate across the square at the Bank of Credit and Commerce. At the rear of the tellers' cages are windows with Venetian blinds half open looking out onto the square. A woman in a beige shirt and brown pants was holding down the blinds with her fingers to get a better view. Who was she?"

"Ah yes, that creature was one of the Committee for the Defense of the Revolution or CDR employees, the dreaded snitches of the Ministry of the Interior.

"Sounds like a scary bitch."

"That she is; she is one of the mother's of the Cuban people—molding a utopian society. There are more than one hundred thousand CDR offices across Cuba—one just around the corner in everyone's neighborhood. They spy on the populace and take action on those who would threaten the revolution or get ahead financially or independent of everyone else. They and the Ministry of the Interior prosecute for the slightest infractions of the party's righteous path. Everyone is kept in place by terror."

"Yeah," Jonathan said, "I had an experience with them in Havana. They were doing their dirty work on some friends of mine."

"When you saw her she was probably watching that group of men gathered at that bench," he pointed to a very verbal group of men talking loudly and gesturing with their hands, "they are arguing about football or maybe politics. There are others she watches like hustlers and jineteras that go after the unsuspected to divest them of their foreign dollars. She is not likely to pursue those individuals unless there are complaints—after all the state needs the cash."

"There is confusion about everything in this country. Take for instance that group of backpackers and hippies wandering back and forth across the square. They are trying to figure out where they are. There are street names in their guidebooks but there are very few street signs in the city. They have been removed or painted over; some are renamed after the leaders of independence and the revolution."

A huge unmarked Ford truck, hand painted blue, roared down the street below the terrace; it belched a thick black smoke that billowed over the street and up the walls of the hotel. It was packed with people to bursting, perhaps a hundred or more going someplace; there were no signs or writing on the fiery dragon to say where. Schoolgirls in white shirts and mini skirts walked across the square. They did not carry books; nobody carried books, magazines or newspapers—no reading material and Jonathan wondered what they meant about the country being literate. At one of the corners of the square two raggedy boys played bottle cap baseball.

The sun was going down and it shone on them. It was not hot; a cool breeze came across the square and up the side of the building, under the awnings and between white ionic columns. With it came the beautiful sound of an old boys band—from where Jonathan did not know.

"The Cubans have music that is magical," James said, "full of passion and Africa—the government cannot take that away from them. Besides it is all they have left." But rising above it were the screams of some crazy toothless man trying to get their attention—he is hungry. The eyes and smiles of young black women wanting other favors darted like arrows up from the street and the tables around them. Some stared in awe at the white men from the north and wondered if it was true what they see on TV.

There were flies landing on their table, some in their drinks. The waiter warned them and gave them fresh ones. He came back a short time later and asks them to pay their bill; there was a shift change. The staff of the bar and people in the square were not smiling, laughing or talking about the evening to come with family and friends. They suddenly became serious; they were in search of convertible pesos for their next meal. Jonathan tried his best to see something positive out there in the square where people gathered long ago with hope in their hearts, but there was nothing.

"Do you think you will find your love that you talked about on the bus?"

"I don't know. It is unlikely but I will try."

"You and her sound like a bad Shakespearean tragedy. Be careful the ending could be a heartbreaker. Keep your mouth shut and stay in the shadows, as you know there are spies all over this country."

"I will James, thanks for the advice and all you have told me about Cuba."

James stood up on his crippled leg and said: "It is fifty years plus a day when once there was a door open to a dream. It is time for me to be on my way. I have relatives to meet. Take care, Jonathan, good luck in your quest."

"Goodbye James." And he stood and shook his crippled hand. James walked out of the Grand Hotel, down the steps and across the square. In James, he saw what happens as we move from one era of our lives to another. He is old now and his body will not recover fully from his injuries and the stress on his mind will not go away. No longer will there be the flamboyancy and vigor of youth but there will be something else; dignity, the kind that comes with an aging mind and the passing of time. He watched him, on his cane, limp across the street and into the square; his crippled hand close to his body and as he disappeared into the mass of humanity. Jonathan noticed he walked tall, his head in the sun.

With much difficulty and frustration, Jonathan found the Archives of History. He had been in and out of administration offices, tourist centers and museums all day. He approached the receptionist's counter and showed Tula's picture to a young black woman. "Did you seen this woman come through here in the last few days?" he gently asked.

The young woman was startled by the image. She took the picture and said, "One moment please." she got up and went to an office in the back. A large well-dressed black man came out quickly and walked over to him.

"Sir," and he extended his hand and Jonathan shook it," I am the Director. Would you come to my office please?" They walked down a hall to his office, "This woman in the picture is important to us." Jonathan looked surprised. The director had a file on his desk with Tula Muginga scrawled across the cover.

"This woman is she a friend of your?" queried the director holding the picture in his hand.

"Yes, actually a bit more than a friend," and they smiled at each other.

"Please sit down for a moment," and he took a seat in front of the director's desk and the director sat in his chair, leaned forward and explained his strange encounter with Tula: "She came into the archives yesterday and gave me twenty thousand American dollars as a donation to the archives to assist our research department. It is a very generous donation so I offered her my assistance. She asked for help in finding the name of a slave. I asked her where we should start and she said three hundred years ago. That would take many hours, I said. But she insisted that she must check that far back. We checked through dozens of slave owners' rosters and shipping records. This is the one we found," he pointed to the name on the file cover, "that is her ancestral name." The director opened the file folder and pointed to a faded ink description on a fragile sheet of stained paper in a plastic folder. He handed it to Jonathan who gently took it:

From: Sierra Leona, Africa; Destination: Santiago de Cuba; Baptism none; Sex: male; African name: Ub Muginga; Given name: Joseph Muginga.

"Impossible!" said Jonathan, "all those years ago, im—"

"Does it really matter if it is the name of her ancestor or not? She is from Africa." and the Director pointed to his chest, "We all came from Africa. It is the cradle of the human race, the original Garden of Eden. We were cast out many years ago to populate the world, and what a great suffering that journey has been. She, like many of us, is finding her peace and place in the world. I did not argue the name because it probably is her ancestor."

"That is her last name, although I've always called her Tula and haven't heard or seen her last name in years.

"Oh boy." he sighed, "This does change everything. Poor Tula, will anything be right for her?"

"Yes, someday," the Director said with a spark of enthusiasm in his voice, "she is on her way there." And he knew then why he was the Director of the Archives and responsible for these precious records.

He studied the name on the faded roster, could it be true. Was that the name of her ancestor. He felt so inadequate and sad for Tula, he felt sad for all those who arrived here in chains over the hundreds of years. They were brutalized and worked to death in the cane fields and mines. He saw in his mind images of her in the rigging of pirate ships; hauling in fishing lines; making her way home tired and filthy from the cane fields; dancing before a blazing fire to the sound of African drums; softly singing a song to her sleeping babies as she washed her master's clothes; fleeing from soldiers and killers as war ravaged her country; standing strong in the line with her man in the fight for independence and, the hardest chore of all, murdering to stay alive. He imagined her race beaten, whipped, tortured, abandoned and controlled up to the present day. He knows they are still not free; there has always been a master. Three hundred years of oppression, fifteen generations of Tula's family, split apart and scattered across the Caribbean, South and North America.

"This is very difficult for me. I must see her again. You understand?"

"Of course."

"Where do you think I can find her in Santiago?"

"I would try the docks," the Director said.

"The docks?"

"Yes, I can not see Tula leaving Cuba by any conventional way. I doubt she came here in a conventional manner." And he gave Jonathan a knowing smile. Jonathan sensed the Director knew more than he was letting out. He was protecting himself and Tula, which Jonathan thought was a wise thing to do.

"Thank you, director, for your time," he shook the director's hand who gave him back his picture of Tula.

And as he was about to leave the director's office, the director said, "Mr. Owen, find the ships that are leaving for Africa."

He left the director's office.

He looked over an exhibit in the archives foyer and read about Tula's people. Dancing in Tula's blood and bones was the stuff of generations past, the genes of her ancestors—the essence of her soul. They came across the years and a huge ocean to a dock in the harbor of Santiago de Cuba. They had survived all those years building a new host one after another all the way to Tula, the fiercest most powerful human Jonathan had ever encountered. He knew now he could never understand her fully or go with her on her journey. She was not running from him, the law or of anything. She was running *to* something, something only she understood. She was much like him and more, a loner out there in the world of adventure. She was embarking on something new that would take her to exciting places with strange customs and people. He suddenly felt joy for her. He put her picture in his pocket and left the Archives. He made his way to the docks, and if he finds her he would say one last goodbye.

At the harbor of Santiago de Cuba he rented a motor scooter. He started his search at the north end and worked his way south. He showed Tula's picture to security guards, longshoremen and anyone who looked like they worked on the docks. Nobody had seen her and ships going to Africa were few—many had left. He was becoming discouraged and about to give up when he arrived at a gate and a mulatta security guard in a Ministry of the Interior's drab green uniform.

"Is there a ship or freighter leaving for Africa?" he asked the guard. The guard looked at him with suspicion. Jonathan knew instantly by his demeanor he knew something so he produced an American twenty-dollar bill.

"Yes there is," he replied, "it's about to leave for West Africa. It's moored to the pier just beyond that shed," and he pointed across a storage compound to a blue warehouse.

"Gracias," and he shoved the twenty into the guard's hand, drove across the compound to the other side of the warehouse and parked the bike. A number of longshoremen where lined up at the dock, each at a cleat holding hawser lines of a rusting gray ship. She was a medium size old girl who had worked better days but now she was a rusting hulk. She flew the British flag at her stern and her name was The Joan, registered in Monrovia. She belched out black smoke as her engines came up.

"Let 'er go!" shouted the captain from the bridge and each man let his line go. Crewmembers quickly pulled them aboard. The captain barked some orders to the helmsman. The ship's bow slowly swung out, her stern gently bumped the dock and the rusting old freighter slowly moved. She was running light; her prop was part way out of the water and it throbbed with each revolution.

Jonathan froze, the gods of many countries were with him today and his heart ached from his loss and joy—at the stern of the upper deck stood Tula. The sun was hidden over the horizon, the moon's sliver was high in the sky and Quetzalcoatl hung brightly below. Tula's flowered dress gently moved in the breeze; her black curls caressed her brown shoulders and cheeks. For the first time in all the years that he had known her there was peace and tranquility on her face. There were no angels dancing today. With both hands on the railing she looked out to the harbor at other ships from around the world who where waiting their turn to leave. She slowly swung her head and saw him; her right hand moved up to her heart and her lips parted into a smile.

He shouted, "Good for you, honey!" He waved and clapped his hands, "I love you!" and she shouted the same back but they could not hear each other over the ships horns but they knew what each other had said. Jonathan laughed and threw her kisses, her hands went to her face and she cried. After three hundred years, Tula Muginga was going home—home to Africa. The ship moved out into the bay and they watched each other close this book on their lives.

THE END